The Hut

The Hut

Zeeba Ansari

Matador
9 Priory Business Park,
Wistow Road, Kibworth Beauchamp,
Leicestershire. LE8 0RX
Tel: 0116 279 2299
Email: books@troubador.co.uk
Web: www.troubador.co.uk/matador
Twitter: @matadorbooks

ISBN 978 1800462 458

British Library Cataloguing in Publication Data.
A catalogue record for this book is available from the British Library.

Printed and bound in the UK by TJ Books LTD, Padstow, Cornwall
Typeset in 11pt Minion Pro by Troubador Publishing Ltd, Leicester, UK

Matador is an imprint of Troubador Publishing Ltd

for my mother and father,
who made it possible

Part One

Part One

Chapter One

Night is in a strange mood this evening. Shadows loom and deepen; the flame in the lamp on the wall flutters and dims.

'Stop fidgeting,' Arun says irritably. 'And it's your turn.' A domino tile inches forward to sit at right angles against the tile he has just laid down. The black spots blur and shift. 'What have I told you? They move, I don't play.'

'You're such a joy to be with,' Night remarks. 'First you turn up empty-handed – it was your turn to think of a topic for this evening's discussion – then you accuse me of cheating. I don't know why I bothered to come.'

'Then why did you?' Arun asks.

There is a frosty pause as a serving-man brings food. Arun spreads butter thickly on the bread, dips it in the lamb broth, and starts eating. The broth is good, though not as good as Lia's.

'You've been like this ever since she left,' Night says. 'All this running round in circles – *Shall I? Shan't I?* – is wearing me out. If you don't decide soon, there'll be nothing left of me. And then what will you do?'

'Have a peaceful life,' Arun says. 'And it's rude to eavesdrop.'

'Samiros will be in ruins by the time you make up your mind. And Lia won't wait forever. Although if she did come back, she'd know where to find you.'

Ignoring the gibe, Arun glances out of the window of the inn at the round spring moon. He can almost feel its weight. At the hut he works hard to keep out the light, plugging the smallest gap with rags, stuffing a cloth under the door.

'It's not that simple,' he says eventually.

'No,' Night agrees, 'not if you don't want it to be. And it's your move.'

Arun stares blankly at the tiles. Lia's absence affects him more than he will admit. Suddenly he has had enough. He finishes his beer and pushes back his chair, swaying a little as he gets to his feet. People glance up as he makes his way through the common room of the Willow. He nods to Olti as he leaves; the innkeeper looks faintly surprised, then wishes him a good evening. Normally he stays until the hours are so small he can almost forget them. But tonight –

He walks briskly through the chill of early spring. Moonlight clears a path in his head. He closes his eyes, stumbles, swears, and stares up at the moon. Her brightness runs into his eyes, his open mouth. He is drowning. He runs the last few yards to the hut, slams the door and throws himself down on his bed.

Sleep takes time to come, but when it does he dreams he is walking beside a stream whose banks are covered with flowers. The flowers are white and gold. No, that isn't right, there were no flowers around his family's hut, only scrubby ground. In front of the hut, a wheatfield; to the side, plots of dark-brown earth planted with potatoes, onions, carrots, lettuces, cabbages, squashes. There were hens, too, and goats.

He opens his eyes on darkness. Not for the first time, he wonders if there is an exam to be taken, a certificate he needs, to pass beyond memory. Abandoning his bed, he goes to the cabinet, takes out a flagon of beer, sits at the table and drinks until it is empty. Getting up, he paces back and forth, brooding. *If she did come back, she'd know where to find you.* He is used to Night's insults by now, but the words are like a stone in his boot.

He goes to his bed, ducks down and drags a large leather sack from underneath it. From the bread crock he takes a passably fresh loaf, wrapping it in a cloth with a small wheel of sheep's cheese and some dried fruit. Unhooking his satchel from the nail beside the door, he stuffs the bundle into it. The dagger Yorin gave him hangs on the other side. For a moment he looks at it, remembering the last time – the only time – he used it, then slips the sheath onto his belt, pulls on his cloak, and goes out.

A light wind stirs as he fills his water bottle from the barrel beside the door. An owl cries; a shiver in the darkness. He thinks of Mirashi's lines about the soul

> moving through twilight
> to the owl's dark measure
> before that last rest
> deep in the wing.

He wonders where she was when she wrote them. Was she alone, like him?

5

He walks steadily, following the track past the well, away from the village.

'Going somewhere?' Night asks.

'Leave me alone.'

'That's a nice thing to say when we've been friends for so long.' Night sounds hurt, but Arun knows better. 'You should be flattered. I don't talk to just anyone, as you very well know. I can't remember the last time, and my memory is long.'

'Of all the people in the world, you had to pick me.'

'And I couldn't have made a better choice. In spite of the fact that when we first met you were awash with beer and flat on your back gazing up the stars, I knew you were the one. I could see your potential. Look how far you've come since then, doing everything you can to avoid the light of you-know-what. It's really rather gratifying, but then, I'm never wrong.'

Arun walks faster.

'Still here,' Night says after a long silence.

Arun stops dead. 'Haven't you got better things to do? Like working on your masterpiece?'

A few evenings ago, Night announced the intention to write a book. Arun was silent for several minutes before making a response. He could sense Night's anticipation; the flame in the lamp flickered wildly.

'A book?' he said carefully.

'Why not? I've seen it all, every kind of madness, civilisations coming and going, the world at peace and war. Like the time I was dozing in the desert and an army caught me full in the face. A host of glittering men and horses, swords and helmets, making their way to a great walled city. When they reached it, a man on a magnificent horse raised his moonlit arm as if he were going to throw a spear. Then a cloud covered the moon, and when it came out again they'd all disappeared. When the wind blows across the dunes you can still hear their voices. Every grain of sand holds something of the world. You should know that.'

Arun refused to be drawn. The Haruan Desert was far behind him now. 'A mouthful of beer holds nothing of the world,' he said flatly. After a prickly silence he relented, asking Night what kind of book it would be.

'An epic romance?' A crumb caught in his throat and he started coughing. Wiping his eyes, he asked who the hero would be.

'I've given it a lot of thought,' Night said. 'There's the captain at the crescent spring, the one who filled Lady Asai's water bottle. You know who I mean.' Arun stifled the memory and countered with the chickpea farmer Night told him about some time ago.

'That man was heroic in an entirely different way, as you well know,' Night said primly.

Arun started laughing; Night accused him of not taking the idea seriously and refused to tell him any more about it. Arun finished his beer very slowly, put down the empty mug and studied it as if searching for an answer. When the atmosphere was wound so tight the flame in the lamp stood rigid, he asked if Night had anyone particular in mind.

'Well, since you've asked,' Night said grudgingly, 'I thought – don't laugh' – Arun promised not to – 'well, me.'

Arun clutched his beer mug. 'Go on.'

'Think about it.' Night's voice was full of enthusiasm. 'I'm the silent watches, the ultimate shadow. I soothe people's hearts by taking away the troubles of the day' – Arun thought of the hours spent tossing and turning while the troubles of the day lay sleepless beside him – 'I give hope, make people want to begin again. I don't need to work under cover of me because I provide my own cover. I'm shield and shelter, not to mention invincible. In short, I'm perfect.'

Arun thought it best not to bring up the fact that the whole world witnessed night fall. For a while he sat running through the many flaws in Night's proposal, not least the inconvenience of daybreak. He could sense Night's attention. 'It's just –' he began, and stopped.

'I know,' Night said gloomily. 'I don't have the face for it.'

Arun walks on, smiling a little.

'You're out of shape,' Night observes. Which is true; for a long time now his only exercise has been the walk from the hut to the inn and back. Even now his feet keep trying to turn around, like old and faithful horses accustomed to seeing their master safely home.

As he suspected, Night can't resist returning to the subject of the book. 'You know when a chapter ends on a note of suspense? How am I supposed to do that? I mean, I can hardly run out into me, can I?'

Arun comes to a halt. He has reached the boulder he once sat on as the sun came up. He has never gone beyond it. He has in fact hardly left Kandra since he came here.

Just once, to see Fulda. Someone else he let down. He leans against the boulder, suddenly exhausted.

'No stamina,' Night says. 'Too much beer.'

Pushing himself up, Arun walks on. He takes a left-hand fork and continues in dogged silence, thinking about when he first came to the village. He'd finished the last of his bread, and his water bottle was empty. At the time he neither knew nor cared where his next meal would come from.

'And now you've made a career of it.' Night says, looming again. 'Not caring, I mean.'

'Don't do that,' Arun snaps. 'I can't see a thing.'

The darkness thins, sketching the track, the dark bulk of grasses at either side. A breeze noses through. He looks up, suddenly aware of the breadth of the sky.

'Can you see them?' he asks.

'See what?'

'The stars, the moon.'

'I am not a pond with fish in it.'

'You're very touchy tonight. I think I liked you better at the inn.'

'That,' Night says with dignity, 'is because we never talked about anything personal. Remember the Rule.'

When they were first introduced, Night explained that while no topic was out of bounds, there was one fundamental rule: Arun was never to ask anything personal.

'About you?'

'About you.'

Arun retorted that he knew far too much about himself already – why would he want to know more? With a suffering sigh, Night explained that it referred to 'anything relating to your life. You can ask, but you won't get anywhere. My lips are sealed.'

Arun's first impulse had been to protest, but what was the point? He had no doubt Yorin was doing very well without him, and as for Lia –

'The Rule,' Night said severely, 'is not to be broken. And note the initial capital.'

'Oh, I Do,' he says now. The beer at the Willow is singing a song of such sweetness he almost groans. There was a time when his body did what he asked, without complaint. He wonders if he has grown old.

'Hardly,' Night says. 'I know places where people live a hundred years or more.'

The thought of all that life is too much. Arun turns off the track and pushes through the grasses. A flake of silver catches his eye. It belongs to a pool in a tree-lined clearing not far ahead.

Within the pool the moon sits full and radiant, deepening the surrounding darkness. Arun drops the sack and satchel on the ground, leans back against the trunk of a tree, and closes his eyes. A small breeze makes the leaves whisper. He wonders what they are talking about.

'You could try asking them,' Night says, 'or we could talk about you. And before you quibble – I've never known anyone so dedicated to sucking the marrow out of an argument – it isn't breaking the Rule. The Rule is about asking, not telling.'

'Thanks for pointing it out. Although when I asked if you could see the stars, that was about you, not me. Just making sure there's no marrow left,' he says in response to Night's derisive snort. 'Anyway, I thought you knew everything. As you never fail to remind me.'

A short silence. 'I do. Everything that happens in me. I can't speak for' – a disdainful sniff – 'the other half.' Arun found out early on how sensitive Night was to any mention of daytime, and has at times used it to bring an argument to a chilly end.

'Besides,' Night adds, 'I'm in the mood for a story.'

'Well, I'm not.' Arun stares into the rush-fringed pool. Small fish dart across the face of the moon. They remind him of the fish trap, and his father, who sometimes took Arun with him when he went to the stream to check it.

He presses down hard, but the memory struggles out.

'That's it,' Night says encouragingly.

He is six years old, a boy in midsummer. The air is sweet, the sun walks in flowered fields –

'Stop it,' he says.

'What?'

'It isn't a saga written three thousand years ago by a man with a little help from his camel. It's just me, sitting beside a pool hogged by the moon.'

'But isn't that how they start, the single act that sets the snow falling?'

An image of snow-covered mountains shimmers in Arun's head, white peaks surrounding the valley like frozen light.

'And you think you don't have a poetic soul,' Night says.

Arun shifts; a tree root is pressing into his leg. He settles into silence.

'Oh, all right,' Night grumbles. 'It's plain old midsummer – you could have chosen a better season – and you and your father are going to the stream to check the fish trap. Your mother –'

'No. Don't bring her into it.'

'If it's a tale about your family, your mother should be involved. You didn't drop from the nearest tree, after all.'

For a moment Arun bows his head. 'It was an almond tree. It blossomed every spring, and my mother loved it.'

He sees her now, making bread, kneading to an inner rhythm. She is wearing her green dress, her hair blue-black as a bird's wing. And there is his father, standing at the fish trap. His brooding aspect, his way of studying aslant, remind Arun of a heron. The trap simmers with fish of middling size, but Arun knows what he is looking for. The one he hasn't caught yet, old and crafty, whose reputation and size grow by the year.

He remembers his father straightening up, turning to him and saying, *One day that fish will swim up to me and say, 'All right, Ned, it's time.' That's what happens if you don't give up, you see?*

Arun shakes his head. 'I was a child. I saw nothing.'

He turns his face away, but he can still see his mother wiping her hands on the apron she wore every day, except when she went to the village. When she took it off, there was singing. The memory stings.

'You see,' he says angrily, 'this is what happens. When people go away they leave time behind them, stuck at the moment of departure. But it goes on without them too.' He wonders if they ever meet, the time turned to stone, the time like water flowing.

'Is it a rhetorical question?' Night asks.

'It's my question to me.'

'Which means it'll probably never be answered. I have another one. About where you're heading.'

'Nowhere. That's what my father said, though not in so many words. I don't think he meant it unkindly; he just didn't put things very well. Talking to him later helped me see that. I was eleven years old, playing skipstones with my sister, when he called me into the hut.'

He sees his sister deploying a pebble with quiet precision, her hair as blue-black as her mother's. 'She always beat me. At the time I found it infuriating. I probably accused her of cheating, which is the last thing she'd ever do.'

'She?'

'You know who,' Arun says. Then, more softly, 'Kara.'

It has been a long time since he said her name, but the pain is still as fresh, the image it prompts – a small, windowless room – still as clear.

He closes his eyes and hears his sister telling him to hurry up, their father is waiting, 'and it's no good looking like that, you were just about to lose, anyway.'

The boy pulls a face as he gets to his feet. He thinks he knows what it is about. The poet.

Arun's hand goes automatically to the pocket of his tunic. Mirashi is still there.

'The poet?' Night says.

'My mother went to the market in Bishra – our village – most days to sell things, milk, cheese, eggs, bread. This time I was with her because' – he thinks for a moment – 'she needed help carrying the baskets.'

The boy stumbles a little, but carries his basket proudly. They take the path to the village and reach the market square early, before the heat. At the head of the square is the inn, the White Poplar. His mother puts down her baskets and gives him a drink of the cordial she always brings with her. He helps her lay everything out on a large cloth, hoping for a taste of cheese – it comes from their goats, and is salty and creamy and sharp – but his mother tells him they will have something afterwards.

When everything is sold, they sit on the bench outside the inn to eat their lunch. And then he hears a man speaking.

'It was more than speaking, it was words made into song, and song made into words,' Arun says. 'When I asked my mother what it was, she told me the man was a poet, and that he was reciting poetry. There was a strange look on her face as she said it, but I was too busy listening to take much notice. I remember . . .'

. . . getting to his feet as the words of the poet turn in the air like – what? – glittering jewels, the ones in the storybook his mother reads to him and his sister? No, like taking flight. As the poet finishes speaking the boy turns to his mother, but her eyes are distant. He can almost sense her walking back down a long road until she stands next to him once more.

'I lost her for a moment,' Arun says. 'And I felt lost and found at the same time. When I got home, I couldn't stop thinking about this magical thing, poetry.'

His throat tightens. He knows the boy's heart was never the same after that. After a moment, he looks back to where he is following his father into the hut.

His mother's face is unusually grave. Did the fish trap give him away? Did they overhear him as he stood trying words in his mouth, adding cloud to sky, mountain to valley, hoping they would flower? Maybe Kara told them. The boy glances around crossly, but she is nowhere to be seen. Then he finds out it has nothing to do with the poet. His father is saying it is time for him to start learning a trade. He is to be apprenticed to a man in the village, Liso, a leatherworker. He expects the boy to work hard and do what he is told. When he is done he gives his usual nod to indicate the end of the conversation, and goes out.

The boy stands very still, stunned and bewildered. Doesn't he work already? He looks after the chickens, feeding them, collecting eggs, avoiding the one with the sharp beak. He helps with the vegetables, too, digging for potatoes and pulling up carrots. And he does his chores. Well, only when reminded, but it still counts. He looks to his mother for help, but knows instinctively that in this matter there is no gainsaying his father's word.

Two days later, he walks by himself into the village and goes up to a door bleached by the sun. His knock is answered by a man wearing a leather apron. He fills the doorway, outlined against the room behind.

'Yes?' he says.

The boy can hardly speak. Behind him is a sunny day; ahead lies doom. 'My father sent me,' he manages, his voice thin and high.

The man looks him up and down. 'You must be Arun. Well, Arun, I'm Liso, but you already know that. You'd best come in.'

It is dark in here, and smoky. Liso takes him through

to a larger room with a long workbench cluttered with tools and pieces of leather. Lengths of folded leather fill the shelves, and leather shavings litter the floor. The smell is not unpleasant. He is told to sit on a stool while Liso tells him about his trade.

'My father was paying him to teach me and I was supposed to be grateful,' Arun says. He smiles slightly, remembering what Yorin said about gratitude. He'd called it a lingering illness. 'Liso wasn't an unkind man. He just had work to do, and money to worry about. He was a good teacher, and he taught me well, although I didn't appreciate it at the time. I cared more about the fact that my back was aching and I'd rather be playing outside.'

He watches the boy bending over the bench, trying to write as fluently with his tools as Liso does. From time to time he looks up at the sound of passing voices, sighs, and returns to his work.

'After that, I tried not to think about poetry,' Arun says. 'What was the point? I'd almost succeeded when I heard the poet again. He returned to the village that autumn. I was getting ready to walk home when I saw him in the square. He was sitting by the well, with people crowded round him. I stood at the back, hoping no one would notice. When he began to speak, I was filled with grateful wonder.'

For a moment he is silent. 'There aren't words for it, because the right words were the words of the poem, and I can't remember them all. But he spoke to me afterwards, when everyone else had drifted away to their houses and their evening meals.'

His thoughts are falling from memory's height, the words of the poet rising to meet them. *Don't just look – see. Don't just listen – hear.* For a moment he is a boy scuffing the dust, squinting up at the tall man who nods and walks away, back to the inn. He smiles wryly. 'I didn't really know what he meant, but it felt as if I'd been given something extraordinarily precious. I had to tell someone, so I told my sister. I'm not sure she understood either, but she came up with a game called *Don't*.'

He laughs. 'One of us would point to something – a flower, a stone, a chicken – and the other would have to try and describe what they saw or heard. We probably thought we were marvellous, and why not? We'd invented imagination, and nothing could stop us.'

As he stares into the pool, he is returned to a day in spring where he is standing beside the almond tree and his mother is kneeling, talking to him quietly. She is explaining why he can't go to hear the poet in the village that evening. His father waits in the doorway of the hut.

That's it; the festival of *fahruz* is here again, in praise of green shoots, leaf and flower. When the boy found out the poet had returned for the festival, he asked to be allowed to attend the midnight recital. His father refused, saying it was too late, although it was a holiday and there was no work the following day. There was shouting, and tears. As day cools into twilight, the mood lingers like mist.

His sister is nowhere in sight. He suspects she is in her house in the shrubs, a small cluster of bushes not far from the hut. He tried knocking once, feeling silly, but there was no answer, so he pushed his way in. There was no sign of his sister, but on the ground he found a small stuffed animal and a red button in the shape of a bird. He had never seen the button before, and wondered where it came from. When his sister found out, she went to their mother and told her. The boy was made to apologise and promise not to do it again.

Arun takes a deep breath. He knows it wasn't a proper apology, that it hurt his sister's feelings. He thinks of the red button, and what it must have meant to her. What it means to him. He wishes he could ask her forgiveness.

Through half-closed eyes he sees the boy creep out when everyone is asleep. He takes the path round the wheatfield, to the village. He has never been out this late before. The night sounds have him half out of his skin; soft movements, a rustle, a shriek. By the time he reaches the edge of the village, his shirt is wet and he is panting with the effort of not running.

The market square is crowded with people. There are spiced cakes, grilled meat dripping with juices, jugs of apricot cordial. Torches blaze and eyes are shining. As he moves closer to the middle of the square, he looks around to make sure Liso isn't there.

A sudden rise of sound. The poet has emerged from the inn. The boy cranes through the crowd, trying to catch a glimpse, then slips through to the front. The poet is seated at the well, his flowing robes gleaming with gold. He scans the crowd, a half-smile on his face. The square falls silent, and he begins.

It is a full-hearted story of love, desire, loss and finding. It involves a red jewel, a magician, and a pair of lovers. As the poet speaks, threads gather and a pattern appears, delicate, then dazzling. When he reveals the magician's plot and the way the lovers confound it, the crowd becomes one body, enchanted. The sky fills with a shower of stars and a golden moon made from nothing more than a kiss. In utter silence he brings the tale to an end. Then, uproar. He is raised on the shoulders of village men and paraded round the square. Flowers are thrown, and coins. The boy thinks there can be no finer moment than this.

He walks home spellbound, forgetting to be scared. When he reaches the hut he steals in quietly, going to the corner where the curtain is drawn across two low beds. His sister doesn't stir. Just as he is falling asleep, he remembers to worry about being found out.

Chapter Two

As the week passes, the boy's sense of unease begins to fade. He walks to Liso's house each morning, returning in the evening with pricked fingers and words running through his head. He loves this time of year, green tips misting the wheatfield, buds starting to open on the almond tree.

It is his day off, and he is helping his mother peel apples for a pie when his father returns from the village. He is not a big man, but he seems to fill the doorway of the hut. He has found out. The boy knows it from the look on his face. His mother puts down the peeling knife. In a quiet voice his father says that one of the village women saw him at the *fahruz*, and what does he have to say about it?

'There was no point denying it,' Arun says. 'He was furious. When he finished shouting, I was told that as I clearly couldn't be trusted, he would walk me to Liso's house each morning, and my mother would walk me back. This would cause a great deal of inconvenience which – in case there was any doubt – began and ended with me. Then he gave me a look of utter disgust, and went out. My mother tried to comfort me, but I was too angry and upset.'

He shakes his head. 'At that moment I decided I was going to run away, find the poet and follow him.'

'But you didn't,' Night says.

The memory turns stiffly in Arun's mind. 'No, I didn't. Something happened.'

That evening, a man from the village calls at the hut with a letter. It is such an unusual occurrence that the boy and his sister stand rooted to the spot, but are shooed out by their father. They hover at the door, trying to listen, but the voices inside are too quiet to make out.

Dinner is eaten in silence, but later the boy's mother calls him and his sister to her side. She tells them their grandmother – their father's mother – is ill, and is asking for their father. To the boy, his grandmother is someone remote, in age and time. Fish traps and grasshoppers, almonds and honeycakes hold more interest than someone he has never met. All the same, he feels a sense of occasion the following morning as his mother packs a bag with a whole cheese, a loaf of bread, dried meats, some fruit. She fills a water bottle with peach juice, and gives his father a small trinket for safe travelling.

His father gives him a nod and kisses his sister before setting out. As they watch him walk away, the boy realises he has no idea where his grandmother lives. Until now, he hadn't quite believed she was real. When he tells his mother, she smiles, saying of course his grandmother is real, or how would his father have been born? The boy goggles at his sister. Their father, with his calloused hands and sun-creased eyes, a baby?

Their mother starts laughing at the look on their faces. 'I was a young girl once,' she says.

'Tell us,' his sister says eagerly.

The boy is due at Liso's, but they plead so hard their mother relents. She tells them she was brought up in a village far away by her mother, who was strict but kind. She was made to work for her keep, and that was a good thing. She never felt she was a burden because she was able to help her mother. Her gaze rests briefly on the boy.

'My mother raised me well,' she says. 'She was there for me, even if I didn't always appreciate it at the time.' She smiles at them, but there is faint sadness in her eyes.

'My father was away for a week,' Arun says. 'My mother walked me to and from Liso's house, and the time I spent with her felt not like a punishment but something special, shared only by us. When my father returned he hugged me and my sister, which was unusual. We sat at the table, waiting to hear his news, but all he said was that his mother had left him some money, enough for new seed, a few more chickens, some things for the house. That was it. Nothing more.

'One good thing came out of it, though.' He smiles briefly. 'Either my father had forgotten about escorting me to Liso's, or it no longer mattered. Whatever the case I didn't mention it, and nor did my mother. But I went there every day for just over two years. Apart from my one day off a week, of course. It might have been my life, if it hadn't been for –'

He stares off into the darkness.

The boy is perched on his stool at the workbench, mending the strap of a leather bag. His stitching is as good as Liso's now, neat and even. His mind is wandering in the crisp autumn air when he hears a gasp, and turns to see Liso with a strange look on his face. One hand holds an awl, the other clutches his chest as he falls slowly forward onto the bench.

After a moment, the boy gets up and looks at him. He knows men can sometimes end up face down when they spend too long at the Poplar – he has heard his father complaining about them – but, as far as he knows, Liso doesn't go to the inn. 'Keeps himself to himself.' His father's approving tone made the boy think it could only be a bad thing.

Cautiously, he approaches. Liso seems to be keeping very much to himself. There is a quality to his stillness the boy has never experienced before. He thinks of his father's silent concentration as he stands on the bank of the stream, watching for fish. It is as if something has been suspended, but can at any moment come back to life. When his sister sleeps it is a living pause, returned in an instant when he tickles her nose with a feather or a blade of grass.

This is different. Not a suspension or a pause, but something that cannot be resumed. The boy has never witnessed a death before, but he feels its presence now. A wave of sickness comes over him. He slides from his stool and stumbles out of the house.

People soon come running. He is vaguely aware of someone putting an arm around him, a woman leading him away. She takes him past the well to a house beyond, sits him down and gives him something to drink. He sips numbly as she talks in a soothing voice, telling him the grace of a quick taking is better than a lingering one.

And now someone is kneeling in front of him, taking his hands and talking quietly. His mother. A man has run from the village to fetch her. Her quiet voice is drawing heat from the wound. When they leave, he does his best not to look back across the square.

At home, his sister is full of questions about what happened, but his mother hushes her gently. When his father returns – he has, his mother says, been to Liso's house – he looks at the boy and puts a hand on his shoulder. Only for a moment, but the boy never forgets.

The funeral is held later that week. He has never been to one before, and stands close to his family as he listens to what is being said by Iden, the headman. The tone is as grave and beautiful as the words, which are neither prose nor poetry but the sum of both. There is talk of creation, of how the world is full of the living and the dead, of hope and peace. The boy wonders if Liso is at peace, and if he is still working on the belt he was finishing just before he died. He feels a rush of affection for him, made from the place and the moment, but real nonetheless.

At home, the family are quiet. The boy's mother hums softly as she prepares dinner, his father works in the vegetable plots. He looks for his sister but she is not there, so he goes to the house in the shrubs and asks to be let in. When he crawls into the dim green space and sits back on his haunches, he sees she has been crying. His sister never cries. Confounded, he asks why.

'Don't you know?' she says accusingly. He shakes his head. 'It'll happen to all of us. We're all going to die. You, me, Mother and Father.' She chokes back a sob.

The boy saw a dead bird on the riverbank once; he and his sister took it away and buried it. It never occurred to him that the same thing could happen to the people he loves. Shaking his head angrily, he leaves the shrubs.

Arun takes a deep breath. 'It was as if a shadow had fallen. I haunted my mother's footsteps for some time afterwards. I think she understood, because that was when she told us the story of the fisherman, his wife and the sea-child.'

'And did you write it down?' Night asks.

Arun closes his eyes and sees a dark-blue leather notebook embossed with golden suns and silver moons. He stares into the pool. Then he says, 'A few days after the funeral, I slipped out of the hut one night and went back to Liso's house. I don't know why; I just felt drawn to it. Everything was untouched: the sheets of leather, the tools, all gathering dust. For some reason, it moved me more than the funeral. The bag I was mending when Liso died was still on the floor, so I picked it up and started stitching. When it was done and the strap was secure, I laid it on the workbench, went out, closed the door, and started walking.'

The boy walks rapidly past the village houses with their lamplight and cooking smells. Music is coming from the Poplar, and he stops for a moment to listen. The door opens, light spills out and a man lurches into the market square. The boy presses into the shadows as he passes, then crosses the square, staying close to the houses. He has never gone this way before, through the village and out to who knows where, but as he walks an idea forms in his head. The decision to go looking for the poet –

25

so long ago, it seems – was taken out of his hands and subsequently forgotten. Why not now?

A bird shrieks in the moonless night, and his heart contracts. He falters, then pushes on, increasing his pace. Another cry, this time from the other side of the path. He stops dead. Something rustles in the shadows; terror floods in. He turns and starts running, back through the village, on to the path to the hut, tripping and stumbling, until he reaches the door and stands gasping and soaked in sweat.

It is a strange feeling, being on this side of the door at night. He remembers the last time, coming back from the *fahruz*. Slipping in, he creeps across the floor to the corner. He is settling down when a whisper makes his eyes fly open.

'About time,' his sister hisses.

In the morning – blessed day, the boy thinks as he wakes – his sister says nothing about what happened. He is so thankful to be under the sun, beside the stream, looking up at the ever-present mountains, that he forgets to mind.

After a drink from the water bottle Arun says, 'She waited until the next day before asking me about it. We were in the house in the shrubs, and she asked me where I'd gone. I could never lie to her – her eyes were like lamps that shone into you. So I told her I'd tried to run away to find the poet. I expected her to laugh but she didn't, she just went very quiet, then asked how I thought our parents would feel when they found out I'd run away.

'She went straight to the point, as always. She may have been younger than me, but she was much wiser. She told me to wait until the poet came back to the village, and ask him.' He smiles briefly. 'It hadn't occurred to me. And then we started arguing about where poets live. She said it would have to be somewhere beyond the mountains, because that was where those kinds of words came from.

'When I asked her how she knew, she said, as if explaining to an idiot, that we only heard them when the poet came. Or the singers and musicians at the winter *tyrianth*, "when the flower blooms in the fire". And they all came from somewhere else, didn't they?

'At that point I was probably feeling so many things I was in danger of bursting. Astonishment – where did the quote come from, and how did she know it? – resentment, for the same reason – jealousy, ditto – outrage – why should we live in lyrical darkness? – and, above all, bitter disappointment. If it was true our valley had no such words, that they had to be carried over the mountains from who knows where, what hope was there for me?'

He clears his throat. 'Life went on, but the idea wouldn't leave me. If anything, it grew stronger. I tried to shake it off, but I couldn't.' He sighs. 'It's a cliché – and I know how much you like clichés,' he adds before Night can interrupt, 'but I never appreciated how lucky I was. Until the apprenticeship, I was never really put to work. There was always time to play with my sister, to sit beside the stream. I think my mother had a hand in that.'

After a long silence he says, 'I remember the winter being unusually cold. Which meant, for me and my sister, warm milk and games indoors. From time to time I wondered what apprenticeship my father would come up with next, but I soon forgot about it. But I couldn't settle. Sometimes I'd go out early, stand beside the almond tree and look up at the mountains. Dawn gave them colours I couldn't find words for, and I'd be reduced to thinking *red, orange, pink*, and feeling like a failure.

'When I told my sister I wanted to be a poet she didn't laugh or mock me, she just looked sad. At the time I didn't know why, but I think it's because she thought it would take me away from our family. That because of it we'd end up broken.'

He takes a ragged breath. For a long time he stares at the moon in the pool, but finds no comfort there. When he looks up again he says, 'Things were much simpler then. Happiness was a full stomach, a warm bed, my mother's cream sauce.'

The boy's mouth is watering as his mother stirs the pot carefully since, she tells him, cream is like silk. Too heavy a hand and it will tear. He has never seen silk before. He asks his mother if she has, and she nods.

'My mother gave me a piece. It was only a scrap, but it was lovely. She kept it in a box under her bed. She didn't think I knew about it.' She smiles. 'I must have been about seven years old, playing hide-and-seek with my friends, and I crawled under the bed to hide. It was cramped, and after a while I stretched out, trying to get comfortable, and touched something with my foot. I was reaching back to feel what it was when a hand came groping under the bed, so I had to come out.'

The boy has forgotten about the cream sauce. 'I was determined to find out what it was, of course,' his mother says. 'It wasn't easy – my mother was usually in the house, and she took me with her to market. But this time, when I said I had a bad headache, she believed me. She never normally did – you were either healthy, or dead.' They both laugh. His mother grows serious again. 'You have to remember that if I was ill it could mean not only the expense of a healer, but that my mother would have to do all the work herself. So she wasn't really being unfeeling.'

The boy nods gravely, feeling very grown up.

'When she'd gone out, I crept back under the bed, and found a wooden box. I don't know what I expected, treasure, perhaps, but inside' – his mother looks away for a moment, remembering – 'I found a button in the shape of a bird, and a piece of cloth. The button was made of red coral, and the eye was a tiny pearl. It looked almost real. The cloth was very fine, sky-blue with sprays of silver flowers, each with a sequin like a mirror at its heart. I didn't know it then, but it was silk of the finest weave, worked with silver thread.'

She stirs the sauce thoughtfully. The boy thinks of his incursion into the house in the shrubs. Now he knows where the button came from.

His mother puts down the spoon and wipes her hands on her apron. 'I didn't know what to do about it. I couldn't ask my mother because she'd know I'd looked in the box. When she died, she left it to me. But it couldn't speak to me.'

She looks at the boy. 'Don't be a servant of silence,' she says, and reaches for a cloth to lift the pot from the fire.

Arun looks thoughtfully into the darkness. 'At the time, I didn't understand what my mother was trying to tell me. I thought she meant I shouldn't let it get the better of me, so I decided the best way to send it packing was to be noisy. So I was, and was probably insufferable, because a few days later she took me with her to market. My sister refused to come because' – he smiles slightly, but his eyes are sad – 'she said she didn't want her nose to drop off with the cold. I think she just wanted a bit of peace and quiet.'

He watches the boy and his mother set off down the path, laden with baskets.

When they reach the square, there are men outside the inn. They are mounted on hardy little horses and wear heavy furs. As the boy helps his mother set out her goods, he asks who they are.

'Men who have no business to be here,' she says. The boy is shocked. He has never heard his mother say anything bad about anyone, and certainly not about strangers.

'Why?' he asks, but his mother shakes her head.

Business is brisk, and they pack up early. As a treat, his mother buys meat patties. As they sit on the bench outside the Poplar to eat them the boy glances about warily, but he can't see the riders.

'Why don't they have any business to be here?' he asks.

'They're not peaceful men,' his mother says. 'They take what they want, and they leave.' She strokes his face reassuringly. 'They've gone now, and that's all that matters.'

But later that day the boy and his sister are called to the table, sat down and told that from now on they are not to go into the village on their own, but are to stay close to the hut.

'Do you understand?' His father looks at him sternly, and he gives a sullen nod.

His mother is watching him. 'Promise me,' she says.

Grudgingly, he does. His sister seems unconcerned. She has always been happy to remain within the locality of the hut.

'I think she knew what mattered to her, even then,' Arun says. 'Unlike me. My father's edict made me resent him even more, but for once I obeyed – not for him, but because of the look on my mother's face.

'By the following spring, my parents must have decided the riders weren't coming back – Leta, the innkeeper's wife, seemed to know about these things, and my mother often stopped for a chat when she'd finished at market – because my father finally sent me into the village on my own. He told me he was trusting me with a very important errand, a great responsibility. I was to collect some seeds.'

He gives a short laugh. 'Hardly something a thirteen-year-old boy would consider important, but it didn't matter. I was just happy to be allowed out on my own again.'

It feels good to be walking along the path, listening to birdsong, snuffing the air. When he reaches the village the boy stands in the market square, breathing in woodsmoke and roasting meat. He has strict instructions not to dawdle but to go straight to Kerel's house, get the seeds and give him the money, in that order. On no account is he to hand over the money first. If Kerel quibbles, the boy is to give back the seeds and come straight home.

He finds Kerel's house on the corner of the square, and stands looking at the peeling front door.

'Going to see old moneybags?' someone passing says with a laugh. 'He'd give it all up for a perfect rose.'

The boy is too busy staring at the door to wonder what he means. When he knocks, a chair scrapes across the floor. The door opens. The man standing before him is tall and broad, with a large belly and a frown.

'About time,' he says. 'Well, come in then.'

The boy's mouth is dry, but he is determined to show his father he can get something right. He is ushered into a room, directed to a chair and told to sit. He sits, looking about. A fire blazes in the hearth. The room is very warm, cluttered with books and sheaves of paper, cloaks, boots, sacks and pouches, but what catches his attention is a large cabinet occupying most of the left-hand wall.

'The money?' Kerel says.

The boy holds out the pouch. He can't bring himself to say what his father told him to say. Kerel takes the pouch, unties it, tips coins into his hand. He nods. 'Good. Want a drink?'

The boy mutely accepts the beaker he offers. The apple juice is cool and spicy. He starts to breathe again, his eyes drawn irresistibly to the cabinet. The doors are carved with animals he has never seen before.

'Come and see,' Kerel says. Clutching the beaker, the boy stands looking.

'See these?' Kerel points to a pair of long-necked, big-eyed creatures. 'Like swans of the earth. And this' – a heavy beast, wide and tall, with large ears and a nose so long the boy wonders how a sneeze would ever get out – 'it's like a moving house.'

When he opens the doors the boy sees many small drawers, each with a label on the front. Kerel pulls out a drawer and removes a paper envelope. 'Tell your father they're the best he'll get.' He gives the boy an appraising look. 'Hasn't told you what they are, has he?'

The boy shifts awkwardly. Kerel opens the envelope, selects a seed and puts it in his hand, thrusting it under the boy's nose. There is dirt in the creases of his palm. The seed is large, green-black with ivory stripes. 'Sunflowers,' he says. 'For your mother.' He puts his nose to the seed and sniffs.

In spite of his nervousness, the boy asks what he is doing.

'Haven't you ever used your nose? It can tell you a good deal.' The boy, sniffer in the hoof of morning, breather-in of sunset like a flower, nods. Kerel tips the seed back into the envelope. 'Seeds have their own smell. It tells you what's green and growing, and what's not up yet. If you know what you're doing, of course. There isn't a plant I can't read.'

He opens another drawer. 'These, for example' – he shakes fine black grain into his hand – 'they're almost ready for planting, but not quite. They're temperamental.' He cups his hand and tips the seeds back into the envelope. 'They'll stay there until I find the right buyer.' He laughs at the look on the boy's face. 'What did you expect? It's hard enough to make a living. I can't afford to go soft over flowers.'

The boy blinks. The room is beginning to darken. He blinks again. Everything is swimming around him.

A hand clasps his shoulder. 'Best sit down,' Kerel says, and leads him to a chair. He leaves the room, returning with a jug and a slice of cake on a plate. He fills the boy's beaker. 'Drink up.' The boy drinks. 'You'd better eat this, too.' The cake is heavy and rich. The boy eats it all, takes another drink, and wipes his mouth.

'Hunger can do that to a man,' Kerel says. 'Feeling better?' The boy nods. Kerel jerks his head towards the cabinet. 'Want another look?'

Each label has writing on it, some almost too faded to read. 'Names and dates,' Kerel tells him. 'Some of these seeds keep for years. They're much wiser than we are. If the time isn't right, they won't germinate. They go into themselves for a long sleep. And when it is, they feel it, and start to wake up.

'It's true, boy. Just because we keep going in all weathers doesn't mean other things have to. This one' – he points to a drawer – 'has been here for two years. Someone kept promising to pay me. They never did. Maybe I'll plant it myself one day. The scent's supposed to be so intoxicating no woman can resist it. Must be worth the price, eh?'

The boy blushes, and asks where he finds the seeds. With an appraising look Kerel pulls up a chair, and nods to him to do the same.

'All sorts of places,' he says. 'Places you haven't heard of – places I hadn't heard of until I got there. There's a river valley' – he leans back with half-closed eyes – 'where lilies grow. Not the biggest, but the finest – petals soft as

34

air, scent so alluring a man could forget everything and just lie there, day after day, transported. A man told me where to find them. Bit of a villain, I didn't really believe him, but I paid him anyway, and off I went. My horse wasn't happy about it – we had to cross a pass infested with those black-and-white creatures that tear the heart out of you when they call to each other – and skipped up the rocks like a mouse.

'My horse is something of a coward. Fine on the road, with the sun leading the way and nothing in front but a parcel of pilgrims, but take him off the path and he goes to pieces. I've tried schooling him, showing him the stick, bribing him with apples, but nothing works.'

He shakes his head, smiling wryly. 'We got through the pass, and up we went. When we reached the top – there were times when I had to get off and walk because we were nearly vertical – both of us stopped, me because I was dumbstruck, my horse because he'd run out of steam.

'Imagine this, boy, you're up on high, nothing around you but walls of stone, then the sky opens and you find yourself eye to eye with clouds so close you could step onto them, and the land drops and keeps on dropping, and far below is a river, silver as your mother's bangle, laying down in pastures and flower meadows, and beyond it great cliffs carved with the figures of giants. I could almost fancy them watching me make my way down as the heat rose and perfume gathered in seams of air, and I had to hold on to the front of the saddle to stop myself falling. I was falling through the air, see, in my head.

'When I reached the valley floor, I don't know what came over me. I got off my horse, flung myself on the ground and lay there staring up until I nearly floated right out of my head. My horse put a stop to it, gave me a hard nudge and reminded me why I'd come. So I got up, brushed down my clothes, and looked about. The grasses were taller than they looked from above, thigh-deep. All I could hear was my beating heart and the swish of grass as we passed.'

The boy listens, captivated. There is a strange, almost private smile on Kerel's face.

'As we made our way across the valley I knew I was going to find something special. The further I went, the taller I seemed to get, but it was only the grass getting shorter. And then I was in meadows of flowers that only grew in that place, at that season, and I was trying to look everywhere at once, at the flowers, at the river beyond with the sun breathing off it, making the air quiver. I was looking so hard I tripped, fell face down, and started to laugh. And I'm not a man much given to laughing.

'And then I sobered up. Or remained drunk. All I know is I got up, made my way to the river, knelt on the bank and looked across. Out in the middle was a small island. In the centre, like the island's eye, was a stand of lilies. Not white, not ivory or pearl, but a colour you can only imagine. I could go into rhapsodies, make comparisons, but this was a flower, not a woman, without all the problems that go with them.

'I sat down on the bank and stared. The harder I looked, the more I became convinced the stone giants were coming closer, the cloud ceiling was lowering, the grasses were on the move. I don't know what it was – the heat, the beauty, the stillness – but I found myself unable to get up. I started thinking about a girl I'd known once, and almost married. Her parents weren't impressed with me, and didn't bother to hide it. A wanderer, a man who hunts plants, not someone who plants seed in his own fields. They told me if I wanted to marry their daughter I'd have to settle down, give up plant-hunting, find a plot of land and cultivate it. The making of bread, the tucking-in of hens at night, that was what made the days turn.'

Kerel looks sombre. 'I talked with her about it. I hoped she'd see that what I was offering was also a life, not bread or hens, but still worthwhile. I asked her to go with me on my travels. She said – it was that part of evening falling into night, the first stars coming out – that although she loved me, she also loved her parents, and because of that she couldn't go.

'Ah,' he says, 'I was so sure of myself. So sure she'd see the fairy tale in what I did, not the flies or the heat or the filthy clothes. I kept trying to persuade her, with words that did their best to turn into flowers. With tears, eventually. Yes, boy, I cried, and I'm not ashamed to say so. If your feelings are true, why not? Men have cried over worse things.'

He is silent for a moment. 'I left her parents' house, went to an inn and proceeded to prove them right. When I woke up in a patch of weeds, I thought I was dying.' He makes a face. 'That, boy, is what it's like to be in love. And beer. I could hardly stand; a merchant and his wife who were taking the air gave me a wide berth. I can still see her face, one eyebrow lifted, pretending I wasn't there.

'That was the day I gathered up my things and got on my horse, who hasn't stopped complaining since. That's the way of horses, and if you're wise, you'll ignore them. Otherwise, their aching hooves and heaving flanks will convince you to carry them on your back. And that, boy, is something you should never do. Life's hard enough.'

He shifts a hip, stretching slightly. 'I travelled,' he says, 'as long and hard as I could. There were times when I thought of her, I couldn't help it, the night does that to you. But it made me what I am, for better or worse. And put me on a riverbank, on the ground, staring at a bunch of lilies.

'It was my horse who saved me. He stuck his head in the river. He's a snorter when he drinks, smacks his lips and shares it around. Being pelted with river water and drool brought me to my senses. I took off my boots and waded in. It wasn't too deep, and there was sand under my feet, not mud, thankfully. I've never been able to stand mud between my toes. I went forward, holding up my arms, until I couldn't feel the bottom, and then I started swimming. It didn't take long to get to the island, and when I reached it I realised I'd left my collecting-bag on the bank.

'I had to swim back, of course, and lay on the bank letting my clothes dry in the sun. When I'd got to the island, one touch had set it bobbing. It was no more than a confection of rushes laced together with roots, hardly strong enough to hold a man. Getting on, and staying on, was going to be tricky. I thought about throwing a rope around it and dragging it back to the riverbank. Then I felt ashamed of myself. Here I was, in this enchanted place, wanting to tie off the magic and let it die.

'I sat up and saw the stone giants watching me. I told myself they couldn't do anything, they were carved into the rock. Then I started wondering, if you're set in stone, only able to look one way, does it make you think in one direction as well?

'At that point I splashed my face with water. Something about the place was making me feel sleepy. I lay back down and told myself I'd have a doze, just for a bit. I don't know how long I slept, but I woke with a start because something bit me. I thought it was a midge, or one of those flies that get redder as they fill with blood, but it wasn't. It was my horse. I was so angry I jumped up and started to tell him what I thought of him, but the beast stood his ground. He looked from me to the river, then back again. And again, from me to the river, and back. It was only when he knelt down that it finally dawned on me. I got on his back, and we swam across.

'After that, it was a matter of slipping onto the island, trying to keep my balance as I walked over to the lilies, feeling under the squelch and reed-straw for bulbs. When I found one I lifted it out as carefully as I could, wrapped it in a damp cloth and put it in my collecting-bag. Just one – no need to be greedy. I held that bag tight, and when we got to the bank I laid it on the ground and made a prayer in front of it.

'Yes, boy, I made a prayer,' he says without embarrassment.

'What did you pray for?' the boy asks tentatively.

Kerel eyes him for a moment. 'I could have asked for the bulb to grow into a queen of lilies whose offspring graced a palace and filled my pockets with gold. I could have prayed for fame and glory. But' – his mouth twists slightly – 'I prayed for the strength to return home. There are times when what's offered can seem irresistible. That's when you need to turn around and leave.'

Whichever way he looks at it, the boy can't work it out. 'You'll understand one day,' Kerel says. 'I got out of that place in the nick of time. I kept feeling something wasn't right. At the top of the hills I stopped and looked down. The valley was full of mist, moving as if it knew what it was doing. I turned away, and never went back.' He shivers. 'Still does it, after all these years.'

'Can I see it?' the boy asks eagerly. 'The bulb, I mean.'

Kerel laughs. 'Sold it, and made my fortune. It's perfuming the chamber of some rich man's wife, no doubt – not just rich, mind you, but possessed of so much gold he had to have his treasury floor strengthened.'

The boy looks at him in wonder. 'Sounds good, eh?' Kerel says. 'It means nothing in the end. What matters is what can't be bought, like kindness. I know you don't believe it now, but you will. And one person who knows all about kindness is your mother.'

He smiles at the boy's bewildered face. 'As soon as I sold the bulb I came back here, and all the things I'd stuffed under the bed started coming out.'

The boy doesn't understand.

'The girl I told you about. I'd put it away and thought that was that. Looking back, she'd never have survived a life with me, but at the time I was too much in love, and too selfish, to see it. Love can do that, make you selfish. You think you're offering something so wonderful she'll jump at the chance of sharing it, and it's only later –'

40

He looks down at the floor. 'When I got back, that particular ghost was waiting for me. There I was, standing in my house with my satchel in one hand and a saddlebag full of coins in the other, and it wasn't the weight of the gold that made me sink to my knees. You can't imagine what it's like, boy, and I hope you never have to. Four walls and a roof, but no home.'

Beside the pool, Arun briefly closes his eyes. When he looks back again, the boy is asking Kerel about his mother.

'It was market day,' Kerel says, 'and your mother was passing by my door. She must have heard the racket I was making. The next thing I knew, she was sitting me on a chair and making tea. She stayed for quite a while, talking to me, not about anything in particular, just little bits of news, but a comfort nonetheless. When I'd drunk my tea, she washed up and said she'd be back tomorrow. And she was, with a basket of food, and cloths for cleaning. Dust was the least of my worries, but a clean floor and a bright fire make a difference. I was never one for hearthsides, mind you, but it kept me from myself. Don't look for enemies beyond the mountains, boy, guard against those inside yourself.'

Before the boy can give the words due consideration, Kerel says, 'Your mother visited me regularly for some time after that. I found myself telling her about the girl and her family. She was good listener, patient and understanding. It all came out, including a good deal of anger and pain. My parents had given up on me when I was a boy – looking back, I can see why. I wouldn't do what they asked, had no friends, just wanted to be left alone. Maybe I thought I wasn't worth more than that, I don't know. But the more they scolded, the more I fought.

41

'Eventually I ran away. I don't know if they tried to find me, and I wouldn't blame them if they didn't. I got by doing odd jobs, bits and pieces of work, never apprenticed – no one would take me on.' He glances shrewdly at the boy. 'You don't like the yoke either, but you're fortunate. You have people who care. I had no one, and that was the way I liked it, or so I thought. Until I met –'

He looks away for a moment. 'Your mother put me right. She made me see that the past was the past, and if I kept blaming what I did for what happened, I'd never get on with my life. It took a while for it sink in, but when it did, it was as if a burden had been lifted. My work became an adventure again. Some people are scared of that, I know, and fair play to them. But I suppose I can say I know the value of wonder, now. Amazing what it can do to an angry soul, like a soft word in the ear of the wild. I have my moments, especially when I'm here too long, but I'm more or less content.'

He sits back in his chair and looks at the boy. 'Your mother will be wondering where you are.'

The boy has forgotten about the village, and the valley beyond. 'Please,' he says impulsively, 'take me with you next time you go.'

Kerel laughs. 'I doubt your father would like that. Besides, I'm better off on my own.'

At the door he tells the boy to make friends, play games, be young. 'That's an adventure in itself.'

The boy blinks in the sunlight, surprised to see nothing has changed. He turns back, remembering something he meant to ask, but the door is closed. Half dreaming, he wanders away, thinking about lilies and rooms full of gold. A man on horseback nearly knocks him down, and scolds him for not looking where he is going. Rubbing his arm, he leaves the village in a daze, setting off down the well-worn path.

Chapter Three

When he gets back, it is almost dinner time. He had no idea he'd stayed so long at Kerel's house. As he dries his hands, he can't help comparing the plant-hunter's cluttered room with the clean, cosy warmth of the hut.

'These, please,' his mother says, handing him plates. He watches her move about, testing the meat for tenderness, checking the vegetables, singing softly.

Rose in the garden, bird in the tree,
Love in my heart when he comes to me.

When he asks her to sing more, she tells him it is all she remembers. 'Perhaps you can make up a verse of your own,' she says, turning back to the pot.

Before he can explore the prospect further, his father comes through the door. His clothes are dusty, his face tired. He washes his hands in the bowl his wife has put out, sniffs the air, and smiles. 'Smells good. I could eat an ox.' He dries his hands, pulls out the chair at the head of the table, and sits down. The boy's sister shuffles up the bench until she perches next him. 'Yes, yes,' he says, letting her kiss him. Then he looks at the boy. 'Did you get them?' The boy passes him the bag of seeds, and he calls his wife to his side.

Sensing the importance of the moment, the boy and his sister sit very still. 'You told me once that your favourite flower was the sunflower,' his father says to his mother. 'We've been here ten years now, and I wanted to mark it in some way.'

He asks her to hold out her hand, and tips the seeds into her palm. The boy is watching her closely. A faint blush rises in her cheek, and her eyes are soft. She looks down for a moment, murmuring something. 'Yes,' his father says in a low voice, 'I know. And they'll be the finest in the province.'

The boy is about to take a mouthful of stew when his father turns to him and says, 'It's high time you started earning your keep, Arun. You've been idle too long. I've given it some thought, and you'll be working with me from now on.'

He seems unaware of his son's pale reaction as he dips thick slices of bread into his stew, eating steadily, thanking his wife as she fills his bowl again. 'See this,' he says, gesturing with his spoon, 'it comes from hard work. Your mother's, mine. Now it's your turn. And I mean proper work, none of this dawdling about. You're thirteen, nearly fourteen. Time to make your mark, show me what you're made of.'

The boy wonders miserably if stew is an appropriate accompaniment to the loss of one's dreams. Surely it should be something grander? Fine white bread, rice perfumed with spices and gleaming with flakes of gold leaf. He has learned of such things from the stories his mother tells him. But he is a boy being told by his father that his life will be measured by seed and season, by the onions and potatoes stored in the shed behind the hut. He and his sister have spent many happy hours in the musty quiet, as diamond merchants or pirates. Now it seems like a tomb.

'Well?' His father seems to be waiting for something.

'Let him be,' his mother says gently. 'It's a lot to take in, and it's late.'

But the boy has taken it in and is having difficulty keeping it down. To his father's surprised face he excuses himself, slides off the bench and leaves the hut. He makes his way to his sister's house in the shrubs and drops to the ground, seething with anger. Only that day he travelled far beyond his father and the mountains, and now there is no way round either of them.

A rustling sound makes him turn his head. His sister crawls in beside him. He wipes his face fiercely, and sniffs.

'Look,' she says, but he turns his head away. He knows that tone of voice. The moderator, the writer in sensible ink. 'Father needs help. You know he has trouble with his knees.' The boy wonders if giving them a talking-to would help. 'Besides, you might enjoy it.'

He gives her an incredulous look. Enjoy being chained to the land the whole year round? An image comes to mind, a shining sphere turning the seasons within it. A rose-and-green spring of almond blossom and early lettuce. A summer as golden as wheat. Flame-coloured autumn ripening like pumpkins; silver-black fish in the winter stream. Maybe it won't be so hard, after all.

Bracing his shoulders, he says, 'Did you know that Kerel – the man I got the seeds from – found the most beautiful flowers in the world?'

His sister looks thoughtful. 'You can't eat flowers,' she says.

He stares, thinking her heart has been planted with rows of beans that will keep growing until they smother her, and she will never again give thought to anything but kneading bread and mending clothes.

She is watching him closely. 'You're not going to run away again, are you? There are wolves in the hills, and they'll follow you until you die of tiredness. Then they'll eat you, and Mother will be sad.'

He grins suddenly. 'No. Not today, anyway.' She is his sister, after all. It wouldn't do for her to forget to worry from time to time.

When they return to the hut, their mother is waiting for them. 'Time for bed,' she says. 'I've made some warm milk.'

As she takes away their empty beakers and turns back their blankets, he waits for her to say something about what has happened. She kisses him on the forehead, wishes him goodnight, and draws the curtain across. He is filled with confusion. Where is the thread of sympathy for him to climb up, the words of reassurance?

Arun is silent for a moment. 'I came down to earth with a bump that day,' he says. 'I realised my father's will was what was said and done. The business with Liso began it, and this confirmed it. Perhaps my mother thought she was making it easier in the long run, but it was clear there was nothing more to be said.' He sighs. 'In the end, it didn't matter.'

The next day is market day, and the boy goes with his mother and sister to the village. His mother has persuaded his father, saying that since he will be starting work tomorrow, one last time won't hurt. The air already holds a promise of the warmth to come, but all he can think is that today is his last day of freedom.

The morning moves remarkably fast; too soon, it seems, they are packing up their things and getting ready to go back to the hut. Their mother sits them on the bench outside the Poplar with cups of peach juice. 'I won't be long,' she says, 'I just want a word with Leta.'

When she comes out of the inn, her cheeks are flushed. 'Time to go,' she says, hurrying them away.

She sees them into the hut, goes to the door and calls to their father. He comes at once, stamping his feet, wiping his hands on his trousers. She glances at the boy and his sister, telling them to stoke the fire and put on the kettle for tea. As they work, the boy furtively watches his parents. They are standing close together, his mother's dark hair brushing her husband's shoulder.

At the table, his mother gives them sweet biscuits usually reserved for special occasions. The boy glances at his sister, who raises her eyebrows. His father clears his throat. 'We'll be moving to the village tomorrow,' he says. 'Staying at the Poplar. Just for a while.'

The boy drops his biscuit into his lap. He had always hoped for change, but –

'But what?' Night prompts.

Arun stares at the moon in the pool. '*"Almond blossom will suffice for us."* It was what my mother said when we left. I never found out where it came from. She had her hand on the trunk of the almond tree. As we walked

48

away, I kept looking back. I don't know why. All my life I'd wanted something different, and now I was trying to commit hut, wheatfield, vegetable plots, to memory. Then we were on the village path, and they were gone.

'I found out later that riders had been seen in the area, the ones who'd been in Bishra that day when I went to market with my mother. My parents thought we'd be safer in the village.' He lowers his head.

The innkeeper, Rahn, is waiting for them at the door of the inn. He is small and round, and greets them with a smile. The boy has never been allowed inside the White Poplar before but now here he is, crossing the threshold into a large, clean room with a wooden floor and a fireplace large enough for him to stand in. Leta shows them to their rooms. She is taller than her husband and equally round, with an air of great energy.

'You and Kara are in here,' she says to the boy's mother, 'and Nedrin and Arun are in the room next door.'

The boy hovers in the doorway, watching them unpack. His sister has brought the small stuffed animal from her house in the shrubs, and it perches on the pillow of the well-padded bed.

'Have you unpacked yet, Arun?' his mother asks. 'Good. Now, let's go downstairs and have some lunch.'

The boy and his sister have made a home in a corner of the common room, and play at guessing what people do and where they come from. Some are easier than others: a man in a long black coat and trousers puts a basket on the table and takes out needles, scissors, thread.

'A tailor,' his sister whispers.

'But where from?' he whispers back.

'Ah,' she says mysteriously, 'what if he's not from anywhere?'

'How can he not be from anywhere?' he says, forgetting to whisper. 'He has to be from somewhere.'

'But if it's somewhere we don't know, that makes it nowhere. Which isn't anywhere.' She gives him a smug look.

One of the serving-men brings bowls of chicken broth and he eats, thinking hard. He is about to open his mouth when his mother returns from an errand. Her warm scent mingles with the heat of the common room.

'Don't think I've forgotten,' he hisses. His sister smirks.

His mother secures a strand of hair with a copper-coloured hairpin set with a blue stone in the shape of a flower. She sees him looking. 'Your father gave it to me,' she says, brushing the boy's hair back from his face.

After nearly six weeks at the inn, the novelty is wearing off. The boy finds himself longing for a game of skipstones with his sister. At breakfast that morning, his father announces they will be returning to the hut tomorrow.

'All this coming and going, making sure everything's still in one piece – I'll be glad to get back to normal.'

Arun shakes his head. 'No explanation, no reason why, but that was his way. We were children and didn't need to know, we simply did as we were told. It didn't matter, though. I was going home, and even the thought of working with my father couldn't spoil it.'

For a moment he stares into the water. 'It was also his way of protecting us, although I couldn't see it at the time. But in the end it wasn't enough.'

That afternoon they are standing by the well, waiting for their mother to finish talking to someone she knows, when a man stumbles into the market square. His shirt is stained with sweat and he is gasping for breath. The boy recognises him as a farmer who always buys his mother's cheese when he comes to market. He runs past them to the house where the headman, Iden, lives. People stop and watch as he thumps on the door. It flies open; an exchange of words; Iden bursts out, runs to the well and shouts for everyone to gather round. The boy's mother is calling to his father as she tries to push through the crowd.

The news is brief: a large group of riders is coming through the valley. There is no time for possessions; everyone must leave now, quickly. A great noise breaks over the square. People start shouting and screaming and running. The boy's world turns on the axis of his mother's hand, and he clings to it desperately. Horses are running into the square; metal flashes; hooves pound the dust. He hears his mother cry out, then her grip is broken, and the world's grip breaks too.

Arun bows his head. He can still hear the screams of voices torn from their owners. He closes his eyes and sees a boy being hauled up onto a horse, the horse leaving the village and galloping through the valley. He remembers thinking wildly that he'd always wanted to explore it, and now he is going through so fast he can't see a thing.

Chapter Four

They ride through the valley and into the foothills at a furious pace. The ground rushes past sideways as the horse climbs the slopes without breaking a stride. Everything is sliding away, and all the boy has to hold on to is a stirrup iron and a madman's knee.

Halfway up the mountain, on a small ledge, the man reins in the horse with a jerk, jumps down, spits, walks a little way off, takes something from his pocket and tears off a piece with his teeth. The boy squeezes his eyes shut, trying not to cry. When he opens them he sees, far below, his valley. It is patched with trees and shrubs, and is smaller than he imagined it would be.

When the man returns the boy catches a glimpse of his face, weather-beaten, seamed, unreadable. They set off again, the boy's head and feet bumping against the horse's flanks, the mountain path a swift grey stream.

For a night and a day they travel with barely a break. Every inch of the boy burns with pain. His throat is raw, his stomach cramped with hunger. Birds keen high above, reminding him of a story about an eagle that lived in a cave. He'd forgotten his father told them stories when they were small.

They come down into the foothills at dusk. The slopes are levelling out, the horse's pace steadying. When they finally reach a village, it is dark. The man dismounts, pulls the boy off the horse, sets him on his feet and pushes him into a lamp-lit inn. He gestures to a chair and the boy sits down, looking around warily. The inn is similar to the Poplar, but the people seem harder at the edges, their voices harsher.

A serving-man is putting something down on the table, a wooden bowl with some kind of food in it. The boy looks at it suspiciously. The man stares, picks up the spoon and makes scooping gestures. It is clear he thinks the boy has no idea how to use it. Filled with indignation, the boy snatches it back and digs into the bowl. The food is good, hot and flavoursome, and he eats quickly, then sits staring into the empty bowl.

After a night spent tethered in the corner of a room listening to the snores coming from the bed, he is back on the horse again. As they ride away, it occurs to him that no one has asked why he is being treated this way. Does it have something to do with the sword at the man's side? Clinging to the stirrup, he remembers playing bandits with his sister. When he rode to the rescue, she told him she would have done it better. They argued; she became the bandit and he the sullen prize. Longing comes over him like a sickness.

They travel for some days, passing through canyons, camping on plains. The boy has lost any sense of direction, though he later finds out they were heading south-east.

One morning, on the outskirts of a city, they come to a halt. He has never seen anything like it. Towering stone walls throw shadows out to meet them; banners fly above great bronze gates barred with steel. He is pulled from the horse, set on his feet and pushed into a walk. The guards at the gates have hard, closed faces; metal gleams on their clothes, swords hang at their sides. They barely give him a second glance.

The city stretches beyond the corners of his eyes, filling them with tall stone houses, some white, some washed in soft pastels, with streets leading off in every direction. When they come to a large house with wooden shutters, the man tugs his elbow and he stops. The sign above is decorated with a cluster of red grapes. A serving-man comes out of the door, exchanges a few words with the boy's captor, and leads his horse away.

As they go inside, the man's hand grips his shoulder. In spite of the warm day a fire smokes in the hearth, throwing heat into the gloomy room.

The man gestures, and he sits down. 'Name,' he says. His voice is harsh, and heavily accented. The boy stares at him. 'Name,' he says again, prodding his shoulder roughly.

'Arun Persaba.'

'From?'

'Bishra, in Sund province.'

'Wait,' the man says, and leaves him.

For a moment he thinks of running for the door. Glancing around, he sees a man watching him. Slung over the back of his chair is a cloak of heavy fur. A sour taste fills the boy's mouth. He stares blindly at the table. He is starting to hope his captor has forgotten about him when he becomes aware of someone standing beside him. His first impression is of embroidered robes and a magnificent beard.

'You are Arun?' The man's accent is strange but not unpleasant, his voice as rich as his clothes. The boy nods miserably. 'I am pleased to meet you, Arun. You have had a long journey. You must be tired.'

His apparent concern reduces the boy to sudden tears. Embarrassed, he wipes his face and looks up into small, shrewd eyes. 'I am Kumbar,' the man says, 'the finest merchant in Harakim. You are coming to work for me. It is a good house, and you will learn much.'

The boy tries to speak. He has no desire to work for this man, no matter how kind he seems to be. 'But –' he begins, his voice breaking.

'There is a problem?' Kumbar asks.

With a rush of desperate hope the boy says, 'My family – do you know what happened to them? Do you know where they are?'

The merest pause, then Kumbar says delicately, 'Ah. I am sorry, but they are no longer with us. I am your family now.'

As he follows the merchant through winding streets, the boy sees nothing. He is trying to make sense of Kumbar's words. *No longer with us.* He once overheard someone in his village using the same expression. When he remembers why, a blackness covers his eyes and he stumbles, causing Kumbar to give him an appraising look and take him firmly by the elbow.

'Here we are,' the merchant says, stopping outside an ornate door set in white walls. 'My house.' He ushers the boy into a long, light-filled hall. 'You've never seen any so fine, eh?' he says, nodding at walls hung with carpets woven with elaborate designs of flowers and birds. He leads the boy down the hall to a door set in the left-hand wall. Beyond is a flight of stairs inlaid with jewel-coloured tiles.

'Come,' Kumbar says, and the boy follows him up into a high-ceilinged corridor, its floor covered with a long, flower-strewn rug. Small tables stand at intervals against the walls, and at the far end an arched window of coloured glass rises to the height of the ceiling. The boy is shaking as he follows the merchant into a small room at the end of the corridor.

'This will be your room,' Kumbar says.

Later, when the boy is alone, he will sit on the bed and look at the chair, the chest of drawers, the large blue rug and the high, recessed window.

'You will be well fed, and well clothed. I have my reputation to think about.' Kumbar smiles briefly. 'You are welcome in my house, Arun. Now, let us go downstairs. My stomach tells me it is time for something to eat.'

They sit in a sumptuously furnished room towards the back of the house. It is, the boy will learn, Kumbar's private sitting room. A white-haired woman appears in the doorway. Her dark-green dress, embroidered in yellow at collar and cuff, is immaculate. She looks sharply at the boy.

'Would you bring us some food, please, Tir,' Kumbar says. 'We have a new member of the household, and I am sure he must be hungry.'

Turning to leave, Tir sidesteps to avoid a small girl, who rushes at Kumbar like a whirlwind. He opens his arms and folds her in his robes. She peers out at the boy with no trace of shyness, ducks free, seats herself in a plump armchair and settles down among the cushions to stare at him. He is aware of being weighed up by unblinking cat-like eyes.

'You're scruffy,' she says, twirling a strand of dark-brown hair round her finger, 'and skinny.'

'Now, now,' Kumbar says indulgently.

'Well, he is,' she retorts. 'Never mind, you'll soon get fat. Adara will kill you if you don't finish everything on your plate.' She gives him an impudent smile.

Kumbar is laughing. 'This is Nissa. My daughter. And a public nuisance.' His eyes are filled with affection. The boy bites his lip, determined not to cry in front of this girl.

Tir returns, and starts setting out platters of food. She is accompanied by a young woman carrying a tray of goblets.

'Drinks, please, Tama,' Kumbar says. She fills a goblet of tinted glass with juice from an earthenware jug, and offers it to him. The blue glaze reminds the boy of the colour of the sky above his hut.

The merchant surveys the selection of meats and cheeses, the different types of bread, the clusters of purple grapes. 'Ah,' he says, 'we have been parted for too long.' Before he eats, he dips his fingers in a basin held out by Tir, and dries them on a white linen cloth. Tir offers the basin to Nissa, then the boy.

Breaking off a branch of grapes, Kumbar holds them up to the light. He tells the boy they come from Datur, where the slopes are golden for three-quarters of the year. To drink the wine is to drink sunlight. 'Eat, eat,' he says, but the boy's mouth is dry, and he can feel Nissa looking at him. She manages to eat and watch him at the same time, unabashed in her scrutiny. To escape her gaze, he takes some cheese and sits nibbling unhappily.

After the meal, Kumbar sinks back contentedly in his chair. Tir offers him a fresh basin and he washes and dries his hands. Nissa follows, then the boy. He never washed this much at home. He stares at the floor, gulping back nausea.

'Now,' Kumbar says, 'I told you I am the finest merchant in Harakim. You will come to know this.' He nods at the boy as if agreeing for him. 'You are to be my apprentice.' The boy thinks of Liso, and swallows the lump in his throat. 'Come. Let me show you something.'

The boy follows him down the corridor to a carved wooden door, half-aware of Nissa in train behind. He finds himself in the middle of a large room lined floor to ceiling, wall to wall, with shelves of books.

'This is my accounting room,' Kumbar says, 'and these' – he makes a sweeping gesture with his arm – 'are my treasures. That is how you should think of them. Each is worth more than the labours of many men. Why do you think that is?' The boy stares at him numbly. 'Because they contain information. *Knowledge*. It is this, not gold or silver, not all the jewels in the crowns of kings, that has value beyond price.'

The boy says nothing. Much later he will accuse the merchant of overstating his case and they will argue about it, amicably.

Kumbar takes a black leather book from a shelf. It is tall and rectangular, with gold letters stamped on the spine. He shows it to the boy, who notices stubby fingers enriched with rings. Marks of black ink cover the page. He thinks it must be writing.

Kumbar studies him for a moment. 'Of course you will have to learn to read and write.'

The back of the boy's neck prickles. Humiliation warms his misery as the merchant tells him it is last year's cloth ledger. How many bales were sold each quarter, where they came from, who bought them, how much they cost. He listens without hearing. Bales of cloth mean nothing to him, nor do quarters or costs.

Kumbar is watching him closely. He is not, the boy will learn, someone from whom feelings can easily be concealed. 'This is what matters,' he says, tapping the ledger emphatically. 'Trade is the gut of every city. It enables goods to pass through the body of the world.' The boy makes an involuntary grimace. Kumbar laughs. 'It is a necessary function, essential to the health of commerce.'

Behind him, Nissa is pulling faces. She has clearly heard the speech before.

Arun looks into the darkness. Over the years he has tried to purge his mind of the merchant and his name. Returning to this house is hard, for many reasons. He knows what is going through the boy's head, and feels ashamed.

'I blamed them for a long time afterwards,' he says bleakly. 'My parents. For not teaching me my letters. For showing me up. It didn't occur to me before, but now I couldn't understand why they hadn't. I know now, of course, but then – then, it became something to hold against them, to resent them for. It was a kind of protection against the pain of losing them.'

He shakes his head. 'I became obsessed with learning everything I could. That book was the cry that starts the mountain falling.'

The boy's education begins that afternoon. He is taken to the sitting room to learn how to read and write. He is taught, to his red-faced chagrin, by Nissa. She is younger than him – nearly thirteen, as she informs him – and, worse, a girl. As she opens a book, he burns with resentment. This, she tells him, is the first letter of the alphabet. She makes a sound, and waits expectantly. He sits in mulish silence. She raises her delicate eyebrows and treats him to a look of such superiority he bends his head, stares at the letter and copies the sound, feeling like a sheep in a field.

'Again,' she commands. With a surge of anger he gathers himself, and tries harder. A smirk twitches the side of her mouth. She moves on to the next letter, and the next. When all the noises are beginning to sound the same, she holds up her hand.

'Time for tea,' she says. 'Go and tell Tama. And tell her we want cakes.'

That night he lies awake, staring up at the window. He thinks about trying to escape, but where would he go? No one is waiting for him. He curls into a ball and pulls the covers over his head to muffle the sound of his crying.

The days that follow are busy and full. Each morning, after breakfast, the boy studies with Nissa in the sitting room. She seems to have an endless variety of pretty dresses but her slippers, embroidered with silks of various colours, are always red. He has been given several sets of shirts, tunics and trousers, much finer than his own. At first he resented them. He would rather wear rags and see his family again. Then, with a rush of anger: if he is to be here, in an unknown and unwanted city, trying to learn something

60

designed to torment him, he will not disgrace himself or his family. If fine clothes make him a better scholar, so be it. He will push against the letters until they open.

And, one day, they do. His head is aching, and he feels thick as mud. Nissa has been drilling him over and over again. Behind the wide eyes and dainty features lies a will of iron. He sometimes wonders if she sees his mind as something to be hounded relentlessly until it drops dead, and she can dance on it. He sits staring at the page until a black shape begins to change before his eyes. And then it speaks, saying, *This is what I am.*

He blinks, rubbing his eyes. The shape is forming into a letter, and the letter has a sound, and he is making it without Nissa's prompting. He watches as shape after shape wakes in miraculous transformation until he finds himself in a meadow of letters, running and sniffing the air. He is overcome with dizziness and pride.

'Look,' he says, pointing at a letter and saying it aloud. Nissa seems unimpressed. 'No, look,' he says, going back to the beginning and reading all the letters, up and down, back and forth, faster and faster until she starts giggling. Her laughter is so infectious he can't help joining in. They start chanting, louder and louder, until they make so much noise Kumbar bursts in and stands with his hands on his hips. The boy stops laughing immediately.

'I am trying to work,' Kumbar says, 'and your racket is making it impossible.'

Nissa runs to her father, taking his hand. 'I have taught Arun the alphabet,' she says proudly.

The merchant frowns. 'Show me.' The boy returns to the book and reads the letters again. If Kumbar is

61

impressed, he hides it well. 'Now you must learn to read and write. And quickly.' He turns and leaves the room. The boy suppresses an urge to throw the book after him.

Nissa is undaunted. She knows her father well. 'It took you long enough,' she says. 'Now you can start reading.'

He devours all the books she brings him. For the time he is with them, he almost forgets where he is. If he comes across a word whose meaning he doesn't know, he guesses. Sometimes Nissa scolds, sometimes she creases up with laughter. And when he starts to write, it is a kind of magic to watch the ink form letters that grow into words. It means something else, too, although he can hardly admit it to himself. If he can write, he can write poetry.

But at night he is defenceless against the evils that crawl from under his bed and work their way up his blankets, into his head. Screams, shouts, cries for mercy. He crushes the pillow against his ears, but he still hears them. Sometimes, in dreams, he sees his family, but every day, when morning comes, he loses them again. His heart feels hollow, and at the same time filled with ash. There are sooty marks under his eyes, and he yawns his way through breakfast. If Kumbar is aware of it he says nothing, but keeps the boy busy from light to dark.

Every day, after his lesson, he is sent out for groceries, although Tir and Tama do most of the shopping. At first he resisted, thinking it no task for a boy. Kumbar knew this and sent him anyway. Nissa accompanies him as they walk down the long street to a large market square.

It is much bigger than the one in Bishra, so big the boy can see no end to the stalls of goods or the people surrounding them. Nissa plucks at his shirt – he has grown not to mind – and swoops down like a little bird with a sharp beak and claws. If she wants milk – sheep's milk, which takes some getting used to – she will try first one seller then another, making sure they are watching as she skips from stall to stall.

At first the boy expected them to dismiss her as a small and flighty girl, but he soon learned that each was keen for her custom. This, he worked out, wasn't just because she was Kumbar's daughter; it was a mark against their reputation if she passed them by. To Nissa, it was a game. In the end, she always got the price she wanted. When the boy asked why she couldn't just accept the first one and save her slippers, she stared at him as if he were mad.

'Haven't you learned anything?' she said incredulously. Then, with a toss of her head, 'Besides, it's more fun this way.'

He wondered at Nissa's endless confidence, and how much – how little – thought she gave to the wider world. Deep down, he envied it.

Afternoons are dedicated to numbers. Kumbar emerges from his office to teach the boy himself. On his first day he sat beside Kumbar, impatient to show him what he knew. His ability to add and subtract with his fingers would, he was sure, put Nissa in her place. Taking more interest in the fine cloth of Kumbar's sleeve than the book in the merchant's hand, he waited to impress him.

Kumbar was explaining something to do with multiplying loaves, or barrels; the thread was already lost. Nissa, who had it firmly in her fingers, twitched it expectantly. 'So how many barrels am I left with, Arun?'

the merchant asked. The boy quickly made up a number. 'That would leave me with minus one hundred and sixty barrels of flour. Do you know of anyone who would buy minus one hundred and sixty barrels of flour?'

The boy blushed, and stared at the cool white walls. In bed that night he would wonder why his parents didn't teach him these things, and feel hot and cold with anger and shame.

'Life is made up of many things,' Kumbar was saying, 'the most important being food and shelter. There is nothing better than being able to provide these things for your family, and those who do so should feel proud. Numbers know how to wait their turn. They are wise; they have patience.' Recognising the small kindness, the boy sat more attentively in his chair.

'It is a difficult thing,' Kumbar continued, 'to learn so much so quickly. As a boy I always tried to start in the middle of things, and found it was a good way to get lost.' He summoned Tama for cups of milk, and began again.

What the boy doesn't know, and what Kumbar doesn't tell him, is that he is a fast learner. The merchant is a hard taskmaster, but he flavours the work with real things – rice, wine, timber, grain, goods that keep the port of Harakim turning. The boy doesn't yet know it as a port city, since all he has seen is Kumbar's house and the market square, but from time to time a brisker air blows down the street, making him wonder.

Arun stares out across the clearing. 'Nothing can stop the world from turning,' he says.

'In spite of your efforts,' Night remarks.

'Yes, in spite of them. But it stopped me from dwelling on what I'd lost – for a time, at least. As the months passed, I became better at reckoning than Nissa. Instead of being cross she was pleased, which surprised me. If I'd been in her shoes – her slippers – I'd have been jealous.

'In the evenings, if the merchant was at home – he often had business abroad, as he called it, or visited friends – he'd tell us stories. Not tales of thieves or jewels or magic rings, but commercial triumphs. At first, when he announced the title, my heart wanted to fly out of the window like Prince Yasef's horse. But the window had bars on it called duty. The merchant would raise his index finger and begin the story of Halla the Wily. Or Markas the Cunning. Or Urvic the Shrewd. That was my favourite. It conjured visions of a beady creature with a lot of native wit. Nissa, of course, gave it whiskers and a squeak. After that, whenever the merchant mentioned Urvic the Shrewd, we avoided each other's eye. I think he knew, but he indulged Nissa and, because of her, me as well. No, I didn't write them down,' he says, anticipating Night's question. 'They were' – he pauses – 'done with when I left.'

He shifts into a more comfortable position. 'One afternoon, instead of teaching me numbers, the merchant summoned me to his office. I waited in front of his desk – beautifully carved and very imposing, of course – staring at a painting of a frog and water lilies. He told me to come and stand beside him, and showed me the book he'd been looking at. The pages were filled not only with columns of numbers but with names, dates, notes. The paper was creamy white, and when he held it up to the lamp I saw it contained the ghost of a sign.

'He said it was the symbol of his house. When I looked closer, I could see a circle from which seven lines radiated, with five wavy lines underneath. He told me the circle was a pearl, symbolising wisdom and wealth. The lines coming from it were the seven sacred rays of the sun. They symbolised good luck, and a long and fruitful life. The lines beneath were the waves of the sea. They represented the crossing his grandparents had made to come to this country and, now, his own ships.

'Every page of his ledgers was marked with it, and so was his writing paper. It must have cost a fortune. He told me it was a mark of continuation, a sign that his house would endure. Then he began teaching me how to read the ledger. To me, the word sounded like a flight of stairs I was about to fall down.'

The memory prickles like a small headache. He takes a drink from the water bottle. 'Where was I?' he asks.

'Falling downstairs,' Night says, 'and you really don't like saying Kumbar's name, do you? Don't you think it's a bit –?'

'No, I don't. And if you want me to continue, you won't either.'

'It will never be mentioned again. Not by me, anyway. I don't have the power to invoke catastrophe whenever it comes up, although it could be rather satisfying. I notice you don't have the same problem with his daughter.'

Arun is silent for a moment. Thoughts of Nissa stir none of the feelings he associates with her father. Her spirit and her endless baiting kept him going when all he wanted was to give up, and for that he will always be grateful. And – but the other reason is yet to come.

'I came to like the ledgers,' he says. 'Not at first – all I saw was row after row of numbers. They meant nothing to me. They could have been figs, or mice, it made no difference. I sweated over those pages, trying to understand them, but it was no good. Night after night I'd lie awake, crossing chickens with olive oil and coming up with insomnia. In the end, it was Nissa who gave me the key. She saw much more than I gave her credit for.

'She came to me when I was sitting glumly staring down alleys which always led to the wrong answer, and said, "Don't you see?" She tended to start conversations like that, a question that was really a solution saddled up and ready to ride. I was tired, grumpy, and probably rude. Instead of getting annoyed, she said I had to think of the stories. I had no idea what she meant. She told me everything came from somewhere, that people had made it or grown it, and there was a history to it. She was trying to tell me to look at it as a journey, from where it began to where it ended up. The life of a commodity.'

Arun smiles briefly. 'It was as if the sun had breached the ceiling of the sitting room. All of a sudden, I saw. Here was a column on which words had been inscribed in memory of what had passed. Not great deeds or battles, but the sweat and hope of people whose lives were no less real for having been lived beyond the reach of the scribe's pen.

'That, for example' – he points to where the boy's head is bent over the ledger – 'is where one of the merchant's ships finally made it into port after being lost in a storm. And that one is the grain that saved the city during the great drought. Work it back, like a thread through a maze, and it brings you to a man standing at the wheel of his ship, wondering if he'll ever get home. And a woman going down to the harbour every day, wondering if she'll see her husband again.

'Those ledgers, stiff with ink, worn with handling, contained as many of the trials and joys of life as any other book. If,' he adds, 'you knew how to read them. The merchant was wily – you had to know how to interpret his records. It didn't take long to understand how necessary it was. Things of great value can turn men into swindlers and thieves. Not all, of course, but the temptation's always there.' He thinks of Kerel, who chased the rare and beautiful, and turned them into coins.

'Kerel didn't swindle anyone, as far as I know. And he showed me a whole new world. But Harakim wasn't a safe place if you had a secret, whether it was the time a ship was supposed to arrive, or what it was carrying besides the cargo on the inventory. It always amazed me that Nissa was a skilled keeper of secrets. The merchant trusted her with most things. She'd sidle up to someone with a look of such innocence they'd end up giving her a ribbon, or a cake. I wondered at first if he truly cared about his daughter, letting her run about the city like that, but I was soon put right.'

The boy closes his book and looks up. Nissa is out on an errand, and the sun is shining through the window. For the first time he considers exploring the city on his own. He hasn't yet, not because it is forbidden but because Kumbar's house has become a sanctuary for him. Loss has stripped away his certainties, and here in the sitting room, surrounded by now-familiar things, he feels safe.

Something catches his eye; a bird flashes past. He finds himself standing at the window, looking out. Leaf-shaped tiles of faded yellow and red cover the roof of the house opposite. The sky seems endlessly deep. As he stands mesmerised, the door bursts open and Kumbar rushes in. The boy whips round, loses his footing, and slides smartly down onto his backside. He scrambles to his feet.

'Have you seen her?' Kumbar demands. 'Is she with you?'

The boy rubs his behind. 'Who?'

'Nissa!' Kumbar's cheeks are red and wobbling.

'I thought she was on an errand.'

'Yes, yes, but she should be back by now.' Kumbar makes a helpless gesture with his hands and sits down heavily on the sofa.

Tir is hovering in the doorway. She gives the boy a severe look, as if he is to blame for the current situation.

'Well?' Kumbar asks her.

'Nothing so far, *Irthan*.'

'Go, go, keep looking.' He gets up so quickly the sofa skids sideways. 'You' – he points at the boy – 'where do you go when you go to market?'

The boy considers. Is it a trick question? To repeat 'to market' might be seen as insolent; on the other hand, now is not the time for silence.

He frames his reply carefully. 'Do you mean what stalls we go to, or afterwards?'

Kumbar flaps his hands. 'Afterwards.'

The words *come straight back* float on the boy's tongue. He closes his mouth and they pop like bubbles.

'Well?' Kumbar says loudly, turning back and forth, his hands sweeping the sides of his robes as if he might find his daughter concealed there.

'We – er – sometimes take a detour on the way back.'

'Where?'

'Just around the houses.'

'But where?' Kumbar almost shouts.

'Through the streets. We count doors and shutters.'

Kumbar stares at him. 'Doors and shutters?'

'The colours,' the boy explains. 'How many blue, how many green, how many . . .' He trails off as he reaches the look on the merchant's face.

'Show me,' Kumbar says, taking him by the arm. His grip is not unkind, just fearful.

The boy blinks against the midday sun as they hurry through the market square and into Nissa's favourite street. Kumbar immediately starts knocking on doors.

On the whole, the inhabitants seem disposed to help if they can, in spite of the fact that Kumbar is a merchant. The boy has noticed that those who make money are rarely looked upon kindly. He has also come to understand, through Nissa's shrewd comments, that if the tables were turned, others would welcome the opportunity not to be looked upon kindly.

He trails from door to door in the wake of Kumbar's robes, meeting with shaking heads, voices saying, 'No, I'm sorry, I haven't seen her, I'm sure she'll turn up. You know what children are like.' Kumbar is growing redder by the minute. The boy wonders how much more he can expand without bursting.

A stableyard lies at the end of the street. Kumbar calls

out to one of the stablehands; the man turns, sees who it is, and starts smiling and beckoning. He directs the merchant into the large, high-ceilinged barn where horses stand patiently in stalls. Kumbar hurries to the far corner. Moments later the boy arrives to see Nissa rising from the straw.

Kumbar seems to burst like a dam. '*Maranissa!*' he cries.

The boy's heart jolts in his chest; it flutters in his mouth; it leaps in his throat. He is amazed it can be in so many places at once. As the merchant folds his daughter in his robes and hugs her, the boy is astonished to see tears running down his face. He stands stiffly, not knowing what to do with his arms, wondering how such a long name can belong to such a small girl. When Nissa untangles herself from her father's robes, her face is bright, expectant.

A mess of feelings churns through the boy. While relieved to find Nissa in one piece, he is reckoning the amount of anxiety spent on worrying about her fate, and ending up out of pocket.

'See, Papa,' Nissa is saying, 'how pretty they are – and this one, with the spotty paws – oh, *please*, Papa . . .'

The boy's mind has lost its footing. Do horses have paws?

Kumbar is turning and smiling at him, a beam to flood the harbour and enough left over to ripen the crops. 'I should have known. Once she heard about it, I should have known.'

The boy remembers someone in his village talking about cats, about a time that was near, and a wish for good mousers. They called it *the happy event*. From what he can gather, a stable cat has had kittens, and Nissa has heard about it. It seems the event really is happy, having restored Nissa to her father, and her father to a calmer state.

As they reach the house Adara runs out, red-cheeked and tearful, and gathers Nissa in her apron. 'You gave us such a fright!' she exclaims. 'We had you halfway to Krystana.'

The boy trails along behind. When the household has finished celebrating Nissa's return – with, he notes resentfully, no scolding – he goes up to his room and sits on his bed.

There is a tapping at the door. Nissa's special knock. He waits. Her face appears, behind a very neat nose. For someone who pokes so much of it into other people's business, it should be much longer. 'Papa says I can have her when she's old enough to leave her mother,' she says, looking pleased with herself. 'I'm going to call her Minu.'

He wonders if he should try it: disappear, cause mayhem, reappear in a shower of glitter and be given whatever he wants.

'Well?' she says, sitting on his bed. He wishes she wouldn't. It isn't his, exactly, but it belongs to him more than anything else in the house.

She nudges him impatiently. 'What?' he says sulkily.

'Aren't you pleased?'

His reply is short and cross. Her mouth starts to quiver and he says quickly, 'I'm just tired.'

'Of what?' Her voice is sharp.

'Of being tired,' he improvises.

She accuses him of not making sense. 'Besides, you don't look it. Not with all the food you put away.'

For a moment he stares at her, dumbfounded. 'Are you saying I eat too much?' he says indignantly.

When she doesn't answer, he realises she is genuinely taken aback. She knows something of the world, of how its open hand can suddenly close, and while to her it remains a theory with no true weight to it, it is something she respects.

'You should always eat when you can,' she says decisively. 'Look at Papa –'

She closes her mouth abruptly. Kumbar's roundness is not easily circumnavigated. They start laughing, each secretly relieved to be climbing out of an awkward place. When they are calm again Nissa says, 'You can share Minu, if you like – part of her, anyway.'

Which part? he wonders as she slides off the bed and darts through the door.

Chapter Five

On the eve of the new year, the household gathers in the dining room. It is a large and splendid room at the front of the house, adorned with tapestries and ornaments. It is well-known in Harakim that Kumbar marks the passing of the year with a feast of great magnificence, and Adara and Tama have worked tirelessly to produce sweetmeats, pastries, cakes and extravagant breads for the merchant's many guests.

The boy has never seen a loaf in the shape of a ship before. Kumbar tells him it represents his very first ship, whose cargo was rice. Following reports of a bad storm, he went down to the harbour every day to watch for it. Just as he had given up hope, the ship crawled in. The planks were leaking like sieves, the crew more dead than alive, but they made it.

'I made sure I was there to greet the captain. People were watching, and I had to make a success of it. People are always watching, Arun, always waiting for you to fail. The captain didn't let me down. He said they had had a terrible time, pirates trying to board them, a great fish trying to eat them, the drinking water running out, but luck was with them in the end.' He smiles complacently. 'It did wonders for my reputation. I stood at the top of the gangplank and gave thanks to the god of cargoes. Never give up,' he says impressively, his gaze encompassing not just the boy but the audience gathered round him.

It is a source of constant wonder to the boy that no matter how much she eats, Nissa never seems to fill up. He watches as she embarks on a dish of chestnut cream. 'Try some,' she says through a sticky mouth. 'It makes you feel sick, but it's delicious.' She lets him have a spoonful. 'There's more over there, in the big red dish.' He hides a smile. Nissa's limits are carefully set; she gives only and exactly what she wants to give.

The level of noise is subsiding. People sit at tables drinking coffee, eating one last cake. Kumbar beckons the boy over. 'Arun,' he says, belching – he has consumed so much lamb the flocks in the hills around Harakim will take time to recover – 'come over here.' Among plump cushions, he shifts and groans. 'Every year I promise myself I won't get fatter. And before I know it, another year has passed and I see even less of my feet.'

He sighs, and looks at the boy. 'Yes, I have brought this on myself. My eyes are the culprits. Would you have me pluck them out just because they look upon good things to eat?' The boy, who is thinking nothing of the sort, looks startled. 'There are things in life that cannot be changed,' Kumbar says, 'and it is well not to lose your hair over them. When I was a child, my mother told me food would be my downfall. She was wrong. Bringing food from far to near, from hand to mouth, has been the making of me. Remember, Arun, you must think about what people want, rather than what they need. Need is the first step; want is the ladder.'

The boy nods, committing it to memory, while part of him feels there is perhaps more to need than Kumbar allows.

The merchant holds up his arms, and the room falls silent. 'Now,' he says, 'I have made a decision. You are to have your first cargo. Sacks of rice, just like mine. I want you to meet the ship when it comes in, and see it unloaded.' He sits back, and everyone claps.

The boy blinks, unable to speak. Rice, he reasons, seems safe enough, especially when cooked. All he has to do is unload it. He becomes aware of people looking at him, of Kumbar waiting for a reply. 'Er,' he says, then, 'rice, yes, that's very – um – thank you.'

'Excellent,' Kumbar says expansively. 'I am expecting it in a few days, perhaps a week, depending on the weather. We will go down to the harbour tomorrow. It is time you became acquainted with it.'

The boy's stomach lurches. He has heard the screaming of gulls as they land with a clatter on the roof tiles, is aware of the sea at the end of the street, but has not yet visited the harbour. Nissa has been forbidden to go, which means she knows every inch. She has also tangled with the gulls more than once, throwing bread rolls to make them fly away.

'But,' she said crossly, 'they cheat. They have wings. That means they can fly back.' The boy thought it might have more to do with the bread rolls, but knew better than to argue.

Nissa pulls him through the crowd to a laden table. 'They're very good. Try one,' she says, pointing to the platter Adara is refilling with sweet pastries. The cook's face looks even redder than usual, and she is laughing a lot. The boy suspects it has something to do with the goblet at her elbow, which must be where she keeps her humour. He has noticed it before on such occasions.

'It's a great honour. If you do well, who knows what else Papa will trust you with,' Nissa says, munching. 'Your own ship, perhaps.' The boy stares at her. Her eyes are wide, the room too warm. He looks away, not wanting her to see his fear.

As the meeting-house bell booms out, everyone starts clapping and cheering. The new year has arrived. Nissa kisses his cheek, and he forgets about sacks of rice. Then Kumbar is there, lifting her up for a kiss.

'*Yafkia*,' he says, 'prosperity to you both.' He motions to someone nearby and the gardener, Ketta, hands him a basket tied with a crimson bow. With an exclamation Nissa pounces, drawing out a black-and-white kitten with white-spotted paws.

'*Minu!*' she cries, kissing first the little cat and then her father.

Kumbar nods briskly, radiating delight. 'Now, now, it's nothing, it was simply ready.' The boy wonders if cats ripen like fruit.

'And this is for you, Arun.' Kumbar hands him a tissue-wrapped parcel. It contains a handsome belt made from tooled dark-brown leather. The silver buckle is fashioned in the shape of Kumbar's symbol. The merchant explains that it represents a beginning: the boy is part of his house now, and the buckle will hold him steady as he sets out on his new path.

He is confused. If Kumbar is making a point, he would rather it were done somewhere other than around his waist. But he thanks the merchant politely, and puts on the belt.

Nissa nudges him impatiently. 'This is from me,' she says, tucking Minu under her arm and fishing in the pocket of her dress. As she hands him a package, he is torn between embarrassment and embarrassment.

'I didn't know you gave gifts at new year,' he mumbles, but Kumbar waves an airy hand.

'When you are rich, you can give them too,' he says.

The package contains a green leather notebook. 'There wasn't any point in giving it to you before because you couldn't write,' Nissa says matter-of-factly.

The boy turns the creamy pages carefully. When he looks up she has gone, lost in the crowd of dancing people holding scarves and ribbons whose colours stream through the soft light of lamps and candles. He watches for a moment, then runs out of the room, through the front door and into the street, where he empties chestnut cream onto the boots of the new year.

Afterwards, he stands in the doorway, fingering the silver buckle. He doesn't know what to feel. He had his own house, his hut. And now he is part of Kumbar's house, whether he wants to be or not. He thinks of the task ahead, and his stomach tightens. He has seen pictures in Kumbar's books of adventurers in heroic vessels that ride the highest waves, slip from the jaws of sea-monsters, and come crashing triumphantly to shore. As for the men who captain them, their hides must be cured in fires deep in the earth. Hell-places, underworlds from which they burst out to tower black-haired at the wheel of their ship in sleeves of billowing white. And here he is, fourteen years old, in well-made but unexceptional clothes, hair and eyes an unremarkable brown, and not a breeze in sight.

He closes his eyes. The city is in celebration, and he is in despair. If he were with his family, his mother would comfort him, his sister would tease, but he is not, and now he never will be.

Then Nissa is beside him, gazing at the moon and singing. Her voice is light and sweet. It is a song about a flower opening in a garden, and the soft hand of a woman caressing the petals. When she finishes she says, 'I'm sorry about your stomach but you ate far too much, you know. Minu agrees.' She holds up the purring kitten, smiles and disappears inside, leaving him staring after her.

The boy wakes early, groaning. The pain in his stomach has nothing to do with chestnut cream. The ship. He wishes his mind were detachable, so he could take it out and lock it in a cupboard for a while. Groaning again, he gets up and goes in search of Nissa.

The front door is open and she is sitting just inside, playing with Minu. Last night the kitten frisked madly, then suddenly collapsed. He'd stared in horror – was the trail of thread too much for her tiny heart? – but Nissa laughed, picked her up and showed him the rise and fall of the furry sides. 'See,' she said, 'she's sleeping.'

His mother used to check on him and his sister sometimes, to make sure they were asleep. Something filled his throat, and he had to look away.

A woman comes out of the house opposite, yawning and stretching. When she sees them she makes a courteous gesture, wishing them a blessed new year. Nissa returns the gesture but the boy, who finds such things awkward, just nods.

Nissa scrambles to her feet. 'It'll be a quiet day,' she says. 'Papa always needs quiet after parties.'

He grins slightly. Kumbar smiled more broadly, sang more loudly, clapped more enthusiastically as the night wore on. Even with a pillow pressed to his ears, the boy could still hear him. This morning, the entire household is wincing.

He follows Nissa into the sitting room. The curtains are still drawn. With a tutting sound, she pulls them open. Minu jumps onto a table and starts patting an ornament, but Nissa scoops her up and reverses into an armchair where she curls up, scolding the kitten fondly. She knows this house so well, he thinks. He is familiar now with the layout, the pieces of furniture, the corner where a mousehole has been blocked up, the way the sun makes its rounds from front to back, but he will never be part of its flesh and blood. He wonders if a map of his valley is written inside him, and if he will ever again find a home.

'Why are you looking like that?' He starts at the sound of Nissa's voice. 'You shouldn't be sad. You've been given your first cargo. You'll be going down to the harbour today.' The boy says nothing; he doesn't think Nissa will understand.

Suddenly she says, 'I'm sorry you lost your family, but you're very lucky, you know. If Papa hadn't taken you in, you wouldn't have a roof over your head.' It sounds suspiciously as if she is repeating what her father has told her. 'When you came here, you didn't know anything. If it wasn't for Papa and me, you still wouldn't. And your clothes were a disgrace.' She smiles brightly, as if sharing his gratitude.

It is too much. The boy jumps up, goes to his bedroom and closes the door. He sits staring at the wall, twisting the tongue of his new belt until his knuckles turn white. Nissa knew his family were dead, and up to now she hadn't said a word. He swipes his cheek with the back of his hand, sniffing. He wonders what Kumbar told her about how he came to be here. Does she know what really happened? Tugging down his tunic, he resolves to tell her. It'll serve her right, he thinks angrily.

The door opens; Minu is being propelled into the room on her bottom and trying to row backwards with her claws. On her face is a look of surprise and indignation. The door closes behind her; she gets to her feet and wanders over to him. He picks her up and puts her on his lap, where she curls up and begins to purr. He finds it soothing, a song without words.

'Well,' he says to the little cat, 'here we are.' He takes her purring as agreement. After all, where else would they be?

He sits stroking her gently until she lifts her head, making a small trill of recognition. Nissa slips in and sits on the bed, nudging him to make room. Before he can speak she says, 'My mother died when I was little. I don't really remember her. Papa never talks about her, but he keeps her portrait in the ivory cabinet in his office.'

Words of anger and accusation die in the boy's throat. Even in the depths of his pain, he knows he can't tell Nissa the truth. There is misery enough in the world without him adding to it. Besides, what would it achieve?

'Papa said she looked just like me,' Nissa continues. She frowns at his silence. 'Well?'

'Well what?'

'You're supposed to say how lucky she was.'

'Why?' he asks, bewildered.

'Because,' she says as if lending him the words, 'she was very beautiful.' She sits back. Minu blinks up at him.

Something is required of him, and he has no idea what it is. Feeling cornered, he stares at his feet.

'She looked like me,' Nissa repeats slowly. As the words plod into his ears, he senses a *therefore* in the background. 'If she looked like me, and she was beautiful . . .'

He is suddenly in daylight. His cheeks redden. 'My mother was beautiful,' he says desperately.

'We weren't talking about your mother,' Nissa retorts, then stops. He is on the verge of tears, and she is not an unkind girl. 'I'm sure she was,' she says. 'Otherwise why would your father have married her?'

The boy stares. Such an equation has never occurred to him before. 'Never mind,' Nissa says, 'you wouldn't understand. I know about these things. I've lived in three different places.' He gives her an incredulous look. 'It's true. Ask Papa.'

The boy finds out later from Adara that it is indeed true. Nissa was born in Cidea, a town to the far south of Harakim. When her mother died, Kumbar took her to Kuchan, a larger city, where he began to expand his business. Then, six years ago, they moved here.

Nissa regards him steadily. 'Well,' she says finally, 'do you think I'm beautiful?'

The question leaves him speechless. Almond blossom

is beautiful. The words of the poet who came to his village were beautiful, as is the painting of the frog and water lilies in Kumbar's office. But a girl . . . He shifts uncomfortably, aware of the scent of cinnamon, the faint dusting of sugar on Nissa's upper lip.

He is rescued from silent agonies by the door opening and Kumbar coming in. He is sipping from a small goblet, glancing at a sheaf of papers, and groaning. 'Come, come,' he says, waving the papers irritably. 'Time is money, haven't I taught you that?'

The boy's heart races him all the way down the street. A breeze brushes his face and he tastes salt.

For one so laden, Kumbar moves very quickly. The boy glances about. Many of the shutters are closed. It seems the first day of the new year must be treated with care.

The street widens, and suddenly there it is, the harbour. He hadn't expected it to be so big, its crescent-shaped breakwaters tapering into long, horn-like piers facing each other across dark-grey water. Great ships and smaller ones cluster up against the quay. Even today it is crowded with men loading and unloading cargo, sitting on barrels, smoking pipes, observing the activity. Dogs run about; gulls fight over scraps of fish. Wind plucks the ropes of the rigging, making them sing. Their coarse harmony excites and terrifies him. And beyond the harbour walls, so vast he can hardly meet its eye, is a sight he has dreamed of many times. The sea.

'So.' Kumbar opens his arms as if offering him the port of Harakim. 'Money comes in, money goes out.' He laughs. 'Now –'

The boy follows him to a group of men talking and laughing. They break off as soon as they see the merchant. He introduces the boy as his apprentice, and they nod politely. He tells them the boy will be meeting the *Silver Falcon* when she comes in. If they are surprised by the news, they are too well-paid to show it.

'These are my dock labourers,' Kumbar says. 'Good strong men. They will unload the rice.' The boy shakes each hand in turn, wondering if the sea air creates giants. 'And this is Arik. He is in charge.' Kumbar nods to a stocky man with broad shoulders. 'Any news of the *Falcon*?'

Arik shakes his head. 'Reports of storms, but that's usual for the time of year.'

Kumbar seems unconcerned, but the boy knows he has a number of faces. To his customers he is bluff, confident, a man of substance. To his servants he is genial, strict but fair, a rule-maker and, at times, a benefactor. To his daughter he is the great bear she teases, delving into his pockets for treats, jumping into his lap and wheedling out silk ribbons. To the boy – What is Kumbar to him? he wonders.

'Well?' The merchant is looking at him, and he tries to remember the question. 'The names of my ships? Too much chestnut cream last night,' he says to Arik, who laughs.

The boy's face grows hot as he recites the names of the merchant's ships: the *Silver Falcon*, the *Golden Lark*, the *Blue Hawk*, the *Mirina* and the *Maranissa*. On discovering Kumbar had named one of his ships after his daughter, it seemed that here, finally, was the perfect means of exacting revenge. When he introduced it clumsily into

84

the conversation, Nissa said with satisfaction, 'Yes, and she makes the most money. The *Mirina* is named after my mother because she's the most graceful.' Any weapon the boy might have made fell to pieces in his hands.

'Good, good,' Kumbar says. 'Now, when the *Falcon* comes in, I will introduce you to Rafiz. He is the captain. He has worked for me since I came here, and he is reliable and trustworthy. Your cargo is only as safe as your captain, remember that.'

He takes a deep breath and looks out across the harbour, coughing. 'Too much fresh air,' he grumbles. Dismissing Arik with a nod, he turns away. As the boy follows, he catches a slight movement to his right. Nissa is sliding round a stack of crates. The boy glances at Kumbar. The merchant is smiling. 'My daughter,' he says with rueful pride.

In the last four days the harbour has grown, in size and noise. The *Silver Falcon* came in this morning, scarred but intact. The boy shifts from foot to foot and looks around, trying not to panic. A man about a hundred feet tall is walking towards him, holding out his hand. The boy offers his own and the man shakes it, smiling. He stands on the stones of the quay as if he owns them.

'You must be Arun,' he says. 'I'm Raf, captain of the *Falcon*.' He glances at the vessel towering behind him. 'Kumbar's fastest ship, but I expect he's told you that.' He grins at the boy, who wishes the ship would follow its namesake and fly away.

'We've got the rice,' Raf says. 'I'm told you'll be handling the shipment.' The boy clears his throat. Out of the corner of his eye, he spots Nissa half-concealed behind a row of barrels. She is mouthing something, but he can't make out what it is. Raf, who is a courteous man but a busy one, says, 'Well, *Irthana*, you want the rice unloading?'

The boy blinks at the title. Little master. 'Er, yes,' he manages, 'twenty sacks.' Raf murmurs something to a man standing beside him, who runs up the gangplank of the *Silver Falcon*.

The boy pushes his hands into his tunic pockets, wondering why his arms are so long. He clears his throat again. 'Have you got the docket?' he asks. Raf hands it to him, his face polite and faintly amused. The boy finds himself wanting it to show respect. As he watches sacks being carried down the gangplank and dumped on the quay, he thinks about staring moodily out to sea, but a gull lands beside him and screams so loudly he jumps. A movement catches his eye; Nissa is waving her fingers at him. Why is she distracting him? he wonders crossly, until he realises what she means.

When the rice is unloaded, he asks Raf's men to wait while he counts the sacks. His face burns, but it is worth it. Raf says nothing, but the look in his eye changes slightly. When the boy has finished, he takes out the small leather pouch Kumbar gave him. He is ready for this, at least. 'For you and your men,' he says, aware of how thin his voice sounds.

Raf bows gracefully and thanks him. 'We'll drink to you,' he says, and they shake hands. Tar and fish. It is a smell the boy never forgets.

Raf turns back to the *Falcon* as Arik and his men start hefting sacks of rice. For now, they will be stored in one of Kumbar's warehouses. The boy watches for a moment, gives what he hopes is an authoritative nod, and flees as slowly as he can. He knows Nissa isn't far behind.

When he reaches the house, Tir is at the door. She tells him to go into the sitting room, that Kumbar is waiting. Nissa is already there, with Minu on her lap. How she managed it is one of her mysteries. Someone has left a jug and goblets and a bowl of pomegranates on a table. Kumbar fills a goblet with warm spiced wine. After giving thanks to the god of cargoes, he tells the boy his work is not yet done. He has to find a buyer for the rice.

The boy stares at the merchant. His stomach turns like a slow wheel. He is beginning to hate rice.

'Remember,' Kumbar says, 'you must never leave a task unfinished. Go now, think about what you must do, and come back to me this afternoon. And take a pomegranate. They are very good.'

The boy sits on his bed, turning the pomegranate in his hand. The skin is leathery, with a faint blush. He runs his nail lightly down the side, but it leaves no mark. He wonders if he should slit it open, but he doesn't have a knife. Other boys have them – Nissa told him so – but Kumbar won't allow him one. He looks at the pomegranate, which gives nothing away. He thinks about smashing it, stamping until the juice runs out, but it would achieve nothing and his stomach would still be empty. As he stares up at the window, it occurs to him that when he went down to the harbour, a place he'd wanted to see for so long, his fear and the hundred-foot man took the sight away from him. He gets up, marches down the stairs, through the hall and out into the street.

His heart marches alongside him. He isn't sure if he is allowed to go by himself, and Nissa is nowhere to be seen. Although she is first cousin to a nuisance she knows how to get out of trouble, but pride keeps him going until the street opens on sea and sky. He stands very still. This, for the moment, is his view. No one can tell him not to look.

He gazes slowly from side to side. There is the sea, cradled in the stone palms of the harbour. He walks forward, and looks down. The harbour wall is green with slime, the water dark and deep. He lifts his head, and light dazzles him. A little distance away he sees the *Silver Falcon*. He takes a deep breath, and his nostrils fill with the smell of stale crabmeat and seaweed. Turning, he almost treads on Nissa.

They stand looking at each other. 'Have you ever been on a ship?' she asks.

From experience, the boy knows the question comes with an answer sewn into it. 'No,' he says, counting in his head. *One, two, thr –*

'I have,' she says, and he hides a smile of satisfaction, remembers his duty and asks her when. 'Yesterday. Rafiz showed me around. He was very helpful. He let me turn the wheel. It was heavy, but I managed it. And I saw the ropes the men run up.'

She wrinkles her nose. 'Actually, it was boring. There weren't any silks or flowers, or jewels of great size.' This, the boy thinks, is what comes of reading too many storybooks. The plain span of a ship's deck, its cargoes of currants and lice, fleas and timber, lacks romance. But, he reminds himself, she also has the same shrewd turn of mind as her father.

Nissa laughs. 'You look so grim. Just because you have to find a buyer for your rice. I know a dozen people who'd take it.' The boy glares at her. A dozen sounds far too patronising. He opens his mouth but Nissa is turning away, saying, 'Come on, it's almost time for lunch. Papa will be –'

But the boy isn't thinking of the scolding to come. At this moment, all over Harakim, people are sitting down to a meal of what this city seems to live on. Rice. And Kumbar's house is no exception. Fired with an idea, he turns and starts running, leaving Nissa in his wake. When he reaches the merchant's house, he slips in quietly and makes his way to the accounting room. Then he goes to the kitchen and stands on the threshold, watching Adara stirring a large pot over the fire.

He gives a small cough. She starts, and turns. 'You gave me a fright!' she says, but her face isn't cross. 'Lunch isn't ready yet, you'll have to wait. I've got this to prepare first. It was bad enough cooking for the new year but no, he has to entertain his friends this evening as well. Well, it won't be as much, or as fine, I've told him so, and he'll just have to put up with it.'

The boy, who knows it is Adara's duty to complain, waits patiently. She stirs the pot and out holds the ladle. 'Taste,' she says. He takes a mouthful and declares it delicious. She looks flattered. 'Now, what is it you want, Arun? Make it quick, I haven't got much time.'

He thinks fast. Adara's relationship with Tir is a delicate one, each believing herself to be in charge of the running of the house. If he weighed their tempers in a balance, he reckons Adara's scale would come up lighter.

'Kumbar buys rice in the new year, doesn't he?' he asks. It is still something of a wonder to him that the merchant imports rice in quantity but insists on buying for the household from another source. He suspects it is because he can't resist a bargain. Adara nods. 'Well, I've found a merchant who'll give you very favourable rates.' She looks dubious. 'Think how pleased Kumbar would be if you bought it. It'd be a real saving. And the rice is finer.'

Adara stirs the pot steadily. He knows she is weighing Kumbar's appreciation of a good deal against his disapproval of her acting without his sanction. After a moment he says, 'I know that Tir' – Adara's back stiffens, but she keeps stirring – 'is going to recommend buying from –' He names a merchant he knows the household has used before. 'I've heard' – he lowers his voice – 'he's charging more this year.' He waits, holding his breath.

Adara straightens up. 'More?' she says, her voice rising slightly. 'That man has more new cloaks than he'll ever wear. His wife bathes in dew sprung from morning's first breath. His daughter –'

The boy listens as she runs through a list of the family's indulgences. When she reaches the carpet sewn with stars from the same sky that witnessed the princess of Hyan bathing on her roof, she finally runs out of steam. '*Tcha!*' she says, turning back to the pot.

Patience bears fruit. He has learned this from Kumbar. 'The rice is finer?' Adara says eventually.

'Yes, and it's still at the harbour. It hasn't been taken to market yet, but when it is . . .'

Adara looks at him. 'You know this merchant?' she asks, narrowing her eyes.

'Yes.'

'And you trust him?'

'Absolutely.'

'How many sacks?'

'Twenty.'

'How much?'

He names a price. She thinks with her fingers. 'That will keep us going until – next time. And Tir doesn't know about this?' He shakes his head. She considers for a moment, then cuts an inch or two off the price. He has anticipated this, and frowns, looking doubtful. 'Tell him it's my final offer,' she says sharply. 'But he has to bring it here, mind, and take it through to the back. I'll square it with Kumbar afterwards.'

'Done,' he says with a nod.

'Well' – she flaps her apron at him – 'what are you waiting for?'

He races through the front door, narrowly avoiding Nissa, who turns like a weathervane as he passes. At the harbour he looks around for Arik, who walks slowly towards him.

'Yes, *Irthana*?' he says.

The boy ignores the insolence in his voice. 'I've found a buyer for the rice. I've told her your men will deliver it.'

He has no idea if he has the authority to ask, or if Arik will agree, but he is determined. Perhaps Arik senses it because he shrugs, calling to his men. The boy follows them to the warehouse and watches them load sacks into a large cart. Two men take up the handles, their faces giving nothing away. It is a fine procession: the boy, Arik, the cart, Nissa – who has just caught up and glares at him as she turns around again – and the dock labourers, grinning and jostling each other.

As they approach Kumbar's house the boy's heart is coming and going. He wants to flee, but he can't turn back.

At the door, he stops dead. The procession halts behind him. Arik looks from the boy to the house and back again. 'Here?' The boy nods. 'You're sure?' Again he nods. Arik whistles, then grins widely. 'After you.'

Tir answers his knock. She looks from him to the small caravan beyond. When he tells her he is delivering rice she stares for a moment, then says, 'I'm getting the master.' She turns away, bumping into Adara, who bends her aside like a blade of grass.

The boy takes a breath. 'I've brought the rice,' he says, and nods to Arik.

Still grinning, Arik jerks his head, and his men start unloading the sacks. Adara stands as if entranced, her eyes following the passage of the rice through the house. The boy watches, rooted to the spot. Then, finally, the voice he has been expecting and dreading. Kumbar.

Chapter Six

The hall is empty except for the merchant and the boy. His nerve suddenly dies. At least it won't take him long to gather up his possessions. He hopes he will be allowed to leave in one piece.

Kumbar's face gives nothing away. Which, the boy thinks wildly, isn't surprising, since Kumbar never gives anything away if he can help it. 'Well?' the merchant says. The boy shuffles on the spot. In years to come, will people visit the place a disobedient boy drew breath for the last time? 'Well?' Kumbar says again.

His heart in his mouth, the boy starts to explain. He begins with how the idea came to him. Then the kitchen, and Adara. The harbour, and Arik. Kumbar's eyes narrow. He forces himself on until he reaches the merchant's house, and stumbles to a halt at the door.

There is only one thing left to do. With a shaking hand, he presents the merchant with a bill of sale.

Kumbar stares at the paper. He makes a strange choking noise. His face, always red at the chops, grows redder. The boy wonders if he is about to explode, and whether he will have to clean it up. The merchant takes a step towards him and he backs away in alarm. Then Kumbar grasps his hand

and starts shaking it. To his astonishment, the boy realises he is laughing.

'My own rice!' he gasps. 'You sold me my own rice!'

There is no escaping the truth of the matter. The boy starts to apologise, but Kumbar waves it aside. As his laughter subsides he wipes tears from his face, rubs his sides, and claps his hands. Tir appears, glancing at the boy as if she is surprised, perhaps a little disappointed, to see him intact.

'Yes, *Irthan*?'

'Bring wine and cakes,' Kumbar says. 'We have something to celebrate.'

Tir has both eyes on the boy as she departs.

Arun smiles bleakly. If he didn't know what was to come, he could almost envy the bravado of his younger self. 'That,' he says, 'was when the merchant made me his assistant. He told me he'd have to check his back in the mirror every day from now on, to make sure it was free of wounds. Nissa managed to involve herself, too – from the way she told it, you'd have thought she'd arranged everything. But I didn't mind. Success can make you generous. That evening, as guests arrived for the party, the merchant made a point of introducing me to everyone himself.'

He looks thoughtfully into the pool. 'At the time I couldn't work out why the merchant didn't order Arik to take the rice back again, but I understood later. Loss of face. He couldn't allow his men to know I'd acted independently of him. I'm sure Arik guessed, and for a while afterwards I worried if he'd use it as a good story in the taverns of Harakim, but there was no need. The merchant's influence was far-reaching, and Arik knew it was more than his job was worth to gossip. As far as I know, he never did.'

He leans back against the tree. 'That evening was a new beginning. It was as if someone had taken a broom and swept away the path to my village. Not entirely, but it began to fade. I was up to my eyes in commerce; every day I sat with the merchant as he updated his ledgers. He taught me about the traders of Harakim, their strengths and weaknesses, who to trust, who to avoid. He told me about the foibles of his customers, what to look out for, what to exploit. I came to know every ledger in the accounting room.

'This, for example' – he glances down – 'belonged to a well-to-do family who depended on the merchant for lace and silk – fancy goods, he called them. He delivered their order himself, which was unusual, but it kept them loyal. His bones may have been housed in abundant flesh, but his mind was tipped with a needle. It was no good trying to shuffle something past him, a penny here, a penny there. Every coin was a seed, he said. The ground they grew in was human ground. The tree they produced was a tree with a human face.'

He breaks off for a moment. 'The image haunted me. It reminded me of a story my mother told us, about a *gohi*, a stone devil. Yes, it's in the notebook,' he adds, 'and that's where it's going to stay.'

Night's silence is wise and old, and for that Arun is thankful. Devils in the dark are nothing compared with those inside his head.

He stretches, rolling his shoulders. 'Of all the jobs I had to do, my least favourite was collecting money. I got to know Harakim very well, going from street to street, knocking on doors. I developed a knack of being able to sense if someone was inside. An empty house has a certain atmosphere. I learned to knock, step back, and listen. Which taught me patience. It wasn't something I particularly wanted to learn, but I did. I also discovered that excuses come in many shapes and sizes.

'There was one particular man, Rashu, whom the merchant called the inveterate debtor. This man, he said, had the ability to transform himself in order to avoid his creditors. If a rat hurried along the shadow of a wall, he'd become the rat. If a woman called her husband to dinner, he'd sink into her voice and vanish. Whenever the merchant called on him, he disappeared so quickly only his beard was left behind. Or so I was told. In my head I called him the shape-shifter. His ledger' – Arun thinks for a moment – 'was large and faded, marked with a stringy brown ribbon. It had scalloped edges that looked like teeth marks. They were probably made by the merchant.

'I was asked to call at Rashu's house for payment of a bill that had become a fully grown bird – the merchant's joke; I laughed dutifully every time. He impressed on me that I wasn't to return without payment. Coin, mind you, not a promissory note or goods in kind. And absolutely no second-best teaspoons bequeathed by an aunt who was too mean to leave him her finest.'

The boy walks the streets of the city with feet that drag every step of the way. From time to time he looks around to see if Nissa is following, but she is too crafty. Even though he tells himself it is just superstition and therefore nonsense, her presence has become something of a touchstone.

As he approaches Rashu's house, his heart is racing. He wonders if he has pushed it too far and will now drop dead. If he does, it will at least have been in Kumbar's service. The merchant could hardly accuse him of not giving everything to the job. He glances about for signs of the debtor; a shadow out of place, a rat with the face of a villain. At this point he is close to believing Rashu could place himself out of time. A little way from the house, he stops.

The door opens. A woman comes out. She is holding the hands of two children dressed in matching tunics and trousers. They look as if the word *misdemeanour* could never be applied to them. The woman has a basket in her hand, much like the one his mother used to carry. It is empty; they must be going to market. He watches them, turning it over in his mind. Markets contain goods that require money to purchase them. If they are going to market with an empty basket, they have money to fill it. So why has the inveterate debtor not paid his debt?

As they pass by, the woman gives him a pleasant smile. He steps back into the shade, trying to work out what to do. When they are some way down the street, he decides to follow them. At the corner the woman turns right, into a wider street. The houses are well-kept, their doors flanked with tubs of brightly coloured flowers. She stops at a yellow door, her children tucked at either side like cygnets under a swan's wing. She knocks, and the door opens. They go in.

The boy comes to halt. What is he supposed to do now?

Listen at the window, the street says in a whisper.

Startled, he looks around, and almost falls over Nissa. Minu shadows her heels.

He glares at them. 'I can't,' he whispers back, 'it's not right.'

'Then you can tell Papa,' she hisses.

He looks at the open shutters of the house. A few steps forward . . . a few steps more . . . Glancing up and down the street, he crouches under the window. He can hear two voices, one louder than the other. Unbending a little, he strains to hear. Though desperate to succeed, he feels like a snake gliding past the hole of a small animal in order to taste its fear.

The woman is talking to her mother; that much the boy has worked out. Her voice is high and tearful. Her mother's voice is calmer, with an undertone of anger. The woman is building up to something – the whole house seems to be building up with her – and finally she comes to it. It is about her husband, and money. This, the boy gathers, is not a new state of affairs. Her mother starts speaking; he makes out the words *useless* and *not even the sense he was born with*. The woman starts crying.

The boy and Nissa stare at each other. While relishing the highs and lows of daily life, Nissa has never taken pleasure in the pain of others. When the children start to cry she turns her head, as if hoping her ears will look the other way. The boy is horrified. He feels grubby, as if there is dirt on his hands.

Then, abruptly, a change. The woman's mother is

talking to the children in a soothing voice. The room brightens; the boy can almost feel it. She says something that causes her daughter to thank her again and again. Then silence, the restful, easy silence of families at peace with one another. No resentment, no sulks, no secret anger. The boy is bewildered. When his father had a grievance he took great care of it, carrying it around for days like an injured bird. It was a time of silences for all of them. His mother was the one who healed it and helped it fly away.

An aromatic scent drifts through the window. Someone is making tea. 'Let's go,' Nissa whispers. 'They'll be there for hours.'

When they reach Kumbar's house, the boy goes straight to his room. For once, Nissa doesn't follow. He sits on the bed, thinking about the inveterate debtor. There is a cold feeling in his stomach, and not just because Rashu eluded him. He can still hear the children crying.

A knock at the front door makes him look up. He has been sitting for so long his window is dark. He hears voices below. Tir, welcoming someone into the house. A muffled reply. Footsteps – Tir running to fetch Kumbar. Kumbar coming out of the accounting room. A voice the boy doesn't know. More footsteps, a door opening, closing. A long silence. A door opening again – two voices – someone walking down the hall to the front door. The door closing. Silence again. He has, he thinks, just witnessed an invisible play, but has no idea how it ends.

He looks up to see Nissa in the doorway. 'Papa wants to see you,' she says.

The boy's heart sinks. He follows her downstairs, wondering what Kumbar will say about his failure. He has been disgraced, thrown out, wandered, starved and died before he reaches the merchant's office. As Nissa goes in, Kumbar looks up from his papers. The boy can't make out his mood. He waits, as he has learned to do.

Kumbar studies him thoughtfully. Heat prickles the boy's neck. Another moment and the merchant breaks into a wide smile, leaves his desk and clasps the boy's shoulders.

'A triumph!' he says. 'I have just been speaking to Rashu. Well, well, well.' The boy thinks three wells must be very deep. 'The inveterate debtor. Can you guess why he was here?' The boy shakes his head. 'So modest!' Kumbar exclaims. 'We will have to think of another name for him now.'

The boy looks confused. 'He has paid his bill,' Kumbar tells him. 'Every last penny. In full,' he concludes, as if making sure there is no confusion.

'In full!' Nissa chimes.

'In full!' her father agrees. The boy wonders if he is trapped in a drama in which all the characters keep reciting the same line over and over until the world ends.

Kumbar pours something from a silver jug, and hands the boy a goblet. '*Altien!*' he says. 'Good health!' The boy takes a gulp, and chokes. Kumbar laughs, patting his back.

'Can we have cakes, Papa, to celebrate?' Nissa asks. Smiling, the merchant gathers her in the crook of his arm. Minu, who has tripped over the boy's foot and is washing vigorously, gives a loud mew.

'You see,' Kumbar says proudly, 'this is what success brings – incorrigible children with cats demanding cake.' The boy wonders what kind of cakes Minu likes.

The jug is soon empty. Kumbar's cheeks have taken on the colour of the wine. He calls for more. As he sips, the boy is aware of a sense of growing discomfort. Something is not right. He has done nothing to deserve this. Kumbar should be sending cakes to the mother of Rashu's wife. He glances at Nissa, who seems to be assessing him.

'Kumbar,' he begins, and breaks off with a yelp of pain. Nissa has pinched the back of his arm. Kumbar seems to think the boy has been bitten by a mosquito, and swats it away.

More cakes, more wine. Finally, when the boy's head is spinning, Kumbar lets him retreat to his room. He lies on his bed watching the ceiling swirl above him. His pillows are swelling into giant puffs of cotton, and he is sure the chair is dancing. He groans, turns over and falls asleep.

He wakes with the mother of all headaches. His tongue has been replaced with sand. But he is young, and is soon up and thinking about what Nissa did. In the back of his mind his arm still smarts. He rolls off the bed, washes his face, and goes in search of her.

He finds her in the kitchen with Adara. Minu is curled up on a chair, apparently fast asleep. He has learned how false this impression can be, having once tried to measure the width of her whiskers with a piece of thread, and ending up with his fingers attached to her claws.

Nissa has made herself comfortable in the corner next to the fireplace, watching Adara put the finishing touches to a large pie. It is a plum pie, one of her favourites. The boy jerks his head meaningfully, but her ears seem to be stuffed with fruit. When she sees the boy Adara opens her

101

arms, smiling. 'Here he is,' she says, 'the conquering hero. You've made your mark, and no mistake.'

But the boy is impatient to talk to Nissa, who knows it and does everything she can not to meet his eye. She dances out of the kitchen with a piece of pie in her hand, throwing a glance behind her. Minu springs from the chair and bounds after her. In the hall, the boy skids to a halt behind them.

'Why did you pinch me?' he demands. His patience and his conscience are being tried, and he is struggling under their weight.

Nissa looks at him in surprise. 'You were going to tell.' He stares. 'It's the first rule of miracles,' she explains with exaggerated patience. 'Never tell.'

The first rule of miracles? 'We were never outside the house of the mother of the wife of the inveterate debtor, and we didn't hear the conversation inside,' she says.

'But we didn't, not really,' the boy points out.

'What's that got to do with it?'

He is even more confused. 'So we say nothing?' She rolls her eyes. 'Isn't it –' He breaks off. The word *dishonest* stains his mouth.

Nissa glares. 'Promise,' she says. He hesitates, takes a deep breath, and makes the promise.

A faint breeze stirs the surface of the pool. 'The merchant never found out,' Arun says. 'It taught me that the value of success often depended on the manner in which it was presented. After that, I was given more responsibilities. I became known for chasing debts – the mere rumour of it proved effective. The merchant presented me with my

102

own quill, and my own ledger. That was an important day – more wine, more toasts, more headaches. My clothes were promoted, too, from cotton to fine linen. I went to the harbour regularly after that to oversee the unloading of cargo, the tallying of goods and money.'

For a moment he watches the glimmering moon. 'The merchant was beginning to treat me like a son. I was trusted by him, as far as he trusted anyone, and respected by the household, even Tir. Nissa continued to tease and torment me, but that was just how she was with me. But I wasn't content.'

He sits back, taking a breath. 'Mirashi understood. She calls it

the rising, terrible instinct of home.'

He sighs. 'It can be a place of dust and desert, a time of famine, the least chance offered, but it's still home. Even though I knew mine had long gone, there were times when the need for it was so strong I had to get out of the house, go to the harbour, the market, anywhere, really, to get away from it.'

He drinks from the water bottle. 'We'd seen in another new year, and it must have been late summer – I kept coming across Minu stretched out in the coolest spots – when the merchant told me to pack some things, I'd be going with the *Falcon* to Krystana. He gave me a long lecture about the importance of my position as his representative, and how he was relying on me not to let him down. That if – he stressed this many times – I lost him money, no matter how small a sum, it would bring shame on him and his house. My mind was spinning. The *Falcon* was sailing to Krystana, the main port of Jedea, across the Gulf of Harakim. It might as well have been sailing to the moon.

'The merchant went with me to the harbour, and so did Nissa, with Minu in her arms. The farewells were brief. To the merchant it was just another journey; to Nissa I suspect it was out of sight out of mind, not to be dwelt on for very long. But to me –'

Arun shakes his head. 'Can you imagine the fear I felt? If the city had been a cage, it now seemed a welcome one. The bars were daylight and moonlight, the lock was three good meals a day and a soft bed. And now the key was turning, and its movement was water and never stopped.

'I didn't leave my cabin for three days. I couldn't believe how badly my stomach was behaving. Although I was well looked after, with cool cloths, plenty of water, a bowl by my bunk, I think I'd have swum for shore if I could. I groaned all the way to the open sea.

'I spent those days and nights waiting to die, wondering if I'd be buried at sea. I'd heard of such things, and it bothered me because I'd also heard about restless souls drifting with the currents. In the end, though, I hardly cared. I'd never really thought about death before, and now I felt so rotten I wasn't even scared. I closed my eyes and prepared myself for whatever lay ahead.'

Which, the boy finds as he opens his eyes and looks about him, is a bowl of broth and a grin from Raf, who is standing beside his bunk. 'Here,' the captain says, 'eat this, it'll make you feel better.' The boy thinks he must be a ghost, and Raf a fellow spirit. He takes the bowl. There is nothing spectral about the meat, the vegetables or the thick brown bread.

When he puts down the spoon, Raf gives him a smile. 'I expect you'll want to wash,' he says. It is possibly the one thing, apart from a good meal, the boy desires most in the world. He spies a basin sitting on the chair, the steam more intoxicating than the costliest oils. 'I'll leave you to it,' Raf says. 'I'll be on deck if you need me.'

The boy slides out of the bunk and stands gingerly on the floor. He takes a few shaky steps. The air in the cabin is woolly and stale, but he drinks it in.

Washed and changed, he leaves the cabin and looks about. A sailor approaches, offering to show him around. As they walk the quarters of the ship, the boy is overwhelmed by the feeling that there is nothing in front, nothing behind, only the endless sea. It confounds and exhilarates him.

Sailors nod respectfully as they pass, and he nods back, feeling vaguely uncomfortable. He hears Nissa's voice saying, *This is how it is, shut up and accept it*, and grins slightly. As he stands at the bow, looking out over the water, Raf joins him.

'No matter how many times you're out here, you never get used to it,' he says, shading his eyes with his hand.

The boy thinks of the carving of the bird and turtle in Kumbar's sitting room. The turtle is made of mother-of-pearl, the bird of lapis lazuli, but they can neither swim nor fly. Here on the deck of the *Silver Falcon* he rides a great beast, alarming, unpredictable, magnificent.

Chapter Seven

Today the air feels different, as if sensing land. And there it is before them, the coastline of Jedea. It is a tricky stretch to navigate, and full of rocks. But Raf and the *Falcon* know their way in the dark, and a great harbour is growing before the boy's eyes. He stands helplessly looking until Raf claps him on the shoulder and tells him it is time to get ready. Until now, he hadn't really thought about what would happen when they reached Krystana.

At times it has been a lonely voyage. The crew were generally kind, but he was Kumbar's assistant, so there was always a gap between them. To pass the time, he walked the deck until he knew it like his own teeth. He watched the men at work, noting that talk about women and beer tidied up when he was around. He put it down to Raf, though he did overhear one song. It began in praise of a lady's eyes, her lips, her neck . . . As soon as he realised where it was heading, he fled.

And then there were the stories, monstrous and beautiful. The sailors seemed to have an endless supply, and the boy drank them in. One in particular stayed with him, the tale of a young man ensnared by a *moali*, a sea-demon whose voice lured sailors to their death. Only the intervention of an older, wiser man saved him.

In his cabin that night, he finally found the courage to open the green leather notebook Nissa had given him that first new year at Kumbar's house, and write the story down.

Once he started, he found he couldn't stop. He wrote and wrote, never minding what it was. It became something of an obsession. The sailors had their superstitions – one always turned three times before sitting down, another polished his left boot first – but it was the boy, with his notebook and pen, who caused the most muttering and scratching of heads. He wasn't sure why, but he knew it disturbed them. Instead of putting him off, it made him more determined. He couldn't leave a footprint on the sea. No matter how many times he crossed it, he would never leave a mark. Writing was a way of keeping his balance.

One evening, as he stood at the prow watching the moonlight on the sea, Raf came to him and told him they were almost there. 'Well, my friend,' he said, 'we made it.'

When he went to bed that night, the boy noted down that Raf had called him his friend.

As the *Falcon* enters the harbour, the boy is looking everywhere at once. After so long at sea, everything is almost too substantial; the stones of the quay, the soaring watchtowers, the ships weighting the water. He gazes at flags tugging masts, at men unloading goods, breathes in the smell of tar, oil, spices. And the noise . . . it is as if a keg has been breached and out of it roars every sound ever made. He feels almost sick with it. Raf gives him a shrewd look, steers him towards a barrel and tells him to wait

107

while the cargo is unloaded. He sits in a daze, still rocking in the arms of the sea. When the last of the cargo has been unloaded Raf says, 'Well, my friend, it's time.' The boy's stomach turns. There is no putting it off any longer.

On the quay a group of men stand talking and laughing. All are well-dressed, imposing. A thought occurs to him. Will they speak his language? If not, will Raf be able to translate? Part of him hopes not, so he can return to Kumbar and plead a breakdown in communication.

As he leaves the ship, he glances back. The gangplank offers a bridge to a safer world. Over the past year he has grown rapidly – 'like a weed,' Tir said with a sniff – but he is still sixteen years old, smoothing down his best tunic and clutching a batch of papers the wind keeps leafing through. Gulls are calling high above, and he is sure they are crying *doom, doom*. Surely the word should be sung in a lower pitch, and not by tongues sharpened on wind and salt?

Raf's voice brings him back to the waiting merchants. He thinks of retreating, but it would mean a walk up the gangplank and into the sailors' laughter, so he looks down at the papers in his hand, selects a name, and says it aloud. With an obedience he can scarcely believe, a man fits himself to it. He is tall and burly, his tunic pulled in at the waist with an embroidered belt. The belt holds an elaborately decorated sheath containing a dagger. The boy wonders if he will see the dagger if the merchant doesn't agree to the price he asks.

When Raf has made introductions the merchant bows, and proceeds to speak fluently in the boy's language. He keeps talking as he looks over his goods: 'Bales of cloth, yes; baskets of ginger, good; and where are the – oh yes, you managed to get them, then?'

The boy's eyes and ears are one instrument, hearing the goods, seeing the voice of the merchant. If he is going mad it doesn't matter, as long as he makes a good sale. The merchant finishes his inspection and steps back, appraising the boy. His face is impassive, but an eyebrow twitches. The boy braces himself and looks him in the eye. As they start to haggle he finds he is enjoying himself. He has been trained by Kumbar, honed by Nissa. *This man is made of milk*, as she would say. It is a game he can win.

And he does, time and again. There are harder opponents, certainly, and not all of them have a wife who is pregnant again and desperate for the candied fruits the fourth merchant requested. One man gauges him frankly, up and down, with an almost visible measure. He ponders, pauses, walks away, returns. But the boy will not be moved. The merchant seems to know it too, in the end. When the sale is finally agreed, he bows deeply. With no awkwardness, the boy bows back.

Eyes, ears, tongue and hands; all are put to work on Kumbar's behalf. If anyone had told him he would still be standing at the end of the day, he wouldn't have believed them. But he is driven by the whip of the wind, and by something more. He has carried the merchant's reputation across the sea as carefully as if it were the last egg of the rarest bird, and he will return it intact whatever the cost.

One merchant remains. The boy knows what he is waiting for. The most valuable item, the one thing missing from the inventory. Before they left, Kumbar gave Raf a box to which the boy has the key. He told the boy that box and key were not to meet until the *Falcon* reached Krystana.

The boy meets Raf's eye, and gives a brief nod. From his pocket Raf takes a small rosewood box decorated with garlands of pearl and ivory. He hands it to the merchant with a bow. The boy takes the key from its pouch and, as instructed, gives it to the merchant. This, Kumbar told him, is a mark of trust. It shows he believes the merchant won't try to run away without paying. *If he does, Raf knows what to do,* he added with a hard smile.

The merchant presents the key to the lock; the box opens. He looks inside, and nods. The boy hands him the bill of sale. There is no need to negotiate; the price is already agreed. He takes the pouch of money the merchant offers and counts it as Raf looks on. When he has finished, inwardly marvelling – what could possibly cost so much? – he bows. The merchant bows back, and departs.

All is finally said and done. The boy tells his heart it may now revert to what it is meant to be, a regulatory instrument for the breath and body of its host. It is to cast off any notion of living in his throat. When Raf says, 'Let me take you for a drink,' he is prepared.

'Thanks, but I have to get back to the *Falcon*. I need to do the accounts.' He may sound like a pompous child, but he knows no other way to bridge the gap between his age and his duty.

He leaves Raf on the quay with his men, goes to his cabin, unlocks the chest he brought with him and spreads shipping orders, bills of sale, inventories, ledgers and money bags on a table. At this moment the table contains his whole world. He bends to his work, tallying, ticking, signing, checking and rechecking, stopping only to light the lamps. When he lays down his pen he stretches, yawns, and locks everything away.

He wakes in the middle of the night in utter panic. Wrapped in blankets, he falls out of the bunk, inches his way like a grub to the chest, unlocks it and looks inside. Everything is there – ledgers, bills of sale, inventories, money bags – so he hatches himself and returns to the bunk.

He walks down the gangplank more readily this morning, knowing what he has to do. The merchants are already there, talking loudly, gesturing, trying to catch his eye. Today he is buying for Kumbar, and the world seems to know it. The merchant warned him many times about buying *only first-rung goods. Second-rung will not do.* If he fails, he will have to make himself walk the plank. He takes a breath, sets his face, and wades in.

By the end of the day he feels like a bundle of goods that has been opened, inspected and quarrelled over endlessly. He also burns with energy. All day he saw Nissa darting ahead of him, pulling cloths from a bale, turning a trinket in her hand, throwing it down, tasting the black salt Kumbar instructed the boy to bring back. She danced from merchant to merchant as he scrutinised, haggled, made faces of surprise, incredulity and scorn until his cheeks ached. It has been a long day, but a good one. The hold is full, the money bags empty. But he kept back some coins to water the goodwill of the crew, who toasted him from stem to stern and back, twice, for good measure.

There has been no time to visit Krystana. As they left the harbour he briefly glimpsed a graceful city whose banners drifted on the air. Another time, he thinks, as he stands on deck watching the moon. For a moment he wishes it were the same moon he and his sister saw when they stole out late one night, at harvest time. The thought fills him with sorrow. But how can it, since sorrow seems more of an absence?

He notes it down that night, and shakes his head over it in the morning. As he sits on a barrel, his face lifted to the wind, he wonders if he will ever be able to set words to what he feels in a way that relieves his senses of their burden.

At last, land. He has survived. For a time, the ocean was his country. He has been away for only two weeks, but it feels as if everything has been turned upside-down. As he watches the gangplank being lowered, he shifts uneasily. Raf comes to stand beside him. 'After you, *Irthan*,' he says.

Kumbar greets him with a shout, clasping him by the shoulders and studying him for a moment. 'You've been caught by the sea, eh? Let us hope you have done some catching yourself. Come, we have much to talk about.'

All the way back, the boy feels the pitch and saw of the ship. His ears ring with the cries of seabirds. He wonders why he is nervous. He knows he has done well. Investigating further, he finds it has more to do with what he will find at Kumbar's house than the tallying of sums in ledgers. By now he has become accustomed to the house. He knows its rooms, how they are arranged, who is in them, generally, and at what time. He knows the vase in the hall that Tir fills with flowers, the red-and-gold cloth covering the large table in the dining room, the way the tiles of the sitting room floor echo the light. And he is filled with fear that they have changed.

When they reach the house, Kumbar stands aside to let the boy go first. It is an honour, and he doesn't want it. But he also doesn't want to offend the merchant. In the hall he pauses. Kumbar seems to understand. He waits in silence, letting the boy look around. Everything is the same, the vase of flowers, the carpets on the walls, the little tables. He follows Kumbar and Raf to the sitting room, where a jug and goblets are waiting. Nothing has changed here, either. A few new ornaments, but Kumbar is like a bird with an eye for pretty things. He pours wine – made, he says, from the blush of the grape – and toasts the boy, Raf and the *Silver Falcon*.

More toasts, more wine, until the room begins to pace around him. Laughing, Kumbar says that hospitality begins and ends with food and drink, with space between for laughter and song. The boy is beyond either. His eyes can barely focus.

'Yes, yes, you are tired, but it is not yet time to rest. There are matters to attend to.' Kumbar takes him by the elbow and guides him to his office. Raf carries the chest the boy kept in his cabin. Seated behind his desk, Kumbar waves the boy into a chair. Raf bows, winking at the boy as he leaves.

'Now,' the merchant says briskly, 'it is time to reckon everything. Now, not later, you understand?'

They bend to the task, working steadily through bills of sale and inventories until all is tallied and Kumbar is satisfied. Only then is the boy allowed to go to his room.

He flings himself down and tries to sleep. But his bed is still at sea, rocking until he wakes and finds himself clinging to the sides. He throws back the covers, gets up, paces about, lies back down. He can hear noises outside: insects praying, dogs barking, the low growl of a cat. A donkey brays; a man shouts. A minute's silence, then a woman singing, someone dropping a plate, hooves beating the dirt . . .

He sits up angrily, scrubbing his face with his hands. While he was away, did someone pass a law making it the duty of every citizen to persecute his sleep?

Yawning, he rolls out of bed and splashes his face and neck with water. Something occurs to him. He hasn't yet seen Nissa.

And there she is as he leaves his room, chattering as if he has never been away. His mouth is suddenly dry, and he can't seem to hear properly. She is telling him he is early, why couldn't he have waited, she has just returned from market, and are the traders of Krystana as villainous as ours? Half listening, he wonders what has happened in the time he has been away. It is Nissa and yet not, quite. Why has he never noticed that her hair, darkest brown with copper lights, reaches her waist? And when did other parts begin to announce themselves?

She comes closer and peers at him. Her eyes are the colour of agates; he knows this because he has seen pictures of gemstones in one of Kumbar's books. But agates don't tilt at the corners, nor do they sparkle. He wonders if he has spent too much time counting coins. His face begins to heat up, and he turns desperately to see Kumbar coming down the corridor, saying proudly, 'It is the other way round, my love – the traders need to watch out for you.'

114

Nissa stands back and considers the boy. 'Well, at least you've learned how to brush your hair.'

He reminds himself that Raf called him *Irthan*, that he faced down the bellies of numerous merchants, sang songs with a crew who drank more than the contents of an inn at one sitting, returned with a first-rung cargo and a chest full of coins that are not shaped like Nissa's eyes.

She catches his hand, saying, 'Minu wants to see you.' Awkwardly he pulls away, telling her he has things to do. He bows to Kumbar and goes downstairs.

Alone in the sitting room he stares at the floor. Tir is striking the gong for dinner and he stirs, shivering. In his absence, autumn has arrived.

In the dining room everyone is assembled: Kumbar, Nissa, the household, friends, fellow merchants. Kumbar holds up a gold-rimmed goblet and says, 'A toast, *pareilla*, to you.' The boy blinks. It is an old-fashioned term denoting respect. It means one who has triumphed, but also one who has survived. Kumbar is looking at him with an unusually serious expression on his face. Something inside him shrinks away as the merchant starts to speak.

Arun lifts his head, breathing deeply. He can still hear the words. *You have crossed the sea and returned. From country to country you have done what is best for my house. Let it be remembered. From today, you are as a son to me.*

'The merchant was trusting me with something far more valuable than treasure,' he says. 'His good name.' There is a bitter gleam in his eye. 'He called me his son, but in the end that was what really mattered.'

Bowing, the boy thanks the merchant, who introduces him to the household as if new-born. Nissa is watching him. The smirk on her face tells him she is, after all, still Nissa. The relief is such that he is hardly aware of people coming up to him, bowing, shaking his hand. Soft lights shine in lamps on the walls, and musicians play. For a second, he is somewhere else. Then someone offers him a drink, and he is returned again.

Kumbar is talking about the next shipment, expected at the end of the week. 'You will see it in,' he says. The boy listens, nodding, but has Nissa in the tail of his eye. She is standing with a friend of Kumbar, and he wonders what they are talking about. The dress she is wearing seems unnecessarily elaborate. Her hair is braided with ribbon whose colour he feels silently compelled to criticise. Minu, who also seems to have grown, wears a matching emerald bow around her neck. As Tir supervises the clearing away of plates there is more wine, spicy and sweet. He sips cautiously.

The lamps have become stars, the music is the sound of the sea. Nissa tweaks his sleeve. 'You can't go to sleep now,' she whispers.

'I'm not,' he mumbles, then sits upright with a gasp. Minu has killed her ribbon and is using him as a ladder. He shakes his leg, she slides down, Nissa gives a cry and gathers her up. They stand before him with accusing eyes.

He opens his mouth but Kumbar is saying, 'It is time to go to your bed now. You will need a clear head for tomorrow.'

The boy lies awake for a long time, and falls asleep wondering why Nissa torments him so much.

Chapter Eight

He runs without stopping. There is too much air in his lungs, and not enough. His feet are aching, his eyes stinging. He runs until he can go no further and collapses against a wall, gasping for breath. The rough stone catches on the back of his shirt as he slides to the ground with a bump. He kicks off his boots – leather so soft a lady could sleep on it, as Kumbar once told him – and closes his eyes.

Kumbar. Fury rises hard and fast. Images flash through his head, of sea crossings and open skies, of Kumbar at his desk, looking up at the boy and nodding with satisfaction. Of new year celebrations, each more extravagant than the last, of gifts and praise and a hand clapping him on the back. *An asset to my house, a better-than-son . . .*

The boy clenches his fists. 'You bastard,' he mutters, 'you two-faced –'

He stares at the ground. It started off as another pleasant morning, the air of early summer clear and warm. A morning in which, after finishing his work, he took his lunch into the accounting room. Nissa found him, as she always did, and teased him about turning into a ledger.

'A dry old book. A book no one will want to open.' The way she said it, leaning against a shelf, the curve of her hip more pronounced, made him swallow.

Celebrating her eighteenth birthday at the end of last month had only increased her teasing. He sometimes felt as if he were something to practise on, without risk or consequence. He had taken to having lunch in the accounting room or the office, but she always found him.

'Did you know Solla made an offer for me? I knew he would. Papa refused, of course. If he hadn't, I would have.' She gave the boy a challenging look. 'When I marry, it'll be to someone I choose. Papa doesn't know it yet, but I will.'

'I have no doubt,' the boy said feelingly. The movement she made as she pushed lightly away from the shelf with her hip made him swallow again. As she came towards him, he took a step back.

'Papa's had lots of offers. Which isn't surprising. After all, everyone wants to be a part of his house.' She was very close now, her eyes sparkling with mischief, her lips curving upwards with amusement. He took refuge in silence.

She lifted her hand and, with her thumb, softly rubbed his cheek. 'Always smudged,' she said. He stood very still. She was so close he could see a tiny freckle at the side of her mouth. As if through someone else's eyes, he saw himself slowly lean forward and –

Nissa stepped back, a look of delighted horror on her face. 'If Papa finds out you tried to kiss me . . .' She let the implication fill the room. 'Besides, you could never marry me.'

He stared at her, willing himself not to take the bait. 'Why not?'

'You work for Papa. He'd never allow it.' With the same impish smile she wore when she first met him, she skipped out of the room.

He sat on his bed burning with humiliation. How could he have let himself be manipulated like that? Never mind the fact that he had no intention of marrying her – she was the most contrary person he'd ever met.

A shadow in the doorway. Nissa stood there, Minu at her side. For a moment they looked at each other. Mustering his dignity he said, 'I am not a game.'

'If you were, I'd always win.'

He looked away, trying to keep his anger in check.

'I've got something to show you. It's very special. I think you'll like it.'

It was, he knew, as near to an apology as he would get. Not that she thought she had anything to apologise for. He sighed. Years with Kumbar had taught him the art of pragmatism. If he were to stay in the house – and where else could he go? – he may as well accept the peace offering.

They stood in front of the ivory cabinet in Kumbar's office. The boy had never seen inside it before. When Nissa produced a key, he knew better than to ask where it came from. Unlocking the cabinet, she opened a drawer and took out a white velvet pouch.

'Hold out your hand,' she said, and tipped something into it. Pink and iridescent, the length of his thumb, the pearl was an almost perfect teardrop. The lustrous sheen held tints of silver, blue, lavender and green. He could feel it warming to his palm.

'It's worth a fortune,' she told him. 'There's only one other like in the world, and it's not as big. You took it to Krystana on your first trip.' He thought back to the locked box, the key. There was no point asking how Nissa knew. 'It'll be mine one day,' she said smugly.

A voice echoed in the hall, and the boy jumped. Nissa laughed. 'It's only Tir,' she said. 'I'll go and see what she wants. You'd better put it back. And don't forget to lock the cabinet.'

He wondered if he should feel flattered or insulted. Did Nissa think he lacked the nerve to tuck it up his sleeve? He made a face. She knew him too well. He would never do anything to disgrace Kumbar. As he replaced the pouch, his hand brushed against a piece of paper. Catching it between two fingers, he pulled it to the front of the drawer. An envelope. Kumbar kept his most precious possessions in the cabinet. Whatever it contained must be of great importance.

Knowledge. It is this, not gold and silver, not all the jewels in the crowns of kings, that has value beyond price. Hadn't Kumbar told him that when he first came here? Aware of shaping the argument to his purpose, he opened the envelope. It contained a bill of sale. For himself.

He stood motionless beside the cabinet, hearing once more the harsh voice, feeling the finger jabbing his shoulder. *Name? Arun Persaba. From? Bishra, in Sund province.*

In that instant, everything fell away. He was no different from the bales of silk Kumbar sold, the perfumes, the rice flour. He had been fed, clothed, educated, trained, but he had also been bought.

He shook his head angrily. Hadn't he known it, deep down? Hadn't he chosen not to see, to take what was offered because there was nothing else? Looking again he noticed, at the bottom of the page, a note in Kumbar's hand. *The boy has family. Whereabouts unknown.*

120

He staggered slightly, gripping the side of the cabinet. *They are no longer with us.* That was what Kumbar said when they first met. As the true nature of the phrase became clear, an icy feeling spread through the boy's chest, and he began to shake. A lie disguised as a statement of fact, relying on inflection, on tone, to do the rest. But not an outright falsehood. Kumbar was as calculating in his form of words as he was in every other transaction.

Bile rose in the boy's throat as he remembered his trusting acceptance of what Kumbar had told him. Hearing footsteps, he locked the drawer, left the room and went out of the house.

As the fact of Kumbar's duplicity overwhelms him again, the boy's gut twists, and he slams his fist against the wall. He has been here for five years. Years in which he could have been looking for his family. The thought of so much wasted time has him up on his feet, ready to confront the merchant, tear down the cultured facade, shake the bill of sale in his face.

He takes a step forward, and stops. Of all the lessons he has learned in Kumbar's house, one of the most important was the need to be prepared. To know your enemy, to anticipate their actions. Confronting Kumbar directly will achieve nothing. The merchant is too clever, too guileful, for that. He needs to be patient, to plan. He looks around. This part of Harakim, its unpainted doors, its flaking walls, is unfamiliar to him. A fitting place for a servant.

He sits on the edge of the bed, having forced down his meal and excused himself as soon as he could. That he succeeded in concealing his feelings from Kumbar gives him no satisfaction. He learned from the merchant, after all. And Nissa was too busy feeling pleased about her earlier triumph.

The knuckles of his fist gleam white. He examines the bill of sale, hoping to find what he failed to discover before: the name of the seller. As before, it offers no answers. It is getting dark, so he lights the lamp and sits in exhausted silence. As lamplight illuminates the paper, he notices a tiny mark in the bottom right-hand corner. Dismissing it as a fleck in the weave, he is about to give up and go to bed when he remembers Kumbar showing him how his paper was impressed with the symbol of his house. Holding the bill of sale up to the lamp, the boy peers close and sees a mark so small he can hardly make it out. Frustrated, he sits back, thinking.

When he is sure the household is asleep, he slips downstairs to Kumbar's office. He knows what he is looking for: the ivory-handled lens Kumbar uses to interrogate trickier contracts. In his room he holds the paper to the lamp, the lens to the paper. The mark becomes clear: a square-cut spiral surrounded by dots, like a swarm of gnats. For some reason it makes him feel uneasy. Looking more closely, he sees the dots are more square than round, as if made by a tiny wedge-shaped brush.

Is this the first step to finding his family? He stares at the paper, his breath crowding his chest. Then he gets up and leaves the room. His heart may be sore, but he won't forget to replace the lens.

He goes about his business the following day, working hard, thinking harder. When Kumbar has gone to a merchant's house for dinner, he slips into the office and takes a book from the shelf behind the desk. It contains information about the various people Kumbar does business with, including the symbols of their houses. The merchant has written comments beside some of them, in the same vaporous script as the note on the bill of sale.

The boy fans the pages open. Here is a particularly fine device, in which gold has been melted over a background of indigo so the sun stands in a night sky. Reminding himself what he is looking for, he turns the page. Finally, at the very back, he finds it. A square-cut spiral attended by gnats. Two sentences are written below. *The symbol of the tribe of the House of Goash. This tribe of camel-traders* – Kumbar's shorthand for every sort of thief and villain – *flourishes in the south-west corner of the Haruan Desert basin.*

He searches other books, but finds no further information. He tries the drawers of the desk but they are locked, as he knew they would be. As he steps back, wondering what to do, Nissa comes in.

He is on the wrong side of Kumbar's desk, behind a stack of books. Nissa's eyes narrow. 'What are you doing?' she asks, advancing. The failed kiss, all but forgotten, comes back to him. Perhaps he can use it to his advantage.

'Nothing,' he says stiffly.

'You're not still sulking, are you?'

'Of course not.'

'Yes, you are.' She glances at the books. 'What are you looking for?'

'Nothing.'

'Don't tell me, then. But I bet I'd be able to find it.'

He pretends to consider, shrugs, and shows her the symbol. She studies it for a moment, tapping her fingers lightly on the desk. 'I've seen it somewhere before. I think it's in a book Papa keeps in one of his desk drawers.'

His heart sinks. 'We don't have the key.'

She smiles. 'Not yet,' she says, 'but we will.'

It feels almost as if someone else is doing it – the door creaking open, the tiptoeing in, the trembling hand searching for keys. Nissa told him that when Kumbar came home he would fall into bed and go straight to sleep, as he always did when he dined at Yassa's house. When he started snoring, the boy was to sneak in and take the bunch of keys from the bedside cabinet.

When he comes out, he is shaking all over. In Kumbar's office he lights a lamp, keeping the flame low.

'Which one is it?' he whispers, holding out the keys. Nissa shrugs. Glaring, he starts trying them in the top drawer of the desk. Time and Kumbar are pressing heavily on his chest.

Why is it always the very last one? As they work their way through the drawers, unlocking one after the other, he is almost frantic. When they reach the bottom drawer Nissa burrows in, fishing out a small black book with no markings on the cover. Holding it up triumphantly, she puts it on the desk. The boy pulls it towards him; she pulls it back. They tug until she lets go, and he falls back against the wall.

'Ow,' he says, forgetting to whisper. She raises an eyebrow and puts a finger to her lips. Biting his tongue, he places the book on the desk. Together, in the lamplight, they look.

He didn't know what he expected – dark secrets, grudges, old bones – but the pages hold nothing but symbols. He skims through quickly, searching for the square-cut spiral. Nissa finds it first. He is too busy looking to pay any heed to her smug remark. Next to the symbol is a number. She frowns, then turns to the back of the book.

'Look,' she whispers. There, next to a corresponding number, are notes in Kumbar's hand.

The boy reads aloud, very quietly. '"The tribe of the House of Goash. The spiral represents invincibility and life without end. The lozenge-shaped dots represent a cloud obscuring their tracks. They are the tribe who leave no trail."' He can't go on.

Nissa continues. '"They trade mainly in human currency. They cannot be beaten down in price. Do not deal with them again. It is too costly."'

Human currency. He clenches his fists. Nissa seems not to have grasped the implication. Briskly she says, 'You'd better return these before Papa wakes up,' and hands him the bunch of keys.

The sun is a weight on his chest. As he moves, it starts purring. Minu. Her whiskers are like quills made from mother-of-pearl; her ears have an air of privilege. He feels exhausted, and his eyes are hot and sore.

'If you wouldn't mind,' he says politely, 'I need to get up now.' Minu looks at him unblinking. Never try to outstare a cat. It is something his mother told him. 'You win,' he says. Minu stirs, rises into a shuddering arch, and jumps off.

All that day he does his duties, standing on the quay, speaking with the sailors and dock labourers, looking out at the hazy brightness beyond the harbour walls.

When he returns to Kumbar's house, Nissa is waiting in the sitting room. Beside her on a small table is a tray of tea and cakes. An aquamarine ribbon is twined in the soft darkness of her hair. A frayed ribbon of the same colour encircles Minu's neck. Kumbar told the boy once how costly aquamarines are, and how the stone, worn in the heel of a shoe, prevents sickness at sea. He clenches his jaw. There is, as far as he knows, no cure for sickness of the heart.

Nissa glances at the teapot. 'It's your turn to pour,' she says. She takes a sip and puts the cup down. 'Why did you want to know about that symbol?'

He is prepared for this. 'So I can look for whoever it belongs to.' As expected, she asks him why. 'Because they owe your father money, and he's never been able to find them to recover it. I wanted it to be a surprise, a way of thanking him for everything he's done for me. That's why it has to be a secret.'

It sounds even more improbable than it did in his head. He holds his breath. To his amazement, Nissa seems to accept it. 'Of course you must go. And I'll go with you.'

He stares. Images storm into his mind: going to bed, getting up, changing clothes, washing, sleeping . . . 'No,' he says quickly, then, seeing her face, 'it wouldn't be fair to your father. You know how much he depends on you.'

'Yes,' she says, 'he does.' She frowns. 'We'll need a plan. And maps.' He waits. 'There are maps in the accounting room.'

'Over here.'

In the stillness, Nissa's voice is very clear. She pulls a scroll from one of the shelves, puts it on the table, unties the ribbon and unrolls it; it curls up smartly. She tries again; it does the same. She giggles. Frowning, the boy looks around and finds two large glass weights, one containing the head of a flower, the other an infusion of silver leaf and powdered crystal, like petrified frost. He sets one at either end of the scroll, and together they bend over the map. It is faded, and detail is sparse. Nissa's finger takes the black ink road away from Harakim and follows it into the bottom left-hand corner, where it ends in the words *Haruan Desert*. The boy wonders if the map-maker ran out of room, or hope.

A scuffling sound makes them look up, but it is only Minu, chasing a scrap of paper across the tiles.

'You'd better take it before Papa comes in.' Nissa removes the glass weights and lets the paper spring back. She watches the boy fold it up and cram it under his tunic. 'You'd make a terrible burglar.'

In every spare moment, the boy studies the map. The few scattered oblongs give no clue as to whether they are single dwellings or villages. The V-shaped clusters are probably shrubland. He wonders about the man who drew it. Did he know the area, or was he relying on the reports of others? It doesn't matter. All he wants is to find his family.

Arun stares into the pool. 'I was grateful to you,' he says to the moon. 'Your light gave me something to read by. I couldn't use the lamp too often because the merchant kept a tally of how much oil was used, and how often it was replaced. Every lamp in the house, mind you. So I travelled the road by moonlight.'

He takes a breath. 'It was all very well making plans. Plans are safe. But I couldn't put it off forever. Nissa became my personal provider of goods and foodstuffs. I don't know how she managed it, but she did. It's the other reason why I'll always be grateful to her. That, and the fact that she helped me find the information I was looking for. I'm not sure I could have done it without her. Certainly not as quickly, anyway.

'One evening, when the merchant had gone out, she called me into her room. I'd never been in it before, but I don't remember much about it, only that I was astonished at what she'd managed to acquire. She even had some of the merchant's candles, which were kept under lock and key in a chest in Tir's storeroom. And money, too, in a blue velvet pouch. I told her I didn't need it, I had enough of my own, which was true. The merchant may have been short on praise but he rewarded success, and I'd had no time to spend it. She shook the bag at me and told me not to be silly. There was no point arguing.'

He falls silent. The money is long spent.

At dinner that evening the boy concentrates on his food, avoiding Kumbar's eye. He and Nissa have made a plan, more three legs than four, but better than panic. That night he will leave Kumbar's house. He will turn left and walk through the streets, avoiding dogs, and leave by the city gates.

Nissa is passing Minu titbits under the table and the merchant is pretending not to notice. A warm breeze steals through the open window, stirring the flames in the lamps. The boy takes in the scene: Tama, always nervous, twisting her napkin, hoping not to be spoken to; Adara, trying not to look too pleased with the compliments Kumbar's friends are giving her; Tir, picking at her plate; Ketta, the gardener, whose hands are unusually clean. The boy can hardly look at Kumbar, expansive in girth and gesture, commanding from his throne-like chair.

There is nothing more to do. Everything is packed and ready. His room has never looked more welcoming. He has never been more ready to leave it. He sits and waits as the hours deepen around him.

His foot has fallen asleep. He gets up from the bed, stamping quietly. A knock at the door. Nissa's knock. 'Are you there?' she whispers.

'Where else would I be?' he whispers back.

He lights a candle, and her eyes gleam. She tells him everyone is asleep, and her father is snoring. He drags a large pack from under his bed. The lantern hanging from the strap clinks faintly.

Nissa opens the door and looks out. 'Don't fall over Minu.'

He follows her downstairs, through the hall, to the front door. A lamp glows on a table; it is lit at night, to guide spirits out safely. The door is locked. Nissa takes a key from her pocket and opens it.

He is silent. While he has visited this moment many times, he still doesn't know what to say.

'When you get back, don't forget to tell Papa I helped,' she whispers.

There is something painful in the boy's chest. He can hardly speak. Nissa reaches up and kisses his cheek. 'Follow the map,' she says, and turns away.

Chapter Nine

Night closes like a soft wall around him. The road strikes the underside of his boots. Nissa's preparations paid off; leaving Harakim was easier than he thought. Two bottles of good wine, a nod from the guard, the postern gate opening and shutting.

From time to time he stretches out a hand, as if the darkness might condense into a full stop. When he judges it safe he stops, slides the pack from his back, unhooks the lantern and fishes for the tinderbox. The sudden light makes him nervous. If there are thieves, brigands, murderers, they will surely be flying towards it. Reminding himself why he left, he walks on.

A rustling noise makes him freeze. Steeling himself, he turns the lantern slowly, showing it to the shadows. At either side of the road, low grasses flare softly. He hoists the pack higher and walks on. After a while he tries singing, but his voice sounds thin and uncertain, and he trails off. Nissa pointed out that adventures always began under cover of darkness, but he feels nothing like a bold adventurer. There is no need to wonder why. The reasons are behind and in front of him.

There are open shadows on either side now, and the lantern is looking both ways. At a fork in the road he stands with closed eyes, visualising the map. He turns left and walks a little further, but his legs are telling him he needs rest. Reluctantly he leaves the road. In the short time he has known it, it has become a companion. A bird shrieks in the treetops. As he pushes through tangled grasses he hopes it isn't an *ishratur*, a bird that feasts when people die. He shrugs the pack from his back, props it against a tree and tries to make it into a pillow. Exhausted, he closes his eyes.

Harakim was never this noisy. The treetops are louder than the market square. Strings of noise – trills, hoots, cackles – run from branch to branch. Every sound is like a lamp flashed in his face. When he finally resigns himself to wakefulness, he sleeps.

It is, inescapably, morning. The boy's trousers are soaked with dew, and a very small frog is sitting on the tip of his boot, staring at him. He studies the greeny-brown skin, the black eyes. The frog shuffles, its splayed feet gripping his boot. There is every chance it will leap straight into his mouth. Without taking its eyes from his face it springs forward, over his head, and onto the tree trunk.

He sits up, rubbing his face. No matter that he has no idea where he is, or that his feet have died of cold, his stomach has first call. The dried fruit he takes from his pack tastes better than all the seeded breads at Kumbar's table. The memory makes him tighten his jaw.

Before he sets off again, he unbuckles the belt Kumbar gave him and flings it as high and hard as he can. He is done with the merchant, his house and his name. The silver buckle flashes as it catches in the branches of a tree. He doesn't look back.

All day the boy walks. The road is part of his feet now. He couldn't turn off it if he tried. Dust travels with him, on his boots, in his clothes. People pass by, going to and from Harakim. There are parties on foot, laden with baskets, men on horseback, one galloping so wildly he is either a messenger or a guilty man. A family of three perched on the seat of a wagon, the child complaining, the mother giving it an apple. Each time the boy steps to the side of the road, pretending to be looking for something in his pack, reluctant to show his face. While he doubts anyone will come after him, he can't take the risk. He was one of the merchant's possessions, after all.

Another night, this time on the other side of the road. He lights the lantern and watches moths gather with loving urgency, heartbreaking in their need. The largest, the colour of dust with markings like the footprints of a bird, flutters against the panes of the lantern. He cups his hand over it, peering through the gentle cage of his fingers. It has fine, feathery antennae and a woolly body. Against the spray of lantern light he can imagine it a giant moth, viewed from far away.

'If you were,' he tells it, 'I'd be running as fast as I could in the opposite direction.'

He removes his hand and the moth blunders into the pane. He can stand no more of its self-destructiveness, so he opens the door and pinches out the flame.

The landscape is slowly changing, the trees growing taller, the grasses thinning. The early sun steams warmth from the air; mist rises. As a group of merchants approach the boy steps back from the road, turning his head to watch

133

them pass, their horses snorting and flicking their ears. When the dust settles, he sets off again. Enough, he tells himself. This time he won't hide, no matter who comes his way.

He is beginning to suspect he has been passing the same tree over and over again. Taking the map from his shirt, he stares at it accusingly. No one has written *Here I died of boredom* or *In this place I waited for grass to grow*. Closer examination of the bottom left-hand corner reveals that a mark he dismissed as a stain or a crease is, in fact, part of the map. A vertical black line. Will he at some point encounter a wall of ink blocking his way? It would make a change, at least.

His irritation rises. Did the map-maker not know the responsibility he had? It is more than ink and parchment; it is faith, and hope. He is so stirred up he nearly walks into a horse. The horse bridles; the rider laughs.

'Careful, my friend,' he says, 'he isn't famed for his good nature.' The boy looks up at a man dressed in a green cloak that covers the horse's hindquarters. He catches a gleam, like a pool glimpsed at distance through trees. The hilt of a sword. Once again he feels his lack. He'd argued for one, but Nissa said he would only cut himself.

'Going far?' He doesn't reply. 'Fair enough,' the rider says. His long red-gold hair and blue eyes are a combination the boy has never seen before. His lean face looks humorous and ready to be amused. 'Are you hungry?' he asks.

'Maybe,' the boy says warily. The rider nods, opening a saddlebag of tooled leather. The boy recognises the hand of a craftsman in the scrolls and flowers, and thinks of

Liso. When he is offered a piece of pie he hesitates, but his stomach speaks for him.

The rider laughs, slipping down from the saddle. 'Eat,' he says.

Hunger makes it the queen of pies. When he has finished, the rider gives him a cloth to wipe his hands. 'I'm Yorin,' he says. The boy introduces himself. 'Well, Arun, as we both seem to be going the same way, why don't we travel together for a while? I'm heading for Gali.' The boy recognises it as one of the few names on the map. 'There's a passable inn, and Tobi needs a rest.'

The boy realises he is referring to the horse, who stands very tall in his dark-brown coat, twitching his coarse black tail. 'Have you come far?' he asks.

'Too far,' Yorin replies with a smile.

'And where are you going?'

'Here and there.'

The boy is beginning to feel irritated. 'Fine, don't tell me.'

Yorin grins. 'I seem to remember asking you a similar question, and that one ran into a wall, too. Which isn't a bad thing. Best keep your wits about you when you're on the road.' He studies the boy for a moment. 'You don't know whether to trust me or not, which shows you haven't entirely abandoned common sense. But' – another grin – 'if I were you, I'd be more concerned about Tobi. He gets nippy when he's hungry.'

The day heats up as they walk, Yorin leading Tobi, the boy at a safe distance from the horse. After a while Yorin says, 'I'm guessing you've come from Harakim?' The boy's heart beats faster. After a short silence Yorin says, 'Peace, my friend, I'm not interested in why you left. That's your business, not mine.'

The boy's head is suddenly spinning. Yorin catches his arm. 'You've been out in the sun too long. Come on.'

He finds himself sitting under the shade of a tree, drinking from the water bottle Yorin hands him.

'I think you need something to eat.' Yorin opens the saddlebag again. He gives the boy a thick slab of fruit cake. When he has eaten every crumb, Yorin says, 'You'd better rest for while. If you want to get to wherever you're going, you need to look after yourself.'

With a stab of pain, the boy realises he has always been looked after. By his mother, his sister, the merchant's household and, whether he likes it or not, by Nissa.

Yorin sits down beside him, his cloak falling away from his tunic. The boy's eye is drawn irresistibly to the sword's bright hilt, the downward-curving crosspiece. The pommel is round as a peach, and gilded. It is not a sword to be taken lightly. Spy or assassin? he wonders as his eyes begin to close.

When he wakes, it is late afternoon. The sun has shifted a tawny haunch, nudging the tree's shadow. He shakes his head, coughs and glances around, but Yorin is nowhere to be seen. A little way off, dust is settling on the road. His pack – he looks around wildly but can't see it. With a rush of cold shock he thinks it has been stolen, then realises he is leaning against it.

The shrubs rustle and part. A horse's face peers through. 'He's getting fatter,' Yorin observes as he squeezes past. 'Feeling better?' More relieved than he will admit, the boy nods. 'Good. If we're going to make Gali before nightfall, we'd better get moving. Here.' He throws the boy a patty made from rice and meat. It is sticky and delicious. 'One of the first rules of travel,' Yorin says. 'Always have enough to eat. Give me the name of a village,' he adds as they walk back to the road, 'and I'll tell you what I ate there. I have a particular fondness for figs.' There is a glint in his eye as he says it.

The trees are growing broader and taller. 'Only for a while,' Yorin says. He is leading Tobi, the boy walking beside him. 'It doesn't take long for them to give up. The Haruan Desert,' he explains. 'It sets to work on the plants and flowers long before you see it. They start off in good health, sure that nothing will take the greenness out of them. But the desert knows better. The closer it gets, the stronger its spirit becomes.'

The boy shoots him a sideways glance. Is he travelling with a poet, or do journeys have this effect on people? If so, will he be able to walk himself into poetry? He asks Yorin how far it is to the desert.

'Another five days, maybe. Tobi's inclined to break down at times, just to keep me grateful. And there are people you don't want to meet on the road. All being well, we'll reach Gali tomorrow.'

The light is fading, the air growing cooler. People approach; two women, a man, a child leading a small goat. They pass with a courteous greeting. The boy wonders if poems have been written about such everyday things. If not, they should be. Perhaps he will turn out to be a poet of people and their lives, not cushioned palaces or sun-dazzled fountains. He isn't sure how he feels about it. Palaces and fountains seem more appealing.

'Off again?' Yorin grins.

The boy returns with a start. Imagining seems to throw a veil over things, as if the thought is real and the real is not. He stares up a little giddily. Yorin's blue eyes are amused. 'You're not from Harakim originally, are you?'

It is not quite a question. The boy finds himself unable to reply. The further he travels from his valley the smaller it seems, and yet also more dear. He has learned to keep it at bay but, like a tide, it won't be bidden. 'You're not obliged to answer,' Yorin says. The boy looks away from the understanding in his face.

The road is softening into dusk when men on horseback approach them. Yorin's face remains unchanged, but the boy senses his attention. The men are all dressed in similar fashion – leather jerkin, knife at the belt, boots of scuffed and dusty leather – and sit very straight in the saddle.

'*Kahrien istra*,' Yorin says as they ride up. With equal courtesy they return the greeting. The tone is familiar to the boy, but the dialect is not. He wonders if there are invisible boundaries at which one tongue ends and another begins. But then, he reasons, language rides a horse and crosses a boundary; it boards a ship and anchors in another country.

In a short while the horsemen are riding off down the road. 'What was that about?' he asks.

'Well,' Yorin says, 'I could make something up, and you'd be none the wiser.' The boy glares. Yorin laughs. 'They were speaking Fezuli. The Fezul are renowned thief-catchers, and they're heading for Harakim. They've heard of a young man who's escaped with a good deal of his master's treasure, and there's a huge reward for his head.'

The boy stares up at him. Yorin holds his gaze for a moment, then starts laughing. 'Too easy,' he says. 'They're thief-catchers, but they're not after you. Besides, I know an honest face when I see one. Here.' He offers the boy his water bottle. 'It'll take the edge off your indignation.'

In spite of himself, the boy grins.

'The world isn't as easy to read as you are,' Yorin says after a while. 'If I had to guess, I'd say you've not long left a rich man's house where you worked in a position of some responsibility, that he probably taught you all he knew and wouldn't be best pleased to find you gone. How am I doing?'

The boy opens his mouth, closes it, opens it again and says curtly, 'Anything else?'

Yorin shrugs. 'Just that there's a reason for you being here, rather than simply running away. You're looking for something, or someone.'

The boy takes a breath. Facts derived from the observation of details – the soft linen of a shirt, the subtle stitchwork of a pair of boots – are one thing, but Yorin has no right to look any further. His shoulders sag. There seems little point in denying it. He nods.

'Have I earned a reward?' Yorin asks.

'What kind of reward?' the boy says suspiciously.

'Information. I'd like to know where you're going.'

The boy eyes him for a moment. 'I am going into the Haruan Desert to find the tribe of the House of Goash,' he says formally.

Yorin sits back in the saddle and whistles. 'You don't do things by halves, do you?' The boy narrows his eyes. Is he being mocked? 'Peace,' Yorin says, his face serious now.

'You've picked two things I wouldn't advise anyone to do. The desert will suck the life out of you if you don't know how to look after yourself. And the tribe of the House of Goash . . .' He shakes his head. 'Do you want to tell me why?'

Sunset highlights the contours of the trees as they come to a deep bend in the road. Telling Yorin the reason for his journey was easier than he'd thought. He kept it brief, and at the end Yorin merely said, 'Fair enough.'

'Ah, here we are,' he says, pointing. The trees are dwindling; they follow the road until it becomes a street running through a village. The boy looks around as they pass the houses, but no one is about. The sun quivers behind the roof of the furthest house, which stands on its own.

'The Damson,' Yorin says. 'The finest beer in Gali.'

As they approach the inn, Yorin advises the boy not to mention the desert. 'Or the tribe of the House of Goash. Keep your wits about you, and keep quiet.'

'Anything else?' the boy asks. Yorin laughs.

When Tobi has been stabled – Yorin insists on doing it himself – they go into the Damson, where the innkeeper, lean and nervous-looking, welcomes them.

'From –?' he asks, but Yorin waves him aside. 'Of course,' he says smoothly, and shows them into the common room.

Although the evening has not yet cooled, a fire murmurs in the hearth. They find a table beside it, and order dinner. The food is good and, Yorin says, the beer even better. Afterwards they sit quietly as the fire, tired of casting itself afresh, begins to sink down.

Stirring, the boy says, 'You said those men were from Fezul. Where is it?'

'North-east of here. The dialect isn't hard to pick up, but it's not very elegant.' Images of words clothed variously in cottons, wools, silks, come into the boy's mind. Yorin's face flickers in the firelight. 'You're thinking again,' he says, putting his feet up on the hearth.

'What's wrong with that?'

Yorin smiles. 'Nothing, in moderation, but it can be disastrous. Look what happened to the *dhaerna.*'

The boy waits, but Yorin seems content to watch the fire. 'Well,' he says crossly, 'what did happen to it?'

Yorin puts his hands together and raises them to his face, as if in contemplation. After a moment, he begins a story. The boy discovers that the *dhaerna* is one of the greatest thinkers in the Greworld, a place between this world and the next. In the story it encounters a fox. In the resulting battle of wits, the fox comes off best; the *dhaerna* meets a noisy end.

Yorin tells it, the boy acknowledges grudgingly, with humour, invention and style. Afterwards, he is quiet for a while. 'An exploding goblin isn't going to put me off thinking,' he says.

'I never thought it would,' Yorin says with mild surprise, and returns to his contemplation of the fire. The boy has a sense of something unscrupulous being performed on him, but he can't quite put his finger on it. When they go up to the room they will be sharing, he is still trying to work it out.

'The cham is very good,' Yorin says at breakfast. 'I think they make it with cream instead of milk. Careful, though, it's hot.'

141

The boy concentrates on his bowl. The thickened meal is sweetened with honey. Yorin is right. It is very good.

'If you want company, I'll come with you as far as the desert,' Yorin says. 'I haven't got anything better to do at the moment. Besides, you'll probably get lost otherwise, and I don't want that on my conscience.' He pushes back his chair, yawning.

'Fine,' the boy says shortly. Yorin grins.

Heat builds as they set off again. From time to time, Tobi sighs gustily. Yorin rummages in a saddlebag and fishes out a wrinkled yellow apple. 'Here,' he says, throwing it to the boy, 'it'll put you in his good books.'

Mindful of the size of Tobi's teeth, the boy dusts the apple carefully on his shirt and offers it to the horse. His lips feel their way around it with surprising delicacy. When he crunches down, the heat of his breath covers the boy's hand.

'Catch.' Yorin throws him another apple. He eats half and offers Tobi the rest. 'If you do that every time, you'll starve,' Yorin says. 'He's a master of guilt.'

The boy wonders how he knows. A horse is simply a horse, a creature whose beginning and end offer neither enlightenment nor, if his only experience is anything to go by, comfort. If he were forced to ride, he'd invent a saddle that was part cushion, part water. That way, it would follow your movements. On the other hand, you'd probably end up seasick. He thinks of the swift grace of the *Silver Falcon* as she ran with the wind.

'See that?' Yorin points at a huge slab of glittering black rock, taller than a man on horseback, standing at the side of the road. It is incised with markings like the spines of a small fish. There is something familiar about them. 'It's where traders used to meet. The stone came first, the writing later, courtesy of your friends.'

It takes a moment for the boy to realise that Yorin is referring to the tribe of the House of Goash. This must be the vertical black line on the map. 'What does it say?' he asks as they reach it.

'It's a warning.' For once Yorin isn't smiling. 'If you go back on a promise, you'll suffer in a great many ways, all designed for maximum discomfort.'

'Used to meet?' the boy asks.

'Would you come back after reading it?'

'But surely –' the boy begins, and stops. Surely what? Surely if you keep your promise there is nothing to fear. But he knows a promise sometimes falls short of its reach. And there are men who simply want more.

As Yorin predicted, it takes five days to reach the desert, with overnight stops at inns of increasing shabbiness. In spite of his initial misgivings, the boy is grateful for the company. Yorin's good humour, his cheerful manner, stop him from dwelling too hard on what he discovered at Kumbar's house. But he will never forgive the merchant, and cannot even bear to think his name.

The trees have vanished. The world has turned to sand. The Haruan Desert. The boy can only stare. Nothing could have prepared him for such vastness. But it isn't simply a blank page; it dips and swells, rising into great dunes that hold within them deep shadows. In the far distance there are mountains.

Yorin waits quietly as he takes it in. If he wished for nothingness, he has found it. A communion of sky and sand and heat. His stomach quakes. What now?

'Well, we got here,' Yorin says airily. He unbuckles a saddlebag, pulls out a length of material and throws it to the boy. The light-coloured cotton scarf is fringed with small tassels. 'The sun's pretty fierce. Best keep covered.' He pulls out another scarf and winds it round his head. 'Ready?'

So he is coming too. Relief overwhelms the boy. 'Yes,' he says.

Chapter Ten

Arun coughs, as if clearing sand from his throat. 'It gets everywhere,' he says. 'In your hair, your clothes, your eyes. But that's not the worst of it. In the desert, there's nothing between you and your mind. At the time I didn't realise how lucky I was to have Yorin with me. He told me a saying: the only way to conquer a desert is to live in it. The deeper I went, the more desperate I was to come out again. But I took that first step. I had to.'

He closes his eyes, letting memory find its way.

The boy's legs are aching, his throat parched. His eyes swim, with sun, with sand, with heat that has a presence all its own. Tobi slides a little and tosses his head, snorting. Yorin, who is leading him, pats his neck reassuringly. For some time they travel in silence. The only noise is the wind. A little way off, the boy sees a stand of trees, small, twisted, defeated.

When they reach them, Yorin takes a knife from his belt and shears off a branch. A clear liquid seeps from the cut. 'Try it,' he says, offering it to the boy. The liquid is cool and sweet as it drips into his mouth. Yorin sets his foot in Tobi's stirrup and swings lightly into the saddle. 'We're lucky. You can travel for days and never find one.' He tells the boy it is *osarian*, which means 'life of the water in the tree'.

'I thought deserts, were, well, deserted.'

Yorin smiles. 'Yes, and no. Plants do grow here, wherever they can find a foothold. Vines, shrubs, anything with a long enough memory for water. Sometimes people manage to cultivate crops, but it takes a lot of work. Animals fare better, so mostly they herd goats and cattle. Others, of course, have made a different way of life.'

The boy looks at him; under the hood of his scarf his face is unreadable, his eyes narrowed against the sun.

The light is beginning to fail. 'We'll stop here for the night,' Yorin says. Rising before them, improbably, is what looks like a sculpture of stone. It is as if a great wind once drove the sand into a towering crest that froze as it broke and fell, a stilled wave holding within it the cup of a cave. The boy is not entirely persuaded about its suitability as a shelter. There is something unnerving about it.

'Don't worry,' Yorin says, 'it's not going anywhere.' He jumps down from Tobi and tugs a couple of rolled-up blankets from the back of the saddle. 'Believe it or not, that was a plum tree.' He points to a withered stem. 'There was a tribe here once, famous for cultivating fruit trees. Every year they found just enough water for the trees to survive, and when it finally dried up, they left. The plums were magnificent, apparently.' He glances at the boy. 'They'll remain that way as long as the trees never bear fruit.'

Ducking into the stone shelter, he throws down the blankets. When he comes out he unbuckles Tobi's girth, hauls the saddle from his back, and slips off the bridle.

Tobi lowers his head and shudders luxuriously from nose to tail. Yorin takes a leather bowl from a saddlebag, fills it with water and offers it to the horse, who gulps it noisily.

The boy settles himself on a blanket and sits looking out. Someone standing above would have no idea he is tucked underneath. The mouth of the shelter darkens; Yorin is leading Tobi in. The horse's nostrils flare and he shies a little, but once inside he stands placidly, his head lowered. The boy eyes him warily.

'Don't worry,' Yorin says, 'he doesn't snore.'

Dinner is a slice of pie, some dried fruit, a few mouthfuls of water. Yorin tells him they should have enough, as long as they are careful. Enough for what? the boy wonders as he looks out on a sunset of extravagant beauty. He has never seen such colours, violet deepening into mauve streaked with lavender and rose. He thinks of writing it down, but is aware of Yorin beside him.

'You can try,' Yorin says, 'but you'd be joining a very long line.' The boy looks at him. 'Of fools who write about sunsets. Not that I'm including you in their number, of course. You do write, don't you? Don't worry, I won't tell anyone.' The boy looks out at the huge moon hanging above, and says yes.

Yorin claps him on the back. 'That wasn't so hard. So, what have you written?'

The boy stares out at the sky. 'I've only really jotted things down. Bits and pieces.' He hesitates. 'When I was younger, I wanted to be a poet.' He holds his breath. If his father's reaction was anything to go by, he has just declared himself to be of no use to the world in general. But Yorin sits up, interested, and the boy finds himself telling him about the poet who came to his village, and his disobedience in going to the *fahruz*.

When he has finished, Yorin nods. 'Why not?' he says.

Evening wastes into night. The boy shivers. It has become very cold. When he asks why they haven't lit a fire, Yorin tells him many things are drawn to the light.

Whether hours have passed, or a single stubborn minute, he can't tell. He has never been this cold before. His feet have passed out. He groans, turning over. Yorin appears to be sleeping. Tobi is standing with one hip relaxed, a hoof-tip resting on the ground. The boy shuffles to the edge of the shelter and looks out.

The sky is spattered with stars in clusters and brilliant sprays. They shimmer and quiver and wink. There are shapes and forms, too; the more he looks, the more he sees. That one, to the left, is a sheep or a dog. A radiant goat, perhaps. The one just above him is a snake. There are people, too – he recognises the warrior with the sword because his father once pointed it out. Those, like a pair of rushes bending towards each other, are the Lovers. He knows this because his mother showed him. And that one is Yaria, the Ring, which his mother called the Pledge. He blinks, because the stars are weeping.

He must have fallen asleep. His bones are frozen to the sand. Every inch of his body aches. It is early; daybreak moves slowly across the sky.

'How did you sleep?' Yorin asks. He is already up, looking fresh and rested. The boy pulls a face, and he laughs. 'Give it time,' he says.

They breakfast on bread, dried fruit and a couple of

apples. The boy devours the food gratefully. Here in the desert, appetite sharpens itself on anything it can get.

'That's better,' Yorin says, stretching and yawning. 'It's going to be another hot day. Best get going.'

The boy covers his head with his scarf and follows him out of the shelter.

Light in the desert is without tenderness. At home, in idle moments, the boy watched the tree's shadow walk around the almond tree. He watched the shadows of fish moving over the bed of the stream, slipping over pebbles and lying quiet under the bank. When they had fish for dinner, he wondered if he was eating the fish's shadow as well. He finds the thought disturbing now, since following it to its natural end means he has shadows inside him, too.

Yorin leans down from Tobi and hands him a water bottle. 'It'll probably take another couple of days to find them,' he says.

The boy drinks, and wets the neck of his shirt. Having bent his nose on Yorin's polite and cordial walls before, he doesn't ask how he knows. 'You didn't have to come with me.' It is out and naked in its rudeness before he can stop it.

'I know,' Yorin says, grinning.

Tobi turns his head and gives the boy a long stare. He thinks he may as well finish the job. 'Then why did you?'

Yorin considers for a moment. 'Perhaps I needed a change of scenery, perhaps I needed to see the desert again. Perhaps –'

'Just tell me why.'

Yorin gives him a steady look. 'Do you eat a peach quickly or slowly?'

The boy takes a deep breath. He is beginning to feel he needs markers to keep the place in the conversation. He considers the peach. Resplendent, it shimmers in front of his eyes. If he could, he would reach out and cram it into his mouth until they both burst with sweetness. 'It depends,' he says.

Yorin gives an approving nod. 'Fair enough.'

The boy shakes his head in exasperation. 'I'm not like you. You'll never get caught out because your feet hardly ever touch the ground. Nor does your tongue.'

There is a brief silence, and they both start laughing.

His eyes must have been replaced with sand, since it is all the view he has. The novelty of feeling his feet sink, roll, pull up again as his ankles protest has long since worn off. At this moment he would sell his soul for solid ground.

Yorin gives him a shrewd look. 'People come into the desert to think,' he says. 'Some of them go mad when they find themselves with only their thoughts for company. No friends, no beer.'

'Do you have friends?' the boy asks.

'I have acquaintances. In some languages, of course, friend can mean anything from confessor to wife. It depends on the context, and the nuance. It can come as a bit of a shock. But' – he glances at the boy – 'some things are the same wherever you go. Being swindled, for instance. I once found myself part-betrothed.'

'Part-betrothed?' The boy looks sceptical.

'It's true. I was a cloth-seller at the time. I'd met a merchant in Veshar who was looking for a particular type of scarlet cloth. It's hard to come by, but I had my sources.' He smiles. 'The merchant invited me to his house to discuss his requirements, and after we'd passed the time of day, he told me he had a price in mind. The piece of paper he gave me contained a sum well below the value of the cloth. He said he knew it was low but that if I agreed to it I might, if I wished, also have his daughter's hand in marriage.

'It seemed a strange thing to say. If the merchant was so anxious to marry her off, surely he'd make me a good offer, rather than the insult he'd written down. But it also intrigued me, so I told him I'd consider it. I could hardly leave without having tea, of course, so I sat and waited politely. When the door opened, a woman came in. He introduced her as his daughter.'

Yorin pauses, looking into the distance. 'She was so beautiful that when she poured my tea I had to hold the cup with both hands to stop it from shaking. When she'd gone out again, we talked for a while about the weather, the city, the usual things. Before I left, I said I'd give his offer some thought, and went back to the inn where I was staying.

'Inns are a good source of information. I sat in the common room, ordered a drink, and waited. It didn't take long before I heard the merchant's name mentioned by a group of men at a nearby table. They were well on the way to being drunk, so I decided to help them along. They asked me my business, which was customary; I lied, which was also customary, said I was new to the city, and offered to buy them drinks. Sons of camels the lot of them, left my purse considerably lighter, but I got what I wanted.

'One of them asked if I'd come across the merchant. When I said I hadn't, he told me it was my lucky day, that

I'd had a narrow escape. That was all he could manage before his head hit the table, but another man told me to take no notice, his heart was broken. The rest of them started laughing and I asked them why, since a broken heart was no laughing matter. That's when they told me about the merchant's way of doing business.'

Yorin drinks from his water bottle. 'He fished in a particular way. He baited his hook with beauty. Which,' he adds with a rueful look, 'makes fools of us all. He'd invite a seller to his house, offer a ridiculously low price for their goods, and throw in his daughter's hand in marriage. While they were smarting at the insult, his daughter – did I mention she was gloriously beautiful? – would serve them tea. The seller was generally so stunned that he agreed to the merchant's price. If he was unmarried, of course. Sometimes even if he was. They'd sign the contract – legally binding, naturally – and the seller would go away thinking the merchant short-sighted and himself a lucky man.

'There was a catch, of course. The next day, when the seller turned up with his goods, the merchant would appear at his door in great distress, full of apologies. He'd tell the seller his daughter had run away, she'd made a secret engagement, and he had no idea where to find her. He, on the other hand, knew exactly where to find the seller's signature. He'd tell the man – with great regret – that the authorities took a rather painful view of a broken contract. They both knew there was nothing the seller could do but accept the price for his goods.

'One part at least was true. His "daughter" was engaged. By the merchant. To reel you in. She was no more his daughter than I'm a member of the guild of carrot merchants.'

'What did you do?' the boy asks.

'I could have walked away. I hadn't signed anything, and I'd had enough of the place by then. But honour' – he grins at the boy – 'had to be satisfied.

'When I went back the following morning, I was shown into the merchant's garden, offered fruit, sweet biscuits, tea. We sat drinking tea, admiring the roses, talking about everything except the contract.

'When I'd drunk so much tea I could have watered the roses myself, he asked me if I'd thought the matter over. I said how could I not, having seen his daughter. He got up, walked about a little, and said I would understand how difficult it was for him to part with her. But he could see I was a good man, and if I accepted his offer he'd be content. I took another biscuit and gave it my undivided attention. When I'd finished, I told him it was very good. But not quite as good as the ones my wife made.'

Yorin smiles at the look on the boy's face. 'The temperature dropped rapidly. The merchant pretended to examine a rose. When he came back to the table he cleared his throat, asked my forgiveness and said he hadn't understood I was married. I said that marriage was indeed a difficult thing to understand, and I hadn't said so because I hadn't been asked. Note the form of words. I didn't say directly, "You didn't ask me", nor did the merchant say, "You didn't tell me." We were both walking down the tunnel leading to the arena of utter politeness. It was to be death by courtesy.' He grins broadly.

'It took him a while to come up with a reply, but when he did he said that if I were married, how could I marry his daughter? I took another biscuit – they really were very good – and said, "Let us agree that if I am married, the lady I met yesterday is your daughter." I could feel him thinking that something was being done, and it wasn't by him.

'I wasn't unreasonable. I told him that if he was willing to buy my cloth – I showed him a piece of paper with a very complimentary figure on it – all would be forgotten. His eyebrows told me what he thought of it, but we both knew he was sunk. He signed, I made a profit, I left.' He shrugs almost helplessly.

The boy is thinking hard. 'But you weren't really part-betrothed,' he says.

'You never give up, do you? There I was thinking you'd be full of admiration for the way I got out of it, but no, you head right back to the beginning. Although,' Yorin adds with a sidelong glance, 'we were engaged, after a fashion. Later on that night.'

He bursts out laughing at the look on the boy's face.

When they stop later for a meal, the boy is still turning over what Yorin said. Is it a good thing to be someone who never gives up? Is it a form of courage, or patience? No, he thinks, it's persistence, surely?

Yorin is leaning against Tobi's side as he eats. 'Go on,' he says, 'I'm waiting.' When the boy tells him, he looks thoughtful. 'There are times when it's not a bad idea to cut your losses. Like when you're facing a snake in the desert. Never mind the desert, whenever you come across a snake. Landscapes change, but a snake's temper never does. They're always in a bad mood. I wonder why.'

He wipes his hands, takes a drink from the water bottle, offers it to the boy, and hoists himself into the saddle. 'It wasn't rhetorical,' he says as they move off.

Beside the pool, Night darkens in anticipation.

'No,' Arun says, 'we didn't argue about the form and substance of rhetoric. I was too busy thinking about snakes. My childhood was relatively snake-free. My mother was quick to show them the door; my father was a less generous host. The only one I can remember seeing, apart from tails disappearing into the grass, was the one he killed. He hung the body on the almond tree, and my sister' – his breath catches in his throat – 'was furiously upset. The noise brought my mother out of the hut. She told my sister to go indoors and called my father over from the vegetable plots. I'll never forget what she said.

'"*Not this tree.*" Her voice was soft – she rarely raised it – but her eyes weren't. For once, my father didn't say anything. He went over to the almond tree and pulled the snake's body from the branch. I watched with a kind of sick fascination. It seemed to take forever to unwind until, at the very end, the tail whipped round the branch. If ever a snake had reason to be bad-tempered, it was that one. No,' he says to Night's unspoken question, 'I didn't come up with anything for Yorin. That came later.'

He stares across the pool, pierced by the memory of a story told beside the fire in a white house, on a winter evening.

Chapter Eleven

Morning brings a drifting mist. The boy wakes, turns over drowsily, rubs his hip, and groans. Hoisting himself up on his elbow, he looks out of the makeshift shelter. Yorin is nowhere in sight but Tobi stands a short distance away, head down, munching on something. He crawls out of the shelter, coughing as he gets to his feet.

'Morning,' a voice calls, and he turns to see Yorin coming towards him. The horizon is piled with yellow and purple clouds. The sun will shortly take its place among them.

'If we meet anyone, leave the talking to me,' Yorin says, heaving the saddle onto Tobi's back. The horse regards him gloomily as he wraps his scarf around his head, his hair glinting in the early sunlight. The boy has no idea how his own – a little too long, a colour not worth mentioning, as Nissa always told him – looks, since he has never been able to stand behind himself.

He ponders as he walks alongside Yorin and Tobi, his pack pressing damply against his back. If someone came up to him in a market, say, or on a road, what would they make of him? Does the way he walks give a clue to his character? Some people, women in particular, move a certain way. Were they born like that, or did they learn?

Sailors on the quay walked with the sea in their heels. He tried it in his room, but fell over. And Yorin – but Yorin is almost always on horseback. He has seen men wince as they dismount, grumbling about long journeys and being married to the saddle. It isn't the sort of marriage he has in mind. Up to now, he has rarely thought of marriage at all. It is an unknown land.

A few times in his village he witnessed two people standing in front of the headman, Iden, exchanging words to the ringing of little bells. Beyond that, he has only his parents' marriage as a guide. Only once did he and his sister talk about it. One morning, after feeding the hens, she announced that she was never going to agree to an arrangement in which a woman gave and a man took. Her eyes flashed as she told him it wasn't fair or right. It had puzzled and bewildered him. His mother and father came as a pair, and would end as one. That was that.

He said as much to his sister, who snorted. 'Would you bring me tea when I told you to? Would you clean my boots, mend my shirts, bake my bread and' – she swelled in preparation for the finale – 'would you accept it when I told you my word was final, and that was that?'

Her eyes were huge as she stared at him. The boy needed no time to think about it. 'Of course not.'

'*Ha!*' she said. He wasn't sure what truth was contained in this third cousin to a word, but she said nothing more. They were clearly so much in agreement with themselves that neither felt the need to continue. The battle had ended. Both sides had won.

He remembers it clearly: hens bustling in the dust, a

soft wind brushing his cheek, the air tasting sweet. Pain fills his chest. The argument seems very dear to him.

'Off again?' Yorin asks. The boy looks at him, dazed. 'Time for a rest.' Yorin jerks his head towards a stand of trees, some bushes, a drop of shade. He loosens Tobi's girth, and they sit under the trees watching the horse drink from the leather bowl. The boy wishes it were large enough to dive into. After a meal of meat patties and cheese Yorin leans back, closing his eyes. 'Just for a moment,' he says, relaxing from crown to sole. This letting go of his body is a knack the boy admires, while calculating the risk of it failing to return.

The silence lengthens. He shades his eyes and looks out, wondering how big the desert is. If he can't see it all, it must be vast. But then, he reasons, he couldn't see the end of his valley, and it turned out to be smaller than he thought.

Heat swims in front of him, and he pushes the sand with his boot. Grains glitter and slide. Sweat trickles down his back. He imagines frost, his own breath in winter air, but it only leaves him hotter. In the past, some of his dreams involved billowing tents among shimmering sand. Here in the only desert he ever wishes to know, he is glad they were just dreams.

Yorin stirs, opens his eyes, and stretches. 'That was good. I'd made a house of ice and was living in it happily. Although the heat makes some things easier.' He grins at the boy, who blushes and glances away at the sky. The sun is caught in a blue haze, a gold coin slowly melting.

'Time to move on,' Yorin says, getting to his feet.

Two days pass. He knows this because the sun rises and sets. Other than that they look identical. He is so deep in thought that he jumps when Yorin says urgently, 'Over there. Can you see them?'

The boy shades his eyes. The desert has a way of making solid objects lose their senses. Heat glides like water over the sand, catching three reflections in the current. Slowly they resolve into camels bearing robed figures. Under his breath Yorin says, 'Let me do the talking.' The boy is too nervous to argue.

Yorin calls out a greeting. The camel riders stop a little distance away and he urges Tobi forward, making a gesture of welcome that is not returned. As he talks with the riders, the boy takes a closer look. Swathed in robes of pale blue and green, they seem very tall. One man lifts his arm; his robe shifts, and a curved sword strikes silver from the air. The boy wonders how much damage a water bottle could do.

Yorin is making broad gestures, sweeping the horizon with his arm. One of the camel riders laughs. A few more words, and Yorin bows deeply in the saddle. The camel riders bring their hands together, bow their heads briefly, and turn away. Yorin watches them go, shading his eyes. Only when the heat has drunk them up does he ride back to the boy.

'That was lucky,' he says, pulling out a water bottle and taking a long drink. The boy gives him a questioning look. 'Let's just say they wouldn't normally leave travellers overburdened.'

It takes a moment for the boy to realise what he means. 'They were thieves?' he says, shocked.

'They have a different attitude to ownership.'

'Why didn't they try to rob us? There were three of them, and two of us.'

'I implied we were known to the tribe of the House of Goash, and that if we were allowed to pass it would be no bad thing.'

The sun is beginning to dream itself away. 'We'll stop there for the night,' Yorin says, nodding. In the distance, clustered round what looks like a dried-up pool, is a small group of palm trees. Flowers grow round the pool, yellow and tall.

'The desert may be silent but it isn't dead,' Yorin says as they reach it. 'There's water under there, waiting to return when the time's right.'

The boy looks at the sun-baked mud. 'How does it know?' he asks.

'It knows.'

Unfolding blankets, they settle down to dinner. 'This reminds me of something,' Yorin says through a mouthful of bread. 'A long time ago a lady was travelling in the desert, on the way to meet her bridegroom. Her name was Lady Asai.

'Ah,' he says, shaking his head as if remembering, 'if you could have seen that caravan. A hundred camels bearing chests of treasure packed so tight that if you sliced through you'd see veins of ruby and emerald, diamond and sapphire. Hand-picked members of the lady's guard riding sixty horses of such delicacy they wore special boots to protect their hooves from the heat of the sand. Forty handmaidens in litters drawn by white horses. Banners of gold and silver, decorations of turquoise and ivory, filmy silks fluttering from the carriage of Lady Asai.

'The desert had a spring whose fame went before it. Which, if you think about it, wouldn't be hard since a spring, contrary to its name, isn't the speediest of things. Fame, on the other hand, has a tendency to sprint and expire. That's been my experience, at least.' He makes a droll face. 'The spring is shaped like a perfect crescent moon. If you stand on the high dunes at sunset, it looks as if the moon is lying down on the sand.

'That night, when the caravan stopped beside the crescent spring, Lady Asai asked the captain to fill a bottle with water. She intended to present it to her bridegroom. If he hadn't the wit to recognise its worth, she said, he wasn't worthy of her hand.

'At dusk the following day, they reached the watering-place where Lady Asai's bridegroom and his very grand entourage were waiting. Lady Asai was handed out of her carriage by the captain of the guard. In a simple gown the colour of peach blossom, she put the light of the sun to shame. When her bridegroom approached, he bowed and took her hand. For a moment it seemed as if he were going to read her fortune, but instead he kissed her palm. She offered him the bottle filled with water from the crescent spring. He took it, glanced at it, and handed it to one of his men.'

For a moment Yorin is silent. The boy looks into the dusk, and shivers. He is still getting used to how hard the temperature falls in the desert.

'The next morning,' Yorin says, 'when Lady Asai's handmaidens went to her tent, it was empty. The bridegroom's men and Lady Asai's personal guard searched everywhere for her. When the sun set on the third day, it was agreed she was lost to them. The next morning the bridegroom and his men returned to their country, Lady Asai's caravan to theirs. On the way back, on the orders of the captain of the guard, they stopped at the crescent spring.

'That evening, a scream brought the captain of the guard running to the spring. It was one of the handmaidens, in great distress, crying that she had seen her lady. When he asked where, she pointed to the water. The captain looked; there, indeed, was the lovely face of Lady Asai. He blinked in astonishment; a small wind piqued the water; the lady was gone. It's said you can hear her singing sometimes, when the spring holds the crescent of the true moon in its arms.'

As Yorin ends his tale they sit quietly for a while, the boy still gazing into the crescent spring.

'Yorin was a born storyteller,' Arun says, 'and part of me envied it, but mostly I was content to sit and listen. That night I lay looking up at the sky, feeling overwhelmed. I'd never seen such a beginning. Mirashi writes about

> the forecasting stars
> she doesn't quite believe in

but that's what it felt like: the stars were a road, and I was ready to go wherever they took me. I'd never felt closer to my family than there beside that dried-up pool in the desert. Maybe it was because I knew that tomorrow we might be meeting the tribe of the House of Goash. The thought played tunes in my stomach all night. When I woke in the chilly dawn I was glad, but fearful too.'

Tension is growing in the boy's head and stomach. He rinses his mouth with lukewarm water tasting faintly of goat. He trudges on, feeling as if he is burrowing ever deeper into the sun. At last, when he thinks no part of him will ever be free of this place, Yorin reins Tobi in. They have reached the foot of a high dune fluted by the wind. It looks like the spine of a gigantic slumbering creature.

'It's called *Menharva*, "the Last Dune". That's where their lands begin,' Yorin says. 'We need to be careful. They're here, even though we can't see them.'

They toil up the towering dune. At the top, the boy stands staring in astonishment. Within a great basin lies a vast settlement. There are flocks of goats, camels folded down into angular mounds, fruiting orchards, vegetable plots. And beyond, as far as the eye can see, a city of tents. Slowly they make their way down the slope and into the lands of the tribe of the House of Goash.

As they pass groves of nectarine and peach, the boy wonders how they find purchase in the sand. Here is a knowledge that has learned to outwit the desert. The thought unsettles him.

'The first time I saw them I couldn't believe it, either,' Yorin says. His face suddenly changes. A horseman is coming towards them. 'Leave the talking to me,' he says in a whisper.

The horseman halts a short distance away. He makes a bow, supple and light. Yorin returns it, riding forward until their horses are nose to tail. The boy can't hear what is being said but the tone is not hostile, more a sounding-out, an enquiry. He waits, hoping the horseman's eyes, which are all he can see behind a sand-coloured scarf, won't fall on him.

When Yorin returns he says, 'He'll take us in. When we get there, expect to be questioned. Be careful. Don't say more than you have to.'

The horseman turns and they follow, past flowering vines, the green dishes of gourd leaves. And, unmistakably, the sound of water. Stretching into the distance, breaking into separate digits as it reaches the crops, is a watercourse composed of a line of wooden half-moons.

'It's called a *shapanah*,' Yorin says. 'It means "resurrection". They're renowned for them. I've no idea how they find water in this place, but they do.'

A tribesman is coming towards them, tall, robed in red and black, his face obscured by a black scarf. The horseman dismounts; Yorin does the same. When he reaches them, the tribesman gives them a long, cool look. The boy shivers. There is something disconcerting about his eyes. Pale yellow. A viper's eyes.

The tribesman bows, making a gesture with his hand. 'Take off your scarves, please,' he says. His voice is soft, and lightly accented. The boy feels suddenly naked, standing bare-headed in front of a man who may or may not know how to smile. 'Your sword,' the tribesman says. After a moment Yorin unbuckles his sword belt. The tribesman nods. 'Come.' They follow, leaving the horseman behind.

The settlement is home to many horses, stabled in the shade of open-sided pavilions. There is a grace to their head and limbs the boy has never seen before. He glances at Tobi, who glares back. He sends the horse a silent apology, but knows that if he spent all his days feeding, grooming and caring for the animal, it would still hold to its first opinion of him.

'No wonder they guard it so well,' Yorin murmurs. 'They prize their horses above all things.' He indicates with his head. At first, the boy sees nothing. Then the faintest movement, a man in robes the colour of sand. As his eyes slowly adjust, the boy begins to spot men everywhere, ranged across the dunes. They seem to disappear into their stillness.

The tents of the settlement are arranged in orderly rows, divided by streets of sand. They shimmer in the breeze, blue, green, lilac, white. No one stirs, not even dogs. The boy tells himself that in the high afternoon only fools and those searching for their family would be abroad. Looking down the streets as they pass, he begins to notice men in sand-coloured robes standing at intervals too regular to be accidental.

They are coming to the largest tent of all, crimson, with swags of silver and gold. The tribesman holds out his hand. 'Your horse.' The boy looks at Yorin, who looks at Tobi. Leaning over, he murmurs something in the horse's ear. When he starts to unbuckle a saddlebag, the tribesman shakes his head. Yorin opens his hands and holds them palm up. After a moment, the tribesman nods. As if conjured, a man appears beside him, takes Tobi's reins, and leads him away. Yorin's face remains unchanged, but there is tension in his silence.

'Wait here.' The tent flap opens, and the tribesman goes in. The boy wonders if the House of Goash has a means of silent communication. He has heard of such things, especially in places where distance and hazard make it desirable. He glances at Yorin, thinking he looks pale.

The tent flap opens. 'You may go in now,' the tribesman says.

After the raw desert sun, it takes time to adjust to the light. The folds of silk, the rich hangings, give the impression the tent is an inch away from floating. The boy takes in little tables of scented wood inlaid with jet, ivory, mother-of-pearl; cushions so big you could lose yourself in them; swords displayed on an ebony rack like sentences in a book of steel and gold; ornaments of silver and precious stones; salvers inlaid with garnet and opal; pipes of jasper and jade. Underfoot, carpets the colour of cinnamon, soft as spice.

There is so much to see he feels faintly nauseous. Beside him, Yorin draws in a wondering breath. The tribesman makes a bow to a man coming towards them, his white robes whispering softly. His head is uncovered; the dark eyes in his lean face have the mineral glitter of stone.

'Welcome,' he says. 'I am Drasta, head of the tribe of the House of Goash.'

Yorin bows deeply; the boy does the same.

'Please, make yourselves comfortable.' Drasta indicates two huge cushions of indigo silk embroidered with gold thread. As the cushion devours him, the boy tells himself to stay calm, that self-control is essential. Fear pins his heart to the inside of his shirt.

Drasta seats himself. Beside him, the tribesman remains standing. A shudder runs under the boy's skin; he glances up, but the yellow eyes look straight ahead.

'You must be thirsty.' Drasta claps his hands, the tent flap opens, and men file in. They are not, the boy thinks, of the same tribe, the distinction not in the robes of undyed cloth but the way they keep their eyes fixed on the ground. Drasta gives orders and food appears, platters of meat, fruit, moist white cheeses. Drinks are offered; steaming tea in tiny silver cups, engraved glass flasks of yellow wine. And bread, warm and white, accompanied by golden pats of butter in jewel-coloured bowls.

'Please, eat,' Drasta says.

When they are done, a man offers the boy a silver bowl of perfumed water. His fingers come out smelling of roses.

'The meal pleased you?' Drasta says.

'It is the only food I ever wish to eat,' Yorin replies.

'It is a pleasure to entertain you.'

'Your hospitality is more than we could have hoped for.'

The boy is almost frantic with agitation. When will they come to the point?

'Then let me increase it,' Drasta says, 'by knowing what you need.'

Yorin glances at the boy. Although they have rehearsed this, his stomach contracts.

'We're looking for someone,' Yorin says.

Drasta inclines his head courteously, his face impassive. 'If it is in my power to help, I will.'

The boy can hardly breathe.

'Some time ago,' Yorin says, 'my friend was separated from his family. He is looking for them, and his search has brought him to you. I'm sure you will understand his desire to find them.' There is a polite silence. 'You are the eyes of the desert, and its memory. I am sure if anyone can help us, it will be you.'

Drasta remains silent. The boy finds himself growing angry. He knows what happened – this tribe abducted his family. He opens his mouth, and Yorin's voice comes out. 'May we tell you which village they came from?'

Drasta nods. Yorin looks at the boy, who says after a moment, 'Bishra, in Sund province.' The words blossom into a marketplace, a well, the White Poplar. He glances at his boots. When he lifts his head, one of the serving-men quickly looks away.

Drasta appears to be considering, his fingertips pressed lightly together. His fingers are slender, with well-kept nails. At last he says, 'These people, who are they?'

These people –

Yorin is speaking again. 'A man, a woman and a young girl.' He gives their names.

Drasta nods, and glances at the tribesman. 'Magra will look into it,' he says.

The boy is hardly aware of leaving the tent and being shown into another, further down the sandy street. The ceiling is composed of silks of rose and cream falling in light clouds around a central pole. The floor is thickly carpeted, and strewn with cushions. In the corner, a low table holds a large shallow basin of steaming water and a pile of soft towels.

'Well, that was a start,' Yorin murmurs. 'At least we still have our heads.'

'Why are you –' the boy begins, but Yorin puts a finger to his lips and jerks his head towards the entrance of the tent. 'That was a good meal,' he says in a normal voice.

'And now for a good wash.'

He strips off his shirt. A scent of roses fills the tent. The boy sinks into a heap of cushions, tempted to bury his head and keep it there. Yorin comes over to him, rubbing his hair with a towel. 'Don't expect too much,' he whispers. 'He may not even remember.'

The boy stares at him. He will never forget.

Later, he lies looking up at the soft canopy, going over what Yorin said earlier, belatedly acknowledging his tact. He would, he knows, have rushed in with questions and anger, and found himself out in the desert. If he was lucky.

He glances over but Yorin seems to be sleeping, so he goes to the entrance of the tent and opens the flap on a tender pink dusk. Men stand silently watching it. Something tells him they have also been watching the tent. He ducks back in.

Yorin is propped up on his elbow, yawning. 'Well,' he says, 'that was a good dream, although at one point I thought I was being smothered. Must be all this froth.' He gets up, straightening his clothes. 'This place is enough to make anyone feel underdressed.' He tugs down the cuffs of his shirt and rubs one booted foot over the other. 'We should be summoned to dinner soon. You might want to have a wash. It'll make you feel better.'

'Fine,' the boy says crossly, but afterwards, in fresh clothes, he feels more comfortable. He is beginning to appreciate such small graces.

'Look,' Yorin begins, but before he can say any more the tent flap opens, and Magra comes in. He is wearing the same robes, but has removed the scarf from his head. The planes of his face hold none of the sculpted softness of the dunes. The high cheekbones, the line of the jaw, the fierce arch of the nose; all is angular precision. He jerks his head, and they follow.

Night has already fallen as Magra leads them to the crimson tent. The boy's mind is racing. He is about to find out if these people know what happened to his family. Of course they do. They took them, after all. He is also terrified of what he might learn. He has been so caught up in finding the tribe of the House of Goash that he has given no thought to what might happen if he did. He feels wrong-footed, and wrong-headed, too. It is hard to reconcile this lap of every luxury with the riders who came to his village.

Drasta is not alone. Other men in robes of lesser magnificence are seated on cushions around a large, low table. Magra takes his place at Drasta's side. The boy wonders if he ever eats.

They are offered what Yorin later calls a dinner of superlatives. The boy eats without tasting it. Throughout the meal, Drasta asks them nothing. When the dishes have been cleared away he claps his hands, and silence falls.

'Magra has made enquiries,' he says, looking at the boy. He lowers his head and opens his hands, showing his palms. 'Alas, he has been unable to find out anything about your family.' After a pause he says, 'I am sorry I can tell you nothing more. Perhaps it is best to remember well.'

Arun stares blankly into the pool. 'A great black cloud smouldering with lightning. And then nothing. The extinguishing of hope. That's how it felt. Call me fainthearted, but I was stuck in the middle of the Haruan Desert with men whose manners were so smooth there was nothing to hold on to, nothing to fight against. I felt utterly alone.'

'Yorin was there too,' Night points out.

Arun shakes his head. 'Grief makes us alone. At that point I just wanted to walk out into the desert, forget I'd ever been there. I could feel Yorin willing me to stay calm. All I could do was thank Drasta, and return to the other tent.'

He bows his head and closes his eyes.

As the flap closes, the boy's composure leaves him. Someone has lit the lamps hanging above, and they make of the tent a soft and silken chamber. He finds himself on the floor, fighting down his anger. Yorin lowers himself onto a cushion, watching him.

After a moment, the boy looks up. 'Maybe it's not the right branch of the tribe,' he whispers. 'Maybe there's another one.'

Yorin nods at a symbol woven into the carpet. A square-cut spiral bothered by gnats. Perfumed candles, candied fruits swim before the boy's eyes. A thought strikes him. 'What about the men who came to our village? They weren't from here.'

Yorin tells him they were probably northern mercenaries. 'People go to great lengths to distance themselves from what they do. And I'd guess this lot are experts at it.'

An image rises in the boy's mind, of scented water and fingers rinsing off blood. After a short silence he says, 'If this is the right tribe, and' – a glance at the carpet – 'we know it is, then they, or people acting for them, came to my village and took my family. Therefore they know what happened to them.'

He doesn't realise his voice is rising until Yorin puts a finger to his lips. There is sadness in his face. 'Look,' the boy says with a rush of guilt, 'I'm really grateful for what you've done, but you don't have to be part of this.'

Yorin makes a wry face. 'It's a bit late for that. Besides, I've seen that look before. That fire. It was in me too, once.' He studies the carpet for a moment. 'I've been thinking,' he says, but the boy is ahead of him.

'They must have accounts,' he whispers, 'and records. If they've done this well for themselves, it won't be because they're disorganised.'

'So they must be here somewhere,' Yorin concludes. 'All we have to do is find them. Simple.'

They look at each other, and start laughing. If there are guards outside the tent, and the boy is sure there are, he doesn't care. It is a relief to let go.

In the end, having whispered plan after plan to each other, there is only one thing to do, and that is to go and do it. First, they need to find out where the records are kept.

'I think it'll be somewhere near Drasta's tent,' the boy says. 'He'd want to keep it close to him.'

Yorin frowns. 'I didn't see anything.'

The boy closes his eyes, imagining the shape of the tented city, row after row, like the beads on a counting device. 'What about behind it?' He is on his feet, reaching for his cloak.

'No,' Yorin whispers, 'you can't just walk out of here.'

The boy glares at him. 'I've done this before. Besides, your family need you alive.'

Before the boy can reply, he ducks down and pulls a small knife from his boot. Covering his head with his scarf, he pulls on his cloak and makes a slit in the back of the tent, exposing a seam of darkness. With a grin, he slips through.

The boy waits. And waits. He thinks of going to look, but worries about putting Yorin at greater risk, so he sits and fiddles with the frayed edges of the fabric. The body of the tent is a soft, wadded material over which silk has been stitched. The sewing is skilful, looping and curving in flower-shaped patterns. He follows it mindlessly with his fingertip. It is a strange, almost hypnotic sensation, and he is half dreaming when he hears something – not words, but uttered from the throat. Then, silence. In spite of Yorin's warnings, he looks out.

The darkness is so thick he almost bumps into it. Ducking back in, he paces about. His agitation grows. Telling himself to be patient, he fixes his attention on a jug and beakers. The jug is made of thick red earthenware, which surprises him. Where is the silver for fingers to cool on, the eye to delight in? He later learns that many desert tribes keep their water in plain vessels, regarding it as more precious than gold. He fills a beaker and drinks. Then he stretches out on a low couch and tries to sleep.

When he wakes, he scrambles up, looking around. Judging by the light in the tent it is morning. There is no sign of Yorin. Gripped with sudden dread, he goes to the entrance, where two men are talking quietly. They turn when they see him, and bow.

'You slept well?' one of them asks. He nods, wanting to ask about Yorin but not knowing how. 'Please,' the man says, 'go back inside. Food will be brought to you, and water to wash in.'

He paces about on bare feet. Where is Yorin? The tent flap opens, and men carry in platters of bread, fruit and cheese, an earthenware jug. A basin of steaming water, a white cloth, perfumed soap. As they leave, one of them briefly catches the boy's eye. He thinks it may be the same man who glanced at him when he was introduced to Drasta but is too distracted, too full of foreboding, to give it any thought.

He makes himself eat as much as he can, telling himself he doesn't know what the day will bring. Afterwards, he washes, finding the scent of the soap cloying. It has no business smelling so lovely when he is trapped in a tent in the desert wondering what has happened to his friend.

In spite of his growing fear, he realises it is the first time he has thought of Yorin as a friend. In the short time he has known him, he has grown to like and trust him. It is a hard thing to acknowledge, easier not to care, because caring leads to hurt, and hurt is something he has spent his time running away from. Here among people who make hospitality an art form and, he is beginning to suspect, a prison, he finally looks it in the face.

Chapter Twelve

He sits opposite Drasta, having been escorted by Magra, who told the boy *Inali-Sumas* would like to speak with him. The boy discovers later that the title means 'the sun bows its head'.

Drasta is watching him. 'But where is *harrefa-rulla*, the man with red hair?'

The boy stiffens, thinking quickly. 'I thought he must be with you.'

'And I thought he was with you,' Drasta says, 'so what are we to make of it?'

The boy feels suddenly unequal to the mountain of manners confronting him. He forces himself to stay calm. 'Perhaps he's checking on his horse.'

Frowning, Drasta turns to Magra, who whispers something. 'His horse has been fed and watered. There was no sign of him. I will make enquiries.' He nods to Magra, who bows and leaves the tent.

Although they are not alone – men sit on cushions and low couches, talking quietly, and serving-men stand at a discreet distance – the boy feels very much on his own. Instinct warns him to say nothing, to wait.

Drasta regards him steadily. 'You need not worry.

We will find him. Now' – he gets to his feet as the boy struggles up – 'you would like to see something of my village?'

Drasta's village, as he calls it, seems endless. There are tents of clothing and equipment, tents for the harness of horses, tents stacked with barrels of salt, dried meat and fruit, tents containing rolls of material, from workmanlike cottons to finely embroidered gauzes . . . The boy's eyes are becoming uncomfortably full, and all the time he is worrying about his friend.

As they walk through the sandy streets, he tries to remember as many markers as he can. He isn't entirely sure why, but he thinks it is something Yorin would do, so he commits to memory a tent with a small dome and sides curving slightly inwards. Two painted barrels outside a tent to the left of the main street. A right turn into a row of dwellings made of plainer material.

Drasta stops outside a small tent the colour of coral. 'Some refreshment, I think,' he says. 'Please, after you.'

Inside, a robed man serves tea made with ginger and fresh lemons. The boy wonders if it is safe to drink, but Drasta is watching, so he takes a sip. Faced with Drasta's silence, he feels compelled to speak.

'How long have you been here?' he asks.

'Forever,' Drasta replies. 'We are an ancient people. Our origins are forgotten, and this allows us to have no beginning.'

'And you're traders,' the boy says carefully.

'Indeed. We work hard for what we have. And, as you see, we want for nothing.'

He studies his teacup. It was, he says, made many years

ago by someone who dedicated his life to creating objects to please the eye. The style looks familiar to the boy. If it is original – and he has no doubt it is – the cup is probably worth more than his family's annual harvest.

'Ah,' Drasta says, 'you know about such things?'

'A little.'

'You were taught by . . . ?'

'My master.'

Drasta sets down his cup. 'It is almost time for lunch. Come.'

After what seems like an endless meal, Magra escorts the boy to his tent. He is beginning to feel as if a very fine cord is slowly tightening round his neck. He is sure something has happened to Yorin, but has no idea what to do. Sitting on the low couch, he wonders if this is to be his fate, trapped in a cage of exquisite taste, choking on carpets and canopies of silk.

Human currency . . . too costly. The merchant's words come back to him, and with them bitter fury at the memory of his deceit. He clenches his fists. The merchant's only thought was of making a profit. What about men shouting, women crying, a child stumbling as a hand sweeps down and catches him up? And, afterwards, endless days and nights in which the heart feels like a ghost-in-waiting.

Hearing voices outside, he looks up. Drasta is coming into the tent. Magra is close behind. He scrambles to his feet.

'I have some news,' Drasta says. His face is grave. The boy feels suddenly cold. Drasta glances at Magra, who takes from his robes the scarf Yorin was wearing when he left the tent. It is bloodstained.

'My men have looked everywhere for your friend,' Drasta says. 'We know the desert like a mother's face, but found only this.' The boy is silent, aware of something caving in. 'The desert can do strange things to men. It is not a friend to those who do not know it. And it is not a friend, sometimes, to those who do. We are its children, and it scolds us at times as a parent would. We have a saying, "The desert is patient. The desert can wait." But it shows no pity to those who are not its kin.'

He nods. Magra hands the scarf to the boy. 'I am sorry,' Drasta says. 'Please, rest now. Tomorrow we will take you wherever you wish to go.'

Afternoon slips by. Magra escorts the boy to Drasta's tent, where another elaborate meal has been prepared. He picks at his food, barely listening as men talk, debate, consult Drasta, who sits at the head of the low table as if in counsel. He asks the boy no more questions; it is as if in some way he is done with him, though his courtesy remains irreproachable. Once, looking up, the boy thinks he sees a flicker of contempt on Magra's face.

Returned once more by Magra to his tent, he sits with his head bowed, desperate for a plan. His eyes are beginning to close when he hears a rustling noise coming from the back of the tent. He looks up, noticing what he hadn't before, that the tear Yorin made has been sewn up. A glint of silver, the tip of a blade: a knife is working the gap wider. He looks around for a weapon, but even as he does a man starts shouldering through, straightening up to stand before him. It is the serving-man who looked away when the boy sensed him watching.

He looks at the knife in the man's hand. He has never fought anyone before, and is unarmed. The man seems to know what he is thinking because he lowers the knife and raises his other hand, palm upwards.

'I'm not going to hurt you,' he whispers.

'Then what –?'

'We don't have much time. Your friend is alive, for now, and you are in great danger. They won't let you leave here alive. If you trust me, I may be able to help you both.'

The boy struggles to gather his thoughts. 'Why?' he asks.

'I never saw my family again. If helping you means you have a chance of finding yours, then so be it.'

The boy stares at him. 'But if they find out –'

The man shrugs. 'I have nothing to lose. I'd love to see those bastards' faces when they discover you've gone.'

He freezes suddenly, holding up his hand. They stand motionless, listening to voices outside. When they have died away, the man says, 'You've got a horse, haven't you?' The boy tells him Tobi's name, and what he looks like. 'He shouldn't be hard to find among those beauties. They mean more to them than their own children.' For a moment the man's face is bitter. 'Get your things and wait here. When I come back, be ready to go.'

The boy stands in his cloak, holding his pack and Yorin's saddlebag, waiting as time crawls by. Did he dream it? Was the man really here? If he was, how can he possibly get past the tribesmen who are surely concealed in the darkness?

He has almost given up hope when the night erupts, as if someone has set fire to the silence. He can hear horses whinnying with alarm, the rising thunder of many hooves. Men's voices, urgent, shouting; many footsteps running past. In moments, it seems, the whole village is awake and on the move. Before he can work out what is happening, the gap in the tent opens.

'I've got your horse,' the man whispers. 'Come on. Quick, we don't have much time.'

Above them is a garden of stars, white and pure. The man leads Tobi, the boy walks on the other side. Voices echo in the darkness; horses neigh and cry. With every step the boy expects to be grabbed by the arm, hit on the head, dragged back.

The man comes to a halt. A tent looms in front of them. There are no lamps burning inside. If there were, the boy would see their light as he would the blood in a hand held up to a candle in a darkened room. Tobi stamps softly, whickering.

'Your friend's in there,' the man whispers. Crouching, he cuts the rope lacing the front of the tent. There is no time to wonder how he knows. Perhaps he was brought here once, too. The boy waits, struck with fear, straining for the slightest sound.

'It's up to you now,' the man whispers as he straightens up. Giving the boy brief directions – 'you're less likely to be seen, but you need to go quickly' – he wishes him luck.

The boy grasps his hand. 'How I can ever thank you?'

'Find your family. That's all the thanks I need.'

He vanishes into the darkness. The boy listens for a moment, then goes into the tent. He can hear someone breathing. A guard? He freezes to the spot, takes a breath and says Yorin's name.

A muffled sound, as if someone is speaking through a closed mouth. The boy moves forward, tripping slightly, stumbling into something. Muttering a prayer, he reaches out. A shoulder. A little further up, a band of cloth. His hands are shaking as he pulls off the gag.

'Hands and feet,' Yorin says in a hoarse whisper. With clumsy fingers, the boy unties the knots.

As they slip out of the tent, Tobi pushes his muzzle into Yorin's hand. 'No time, my friend,' Yorin whispers. He scrambles onto the horse's back and pulls the boy up behind him.

As Tobi starts walking, the boy is seized with an urge to kick him into a gallop, but knows it would be madness. It feels like a kind of madness already, perched on a horse guided by the hands of night.

Every step is a lifespan. The boy's ears are making sounds out of nothing; he can almost hear people following. Will two more steps take them to the point of a sword? He is, he realises, waiting to die. It isn't the great moment he thought it would be. It has sweaty palms and eyes frantically trying to drill through the darkness.

Far away a dog barks, and his fear suddenly shifts. There are still such things as dogs, and people shouting at them to shut up, don't they know what time it is? He is overcome with a sudden urge to laugh. He is a boy in the desert, and the desert may cover him if it will. But he is with someone – two someones – and he is not alone.

Arun takes a deep breath. 'It's funny,' he says softly, 'I hadn't realised until now that what I feared most wasn't death, but being alone.' He stares at the moon in the pool, so close, so far away.

And far away they are travelling on and on. The boy's only sense is the night, the rhythm of Tobi's galloping hooves the heartbeat of the desert. They have left the tented city behind them. Before them looms a mass of deeper darkness. He is half dozing when Yorin says, 'I don't think they're coming after us. If they were, they'd have caught up by now.' There is such relief in his voice that the boy starts to smile.

The sky is beginning to grain with first light. When it comes they will be unhidden, running on sand.

'One last push, my friend,' Yorin tells Tobi. 'You can rest when we get into the hills.'

Which start to reveal themselves as the sky waxes indigo and amber, purple and pale gold. The colours remind the boy of the tented city, and he wants to cry, *This is what's real, not the dyed fancies of a man who calls himself head of the tribe of the House of Goash. Your silks will catch on the thorns of the desert and turn to rags, and the morning sky will look down as they rot away and are forgotten.*

He feels his heart exulting because he is here, and the sun is rising, and every part of him is thankful.

If Yorin feels the same, he doesn't show it. Slowing Tobi to a walk, he dismounts and stands quite still. As the boy slides off, the horse lets out a deep, whooshing sigh. The sun settles in the sky and sends light flowing like cool water across the desert. The boy's legs are starting to shake. During the ride he made many bargains, not least of which was the letting go of hope in order to double back into it again.

Arun gives a short laugh. 'It made sense to me at the time. During that ride I donated all my money to good causes, became so upstanding no self-respecting city would have me, doused myself in patience, dined with understanding and peace, and helped everyone who crossed my path whether they wanted it or not. It didn't last, of course, but I learned one thing.'

'Which is?' Night prompts.

'The sun always rises in the morning.'

If the tribe of the House of Goash were coming after them they would, as Yorin said, know it by now. The boy lets out a breath, glances at his friend, and gasps. The left side of his face is a mess of bruises, his eye bleeding and drooping slightly.

Yorin dismisses it with an airy wave. 'I've had worse,' he says. 'And women find it irresistible.'

They begin the slow climb up a slope covered with shrubs and sedges. 'The Marimvara Hills,' Yorin says. 'Breaking us in gently.'

Halfway up he stops, picks a yellow flower and threads it through Tobi's forelock. '*Kariesh*,' he says. '"Flower of morning." I never thought I'd see it again.' His face is expressionless, but the boy is learning to read the fine print of his voice.

They stop for a break in a shady hollow. The boy throws down his pack and hands Yorin his saddlebag. 'At least one of us had his wits about him,' Yorin remarks as he digs around and comes up with a water bottle and some crumpled packets. He sniffs one, making a face. 'Cheese, on its last legs. Well, it's better than nothing.'

He shares the food between the three of them, smiling at Tobi's face as he chomps dried fruit. 'I'm sorry, my friend,' he says, trickling water into his hand and letting the horse drink it. 'When we're through the hills, I'll treat you to the best breakfast you've ever had.'

When the meal is over, Yorin stretches out gingerly and closes his eyes. The boy sits with his knees drawn up to his chest. He reaches out and strips leaves from the stem of a small bush. They sit in his palm, tiny ovals frittered by a breath.

'I think I owe you my life,' Yorin says after a while.

'No,' the boy says, 'it wasn't me.' He tells Yorin what happened, briefly, not wanting to dwell on the gut-freezing terror, the thought of dying without ever seeing his family again.

Yorin opens his eyes. 'Whoever he is, I'd like to find him and buy him a lifetime's supply of beer. But you came looking for me, and I won't forget that. It amounts to the same thing, in my book.' He closes his eyes again.

Reluctant to disturb him, needing to know, the boy says, 'What happened?'

'They caught me. I think I'm a bit rusty.' The boy senses it is all he will say on the subject.

'Do you think we should get going?' he asks after a while, trying to dispel an image of cold yellow eyes. Yorin waves a vague hand, but remains where he is.

Tobi is resting in the slouching position he favours. 'What do you think?' the boy asks. The horse raises his head, walks over to Yorin, and nudges his shoulder.

Yorin groans. The horse nudges him again. 'Fine, you win,' he grumbles. Someone has removed Tobi's bridle and replaced it with a rough rope halter. Before they set off, Yorin throws it away and fashions a halter from the boy's scarf. The horse shakes his head, and little tassels dance beneath his jaw.

All that day they journey into the heart of the hills. As evening falls, they drowse peacefully in cool shadow until the thought roosting on the boy's shoulder finally crows.

'Why did no one follow us?' he asks.

Yorin is silent for a moment. 'If I had to guess, I'd say it was all about reputation. They live and die by it. The last thing they'd want is for word to get out that they'd let someone escape, and coming after us would only make it obvious. Not everyone was there by choice' – the boy thinks of the man who saved them – 'and I'm sure they'd be only too ready to spread the word. Not forgetting the arrogance that comes with being the most feared people in the region. Better to write it off as a necessary loss than risk it getting out.'

The boy hopes Yorin is right. He shivers, remembering something Drasta said. *The desert is patient. The desert can wait.* He rubs his arms. Something else occurs to him. 'Don't take this the wrong way, but why did they keep you alive?'

'I could say it was my sparkling personality,' Yorin says lightly, 'but I don't think they'd finished with me yet.'

Just as the boy is leaning back and closing his eyes, he is overwhelmed by the realisation that, in the rush to escape, they failed to get what they came for. It has all been for nothing: the merciless desert, Drasta's elegant duplicity, the fear that has followed him into his sleep.

Yorin is grinning. 'You didn't think I'd leave empty-handed, did you?' He pulls a piece of tattered paper from his bloodstained shirt, and hands it to the boy.

'How did you –?'

'They thought they caught me going into the tent, but I was coming out.'

The page is set out in a familiar way, like the workings of a book of accounts, but instead of words there are symbols the boy can't read. Except for the heading. *Bishra*. The name of his village. He catches his breath. 'What does it say?' he asks.

'No idea. It's in code. Which is what you'd expect. They cover themselves in layers of secrecy.'

The boy looks again. His home, reduced to a few strokes of a pen. He feels sick with anger. The people who took his family cared nothing for the fact that it wasn't just another village. It was a valley with a stream running through it, and mountains that looked like a series of smoky triangles as the sun rose behind them. And in the valley was a hut with an almond tree, a wheatfield and a fish trap.

He is silent for some time. Yorin sits calmly looking out.

'Is there any way to find out what it means?' the boy asks eventually.

'Well,' Yorin says slowly, 'there may be somewhere that can help us. We'll rest here tonight, and see what tomorrow brings.'

The boy fights down frustration. He has in his hand a piece of paper containing the fate of his family, and once again he has to wait. 'Look,' he says belatedly, 'I can't tell you –'

'No need, it keeps things interesting.'

The boy's stomach grumbles, and he realises how hungry he is. 'My sentiments exactly,' Yorin says, opening his saddlebag.

The boy is beginning to lose patience with the word *up*. Since setting off this morning, they have climbed ever higher. He also worries about finding water. They came away with their lives which, in the face of it, is a good bargain but, without enough to drink, could prove a costly one.

The path winds steeply, and Tobi stumbles on loose pebbles and grass. One slip . . . The boy glances down and wishes the sight away. Then, almost without warning, they come out onto a wide plateau.

All around them, stone pools brim with water. Light lies fresh and sweet in each, and in them the sun is golden. Yorin dismounts, leading Tobi to one of the pools. The horse takes deep gulps, his sides pulling in and out like a pair of bellows. With a joyful laugh Yorin shrugs off his cloak, kneels down, scoops up water and throws it over his head and shoulders. Taking off his cloak and boots, the boy slips into a pool, lies back and closes his eyes, letting water fill his ears, listening to what it tells him.

It speaks of a time when the hills were young. They began in the freshness of the world, the long cradling of wind and rain and sun. They weathered the years, growing and changing as men came and went with their goats and sheep until they moved beyond mortal sight. In this moment the boy feels as if he too is a part of the going-on of the world, lit with soft lightning that runs from hill to hill, around and beyond and within him. He feels no shame as his tears mingle with the water of the pool.

Yorin is pulling himself up, shaking his wet hair. Some of the blood has washed out of his shirt. 'Much better,' he says. 'I feel as if I've been thoroughly watered.'

The boy gets to his feet and shakes himself like a hound. They look at each other, and grin. They are alive, and beyond the reach of the tribe of the House of Goash. For now, it is enough.

Yorin glances up at the time-keeping sun. 'First things first.' Taking the water bottle from his saddlebag, he immerses it in the pool. The boy does the same. 'That should keep us going for a while,' Yorin says, picking up his cloak and shading his eyes. He nods to where a skinny track winds up a steep incline. 'Up again.'

As they set off, the boy makes a gesture of thanks. 'When you've finished, holy man,' Yorin laughs, but he glances down and murmurs something under his breath.

They have reached the highest point of the Marimvara Hills, whose green pastures roll away on every side. 'It's called *Tharin-en-Pirin*,' Yorin says, 'which is a fancy way of saying "place of hope". Herders used to come up here every year in high summer; there's grazing even when the lands around have burnt up. That's something to add to your map.'

'And the rock pools?' the boy asks.

'Not on any map I know of. You have to find them yourself. And when you do –'

He breaks off, and the boy understands. Would he want to share the wonder? With his family, perhaps, but . . . He

188

has a sudden vision of Nissa standing at the rim of a pool, testing the water with her toe. She'd wrinkle her nose and make a comment about the boy needing a wash. His sister would take everything in and carry it back to her house in the shrubs, to gaze at in peace.

Yorin is a little way off, rubbing Tobi down with a damp cloth made from the hem of his cloak. Kneeling, the boy places his hands on the ground, feeling its warmth. He thinks of making a garden somewhere, from earth and water, light and shade, to walk in when it is hot and when it is cool. A quiet place, somewhere to be alone if he chooses, but never lonely.

Yorin's shadow is growing long; evening is coming. 'We'll rest here until morning,' he says. 'It'll take about a day or so to get there.'

'Get where?' the boy asks.

Yorin lays down his cloak like a blanket. 'You'll see,' he says.

The boy wakes to a mist of dew covering the grass. Yorin is already up, bright-eyed, smiling. 'How did you sleep?' he asks.

'Very well.'

Yorin rolls his shoulders and takes a deep breath. 'Downhill all the way now.'

At the mouth of a small ravine, he dismounts to lead Tobi through. The horse picks his way daintily over the scurf of decayed rock. A sudden noise stops the boy in his tracks. He glances up. It sounded like pebbles slipping underfoot. He scours the ravine, but sees nothing.

'Everything all right?' Yorin calls back.

'Yes, fine,' he says. Feeling sheepish he walks on, determined not to let groundless fears get the better of him.

Stone gives way to sunlight as they come out onto a broad ledge overlooking a great plain of sand. It is lit by a vast, crescent-shaped oasis lying silver-blue in the late afternoon. Tall palms surround it like a crown. Beyond is a bank of high cliffs backed by mountains. The boy stares at the oasis, then at Yorin.

'You thought I'd made it up, didn't you?' Yorin says. 'Well, here it is. *Riallin-en-Asai*, "the voice of Asai".'

The boy keeps it in sight as he follows Yorin and Tobi down the long steep slope and across the desert plain.

Yorin waits for Tobi to drink, then fills his water bottle. The boy settles against the trunk of a palm tree, shading his eyes. It seems incredible that here, in the middle of nowhere, is a place of such beauty. The spring makes a lovely curve, the water a million sparks of light. Beside the tree a small shrub grows, its milky flowers the size of his thumbnail. The scent is spicy and sweet. He finds it intoxicating.

Yorin's look is knowing. 'That scent,' he says, shaking his head. 'I knew a lady once – but that story's not for the light of day, or for boys who look soppy when they sniff a flower.'

A blush warms the boy's face. He looks across at the mountains, receding like folded paper. At their feet is the bank of cliffs he saw from the ledge.

'The library caves,' Yorin says, and the boy's eyes widen. In spite of himself, he remembers the merchant telling him about scrolls whose knowledge was beyond price, and paintings of astonishing beauty. He was, the boy reflects grimly, both shrewd and sentimental. When he mentioned it to Nissa, she said it was like the tale of the tender-hearted tyrant, and darted away before he could question her further.

'The Tale of the Tender-Hearted Tyrant?' Yorin's expectant look fills him with panic. In daydreams he has written stories in private, by a fireside perhaps, with time afterwards for improvement. 'Don't worry,' Yorin says, making himself comfortable, 'I'm not going to give you marks.'

After a false start, a croaking throat and an apology, the boy begins. As he talks, he slowly loses himself in the story. He tells it not with Yorin's wit or Nissa's dramatic asides, but a full and ready heart. Little by little he makes it his own, and becomes so much a part of it that by the end he is completely absorbed.

It takes time to return to the crescent spring and the moon now risen above. When he does, he can hardly look at Yorin, who stirs and slowly opens his eyes. The boy thinks his timing would reduce a hardened storyteller to a nervous wreck.

'That wasn't bad at all,' Yorin says, nodding. 'Here.'

The boy takes the water bottle and drinks. His hands are shaking. Getting up, he goes to the edge of the spring and sits down, his arms clasped round his knees. Through the darkness he can hear Yorin settling under the palm tree, Tobi fidgeting softly. The moon is hidden behind the only cloud in the sky. *Go*, he thinks, and the cloud drifts on a breath of wind, leaving the moon naked before him. It is a water-moon, huge and radiant.

'Are you there?' he asks softly. Wind stirs the leaves of the palms. Somewhere in the night a bird croons, warm and nest-bound.

When he finally sleeps, he dreams of silver water and a face he can't quite see. In the middle of the night he wakes, sits up, and sees on the surface of the spring a cloud of mist. Within it he can just make out the graceful form of a woman. He watches, entranced, as she approaches, holding out her hands. Getting up, he walks towards her. Only when he feels someone pulling him back does he realise he is ankle-deep in water.

'It's not your time yet,' Yorin says. He watches until the boy falls asleep and sits, wakeful, until morning.

Arun stares into the pool. 'Was it her?' he asks. Night is silent. 'If it was, why would she want me to go to her? If I'd been on my own, I could have drowned. No,' he says, with sudden understanding, 'it was something in me. Yorin saved me. He knew the heart can starve for the simple bread of loving.

'In the morning he made sure I had the last of the food, and watched over me while I ate it. Before we set off, he picked a flower from the rushes and floated it on the water. It was deep pink.'

He bows his head, remembering.

Chapter Thirteen

By late afternoon they have almost reached the bank of cliffs. As they approach, the boy sees cavities in the rock too uniform to be the work of time and weather.

'The caves were made many years ago by people who wanted to study in peace,' Yorin says. 'There was a community here once, of scholars and holy men. They've mostly gone now, but the place seems to inspire dedication. There are always people to keep things going. And, hopefully, he'll still be here.'

'Who?' the boy asks, but Yorin just smiles.

As they reach the front of the cliffs, the design of the caves becomes clear. They are not crude, hollowed-out holes but have doorways and porches whose fretwork, set against the great stone breast, is fine as old lace. A little further down, a series of stone terraces rises to the height of the cliffs. Each has five pillars set back from a balcony, creating a portico covered by a fluted roof, like graceful wings. A carved stair winds up to the topmost building. The boy wonders about the hand that drew on the stone.

'One for each of the four winds, the middle for the sun,' Yorin says, nodding at the pillars, shading his eyes even though the cliff makes its own shadow.

'Who built them?' the boy asks.

'Men with a wish for immortality.'

The boy wishes his sister were here to see them. She would have something to say, and something more again. A movement catches his eye, and he looks round. Coming towards them is a very old man in a rust-red robe. His arms are bare, thin and withered.

'*Dhisava*,' Yorin says, bowing. It is, the boy learns, a term of the greatest respect, meaning master and teacher and guide.

'Welcome, my friends,' the old man says, 'to the caves of Linshafan.' If he is curious about the stains on Yorin's shirt, the fading bruises on his face, he shows no sign.

When Yorin has introduced them, the old man beckons to a man standing to one side. 'We have stables,' he says. 'They are quite comfortable. Will your horse be led?'

Yorin murmurs something to Tobi. 'I've told him food's on its way.'

'I am sure you must be hungry too.' The old man smiles. 'Please, come with me.'

They follow him to an enclosure surrounded by a wooden fence. Within the enclosure are a table and chairs, the table set for a meal, with plates of fruit, cheeses and bread. The old man pours water into a basin, and invites them to wash their hands.

The fruit is delicious, fresh and sweet. 'Grapes from Hanarvel,' the old man says, 'and plums from the orchards of Karishvar.' Yorin nods. Experience has taught the boy that pretending knowledge often ends badly, so he contents himself with looking polite.

They take time over their meal. Afterwards, the old man sits back comfortably. 'Well, my friends, you have come a long way.'

The boy wonders how he knows. His eyes, with their faint blue film, must see beyond the normal range of things. When he asks them their purpose in coming, Yorin hands him the piece of paper, telling him where it came from. For a while the old man studies it in silence. Then he lays it on the table and wipes his hands together, as if ridding himself of something. The boy understands. He felt the same way when they escaped the tribe of the House of Goash.

'Can you help us?' Yorin asks.

'It is in code, as you see. And constructed with particular cunning. But there is a book –' The old man smiles. The boy is startled to see he has all his teeth. 'Come,' he says, rising.

For someone of great age, he is very nimble. The boy finds himself puffing as they climb the winding stair. The uppermost house has a smaller facade but is intricately decorated, each pillar twined with vine tendrils and tiny flowers. He wonders what would happen if someone cut them away, imagining pillars floating up to the peaks of the mountains.

In front of the door the old man bows low. It is carved with flowers through which peep little birds with long, curved beaks and outstretched wings. The boy can almost hear them humming. How did the woodcarver discover their grace-lines?

The old man is watching him. 'Before you go in, it is customary to offer something to the goddess,' he says.

Yorin seems to have expected it; he brings out a small piece of cloth on which a letter is embroidered. The boy wonders where it came from. They fled the tented city with barely the clothes on their backs.

The old man takes the cloth and bows. 'You know the Galanthir script?'

'I was in Rocabar once,' Yorin says, and the old man nods.

The boy feels as he once felt when his parents were talking and he was in the room, but not part of the conversation. He'd tugged his mother's sleeve and she looked down, smiled, and told him the fish were waiting in the trap. It was a loving dismissal, but he took it away to brood on by the stream. She explained later that some things were not for the ears of a small boy, and some things a boy did were not for the knowledge of his mother. He'd stared at her, wondering if she knew about the piece of pie hidden under his pillow. By bedtime it was forgotten. In the morning he managed to scrape it off, but the blue stain never came out.

The old man is waiting. Yorin's face gives no clues. The boy pats his pockets anxiously. What if he isn't allowed to enter or, when he does, a pillar falls on him as punishment for his impiety? He looks out over the desert plain, takes a breath and says, 'I offer my thanks.'

The old man studies him for a moment, and bows. 'Please,' he says, stepping aside to let them enter. Yorin goes first; the boy follows, and stops.

The chamber is vast, high-vaulted, broad and deep. The air is cool, the stone floor dry and even. The walls are layered with stripes and folds of grey and dark-red rock seamed with sparkling quartz. The boy gazes, enchanted, at the colours of the earth. Later he will understand the persuasion of water, the mineral acceptance, the enduring marriage.

Smiling, the old man says, 'There is more, look.'

The walls are pierced with hundreds of holes: a stone hive. Every hole is filled with a scroll or a book; beside each one is a charcoal mark. Only the back wall is untouched. On it, to the ceiling's height, is a painting of a woman on a throne, surrounded by a garden. It is so large it seems to belong to the heavens. The boy makes an involuntary bow.

'The Goddess of Eternal Spring watches over our caves, and keeps us safe,' the old man says. 'This is the main cave; there are many antechambers.' He indicates an arched doorway leading into a smaller cave also pierced with honeycombs. At the far end is another doorway. 'They run for quite a way through the cliffs.'

'Are they are all full, like this one?' the boy asks. The chamber seems to be absorbing him; he feels strangely calm.

'They are. And I am their Keeper.'

'Did you make those?' The boy nods at the charcoal marks.

'They were made by my predecessors. It has taken me many years to understand what they mean.'

Codes and riddles. The boy sighs.

'It seems a waste of sun and air, perhaps, toiling here year after year?' the old man asks.

'Not at all,' he says quickly.

The old man smiles. 'I felt that too, when I was first brought here by my father. He was Keeper of the caves before me. I was ten years old, and only interested in lizards.' He rubs his arms. 'That was a long time ago, and my father walks beside me now. I have lost count of how many years I have spent here. That is why visitors are always welcome. Company refreshes us. People come from many places to study. Some know what they are looking for, others do not. Perhaps it is a good way to conduct oneself.'

He looks at the boy, and his eyes crease at the corners. 'Now, let me find the book, then we shall see. Please, look around.'

The boy stands in front of the painting of the Goddess of Eternal Spring. The garden is a fantasia of flowers. Paint has been nimbly applied to create a work of glowing depth and colour. A long-fingered plant, silvery green, bursts into bells of pink and white, providing a soft footing on which other flowers tread. They are washed in lavender, rose and deep pink, tinted with violet and creamy pearl. Among the flowers he begins to make out birds, none of which he has seen before. Their feathers are scarlet and orange, coral, jade green and marine blue, like a stone he found once at the harbour in Harakim.

As he looks more closely he spots something in the corner, near the back wall. A tiny beetle, painted so precisely he can see every leg, each feeler. He examines the green shimmer on the black wing cases, but it is all of a piece, no obvious overlaying of pigment or sprinkling of glitter. Absorbed, he stands looking until he senses the old man beside him.

'You found it,' he says. 'Each Keeper puts his mark on the chamber when he begins his service here. This was made three hundred and forty years ago.' The boy wonders if beetles live that long.

'It's beautiful,' Yorin says. 'It looks so real.'

'We have never found a way to reproduce the colours our brother made,' the old man tells them. 'If he wrote it down, I have not yet come across it. But there is still time.'

'Have you made one?' the boy asks.

'I have,' the old man says. 'That reminds me –' He touches the boy's arm. 'I have found what I wanted. Come, let us see.'

He takes them to an area near the doorway, set with a table and chairs. On the table he puts a small brown book. 'Please, sit, my friends. Now –'

He opens the book at the first page. The index is written in a script unknown to the boy; numerals run down the side. 'I am happy to find it still here,' the old man says as he studies it. 'It has been stolen three times. It is a valuable book. It contains many of the codes and secret writings of the tribes who flourished in this region. Some of the codes have taken scholars many years to decipher, and others remain a mystery.'

The boy frowns. The thought of it being stolen – of a person harbouring such intentions even as they are welcomed and shown around – is shocking to him. The old man's glance is understanding. 'As you see,' he says, 'it found its way back.' He scans the index, murmuring to himself.

The boy's mouth is dry, his stomach churning, as the old man turns the pages. Finally he stops, laying his finger along the seam of the book. It is a curiously intimate gesture. 'Here it is. The tribe of the House of Goash has many codes, and this seems to be the most recent.'

There are, the boy sees, two columns, one with symbols similar to those on the piece of paper, the other containing what looks like a list of characters. The old man lays the piece of paper beside the page, glancing from one to the other. The creases in his face deepen and he begins to rock back and forth slightly, his eyes half closed.

When he opens them, he is smiling. 'You see where it begins? These symbols' – he points to a horizontal line cut across with a curve, and a leaning staff above which two gnat-like marks hover – 'are the path. If you follow, they take you to the door. Then it is simply a matter of finding the key.'

The boy feels lost, and too tired to pretend otherwise. 'It may take a while,' the old man says gently. He gestures to an alcove behind them, curtained in loosely woven cloth. 'Please, help yourselves. Then perhaps a breath of air?'

Within the alcove is a stone flask, earthenware beakers, a plate of bread and cheeses. Yorin fills a beaker and hands it to the boy. It is spiced water, neither sweet nor savoury, cool and tingling in his mouth. Yorin puts a beaker on the table for the old man, who nods absently. He is humming to himself as he works. It reminds the boy of Liso, sewing the sound into the leather, the thread coming out like a breath.

Putting down the beaker, he leaves the chamber and stands on the balcony, looking out. Immediately below him is a roof, its fluted tiles like waves. Far below and to his left is a stand of dark-green trees. Some, he sees, have seats wrapped round them like a wooden belt. One of them is occupied.

His gaze is no longer idle. What is a girl doing here? And why is the evening sun finding gold in her tawny hair? She has a book in her hands and seems absorbed in it. He wants her to look up; he doesn't want to be seen. Stepping back, he almost collides with Yorin, who has a slight smile on his face. 'Enjoying the view?' he asks. The boy's face burns as he mutters something about trees. At a sharp exclamation from the chamber, they go back in.

'Come, my friends, come!' The old man beckons, the shoulder of his robe slipping down in his excitement. 'I have it,' he says, beaming at them. He makes two marks on a separate piece of paper. The boy recognises them at once, two of the most common sounds in his language. Why couldn't he see it?

The old man smiles. 'It is often the best way, to hide among what you know. Rarely have I seen a code so intricate. But since it has been made by the thought and hand of a man, the thought and hand of another may follow. So, when you put these together, they make –'

A name. The sound is loud in the quiet chamber. There is kindness in the old man's face as he says, 'Would you like me to read them?'

The boy's throat swells, stifling his breath. Here are people he knows – knew. As each name is read out, he sees their faces. The woman selling milk at the market; the weaver and his talented wife who did most of the weaving and raised three – no, four – children; the corn merchant, who grew fatter after each harvest and leaner when his wife took an interest in a man who made barrels; Rahn, the innkeeper of the White Poplar, and Leta his wife . . .

For a moment he closes his eyes. It is only a matter of time until – and here they are, the names of his father and mother. His own. Kumbar's name – there is no avoiding it this time – and the city of Harakim. The old man's voice is very gentle as he reads, '"Apprenticed for life."'

Apprenticed for life. Not abducted and enslaved. Even in code, the construction of a city of symbols so fortified the tribe of the House of Goash believed it could never be overthrown, they still won't admit the truth. A fever of anger consumes him. Yorin offers him water but he looks away at the walls, which are beginning to contract.

The old man touches his arm briefly. 'Would you like me to stop?' he asks, but the boy shakes his head.

'What about Kara? What about my sister?'

The old man looks again. 'There is an entry for a girl-child in your family group, but no name, just some initials. PG. Perhaps they mean something to you?' The boy shakes his head.

After a moment the old man says, 'Your father was sent to the mines of Chanlin. Your mother went to Dhurkana, to serve in a family.'

'What kind of mine?' the boy asks.

'A copper mine.'

'And my sister?'

The old man checks the page. 'She was taken to Kerizon. There is no further information.' He looks at the boy, and his face is sad.

The boy is silent. He sees his sister's eyes, his mother's smile.

'Come,' the old man says, getting to his feet. 'We will eat, and you will rest, and we will know what to do tomorrow.'

The boy lets Yorin guide him out to the stone balcony, where the sky is dark blue. The seat under the tree is empty, and he wonders briefly where the girl has gone. Then he wonders where everyone has gone, and is filled with such grief he wants to empty the contents of his heart until nothing is left.

Lanterns light the enclosure against the dusk. When they are seated, a man comes out of a small cave. His robe is the orange-yellow of the saffron sold at the market in Harakim. The boy watches in silence as he sets the table.

'How many others are here, *Dhisava*?' Yorin asks.

'Numbers vary,' the old man says. 'People come and go, but generally we are a small community, ten or so. Ah –' He looks up, smiling. 'Please, come and join us, my dear.'

The boy watches as the girl he saw sitting under the tree crosses the sandy ground with easy grace. He tries not to scowl. In spite of being here for less than a day, he feels slightly possessive. Girls, especially girls who look like this, shouldn't be allowed. The old man introduces her as Talaia, which, he grudgingly concedes, is a pretty name.

'Talaia is travelling to Kushtar,' the old man says. 'She will live there with her aunt and her uncle-in-marriage, as part of their household.'

'It's good to meet you,' Yorin says, nudging the boy with his foot. He gives a curt nod, briefly meeting Talaia's gaze. Her eyes are like dark-grey smoke flecked with amber. He looks away.

'Now,' the old man says, 'let us give thanks for our food. To the earth that held the seed, to the rain that fed it, to the sun that grew it, to the hand that made it, we offer our gratitude.' He opens his hands. 'Please, eat.'

It is a good meal of delicately flavoured rice, spiced meat and crusty bread, but the boy has little appetite. He keeps thinking of the names on the piece of paper. Of the tribe of the House of Goash.

After the meal, the man in the saffron robe brings out a large platter of fruit. The water they have been washed in sparkles in the lantern light. The boy selects some grapes and wishes he wasn't sitting opposite this girl with grey eyes, who is proving to be self-assured and well-educated. She is saying something about the scrolls in the third chamber, and the old man is answering.

'Yes, at first we thought they must be much later because of the technique. Then to find out they were over a thousand years old – imagine!'

He smiles at Talaia, and the boy feels suddenly excluded. Rising abruptly, he says, 'Forgive me, *Dhisava*, but I'd like to walk for a while.'

The old man's face is understanding. 'Of course, my friend. I have been talking too much. I can only plead the fault of solitude.' The boy is immediately ashamed but can find no words to express it, especially in front of this girl. 'Perhaps you would like to walk among the trees?' the old man asks. 'Imbul will show you the way.'

The boy follows the man in the saffron robe along a narrow path. The trees are in full summer leaf, broad

204

and tall. 'How did they come to be here?' he asks. Imbul glances upwards without explanation. The boy wonders if they were dropped by giant birds.

When he is alone, he bends down and scoops up a handful of earth. The mixture of sand and soil rasps softly in his fingers. Letting it fall, he sits down heavily on a curved wooden seat. He lowers his head, and closes his eyes.

How can people be forced to do things they don't want to? Even as he thinks it, he knows it is a naive question. He has seen enough of the world to know how it works, sometimes with a handshake, sometimes with threats. He thinks of his father, a proud man, being put to work by someone else. From the arguments he overheard, it was something he resisted all his life. He tended the wheatfield and the vegetable plots, calling for water, a scarf for his head, until night fell. In the stories he would be a legendary tiller of the soil, working under an eternal sun, fading to a black shadow as it set, coming to life as it rose again. The idea of him toiling in a mine, in darkness, is almost more than the boy can bear.

His mother, taken to Dhurkana to serve in a family. He has no idea where Dhurkana is, and no faith in the kindness of its people. He hopes the family recognise what a rare and precious person she is. She served her own family lovingly, without complaint, and he never told her how much he appreciated her. He feels a guilt so quiet and cold it is almost petrifying.

His sister, taken to Kerizon. Do the initials PG belong to the person who – he can hardly face the word – bought her? He thinks of her house in the shrubs, her observations, her brightness. They wouldn't know any of that; they wouldn't know her.

He shivers suddenly, gripped by the feeling that someone is watching him. He looks up, but sees only shadows among the trees. He stares at nothing until a noise makes him wipe his face and straighten up. The old man is coming towards him, a beaker in his hand.

'I thought you might be thirsty. May I?' He sits down. 'It is a great deal to take in, I know.'

The boy can't reply. It is too difficult.

'I have a suggestion,' the old man says. 'You are most welcome to stay here while you think about what to do. We live quietly and our food is simple, but you could explore the caves, which interest you, I think?' He pats the boy's arm. 'We have beds prepared for you whenever you are ready.'

The boy watches him wander slowly away. He sits for a little while longer, listening to the calling of birds. Then he gets up, making his way through the trees and the last of the light.

Yorin is still at the table, replacing the lid of a small wooden pot. Talaia has gone. The boy is mostly relieved. He glances at the pot enquiringly. 'Ointment,' Yorin says, 'for the bruises. *Dhisava* gave it to me. It seems to be doing the job.' He studies the boy for a moment. 'Take a seat,' he says, leaning back in his chair. For a while they look out over the darkening plain.

'*Dhisava* suggested I stay here for a few days,' the boy says. 'To sort things out.'

'There are things that need sorting out,' Yorin agrees.

'You don't have to –'

Yorin laughs. 'I think we've been here before. Besides, I've always wanted to explore the library caves.' When the boy asks where Tobi is, he nods at an opening a little way down. 'Oats, and plenty of hay. He'll never want to leave.'

The chamber is snug, warm and dry. The blankets are thick, the pillow soft, but the boy can't sleep. Seeing Yorin outlined the doorway, he gets up and joins him. The moon hangs like a lamp among the stars, and he wonders if the crescent spring is brimming.

'See that one?' Yorin says. 'Mesara. The Weeper.'

Tilting his head, the boy sees the outline of a face. One bright star trembles on its cheek. Yorin leans against the wall and tells him a story about a woman who finally found love but was forced to choose between her heart and her family. Before she left her home for good, she gazed into the well behind the house and shed a single tear. The next morning she was gone. The family never spoke of her again, but that night a new constellation appeared in the sky, the face of a woman with a teardrop on her cheek.

As Yorin finishes the story, the boy is frowning. It wasn't the ending he expected. If she ran away to be with her true love, why didn't she have a smile on her face?

'Love,' Yorin says wryly, 'is rarely what we expect. Get some sleep.'

When he does, the boy dreams of falling stars.

Chapter Fourteen

They find the old man in the enclosure, having breakfast with Talaia. The boy gives her a brief nod. Although ravenously hungry, he finds the warm rolls and honey hard to swallow. He looks out towards the trees as Yorin asks Talaia a question.

'A few days,' she says. 'I've always wanted to see the library caves, and I knew they were on the way to Kushtar.'

The boy stares hard at the trees until Yorin nudges his elbow. Talaia is speaking to him. 'You've come from Harakim, haven't you?'

He wonders how she knows. Yorin must have told her. 'Yes.'

'How did you find it?'

He wants to say it wasn't a matter of finding it; he was introduced to it against his will. 'It was fine,' he says.

Nodding, she breaks open a roll, butters it and heaps it with amber-coloured honey. He realises he has been dismissed. He is so busy smarting at her rudeness he doesn't realise he is staring until the old man says, 'When you have finished, there is something I would like to show you.'

The boy follows him up the stone stairs, aware of Talaia behind him. Why did she have to come? As he reaches the door of the main chamber, the thought strikes him as small and mean. In the chamber, the old man leads him over to a niche marked with a charcoal number. With great care he removes a scroll, which, the boy sees as he unrolls it, is not one unbroken length of paper but sheets stitched together at intervals with black thread.

'Come, see,' the old man beckons.

The boy is amazed to discover it contains a history of Sund, his province, documenting the people who settled there, their lives, their work, the changes in agriculture and building that took place over hundreds of years.

'Who wrote it?' he asks.

'We don't know,' the old man says. 'Someone began it, another took it up, and so on. It passed from hand to hand, you see? Have a look. I think you will find things are much as they always were.'

Bending over, the boy reads aloud. '"It was a good year for apricots and walnuts. A bad one for beer, with barrels reaching exceptional prices. There were many complaints at the weekly meeting. The innkeeper had to defend himself against the bad feeling of the villagers."'

A comment has been squeezed into the margin. *If Basa stopped drinking for a week, there would be no problem with supply.* The boy stares indignantly, wondering what manner of hooligan wrote it. To his surprise, the old man chuckles. 'There are many forms of history. Who is to say which is more important than the other?'

Lost for an answer, the boy imagines a small man with a long nose observing another, larger and red-faced, downing yet another mug of beer. The old man is watching him. 'The things we think and do are part of us,' he says. 'Everything is part of us.'

Talaia, who has been examining a row of scrolls, says, 'And we're a part of everything, too, aren't we, *Dhisava*?'

If he'd known he'd be taking part in a philosophical discussion he should at least have been given time to prepare, the boy thinks irritably.

'What about you, Arun?' the old man asks. 'What do you think?'

Cutting Talaia out of his field of vision, he starts to say something he hopes won't disgrace him. Then he stops. 'I'm sorry, *Dhisava*, I don't understand.'

The old man smiles. 'If we understood everything, where would the wonder be? There are things we need to know – the planting of crops, the milking of a goat – and things that are happy to go on being themselves whether we understand them or not. When you see an apple tree, what do you think? Please, I would like to know.'

'I wonder what the fruit will taste like.' It is, he thinks, a far from adequate answer.

The old man smiles. 'What more is there to know?'

Aware of Talaia's eyes on him the boy says wildly, 'Everything.'

The old man laughs. 'Perhaps, but there are other reasons to live too. Only we can find out which is right for us.' The boy says nothing. His reasons were taken from his home and sold.

The old man takes his arm. 'Come,' he says, 'let me show you something.'

At the back of the cave he takes from a niche a small, rectangular book. A title is inscribed in silver on the dark-blue leather cover. *The Book of Light.* 'These are the poems of Mirashi,' the old man says. 'She was born three hundred years ago, in Lar'kan.'

The boy is astonished. It is a town just beyond the mountains that overlooked his valley, and yet he has never heard of her.

'She was the daughter of a goatherd,' the old man says, 'one of four children, all working hard to help their family. But when the wind swept the fields and the eagle cried, she heard a different song.'

The boy swallows. The old man could be talking about him.

'Mirashi tried her best, but as she wrote in her notebook, it was not enough. She spoke of being bound even though she was free. In the end her family sent her away, or she left, there are differing accounts. She went from Lar'kan to the city of Kembla, where no one knew her. Her notebook records the trials she faced trying to make a living.'

The boy frowns. Surely such things shouldn't concern a poet? The old man smiles. 'Everyday life can be just as demanding. My knees, for example, are not what they used to be. Shall we?'

When they are settled at the table by the doorway, he begins again.

'Mirashi found a place to live, a small dwelling on the outskirts of Kembla, among those the city would rather leave behind. The poor, the sick, the desperate. She found work with a man who made shoes. For months she rose with the light, and slept when it became too dark to see what she was doing. The shoemaker was a hard taskmaster but, by her own account, not unkind. Every seventh day was hers; she used the time to go walking unaccompanied in the hills. It was not the custom of the city, but since she lived in a place it chose to forget, who was to know?

'In the hills she found a certain kind of peace. Not the true peace of the heart, but the temporary removal of care. The hills were green, with white rocks and small trees. Goats roamed freely, cropping the grass, nibbling leaves. There was a particular rock on which Mirashi would sit, an outcrop from which she could look down over the dusty city. She wrote about being in a place that belonged neither to heaven nor to earth, about the light rising up her body at sunrise, like water. A moment like this, she said, gave itself many times to the one remembering.'

The old man clears his throat. 'Can I get you some water, *Dhisava*?' Talaia asks.

He drinks from the beaker she offers him. 'Mirashi began to spend more time in the hills,' he says. 'Eventually, the shoemaker told her that unless she worked harder she would have to go. So she went. Up into the hills, to sit with the goatherds, walking for hours, watching and listening. The eagle soaring above was neither kind nor cruel, she wrote; it saw everything, and in seeing all it saw nothing, too.'

The boy frowns. Understanding has once more turned a corner and left him behind.

'She meant that you can sometimes lose sight of what matters,' Talaia says.

The old man smiles at her, and the boy feels annoyed. Part of him hoped she would be told she was wrong. He is faintly ashamed of himself.

'Mirashi spent two years in the hills,' the old man says. 'In her notebook she calls it the time of silence. Goatherds made a small hut for her to sleep in. They gave her meat and milk from their goats, and showed her which berries and fruits were good to eat.

'When Mirashi came down from the hills, she had a satchel full of poems. She had no idea if they were good, or simply the thoughts of someone to whom they mattered. But she also knew she wanted people to hear them, so she took them to a poet in Kembla, a man of some standing who, it was said, had read at the marriage of the king. She had to wait for some days before he agreed to see her. When he did, he took the poems and promised to look at them. When she returned the following day, he was gone.'

The old man sighs. 'When he read Mirashi's poems, the poet saw they were unlike anything he had read before. So he left the city and took them to the palace of the king in Gornai, where he presented them as his own. They were received with great acclaim, and he was given many gifts and honours.'

The boy is almost exploding with fury. How could this be allowed to happen? Surely justice, in full armour and with a freshly sharpened spear, should be waiting round the corner for the fraudulent poet?

The old man smiles at him. 'Ah, my friend,' he says, 'what we do makes a home inside us. When Mirashi discovered what had happened, she left the province and was lost from history until many years later, when her notebook was found. A man travelling in the hills came across her hut, which was in a state of such ruin that he began to collect the wood for a fire. When he did, he found a small cloth-covered book. For some reason Mirashi had left it behind, whether to forget, or to be remembered, who knows? In it she had written the story of her life, and an account of what had happened to her poems. When he finished reading, the man knew he couldn't rest until he had found the poems and put things right.

'He took the notebook to a bookseller in the city, who said he would make enquiries. At first it was hard to find anyone who knew Mirashi's name, but the bookseller was, like most of his kind, a tracker of lost voices. One man asked another, who asked another, and the river of enquiries flowed. An elderly man brought in a volume containing the proceedings of the court of the king who ruled in Mirashi's time. It was exceedingly detailed. Everything from the purchase of a new parakeet to the number of times a nightingale sang outside the window of the first lady of the court. And, in violet ink, the lines recording the perfidy of the poet.

'Mirashi's poems had been presented to the king, and placed in the royal library. Three kings had since succeeded him. The bookseller said he had a cousin who worked in the palace as an archivist, and would write to him about it.

'Word came from the cousin that the poems were indeed in the royal library. They were not, he explained, allowed to be removed, unless one wished one's head to follow. The man decided there was only one thing to do. He would petition the king.

'He and the bookseller travelled to Gornai, and were received into the king's presence. The king showed little interest in the man's request. He had many petitions behind him, and many more ahead. Old documents, particularly those containing the writings of a woman, were not his concern. He dismissed them.

'They were leaving the antechamber, where many sweltering souls sat waiting their turn, when they were stopped by a footman. He showed them to another chamber, in which a woman was sitting. She introduced herself as the queen. The bookseller bowed so low he saw his nose reflected in the floor; the man told himself consorts did not normally call for the removal of heads, although centuries ago a queen of magnificent barbarity had made quite a career of it.' The old man smiles.

'The queen made them welcome, sat them down and served them coffee. She told them she heard what had been said, and that if a wrong had been done to this woman, she wanted to put it right. She asked them to come with her to the library. Beyond a pair of tall bronze doors, aisle after aisle of bookshelves rose to the ceiling.

'At the back of the library, in a dusty glass case, they found Mirashi's poems. The queen took them out, and left the library. When she returned, her face was inscrutable. She told them they could do what they wished with the poems. The bookseller said they must make announcements, put them on display, let others know about them. The queen promised she would see it done.

'She kept her word. The poems were set between covers of white silk decorated with silver and mother-of-pearl. It became known as the Book of Light, and people came from far and wide to see it. The king discovered that the poems were good for his reputation as a man of culture, and congratulated himself on his decision. The queen merely smiled. She was not in a position to do much else, and wise enough to know it.

'And that,' the old man says, 'is the story of Mirashi. There is a shrine to her in Lar'kan, of rose-coloured stone with open sides for the wind to sing through, a curved roof to support the sun. From ground to sky each pillar is carved with lines from her poems. Perhaps you will see it one day.' He is looking at the boy, but Talaia is studying the cover of the book.

'This is a copy,' she says.

The old man nods. 'A number were made, and this one belonged to the man who found Mirashi's notebook. He came here in old age, and donated the poems and the notebook to the library.' He gives a wry smile. 'The notebook was successfully stolen, but I was lucky enough to read it as a young man. Perhaps this evening we can listen to some of the poems.'

The boy would prefer to take the book to a quiet place and read it in private, but he is a guest, so he nods politely.

As evening comes, they gather round the table in the enclosure. A fire has been built; food is served. There is expectation in the cooling air. When the last of the figs have been eaten, the old man says, 'If you would, my dear?'

The boy stares as Talaia takes the Book of Light from the old man, pushes her hair – such long, thick hair – back from her face, and reads the first poem. When she stops speaking, no one stops listening. The boy can almost feel Mirashi's presence in the words. The old man asks for another, and Talaia starts reading again, a poem about a lost city. In it, Mirashi sits listening as the spirit of the city remembers the people who built it, lived in it, laughed, sorrowed, loved and died. As Talaia reads the final lines, there is utter quiet.

> A city's name is made not of great deeds
> but the leaf that falls, the cloud that travels softly,
> the small flame your hand makes in mine.

The night is so still the boy can hear the velvet thrum of moths' wings. He wants to hear the poem again, but feels unable to ask. Talaia's eyes are shining in the firelight.

'You enjoyed it?' the old man asks her.

She makes a gesture with her hands. 'It was . . .' They exchange a look the boy would like to examine further.

When Imbul has served tea, Talaia reads three more poems. The first is about the doomed courtship of night and day, the second how the hills recall every footstep ever made on them, the last about a nightingale who falls in love with her owner. It is funny, and sad, and full of the discreet music of an unrequited heart.

When she has finished the old man thanks her, and rises from his chair. 'It is time to rest now, my friends,' he says.

As he tosses and turns in his comfortable bed, the boy can still hear Talaia's voice. He thinks of Nissa, and his sister. Each came with her own brand of mischief, which drove him up the wall and over the rooftops. He suspects Talaia is mischief of a different sort, and falls asleep worrying about it.

He spends the next morning in the main chamber, no closer to making a decision about what to do next. He wonders when Talaia will be leaving.

'There is one thing you do know.'

He turns to see the old man coming towards him. 'What is that, *Dhisava*?' he asks courteously.

'You cannot be in three places at once. Would you allow me to make a suggestion? Dhurkana is the nearest, a great city, a crossroads to many things. It would make sense to go there first.'

The boy gives it some thought. It would be a relief to have the decision taken out of his hands. 'Yes,' he says, 'thank you.'

The old man looks pleased. After a moment he says, 'Kushtar is on the way to Dhurkana. It would be a comfort to me to know that Talaia could travel with you and your friend.' He smiles expectantly. Faced with such kindness, the boy can only bow and say it will be an honour. When the old man touches his shoulder briefly, it feels as if he has been paid a compliment.

He remains in the cave after the old man has gone, pulling out books and scrolls, many of which are written in languages he doesn't understand, admiring the little sketches he comes across. He grins at the drawing of a boy showing his bottom in the margins of a set of town records, imagining a bored young scribe noting down the fiftieth interruption of the proceedings by the most pedantic elder on the council. The elder, he decides, has announced there will be no wine festival this year, and is taking pains to list the reasons why.

Before he can elaborate, a footstep makes him look up.

'Is it interesting?' Talaia asks. Her soft ivory tunic and trousers are backlit by the sun. He closes the book, wondering desperately where Yorin is.

218

After a short silence she says, 'You're looking for your family, aren't you?' He stares. How does she know? More to the point, what right does she have to know?

The look on his face must have spoken for him. 'I'm sorry,' she says, 'I didn't mean to pry.'

After stammering out, 'You weren't,' he falls silent.

She studies the cover of the book for a moment. 'If they were my family I'd want to find them. *Dhisava* tells me you're going to Dhurkana?' He nods mutely. 'Kushtar is on the way,' she observes. Determined to change the subject, he asks her where she is from. She tells him she comes from Inishpur, a town close to the edge of the desert.

After a further silence, he asks why she is going to her aunt and uncle's house. She tells him her father died recently, and now she is on her own.

'I'm sorry,' he says tentatively.

'These things happen.'

He wonders if she is pretending to be tougher than she is. 'Are you looking forward to it?' he asks, and cringes inwardly. Why is he using his visitor's voice? Are the library caves invisibly schooling him? He finds himself wondering what would happen if he ate a book. Would the knowledge be absorbed? He shakes his head. It is a dreadful thought, not just because of the indigestion that would surely follow.

'I think you need some fresh air,' Talaia says, leading him outside. From the balcony he can see Yorin at the table in the enclosure. Aware of Talaia's presence beside him, he casts around for something to say.

'My interest in books? It came from my parents, I suppose. My mother began it. She taught me my letters,' she says in answer to his question. He looks at her in surprise. 'What's wrong with that?' she asks in a clipped voice.

He gulps, stammers, 'I didn't mean . . . I meant . . .' and trails off, wondering why most of what he says to her ends up face down on the ground.

Talaia's expression softens. 'Don't mind me. I'm probably a little sensitive about it. My mother began teaching me, and my father continued after she died. He was a scribe.' A scribe? He has never been this close to one before. Talaia smiles. 'It's not as interesting as it sounds. He taught the village children to read and write, wrote letters for people who weren't able to, and read them to those who couldn't. But his real interest was writing about nature. The way leaves change colour in the autumn, the pattern of a spider's web, the different types of rain.'

The boy frowns. Rain was rain. You knew where you were with it. He tries to think of different kinds. All he can come up with is wet, and wetter. But doesn't it become needles when the wind drives it, or tiny sacs bursting on the leaves of a tree?

'What about you?' Talaia asks. 'Where are you from?'

It is a question both enormous in scope and able to be dealt with in a few simple words. 'I'm from Bishra, in Sund province,' he says. 'I left, went to Harakim, and then came here.'

Short, but in essence true. Talaia seems content with it, and asks him what he thinks of the library caves. The boy, who doesn't seem to be thinking about them at all, stammers a reply.

'Yes,' she agrees, 'marvellous. But I wonder how many men have sat here regretting being tied to them.'

The boy feels compelled to disagree. 'I think they're lucky, being able to spend time with things that matter.'

'It depends on how you define what matters. Besides' – she shrugs – 'they have no real need of us. They've been here for over two thousand years, after all.'

Two thousand years seem to him like a vast, unscalable cliff. 'You think I'm disrespectful, don't you?' Talaia says bluntly.

He is silently frantic. They have come to a fork: small, not particularly sharp, but pointing two ways. Honesty, or politeness. 'Yes, a little,' he says.

She studies him. 'I don't mean to be. It just seems a waste of a life. There has to be more to it.'

'Such as?'

'This.' As her arm sweeps the plain and the distant mountains, her sleeve falls back, and the bangle on her slender wrist catches the eye of the sun.

Another, longer, silence. When he asks what she will do when she gets to Kushtar, Talaia grimaces. 'Become my aunt,' she says, and they both laugh. 'I haven't seen her or my uncle for a very long time. They visited us once –'

She breaks off as Yorin climbs the last few stairs and joins them on the balcony. The boy is not quite relieved to see him. 'You're looking very solemn,' Yorin says. 'Cheer up, it's a beautiful day. And' – he looks at the boy – 'we need to talk.'

Ah. He knew it was coming, but it doesn't feel as straightforward as it was before. He excuses himself from Talaia, who smiles rather absently and continues looking out over the desert plain.

Yorin leads him to the trees, and they settle down in

the shade. 'I've been thinking about what to do next,' he says. 'It makes sense to go to Dhurkana. We can go from there to Chanlin, then on to Kerizon.'

The boy shades his eyes against the light. 'You don't mind going with me?'

'I've come this far, no point turning back now. Besides, it'll keep me occupied. I've spent too much time running from irate, er, traders.' The boy is too used to his ways by now to bother filling in the gaps.

'I've been talking to *Dhisava*,' Yorin continues. 'He suggested we take Talaia with us. Kushtar's on our way.'

The boy stiffens. 'Yes, I know.'

'He's already talked to Talaia. She said her uncle will probably insist on paying us, which will come in handy. Tobi eats enough for a herd of camels.'

It hadn't occurred to the boy that Yorin might be short of money because of him. 'As long as you keep it,' he says.

Yorin grins. 'No problem. By the way, *Dhisava* gave me a saddle and bridle for Tobi. Talaia has her own horse.'

'Her own horse?' the boy echoes.

'Women can ride.' Yorin sounds amused.

'But who brought her here?'

'She did. If you don't count the horse. It's unusual, I know, but then, Talaia isn't the usual sort of woman.' The boy is aware of a knot in his chest. 'I take it you'll be using your legs,' Yorin says.

After lunch the boy returns to the library caves, and spends the afternoon there. He finds it strangely comforting to be among people whose hopes and fears

222

have lived and died, and loses himself in imagining who they were. By the time he hears the call for dinner, he feels very tired.

The others are already at the table. He is ravenously hungry. Spiced lamb and olives quickly fill his stomach, and more than a few slices of buttered bread washed down with long, cool draughts of apple juice. When the lanterns are lit, summoning moths, everyone sits back quietly. Yorin sings softly to himself, an evening song the boy vaguely recognises.

In the day I welcome hope,
In the night sadness comes.
Send the night away,
Send the night away.

He sits drowsily watching sparks winking in the bushes. He has always loved fireflies. It is a source of constant wonder that they hold suns in their hands.

'They're like stars on a necklace of leaves,' Talaia says. In the half-dark, her eyes are shining.

The boy finds himself thinking her eyes are also like stars. He stares into his cup of apple juice as the old man says how glad he is that they will be accompanying Talaia to Kushtar. 'I am sure she will be safe with you.' The boy suspects she is more than capable of taking care of herself.

That night, in his dreams, he hears voices he hasn't heard for some time. He listens, but they are light as mist and he can't make out what they are saying. When he wakes, he sees Yorin at the entrance of the cave, looking out at the morning. The boy thinks he could stay here forever, the soft joint of time neither open nor closed. But there is a journey to be made.

The old man and Talaia are sitting at the table in the enclosure. She is wearing a rose-coloured tunic and trousers under a light travelling cloak. The boy dedicates the next few minutes to his breakfast, and is finishing his tea as Imbul comes towards them. He is holding the reins of a chestnut horse whose mane and tail are the colour of wheat. Two cloth satchels hang from his shoulder.

And now Yorin is returning with Tobi, who looks as he usually does, though a little rounder. Beneath his new saddle is a blue quilted cloth. Yorin's saddlebag hangs from one side; a roll of blankets is tucked behind it.

As they leave the enclosure the old man holds out his arms, and Imbul comes forward.

'These are for you,' the old man says to Yorin and the boy. 'There is food and clothing, and a few other things you may need.' Imbul hands them the satchels. The boy remains anchored to the spot. 'I wish you luck in your search,' the old man tells him. 'Trust yourself, trust your friends. Remember that whatever you find, your heart will go with you.' The boy thinks it a strange thing to say. If it didn't, he wouldn't be going at all.

The old man hands him a parcel wrapped in white cloth. He opens it slowly, and stares. Bound in cream-covered leather is a copy of the Book of Light. He doesn't know what to say. He has never been given anything like it before. The old man smiles, embracing him. 'I hope you find your family,' he says.

He turns to Talaia. 'My daughter, do not lose what

224

you have learned. There is a time for words and deeds, for being and doing.'

To Yorin he says, 'When you came here you had one charge. You leave with two. Use your hand to protect them, and your heart to guide them. Or' – mischief touches his eyes – 'the other way round.'

As they pass under the shadow of the cliffs, the boy catches a glimpse of someone looking out from one of the caves. He wonders if they ever tire of being here, and if their spirits linger when they die. If your surroundings become too familiar in life, how must it feel to be committed to them after death?

The thought is too gloomy for such a bright day. With a last look at the library caves he turns away, towards the distant mountains.

Chapter Fifteen

Heat covers the plain like a camel's blanket. Yorin is leading Tobi, Talaia riding her horse which, the boy has learned, is called Ashka. Shadows fall away, morning draws on. There are no more trees; they have all been drunk up by the sand.

'We'll stop here for something to eat,' Yorin says as they reach a deep curve in the cliffs.

Talaia is very quiet as Yorin attends to Tobi and Ashka. The boy thinks about asking why, but isn't sure how it will be received. Questions are like the varying depths of a pool. There are those of the surface: *What do you feel about such-and-such? Did you agree when so-and-so said this or that?* Further down are those not so easily broached: *How do you feel after your husband/wife/child ran off/disgraced you in some unnamed way the whole village knows about?* And, deep down, where the water is cold and nothing lives, the darkest reflections: *Why have you not fulfilled your promise? Why have you wasted your life?* These are the drowned questions, and there is a reason they remain that way.

Instead, he asks Talaia what her uncle does. She turns and looks at him. 'My aunt,' she says in a crisp and clear voice, 'runs the household. She enables her husband to go to his work as the owner of a brickworks, return home and rest.'

The boy looks down at his feet, and up again. If he says anything more he suspects his words would be returned to him dead. He finishes the peach he is eating, and throws the stone on the ground.

'If you keep it, you can plant it and it'll grow,' Talaia says.

'It'll grow here just as well as anywhere else.'

She raises an eyebrow. 'Perhaps.'

He is still fuming when Yorin joins him, throwing himself down, taking a gulp of water from his bottle. 'When we go through the Eye of Jala, we'll wish we were still in the sun. A shortcut,' he explains, 'takes us all the way through the Khat Mountains. *Dhisava* told me about it. He knows many things. For example, that Tobi is really a good-natured animal beset by circumstance.' He glances at the boy, his eyes mischievous. 'If you give him a chance, he might even let you ride him.'

The idea of perching on the back of such a bad-tempered beast even for a moment is too much for the boy. Yorin bursts out laughing. Talaia looks at him coolly.

'If you know how to treat them, they make very good companions,' she says.

The boy bites his tongue. As far as he is concerned, horses are only useful if you can stay on them. He has heard of larger animals serving men in the fields, and imagines them creatures of steadier temperament. Talaia's horse is the giddy kind, with long limbs and a restless eye.

'Have you ever ridden?' she asks.

'Only once, and that was enough.'

'I don't blame you,' Yorin says. 'Plays havoc with the' – he glances at Talaia – 'stomach.'

When they set off again, the boy checks that Talaia isn't looking before retrieving the peach stone.

All day they travel, the sand slowly giving way to a landscape strewn with rocks. The boy is only too glad to leave the desert behind. As the air cools, they make camp in the shade of a large boulder, laying down blankets, sharing a meal. Tobi and Ashka stand nose to tail, whickering softly. The boy lies back, exhausted but unable to sleep. The stars are so close they almost cover his eyes.

Morning is cold, and his back is aching. He rolls over and sits up, groaning.

'Here.' Yorin throws him an apple. Under wrinkled skin the flesh is sweet. He eats it in a few bites, and helps pack up. Talaia, he notices, is a little way off, looking out. Catching Yorin's glance, he concentrates on rolling up his blanket.

By mid-morning they have reached the base of the mountains, more dizzyingly vertical than they seemed at a distance. A little way into their lee Yorin dismounts, nodding at an expanse of sheer rock. 'The Eye of Jala,' he says.

As they come closer, the boy sees that the rock is split all the way up, as if long ago a blade of light was driven down into it. Tobi whinnies, throwing his head back, fretful. 'We talked about this, remember,' Yorin says. 'There's nothing to worry about.' He pats the horse's neck reassuringly.

The gap is only wide enough for them to enter one at a time. Yorin goes first, leading Tobi. Talaia adjusts her silver belt before following with Ashka. As the boy goes in, he hopes Jala never sleeps.

The world disappears. He cranes his neck, trying to see beyond the walls, but the more he looks the more they seem to lean into each other. Something about this place makes him uncomfortable. It is clammy, and far too quiet.

As they go deeper, he starts imagining he can feel the walls closing behind him. He puts his hand against the rock, touching something soft and moist. He quickly removes it. A rustling sound stops him in his tracks.

'Don't worry,' Yorin calls back, 'whatever it is, it has no interest in us. Alive, anyway.'

'What about some light?' Talaia asks.

'Best not, for the moment.'

'Of course.'

The boy suppresses an uncharitable feeling. He wonders if anything ruffles her.

Time, which he has come to know as a temperamental thing, takes its time. They walk for what seems hours. The air is colder now, and he pulls his cloak around him. Just as he is beginning to feel part of the darkness he stops dead, thinking he heard something behind him. Footsteps? His heart races as he strains to listen, but the only sound is the steady beat of the horses' hooves.

He walks a little further and stops again, half-turning. Is it his imagination, or did he hear soft steps following? He waits. Silence gathers around him.

'You all right back there?' Yorin calls.

'Yes, fine,' he says robustly, aware of Talaia up ahead.

'Darkness can do funny things to you. I knew a man who spent a year in a well.'

'Really?' Talaia sounds sceptical. The boy's eyes widen

slightly. She has offended against the first principle of storytelling. Prepare to believe.

'Of course,' Yorin says mildly. 'And when he came out, he was just the same as when he went in.'

The boy can sense Talaia's curiosity. 'Go on,' she says.

'The well was hollow. Not just downwards, but sideways too. There was a tunnel running out of it, right under the walls of the city. So, while people stood around scratching their heads, he was long gone. A year later he popped up again, to instant fame.'

'So he didn't really spend a year in a well,' the boy says.

'No, but they didn't know that. They went away with wonder in their hands, and he got a lot of free meals out of it.'

The boy senses a change in the stifling dark. He thinks Talaia may be smiling.

He would like never to see the Eye of Jala again. From time to time he touches the walls to make sure they are there. The darkness has such presence they feel unnecessary.

'How are you doing back there?' Yorin calls. There is a ripple of mischief in his voice.

'Fine,' the boy says loudly.

'Not far now.'

The boy nods, then realises no one can see him.

Up ahead is a seam of light. Something sparkles: a clutch of crystals in a shallow basin. Their glitter in the not-quite-dark is breathtaking. 'People used to mine for them,' Yorin says, 'until they realised they weren't worth anything.'

'But they're so beautiful,' Talaia exclaims softly.

The boy is quiet as they walk along. The idea that they have no value pricks his romantic soul.

When they come into the light, it is blinding. He closes his eyes, breathing space and air. And birdsong. He hadn't realised how much he missed it. He almost feels like singing himself as he looks around a grassy clearing surrounded by a horseshoe of trees. In the centre, a tall grey stone glitters in the early evening sun.

'A boundary marker,' Yorin says. 'We're about to enter Karez province.'

The boy finds a comfortable spot and sits with his palms touching the grass. Talaia is standing with her hand against the boundary stone, looking through the trees. A light breeze shapes her tunic to the curves of her body. He looks away.

'Well, we got here,' Yorin says, and his grin is very wide. Suddenly they are laughing, at deserts, at tribes, at crimson tents and codes made by men with no sense of humour.

'Sleep well?' Yorin asks, coming over from the edge of the clearing, where he has been grooming the horses.

'I did, thanks.' The boy gets up, stretching, and looks around. Talaia is sitting beside the fire, eating an apricot.

'Time for breakfast,' Yorin says.

In his satchel the boy finds an earthenware pot containing honey. He spreads it thickly on bread, and eats until his stomach groans. As Talaia finishes the apricot she says, 'It would be nice to hear one of Mirashi's poems.' She looks at him enquiringly. He takes the Book of Light from his shirt pocket and offers it to her, but she shakes her head. 'No, you read.'

Yorin seems to be studying the skyline, so the boy turns the pages until he finds a poem about birds. Dawn is a wren flying from the breast of the dark, morning a lark in an endless sky,

rising beyond season and sight.

Self-conscious at first, aware of his thudding heart, he settles into Mirashi's words as a noon-song

warms phrase after phrase into swallows.

By the time evening comes,

swifts, in a nocturne of dusk,

his voice is steady. After a thoughtful silence, Talaia thanks him. Yorin shifts, getting to his feet. 'Time to go. *Dhisava* told me about a place where we can stay. We can make friends with beer again.'

At the edge of the clearing, the land widens and falls away into a valley. As valleys go it is modest, but it is not the desert. They make their way down a grassy slope, following a shallow track. The ground is firm and springy; after the vagaries of sand, it feels like dancing. Across the valley lies a mountain range covered in what looks like green fog.

'The *Verdul Chen*,' Yorin says. 'The Green Mountains.'

By early evening they have reached the foot of the Green Mountains, and climb a steep path slanting round a great hill. A little way above them, a large wooden building stands on a broad, flat sill of grass. The sign is painted with an image of mountains, a golden bird soaring above.

'The Green Mountain Inn,' Yorin says.

As they cross the grass, a man comes out from the inn. He introduces himself as Groshi, the innkeeper.

'Have you come far?' he asks.

'Far enough,' Yorin replies courteously.

'Then you must be ready for a good meal.' The innkeeper beckons, and a man comes forward. As he reaches for Tobi's bridle, the horse throws his head back and rolls his eye in what the boy considers to be an unnecessarily dramatic manner.

'I'll take him,' Yorin says, patting the horse's neck. 'He can be wary of strangers.'

Wary? The boy knows Tobi carries enough weaponry to defeat a small army. Talaia unbuckles a bag from her saddle before handing over Ashka's reins.

At the door of the inn, the boy and Talaia are met by a pleasant-faced woman. Groshi introduces her as his wife, Marisk. She is particularly interested in Talaia, admiring her tunic. It is something the boy has observed when women get together, and finds comfort in its familiarity. Marisk leads them upstairs, chatting as she goes, and shows them to rooms with balconies overlooking the foothills.

The boy stands on the balcony, looking out. There is a knock on the door. Marisk is holding a bowl with a jug sitting in it. 'Here we are, my dear,' she says. 'I thought you'd like to wash off the dust. Your friends asked me to tell you they'll be in the common room. Dinner is ready when you are.'

When she has gone, the boy strips off his clothes and washes all over. He holds a hot towel to his face; it comes away filthy. For the first time he wonders what he must look like. Talaia seems immune to the smuts of travel.

The common room is filled with delicious smells of roasting meat. 'Better?' Yorin asks. He has changed into a clean shirt and trousers, and his hair is damp.

'Much.' The boy looks around. The common room is large and pleasant, with tables and chairs of the same clean-limbed wood as the inn. Sitting opposite, Talaia is surveying the room in a rather queenly way. He eyes her tunic of pale aquamarine and wonders how many outfits she has.

Marisk brings over a tray, and busies herself with dishes and bowls. The boy's stomach growls. He hopes Talaia can't hear it.

'You came over the Great Escarpment?' Marisk asks. It is, the boy learns, the local name for this side of the Khat Mountains.

'No, through the Eye of Jala,' Yorin says.

She stares for a moment. 'You didn't meet anyone, then?'

'Not a soul.'

Her face relaxes. 'That's good. Not that they normally come through. They usually stay that side of the mountains.'

There is no need to elaborate. The boy knows who she is talking about. He feels an urge to return to the Eye of Jala and cause a rockfall.

The meat is tender, the vegetables well-cooked. The common room dissolves around him as he concentrates on his stew.

'You worked for a merchant in Harakim, didn't you?' Talaia is speaking to him.

He wishes her eyes weren't so grey and smoky. It makes them very hard to read. He shoots an accusing glance at Yorin, who gets to his feet with a smile.

'I'm going to check on Tobi. I won't be long.'

The boy watches him go, aware of Talaia's eyes on him.

'It's a port city, isn't it?' she says. 'I've never been, but I've heard it's one of the main trade routes to Jedea. What was it like?'

He grips his cup and stares at the table. Part of him wants to tell her about his journeys, to conjure gulls, billowing sails, clouds running across a wide sky. To see her eyes widen in admiration as he describes his triumphs in Krystana. Another part wants to forget it ever happened. Five wasted years.

'I'm sorry,' she says stiffly, 'I didn't mean to pry.' Before he can reply, she gets to her feet. 'I'm very tired, and there's a long way to go yet. Would you excuse me?'

The boy watches her leave. Heads turn as she passes. The back of his neck prickles. He thinks about going after her, but has no idea what he would say.

'Talaia gone to bed?' Yorin asks, slipping into his chair. He gives the boy a shrewd look. 'I think you're in need of beer.'

The boy finds himself enjoying the aromatic, slightly tart flavour. After two mugs, his thoughts begin to turn golden. After three, he feels inspirational. He vaguely hears Yorin saying, 'I think it's time for bed.'

When he wakes, he can't remember where he is. He is still in yesterday's clothes. Squinting, he pulls himself up on his elbow. Someone has left a jug and bowl on a chest in the corner, so he fills the bowl and dunks his head in. As his conversation with Talaia comes back to him, he wonders if he can remain submerged, but his lungs tell him otherwise and he comes up gasping.

Tidied up and brushed down, he makes his way to the common room. The smell of frying meat reminds him of the night before. He spots Yorin and Talaia sitting near the fireplace.

'Morning,' Yorin says cheerfully, raising a beaker. The boy nods, glancing at Talaia. She doesn't look up. A plate of mutton is put in front of him, and he swallows. 'Just cham,' Yorin says to the serving-woman. 'He's not used to' – he catches the boy's eye – 'fried food.'

The boy gulps tea. He hears Yorin saying, 'The Green Mountains should be safe. As safe as they can be, at least,' before sickness takes him. Excusing himself, he goes up to his room.

Yorin is at the door. He studies the boy for a moment. 'It wasn't a bad attempt. I've seen worse. Here.' He throws the boy a wad of what looks like dried grass. 'Chew it. It'll settle your stomach.'

The boy, who has just finished with the bowl and would chew the sun if it helped, crams it into his mouth. His stomach, recently estranged, begins to find its way home.

'Goldenburn,' Yorin says. 'I always keep some with me.' He glances around. 'We'll be leaving soon. Think you'll live?'

The boy grimaces. 'What did you mean, the Green Mountains are as safe as they can be?' he asks.

'Forests offer plenty of places to hide. Don't worry,'

Yorin adds, seeing the boy's face, 'they won't be coming after us.'

The air is cool, the sky pale blue as they leave the Green Mountain Inn. Yorin is talking quietly with Talaia as they ride along. The boy keeps a safe distance from Ashka, eyeing the shining hindquarters, the dainty hoofwork. He wonders if Talaia knows she is seated on a show-off.

Wispy shrubs with pale-blue flowers freckle the slopes. '*Arylindra*,' Talaia says. 'Maiden's Purse.' She dismounts and bends over a shrub. The boy watches silently as she comes up to him and threads a tiny flower through the top eyelet of his shirt. Yorin is smiling slightly as they continue on up the slope.

As they enter the forest, the light leaves part of itself behind. The boy has never seen such trees before, mighty and ancient mountain firs. When Yorin tells him some of them are over a thousand years old, he finds it easy to believe.

Talaia, now leading Ashka, says, 'There are lots of stories about the Green Mountains.'

'Please,' Yorin says, 'enlighten us.'

She thinks for a moment. 'This is a story about a lark and a jay.' She tells them how the lark, a ground-nesting bird afraid of heights, took to the skies because of the wiles of a devious jay, who coveted the treasures the lark had in its nest. As she comes to the end, the boy is still spiralling with the lark.

Yorin makes an extravagant bow. 'Thank you. That was a good story.'

Arun passes a hand across his forehead. 'It was. In her hands, a simple tale became a thing of beauty and delight. She had a gift for it. To be honest, I was a little jealous. It left me wondering if I'd ever find something I was good at. It was only when I saw both of them looking at me that I realised I hadn't said a word. So I put aside my pride and said how much I'd enjoyed the story, and how well she'd told it.

'I didn't know how it would be received, especially after the previous evening, but the last thing I expected was for her to look embarrassed. I thought I must be imagining it, but I wasn't. I found out later that it was because she felt shy. At the time I suspected she was reluctant to accept my praise because I wasn't worthy of giving it. Ah,' he says with a soft laugh, 'I thought myself into all sorts of situations in those days.'

That evening they make a fire in a small grassy clearing. After a dinner of toasted bread and cheese they lick their fingers and sit back, yawning.

'It'll be harder tomorrow,' Yorin says, stretching comfortably.

'Harder?' Talaia asks. She is sitting cross-legged, eating a peach.

'Steeper. But don't tell him.' He glances at Tobi, who is standing with Ashka, nibbling grass. 'Once we're through the mountains, it's roughly north-west to Kushtar.'

The boy tries to draw a map in his mind's eye, but tiredness is filling the path with clouds.

As the sun comes up, he stirs. In the night he heard the many voices of the Green Mountains. Some were familiar, birds chirping sleepily, the wind in the trees. Others he couldn't place, and they troubled his dreams. One in particular, a low, lingering note, pressed into his sleep so deeply he hears it still. A bird, or something else?

He sits up groggily, looks around, and sees Yorin clearing the fire. The shins of the trees are bathed in mist.

'Morning,' Yorin says. 'How did you sleep?'

'Not bad.'

'I did, too, apart from that plaguey owl.' Yorin laughs. 'Didn't you hear it? Every time I started falling asleep, it went off again. If I'd found it, I'd have taught it a different tune.'

An owl? The boy smiles. Making sense of the night is easier now he can put a face to it. He looks around. 'Talaia's gone to have a wash,' Yorin says. 'There's water in the bottle.'

Taking the hint, the boy splashes his head and neck, wetting his hair.

'Careful!' Talaia cries. She has returned, and he is pelting her with water. To his amazement, she is laughing. She holds out a cloth. 'Here.' He blots his face. The cloth holds a trace of scent, honey and roses. He quickly finishes drying himself and gives it back to her.

The path through the forest is growing steeper. They are leading the horses, who stumble from time to time on thick leaf litter. Talaia murmurs words of encouragement to Ashka. Today her tunic and trousers are pale green. The boy tries not to think she is like a slender leaf among the trees.

'Do you want to stop for a moment? We're due a break.' Yorin glances up at the sky, in pieces among the high branches.

'I'm fine,' Talaia says.

'So am I,' the boy says quickly.

Yorin smiles. The creases at the side of his eyes are more pronounced, and he looks tired. The bruises on his face have faded to yellowish-brown. When the boy asks if he is all right, he waves an airy hand. 'Never felt better. Always ready to see what's beyond the next mountain.'

'And when you get there?' Talaia asks.

'That's not the point,' the boy says.

'So you'd just wander aimlessly?' she asks a little scornfully. She doesn't look at him as she speaks. Travelling with Talaia is, he reflects, rather like sailing unknown seas and hoping the ship will hold its nerve against the weather. He judges it best not to answer.

A short while afterwards, they settle in a hollow of grass against broad tree trunks. After their meal Yorin goes off, 'to see what's ahead.'

With rising panic, the boy watches him go. Why is Yorin leaving him with this girl?

Talaia rinses her hands and tidies herself, although there is no need; everything falls gracefully into place. After a moment she says, 'I'm sorry I was rude earlier.'

He looks at her in surprise. In his experience, those who offend are generally the last to apologise. 'It was nothing,' he says. 'And I'm sorry, too, about how I was at the inn.'

Talaia glances down. The boy finds himself wanting to gently raise her chin. When she looks up she says, 'It was my fault. I don't know much about you, but I should have realised it was difficult to talk about. I can sometimes say the wrong thing. "Think before you speak." That's what my father said. Of course I never listened.' She smiles, and tears shimmer in her eyes.

The boy is quiet for a moment. He knows Talaia won't be with them for long; she will be leaving them at Kushtar. He takes a breath. 'I was always putting my foot it in at home.'

It is not as hard as he thought. Something in Talaia's eyes makes him want to tell her about the hut, his sister's house in the shrubs, the almond tree and the fish trap. She seems particularly interested in his sister, and asks many questions, but not about how he came to be separated from his family. For that he suspects he owes Yorin his thanks.

Beyond the forest, day is wearing on. The silence has begun to feel like a second skin. Once, the boy thought he saw a movement in the shadows, and peered uneasily through the trees.

'Are there animals in here?' he asks.

'Bound to be,' Yorin says, 'but they're mostly harmless.'

'And the ones that aren't?' Talaia asks.

'There are three of us, and two horses. We'll be fine. Even if we come across a *yizuma*.'

Talaia's face brightens in recognition. It is a look that absorbs and reflects things, and the boy finds himself grudgingly admiring it.

'Ah,' Yorin says, 'you've heard of it.'

'I've read about it. But, please, go on.'

'The *yizuma*,' Yorin says with the air of one about to deliver a lecture, 'is neither fact nor fable. For which it has only itself to blame, since it spends most of its time in seclusion. Reports of what it looks like render it, by various accounts, a bear with the head of a chicken, a fox that fell

241

in a river and came up scaled like a fish, a stone giant with detachable arms to throw at people who trespass on its land.'

The boy starts laughing. Yorin gives him a challenging look. 'Go on,' he says.

'A bull with metal horns and a leather hide,' the boy offers. 'When it's angry, it lowers its head and charges at mountains, making rocks fall.'

Yorin looks at Talaia. 'No one has ever seen it because it can't be seen,' she says. 'It takes on the colour of its surroundings, and can be so large it covers the entire forest, or so small it can hide under a leaf. It's with you at all times, although you'd never know it.'

It can't be helped. Everyone looks around.

'Yours is the better *yizuma*,' the boy concedes.

Talaia makes a graceful bow. He wonders if the *yizuma* is watching.

Chapter Sixteen

As they climb higher into the Green Mountains, the boy reflects on the contrariness of human nature. When he was in the desert, he wanted to dive into water and stay there until he became a fish. Here in the cool green light of the forest he wishes he were an eagle, gliding in a blue sky. He thinks he has more in common with forests than deserts, and most in common with valleys. He asks Talaia what her town, Inishpur, was like.

She shrugs. 'The same as most, I expect. People, houses, a marketplace. Nothing special.'

Having shared with her his family and his village, the boy feels snubbed. He wants to say, *If it had been taken away from you, it would become special,* but is struggling with the idea that she sees one place as being much like another. He had thought her more discerning. 'But surely,' he says, 'the people make them different. Or the houses. The markets. The food.'

He waits for another dismissal, but Talaia looks thoughtful. 'Maybe it's that each of us is different,' she says. 'Or think we are. And so our surroundings, our experiences, seem different, too.' She looks at him enquiringly. He is once more at the water's edge, and senses her waiting for him to test it.

'I like it better than the sameness.'

'The sameness?' Her tone is icy. He stares, wondering at how fast the temperature has dropped.

Yorin saves him. 'What about people who go nowhere? Is it because they believe they'd only end up in the same place if they went, and don't want to waste their time? Or is it because they think it'd be different, and that would be like a death to them? Would they mourn the loss of their sameness? If so, what colours would they wear?'

'The same as they always wore,' Talaia says. The sudden mischief in her face is like a light in the dimness of the forest.

'Indeed,' Yorin agrees. The boy feels as if he is missing something. 'It was your idea,' Yorin tells him. 'We're indebted to you for our confusion.'

The boy stares, then laughs. 'You're welcome,' he says, and gives a small bow. Talaia smiles. He trips over a root.

They make camp that night in a small, pine-scented clearing. Yorin makes a fire, ringing it with stones. 'Otherwise,' he says, 'we'll go up like tinder. The needles are very dry.'

In the fresh air of morning the boy feels alive, and full of – sap. 'That's it,' he says, 'sap.'

'I know we're far from civilisation,' Yorin remarks, 'but I didn't think you'd go to pieces so quickly.' His look is ironic.

'What do you mean?'

'You spoke out loud,' Talaia says. 'You said, "That's it. Sap."'

Oh. In the midst of his embarrassment, the boy reflects that it could have been worse. He has heard of people talking in their sleep, and marriages being broken that way.

Yorin and Talaia seem to be waiting for him to speak. 'I was thinking,' he says tentatively, 'that I feel different here, more alive, somehow.' It is the first time he has volunteered his personal thoughts, and he has no idea how they will be received.

'So do I,' Talaia replies. 'I thought I'd be flagging by now, but I just want to keep going.'

The boy is so grateful for her words that he gathers them up and carries them with him as he climbs.

A little while later Yorin stops. 'There,' he says, pointing at a broad flank of grey stone. When they reach it, he takes a piece of paper from the pouch at his belt. '*Dhisava* made it,' he tells them, showing them the drawing. 'It's here somewhere . . .' He looks from the drawing to the rock, and back again. 'I think – yes.' Feeling his way through a tangle of roots and briars, he pulls them apart to reveal a narrow gap. Without the drawing, it would have remained hidden.

He pushes his way through the soft door. Tobi snorts and stamps. 'No need to worry, my friend,' he says, 'it's quite safe.' The horse tosses his head but allows himself to be led in. The boy follows Talaia and Ashka into a deep gully, clean and dry. The stone walls are green with moss, the ground strewn with twigs.

'It's a friendly place,' Talaia says, 'I can feel it. Do you think it knows?' She presses her hand against the stone, listening. 'Yes. It knows.'

It is a surprising detour, an unexpected side to her character. The boy grins suddenly. Here in this sunlit gully they are working their way towards something he'd thought lost.

'Are you going to share it with us?' Yorin asks.

'It's a good day, that's all,' he says. Yorin grins back at him. Talaia shakes her head, but she is smiling.

Evening is beginning to fall as they come out onto a tree-covered ridge above a steep slope. The soft gestures of dusk are all around them, outlining the shapes of the trees, brightening the stars. A light breeze stirs the horses' manes. They make their way carefully down the slope until they reach a rocky basin. Not a shelter, exactly, but in the wild the mind builds a house from very little. After their meal they sit back in the firelight, talking quietly. It is an evening the boy will look back on and wish for, many times.

'We've made it,' Yorin announces the following morning.

They are standing on a vast grey plateau, looking out on a dusty brown plain. After the desert heat and the closeness of the trees, the air seems to glitter and swell. At the far side of the plain, light glances off the towers and spires of a city. Beyond it, a range of hills gently rises.

'Kushtar,' Yorin says. Talaia is silent, but the boy senses a change in her. He wants to ask her about it, but leaves his nerve behind as they make their way down the rocky slopes.

Boulders litter the plain. Patches of scrubby grass grow between stumps of rock. The boy feels suddenly exposed. There is nothing between him and the sky. Will he ever shake off the feeling of being watched?

Talaia turns to him. 'I think it's time for a poem. Would you?'

Leafing through the Book of Light, he finds a poem about a man recalling his first meeting with his wife. He is becoming less self-conscious about reading aloud, though he stumbles slightly on the ending,

when love walked out of the desert
and barefoot by the well stood waiting.

Yorin thanks him. Talaia says nothing.

They walk in silence until the boy says, 'What's it like? Kushtar, I mean.'

'Bigger than Harakim,' Yorin says, 'and smaller than Dhurkana.'

'It's famous for its paper,' Talaia adds. 'It's very fine, and very expensive.'

It strikes the boy as an odd thing to be famous for. Silversmiths or winemakers, yes. Gardens, or architecture. Maybe even prize-winning cheeses.

'I think I've heard about it,' Yorin says. 'Isn't it something to do with the type of reed they use?'

Talaia looks mildly impressed. The boy wonders what would be written on such fine, expensive paper. Not lists of groceries or columns of figures. Love letters, perhaps.

Kushtar is shimmering into shape, its grey stone walls kindled from the rising heat. As they join a broad track, the boy reflects that a moment ago they were walking on a barren plain. As soon as a line appeared in the dust they fell in with it, and with the idea of order.

There are other travellers now, riders, wagons, people on foot carrying baskets and bundles, chatting, laughing, catching them up into the world again. Life, it seems, has been getting on very well without them. They are greeted with nods, with smiling faces, or they are ignored. 'Men of business,' Yorin says with a grin. 'Can't spend a moment. Costs too much.'

Banners fly from turrets above the city walls. When they reach the tall wooden gates, the guards shrug them through. 'An army could pour in,' Yorin says, 'and they'd let them pass. But then, if you're paid less than a racing snake, you wouldn't be inclined to work too hard, either.'

It seems the whole world has decided to visit Kushtar today. There are people everywhere, calling from houses, sitting at tables outside taverns, standing behind market stalls. There are animals, too, some tethered, others running about, especially dogs. As they walk, the boy glances about at the streets, narrower than those of Harakim, twisting away into the distance. Halfway down a long street, they pass under the sign of a goblet held up by a disembodied hand. Round a corner, through a large archway and into a stableyard.

'I'll see to the horses,' Yorin says. Tobi gives him a look.

'I'm sure that horse can talk,' Talaia says as she and the boy make their way to the back door of the inn.

In his room, the boy reacquaints himself with hot water and soap. Scented water runs down his neck, undoing the knots and tangles his body has become accustomed to. When he is dry, he puts on clean clothes and sits on the bed. It is a quiet, extraordinary luxury. The materials of the sheet, the blanket, the pillow – so soft he can sink an elbow into it – feel almost wondrous. Here he is, safe and relatively sound, with clean fingernails and a shirt that smells of something other than himself.

He answers the door to Yorin, also in clean clothes, his hair bright, his face unsmudged.

'It all comes down to this,' Yorin says as they go down the wooden staircase. 'Food, beer, bed. The rest is embroidery.'

After an enormous meal, the boy is inclined to agree with him. Talaia, he notices, has managed to put away an honourable amount. Yorin looks at them mischievously. 'There's one slice left,' he says.

They consider the golden crust of the pie, bursting with apples plucked from a tree whose birth made orchards rejoice. The boy says it aloud, and Yorin laughs. 'And wrapped in a dew of spices,' Talaia adds.

The boy looks at her. Is it a game, a contest of extravagant praises? If so . . . but before he can reply Yorin says, 'If nobody wants it . . . ?'

Yorin and Talaia are already in the common room when he goes downstairs the following morning. Last night, for the first time in many days, he had no dreams. Or, if he did, they knew enough to leave a weary traveller alone.

'We'll go after breakfast,' Yorin says. 'Talaia's sent word; her aunt and uncle are expecting her. I've asked the innkeeper for directions.'

After a short silence Talaia says, 'Could we have one last poem please, Arun?'

He is aware of his hands shaking as he opens the Book of Light, finding a poem in which Mirashi looks out over a sleeping country.

In your arms lie
Bethra of the star-gazers,
sad-eyed Darios, whose perfume tames the thorn.

They walk through a wash of early light. They have left
Tobi at the stables, and Talaia is leading Ashka. As they
pass a street where weapons are sold, a sign flashes silver
as a light wind nudges the wood.

'Good,' Yorin says. 'I need a replacement.'

Another street is full of cloth-sellers. 'They're
renowned for their flower embroideries,' Talaia says. The
boy wonders if it will be possible to slip away later and find
an embroidered flower.

In the heart of the city they arrive in a street with
stone balconies at the upper windows of the houses, gauzy
curtains stirring in the breeze.

'It's that one.' Yorin nods at a house of pale-grey stone.
The door looks very shut. As they reach it, the boy smooths
down his shirt. Talaia knocks.

Voices. Footsteps. The door opens; a woman comes
out and stands for a moment looking at Talaia. 'We've
been waiting for you,' she says. 'You'd better come in.' She
calls a name and a man appears. 'Take the horse,' she says,
glancing briefly at Yorin and the boy. This, he realises, is
Talaia's aunt. She is older than he imagined, and thinner.

'Aunt Ro, this is Yorin, and Arun,' Talaia says. 'They
brought me here.'

Her aunt nods briskly, sweeping them indoors. In a
white-walled room she indicates which chairs they are to
sit on. As she pours tea, another man comes in. Above his
white tunic and trousers, his round face is flushed.

'Uncle Ferec,' Talaia says, getting up and holding out her hand. Bowing, he looks at the boy and Yorin. Talaia sits down again. The boy glances around the room. It is square, with two windows, one facing the street, the other to the side. A cornered window. He wonders if it ever thought of making a run for it.

'Thank you,' Talaia's uncle is saying rather pompously, 'I am most grateful. I understand it is not an easy journey, but you brought our niece here safely. *Yishana*, the thanks of my house to you.' The boy thinks he has had enough of houses, whether made of stone or tented and strung with camels.

'You'll stay with us while you are here?' Talaia's aunt says. Yorin tells her they have lodgings at the Goblet. 'Of course,' she replies. The boy catches the look of relief on her husband's face. He has been glancing, not very subtly, at Yorin, whose red-gold hair seems to inflame the sunlight pouring through the windows.

After a short while that seems much longer, Yorin puts down his cup and gets to his feet. Thanking them for their hospitality, he says, 'We'll be leaving for Dhurkana tomorrow, but we'd like to take a look around the city while we're here. Is there anywhere you'd recommend?'

Talaia's aunt suggests the market, her uncle the Administration Hall. They speak at the same time. It reminds the boy of two people trying to enter a room at once.

Talaia's uncle walks them to the door. 'You will find there is nothing between us and Dhurkana. It is the bigger city, certainly, but not the greater.' He hands Yorin a small pouch. 'For your trouble. Enjoy your stay.'

The boy glances back. Talaia is standing with her aunt, who is saying something to her. He meets her eyes briefly before she looks away.

They have fingered the market from top to bottom, and parcels pile up in their arms. Tobi has a new blanket, and a fine new bridle chased with silver. The sun on his face, the sounds of daily life, swell in the boy like a song. He hadn't realised how much he missed it. He is not a hermit of the ocean or the plains. He is still a part of things.

When they finally collapse outside a tavern, the goodbye that wasn't said fills his throat. Perhaps he can go back, say it properly. But he knows he can't. The door closed behind them, and that was that.

They sit quietly for a while, Yorin observing people passing by, the boy deep in thought. Stirring, Yorin gives a contented yawn. 'Let's go and look for that sword,' he says.

Shadows are lengthening when they finally return to the Goblet. A scabbard hangs at Yorin's belt. The boy can still see the bright arc the sword made as it flashed across his face. 'If he'd wanted your head you wouldn't still be looking,' the swordsmith remarked.

He glances down at the new tan-coloured leather belt at his waist. From it hangs a sheath containing a dagger. He kept offering his thanks until Yorin held up a hand and said, 'I thank you for your thanks, and that's an end to it. Gratitude can be a lingering illness.'

Up in his room, the boy examines the dagger. It is a beautiful thing, the silver hilt chased with intricate patterns of flowers, leaves, and surprisingly, a bee. The pommel is set with a silver-grey gemstone, liquid with light. For a moment he sits with it on his lap, then thinks perhaps he shouldn't stroke it like a cat.

At dinner, he asks Yorin about the pommel. 'It's a cloudstone,' Yorin says. 'It's said to have protective properties. Although you'd believe anything if you got home safely.'

After the meal, they sit watching the fire. Every inn seems to have a fire, the boy thinks sleepily, no matter how hot it is outside. The flames spark gold, reminding him of Talaia's hair. A wave of emotion almost knocks him off his chair. Excusing himself, he goes up to his room.

It doesn't do to dwell on things you can't change, but he lies on his bed and dwells so hard a town grows up around it. They are leaving for Dhurkana tomorrow, and he will never see Talaia again. Even though she can be irritating, and knows far more than she has any business to, the thought is not a happy one. He gets up and goes to the window. As he stands looking at the moon, the thing that has been bothering him all day comes to light. No books. In Aunt Ro's house, there were no books. He tells himself he only saw the sitting room, but he knows it is normally the room where items of learning and beauty are displayed for visitors to remark on and admire.

He is woken from a doze by a soft knock. He sits up, listening. Another knock, a little louder this time. Pulling on his trousers, he goes to the door. Slowly he lifts the latch.

Talaia is standing there and he says nothing, because his mouth is an O and he cannot speak.

Chapter Seventeen

For the briefest moment her eyes flicker to his naked chest. 'I didn't know what else to do,' she says at the same time as he says, 'What are you –?'

The anxiety in her voice pulls him together. 'Come in,' he says, 'sit down.'

She sits on the bed, he puts on his shirt and perches at a safe distance. He waits for her to speak but she says nothing. Her travelling cloak has fallen back, and moonlight illuminates her clasped hands. He wonders if he should offer tea and, if so, where he would get it at this time of night.

'Would you like some water?' he asks.

'No. Thank you.' She is whispering, but her voice in the stillness is very clear.

As the silence lengthens, he realises it is up to him to broach the subject. When he asks what has happened she says stiffly, 'They've arranged a marriage for me.'

Heat flares in his chest. He is taken back to the look in Nissa's eye when she heard Adara telling Tir about such a marriage. 'In our street, among respectable people,' she told him later, outraged. At the time he made the right noises and took very little notice. But now . . .

'It had all been settled before I got here,' Talaia says. 'They told me this evening. Can you –'

No, he can't imagine. He is too busy feeling entirely at sea. As he searches for something to say, it dawns on him that Talaia isn't crying but seems possessed of a fierce calm.

'He's much older,' she says, 'and well off, of course. He's a friend of my uncle's.' The boy hates him, for all three things. 'I thought I was coming here to help my aunt. I also thought I'd be able to continue my studies, do what my father did.' Talaia's voice shakes slightly. All he can do is reach out and touch her hand. She flinches, but doesn't draw away.

'It'll be all right,' he says, 'I promise.'

Another silence, in which he realises they are sitting in the dark. He lights a lamp, his hand shaking as he slips the casing over the flame. There is no sound from downstairs; it is too early yet. He makes a decision. 'I'll fetch Yorin.'

Yorin's eyes widen slightly when he sees Talaia sitting on the bed, but he listens in silence as the boy quickly explains the situation.

'So,' he says cheerfully,' we have a problem to solve.' Talaia glares at him but he smiles and says, 'There's really nothing to think about. Come with us. Better that than –' He shudders dramatically.

The boy wonders if anything ever bothers him. If they take Talaia with them, they will have broken so many codes of conduct, of family, of honour, they can never be put back together. When he looks at her, all scruples fall away. 'Yes,' he says firmly, 'come with us.'

Talaia's eyes narrow. 'Why?' she asks. He is so taken aback he has no reply.

'Because we need you,' Yorin says. 'We'd drive each other mad otherwise.'

Talaia's shoulders sag. With a rush of understanding, the boy realises she can't bear to be pitied. 'Yorin's right,' he says. 'You wouldn't want that on your conscience, would you?'

After a taut silence she nods.

'Right,' Yorin says briskly, 'time to leave. Best pull up your hood. Is that yours?' He nods at the bundle on the floor. As if in a trance, Talaia leans down, picks it up and gets to her feet. To the boy Yorin says, 'Get your things together, I won't be long.'

As they cross the stableyard, it feels as if the eyes of Kushtar are upon them. Talaia is silent, her hood covering her face. The alley beyond is short, and takes them out into the street. When Yorin catches up with them, he is leading Tobi. 'Down here,' he says. When they turn the corner into a broader street the boy glances back, imagining he can hear the feet of pursuing relatives. Yorin glances around, and stops. 'It'd be better if you ride,' he says to Talaia.

The sky threatens dawn as they move quickly on. 'This'll take us to the west gate. Less chance of being seen,' Yorin says as they enter another street. It is empty except for a cat that slides out of sight. Tobi snorts. 'Quietly, my friend,' Yorin murmurs.

They come out into a wide, tree-lined square. Tall wooden gates are set in the wall at the far side. In a small hut next to them someone stirs; a lantern bobs, stops and hails them.

'Your business?'

The boy wonders why the guard bothers to ask, since there must surely be a sign above their heads announcing that here is a girl abandoning her duty in the company of two villains and a curmudgeonly horse.

Yorin is speaking quietly. He is at his most guileful; such innocence radiates forth there is almost no need for a lantern. The guard shrugs, glances up at Talaia, says, 'That bad, eh?' and nods to his companion. A postern opens within the gate and they pass through, Talaia ducking her head, Tobi snorting and jingling his new silver bridle.

The postern closes; a bolt rattles home. They leave Kushtar quickly and quietly until the orange light of the torches on the city walls no longer reaches them. The silence deepens as it carries them into a copse at the side of the path. It fits them closely, a hide of trees with a pool of earth at the centre.

Talaia dismounts, throws back her hood and hisses, 'That bad!' Suddenly she is crying, Yorin is patting her arm, and the boy is wondering if he will ever understand anything about her.

Morning is behind them. No furious cloud of hooves, elbows and spears has come thundering after them. Talaia is composed once more, the belt of her lavender-coloured tunic and trousers sitting lightly on her hips and, to those who might be interested, accentuating her slender waist. The boy fixes his eyes on the country ahead. The land sweeps slowly upwards into rich green downs.

'Where are we?' he asks.

'The Yondra Pass,' Yorin says. 'Gateway to Dhurkana.'

The look on Talaia's face reminds the boy of the relief he felt when he and Yorin escaped from the tribe of the House of Goash. Although, he argues, their threat was mortal, and Talaia's was an unwanted bridegroom. Before he can weigh up their respective claims she points, saying, 'Look, a garahawk.'

The bird high above reminds him of a kite he and his sister tried to fly once, a construction of paper and twigs made by their father. It must have been when they were very young. They'd run back and forth on the bank of the stream until the grass grew hot. The air caught the kite, toyed with it, and let it drop. The boy was downcast but his sister, ever practical, said, 'We'll try again when it's windier.'

They did; the kite embraced the sky so hard the string broke and it soared upward, trod air, and plummeted to earth. To water, in fact. The boy waded in and rescued it, but it dissolved in his hands. Only the twiggy skeleton remained.

The hawk hangs in the air. It needs no strings, and water will not quench it. 'Why is it called a garahawk?' he asks.

'Because it only nests in gara trees,' Yorin says. 'I think there are some further up the pass. People protect them, they believe the hawks bring luck.'

Not to rabbits or mice, the boy thinks.

The downs bear them higher, closer to the sun. In the late afternoon, they stop for a meal before setting off again.

'There was a battle here once, over land boundaries,' Yorin says. 'It was a long time ago. I'm sure they're sleeping peacefully now' – he glances at the ground – 'but I wouldn't like to linger at night.'

The boy looks at the dreaming uplands. The thought of what might be buried here unnerves him. Talaia is frowning. 'Do you really believe in things like that?' she asks.

Yorin shrugs. 'It's in the tales.'

'And that makes it true?' Talaia's voice is dangerously calm.

The boy holds his breath. The further they come from Kushtar, the more argumentative she seems to become.

'Your father was a scribe,' Yorin is saying.

'Yes.'

'And he studied the tales?' She nods, a little stiffly. 'Then –' Yorin holds out his hands as if they contain a conclusion.

Suddenly Talaia smiles, and the boy feels as if he is being hauled up from underwater.

'Fair enough,' she says mildly. He is speechless. How does Yorin do it?

They travel the Yondra Pass for three days, entertained by Yorin with stories of increasing extravagance. On the afternoon of the third day, they reach the high tops. Stirred by a pilgrim wind, the sky sweeps clouds before it. There is a sense of something gathering as the grasses flow downhill again.

Yorin points across the distance. Dhurkana. Green plains spread round it like grass at the foot of a great tree, rising into gentle hills. It is much bigger than the boy imagined. Settlements nudge up against vast walls of golden stone braced with many towers.

'The original part of the city is over two thousand years old,' Yorin says. 'We'd better get moving, we need to get there before nightfall. They really do shut you out.'

He starts singing quietly.

Once I rode, now I walk, once I smiled, now I frown.
Take the miles from my feet and let me lie down.
I am tired, tired, and want to lie down.

Once I was a young man, with a young man's dreams,
Now I sit in my house alone.
Take the miles from my feet and let me lie down.
I am tired, tired to the bone.

'He obviously didn't have a good horse,' he says when he finishes.

They walk on in silence until the boy hears a melody. It is pure and clear as a reed flute. With a start he realises Talaia is singing, about the moon, a river, and a tree. A bird lands in the tree and makes her nest, the river flows by, the moon looks down,

And the land is the white of her eye.
And the bird takes flight by her silver light
And never comes back again.

Why do so many songs have to be dipped in melancholy? he wonders. After a moment's thought, he comes up with a song about an ant and a cricket. Bracing himself, he starts to sing. Yorin, who seems to know it, joins in. Talaia lowers her hood to listen. The tune is a merry one, and the notes chase themselves faster and faster until they come to an end in a breathless heap. Talaia laughs, and claps. The boy feels as if he has made the sun come out.

The day is ending; the air grains with dusk. The boy finds himself walking more quickly, and with rising fear. What will he find when he gets to Dhurkana? He lets the thought dissolve in the waning light, and hopes its ghost won't trouble him tonight.

The guards are sharper and more suspicious than those in Kushtar. Yorin tells them they are looking for employment, that they are good workers, and come from – he names a city known for the quality of its labour.

'You're best off trying the Well, then,' one of the guards says. 'It's a favourite with workmasters.' He glances at Talaia – the boy feels a hackle rise – and says to Yorin, 'She yours?'

'Yes,' Yorin replies smoothly, 'and a good worker, too.'

'You're all good workers.' The guard laughs. It is not a friendly laugh, but he waves them on through the great black gates, into the city.

That Dhurkana appreciates its visitors soon becomes clear. They have scarcely taken two steps before someone offers to sell them a very good carpet. Yorin thanks him, saying, 'Not now, my friend, it's late and we're looking for somewhere to stay.'

'Of course,' the carpet-seller says. 'Please, come with me.'

In a great square already in shadow they come to a halt. The square is lined with shops and larger, more ornate buildings whose business, the boy suspects, is commerce. The carpet-seller beckons them down a side street to an inn, a sturdy-looking building with a large, freshly painted sign. He tells them the Golden Bear is one of the best inns in the city. Yorin thanks him, and gives him a coin.

The inn is comfortably furnished, with deep-seated chairs in honey-coloured wood. After a good meal, the boy climbs the stairs to his room. Sleep brings broken dreams.

The following morning they return to the square. The shops are already open, shaded with coloured awnings and shutters. The boy glances at Talaia. Her grey eyes catch the light; he looks away. To the right is a building of some importance. The early sun carves lineaments from shadow, fluted pillars twined with flowers, walls decorated with garlands and inscriptions.

'Impressive, eh?' Yorin says, nodding at the building.

'What is it?' the boy asks.

'The City Hall. That's where we should be able to find out –' He stops.

It feels as if the whole square has also fallen silent. All the way from the library caves the boy has avoided the subject but it has followed him faithfully, sore of foot and heart, and sits now in the eyes of his companions.

The doors of the City Hall are intricately carved, and bound in elaborate ironwork. Before them stands a man, not quite a guard, asking them their business. 'We've come from the caves of Linshafan, a place of wonders,' Yorin says. 'We're interested in the way you keep your records. We've heard great things about them.'

The man squares his shoulders. 'Come with me.'

He takes them into a cavernous hall whose pillars rise to the ceiling, whose walls are painted with billowy clouds half-concealing small children with fat cheeks, men in impressive robes, women whose glorious hair seems almost to stream in the upturned faces of visitors. Their guide looks smug. 'You see?' he says. 'Our entrance hall is a wonder in itself.'

He leads them through the crowds to a man sitting at a desk. A man of study; the boy recognises the signs. Eyes half lost in a paper quest, the nose of his cloth belt dipped in ink. Their guide introduces him as Sirishasta. 'These people are interested in seeing how we keep our records. They've come from the caves of Linshafan.'

'You saw *Dhisava*?' Sirishasta asks, his eyes lighting up.

'We did,' Yorin says, and Sirishasta smiles.

'He is well?'

'Very well.'

'I am glad to hear it. Now, you are interested in our record-keeping? Then let me take you to the Hall of Records. Please, come with me.'

'We'd particularly like to see how you record your labour transactions,' Yorin says as they walk along.

A little way down, they enter a large chamber. Sirishasta leads them to a bright, spacious area where people are seated at tables, their heads bent over books. 'These' – he indicates the shelves surrounding them – 'are the Registers of Citizens. They contain the names of everyone who comes to live or work here. They go back over seven hundred years. Those' – he points – 'are the most recent.'

The boy's mouth goes dry as he stares at the large brown books, each with a year embossed in white on the spine. 'Now, my apologies, I have duties to attend to,' Sirishasta says, 'but you are most welcome to stay and look around.'

When he has gone Talaia says carefully, 'How long ago – when –?'

'Five years. Late spring.'

She starts searching the shelves. Yorin joins her. The boy finds himself fixed to the spot. Each book contains many names. Only one will do.

'This might be it.' Talaia tugs at the collar of a book.

Yorin helps her lift it onto a table. 'Only one way to find out.' With a heave, he turns it over and opens it.

There are two silences, one in the Hall of Records, one beside the pool. When Arun speaks, his voice is strained. 'Behind every name is a heart. It beats fast when it sees the people it loves the most, faster still when it thinks it will lose them. And when it believes it will be reunited with one of them . . .'

He falls silent, staring out over the pool.

'I think I've found her.' Talaia is bending over a page. The boy takes a breath, and looks down.

Written in a small, neat hand is a date, the statement that Lirriel Persaba, a freewoman of Bishra in Sund province, entered the service of Greus Ranva, a silk merchant of the city of Dhurkana.

Freewoman? Fury boils in the boy's chest. He can hardly breathe. There is no mention of the tribe of the House of Goash. Were the Dhurkanians aware of who they were dealing with? Were they afraid of admitting to it? Or did they simply close their eyes? He wonders if there is anywhere in the world that doesn't have two tongues. Then he thinks bitterly, grow up, this is what life is like.

Talaia touches his sleeve gently. He follows her finger across the page to an address in the city.

They are given directions by a woman in the square, and find themselves in a tree-lined boulevard. The houses are large and elegantly made, its residents clearly well-to-do. A little way down, Yorin stops.

'This is it,' he says, nodding at a door. The boy's stomach turns over.

It is a good door. A sturdy door for whom winter holds no terrors. A green door whose skin is renewed each spring when the silk merchant's servants repaint it. Yorin knocks. No answer. He knocks again, loudly. A window opens upstairs; a woman looks out.

'We're looking for Greus Ranva,' Yorin calls.

'The master's not here. He's at Flavi's house. More problems with the colour of his daughter's wedding coat. He's never satisfied.' The woman speaks as if they are familiar with Flavi and his exacting ways.

'Are you the lady of the house?' Yorin asks.

She smiles, looking pleased. 'Goodness, no, I'm the housekeeper.'

'I thought you must be in charge of things.'

'What's your business with the master?' she asks.

'It's private,' Yorin tells her pleasantly, 'and urgent.'

The woman's eyes widen. 'Wait a minute. I'll come down.'

The green door opens, and the woman introduces herself as Rinn. 'I'm not sure how long the master will be, but you're welcome to come in and wait.'

Yorin bows. 'You are kindness itself.'

Blushing, she shows them into a large hall flooded with light from a round window set in the high ceiling. 'Grand, eh?' she remarks to the boy.

'Yes, indeed,' he says politely.

She leads them down the sunlit hall, through an ornate door, into a large chamber. Everything is designed to be beautiful, from the graceful cabinets to the white wood tables nesting at the side of low couches upholstered in ivory linen. White curtains, perfectly draped, frame tall windows.

Rinn ushers them into chairs. 'I'll bring you some tea,' she says, excusing herself.

They look at each other. 'Well,' Yorin says cheerfully, 'I've seen worse.'

Talaia's face is suddenly alight. Rising, she goes over to a glass-fronted cabinet and looks in, exclaiming softly. After a moment, the boy joins her.

'Look,' she says, pointing to an intricate ivory carving. It reminds him of a verse in Mirashi's poem about a lover trying and failing to please a demanding mistress, who is only satisfied when he presents her with death. They read it in the Green Mountains.

He crafted a country from ivory:
she peered close, saw cranes flying south
and said, 'This is not enough.'

Talaia says the words aloud. Startled, the boy turns to her. There is a brief silence in which he notices her irises are delicately ringed with black.

'It's lovely, that.' Rinn has returned with a laden tray. 'The master collects all sorts,' she says as she expertly assembles tea and cakes.

The boy is beginning to wish that (1) he had never

come here, and (2) that someone would drop something on Greus's foot – nothing too painful – so he has to return home immediately.

Rinn serves them tea in fine white cups, and cakes that melt like a sigh. 'These are excellent,' Yorin says. 'Did you make them?'

'It's an old recipe,' Rinn says, beaming. Somewhere in the house a bell rings. 'It's the mistress. You'll have to excuse me. She has one of her heads.'

Yorin tips some of the cakes into his pocket. Talaia glares at him, but he shrugs. 'For later,' he says. The boy wonders if there will be a later.

They know the front door has opened because the white curtains briefly stir. Footsteps, voices. Moments later the door opens, and a man comes into the room. They get to their feet as he pauses on the threshold before making a low bow and coming over to them. He is dressed in a tunic of embroidered blue silk girdled with a sash of silver tissue. His soft leather boots are the colour of good earth. He is as well made as his house.

'Welcome to my home. I am Greus Ranva. I believe you were looking for me?' Yorin offers his hand, and introduces them. The silk merchant takes a seat. 'So, how can I help you?'

The boy grips the arm of his chair.

'We're looking for someone,' Yorin says. 'Lirriel Persaba. We understand she works here.'

The boy watches Greus. The weather of his face isn't good. 'You know her?' the silk merchant asks.

Yorin looks at the boy.

'She's my mother,' he says tightly.

267

Greus stares at him in astonishment. 'Your mother? I had no idea –' Pain crosses his face, and he looks away for a moment. 'Then I am very sorry indeed. She was a cherished member of our family. She became ill last autumn, a fever. We did everything we could, but we weren't able to save her.'

Chapter Eighteen

No. The word is unspoken but clear as a bell, and the bell is the boy's heart. He wishes it would be silent. He wishes he had never started this journey since it is clear now it will only end in despair. He wishes – but he can only sit numbly as Greus tells him what a much-loved member of the household his mother was, pulling anxiously at his sleeve, his face creased with concern. The boy knows someone else is looking at him, but he can't meet her gaze.

When Greus has excused himself, 'to fetch something', the boy sits motionless, hearing sounds within the house and outside, neither of which has anything to do with him. When Talaia offers him tea, he wants to laugh. He wants to cry. He doesn't know what he wants. Yes, he does. To be left alone. It is a rude thing, grief, immoderate in its need.

Greus returns with a box of dark wood. It is prettily carved, inlaid with flowers of paler wood. 'It was your mother's,' he says, offering it to the boy. Silently he takes it in his hands.

Yorin glances at him. 'We're grateful for your hospitality, but I think it's time to return to our lodgings,' he says.

Greus almost manages to hide his relief. Other people's pain is never the easiest visitor. Talaia leans over and touches the boy's sleeve. He looks at her unseeing. With her hand at his elbow she prompts him gently upwards, and out of the room.

At the Golden Bear he climbs the stairs, goes to his room and sits on the bed. Yorin hovers on the threshold, Talaia at his shoulder.

'Can we get you anything?' he asks. The boy shakes his head. 'No, of course,' Yorin says, and withdraws. After a moment, Talaia follows. He can hear them talking quietly as they go downstairs. Below stairs. The lower city. Names for the underworld. In the stories they went downwards, through fire and torment, into the depths . . .

. . . but his hell is here, it has hollowed out a place in his body and is digging in. It shouldn't be possible to sleep, but he does. The dreams, when they come, take the form of images: a green dress tied with a simple cloth belt; a gold ring glinting as a rolling pin rocks back and forth; a copper-coloured hairpin gleaming in blue-black hair.

He wakes to find nothing changed. Except that an anchor has been cut away.

At dinner, he can feel Talaia watching him as he stirs his spoon around his bowl. He wants to tell her he isn't ill, but in a way he is. It isn't an illness anyone can see, but it is there in his heart and he has no cure.

'Greus said that if you wanted to know any more about. . .' Yorin leaves the question hanging.

Yes. No. He doesn't know. Part of him wants to leave Dhurkana, which is a city of blight for him now. He gulps his broth, burning his tongue.

'At least –' Talaia begins, and is silenced by his look. There is no *at least*, no bringing the good things forward and patting them on the back.

Later, as he lies in bed, he wonders why no one has advised him to dip his heart in wax, to stop it splitting.

When he wakes, he realises where he is and sinks back down. In the room next door, someone is yawning very loudly. It isn't Yorin, who is some way down the corridor, and Talaia would never make such a noise. His mother's box is on the small table beside the bed. He opened it last night and found a necklace of rose quartz, a silver belt buckle, and a letter addressed to his father. He closed it without touching them.

Getting out of bed, he drowns himself in the bowl of water someone has left for him, and wrings himself out with a cloth. His ears smart. His eyes sting. His body still goes on. So he goes with it, down the stairs, into the common room where Yorin and Talaia are waiting.

After breakfast they sit quietly for a while. Yorin tries to smuggle Talaia a look, but the boy notices. They have something to say, but don't know how to say it.

'I think I'd like to go back to see Greus,' he says.

Their obvious relief causes him a pang of conscience. Here they are, saddled with an emotional burden the size of a small town, and they can do nothing to relieve it.

'Would you like us to come with you?' Talaia asks. Her gaze is calm, her eyes without the look that invites tears. Later he will reflect on her understanding that grief, in the early stages at least, cannot cope with too much kindness.

'Yes,' he says, 'thank you.'

The streets are quieter this morning, the day clear and bright. Talaia is walking next to him. She says very little, but he is aware of the softly ordered movement of her clothes. They have once again left Tobi in the stable of the inn, with promises. The horse looked unconvinced, but Yorin rubbed his nose affectionately until his eyelids drooped. The boy wonders what would happen if someone rubbed his nose. Would a genie come out of it? He can't understand why he is thinking this when – but the burden is too great to take up again so soon. It is enough to hold images in his mind. Her hands, her face.

They sit in the same room in Greus's house. It seems less dauntingly magnificent today. Is it the consequence of familiarity? Do palaces become huts to their inhabitants? The boy realises he can't love it, no matter how finely someone has arranged it. It is not his house, his home.

Rinn bends over him, putting a cup into his hand. He sips tea, not tasting it. The door opens and Greus comes in. When Rinn has left, he sits down and begins to explain what the boy has been turning over in his head all night. Whatever his vanities, Greus didn't seem like someone who would knowingly own a slave.

'Your mother came to us from a very reputable agency,' the silk merchant says. 'We've used them for years. We tell them what we're looking for, what skills we need, we pay a fee, and they find a suitable person.' His voice is anxious, but the boy can't feel sympathy. 'I had no idea she had a son. Truly.' Greus looks stricken. The boy's face is frozen. 'Truly,' he says again. 'But it explains –'

Catching his breath his says, 'When Lirriel first came to us, she said very little. My wife and I let her be. We thought she would open up when she was ready. Every evening she would go up to the roof and stand looking out over the city. When she came down she never said anything, just carried on with her work. In time, she seemed to settle down. My wife came to love her – we all did.'

How could you not? the boy thinks angrily. Greus looks wretched. 'If I'd known,' he says, shaking his head. The boy wonders who is worse, the tribe of the House of Goash or the unthinking people of this city. He realises he is boiling with rage. He shouldn't have come.

Silence spreads. Greus shifts in his chair. Finally the boy says, 'Where is she?'

'Yes,' Greus says, 'of course,' and tells him about the cemetery on the hill overlooking the city.

Thanking him, the boy leaves the house.

Yorin and Talaia catch up with him at the corner of the street. 'Do you want to go now?' Talaia asks gently.

'Yes,' he says, 'but on my own.'

The road to the cemetery is broad, lined with tall cypresses like the tails of green foxes. There are people on the road but their heads are not bowed, and they are not silent. They have baskets in their hands, and are chattering to each other. The boy feels a rush of annoyance. This is not what mourning should be. How can you show proper respect when people are swinging children by the hand, calling out greetings, shifting a large jug on a hip? He wonders if he is heading to the wrong place.

But they are here, the dead. The hill is tall and wide, and they cover it. He walks a little way up and comes to a halt, staring in disbelief at people sitting on rugs, talking

273

and laughing, eating and drinking wine. Where are the mourners? They are here too, standing at graves, picking off moss, tidying flowers, adding fresh blooms before rejoining their friends.

In some strange way it feels quite right. To celebrate those who will always be with you, to bring life back to them. As the boy climbs the hill, he hears snatches of gossip – *and her old enough to be his* – and almost smiles. He could be back in Bishra, on the bench outside the White Poplar. But he isn't, and as he climbs higher and leaves the chatter behind, he starts to shake. The stones here are smaller, and whiter. He sees only one other person, some distance away, bent in contemplation before a headstone.

Two rows across, three up, he finds her. *Lirriel Persaba.* A date. He kneels before her. Does she know he is here? If he speaks, will she hear him? He has no idea how long he kneels, only that it is necessary to remain in front of the small white stone.

And now someone is raising him up gently, taking his hand. Talaia says nothing, but stands quietly with him. Later, he will remember what Mirashi wrote about the lost city, and think of the small flame Talaia's hand made in his.

The day is wearing into noon as they walk slowly back to the inn. Yorin is settled in front of the fire, a mug of beer in his hand.

'How's Tobi?' the boy asks.

Yorin looks faintly surprised. 'He's fine. Eating everything in sight.' The boy nods. It is good to know something holds steady. The noise of the common room chafes his spirits, warming him back.

When they have ordered food Yorin says, 'You found your mother?'

'Yes,' he says. Yorin nods, but asks nothing further.

After their meal, Yorin puts down his napkin and clears his throat. 'While you were at the cemetery, I made some enquiries. About how your mother came to work for Greus. About the agent he used.'

The boy sits very still.

'It wasn't easy. No one wanted to talk about it. But I managed to find someone. Well, my purse did. Shall I –?'

The boy nods.

'It won't surprise you to know that the tribe of the House of Goash go to great lengths to keep their hands clean. They hire people to do their dirty work, like the men who came to your village. The way they – for want of a better word – dispose of the people they abduct probably varies from place to place, but here in Dhurkana they generally pass through factors, who have links with various agents. They make sure the agents they choose are very respectable, no hint of anything' – Yorin pauses – 'untoward. The reason your mother never mentioned you –' He stops, as if wondering whether to go on. The boy clenches his fists.

'They try to take families if they can,' Yorin resumes. 'They separate them, and tell them that if they talk about what's happened, they'll –' He shakes his head.

The boy glares at him. In a flat, furious voice he says, 'They'll kill the rest of their family. That's what you mean, isn't it?' He can feel Talaia looking at him but doesn't turn his head.

Yorin nods, and stares into his mug of beer.

As the silence lengthens, the boy becomes aware that Talaia has put her hand on his. It is warm, and gentle. He can't bear it, and yet he can. A serving-man clears their plates, refills Yorin's mug and offers coffee.

After a while Yorin says carefully, 'We were wondering if you've thought about what you want to do next?'

Of course he has. He wants to saddle the nearest horse and ride for Kerizon to find his sister. He wants to run to the copper mines at Chanlin. And whatever is left wants to return to the Green Mountains and stay there, watching cloud and rain and sun wear the past away.

'Sorry,' Yorin says, 'I shouldn't have –'

'It's not your problem,' the boy says quickly. 'You don't have to come with me.'

There is a short silence. 'I'm on the run, remember?' Talaia says.

'And Tobi gets bored very quickly,' Yorin adds.

The boy looks away, unable to speak. 'Which one is nearer?' he asks finally.

Yorin tells him Chanlin is to the north of Dhurkana, beyond the Getar Hills. 'I went to the City Hall while you were out. They've got maps coming out of their ears.'

They are waiting for his decision. 'We'll go to Chanlin.' He says it in a workmanlike way, mortised and tenoned, so there is no chance of anyone thinking he is sagging in the middle.

Although, he thinks later in his room, it wouldn't matter if they did. They have shared so much with him, and they are still here.

Chapter Nineteen

They leave the city by the western gate. Feelings of guilt and relief accompany the boy. He thought about going back to the cemetery, but his courage failed. He promises himself he will return one day.

The road is broad, the landscape populated with stone houses, barns, fenced-off fields. Up ahead, pasturelands rise into the Getar Hills. 'They're famous for their pears,' Yorin says. 'They make a sweet wine, pireem, that's said to be' – he glances at the boy – 'dangerous. One cup and you're off chasing your heart's desire.'

Talaia makes a dismissive sound. 'And what does your heart desire?' Yorin asks.

'I've no idea,' she says, looking straight ahead.

'Plenty of time to think about it now.'

The boy wonders if what Talaia said is true. Has she really never thought about her heart's desire? He knows what his would be.

'Off again?' Yorin says with a grin.

'And why not?' Talaia retorts.

The boy's attention comes racing back. Was she defending him? She meets his stare with a steady look. 'Sometimes, the deeper we go, the clearer the water becomes,' she says.

He frowns. It sounds like something the old man at the

library caves would say, and he isn't sure how appropriate it is in someone with a fondness for embroidered belts. But then, he reflects, if someone met him, would they think him capable of great thought? Part of him hopes not. To be marked in that way would be a burden, a weight of expectation trundling after you like a rolling stone, following devotedly until you slept, then crushing you.

'The countryside is beautiful,' he says with such firmness they both look at him.

Yorin laughs. 'It'd be even better with a cup of pireem, although I wouldn't say no to apple wine. Talking of which. . .' He ruffles his hair, a gesture the boy has come to know as a prelude, his way of clearing his throat before telling a story.

'When I was a boy,' he says, 'there was an apple orchard on the edge of town. It was surrounded by a high wall. Big mistake. Made it irresistible to every boy in the place, including me. It became a palace of apples, with queens on every branch.

'I spent a lot of time working out how to get in, and one night I managed it. Did you know walls grow taller at night? But I'd promised my friends a sackful of apples, and that's what they were going to get. I worried about dogs, but I couldn't hear anything, so I climbed the gate and dropped down on the other side. There I was, a small burglar creeping across the grass to the nearest tree, and there she was, tall, broad-boughed, thick with fruit. I picked as many apples as I could, went on to the next tree and the next, until my sack was full.

'One thing I hadn't counted on, and that was how heavy the sack would be. Apples may be neatly made, but put them together and they're a hell of a weight. Anyway, I hauled the sack through the grass, back to the gate. It took a while to get over, but I did.'

They watch as he creeps back up the street to his house. Silently he enters – he has taken care to oil the latch – slips across the wooden floor and into his room. He counts every apple before hiding the sack under the bed.

The next day he is a god to his friends. The apples go into pies and tarts. They glorify chutneys and preserves. The cook working for the owner of the orchard inadvertently serves him a dish of his most prized apples. The owner's nose instantly detects felony. The cook is dismissed, and leaves to become a pastrymaker whose speciality is cherries. The owner drinks too many apples and takes a tumble downstairs. He sells his orchard to the town. The town's children play in it, climb in it, and steal from it for fun.

'When I left,' Yorin says, 'I took two apples with me and kept their seeds to plant when I found the right place.'

'Why did you leave?' The boy is still getting used to the directness of Talaia's approach. It is an arrow flashing brightly before finding its mark.

Yorin smiles. 'I could tell you tales, but I won't. Like most boys, I served an apprenticeship in the town. He was a saddler, and a hard man. I was in his stables one day, wishing I was anywhere else. There was a particular horse – it really was particular – that I'd been forbidden to ride. I was never sure if it was because the saddler thought I wasn't up to it, or because he thought I was.

'He'd heard rumours about the orchard, and although nothing was ever proved, he had his suspicions. To him, I was a villain in the bud. He lived mainly on jugs of apple wine, and when he'd drunk enough, he'd tell me I was the first and last scoundrel this side of the sea. I found it rather flattering. But one day he went too far, so I used the jug to help him sleep.'

Talaia looks shocked. 'Don't worry,' Yorin says, 'I gave him a headache, that's all. I made sure he was alive before I left, which was more than he deserved. Anyway, I took the horse, and proved him right.'

'Did you ever go back?' Talaia asks. Yorin shakes his head. 'What about your parents? Wouldn't they have been worried?'

'I doubt it. They weren't exactly –' He breaks off.

Weren't exactly what? the boy wonders. Kind, caring, loving? He thinks of Talaia's aunt and uncle, who tried to sell her to a husband. They wouldn't consider themselves unkind or uncaring. They took a path, and it wasn't one Talaia could follow. But he can't forgive them.

Yorin is looking at him. 'Not every parent is good, and not every child is either,' he says. 'We have to make up the balance ourselves.'

'Do you still have them?' Talaia asks suddenly.

'What?'

'The apple seeds.'

Yorin nods, patting the pouch at his side. 'Of no interest whatsoever to the tribe of the House of Goash.'

'You'll have your orchard,' she says, and her voice is surprisingly gentle. Yorin looks ahead, narrowing his eyes against the sun.

As they journey on, the boy thinks it a lonely thing to do, accreting qualities with no hand to guide you. His family weren't like that, but there was no time to appreciate it. His eyes burn, and he blinks.

Talaia touches his arm. 'You were lucky,' she says gently, 'and that's why you're looking for them now.'

The boy looks away. How can he tell her that after what he learned in Dhurkana part of him wants not to go on, to remain in hopeful ignorance? But he will. Talaia is right. He was lucky. The least he can do is repay that love by finding his father and sister.

They camp in a crook of the hills. Cradled in grass, the boy lies awake. He has tried to sleep, but it is no use. During the day Yorin's stories, Talaia's observations, kept him from thinking too much. But grief sees more clearly at night.

He hears Yorin stirring, and props himself up on his elbow. 'Just going to check on Tobi,' Yorin says, moving out of the circle of firelight.

Wrapped in a blanket, Talaia comes over to sit beside him 'Are you all right?' she asks quietly. Her eyes shine softly in the firelight.

His breath catches in his throat. 'I'm fine,' he says.

'No, you're not. I can't begin to imagine what you've been through.'

She reaches across and touches his face. Every inch of his body is suddenly awake. He sits transfixed as she strokes his cheek, aware of the gentleness of her fingers, the closeness of her body. As his gaze moves from her eyes to her mouth, her lips part slightly. Very slowly, hardly breathing, he leans towards her.

A cough makes him pull back guiltily. Yorin is

returning. 'Pretty chilly tonight,' he says, throwing more wood on the fire.

The air is fresh and cool; a light wind swims through shallows of grass. Yawning, the boy looks over to see Talaia sitting cross-legged beside the newly made fire. Having lain awake poring over what happened – what could have happened – he has come to the conclusion that Yorin probably saved him from disaster. Talaia was simply comforting him, and he'd read into her kindness something that wasn't there. Or had he? He wonders about asking Yorin, but it doesn't feel right.

'Good morning,' Talaia says with no trace of embarrassment.

His suspicions are confirmed. He definitely misunderstood. His lack of experience almost led him into making a complete fool of himself. The memory of his only other attempt pricks his mind. No, he thinks, that was different. He was responding to Nissa's challenge. It was almost obligatory. This is –

But there is no time to consider what it is. Yorin is calling them over for breakfast.

'Before we go, could we have a poem, Arun?' Talaia asks. Her tone is polite, her face gives nothing away. The boy opens the Book of Light, choosing a poem at random. It is about a man on a long sea voyage sending letters home to his wife and son.

He sews sea and sky to the spine of the world,
making a scroll whose pages fly open –
horizons unfold in his hand.

Time passes,

> the years turn east; he writes
> with the limitless ink of the sea
> that his heart misses the simple things –

> a shoot of green rice, the delicate claw
> of the first crane touching the fields in spring,
> his boy singing.

The end reveals what was hidden: the letters and their people are long dead.

> The scroll springs back; the ghost ships sail.

Talaia says nothing, but her eyes meet his, and he catches his breath.

After two days the hills are beginning to thin, as if a mighty flint has over centuries patiently knapped the green hide. The small path dwindles into pebbles and dirt. The boy thinks of Mirashi looking out over the city of Kembla in solitude.

'Is there a difference between loneliness and solitude?' he wonders aloud.

'Of course there is,' Talaia says from her moving perch. Height often bestows superiority even when none is deserved, the boy thinks resentfully, remembering a very tall man in Harakim whose trousers, Nissa said, had to be specially made by tailors on ladders. When he told her he didn't believe her, she seemed to regard it as an improvement in his character. *About time*, she'd said. *Your problem is that you believe everything people tell you. But it works. He's a perfume-seller. People go to see his trousers, and then they have to buy something. After all, it wouldn't be polite just to go and stare, would it?*

The boy, as usual, had no reply.

'We've lost you again,' Yorin says.

With a wary look at Talaia, the boy tells them the story. Yorin laughs. After a moment Talaia says, 'Who is Nissa?'

There is, the boy notes, a distinct coolness in her voice. He glances at Yorin, who seems to be studying something on the path ahead. 'She was the daughter of the merchant I worked for in Harakim,' he says.

After a brief silence Talaia says, 'I think to be lonely is to have a choice removed from you. Solitude is different. It can be a gift, not a hardship.' A faint frost lingers in her voice. The boy wonders what offence he has committed this time.

Yorin kicks a large pebble from the path. 'There's a road,' he says, 'between two cities in the south. It's wide and straight, and you'd think it would be teeming with people, but it's not. There's a path through the hills, rough around the edges but quicker, so people go that way. I took the straight road – well, we did' – he glances at Tobi – 'and it was as if I was the only person in existence. There were no houses, no herders, no trees, no wells. It was simply a line between places. I started singing, but eventually I ran out of songs. I started reciting poems – yes,' he says with a glance at the boy, 'I do know some. At one point I thought I saw people coming towards me, but they were made of heat and light.

'I stopped, got off Tobi, and sat down. I could have shouted my lungs out if I'd wanted to, torn off my clothes and acted like a complete madman, but I didn't. I just sat. I don't know how long I stayed there, in the sun, on the baking ground, until Tobi decided things had gone far enough, and bit me. First and only time.'

Yorin pushes back his sleeve. On his right arm is a pale curved scar. 'I've had my fill of solitude,' he says, and walks on.

The boy looks at Talaia, bracing himself for a quelling glance. Instead she says, 'Let him be. He'll be fine.'

They continue on in silence. When they reach Yorin he turns, his face his own again.

'Come on,' he says, 'I've found the way.' He pushes back a curtain of ferns with his foot, revealing a flight of steps cut into the rock. Talaia slips down from Tobi and Yorin talks quietly to the horse, whose ears are pointing the way back. Finally he allows himself to be led upwards.

The steps are broad and shallow, dipping slightly in the middle. Water trickles down the walls, the air brackish and cool. The boy wonders if the dip in the steps was made by water, then scoffs at himself until he remembers his father taking him to the stream, scooping up a handful and letting it pitter down. *This*, he'd said, *is more powerful than this* – pointing at his hand – *or this* – pointing at the ground. *It has all the patience in the world.*

'Not much further now,' Yorin says.

'You've been saying that for ages,' Talaia says tartly.

'Doesn't mean it's not true.'

Talaia glances at the boy with a faint smile. He hopes it means that whatever he has done is forgiven.

There is brightness ahead. Yorin, who has led Tobi up and out, peers down at them. 'I told you it wasn't far,' he says.

Talaia gives the boy a mischievous look, and holds out her hand. He is definitely forgiven.

At the top he pauses, aware of her hand in his. Below them, a plain of white dust glares in the growing heat. A chalky track winds towards a sparse settlement of wooden shacks clustered round shallow cliffs. Chanlin.

The plain is a dry river running between slopes whose feet are black with shadow. They are, the boy sees as they make their way down, the entrances of mines. As they round a shoulder of rock, the track widens and levels out. He has never been to a mine before, but the air feels purged of hope.

A group of men stop talking and look at them as they approach the shacks. They are wearing swords, and their expressions are not, as Yorin would say, an invitation to tea.

'Wait here,' he says quietly, and goes on ahead, leading Tobi.

'I don't see why,' Talaia says indignantly. The boy can think of four good reasons hanging at the men's sides.

'It's fine,' Yorin says when he returns. 'They'll take us to Brundis. He's the mine captain.'

'Can they be trusted?' the boy asks.

'I shouldn't think so, but I've given them money. It tends to make things easier.'

The men make brief bows and lead them past metal tracks curving into the entrances of the mines. On them sit wooden trucks, their metal wheels fitting to the groove of the tracks.

'Do you use ponies?' Yorin asks pleasantly, indicating the trucks.

'No, just ourselves,' one of the men says. He laughs. The other men laugh too, but the boy can't see the joke.

'Is the ore smelted here?' Talaia asks.

There is a brief silence. One of the men says, 'Not just a pretty face, eh?'

The boy starts forward, but Yorin's hand is on his arm. Talaia regards the man steadily.

'No,' he says after a moment, 'we sell it on.' Turning, he walks away. The other men follow.

'I don't need to remind you Tobi's a coward,' Yorin says in an undertone. The boy can't smile. He has come here in search of his father, and the man coming towards them may be about to tell him where he is.

'Welcome,' he says, a smile on his weather-beaten face. 'I'm Brundis.' He looks down at his dusty clothes. 'You'll have to excuse me, we don't get many visitors here. It's not the prettiest of places.'

'But interesting,' Yorin says. 'I've never been to a copper mine before.'

'Interesting is one word for it.'

The boy's patience is worn through. 'I'm looking for someone. I was told he was brought here.'

'Of course,' Brundis says. 'What's his name?'

'Nedrin Persaba.' As he says it, the boy watches the mine captain's face. It gives nothing away.

'Ulaf!' A smudge of a man, dressed in black, comes forward. 'Would you take these people to my office?'

287

The office turns out to be a big cedarwood hut not far from the largest mine entrance. A small veranda is furnished with chairs and a table. When they are seated, Ulaf goes into the hut and returns with a pot of coffee, cups and a plate of fruit. The boy takes a polite sip and puts the cup down.

Brundis joins them. 'You like the coffee?' he asks.

'It's very good,' Yorin says.

'Small things are important in a place like this. You sometimes forget there's a world outside.'

The boy looks out over the white plain. The silence here is very deep. It is like sitting at the bottom of the sea.

Excusing himself, Brundis goes into the hut and returns with a ledger. He seems to know where to look, and before long he says, 'Yes, here we are.'

The boy leans over but Brundis is sitting back, his chair creaking a little. His face has changed, and the boy finds himself unable to speak.

Talaia asks for him. 'Is he –?'

'He's alive,' Brundis says, 'but he had to be retired. There was an accident in the mine – it happens sometimes, no matter how careful we are – and he couldn't work any more.'

The boy mistrusts his composure. 'Where is he?' he asks sharply.

'In Amala Dyssul. It's not far from here. It's a place where –' Brundis clears his throat. 'He's being looked after there.'

The boy is on his feet. 'Can you take me?'

'I'm sorry, I can't spare the time, but I'll ask Ulaf to show you the way.'

Heat shimmers and rises from the white plain. The boy glances into the entrance of a mine as they pass. It is shockingly black in the bright morning. He wonders how long his father worked here, and what the conditions were like. A muffled boom; dust and grit float out. It is like invading a body, he thinks. Again and again the earth is laid open; again and again it gives, until nothing is left.

Ulaf takes them up the shallow cliffs through a wide, uneven cutting. Yorin leads Tobi. They come out onto level ground and a treeless expanse in which are set a number of red sandstone buildings.

'Amala Dyssul,' Ulaf says, and turns away.

As they reach the main building, a woman comes out of the carved stone portal to meet them. She is dressed in a simple white robe. 'I am Pera,' she says, 'Mother of Amala Dyssul.' Yorin introduces them, explaining why they have come. Smiling, Pera turns to the boy. 'Your father is here,' she says. 'Would you like to see him?'

He is suddenly lost for words. Talaia answers for him. 'I'm sure he would, thank you, and we'd welcome a cup of tea. We've come a long way.'

'Of course,' Pera says warmly. 'Please, come with me.'

The boy will later ask about the triangular capstone above the doorway of the portal, inscribed with a wreath of words. He will find out it is written in Vindri, the language of healers, and that it reads *May You Know Peace, In Life, In Death.*

They pass through wide wooden doors, into another world. Stone cloisters enclose a large square lawn bordered by flowers. At the centre, a fountain plays in the light.

289

There is such a sense of peace the boy feels he could sink down, close his eyes and never get up.

Pera is speaking to Yorin and Talaia. 'If you'd like to wait here, I'll send someone to take you to the refectory. You can have tea there. Our cakes are very good. And we have stables for your horse.'

Talaia thanks her, but Yorin is silent. He seems unusually subdued. Pera looks at the boy. 'Arun? Would you like to come with me?' He follows her over the lawn without looking back.

He is barely aware of the softness of the grass, the murmuring fountain. A wooden door in the wall of the cloisters leads into a white-painted corridor whose tall arched windows glitter with light. Doors are set in the right-hand side, some ajar, others shut. The corridor opens into an atrium banked with plants in pots. The floor is stained with coloured light. Beyond is another, wider, corridor with a door at the far end.

When they reach it, Pera stops. 'Would you like me to go with you?' she asks.

Yes. No. He doesn't know. He stands for a moment, unable to move. What will he find? Will his father know him? Will he know his father?

Arun stares into the pool. The moon's cold silver shivers as fish dart and ripple. Night deepens around him. After an endless moment he returns to Amala Dyssul, where the boy is opening the door.

Chapter Twenty

The room is large and bright, with a high ceiling and tall arched windows. Rows of beds are set at either side, each with a small table and a chair beside it. There are tapestries on the walls, and flowered rugs of pink and cream. It is a beautiful room. At the far end, a woman in a blue robe is seated behind a table.

The boy stands frozen. He follows Pera's gaze to a bed in the corner where someone is sitting up, his eyes half closed.

'Go on,' Pera says softly.

At his approach, his father looks up. His face is blank. With shock the boy wonders if his wits have gone. Words choke his throat. He reaches out and touches his father's hand. His father stares for a long moment, then begins crying silently.

Tears run down the boy's face as he leans over and puts his arms around his father, holding the thin body close. Only when his father starts to cough does he draw away, alarmed. His father shakes his head. 'It'll pass.' His voice is painfully weak. 'If you could –'

The boy hands him the cup on the table, and he drinks. 'Now, let me look at you.' He puts out a trembling hand and strokes the boy's face. 'I should have known,' he says.

'You look just like your grandfather. He was a handsome man. And tall, like you, with the same broad shoulders.' His eyes are full of tears, but he is smiling.

The boy looks into his face, wondering at the change. Later he will come to recognise the shadow of deep grief but here, now, the finding is enough.

His head is so full of questions he doesn't know where to begin. His father laughs, and it is a good sound. 'Still looking everywhere at once,' he says. Then, after a short silence, 'I should have done more for you, Arun. I didn't listen. I was too busy, too –'

He stops as Pera approaches, a tray in her hands. She puts it down on the table, touching the boy's arm as she leaves. He pours tea, aware of his father watching him. It is a fruit tea, sweet and refreshing. 'They make it here,' his father tells him. 'From dried berries. There's a room dedicated to the resuscitation of fruit.'

The boy looks at him in surprise. Is he making a joke?

'Without it, Amala Dyssul would grind to a halt,' his father continues. 'I think people pretend to be ill so they can come here and drink the tea. I've talked to Pera about offering it for sale. It could supplement their income which, goodness knows, is little enough. But she said it should be freely given – she put it more tactfully, but that's what she meant, and I respect that. They do all this out of the kindness of their hearts. No one helps them, they rely on donations and goodwill.'

It is the longest speech the boy has ever heard his father make, except when he was scolding. His head is spinning. He can't quite believe he is here, in a room filled with more than light. His father has stopped talking and is looking at him. What he is waiting for is so clear the boy almost has to shade his eyes.

'Tell me you found them,' his father says at last. The boy can't speak. He stares at his hands, then into his father's eyes. In them is all the hope in the world.

He takes a breath, seeing a small white stone on a hillside above a city. 'I came here first. I'll look for them next, I promise.'

His father studies him, then nods and leans back against his pillows. The boy notices deep shadows under his eyes, a hollowness in his cheek. He is suddenly afraid.

'They told me you had an accident,' he says. 'What happened?' His voice is a little too loud.

His father smiles. 'Nothing that matters now. You found me, I know you'll find them. Do you know where they went?' He speaks with desperate eagerness.

The boy takes a deeper breath. 'To Dhurkana and Kerizon,' he says.

His father frowns. 'I don't even know where they are. How did you find out?'

Keeping his voice steady, the boy tells him about the library caves. If his father is curious about the names that keep coming up he says nothing, but seems content to close his eyes and listen.

Pera brings lunch, but neither of them eats much. Afterwards, the woman in the blue robe gives his father a warm drink scented with berries. She waits for him to finish it, then takes the cup away. He leans back, closing his eyes as the boy travels from the library caves to Chanlin, from Chanlin to Amala Dyssul, sidestepping Kushtar and

Dhurkana. He stops talking. For the moment, the road has ended.

When his father opens his eyes, they are filled with tears. Before today, the boy has never seen him cry. If he was angry you knew it, and so did half the valley. He feels almost unbalanced by the change. His father seems to understand because he smiles and says, 'Don't worry, Arun, I haven't gone soft. I've just learned to appreciate what I have. What I had.'

He falls silent. Then he says, 'You were a good worker, you know. I know I was hard on you, but you mostly did as you were told. You'd have made a good farmer.' Something in the boy sings. 'But,' his father adds, 'you always were a thinker.'

'I still am.' He is unable to keep a note of defiance out of his voice.

His father nods. 'Yes, and there was no ploughing it out of you. I should have known. Didn't you make up poetry once, by the fish trap?' The boy stares. He had no idea his father heard. 'I was wrong,' his father says, 'to keep you from it.'

Another silence. Interpreting the boy's look, his father smiles. 'I was a young man once,' he says, 'full of dreams, just like you. I never thought I'd end up a farmer. I grew up in Goshan, not far from the sea, although I never saw it.' The boy frowns. Goshan is a large town in the north of the country. He thought his father came from Utur, an inland village. With shock and some pain he realises he knows nothing of his life.

'Utur was where I was born,' his father explains, 'but I was raised in Goshan.'

'Why did you go there?' the boy asks.

'My father – your grandfather – thought we'd do better there. More people, more prospects. He was a blacksmith, and our village had too many of them. Or perhaps he'd had enough of Utur. My mother didn't want to move. She was a sociable woman, and she cared about putting down roots. My father took us anyway. She never really forgave him.'

He sighs, looking down at the soft white blanket covering him. To the boy's astonishment he says, 'I had a brother and sister, twins. They died before I was born. I think that was the real reason my mother didn't want to go. She didn't want to leave them behind.'

He glances at the tall window opposite. The boy follows his gaze to the green blossom of trees in full leaf, to flowerbeds and people strolling among them. 'There are two gardens here,' his father says, 'one for contemplation, one for conversation.'

'Which do you prefer?'

'Oh, I haven't been out for a while.' He coughs hard, taking some moments to recover.

'Would you like some water?' the boy asks.

His father gives him a shrewd look. 'Your manners are good. You found someone who looked after you.'

It takes a moment to remember his father has no idea what happened to him. 'I'd like to hear about you first, if you'll tell me,' he says.

His father shrugs, but he looks pleased. He drinks from the cup the boy offers, thanks him and says, 'I was expected to follow my father's trade. I tried for a while, but I just couldn't take to it. My father knew, and said nothing. My mother knew, and spoke to him about it, but he wouldn't listen. He said a trade would provide for me and, when the time came, my family. I was fourteen, and the idea horrified me.

'I tried my best to do what he wanted, but the tools must have known my heart wasn't in it. I ended up cutting myself quite badly.' He lifts his arm and his sleeve falls back, revealing a familiar scar. The boy remembers asking about it and being rebuffed.

'It was like a whip to my mind,' his father says. 'I left that night, angry and young, and' – he smiles – 'full of self-righteousness. I told myself they'd be sorry when they woke up and found me gone. Ah, the perils of wounded pride! I went with a bit of food in my pocket and a temper that lasted the night. In the morning I woke up in a thicket outside the town, and found I'd shared my bed with ants.'

'What happened?' the boy asks.

His father gives him a steady look. 'I went home, and if I'd had a tail you know where it would have been. My mother welcomed me with open arms – she always was forgiving – but my father stayed in the forge all day, which was no bad thing. My anger had mostly been stung out of me, but there was still a little to spare. My mother knew it, and sent me on errands, kept me busy, let me cool down. When my father came out of the forge at sunset, he sat down to dinner as if I'd never been away. We never spoke of it again.'

He takes a breath, shallow and ragged. 'The fight went out of me for a while. I kept at it, working with my father. Eventually I became a passable smith, could fit shoes to a horse, work metal into gates, mend tools and knives. But there came a point when I just couldn't do it any more.

'Like many young men before me, I stood in front of my father and told him I needed to go my own way, find out what I was good at.' He gives a flat laugh. 'My father told me to go. He said if I ever found out what it was, I should come back and tell him, as he'd dearly like to know. My mother cried, but I didn't change my mind. Leaving the town was good. Leaving my mother wasn't. I didn't see her again, not until she died. Well, you know about that. And I never saw my father again.'

In a piercing rush the boy remembers the day a man called at the hut with a letter in his hand. Only now can he understand how much was behind it.

His father looks at him with bright, burning eyes. 'Your mother is the best thing that ever happened to me,' he says. 'Apart from you two, of course.' He leans back against his pillows, briefly closing his eyes.

'I first saw your mother beside a well in Prira, a village about forty miles from Goshan. I'd been there a while, making a living of sorts by mending things. I'd taken a room at the inn – it was cheap, and the food was passable. I'd run out of nails and was going to the market to get some more. That's when I saw her. She was talking to someone, a girl about her own age. I noticed her boots first, red leather, embroidered, very fancy. I wondered what kind of person would wear them. Then I saw her face, and –'

He shakes his head. 'Ah,' he says, 'she was beautiful. Not just her face; there was a warmth about her, a true kindness. Call me daft, but I knew it the moment I saw her. I must have stood there gawping because a man walking by murmured, "*Not a hope.*" He did me a favour. When I heard it, I took my courage by the scruff of the neck and pushed myself forward. I kept going until I was two steps away. Then I was struck dumb. Your mother gave me a kind look, and turned back to her friend. Her friend's look wasn't so kind.

'Instead of putting me off, it spurred me on. For a week I went back to the well, living on crumbs your mother didn't throw me, but she seemed to ignore me in a way that meant she was paying attention. Or so I hoped. Then, next market day, I saw something I thought she'd like.'

For a moment he retreats into his thoughts. The boy imagines stalls and booths, many voices, the sizzle of roasting meat. Stirring, his father says, 'It was a pair of slippers, deep-blue silk velvet, embroidered with gold and silver thread. In my head I thought they'd be nice for her to wear when she took off her boots in the evening.

'I bought them, and walked around the market looking for her. I was that nervous, I can feel it even now.' He laughs. 'The best I could hope for was that she wouldn't throw them back in my face. When I found her, she was with her friend again. It took all I had to go up to her. You could have knocked me down with a blade of grass when she told her friend to go away for a moment. Just for a moment – there were proprieties to be observed, after all. Any longer, and I'd be looking at the cudgels your grandmother almost certainly kept for young men like me.

'My heart was in my mouth. I think I said "*Er –*", which wasn't the greatest of openings. The look she gave me! It was a moment of absolute torture. At that point I wanted the earth to open up and swallow me, but as it didn't I offered her the slippers, and hoped they'd make a better job than I had. She looked at them, then at me, dying on the spot.' His voice is a little unsteady as he says, 'She took them from me, and she smiled.'

His face is drawn and weary, but the look in his eyes could conquer any darkness. 'After that, I could face anything. Not,' he adds, 'that your mother was easily wooed. She had her own mind, and her own idea of what she wanted from life. I promised I wouldn't take those things away from her. I broke that promise.'

He looks at his son with shining eyes. 'When you find her, will you tell her I'm sorry?'

The boy can't speak. Finally he says, 'You can tell her yourself,' and swallows the sour yellow taste of the lie.

His father leans back into his pillows. 'We were married in Prira four months later. Most of the village attended the ceremony. I think they wanted to see it for themselves. Your grandmother didn't think I was good enough for her daughter, either, but I was determined to prove her wrong.

'To be fair, she was good to us, gave us a house, and money to put into whatever trade I wanted to follow. And we were happy there. Our house wasn't large, but it was big enough for us, three rooms and a roof terrace. Your mother loved that terrace. She'd go up every evening and sit in the chair she'd brought from her mother's house. I'd leave her for a while, give her time for herself. I was thoughtful in those days.' It hurts the boy to hear the bitterness in his voice.

After a pause his father says, 'When I joined her we'd watch the sunset, sometimes talking, sometimes not. We'd have spiced apple juice to warm us as night came in, and small cakes – you know the ones she makes, with cinnamon and honey. The sky seemed to stretch away forever. And when dusk came, there was a particular cluster of stars – our stars, she said. Yaria, the Ring. Your mother called it the Pledge. It was very bright on the evening I asked her to marry me.'

The boy stares at his father. He knew his mother called it that. Now he knows why.

Arun looks blindly into the darkness. Night is silent; the eyes of heaven are closed.

'Was I right,' he asks finally, 'not to tell him the truth?'

'I hope you're not expecting an answer from me.'

No: he is asking the conscience of the world, and the burden bows his head. He thinks back to the bed, the chair, the light from the tall windows. He sees again his father's face, the hope in his eyes. Here beside the pool, he finally knows the answer.

Chapter Twenty-One

Lying in a comfortable room whose window is open to the night air, the boy can hardly believe he is here, or that his father talked for so long. Where is the man who barely said a word from sunrise to sunset, who seemed to want to be anywhere but in the hut in the valley? At dinner that evening he found himself unable to talk about it. Yorin and Talaia seemed to understand; when she said goodnight, Talaia briefly touched his hand.

Restless, he gets up and goes over to the window. Crickets are singing, small bards of evening, and water murmurs over stone. Fireflies are taking their lamps from shrub to shrub. When he returns to bed, somewhere beyond the scattered lights of thought his mind finds rest.

He stands at the window looking out over misty gardens. Something has been growing overnight until now it is too big to ignore, and yet he has no idea how to say it to his father. He answers the knock at the door to find Pera wishing him good morning.

She tells him there are baths in a room at the end of the corridor. 'When you're ready, there's breakfast in the refectory.'

Yesterday evening he barely noticed the high-ceilinged room, the white walls hung with embroideries, the rows of long wooden tables on a floor of pale-gold stone. Although people are talking freely, it is not in the lively, many-tongued manner of inns or tea houses. The boy senses time matters to them. He sees Yorin and Talaia sitting in cool sunlight, and goes to join them.

'They do an excellent breakfast,' Yorin says as he sits down. Talaia is wearing a pale yellow tunic embroidered with ivory thread. She seems thoughtful. 'They make them here' – Yorin indicates the bread roll the boy is breaking in half – 'and grow their own fruit and vegetables. They keep sheep for milk and cheese, and goats for general nuisance. We had a look around when you were with your father.'

'The gardens are beautiful,' Talaia says. 'You could lose yourself in them. And the people here are very special. They do all this for nothing. They give everything up when they come here, and stay until –' She breaks off awkwardly.

He looks at her, at Yorin. 'I'm going to see my father,' he says.

There is heat in his step as he walks down the room. His father is sitting up in bed, and the boy knows he has been waiting for him. He clasps his father's hands, says good morning and sits down, not knowing where to start.

His father smiles. 'I know that look,' he says, 'same as the one on a minjula's face when it's confronted by a snake. The minjula usually wins. They may be small, but they're very fast.'

The boy stares at him. Then he bursts out, 'Why didn't you teach us to read and write?'

His father's mouth opens slightly, his eyes crease with surprise and pain, but it is too late to take the words back. After a long and difficult silence he says, 'I didn't teach you because I couldn't.' The boy looks at him blankly. 'I couldn't read and write,' his father explains, 'so I couldn't teach you.'

The boy stares in astonishment. 'It doesn't matter,' he says quickly.

When his father speaks, it is as if each word is a thorn in his tongue. 'Yes, it does. It comes down to the fact that I was too damn proud. Your mother could, and she wanted to teach you, but I wouldn't let her. She'd tried to persuade me to learn, but I knew better, of course. When would I ever need it? What good would it do? All it did was make people think they were better than you.'

He asks for water, and the boy fills a cup. After a long drink he says angrily, 'I was a stubborn-headed fool. I should have managed things better. I'm sorry, Arun –'

'No,' the boy says sharply, 'you did what you thought was right.'

The more his father talks, the more he understands. His own father – the boy's grandfather – saw him as a disappointment. The boy's grandmother thought him unworthy of her daughter. Perhaps the feeling of never being good enough followed him through life. Perhaps he feels it still. Looking at him now, the boy sees a man who, in his own way, tried his best. Unable to express it adequately, he touches his father's hand.

After a short silence his father stirs and says, 'What happened was all my fault. I didn't listen to your mother. I thought I knew best, as usual.'

The boy is confused. Is he still talking about reading and writing?

'I made us move to Bishra that spring,' his father says. 'I thought we'd be safer there. Your mother didn't want to, she thought we'd be better off at the hut. She was right. If we'd hadn't gone –'

'You don't know that,' the boy says. 'They could have found us there too. They probably would have. There was nothing you could have done.'

His father's eyes are full of tears. 'I've told myself that a thousand times, and never believed it until now. Almost.'

'What matters is that we've found each other again.'

His father gives him a lingering look in which the boy sees his family clearly, as if in sunlight. It is a peaceful scene, his sister playing with her stuffed animal, his mother at the door of the hut, his father in the wheatfield.

'You gave us a good life,' he says, and means it. His father leans back wearily, his face full of gratitude.

'I'll leave you to rest now,' the boy says. 'I'll come back later.'

They talk again that afternoon. This time the boy tells his father about Harakim. Wanting to spare him pain, he is careful to conceal his anger. He presents the merchant as a generous benefactor, emphasising the education he received, reforming Nissa into a helpmeet and friend. Which is partly true – she helped him leave, after all, and for that he will always be grateful.

His father listens carefully. He is, the boy senses, trying to make pictures with the words. It has always fascinated him how much one word contains within it. If, for instance,

304

he hears the word *house*, he immediately starts building it in his head, furnishing it with inhabitants and sending them into their daily lives. If he hears the word *well*, he will construct around it a market square much like his own, a dog nosing the ground, people stopping to gossip.

When his father asks him what he is thinking he tells him, a little sheepishly. His father smiles, moving his shoulders stiffly against the pillows. 'How one head can hold all that is beyond me,' he says, his eyes filled with affection.

The boy becomes aware of Pera beside him, telling him it is time for his father to rest, that dinner is ready and his friends are waiting in the refectory. He touches his father's hand briefly as he leaves.

The moon is faintly transparent in the twilight. The boy walks in the garden they came through yesterday, flowers pale in their beds, the fountain playing softly.

Talaia joins him. 'I thought you might like some company,' she says. They find a carved stone bench where they sit for a while in silence.

When Talaia asks how his father is, he looks out across the garden. 'Different.'

'In what way?'

He hesitates; the look in her eyes encourages him. 'He was like me when he was a boy. He didn't want to work with his father either. I never knew. He didn't want to be a blacksmith, just like I didn't want to be a farmer.'

'What did you want to be?'

He is silent for a moment, not daring to name it in case she laughs, or looks politely incredulous. 'Something to do with words,' he says eventually.

She doesn't seem surprised. 'You still can,' she says, but he doesn't answer. How can he explain that he can't see or feel more than here and now, that the future is hidden from him and all he has to hold on to is a man with shadows in his eyes?

'It's getting late,' Talaia says gently. 'Shall we go in?' As they walk across the grass, she slips her hand into his.

He stands in the dew-lit garden, listening to the fountain. It is, he learned, the garden of contemplation. The lie he told his father troubles him, but there is no way out of it now. Taking the Book of Light from his pocket, he turns the pages and reads

morning has a pearl in its mouth.

He closes the book. The morning is its own poem.

In the refectory, he finds Yorin finishing breakfast. 'Talaia's already eaten,' he says. 'She's gone off with the healers to learn more about their work. She seems to have taken to it. This place seems to have that effect on people.'

The boy's appetite vanishes. 'I'm going to see my father.'

They greet each other with clasped hands. Shadows linger in his father's face but his eyes are bright as he looks around. 'It's going to be another lovely day.'

'I've been in the garden of contemplation,' the boy tells him. 'It was very peaceful.'

'They do it well here,' his father nods. 'Did you know that Amala Dyssul means "House of Peace"? They took me in when it looked as if I was beyond hope. You can't imagine what it's like in a mine, for which I'm truly thankful. It swallows you, nerve and bone.'

The boy goes still. It is the first time his father has spoken about it. 'I was taken there by men who dressed in fine clothes and spoke elegantly while their palms warmed the money they made from the slaves they sold. But I didn't just lie down and let them take me. I was too angry for that. I had to be' – his fist clenches – 'restrained.'

He takes a breath. 'The will to survive is extraordinary. I'd lost my family, my home, my freedom, but inside something still burned. I'm glad now that I was an angry man. Otherwise I'd have given up long ago. All the time I was working, sweating, toiling – the foremen were merciless, there was no pity for the weak – I held on to what I'd lost.

'It kept me going. Every night I lay in bed and kept going over your faces – your mother's eyes, so dark and beautiful, the colour of your hair, your sister's smile. She'll be – what? – seventeen soon? I'll bet she's the image of her mother. And you –'

'Nineteen.'

His father pats his hand. 'Nineteen,' he says wonderingly. 'You were more real to me in the darkness than the dust in my throat or the ache in my back. When I went into that mine, I took your light with me.'

He starts coughing, hard and painfully. The boy pours him water, and he looks at the cup before he drinks. 'There's something I'll never take for granted again.' For a moment his eyes are distant, and when he starts talking again the boy realises he is back in Prira.

'We lived there for some years, but to be honest, I found it difficult. I tried a few jobs, but never really settled. And your grandmother was always there, arranging things, generally advising the opposite of what we'd decided. Your mother was very patient, kept saying she was just trying to be helpful, but when you were born it got worse. And when Kara came along, your grandmother seemed to be there all the time, making suggestions, interfering. That's how I saw it, anyway.'

He looks down at his hands. 'I gave your mother an ultimatum. I said she had to choose between her mother and us.' He shakes his head. 'When we told your grandmother we were leaving, there was an almighty row. Blames were laid at people's feet, old grievances brought up all over again. In the end, it was your mother who stopped the arguments. She went over to your grandmother's house, on her own. She was there for a long time, and when she came back she told me her mother had agreed to let us go.'

Interpreting the boy's look, he says, 'You think we should have made our own decisions, no need for her approval, but it was necessary to your mother. She was always the peacemaker. I don't know what she said, but it worked. We decided on Bishra, sixty miles south, because I'd heard land was available for those willing to work it. So we went, and I built our hut, and we started making a life for ourselves.

'You're probably wondering why we had a hut rather than a house, especially when your grandmother was well off.' He smiles wryly. 'Pride again. I was setting out on a new life with my family, and I didn't need help from anyone else. When we crossed the mountains into the valley, I put

308

my head down and got on with it. I'd get up, eat, work, sleep. I never took the time to see how lovely it could be, the way the sun came over the mountains on frosty winter mornings, the first time the almond tree blossomed. I was too busy making mountains for myself.

'Your mother understood what I was trying to do, but I know she missed your grandmother. After what happened, there was silence between us. We'd appeared to leave on good terms, but I think it was more about saving face in front of the village. Your grandmother never forgave me for taking your mother away.

'We worked hard, hoping the land would make good, give us enough to live on and a little more, perhaps, to build a house.' He sighs. 'I was no farmer. I did what was necessary, planted and harvested year after year, but the land knew it. It has a way of knowing,' he adds, looking at his son. 'You may not think it – I didn't, at first – but it has. Take your mother – whatever she planted, it grew. I used to joke about it at first, examine her hands, tell her I was sure they were turning green.'

He looks away briefly. 'We – I – kept putting off making contact with your grandmother, until one day it was too late. I've never forgiven myself.' He stares out of the window. The day is brightly gathering, and a bird is singing with great sweetness.

When he turns back, his face is composed once more. 'I wanted things to be better for you and Kara,' he says. 'Doesn't everyone want that for their children? But it came out the wrong way. Instead of encouraging you, letting you find your own feet, I told you what was – as I saw it, at least – because I thought it would protect you from disappointment. I watched you grow, and worried because I could see in you the same restlessness I had in me. I tried to keep you occupied – well, you know what I did.'

He stares down at his hands. 'I was too hard on you. I know that now. Having time to think can be a mixed blessing. You can't run away from it. But I've learned, these past few months, to look things in the eye.'

A thought strikes the boy. 'Do you remember the chair?' he asks. His father made it for his mother, giving it gracefully curving arms and carved flowers on the back. In summer she took it outside when she shelled peas or stripped beans; in winter it sat beside the fire.

His father's face lights up. 'It took a lot of swearing, and I was half afraid that when the wood warmed up the words would come out.' He smiles, but his face quickly sobers. 'Your mother never once complained about what she didn't have, but I know it must have been hard for her to go to market and see other women boasting about what their husbands had bought them, cloth for a new dress, pans for the kitchen, another goat or sheep.'

The boy has no idea how to fill the silence. His father stirs, touching his hand. 'Don't worry about me,' he says. 'Your coming here makes it all worthwhile. Just to see you again is more than I could ever have hoped for. What matters now is you, and your mother and sister.'

The boy looks down at his lap.

'You'll find them,' his father says, 'I know you will.'

The garden of contemplation is quiet, but this afternoon he can't find peace. Talaia is coming across the grass. She sits down beside him.

'How is your father?' she asks.

He doesn't know what to say. That he is and isn't himself? That there is so much he never knew about him, and now there is too little time?

As if guessing his thoughts, Talaia says, 'It may feel like small comfort, but what matters is that you found him. That must mean the world to him.'

'Do you think so?'

'Yes.' She takes his hand. 'I wasn't there when my father died. I was running an errand. I should never have left him.' She turns to him, her face stricken. 'I'm sorry, that was –'

'It's all right, you don't need to apologise.'

Tears stand in her eyes. 'I miss him.'

Very gently, he moves towards her. Resistant at first, she lets him take her in his arms and hold her as she cries.

The day is already warm when he stands at his window, looking out. Last night he slept very little. When he did, he dreamed of the hut, but no one was there. He leaves the room and walks slowly down the corridor, absorbed in thought.

Pera is waiting at the door. 'Your father is a little tired today, but he's awake and looking forward to seeing you.'

His father greets him with a smile and a clasp of his hand. 'Come, sit,' he says. His face is calm, without pain. On the table beside him is a glass of cloudy water. 'It helps when things get worse. It's made from the herbs they grow here. They've never lost touch with the earth. You know, there were times when I saw myself as a farmer, in spite of what I said to you.' He hesitates. 'It wasn't so bad, was it?' His eyes reflect the anxiety in his voice.

The boy thinks for a moment. 'Do you remember . . . ?' he says, and takes them back to a hut that is larger and more elaborate, a stream alive with fish, a flock of plump and glossy hens, to mountains that cradle them like time.

When he stops speaking his father's eyes are wise, but grateful. 'Thank you,' he says, but the boy doesn't want gratitude. He wants his father to be as strong in temper as he always was, recalcitrant, unyielding. 'I've been meaning to ask you what it was like, crossing the sea,' his father says, and the boy thinks back to the harbour, the gulls squabbling and fishy-mouthed, the sailors, the *Silver Falcon*.

'It's where I started writing,' he says, surprising himself. His father looks at him with interest. The boy tells him about the green leather notebook. 'It was mostly about sunsets at first. I could never get them right, no matter how hard I tried. One day I got so fed up, I –' But his father's eyes are closing, so he stops talking and sits watching him.

There is a movement at his side and he turns, anticipating Pera, but it is Talaia. 'Would you mind if I join you?' she asks quietly.

They sit hand in hand until Pera tells them it is time for lunch, that his father will need his sleep this afternoon, but they may return after dinner.

Later, they go into the second garden, where people are reading, talking, walking among the trees. They find a place to sit, a stone bench under a tree whose silvery, fawn-coloured bark glows in the afternoon light.

'It's a water willow,' Talaia says. 'It was brought here by the healers. It doesn't drink very much, and does well in drought.'

'Shouldn't it be called the not-very-thirsty willow?'

She considers. 'Maybe it started life as a greedy camel that drank a lake dry and was punished by being turned into a tree.' The boy eyes it warily, and she smiles.

'Could I ask you something?' she says after a moment.

'Of course.'

'Did you tell your father about finding your mother?' Her tone is measured, careful. He shakes his head, she nods, and he knows there is no need to explain.

'Where's Yorin?' he asks suddenly.

Talaia laughs. 'He's found a card game. They don't play for money, it's not permitted, but apparently they're very competitive.'

The boy smiles. He has a feeling he knows who will win.

Shadows are lengthening into evening. 'You've never said much about your time in the desert,' Talaia says.

The boy stiffens. A familiar feeling crawls across his back.

'I'm sorry, it was thoughtless, I shouldn't have mentioned it.'

He looks out into the darkening air, thinking of the man who almost certainly gave his life to save him. 'Maybe one day,' he says, aware of the implication of the words.

'One day,' Talaia says, and he hopes she understands it too.

After dinner, the boy returns to his father. He is awake, and sitting up. He looks rested and peaceful. A woman in a blue robe pours him a herbal drink.

'It helps me sleep. The pain's worse at night.' The boy shifts slightly, wanting to offer comfort, unsure as to how it will be received. 'It's fine,' his father says. 'Things are as they are.'

The boy stares. Is this the same man who stood in the wheatfield shaking his fist when the locusts came?

'Your face always did show everything,' his father says, smiling. 'Come and sit down, I've got something for you.'

On the blanket is a rose-coloured pouch. He hands it to the boy, who unties the cord and takes out a pair of slippers. They are made of deep-blue silk velvet embroidered with gold and silver thread, and look as if they have never been worn.

'Your mother took them with her when we moved to Bishra,' his father says. 'I was in the Poplar when the horsemen came, and I went back upstairs to get them. I wasn't going to leave them behind. It might sound strange, but I knew that if I had them with me, I'd find your mother again. And I have, through you. Keep them safe, and when you find her, give them to her, and she'll know.'

He leans back, closing his eyes. The boy looks up and Pera is there, saying, 'It's time to rest now.' She glances at the pouch, and smiles.

She'll know what? he wonders as he stands at his window watching stars flicker and dance. But he thinks he understands, and grieves because now there is no time. Perhaps her spirit will know. If he has ever thought of the soul, it is as something with the capacity to fit whatever receptacle it finds. He thinks of the stream in his valley, a moving spirit flowing to meet the sea, of the cloudy souls of the gulls that fly above. He shivers, as if something is passing by.

There is a knock at the door. He opens it to see Pera. He has half-expected her, and wishes the moment could be put off until he is ready, so he could wait forever.

'Your father is asking for you,' she says gently. There is a lamp in her hand; he follows it like a moth, obedient even as his heart tries to fly away.

His father is awake. A lamp burns on the table next to him. 'Come, sit down,' he says, holding out a hand. 'I was thinking' – he smiles – 'about the sunflower seeds. We never planted them.'

His breath is tight as he pulls himself up and leans forward slightly. 'Arun,' he begins, then breaks off and stares at something beyond the lamplight. He tries again, but the effort is too much and he sinks back into the pillows.

'I know,' the boy whispers as his father closes his eyes.

Chapter Twenty-Two

He sits beside his father's bed, outside time. The lamp on
the table flickers, a soft gust making shadows quiver. Pera
is there, murmuring something. He knows they are words
of comfort, but they are of no use to him. They can't walk
and talk, love and sing.

'He is at peace, *dayursi*,' Pera says.

Why she is calling him 'my son' when he is no one's
son any more? It is a courtesy, but he doesn't want
courtesies. He wants his father, his mother, his sister. He
wants the valley, the hut and the almond tree. Most of
all, he wishes for snow to bury his mind until all thought
freezes.

Pera gently releases his fingers from the blanket and
helps him to his feet. 'We'll prepare him now, and take him
to the house of rest,' she says. 'He'll lie there until morning.
Would you like to stay with him?'

The boy stares at her.

'It's customary,' she explains. 'His spirit won't want to
be alone. I'll sit with you, if you wish.'

Her face is so understanding he can't bear it. He turns
and walks off, down the room, through the door and out
into the corridor. The wall is cool and hard and he leans
against it, taking deep breaths, gulping. It is no way to

behave, he knows, and part of him is ashamed, and part is numb.

He stands for a long while, staring at nothing, until a hand slips into his and Talaia says, 'Your father is in the house of rest. Shall we sit with him? He'd like that, I think.'

The house of rest is not what he expected. It is small and comfortable, with rugs and ornaments, paintings of flowers and landscapes. It resembles the room of a moderately prosperous merchant.

'They're gifts,' Talaia tells him, 'from relatives of people who have been looked after here.' Then she says, 'See, he's sleeping, that's all.'

His father lies on a couch draped in soft cloths. Candles burn on a small table beside him. His face is very peaceful.

'You see?' Talaia says gently. 'There's no need to be afraid.'

And he isn't; he sits beside his father with Talaia at his side until the sky slowly changes, and a pale light covers the stars.

Chapter Twenty-Three

They sit in a room reserved for those who have lost someone, which is the meaning of *Ritalshanir*, the word inscribed on the lintel. Gentle light feathers the many-coloured wall hangings. The boy gets up and goes to the window overlooking the field of rest where, earlier that day, he stood beside his father's grave with Yorin and Talaia. There were other people with them, some in blue robes, some visitors wanting to pay their respects.

Pera spoke words of comfort, kindness and love. She asked the boy if he wanted to say something, but no words would come. Instead, he opened the Book of Light at the page he had marked, and handed it to Talaia.

"'Last Thoughts of the Poet Mirashi",' she read, her voice in the still air clear and calm. One of the few poems with a title, it begins

My writing room is the early morning

and goes on to say how Mirashi has tried, like an engraver, to record what she sees around her and how, in her desire to be as faithful as she can,

my fingers shake,
scratching the delicate world.

As she thinks of what is to come, she writes that

the desert lies at the end of every sentence

and that, even as she starts to journey on, she feels pulled
by the beauty of the world.

I have passed the inn of the longest day
in the company of night –
I would welcome the pain of light.

There is a knock at the door and Pera comes in, carrying a
tray. Placing it on the table, she explains it is customary for
her to take tea with them. 'Camomile,' she says in answer
to Talaia's question.

Out of politeness the boy takes a cake, small, round,
studded with lemon peel.

'They're excellent, very light,' Talaia says. 'Did you
make them?'

Pera shakes her head. 'I'm afraid I'm not very good at
baking. The last time I made something it became dinner
for the goats.'

'But your kitchens are a miracle of efficiency.'

Pera smiles. 'When I first came here, they were a
complete muddle. I'm not sure how any meals came to be
made at all. It's taken time to find the best way of doing
things, and I've had a lot of help along the way. I wasn't
always Mother of Amala Dyssul.'

She sips her tea. 'I'm the daughter of a fruit-seller
and a healer. My father had orange and lemon groves
in Duina, about five days' ride from here. My mother

made remedies from the herbs she grew. She taught me about them, although at the time I was more interested in things that glittered, especially, for some reason, silver thread.

'I was probably something of a trial to her, but she was always patient. She made me feel as if I was very special. We lived simply in a one-roomed house with the fruit trees behind it and the herb garden to the side. The sun needs very little to work with, and water came from an underground spring. Every day I learned my lessons, including a list of five healing plants and herbs, with a rhyme to help me remember.

> *Grow, little herb, in sun, in rain,*
> *Bring physic and balm to those in pain.'*

She smiles briefly. 'Time went by, my father grew older, my mother's aches and pains grew worse. They tried to talk to me about what would happen when they were no longer there, but I didn't want to hear it. I'm afraid I was angry with them for bringing it up.

'They died, one after the other, when I was seventeen, and I was left alone. Relatives in a neighbouring village offered to take me in, but the idea of leaving the fruit trees broke my heart, and the herb garden needed to be looked after by someone who loved it. What I hadn't realised was that my parents didn't own their house. It was rented from a local man. So in the end I had no choice. I went with a great deal of bitterness.

'My relatives were kind to me in their way, but they had little to spare, and I was another mouth to feed. I never went hungry, but it felt as if something inside wasn't being fed. It was only when I walked down the lane to their orchards that I found peace. I'd sit dreaming when I was supposed to be doing my chores.'

She sits thoughtfully for a moment. 'They were good people, and I was young. I had cousins – five of them – and aunts and uncles who took an increasing interest in me as I grew up. I didn't know why until I found myself betrothed to a landowner who lived just outside the village.'

The boy glances at Talaia, who stares at her teacup.

'The idea horrified me,' Pera says. 'I think I was a romantic at heart – I'd seen too many suns setting in the orange groves. But' – she shakes her head – 'that man . . .'

She puts her cup down carefully. 'He was the reason I became a healer. I had no intention of loving him. He was a careful, well-planned person, and I was at the harum-scarum stage. He wasn't unattractive, but you had to look to find his appeal. I didn't, at first. I didn't want to. I suppose I thought the betrothal would come to nothing; it was simply a matter of wishing it away. When I realised I had no choice, I promised myself that if it wasn't a good marriage I'd leave it, no matter what. And I refused to wear a wedding ring.'

She looks at Talaia for a moment. 'It crept up on me, which was rather unfair. He was a patient man, and time was on his side, so he waited, and put up with' – she winces – 'the mother of all tempers. It took me two years to realise I loved him. That was a good day. I don't think he ever got over it.'

She smiles, her eyes far away. 'I finally wore the ring

he'd wanted to give me on our wedding day, and I gave him one, too. I know it's not customary but it was important to us, and that's what matters in the end.'

She stops talking. The others prepare themselves. 'He died,' she says. 'I tried to save him, but in the end there was nothing I could do. So now I do what I can to help others, or at least give them comfort. That was his doing.' She looks at the boy. 'Your coming here gave your father such comfort. He wasn't an easy man, he said so himself, but he loved you very much.'

Yes, the boy thinks as the tightness in his chest eases a little, he did.

He is unable to sleep, unable to think of anything but the fact that he has no parents now. Kara is the last of his family, and he should be making his way to Kerizon as fast as he can. But all he can do is sit with an emptiness that feels like a weight he will never put down.

At first he ignores the knock. When he opens the door to find Talaia standing there, he is reminded of Kushtar. She must be thinking the same because she smiles and says, 'Don't worry, I've checked for relatives. May I come in?'

The boy lights a lamp and they sit on the bed, a little way apart. Talaia's eyes shine softly. 'I wanted to see how you are,' she says. 'I hope you don't mind.' He shakes his head. 'I also wanted you to know you're not alone. You have Yorin. And me.'

He looks into her eyes. She is very still. Slowly he leans forward. As their lips meet, a sound rises in Talaia's throat, and suddenly they are kissing, urgently, frantically, struggling with each other's clothes, and he loses himself in the sweetness of her body. Later there are tears and, for a time, peace.

The boy wakes in the early morning to find Talaia gone. After a pang of disappointment he lies thinking about last night, his body as dazed as his mind. A feeling of anxiety begins to gather. Phrases drift uncomfortably in his head. *No better than she should be. Damaged goods.* Euphemisms, overheard in his village and not at the time understood. He sits up, knowing what he must do.

The refectory is quiet. Yorin is sitting by himself, stirring a bowl of cham.

'Have you seen Talaia?' the boy asks.

'I think she's in the garden,' Yorin says. 'She seemed to be miles away.' He grins. 'It must be catching.'

The boy makes his way over the grass, the images in his head so much at odds with the person sitting in perfect composure on the stone bench that he wonders if he dreamed last night. Talaia looks up and smiles.

'Good morning,' she says as he sits down next to her. His heart fights with his breath as he tries to work out what to say.

After a too-long silence, her face changes. 'It's all right,' she says, 'you don't need to worry. It was one night, that's all.' Her eyes are as cool as her voice.

Horrified, he says, 'I wasn't thinking that – that's not what I –'

'I'm sorry, I just wasn't sure what –'

Her smile is shaky, and so is his. 'Nor was I,' he says, relieved. 'It was wonderful,' he adds cautiously.

She takes his hand, and a shudder runs through him.

'It was. But it doesn't have to mean anything. I mean, I hope it does, but I don't want you to feel –'

'It meant everything,' he says fervently. 'Which is why' – he steels himself; it is now or never – 'I think we should get married.'

Talaia looks at him steadily. 'Why?' she asks.

It is not the reaction he expected. 'Well, after what happened last night – I mean, you know . . .' He trails off.

'What do I know?' Talaia asks calmly.

'Well,' he says with a feeling of increasing desperation, 'you know how people talk.'

'Do I?' Talaia's eyes are cool again. Perhaps he should lighten the mood.

'I don't want you to become a euphemism,' he says.

His smile is not returned. The temperature seems to have plummeted.

'So you're trying to save me from public disgrace?' Talaia's voice is polite and very cold.

'No, that's not what I –' All the right words seem to be stuck in the back of his throat.

'Don't worry, Arun,' she says with the same icy politeness, 'I'll save you the bother. You don't have to see me again if you don't want to. I wouldn't want to embarrass you.'

Open-mouthed, he watches her stalk away across the grass. What happened? How did everything go so wrong?

He sits in the garden for a long time. When he returns to the main house he wanders through the corridors, half-hoping to see Talaia. Noise and laughter draw him to a room where he finds Yorin seated at a crowded table, playing cards.

'Come in,' Yorin says, 'you're just in time to witness my moment of triumph.' He grins at the good-natured mutterings, and makes room for the boy. 'Did you find Talaia?' The boy nods. Yorin gives him a shrewd look. 'I take it it didn't go well?'

'It was a complete disaster.'

'Right.' Yorin lays his cards on the table. 'I fold,' he announces to general surprise. 'Make the most of it while you can.' He gets up. 'Come on, your need is greater than mine.'

It is hard to negotiate what should and should not be said, but the boy manages enough of a gist for Yorin to nod thoughtfully. He listens without comment, though at one point he sucks in his breath and winces.

'Can I ask you something?' The boy gives a hopeless nod. 'Do you love her?'

Even though the question is unexpected, it requires no consideration. 'Yes.'

'Just checking,' Yorin says, smiling at the look on the boy's face. 'I have got eyes, my friend. I was wondering how long it would take you to work it out. In which case, there's only one thing to do.'

'What's that?'

'Find her, and tell her.' He glances at the wall of the small room they are standing in. 'Don't waste time. Don't make the same mistake as me.' The boy shifts uneasily, not knowing what to say, but there is no sadness in Yorin's face. 'Go,' he says, 'make it right.'

He is blind to the light patterning the library floor with jewel-coloured coins, blind to everything except Talaia, seated at a table beneath a tall arched window. Pera, who is with her, smiles at him. She says something to Talaia and makes her way towards him, touching his sleeve as she passes.

His footsteps echo as he walks towards the table. 'Can we talk?' he asks.

Talaia doesn't look up.

'Please. It's important.'

'Fine,' she says eventually.

He looks around. 'Not here.'

The garden of contemplation is empty. It seems to have taken a very long time to reach it. The silence Talaia brought with her sits upright on the bench. The boy's heart pounds, his palms are damp. There is only one chance, and this is it.

Her eyes widen in surprise as he kneels on the grass and tells her he loves her, and asks her to be his wife. It is what he wanted to say before, he adds, but it all came out wrong. There was never any question of duty, but he was so frightened she would turn him down that what he really felt got lost along the way. He tells her he cannot imagine a life without her and, if she lets him, he will do everything he can to make her happy. And did he mention he is so in love with her he can hardly see straight?

'I think you might have,' she murmurs, 'and I think you'd better get up now, or you might get stuck like that for the rest of your life. Oh, and yes, I will marry you.'

He meets her shining eyes with a smile so wide she starts laughing, and he scrambles to his feet and pulls her into a kiss that becomes, for the moment, the only world that matters.

They are married in a quiet and lovely ceremony performed by Pera in the garden of contemplation. Pera speaks of the boy's father, and how he is here with them, as are all the people the boy has known and loved. She speaks of Talaia's parents, and how they are here with her, watching in loving spirit. The boy and Talaia turn to each other with tears in their eyes. There is no need to hide them now.

When Pera asks if they wish to exchange rings the boy looks at her in bewilderment, but Yorin steps forward. He hands Pera a small velvet bag, and from it she takes two bands of beaten silver rippled through with threads of gold. Each ring contains three gemstones. Two are blue, the middle one white. She explains that blue is for sky and sea, which are each other's mirror; white is for love. Every day the sky and sea may change, but love remains constant.

There is no time to wonder where they came from. Today is the boy's wedding day, and the only thing that matters is that Talaia is putting a ring on his finger. When he has done the same, Pera joins their hands and declares them *Marisani, Marisana*. To the sound of cheering and applause, they kiss.

Husband and wife. Happiness overwhelms him. The long table in the refectory is decorated with flowers, candlelight and the last of the setting sun. Everyone is talking, drinking, laughing, but the boy is caught in a bubble of something warm and glittering.

'You're very quiet,' Talaia says. 'You're not –' Her face is anxious.

'Not what?' he asks.

'Regretting it,' she says in a rush.

His heart knocks against his chest. 'Not for a second. You're not –?'

'Not for a second,' she says, stroking his cheek.

They sit leaning against each other in peaceful silence until the boy says, 'When did you know?' It is suddenly important to him.

'Know what?'

'That you –' Absurdly, he can't say it.

She smiles. 'That I love you?'

He catches his breath. 'Yes.'

She gives him a mischievous smile. 'I knew when you left the table at the library caves because you were cross with me for talking with *Dhisava*.' He stares at her, remembering it with a twinge of shame. 'What about you?' she asks.

His throat constricts. If he says, *What a coincidence, it's the same for me*, will it look too calculating? Perhaps he should place it a little earlier, just enough for flattery. Or afterwards, as something that took time to grow.

She smiles. It is like a delicate frost being broken by the tread of a waterbird. In a rush he says, 'I've always loved you.'

She looks relieved. 'Me too.' It takes a moment for understanding to come.

At the head of the table, Pera is getting to her feet. 'To your marriage and your life ahead,' she says. As the company raise their cups, Yorin lifts his highest of all.

Pera's words echo in the boy's head as she leads them from the refectory, down a long corridor and into a small area overlooked by an arched window. To the left is a door.

'It hasn't been used as a bridal chamber before, but I

thought it would do very well,' she says, making a gesture of blessing as she leaves them.

They look at each other for a moment. 'It's funny, I don't feel in the least bit tired,' Talaia says as she leads the boy through the door.

On the morning after their marriage, they sit on the stone bench in the garden of contemplation. The sun is a rosy peach in the sky. The ring on his finger winks as the boy strokes Talaia's hand. They learned from Yorin that the rings came from Pera, that they had belonged to her and her husband. The thanks they offered seemed inadequate, but Pera told them there had never been a marriage at Amala Dyssul before, and she knew it would have made her husband very happy.

He holds Talaia's hand as if it might vanish, studying her profile as she basks in the sunshine.

'You're looking at me,' she murmurs.

'I am,' he says, 'and I never want to stop.' Her mouth curves in a smile. He can't resist. He leans in to kiss her.

All that day they wander in the garden, smelling the flowers, passing their hands through the shimmering spray of the fountain. Time, it seems, is on holiday. They are held in the palm of something gentle and good, and it protects and keeps them. Or so the boy thinks as they sit at the refectory table that evening. Yorin sits opposite, a smile on his face.

'So, how are you enjoying being married?' he asks. The boy starts blushing. He'd thought being a husband would put a stop to it. 'I told Tobi about it when I took him for a ride.'

'And?' the boy asks warily.

Yorin looks at Talaia. 'He says good luck to you.'

Later, when Talaia is sleeping beside him, the boy lies awake. That she is here, and she is his, is a marvel to him. Or is she? He has been wary of claims of possession ever since he overheard his father telling his mother that of course she will do it, she is his wife, after all. No matter how fine, to a fly a cobweb is still a prison. He tries to remember what his mother said, but he can't. She would have coped as she always did, quietly working away at things, making them better.

A deep sorrow overcomes him, for his father sleeping in the field of rest, for his mother lying on the hillside above Dhurkana. He slips quietly out of bed and takes the Book of Light from the pocket of his shirt, using the light of the moon to find what he is looking for.

> To make the word *husband*
> you hired a man who broke stone,
> mixed clay, and raised it facing north.

> What you meant was four corners lightly set on grass,
> a silk pavilion under stars.

He wishes he had been able to show his mother the poem. He hopes she knew how much his father loved her.

'I'm sure she did,' Talaia says as she comes to stand beside him. He turns to her, and she takes him in her arms as he weeps.

There are six more days to spend in this peaceful place.

They go often to the stone bench, talking quietly. They say things which make sense only to each other, and it is a good feeling. When the boy tucks a shining strand of hair behind Talaia's ear, he sees it is small and perfect. He wonders if there is anything to find fault with, and suspects not.

It cannot last forever. He knows this, and while he tries to ignore the feeling building inside, it will not go away. In the end, Talaia broaches the subject.

'I could stay here for the rest of my life,' she says as they sit on the bench after dinner, cups of fragrant tea in their hands, 'but I know we can't.'

He watches the play of the fountain in the evening light. He has been wondering how to find out if Yorin still wants to go with him now that he and Talaia are married. It has become a matter of great importance that they complete this journey together.

'I hope you don't mind, but I've talked to Yorin,' Talaia says, 'and he said that while he isn't sure how his constitution will stand up to being around' – she pretends to think – 'two lovebirds, he's never been to Kerizon.'

'Lovebirds?' the boy says, and the look on his face makes her burst out laughing.

Pera stands with them at the door of Amala Dyssul. Earlier that morning, the boy went to the field of rest and stood at his father's grave. He told him that the sun was rising, and that he was married. He hoped his father would love Talaia as he did, and said he knew his mother would have welcomed her with open arms. Kara, he added, would have had plenty to say about it. Before he left, he touched the small white headstone engraved with his father's name.

Arun stares into the pool for a long while. 'It was hard, leaving that place. It was where I found my father again, and where I was married.' He looks blindly across the clearing. 'Part of my heart is there. It always will be.'

He bows his head as the boy, Talaia, Yorin and Tobi set out from Amala Dyssul, to Kerizon.

Chapter Twenty-Four

White dust follows them into the low hills west of Amala Dyssul. Talaia squeezes the boy's hand. 'Are you all right?' she asks.

'Yes,' he says, 'I am. You're with me. And' – a glance ahead – 'so is the grumpiest horse in the world.'

She laughs. 'He's not so bad when you get to know him,' she teases, stroking his cheek.

'Enough of that,' Yorin calls. 'You don't want to make him even grumpier, do you?'

The boy worried at first about sleeping arrangements, suppressing a guilty longing for a soft bed and a closed door, but after dinner on the first evening Yorin simply wished them goodnight, and withdrew to a discreet distance.

Many times the boy has given silent thanks for Talaia, who eases his pain in the bleakest parts of the night. When he confided his fears about what he might find in Kerizon, she said, 'Remember what I told you, my love? You're not alone. I'm with you, and we'll face whatever comes together.'

On the morning of the third day, they enter a misty valley flanked with trees and bushes and threaded with a river.

'The Medin Gap,' Yorin says. 'Gateway to Kerizon.'

The banks are strewn with mossy boulders; water prattles over the rocks. To the boy it feels like a valley of beginnings, formed when the world was setting out to make its fortune. Yorin leads Tobi to the river for a drink. The horse's breath steams; water droplets slip and shiver as he gulps it up. Talaia pushes back her sleeves and dips her arms in the water.

'Oh!' she cries, and the boy starts towards her in alarm. 'It's cold, that's all,' she says. With a mischievous look she flicks water at him, wetting his shirt. He scoops up a handful and advances. 'Mercy!' she cries. They look at each other. They both know he won't do it.

As they walk through the valley, a bird repeats its song. The boy asks Yorin what it is. 'Probably a greenchat. They nest near rivers.'

'They're supposed to make very good pets,' Talaia says. 'They can copy what you say.'

The boy imagines a dinner party attended by guests who disliked each other. The bird could be employed to wreak havoc, and the host would remain blameless.

'I must remember that,' Yorin says thoughtfully.

Day folds into afternoon. Gnats swim in liquid light. The river is wider now, and slower. A little way ahead it loses itself entirely to a lake, on whose surface floats a city. Yorin gives a low whistle. The boy stares open-mouthed at the rose-pink walls of Kerizon, its towers and spires in endless flight.

Talaia stands very still. 'My father told me about it. It was somewhere he always wanted to see.' The boy understands. If she looks hard enough, the image will float away to the place her father is now. As he holds her close, she says, 'I think I'd like a poem. Would you?'

When he finds what he is looking for, he reads

Light is a peacemaker, returning to perfection
the million drops of rain shaken

from the muzzles of mountains
bending their heads to the Talshan River

where all roads find reflection.

For a moment Talaia bows her head.

'We'd better get a move on,' Yorin says, 'we don't want to get shut out.'

Even as the boy is wondering how they are supposed to get across, and whether the citizens of Kerizon walk on water, he sees the causeway. Great slabs form a rosy path melting at the edges in the fading light. As he takes his first step hand in hand with Talaia, it feels as if he is in a dream. Tobi frisks, shies and jinks. Yorin takes him firmly by the bridle and starts murmuring. The horse settles a little, makes an experimental dodge, settles a little more.

It is a long way across, and the walls of the city grow taller with every step. The last of the sun's rays bestow a radiance almost too much for the eye to bear. A horn sounds.

'Must be the curfew,' Yorin says. 'Not that the citizens have anything much to worry about. I think there was a siege here once, but it fizzled out. Fire didn't work, so they tried starving them out, but there's a network of underground tunnels that leads to the other side of the lake. So I'm told.' He grins at the boy. 'It's a great prize. Legend has it that only when the rose sheds its petals will Kerizon fall.'

'The flower of eternity,' Talaia says. 'I read about it somewhere. The rose symbolises eternal love. A rose made of stone is a love that can never die.'

'I'd die for a hot meal and a warm bed.'

Passing through the city gates, they find themselves in what must be Kerizon's equivalent of a village square. It could be the courtyard of a palace but is much larger, a place of marble and water, thronging with people and set with fountains whose liquid diamonds make the air glitter. There are cloistered walkways at every side and, at the centre, a fountain so large the boy could swim in it. Fashioned in the shape of a rose, it rises upwards to an arched trellis of rose-coloured marble over which water breaks in beautiful confusion.

It is a work of such art he can only stand and stare. Talaia is turning in a circle. As she comes back to face him, her eyes are a little dazed. Only Yorin and Tobi seem unmoved, though the horse is eyeing the fountain.

'They must be used to visitors gawping,' Yorin says. It's true; conversations continue around them as if they weren't there. The boy wonders what would happen if an elephant sat in the fountain.

They leave the square, which they later learn is called *Ishnarien*, 'the talking-place', and cross into a wide, empty street. The inhabitants must either all be out, or having their dinner. The boy's stomach rumbles.

'There's got to be an inn round here somewhere,' Yorin says. Halfway down the street they see a sign. 'The House of Roses. Original. At least the painting's good.'

The common room is spacious and light. The furniture is elaborate, carved chairs filled with embroidered cushions, tables decorated with fruiting vines. It is very busy.

'We're lucky, they've got rooms,' Yorin says. 'I think someone's mule took a wrong turn.'

Talaia looks around calmly. The boy resists the urge to ruffle her.

The same attention to detail follows them into their room. 'Thank goodness,' Talaia exclaims, 'a proper bed!' She immediately sets about testing it – 'Look, Arun, feather pillows, and the blankets are so soft' – then slips away from him, saying, 'Not now, we don't have time,' with a look that promises the opposite.

By the time they go downstairs, the blue-shadowed evening is taking the air. Talaia has threaded her hair with silver ribbon, and it falls over one shoulder all the way to her waist. The boy half wishes he had a large cloth, the kind people drape over birdcages.

When the food arrives it is a feast for the eyes, though they are soon deprived of the view. 'Kerizonian lamb,' Yorin says. 'Bathed every day, their hooves oiled and polished, their fleeces combed until they're fluffy as clouds. The shepherds have to tie them to bushes to keep them from floating away.'

Talaia makes a noise of disbelief. 'It's true' – Yorin looks hurt – 'I've seen them myself.'

'When the world was made of sweetmeats, and the rivers flowed with honey,' Talaia says, but her mouth twitches.

The boy wonders how horses would cross them. How people would sit in boats and fish. How, if it came to that, fish would swim. 'It would be a very slow world,' he says thoughtfully.

'And gone very quickly,' Yorin laughs. 'We'd eat our way through it in no time. Then we'd find ourselves falling, into –'

'A trap,' Talaia says.

Yorin fails to look abashed. 'It's a fair question, in a fair city.' He glances at a woman walking by. She looks back, and smiles.

He clears his throat. 'I've been making enquiries,' he says. 'We need to go to the Municipal Hall. We should be able to find out more about your sister there. We can go tomorrow.' He looks at the boy. 'Now, if you'll excuse me, I'm going to join that game of triples.'

The boy sits in silence, a chilly sickness in his stomach.

'Arun,' Talaia says, 'do you think –' Seeing his face, she says quickly, 'Never mind, it doesn't matter.'

'Yes, it does. Please, tell me.'

'It's just that – no, you'll think it's silly.' He assures her he won't. 'Do you think Kara will like me?'

'Of course she will,' he says, surprised.

'I hope so.' She looks worried.

'Does it matter that much?'

'She is my sister-in-law, after all. And yes, it matters to me.'

He sits back, stunned. How has it not occurred to him? In his mind Kara is eleven years old and much too short to have a sister-in-law, when she is in fact nearly seventeen and a young woman.

He takes Talaia's hands in his. 'She'll love you,' he says. 'How could she not?'

'The Municipal Hall.' Yorin nods at an elegant building of rose-coloured stone. Tall doors of chestnut wood lead into an atrium cupped by a great dome inlaid with coloured glass. Small shadows line the dome.

'Pigeons,' Yorin says. 'They nest there. They're supposed to be lucky.'

'Very,' Talaia observes, 'if it saves people from having to climb up and remove them with brooms.'

Yorin touches the boy's sleeve as a man in a dark-green tunic approaches. Introducing himself as Selou, he asks if they are visitors. If so, he would be happy to show them around.

The boy takes a step forward. 'I'm looking for someone. Her name is Kara Persaba. My sister. She came to Kerizon five years ago, in late spring. I was told I'd be able to find out more about her here.'

'Of course. Please, come with me.'

They follow him through the atrium to an ornate doorway. The room beyond is equally impressive, with magnificent carvings, an encircling balcony, another soaring dome.

'These are the archives. Many people come here to research their families,' Selou tells them in a whisper.

At the far side, a man is sitting on a tall chair that has formed an alliance with a desk. On any other day the boy would find it funny. Selou introduces the man as Erza, the chief archivist, and talks quietly with him for a moment.

'I understand you're looking for your sister?' Erza asks. Biting back impatience, the boy repeats what he told Selou. With a nod the archivist steps down from the desk, leading them over to a row of tall shelves filled with large black ledgers. The boy thinks his world is made from them. Paper dissolves in water, and water washes everything clean.

Erza pulls out a thick volume. With growing agitation the boy watches him turn the pages of the book, taking what seems an eternity. Erza is frowning. 'You said late spring?' The boy nods. 'I can't seem to find her. You're sure about the time?'

'Yes,' he says shortly. 'Please, check again.'

Erza runs his finger slowly down the pages. He shakes his head. 'I'm sorry, there is no record of a Kara Persaba.'

The boy thinks back to the piece of paper, the library caves. 'What about the initials PG? They could belong to the person she works for. Is there a name with those initials?'

Erza looks again. 'No, I'm afraid not.'

Heat rises in the boy's chest. The room is beginning to blur. 'She was taken from her family by people working for the tribe of the House of Goash, and brought to Kerizon. You've got to have a record of her.' The words come out in a torrent. He is almost shouting.

Erza takes a step back, an expression of polite bewilderment frozen on his face. People are looking up from tables.

'Arun –' Talaia's hand is on his arm. She speaks gently as Yorin thanks the archivist, and together they steer the boy out of the Municipal Hall.

He stands on the top step, gulping air, shaking with

340

anger. 'They brought her here,' he says furiously, 'it says so on that piece of paper.'

'I know, my love,' Talaia says, 'but they don't have a record of her. Not here, at least.'

Turning away, he stares out into the immaculate square. How could he have been so careless, talking like that with Talaia yesterday evening? He should have known it was inviting disaster.

'Arun' – Talaia touches his arm – 'someone wants to talk to you.'

A woman has come out of the Hall and is looking at him warily. 'I couldn't help overhearing what you were talking about,' she says, speaking so quietly he has to move closer to hear properly. 'I shouldn't really be saying anything – I work in the Municipal Hall, and they wouldn't like if they knew, and I'm not saying it will help you find your sister, but –'

'But what?' He cuts her off impatiently.

'Please,' Talaia says, 'go on.'

The woman glances around nervously. 'It's just that when you said about her being taken from her family –' She breaks off, biting her lip.

'Anything you can tell us would be helpful.'

The woman glances around again. 'There are a lot of things that go on in Kerizon that aren't talked about. If your sister wasn't registered . . .'

'What do you mean?'

'Try the Velvet Quarter. That's all I'm saying. But you'll need to be careful.' Her eyes are fearful. 'I'd better get back. They'll be wondering where I am.'

In spite of its name, the further they go into the Velvet Quarter, the greater the boy's sense of disquiet. The houses are shabbier, their upper storeys leaning into the narrow streets. The famous rose-coloured stone is less in evidence. But it is the atmosphere of watchful stillness that fuels his rising panic. There are few people about, and those Yorin questions give a brief shake of their head and hurry away.

'They probably wouldn't tell you even if they did know,' Talaia says. 'Look at them. They're frightened.'

The boy glances at her. Her beauty is almost luminous in the faintly gloomy light, and it worries him. He wishes he'd brought his dagger. At least Yorin has his sword.

They stop outside a house. On the sign above, a lightly clad woman reclines beneath a gravid moon. The Dreaming Maiden. Even though it is almost noon the shutters are closed, but strains of music come from inside.

'I'm going in,' Yorin says. The boy steps forward. 'No, my friend, it's better if I go alone.'

Talaia holds the boy's hand firmly as they wait. Time slows. Just as the boy is about to open the door Yorin comes out, blinking as if emerging from darkness. A strong, too-sweet perfume clings to him. Talaia wrinkles her nose.

'Well?' the boy asks.

Yorin shakes his head. 'I didn't think it would be easy,' he says with a shrug.

As they work their way down the street, a sudden fear strikes the boy. Every nerve tightens. It is the same feeling he had in the Eye of Jala. He looks up and down, but the street is deserted.

Each time Yorin emerges with a shake of his head; each time the boy's heart sinks. Around the corner, into the next street, no different from the last. The sign above the final door depicts young women bathing in a pool on a flowered lawn. The Perfumed Garden. Yorin stands for a moment, studying it.

'When you've quite finished,' Talaia says, but he frowns thoughtfully.

'You know you asked the archivist about the initials PG?' he says to the boy.

'Yes.'

'What if they stand for Perfumed Garden?'

The boy stares at him.

'Only one way to find out,' Yorin says as he goes in.

When he comes out, the boy knows something is different.

'I've got a name,' Yorin says. 'Ruvek. She seems to know most of what goes on around here. But she wants money.' He names a sum.

Talaia begins to protest but the boy says quickly, 'Yes, fine.'

He starts forward, but Yorin holds up his hand. 'She might lie, or she might not like the questions you ask, in which case you become a problem. There are men in there who'd happily take care of it for her. Are you sure you want to do this?'

The boy glares at him.

'I had to ask,' Yorin says mildly.

The door opens into a small, dimly lit entrance hall hung with cloaks and swords. Two large men are stationed at either side of a door in the wall opposite. One of them has a scar running from his ear to his jaw.

'I expect it back,' Yorin says pleasantly, unbuckling his

sword belt. Neither man smiles. 'Ruvek's expecting us,' he says, and the scarred man shows them through the door.

In the long passage, the thick, sweet scent is almost overpowering. The walls and ceiling are draped with a gauzy fabric that turns the lamplight dusky red. The boy grips Talaia's hand. At the end of the passage is another door, flanked by men who were not instructed to leave their swords in the entrance hall. The scarred man gives a sharp rap and enters. They follow him in.

'Thank you, Voll.'

The room is so cluttered it takes a moment for the boy to locate the owner of the voice. Seated behind a large desk is a woman so old, her skin so netted with wrinkles, it is almost a wonder to find her alive. 'I understand you are looking for someone,' she says. The glitter of her deep-set eyes reminds him of Drasta. 'Please, sit down. You would like some tea?'

What the boy would like is to know where Kara is, but he keeps his temper in check as Voll leaves the room. Among numerous little tables crowded with trinkets and ornaments, they find chairs. Heat from a large fire stifles the air. He waits, looking about distractedly. Filmy hangings cover the walls; a painting of a green bird hangs behind the desk.

Voll returns, accompanied by a girl, barely a child. She puts a tray on Ruvek's desk and leaves the room without looking at them. The boy's fear grows.

'How do you take it?' Ruvek asks. 'With honey?' As he watches her pour, the boy suspects she is enjoying a private game. He tightens his grip on his temper. 'Payment was agreed, I think?' she says. 'And' – she smiles, but her eyes are hard – 'there is no returning it, whether you find this person or not.'

The boy puts a pouch on the desk. She tips it up and counts every coin. 'So,' she says, 'who are you looking for?'

'Kara Persaba.' The boy leans forward as he gives his sister's name. He can hardly breathe.

After a moment's silence Ruvek smiles. 'Then it is easy. I know no one of that name.'

'You must do!' he bursts out.

A movement to his right; Voll steps closer, but Ruvek waves him away. 'Where is your compassion? This man is looking for his sister. It is our duty to help if we can.' She seems to take a malicious interest in the boy's predicament.

Sweat prickles the back of his neck. He tries again. 'She was brought here by men from the north – mercenaries, we think.'

'When was this?' Ruvek asks.

'Five years ago. She was eleven years eight and a half months old.' He struggles to keep his voice steady. The half month had been very important to her.

'You are sure she came here?' Ruvek asks.

'Yes,' he says angrily.

Talaia lays a hand on his arm. 'What if Arun gives you a description?'

'By all means.' Ruvek's voice is polite, but it is clear she regards the interview as over. The boy describes what Kara looked like when they were separated. Ruvek shrugs. 'Girls come to us from many places. I can't be expected to remember every one. Is there anything in particular, something memorable – a birthmark, perhaps?'

345

The boy bites back an angry retort. Everything about his sister is memorable, especially her house in the shrubs and the treasures she kept in it. Her treasures . . .

'She had a small stuffed animal,' he says. 'She took it with her everywhere.'

Ruvek takes a sip of tea, and shrugs. 'Such a thing is easily lost.'

The boy thinks desperately. Time is running out. 'What about a red coral button in the shape of a bird?'

Passed down from his grandmother to his mother, who gave it to his sister. A gift beyond price.

Ruvek's face changes. 'Ah, you mean Luana.' Something seems to amuse her. 'Of course I remember her. She was very fond of that button. She wore it on a thread around her neck. She was quite a favourite with the girls.'

'Where is she?' he says, half-rising.

Ruvek opens her hands. 'I have no idea.'

He sits back down. He cannot form a single useful thought. It is Talaia who says, 'So she was here once?' Ruvek gives her an appreciative look, and nods. 'But you don't know where she is now? Could you tell us why?'

'Of course. She ran away.'

'Do you remember when?' Talaia asks.

Ruvek inclines her head as if considering. 'Now, when was it? Perhaps we should ask Voll. He doesn't forget things like that, do you, Voll?'

'About four years ago,' he mutters, fingering the scar on his face.

'As I recall, it wasn't the only mistake you made.' Ruvek's eyes glitter with spite. 'But you learned your lesson, didn't you?'

346

'What about my sister?' the boy says sharply.

'When Luana came to us she was too young to work, but she made herself useful. She became a very good cook. Trokas taught her.'

Too young to work. There is no need to ask what Ruvek means. The boy fights down nausea.

'Why did you call her Luana?' Talaia asks evenly.

'We had to call her something.' Ruvek's eyes linger on Talaia's face. 'The girls came up with it. Little Helper.'

The boy clenches his fists. 'She already had a name.'

'But we never found out what it was, because she never spoke.' Ruvek smiles at Talaia. 'It's a shame we lost her. I was just about to begin her training. She was going to be quite a beauty.'

The boy is on his feet, lunging at the desk. 'You evil old –'

Voll is instantly between them. Yorin's hand grips the boy's arm. Ruvek remains calmly watching, her eyes gloating.

'Forgive my friend,' Yorin says. 'I'm sure you'll understand it's not an easy time for him.'

'He has a lot to learn about the world.'

'I'll go to the magistrate,' the boy says furiously, 'I'm sure he'd be interested in what's going on here.'

'By all means. Ettu is a good friend. And a good customer.'

The boy's hands fall to his sides. His shoulders sag.

'Would you like to see your sister's room?' Ruvek asks. 'We clothed her, fed her and gave her somewhere to live. I wouldn't want you to think we didn't look after her.'

Voll leads him up a flight of stairs, his footsteps soundless on deep carpets. As they pass rows of closed doors, the boy hears a muffled thud, a shriek of laughter.

At the far end Voll stops. 'In there,' he says.

He stands on the threshold of a small, windowless room. It contains a bed, a chair and a faded yellow rug. He looks around, sensing nothing of Kara's spirit. He goes over to the bed and sits on the thin coverlet. His hands are cold; shivering, he rubs them together, thinking of the girl who invented a rich home life for caterpillars, who claimed to have named every one of a swarm of ants. The same girl who, as he once shouted, never shut up.

He stares blindly at the wall. This room is not someone he knows. There is nothing here for him.

Arun looks into the darkness. 'It finally made sense,' he says. 'The reason why Kara's name wasn't on the piece of paper Yorin took from the tribe of the House of Goash. It was because she never told them. They couldn't make her. I always knew she was a better person than me.'

Fierce pride overwhelms his pain. He falls silent, seeing nothing but the past.

Perfume lingers in the boy's nostrils and the back of his throat. Although the day is hot, it is a welcome change to the suffocating air of Ruvek's house. He can still hear the spite in her voice as they left. *I wish you luck in your search for your sister. But consider this: if we couldn't find her, what chance do you think you will have?*

'So,' Yorin says, 'where shall we start?'

'Here seems as good a place as any,' Talaia says.

A little way down the street Yorin stops. 'Don't move,' he says under his breath.

'What –' the boy begins, but Yorin has already spun round and is facing the man coming up behind them.

'Go on,' he says, 'give me an excuse.'

The man smiles grimly, hefting a thick club. A movement to the side catches the boy's eye, but before he can shout a warning Yorin draws his sword so fast it blurs the air. With a shout of pain another man drops to ground, clutching his shoulder. The man with the club lunges at Talaia but Yorin swings his sword again, catching him on the side of the head with the flat of the blade. He falls to the ground, stunned.

It happens so fast the boy has no time to react. 'Well,' Yorin says, sheathing his sword, 'it's about time it was broken in. Definitely worth the price.'

The boy turns quickly back to Talaia. She is standing very straight, her eyes blazing. 'Why didn't you kill them?' she asks furiously.

A slow grin spreads across Yorin's face. 'I should have left it to you.'

The boy is silent. He failed to protect his sister, and now he has failed to protect his wife.

'Come on,' Yorin says, 'time to go. And you can tell Ruvek' – he addresses the man with the bloodstained shoulder – 'I won't be so polite next time.'

All that day and the next they search the Velvet Quarter for news of Kara – Luana – without success.

'I think it's time to stop now, Arun. You need to rest.' Talaia is speaking to him, but he hardly hears.

'Talaia's right.' Yorin says. 'Let's try again tomorrow. Perhaps further afield.'

In the morning they widen their search, stopping people on the streets, asking in market squares, in shops and taverns. Either no one is willing to talk, or whatever information the city might once have held is lost.

'Don't give up hope,' Talaia says that evening. It is late; only a few people remain in the common room. 'Maybe tomorrow –'

The boy gets up abruptly and leaves the table. Talaia starts to rise, but Yorin puts a hand on her arm. 'Best leave him be,' he says.

The boy sits on the bed, turning the Book of Light in his hands. He opens it, hoping for words of comfort.

You are no longer with me.

He closes it again.

That night he reaches for Talaia in desperate need, seeking the absolution of her body. When he cries out, she holds him close, cradling him in her arms until he sleeps.

The light is barely breaking when he slips out of the room, leaving Talaia sleeping. Through the silent common room, into the street.

All morning he wanders, oblivious to the cries of market sellers, the scent of spices and coffee. Beside a graceful fountain he stops, letting droplets of water touch his face, taking his tears for their own. Right or wrong, he has come to a decision, and there is no going back.

Chapter Twenty-Five

'Arun! Where have you been?'

As he enters the inn, Talaia comes running to meet him.

'I've been so worried! Yorin's out looking for you. I stayed here in case you returned. I thought you might have gone back to the Perfumed Garden. I was frantic.'

He takes her hand. It is shaking. 'I just needed to be on my own for a while, to think. I'm sorry,' he says, stricken with remorse.

'You're safe now, and that's what matters.' She strokes his face. 'But don't do it again. Promise?'

He promises. Then he says, 'There's something I need to talk you about. But not here.'

Downstairs, a chair scrapes back. Talaia shifts on the bed, waiting. How can he tell her he can't do this any more, for two reasons, the first of which he can more easily acknowledge because it concerns Talaia herself? They are barely married, and their life has already been consumed by his search for his family. If he keeps on looking for his sister he knows she will go with him, but he also knows she deserves more, and better.

'It's been four years since Kara left here,' he says at last. 'We've looked for her everywhere, and we haven't found anything.'

'I know, but there's always –'

'Another day? Another scrap of hope? I can't keep doing this, to me or to you. Especially to you. I can't keep dragging you from place to place. It isn't fair.'

'But I don't see it that way, and it's nothing to do with it being fair or not. You're the man I love, Arun, the person I want to spend the rest of my life with. It doesn't matter where we are or what we're doing, as long as we're together. But it isn't just that, is it?' She studies his face.

No. But he would rather not face the second, deeper, reason at all. He knows how he felt after finding out what happened to his mother, and how he forced himself to go on. But now, having lost both parents, he cannot bear the thought of losing his sister too. As long as he doesn't know what has happened to her, he can allow himself to believe that somewhere she is safe and well. And that one day, when the time is right, he will find her again.

He has spent the last few endless hours compelling the logic of emotion into what he knows is a coward's argument, but it is all he has. What kind of brother – what kind of son – it makes him hardly bears consideration.

'Please, Arun, tell me,' Talaia says gently.

So he does, in part. He says that his life is with her, that she is his family now. He is done with the tribe of the House of Goash and with this city, whose beauty conceals a pitiless heart. It is time to look forward, to plan a life together. It is time to let go.

'Are you sure?' she asks softly.

'Quite sure.' He strokes her hair, breathing in the scent of honey and roses as she rocks him gently.

'Arun,' she says after a while, 'what you said about planning a life together – did you have anywhere in mind?'

Something in her voice makes the boy pull back slightly. 'I haven't really thought about it. Why?'

Talaia bites her lip. 'Promise not to be angry?'

He looks at her in surprise. 'Of course.'

'It's just that –' She pulls at the hem of her sleeve. 'There's something I have to tell you. I wanted to in Amala Dyssul, but it never seemed to be the right time. And I didn't tell you before because –' She breaks off.

'Then tell me now,' the boy says, his heart beginning to quicken.

'Aunt Ro and Uncle Ferec – they aren't my only family. I have a cousin in Mudaina, in the Suth Valley. I didn't mention it because I thought – well, I thought if you knew you might feel obliged to take me there, and I didn't want to go. Not just because of what happened in Kushtar but' – she looks at him shyly, defiantly – 'because I didn't want to leave you. And then it became lost in everything that was happening, and it didn't seem to matter so much any more. Please don't be cross with me.'

How can he be, after what she has told him? He pulls her close, and they sit holding each other. He thinks of Amala Dyssul, and their marriage. The brief days of peace that followed. Then he says, 'Your cousin? Mudaina?'

'My cousin, yes. She's called Meriem. Her father is my mother's older brother. I only met her once, a long time ago. She's married. That's really all I can remember. I wondered about going to visit them, since we don't have any other plans at the moment. It would give us time to work out what we want to do. I'm sure she'd make us welcome. But if you don't want to, that's fine,' she adds hastily.

353

The boy considers. Part of him resists, unwilling to share the start of their new life with someone else, particularly someone related to Talaia's aunt and uncle.

'We don't have to decide now,' she says, but the boy feels he does. It is important to put things behind him.

'If we can't stand it,' he says, 'we can always escape through a window.'

Talaia throws her arms around him, kissing him. 'Mudaina is in Hain province, but I've no idea where it is.'

'Yorin will know.'

They stare at each other.

'What are we going to tell him?' Talaia asks.

Yorin is waiting downstairs. He gives them a quizzical look. 'Everything all right?'

With a glance at Talaia the boy says, 'There's something we need to discuss with you.'

'Sounds serious. Do I need beer?'

If he is surprised by the boy's decision not to continue the search for his sister, he shows no sign. 'Mudaina?' He looks thoughtful. 'It's roughly south-west of here, over the northern Tura Lar. I've heard stories about them. As mountains go, they're not to be taken lightly. I'm not sure how Tobi will manage. I'll probably end up pushing him.' He grins. 'But I can't have you getting lost, not when you've come this far. And I've heard good things about the Suth Valley.'

When they leave Kerizon the following morning and cross the western causeway, the boy doesn't look back at the city on the lake. Their reflections ripple on the water as they pass.

Part Two

Chapter Twenty-Six

In Hain province, the new year is celebrated as the week-long festival of Kaba. It is as much a festival of thanksgiving for the year that has passed as a welcoming of the new one. The family's celebrations have always taken place in Meriem's house, and this year is no exception. '*All* my family,' she said. Since it will be the first new year in their own home the boy initially resisted, but, as Talaia pointed out, the family have given them so much it is the least they can do to repay their generosity.

Some weeks before the festival they discussed the issue of presents, given traditionally on the first day of the new year. It wasn't a question of money, since their share of last year's profits was more than ample – due, the boy suspects, in no small part to the kindness of Jabar – but, as Talaia said when they sat beside the fire in the white house one evening, what mattered was the thought that went into them.

'It's not about how much we spend, it's about showing the family how much we appreciate everything they've done for us. I thought we could make most of them ourselves. Don't look so worried,' she added, smiling as she got up.

A drawer in the bedroom opened and closed; she returned carrying a packet wrapped in tissue paper. It contained a piece of silk, butter-yellow, heavy and rich.

'Pera gave it to me before we left Amala Dyssul. It was her bride-cloth. She said I'd find a use for it.'

The boy saw again the red houses on the plain, the stone bench in the garden, a man sitting up in bed.

'I thought of making napkins and a tablecloth for Meriem,' Talaia said. 'There'll be enough left over for a ledger marker for Adri, and a bookmark for Jabar. We'll need something for Yentra and Vezu. And Birith, too, of course. What do you think?'

He hesitated. Talaia had made her feelings about sewing clear on more than one occasion. He hadn't realised he was sitting in silence until she knelt before him, taking his hands.

'You're worrying about me. There's no need, my love. Things change. I wasn't sure if I could do it, but – no,' she said honestly, 'they haven't changed. I'm dreading the idea of sewing, not just because I have a feeling the stitches will end up killing each other' – she made a face, and he laughed – 'but because a needle in my hand might feel like a weight around my ankle.'

He started to speak but she said, 'I've given it a lot of thought, and I want to do it. It's a way of giving something back. Besides, I can always cheat. Oh yes,' she said to his enquiring face, 'you don't think I'd leave it to chance, do you? I've asked around, and I've found a seamstress who will be able to' – she coughed delicately – 'rescue me if necessary. Why are you looking at me like that?'

He couldn't speak. He was laughing too much.

On the eve of the new year they sit beside the fire, wrapping presents. A pot of tea and a plate of taklaris sit on the small table beside Talaia. The presents have taken up most of her spare time and patience, but they are finished. The boy has been making things too, leather pouches for Adri and Jabar. As he worked, the skill came back to his hand as surely as if the spirit of Liso were watching over him. He took great care, making sure each stitch was precise, working intricate patterns into the leather.

As he wraps the pouches, he remembers the story Talaia told in the northern Tura Lar, on their way to Mudaina. About the girl, the miser's purse, and the house of treasure. When he mentions it, Talaia smiles. 'I'd forgotten about that,' she says. 'So much has happened since then. I can't believe it's only been a few months.'

She ties a ribbon in a neat bow, bending her head in concentration. The boy stares into the fire, remembering.

The northern Tura Lar ranged across and beyond the line of sight, buttress and battlement of dark-brown shadow rising to distant peaks of snow. As they crossed the plain the day before Yorin had stopped, whistled and said, 'Now that's what I call mountains.'

How, the boy wondered, would they ever find their way in? It turned out to be surprisingly easy, if you knew where to look. Yorin found the path into the foothills, little more than a thread, after only a short time. 'Instinct,' he said, leading Tobi forward.

The mountains hid their secrets well. They were not, as the boy imagined, a jagged mass of hard-packed rock riddled with paths and tracks, but small kingdoms of unexpected beauty. They stopped for lunch in a broad-sided valley leavened by tumbling streams. Yorin unsaddled Tobi, fed and watered him, then threw himself down on the grass under a small tree.

As they shared out bread and meat, the boy glanced across at the horse and said, 'Do you think he dreams of a flat road leading to a comfortable stable?'

Yorin laughed. 'I'm sure he dreams about many things, all ending in hay.'

That night, they made camp in a small glen whose waterfalls glimmered in the fading light. The boy and Talaia shared a blanket by the fire, listening to Yorin's stories. When Talaia asked for a poem, the boy found one about night,

its quarters of dusk, its dark bazaars.

In it, Mirashi wrote that she finally had time to count the stars, yet never arrived at the same number twice. Later, as Talaia slept in his arms, the boy looked up at the sky and gave thanks for the brightest star of all.

Morning took them into a deep gorge with sides of craggy rock. Catching a sudden movement in the tail of his eye, the boy turned, his heart racing. A small bird passed with the speed of silence, leaving an impression of crescent-shaped wings and bright black eyes.

Yorin was grinning broadly. 'Rock swallows,' he said. Handing Tobi's reins to Talaia, he climbed a little way up the side of the gorge. 'Look,' he called, and they saw, clinging to a low overhang, a little village of gourd-shaped nests. They seemed precarious, fragile.

'How do they stay there?' the boy asked as Yorin joined them again.

'A wing and a prayer.'

The boy wondered what would happen if a swallow grew fat. Talaia laughed. 'The nest would fall down.'

'And how would they get back up?'

'They'd build a ladder, of course,' she replied, her eyes sparkling.

Yorin shook his head. 'You two,' he said, but his eyes were soft, and he was smiling.

Swallows accompanied them as they made their way up the gorge, skimming their ankles, brushing their shoulders. 'They're warning us off,' Yorin said. 'They'll have youngsters in the nest – probably their third brood.'

'Third?' Talaia looked startled.

'You can never have too many,' Yorin said with a mischievous smile. She flushed slightly, looking away.

At the mouth of the gorge, they turned back to watch the swallows. 'It's good luck to have them in your house,' Talaia told the boy.

'Then we'll make them welcome,' he said. Talk of houses felt so responsible, so grown up. Part of him thrilled with delight; another part quaked with constant vertigo.

They came out of the gorge onto a broad sill of rock. Below them, a long slope dropped steeply away. Tobi shied, throwing back his head. The boy silently agreed with his assessment.

'How do we get down?' he asked.

'Slowly,' Yorin said.

Halfway down, a faint sound made the boy glance up. Straining his eyes, he thought he saw a puff of dust, as if made by the displacement of small stones. He froze, listening intently, but nothing moved.

'What is it?' Talaia asked.

'Just a rabbit,' he said. Enough, he told himself firmly. No one was following. He had left them far behind.

At the foot of the slope they pitched what Talaia called a half-tent, a cloth canopy open to the evening air. On the small fire a pan sizzled and spat with browning meats. They hadn't, the boy thought, entirely abandoned the grist of civilisation. Put a man in the wilderness and he will make an approximation of what he knows. He breathed in the smell of smoke, spitting fat, frying meat, thinking that it wouldn't be a bad thing to sit here forever, Talaia beside him, Yorin testing the meat with his knife, Tobi snorting quietly as the nimbus of night grew around them.

'Your turn for a story,' Yorin said after the meal, sitting back comfortably.

The boy's mind went blank. Talaia looked thoughtful. 'This,' she said, 'is a tale about a girl and a miser's purse.'

The miser hid his treasure in a house in a village some miles from his home. The village had been abandoned many years ago, to plague. People called it *Mortuan*, 'place of no return'. No one went there any more – it was rumoured to be full of weeping souls. The boy shivered.

Talaia explained that the purse had been with the miser for so long it was desperate for a change. It dropped from the miser's belt and was found by a young girl, who picked it up and ran away. Then, feeling guilty, she was about to ask around to find out who the purse belonged to when it spoke to her, begging her not to return it to the miser. Being a kind-hearted girl, she agreed. The purse was so grateful it told her about the house of treasure in the plague village. The girl's family were poor; after some thought, she decided to go looking for it.

Talaia's description of the girl's midnight journey, her growing fear as she reached the village and made her way through the empty streets, was so vivid that when a bird shrieked somewhere in the darkness the boy almost jumped out of his skin.

They followed the girl into the deserted house, wincing as she hit her knee on the large wooden chest containing the miser's treasure, the purse directing her to a small niche in the wall where the key was kept.

'She took away as much as she could carry,' Talaia said, 'and used it to help her family, and to set up a school that was open to anyone who wanted to learn.' The boy smiled in the firelight. 'She kept the purse,' Talaia added, 'and passed it down to her daughter. And' – with a smile at her audience – 'they lived happily ever after, naturally. Although I'm not sure what the miser felt about it.'

Yorin started to clap. The boy joined in. The story was told with skill and style, and he told her so. There was no envy any more, only pride in his wife's accomplishment.

'Sleep well,' Yorin said as they settled down later. 'Don't worry, Tobi doesn't believe in ghosts.'

Just as he was falling asleep the boy thought he saw, a little way beyond their camp, twin points of light, like eyes reflected by the fire. He looked again, but the darkness was complete.

He was already awake when the sun, eternal firebird, crested the mountains. Quietly, trying not to disturb Talaia, he pulled the Book of Light from his pocket and let the well-thumbed little book fall open. Talaia stirred, opening her eyes. 'Tell me,' she said sleepily.

Two thousand years from here
Adoula considers the morning.

Sun is her head-note, moon is her spirit,
folding the rich hours round her again
as if they have no shadow.

When he finished reading, Talaia was quiet for a moment. 'You should write one,' she said. The idea excited and appalled him.

'It would be like a buffalo doing needlework,' he said a little wildly.

She laughed. Then, thoughtfully, 'I don't think so.'

After the slope, to walk on level ground was a welcome relief. They followed a small gritty path between towering cliffs. By mid-afternoon they rounded a corner, and the sheer sides fell away. Wild flowers – scarlet, blue, yellow, white – embroidered a meadow of nodding grasses. The air was crystalline, heady.

'Oh,' Talaia said softly. Suddenly she dropped her bundle, raised her arms and turned in a wild circle, her tunic flaring around her. It was a moment the boy would remember for the rest of his life.

'Look.' Yorin was pointing.

'Aren't they –' the boy began.

'Beehives,' Talaia finished giddily.

Only when he had taken in the dome-shaped structures

clouded with bees did the boy see the houses, spread out across a long, shallow slope like a collection of white stone boxes. At the far side of the meadow, a well-kept path took them to the outskirts of the village. A dog started barking. Tobi snorted, tossing his head.

'Nearly dinner time,' Yorin said.

The boy's stomach agreed. Talaia laughed. 'All I have to do to know what time it is . . .' Her eyes brimmed with affection. The boy was overcome with such love he hardly knew where he was. Every time he looked at Talaia was a first time for his eyes. Perhaps she knew, because she reached up and touched his face tenderly.

'Hopefully we'll have a proper bed tonight,' she murmured, and the look in her eyes made him swallow hard.

Someone was coming along the path, a small man with a smile on his face. He greeted them with a bow, introducing himself as Tafu and asking if they had travelled far.

'A fair way,' Yorin said. 'We're tired, and we could do with a good meal. Is there somewhere we can stay for the night?'

'Of course. Please, come with me.' Tafu used his arm as a gate; Yorin, Tobi, the boy and Talaia passed through, into the village of Limora. Fluffy chickens scratched in the dirt; a goat bleated loudly.

'From Kerizon,' Yorin said in answer to Tafu's question. 'And before that, Amala Dyssul.'

'A long way, then,' Tafu said, inviting them to spend the night in his family's house. There was, he told them, stabling for Tobi in an adjoining building.

The main room of Tafu's house was large, simply furnished, and full of people. After introductions – Tafu's wife Rin and their three children; his brother Tarim; Tarim's wife Nir and her sister Zala, who had a small child attached to her trouser leg – everyone began speaking at once. The boy and Talaia stood hand in hand, her calmness like a silver thread between them.

Nir was asking about the embroidery on Talaia's tunic. 'It is very fine,' she said admiringly. 'It must have been made by someone with big eyes.'

Talaia laughed. 'Yes, and a lot of patience. I hate needlework. I could never sit still long enough.'

'It is important to be able to do it,' Nir said. 'When your children come, it will make their clothes pretty.' She tilted her head and her look was warm, appraising. Talaia smiled faintly.

In a short time they learned that Tafu's brother lived in the house opposite with Nir, Zala and her daughter Rosi, that they kept goats for milk, cheese and meat, and were very proud of the honey their bees made.

As they gathered around a large table, the boy returned to what Nir said. If the thought of children had crossed his mind, it was a vague idea belonging to some distant future, no more substantial than mist or gossamer. He wondered what Talaia felt about it, suspecting a sturdier proposition, not mist or gossamer but fruit on a tree, perhaps. He realised, too, that he had no idea what she would want to do when they finally found a home. She was not like the girls in his village. They had been straightforward, like alphabet books for children, a letter to a page, an accompanying picture to remove any chance of misunderstanding.

Was he being entirely fair? All he'd known of them was the ribbons in their hair and their quick laugh when a young man walked past. If he'd stayed, he might have learned their language. But he would never have met Talaia.

'Your husband is a deep one,' Nir said. Her smile was kind, and wise.

'He is.' Talaia took his hand under the table.

As they ate their fill of stew enriched with apricots and sultanas, Tafu and his family asked many questions about where they had been, Amala Dyssul in particular. Their interest was as warm as their welcome. When Talaia told them they were going to Mudaina, Tafu said, 'Ah, the Suth Valley. Have you been there before? No? Well then, I won't spoil it for you.'

The boy lay awake beside Talaia. He had drunk so much coffee constellations were forming in his head. Listening to her peaceful breathing, he thought about where they had been, where they were going, and what would happen when they did. Were their actions entirely their own, or did something else, some other agency, play a part?

Talaia stirred, and he stroked her arm thoughtfully. What did he believe in? What didn't he believe in? He knew the world turned in spite of, went on without need of, him or his beliefs. Then he thought, a coin thrown into a well is still a coin. It was up to him to make it into a wish. The responsibility frightened him.

'I can hear you thinking,' Talaia said sleepily.

'Sorry,' he whispered.

She opened her eyes. 'Tell me.' When he did she lay

quietly for a while, stroking his hair. He could hear the smile in her voice as she said, 'It's the middle of the night and you're worrying about destiny?'

He frowned slightly. Surely one word couldn't cover everything he'd just been thinking?

'In the end,' Talaia said, 'isn't it up to you to choose what to believe in? My father believed that everything he did was determined by him, and he never changed his mind about it. Although I suppose it can be a comfort to think that what happens isn't entirely your doing.'

'What do you think?' the boy asked. It was important to him to know.

'Well,' she said slowly, 'I don't see anything wrong with doing what you can with your life, and telling yourself that if something doesn't work out, it wasn't meant to be. If it gives you peace of mind, what's wrong with that?'

Nothing, he thought, as she put her arms around his neck and began to kiss him.

It had rained in the night, and the air felt refreshed. Before they left, Rin presented them with a basket of food and leather flasks of apple juice. Yorin's offer of payment was waved away and replaced with three earthenware jars of honey. Tobi snorted briskly, none the worse, Yorin observed, for sharing a room with goats.

When they reached the top of the slope, they entered a tableland of grass chomped flat by Limora's goats. Although the ground was level the boy felt as if he were walking downhill, perhaps because the mountains were beginning to fall away.

The path through the foothills was wide and clear, as

Tafu said it would be. Birds twittered and chirruped in the undergrowth. A hawk keened in the late summer heat.

'What is it?' the boy asked.

'Muttonhawk,' Yorin said, glancing up.

'Does it really carry off lambs?' Talaia asked.

'Only if it has a sack,' Yorin said. Tobi whinnied. 'Don't worry, you'd never fit.'

That evening they camped in a small wooded crease of the hills. Yorin made a fire, and they settled on blankets as night came in. Rin's basket contained a large meat pie, a loaf of bread, some cheese and milk. When the pie was eaten, they opened a jar of honey and spread it on toasted bread.

'Those bees deserve prizes,' Yorin said appreciatively.

For a while they sat in restful silence.

'I've given it a name,' Talaia announced. '*Iristelnadomisel.*' The boy goggled at her. 'It means "place of fragrant woodsmoke where three people sit around a fire".' Firelight caught the gleam in her eye.

'It's an excellent name,' he said hastily.

Yorin propped himself up on his elbow. 'What language is it?'

'My own,' she said, her tone faintly challenging. The boy wondered if words were like cheeses, some ready to use, others needing time to mature.

'And some,' Yorin said, 'are real stinkers.' The boy started laughing, mostly at the look on Talaia's face.

A little way off, Tobi snorted and stamped, pulling at the grass. 'Some languages say things without taking all day about it,' Yorin said thoughtfully.

'Such as?' Talaia asked.

'Such as the Mayurs, who use two words to stand for everything. The meaning is in the delivery. It takes from the time you're born to the time you die to master the inflections. They only started out with one, of course.'

'One?' Talaia asked in a dangerous voice.

He nodded. 'Apparently a visitor asked for roasted meat, but it was mistranslated as rhubarb. The Mayurs had never heard of it before, but the rules of hospitality meant they had to provide it if they possibly could. They used a month's grain money to buy it. After that, they banned all visitors unless they could speak the language. That's when they added the second word.'

'I know I'm going to regret it,' the boy said, 'but what was it?'

'Rhubarb.'

The path was bearing them up again, so gradually the boy hardly felt it. The air was misty, the grass damp with dew. Only when they reached the crown of a long ridge did he see how far they had come.

Talaia touched his arm. 'Look,' she said, and together they stood looking out over the Suth Valley.

Although it had been in his thoughts many times lately, nothing could have prepared him for the fair green country laid out before his eyes. Within it lay a sprawling city of light-brown stone. To the east of the city fields of crops, orchards in full summer ripeness, a broad silver river. To the west, wooded grasslands intersected by a great crossroads. North, south and east, the Tura Lar Mountains offered shelter and protection.

'Mudaina,' Yorin said. 'Unsung gem of Hain province.'

Talaia was standing very still. The boy squeezed her hand, thinking of Mirashi's poem about a woman at the end of her life. She described it as climbing a mountain.

At the top she hesitates –
her singing-robes will fill with moths,
she'll become an absent figure,
the blind side of a temple banner.

But this was a beginning, not an end. Or so he hoped, as they made their way down the hillside, to Mudaina.

Chapter Twenty-Seven

The entrance to the city was marked not by imposing gates but two square, red-roofed towers set among the houses in a roughly central position. The towers were linked by a long porch with a shallow, sloping roof. There were no guards or watchmen since, as Yorin remarked, you could get into Mudaina a hundred different ways.

The directions they had been given were clear and concise which, in this city of winding streets and alleyways, had saved them from getting lost. At the head of a pleasant, tree-lined street they came to a stop. Large wooden gates were set at intervals in the walls.

As they stood looking, someone came out of a door in a gate halfway down. It was a woman, comfortably plump in a dove-grey dress, her dark-brown hair caught over one shoulder in a long plait. She made her way along the twilit street, looked up, and saw them.

For a moment she stared, then her face changed. Her voice carried in the still air. 'It's never? It can't be –'

Calling Talaia's name, she hurried towards them. Talaia started walking; they both began running; there was laughter, hugs, kisses, tears. The ring on Talaia's finger was inspected; the boy was introduced, lightly held by two assessing arms, and drawn into a hug.

'I don't believe it!' Meriem cried repeatedly. The boy stood dazed as she shook hands with Yorin and patted Tobi. 'Now,' she said, 'you must come and meet the family.'

Arm in arm with Talaia, she led them down the street. 'You can leave your horse here for the moment, it's quite safe,' she told Yorin as they reached the gate.

'For who?' he asked with a grin, knotting the reins.

The door in the gate led into a large square courtyard where a fountain was playing. A covered veranda skirted the walls. It was deep enough to hold a substantial table and a number of chairs, one of which was occupied by an elderly man with an abundance of white hair. The boy took in a profusion of flowers spilling from hanging baskets before returning to the elderly man, who was regarding them with interest and faint surprise.

Meriem crossed the courtyard, talking rapidly, telling him they had visitors, little Talaia, would you believe it, and with a husband, too? The elderly man rose slowly, smiling broadly, opening his arms wide.

'Uncle?' Talaia took a few steps, and ran to envelop him in a hug.

'My father, Jabar,' Meriem said as Talaia beckoned the boy forward. A little self-conscious, he stood in front of the elderly man, who took his hands and shook them warmly.

'You are most welcome, husband of the cousin of my daughter,' he said. Before the boy could work his way through the tangle of relations, another man came out of the house. He was younger, mild-faced, with light-brown eyes. Meriem flew to him and pulled him towards them. He extended his hand, introducing himself as Adri, Meriem's husband. The boy was beginning to feel overwhelmed. A new family had grown around him in minutes.

Adri gave him a swift, searching look. 'Come and sit down,' he said, 'you must be tired.' He called into the house and a man came out. He was small, with neat features and bright eyes. Meriem gave instructions and the man, Vezu, disappeared into the house as another man appeared, taller and thickset.

'Birith will take your horse to the stables,' Meriem told Yorin. They were, the boy gathered, situated at the back of the house.

'Come and meet them, don't be shy.' Meriem was speaking to someone in the shadow of the doorway. A woman emerged, her short, sturdy form enclosed in a multi-coloured apron. She giggled. 'This is Yentra,' Meriem said. Yentra giggled again. The boy would discover that his first impression of a head full of bubbles was misleading. She was the only member of the household Meriem trusted at market, and salted the traders with her bargaining skills until they stung.

'I think we'll have supper out here,' Meriem said, and Yentra disappeared into the house, returning a short while later with Vezu. Each carried a laden tray. As he filled his plate, the boy tried to remember names. Yentra poured him a large glass of lemon juice – 'from our own lemons,' Adri said – and he sat in half a daze, listening to the chatter and laughter of people who seemed so ready – so happy – to welcome him.

'And where did you two meet?' Meriem asked, with a glance at the boy's wedding ring. Adri and Jabar had heard of the caves of Linshafan, and listened as Talaia told them about the old man, the chambers, the Goddess of Eternal Spring. Meriem's voice wove through it, asking about the food, how Talaia managed in such difficult conditions, complimenting her hair, her clothes, touching her hand fondly.

The hut in the valley had never felt so far away. Hearing his name, the boy turned to see Adri looking at him. 'Once Meriem's off, there's no stopping her,' he said with an apologetic smile. 'What about you? Where are you from, if you don't mind me asking?'

'Harakim,' the boy said. He and Talaia had discussed it one evening in the mountains, whispering in the firelight. It was easier, they agreed, for the time being. Adri seemed content, and asked no further questions.

A natural hush had fallen. The boy glanced at Talaia, who squared her shoulders and said, 'There's something I have to tell you. About Aunt Ro and Uncle Ferec.'

The atmosphere changed. Adri looked down at his hands; Jabar seemed to be studying the scarlet bell-shaped flowers cascading from a hanging basket.

Suddenly Meriem started laughing, a rich, infectious chuckle. The boy and Talaia exchanged startled glances. She laughed so hard she clutched her sides to steady herself, saying in little gasps, 'We already know. They wrote to us. They were furious. We' – she wiped her eyes – 'had to handle the letter with fire tongs.' Jabar shook his head slightly – Talaia's aunt was his sister, after all – but his eyes crinkled.

'So,' Meriem said when she had composed herself again, 'tell us all about it. Don't leave anything out.'

It was late, coffee had been drunk, cakes eaten. Soon Meriem was leading them through the main hallway and up a long flight of stairs. Judging by the length of the corridor and the number of doors leading off it, the house was very large. The boy and Talaia were setting down their things when Yentra bustled in with a bowl of steaming water and towels. Laying the bowl carefully on a cloth on a pretty chest of drawers, she placed towels at either side, twitched one slightly so it aligned with the top of the drawer, and hurried out.

They were alone in the spacious white room whose window let in the drifting pollens of night. The sky-blue coverlet on the bed was heaped with velvet cushions; cabinets at either side held bowls of scented petals. Much of the floor was covered with a thick cream rug whose pattern of russet leaves reminded the boy of autumn woods.

Talaia took his hand and led him to the window. Beyond it, the sky loomed vast. 'It went well, didn't it, all things considered?' she asked.

He had for a moment forgotten where they were, thinking only of being here with his wife, looking at the stars, wondering if he could make them sing for her. 'I wish I could,' he said out loud.

'Could what?' she asked, and smiled when he told her. 'They do,' she said, 'every time you tell me you love me.'

In the gleam of the moon, Arun's eyes are sad. 'When Meriem came into our room the next morning to bring us breakfast, after the initial shock it didn't feel awkward. It was more kindness than intrusion. She was so happy for us, so generously determined to help us out.'

He takes a breath 'It was a good house,' he says. 'Whole-hearted in its making and its living.'

After breakfast, Meriem offered to show them around Mudaina. Yorin was with them as they walked down the long street into a broader one, keeping to the cooler side as the sun's heat warmed the walls. They came eventually into a wide square set about with shops and official buildings. Meriem pointed them out: the City Hall, the library, the covered market, the various guilds of artisans. Then, with a smile and a wave, she left them.

'Shopping,' she said. 'There's a feast to prepare – it's not every day your cousin and her husband come to stay.'

Later that night the boy lay in bed, misty around the edges from the good red wine. As the evening passed, he'd lost count of how many dishes were set before him. The lentils had been a particular triumph, richly spiced in a great earthenware dish painted many years before by Jabar's wife, Sireen. When she came to the city as a young woman, she brought it with her. Jabar told them that the blue flowers were a symbol of her village; the green vines around the rim, clustered with purple grapes, represented her family's vineyards. And the white birds at the centre were birds of peace.

Meriem had touched his arm gently. 'No,' he said with a smile, 'I have no need to mourn her. She is here.' He put his hand to his chest, raised his cup and said, 'Thank you.'

Talaia squeezed the boy's hand; he turned his head to meet her shining eyes. In the glowing lamplight he thought *thank you* so hard she must surely have heard him.

Meriem had gone to market with Talaia. Adri was in his chambers where, the boy learned yesterday evening, he worked as an advocate. He was sitting on the veranda with Yorin, whose chair was tilted back against the wall in his usual fashion.

Stirring a little, Yorin said, 'So.'

'So,' the boy agreed, since nothing else seemed necessary. Tobi was settled comfortably in the stables. They were large and deep, with hinged shutters to cover the top half when required.

The boy sipped his coffee thoughtfully. If Yorin were to lose his horse, would it make him a different person? Slower, of course, but would he still be –

'I can hear you from here,' Yorin remarked lazily. 'One day it'll all burst out, and we'll have a hell of a job putting it back again.'

After a leisurely lunch, Jabar said, 'There's something I'd like to show you both.'

The boy glanced at Talaia, who smiled a little anxiously. Something clutched at him as they followed Meriem and Jabar through the house, into the large, high-ceilinged kitchen where Yentra was working, and out through the open back door. To the left of a large square yard, Tobi looked out from one of the stables. To the right, an open-sided shed housed carts and a wagon. The boy was struck again by how much was concealed behind the wooden gate.

At the far side of the yard, the back gate opened into a long lane. The light broadened as they followed Jabar down the lane and onto a dirt track running into the green country the boy had seen from the high ridge. The track glittered like powdered gold in the afternoon sun. Across the valley, green hills rose into greater mountains.

'The eastern Tura Lar,' Jabar told them. 'The Peluin flows down from the northern range. We've owned land in the Suth Valley for generations.'

People working in the fields stopped to call out greetings as they passed. Meriem pointed out who the fields belonged to. 'And these,' she said, 'are Pangur's. He had more, but he had to sell them. His mother was ill, and she couldn't work any more. He still grows barley, and we help with the harvest.' The boy thought of his father's wheatfield.

As they came to the end of the track and joined the broad path running across it, Jabar stopped, letting them take in the view. Below a shallow grassy bank lay the Peluin River, wide and glittering. And beyond that, the full sweep of the Suth Valley.

'Our land,' Jabar said with pride, his outstretched arm encompassing a good deal of the valley. 'The soil is very good, and we have a long growing season. The mountains give us just the right weather – rain, but not too much, sun, but not too strong. We grow wheat, barley, corn . . .'

He glanced at Meriem. 'Squashes, potatoes, onions, beans, peas, cabbages, tomatoes' – she ticked them off her fingers – 'and, of course, the fruit. Apples, pears, plums, peaches, cherries, apricots, oranges, lemons, melons and pomegranates. I'm sure I've forgotten something.'

'Nuts,' Jabar said with a straight face.

The boy's eye followed the curve of the river. In the distance, beyond an arched stone bridge, he saw a small boat, sketchy in the sunlight. He could just make out two thin lines, one raised at an angle, the other running into the water. Someone was fishing. He turned to find the family looking at him. They seemed to be waiting for something, so he asked if there were many fish in the river.

'Oh yes,' Meriem said enthusiastically, 'lots.' Exchanging a look with Talaia, she said, 'Come on, there's more to see.'

He was silent as they walked along the path, wondering what lay ahead. A little way down Jabar turned right, into a lane. Along it ran a row of white houses, their roof tiles weathered a warm red-brown. The boy counted eight in all. A very short village. Chickens crooned as they picked at the dust. How did their owners know which was which – the arrangement of the feathers, the shape of a beak, the noise they made? If he were the owner of a chicken that refused to shut up, he would quickly fail to recognise it.

Jabar stopped outside the first house. It had the look of an empty place that was still cared for. He showed them into a large, airy room whose dark wood floor glowed in the light of the windows at either side of the door. In the right-hand wall was a fireplace broad enough to duck into, in the opposite wall another window. Chairs, tables, shelves, shutters, created impressions the boy couldn't quite make into a whole.

They followed Jabar through a door at the back of the room, into a spacious kitchen whose fireplace had a sooty hearth flanked by a clay oven and a tall cupboard. A scrubbed table and chairs, a pump and sink, shelves piled with pots and pans, utensils hanging from hooks overhead, and a window at the back, looking out over – the boy and Talaia walked towards it – a walled garden, broad and deep, full of flowers, shrubs and trees, shady places to sit. He found himself noting it all down as if his eyes were a pen, his mind a sheet of paper.

He could feel Talaia's hand trembling slightly as they went into the garden. As they walked, Jabar pointed out cherry, magnolia, fig and plum, roses and flowering shrubs, a magnificent jasmine under which was set a curved stone bench. At the end of the garden he led them to a wooden table and chairs. When they were seated, he explained that the family's storage barns were across the lane. The boy felt calm, yet light-headed.

'What do you think?' Meriem asked.

Everyone was looking at him. He felt as if he were in a pen being stared at by farmers who chewed and scratched and brushed away a fly. The thought was unworthy of these people and their kindness.

'I like it very much,' he said.

Jabar told them that he and Sireen had lived here when they were first married, and so had Meriem and Adri.

'It hasn't been used for some time now, but Vezu comes in to do the garden. Adri and I aren't farmers,' Meriem said. 'We keep an eye on things, and get people in when we need to, but –' She broke off, and the boy wondered if it would be up to him to put the pieces back together.

'We hire people to work the land,' Jabar said. 'Some of them live in Mirza.' Which the boy took to mean the very short village. 'They do a good job, work hard, but it would be better if someone was on hand, to manage things.' He cleared his throat. 'It would be good to know that someone in the family was looking after it again.'

Beside the boy, Talaia is very still.

'I don't know what your plans are,' Jabar continued, 'but we wondered if you'd consider taking it on. We'd show you what to do, of course, you wouldn't be on your own.' After a short silence he said, 'I know it's a lot to think about, and you'll want to discuss it. Whatever decision you make, you're most welcome to treat this house as your own for as long as you like.'

After dinner, the boy and Talaia sat on the veranda as the stars grew bright. Taking his hand, Talaia said, 'Shall we talk about it?'

They talked for a long time and yet there was nothing, really, to discuss. He knew Talaia had been looking for a place to settle and here it was, presented, remarkably, with no struggle or hardship. He also knew that although she wanted it very much, she was waiting to see how he felt. He wanted to laugh, to say, *Don't you know I'd do anything for you?* but understood her need for discussion, negotiation. That way they wouldn't go one-sided into what would become their home.

When he said yes, she kept asking him if he was sure until he held up his hand and declared an end to the subject. She threw her arms around him and kissed him, and pulled him inside to tell the family. The long, happy evening went deep into the night, translated by morning into a dry mouth and a fuzzy head.

The days that followed were full, and good. Only one thing concerned the boy: money. He had some of his own, saved during his time with the merchant, and Talaia had the small amount her father left her, but it wouldn't last forever. The problem was solved when Jabar took him aside, saying he'd like to talk to him. When the boy insisted Talaia was present, Jabar's forehead creased briefly, then he told them he and his wife had shared the decisions in their marriage.

Touching his arm, Talaia said, 'Then you were the wise one.'

It was a good thing to say; Jabar smiled at her, explaining that the family would provide for them in the first year, while they were settling in and getting to know the land. The profits would be divided between them and the rest of the family. This, the boy thought, was more than generous.

In the years to come, Jabar continued, provision would gradually be reduced until the boy and Talaia were able to support themselves. 'Balancing the scales,' he said, using his hands to demonstrate. He had no doubt they'd manage, but if things became difficult they were to let the family know. There was to be no hardship; they were grateful for their good fortune and thankful they could help others.

The boy looked down at his feet. It was as if he had opened his hands and bounty had poured into them. He remembered what Yorin said about gratitude. When he looked up, Jabar was watching him. 'It isn't a favour, Arun,' he said gently. 'The house needs to be lived in, the land looked after. It will be hard work, and we're trusting you with it.'

The migration was gradual. Although the house was well-provisioned, Talaia made it clear she wanted them to put their own mark on it. 'We can have a meadow indoors,' she said when they stood at a market stall in front of a carpet of fine wool. They bought the carpet. They bought other things too; packages and parcels piled up until Yorin made a comment about a sinking vessel, and Talaia glared at him.

'I'm glad to see there's still an edge to you,' he remarked.

At dinner that evening, Meriem required a thorough inventory of what they had bought.

'Going soft,' Yorin commented with a shake of his head. 'Nothing a few months in the fields won't cure.'

Jabar lifted a finger, as if it contained his thoughts. 'It will not do,' he said, 'for Talaia to be working in the fields.' After a crisp pause inclining to frost, Yentra brought out a pudding so deep in cream it created an entirely different silence.

Later, they discussed it. Talaia was frowning. 'Is this how it's going to be? I'm supposed to abide by stupid conventions because they're – stupid conventions? Because I'm Meriem's cousin and Jabar's niece, I should know my place? Which isn't in the fields,' she added with a flash of anger.

The boy stared at her. How could she possibly think that?

'Of course not,' he said. 'Your place is wherever you want it to be. I thought you knew that.'

For a while she looked out of the bedroom window without speaking. 'I sound ungrateful, don't I?' she said more calmly. 'I'm not, at all. But when you're surrounded by people with good intentions, freedom somehow becomes more important.' She sighed. 'Everything has happened so quickly I don't think either of us has had time to take a breath.' She touched his face. 'It won't feel like a prison to you, will it?'

The boy looked into her anxious grey eyes. 'It's a beginning. Our beginning. But we need to talk to each other, tell each other how we feel. Otherwise things become so tangled you can't find your way out.'

'I'm good at undoing knots,' she said with a thoughtful look at the neck of his shirt. 'I think I'll start with this one.'

Two weeks later, they stood with the family outside the white house in Mirza. A dour-looking bay horse stamped in the shafts of a cart filled with their new belongings. The family seemed to be waiting for something.

'My wife was very light; it made things easier,' Jabar said, smiling. It took a moment for the boy to remember the custom of carrying a newly made bride across the threshold. He glanced nervously at Talaia, who was stroking the sleeve of her tunic rather stiffly.

'Go on,' Meriem said, nudging him.

He wondered if a bonfire gave out as much heat as Talaia's eyes. Perhaps if he tried an ambush . . . ?

She glanced sideways, and he caught her secret grin. Pushing up his sleeves, he advanced. She started giggling as he gathered her up, catching her waist, lifting her with a slight jump.

Her eyes were filled with light as he steadied her in his arms and advanced to the front door. Even as his mind was working out how to press the latch while holding the warm, silky weight – which was no weight at all – of the girl in his arms, Adri pushed the door open. Everyone shouted and cheered as they crossed the threshold, then Talaia fell out of his arms, laughing, as the family came through the door.

Chapter Twenty-Eight

'What are you smiling about?' Talaia asks, putting down a half-wrapped present.

'I was thinking about when we first moved in.'

She smiles. 'Has your back recovered yet?'

'You were light as a feather,' he says.

'For that, you can have some more taklaris.'

He watches her go into the kitchen, then turns back to the fire.

The first morning in their new house. Their home. The boy lay drowsing, enjoying the contrast to the bustle and chatter of yesterday.

When everything had been brought in they'd stood outside the door, lifting their faces to the air.

'Time for lunch,' Meriem said. 'We can either go back to our house, or – but you don't want us cluttering up the place. You've probably had enough of us for one day.'

With a glance at the boy Talaia said, 'I think it would be nice to have lunch here, to break the house in.' It made him think of Tobi. At least, he reflected, a house wasn't likely to gallop away.

With a delighted smile, Meriem had immediately started organising. The boy found himself indoors with

Yentra, who was pulling out plates and dishes. When they were all assembled, Jabar brought out a tissue-wrapped package and put it on the table. He looked promptingly at Talaia and she opened it, taking out a length of embroidered white linen. Carefully she unfolded it, laying it lengthwise across the table. A story was stitched into the cloth.

'This is me, and this is Sireen.' Jabar touched two tiny embroidered figures standing hand in hand. 'And here –' The figures walked in green fields, looked out from the arched bridge, stood outside the white house, the woman with a small bundle in her arms. 'You,' Jabar said to Meriem.

'Me,' she echoed, touching the silks of her mother and herself. As they followed the story to Meriem and Adri's marriage, the boy put his arm around Talaia.

Three-quarters of the way across, the embroidery stopped. Jabar touched Talaia's hand. 'It is for you to continue, you see?'

She couldn't speak, so the boy said, 'I seem to remember something about you and sewing?'

She clouted his arm softly. 'I'll learn.'

They had lunch on the bare wood of the table. The embroidered cloth had been folded away because, as Meriem said, olive oil and linen were not good companions. Afterwards, the boy felt as stuffed as the olives he had eaten.

'That,' Adri declared, 'was a good meal.'

Meriem glanced at Yentra, who ducked down and produced a large round cake studded with honeycomb. 'A hearth-cake,' Meriem told them. 'It means you and your house will be blessed.'

'Especially if you manage to eat any of it,' Yorin remarked. As Yentra tipped a large slice onto his plate, he met the boy's eyes with a smile.

The tantalising scent of warm bread and hot coffee made the boy sit up. He looked around the bedroom, a cosy room and now a pretty one, made so by the things Talaia had bought. A sky-blue rug stitched with pink and yellow flowers. A chest of drawers made of pale wood, fretted and pierced with arabesques and scrolls. On it, a cream-coloured jug and basin, Talaia's hair combs and pieces of jewellery. Two low chairs with curved backs and plump cushions, a carved wooden chest for linen, another for clothes.

All this in one room, the boy thought, smiling as Talaia brought in the breakfast tray and fed him apricots until he thought he would pop. Much later, morning began again.

That evening, when Meriem and Jabar had left, they went for a walk. The boy wanted to see the river, Talaia the orchards. Some of the inhabitants of Mirza had already introduced themselves. A family of five, all of whom worked for Jabar. A carpenter and his wife, a candlemaker. A weaver and her husband, whose nose threatened to overwhelm the living room. The boy had focused hard on the man's eyes as Talaia's hand tightened in his.

They made their way to the bridge and ran hand in hand up the arched stone back. There they stood as the river flowed on below them.

'We could almost walk on the clouds,' the boy said as they watched the mountains mirrored in the silver-blue water.

'It's a good thing one of us keeps her feet on the ground,' Talaia remarked.

He threw her a glance. 'Not for long,' he said, scooping her up into his arms before she had time to protest.

Wind stirred the branches as they walked between rows of ancient apple trees ripe with fruit. Their bark was silvery, their leaves curling. Talaia reached up and plucked a rosy-green apple. 'Taste,' she said, and he bit into crisp sweetness. A drop of juice ran down his chin, and she caught it with her finger and licked it up. The low sun tawny in her hair, her face half mischief, half something else, kindled slow heat as she pulled him gently down into the grass.

They had been expecting the knock.

'We've brought breakfast,' Meriem said. 'A good night's sleep gives you an appetite.' Talaia met her gaze steadily, a faint warmth in her cheek.

The boy stood alone in the living room, looking out at the fields beyond. The river would be shining in the morning sun, a boat letting down a hopeful line, perhaps. He wondered if there would be time for such things in his life.

They were coming back in. 'Could you put these out, my love?' Talaia asked, and he laid the table, setting each place with a linen napkin. In the centre Meriem put a plate heaped with golden-brown dumplings. When Yentra had served coffee she nudged the boy's elbow, nodding at the plate. Three pairs of eyes watched as he selected a dumpling. It melted in his mouth like a warm cloud, leaving in its wake a whisper of cinnamon and sugar.

Meriem was smiling, Yentra offering him the plate. No prompting was needed.

'Yentra makes the best taklaris in the country. Yes, you do,' Meriem said, making Yentra beam with delight. The boy was inclined to agree. He had never tasted taklaris before, wasn't even sure if the word was singular or plural, but hoped it would multiply for the benefit of his stomach. In a very short time the plate was empty. They sat back, sipping coffee contentedly.

Stirring, Meriem said, 'My father would like to talk to you later, Arun. You'll be coming over for dinner, so perhaps afterwards?'

'Of course,' he said, wondering if this was the something beneath the kindness, the pit he had been waiting to fall into. Then he reflected that his time in Harakim had carved a road through his trust. But roads could grow dim with lack of use until they existed only in the heads of those who once knew them.

Talaia's voice returned him from the wilderness. 'You did mean both of us?' She sounded strained, defensive.

'Well . . .' Meriem looked uncertain.

'It's what we agreed, isn't it, that we'd share things equally?' Talaia said, turning to the boy.

'Yes, of course.'

After a tense silence Meriem said, 'Perhaps it's different for you – for young people, I mean. I wouldn't expect to be included in Adri's business, but then I probably wouldn't understand it, and I'm not sure his clients would like it either.'

The boy grasped the olive branch, hoping Talaia would too. An advocate undertook years of training, and his skill was singular. Unlike baking, or growing cabbages. As far as he knew, there was no academy for cabbage growers.

'No, of course not,' Talaia said. Her tone was conciliatory, and Meriem looked mollified.

When the family had gone, they stood looking at each other.

Talaia broke first, into a smile, then laughter. 'Your face,' she said, wiping her eyes. 'I thought you were going to run for the door.'

'Never,' he said stoutly. 'Well, it might have crossed my mind.'

'I think we've caused a stir.' She put her arms around him, looking into his eyes. 'Is it too much? The family, I mean, turning up like this. Perhaps if I explain we need some time to ourselves to settle in properly?'

He hesitated, unsure of the wisdom of honesty. Reminding himself of the open-handed welcome they'd received, he told her there was no need, the family were just being kind.

Talaia stroked his hand. 'They all have an opinion about everything, and I know it can be infuriating, but if you put them together they make a pretty good whole, on the whole. Yes, I know I said "whole" twice,' she added with a smile.

'I wasn't counting,' he said quickly, although he was, and Talaia knew it, and the wonder was that she loved him in spite of it.

They were tidying up the breakfast things when they heard hoofbeats. A short silence, then a knock. 'Horses don't knock,' Talaia said.

The boy made a face at her. 'Come in,' he called.

It was Yorin. As he came through the door he took in the scene, and shook his head.

'No way back now,' he said with a grin.

They sat at the table, Yorin without removing his cloak. 'How are things?' he asked as Talaia served fresh coffee and cakes. The boy found himself regretting lost opportunities to have a proper talk. They'd conducted brief conversations across the table at Meriem's house, chatted on the veranda about nothing in particular, but – but, he reminded himself, Yorin was Yorin.

'They're good,' he said. Part of him – the tiny part always threatening to dissolve – wouldn't allow more than that.

'We're very happy,' Talaia said. 'We couldn't ask for more.'

For a while they talked, lightly, comfortably. When Talaia offered more coffee Yorin declined, putting the cup down in a way the boy instinctively recognised. He had been expecting it, and hoping it wouldn't come.

'I've enjoyed being here, watching you settle down, but I think it's time to move on,' Yorin said.

Even as Talaia said 'You're welcome to stay. I'm sure Uncle Jabar would find you work,' the boy knew it was no use. His friend had been with him for so long he could hardly imagine life without him.

'We'll miss you,' he said. 'You've been a good friend to both of us.'

'I hope I still am,' Yorin said with a smile. A short silence fell.

'Where will you go?' Talaia asked.

'The hills look interesting.' Purple-brown, receding

into distance, the Neyma Hills rose to the west of Mudaina.

'Will you ever settle down?' she asked, half smiling, half serious.

Yorin shrugged. 'My feet always seem determined to take me somewhere else.'

'One day they'll take you to someone's door, and she'll open it, and you'll know you've found your place.'

For less than a moment the boy glimpsed sorrow in his friend's eyes. 'Well,' Yorin said, getting to his feet, 'I'd better get going. Tobi will be waiting.'

'You're not escaping that easily.' Talaia went into the kitchen and returned with a cloth-wrapped bundle. 'I know Meriem will have given you enough for an army, but there's bread, a good cheese, fruit and some lamb.'

Yorin took it from her, touching her hand. 'Thank you,' he said. She hugged him and kissed his cheek.

The boy walked him to the door, and they went out together. A light haze lay over the valley; the lines of the mountains were not yet fully resolved.

'We've had some good times, my friend,' Yorin said.

'We have,' the boy agreed. 'And some not-so-good times.' The shadow of the tribe of the House of Goash had never entirely left him.

'But we made them good,' Yorin said, 'and that's what counts.'

Tobi was standing in his usual fashion, his back leg slightly bent, the hoof-tip touching the ground. His skin shivered as the boy gingerly patted his neck.

'Give it another ten years,' Yorin said as he put the bundle into a saddlebag. The boy pulled a face and Yorin laughed, then reached out to shake his hand. The handshake turned into a brief but solid hug, then Yorin was swinging himself into his saddle and looking at the boy, the house, and Talaia, standing at the door, shading her eyes.

'Take care of each other,' he said, nudging Tobi forward. A little way down the lane he stopped, turned his head and called, 'Write it down.'

'What?' the boy called back.

'All of it – the stories, everything. And don't forget the poems. I want to read them one day.'

The boy watched until he and Tobi were out of sight. Talaia came to stand beside him, taking his hand.

'Now,' she said briskly, 'I'm going to try making taklaris, and you're going to help me.'

Over dinner that evening, Talaia told Meriem and the family about the well-cooked stones fished from bubbling oil. Meriem shook with laughter, Yentra sat with a solemn face. She took taklaris-making very seriously, Meriem told them. A family without a taklaris-maker wasn't a family at all.

'In which case –' With a glance at the boy, Talaia produced a small cloth-wrapped bundle, unfolding the corners to reveal a heap of golden-brown dumplings. 'I thought we could have them with coffee.'

Everyone clapped, even Yentra, who declared them acceptable. Which, Meriem told them, was praise indeed.

'I had help,' Talaia said, taking the boy's hand. The atmosphere changed slightly.

'It's good to share things like that,' Adri said thoughtfully. Once again the boy found himself reassessing the quiet, kind-faced man whose intrinsic good nature was slowly coming to light.

Jabar was touching him on the sleeve and saying, 'Arun, could I have a word?' He stiffened, preparing himself, but the word, it turned out, was very brief. Jabar simply wanted to know if they had enough money for the time being.

In bed that night, he reflected on how quickly he'd jumped to the wrong conclusion. Was it because he couldn't quite believe he'd finally found somewhere to belong? And if so, why did he feel an urge to push it away? Was it because he hadn't chosen these people, because they were not, in terms of blood, his family? He tossed and turned so much he woke Talaia, who asked him what was wrong.

When he told her, she kissed him and said, 'No one can ever replace what you've lost, my love. I can't imagine what it must be like for you. Perhaps you feel you're betraying the memory of your family, but I don't think they'd think that, not for a second. I think they'd be happy to know you're safe, and loved.'

Morning came. They woke, and got up. Not immediately – they were too newly married for that – but when they did, they stood in the living room holding hands, watching the risen sun gilding the river as the valley breathed away mist. A knock at the door; they looked at each other.

'Come in,' they called together.

Meriem was accompanied by Vezu, who looked smaller than usual this morning. The boy wondered if he grew taller in the spring. Meriem greeted them with a kiss, telling them she had come to discuss the arrangements for the apple harvest.

The boy's stomach grumbled.

'Oh, I'm stopping you having breakfast,' she said. She didn't, he thought, sound too put out about it.

Talaia's eyes told him she knew what he was thinking. 'Could you set the table, my love?' she asked.

'We thought we'd break you in gently,' Meriem said after her second cup of tea. 'We'll leave the other crops to the usual people this year, while you find your feet. The main apple crop will be ready soon. Don't worry, we'll make sure you know what you're doing.'

The boy imagined a hand reaching up to an apple, twisting the stem, tossing the fruit into a basket, repeating the action.

'It's quite a skill,' Meriem said, 'picking each one at the moment of ripeness, making sure it's not galled or bruised, placing it in the basket so it doesn't get damaged. You'll need to know the names, too, so that when we make the wine each batch will be correctly labelled.' This sounded more promising. 'Now, the pickers. We pay them daily, so we can keep an eye on how much it's costing and, if needs be, we can bring more in.'

'And you keep books?' Talaia asked. The way she said it made the boy suspect the question was not entirely spontaneous.

'That's what I wanted to talk to you about, Arun,' Meriem said. 'You kept books before, didn't you, for a merchant in Harakim?' He could only nod. 'We'd like you to keep them for us. It'll just be the apples this year. At the end of the harvest, my father will go over them with you.'

The boy felt something rising in his stomach, as if he'd slept with his mouth open and whatever he swallowed was crawling up for air. He took a deep gulp of tea. Talaia and Meriem were looking at him.

'Yes,' he said, 'of course.'

'Good. That's settled, then.' Meriem looked pleased.

It was all the more precious, the time before the apple harvest. They used it to make the house properly their own, coming back from market with a cloth for the table, cushions for the chairs beside the fire – 'If Vezu sits down we'll never see him again,' Talaia remarked – a set of silver teaspoons, their handles shaped like roses in bud. And, for Mirashi, a piece of silky dark-blue cloth for a bookmark. Talaia intended to embroider it with their initials. It would, she said, be good practice for the cloth Jabar had given them.

When everything was in place they went into the bedroom, took the Book of Light from the top drawer of the cabinet next to the boy's side of the bed, and opened it at random.

A woman diving for jade
finds love –

she hides it in her hair,
keeps it secret for hundreds of years.

The boy lifted his hand and softly touched Talaia's hair.

There was no putting off the harvest. The apples would go on ripening whether folk were ready or not. So here they were, gathered in the orchards with the pickers as Meriem made introductions. The boy suspected he and Talaia were a talking-point for those acquainted with Meriem and her household, and wondered what had been said about them, two people from far-off places landing like swans on the valley's green waters.

Under Meriem's watchful eye, Vezu demonstrated what to do. Ducking into the broad leather strap of a wicker basket, he came up with the basket resting on his hip. He climbed the ladder propped against a tree, plucking deftly, placing each apple carefully into the basket. His arms were freckled with the sun, his lips pursed as if blowing away an invisible fly.

'Now, Arun,' Meriem said, 'you'll be keeping a tally of how many baskets each person picks.'

The boy glanced up at Vezu. 'I think I'd like to try it for myself.'

There was a short, rather stiff silence. Meriem looked at Jabar, who said nothing. She glanced at Talaia for support, but found none. 'Of course,' she said primly, 'if that's what you want. Come down, Vezu. Let Arun try.'

Vezu removed the basket and held it out to the boy in silence. Pushing through the branches, it felt as if he were climbing above a snowline, with Meriem and the family below. He was concerned about losing his balance but there was no need; he was back on the deck of the *Silver Falcon*, sure-footed above the crowding waves.

Up here, he had a clear view of the grassy lanes intersecting the rows of trees. As he looked down them, something caught his eye. In the farthest corner he saw a figure in a hooded brown cloak slipping away between the trees.

His mouth was suddenly dry. He looked again, but it had gone. Somehow he knew it wasn't one of the pickers. It seemed vaguely familiar, although he couldn't remember ever having seen it before. And with it, flooding back, came the sense of unease he thought he'd finally laid to rest.

That day they picked so many apples he wondered his fingers didn't burst into leaf. His time was divided between picking and counting, sky and earth. Talaia checked numbers, talking with Jabar, who sat in the shade on a comfortable chair. He seemed content to watch, trusting what the pickers were doing.

As he worked, the boy wondered if there was a language for it. So many apples made a – what? A branch? A barrel? A pie? When he told Talaia, she laughed. The sun cast a net of light around her hair; a leaf was caught in the crease of her sleeve. 'Did you know there's a variety called Heavenly Sun, and one called Winter Fool?'

'Is there one called I'm So Hungry I Could Eat An Entire Orchard?' he asked.

Jabar, who had been pretending not to listen, smiled. 'I think you've earned a good meal. The apples seem like you. They come off easily in your hand.'

'They'll be eating out of it next,' Talaia murmured.

In the evening they had dinner in the white house, and afterwards sat by the fire. The boy couldn't settle. His mind kept returning to what he had seen earlier. Talaia looked up from her cup of tea. 'You're miles away,' she said.

He stirred, smiling at her. 'I'm just tired, my love.'

'I think we need an early night.' Her eyes were soft and sparkling.

Later, he lay awake beside her, thinking about the figure in the orchards. Was it one of Ruvek's men? The malevolence he'd felt in that stifling room spoke of someone not used to being thwarted. Was Ruvek hoping to conclude the business Yorin had so deftly frustrated?

He turned restlessly. Whether his fears were imagined or not, he would keep Talaia safe. If it meant making sure she was never on her own he would find a way to do it, although it was best she knew nothing about it. Nothing was going to happen to her. He would make sure of it.

Four days later, they were done. As the final apple was picked, a cry went up and everyone stepped back, wiping brows, clapping backs. Jabar got to his feet, a stone bottle of last year's apple wine in his hand. The pickers stood silent as he sprinkled a little over a brimming barrel, closed his eyes and said a blessing for the harvest. Then they piled forward to a table heaped with food and drink prepared by Meriem and Yentra.

Everyone was invited to dinner that evening, and a long table in the courtyard was filled with an even longer feast. The air was cool as stars began to come out. The boy's head was starry too; as he would learn the following morning, apple wine was fresh, clear, and deadly.

'A toast!' Jabar was on his feet, holding up his cup. 'You have all worked hard, and we are most grateful to you for your help. When you return to your houses, remember we will be starting the wine-making the day after tomorrow, and I expect you to be there bright and early.' There were dutiful groans. 'Yes, yes,' he said with mock severity. 'And now, eat more, drink more, and sleep well.'

He sat down, a little unsteadily. If Jabar pricked himself, the boy thought hazily, he'd probably leak wine. He wasn't aware of Meriem until she said, 'I think someone's ready for bed.'

Talaia raised her head sleepily. Putting his arm round her waist, the boy helped her to her feet.

'Too much apple wine!' someone called merrily.

'No,' he said, 'she's just tired. She's been working very hard.' Meriem looked at him. It was an approving look.

They treated the next day as a reprieve, enjoying their time alone together. Leaves were beginning to turn as they walked in the garden, their faces lifted to the sun. That evening they sat at the wooden table in the crisp evening air, drinking tea. Too tired to cook, they made a cold dinner from a lamb pie left by Meriem.

'Apple wine tomorrow,' Talaia said. 'I'm not sure how it's done. Do we stand on them?'

'On what?' he asked, pretending not to understand. 'Feet? Our own two? Ceremony?' Seeing the look on his face, she lunged; ducking, he slipped from his chair and ran. When she caught him, she pulled him down into the grass and started tickling him mercilessly.

'You don't think the neighbours heard?' he asked as he pulled her to her feet, still laughing.

'They already think we're a bit odd. We can't let them down.' She took his hand. 'Uncle Jabar said the fruit press is in the second barn from the end. Come on.'

They went through the garden gate, into the lane. In the cool blue dusk a star hung above like a bright hawk.

'Arina,' Talaia said. 'When it gets a bit darker she'll be joined by Safia and Amana. The Sisters.'

'How do you know?' the boy asked.

'My father taught me the stars. The alphabet of the sky.'

The barn wasn't locked, so they pushed open the heavy door and went inside. A warm, woody smell nested peacefully in the timbers. The floor had been left as earth, and tools hung on the walls. The main space was filled with a massive wooden structure, great-boned, sitting squarely in front of them. Talaia touched the old, polished wood and looked it up and down, from the hewn horizontal beams to the large wooden tub beneath. She turned to the boy and said, 'I haven't got a clue.'

The look on her face made him burst out laughing.

So now they were makers of apple wine. After a week at the press, they had squeezed the life out of so much fruit the boy felt he should do penance. The wine was standing in earthenware jars in one of the barns, ready to supply the inns and taverns of Mudaina. Not all of it, of course. Some would be kept in cupboards to warm heads and hands when winter came.

As he looked at the jars, it took a few moments for him to work out what he was feeling. A deep satisfaction. It was something he had never felt before. Gold and jewels were surfaces; they could be turned into objects of beauty by those with the skill to do it, but in the end they were held to the value of the market. Living things were the seed inside.

That night, in his dreams, he saw his valley again. His father was in the wheatfield, his mother coming out of the hut like the sun. As light broke over the eastern Tura Lar, he folded his map of the valley away in his heart.

Chapter Twenty-Nine

That evening, wrapped in thick cloaks, they travel to Meriem's house in one of the family's carts. The horse stamps, snorting white clouds. 'You'll soon be in a warm stable,' Talaia says soothingly.

As they turn into the street Meriem is waiting, a lantern in her hand. 'Welcome!' she cries, helping Talaia down and drawing them into the house. The hallway glows with the light of many candles, the walls strung with paper lanterns of silver and gold. Meriem beams as Talaia exclaims with delight.

The dining room is decorated with equal care, and seems to be filled with most of Mudaina. Through the noisy crowd, the boy sees a large table covered with dishes from which delicious scents are rising. In the centre of the white damask cloth is a loaf of such monumental proportions he wouldn't be surprised if a plaque at its head declared it to be of architectural significance. Divided into the four seasons of the year, it is decorated with snowdrops and grapes, pumpkins and roses. At the centre is a representation of Meriem's house. The golden crust shines with egg-wash.

'It could feed the entire province,' Talaia says in his ear.

'Kaba bread,' Meriem explains, offering them glasses of wine from a tray. 'It's an old tradition. We break it at midnight as good luck for the coming year.'

'It's exquisite,' Talaia says. 'And look!' She points to the figure of a tiny mouse sitting in one corner, a nut in its paws.

'It was Vezu's idea,' Meriem says.

'It's lovely,' Talaia says. Then, faintly anxious, 'I hope no one eats it.' The boy puts his arm around her, smiling.

As the new year comes in, bells start ringing out across the city and fireworks burst in showers of glittering rain. Jabar makes a simple blessing, and the Kaba bread is broken and shared among them. The room grows warm and loud with people wishing each other a happy new year as they shake hands, embrace, sing, dance. Through it all the boy is aware of Talaia's shining eyes, her closeness as they sit together quietly talking, part of the shared joy, part of each other's joy, too.

The boy lies drowsing as the household begins to stir. Talaia murmurs something, and he turns to her and kisses her gently. When she sits up, her face is expectant. He knows what she is waiting for. 'Close your eyes,' he says. He takes a rose-coloured pouch from the cabinet next to him. 'You can open them now,' he says, placing it in her hands.

She unties the cord and takes out a pair of deep-blue silk velvet slippers embroidered with gold and silver thread. 'They're beautiful,' she exclaims, kissing him. When she draws away, the look on his face makes her say softly, 'Tell me.'

He takes her hands, suddenly nervous. 'They were my mother's. My father gave them to me at Amala Dyssul. If you'd rather not – if they'd make you feel –'

She stops him with a kiss. Her eyes are full of tears. 'I can't think of anything better,' she says.

Gently detaching herself from his arms, she ducks down and brings up a parcel wrapped in fine patterned paper. His reluctance to spoil it is overcome by curiosity, which quickly tears it off. It is a rectangular notebook whose dark-blue leather cover is embossed with golden suns and silver moons. As his fingers explore the smooth creamy pages, he finds himself unable to speak.

'Remember what Yorin said about writing things down?' Talaia says. 'And' – she bites her lip – 'I know you kept a journal on the *Silver Falcon*. I thought you could start a new one here.' Her face is anxious; there is a slight crease between her eyebrows.

How can he tell her how perfect it is? How perfect she is? He looks at the golden suns and silver moons. 'It'll be a night-and-day journal for both of us,' he says, wondering how he ever came to be given such gifts.

When they join the family in the sitting room Jabar rises from his chair, embracing them both. 'A happy Kaba,' he says, smiling.

And it is. The presents Talaia made are received with enthusiasm. There is real delight in Meriem's face as she strokes the napkins and unfolds the tablecloth. 'You did all this?' she asks admiringly.

Talaia blushes with pleasure. 'Arun helped.'

'If searching for dropped needles and providing cups of tea count as helping,' he says, and everyone laughs.

Jabar and Adri are touched by the time and trouble he has put into their presents. On the front of Jabar's leather pouch he has carved a fruiting vine, on Adri's the words *Light is a Peacemaker*, taken from a poem he read on the way to Chanlin.

When Adri looks up, his eyes are full of something the boy can't make out. 'It's beautiful,' he says and leaves it at that, which, the boy understands afterwards, is where it should be left.

Meriem nudges Adri, her face alive with secrets. 'We have something for you,' she says, and leads them through the hallway to the back door.

The sun is a silver berry in the sky as they pass through the yard and into the lane, where Birith is standing beside a horse and cart. The cart is made of yellow wood, its side panels carved with patterns of leaves. The horse is a handsome bay whose coat is so glossy the groom probably still feels the ache.

'What do you think?' Meriem asks, with a look that anticipates delight.

The boy is silent for a moment. 'It's . . . they're . . .' he starts, at the same time as Talaia says, 'It's a wonderful present, but it's too much. We can't accept it.'

The boy holds his breath, but Meriem isn't frowning. 'Of course you can,' she says. 'It means you won't have to use one of our carts, and it will save you the bother of returning it each time. Besides, there's stabling in the barns just waiting to be used.'

The boy echoes Talaia's thanks as the horse tosses its head and whinnies, making the harness jingle. She is, Meriem says, called Jena. He makes an approach, a brief pat on the neck, and the horse gives him a look he is all too familiar with.

Dinner that evening is taken in the sitting room, with plates balanced on laps and little tables filled with food. They chat quietly, breaking into occasional laughter. Yentra's face is red with happiness as she insists on serving them, even though Meriem says there is no need. Through the heat and the noise and the smiling faces shines something the boy is beginning to recognise as love, the everyday kind that has little need of declaration, but is strong and reliable and quietly real.

He glances at Talaia drowsing beside him. Their love hasn't yet worn itself into the shape of their lives, but is remade each day. If he had concerns about what might lie beneath the bright surface, they are gone now.

Talaia stirs, stretching a little. 'You're thinking again,' she says sleepily. 'Maybe your notebook would like to know what you have to say.'

Tomorrow, he thinks, he will start writing.

Arun looks down at his hands. It is hard, returning from the past. 'I did,' he says eventually. 'Every evening we'd sit beside the fire and write down what we'd done, the journeys we'd made to get to Mudaina, the stories we told along the way. In the back I began writing down scraps of things, images, phrases I hoped might end up as poetry. It was exciting, but terrifying too. They were like plants whose origin I didn't know, and I had no idea what they might produce.'

He sighs. 'Only one thing cast a shadow. I think I expected children to come along fairly quickly, as they did with other people, and I didn't give it much thought at first. It was something we never mentioned, and as time went on it became harder to talk about, then almost impossible. I think she – my wife – probably did, with Meriem. I hope so, because I was no help.'

Night deepens around him, but makes no comment.

Arun's hand shakes as he drinks from the water bottle. 'It took less time than I thought to grow into the land. And yes, I was aware of the irony. I'd become a farmer like my father, and I felt only gratitude. I remember standing at the door one day and sensing all around me the silent music of spring. It had been another mild winter in the Suth Valley, and I was finally beginning to understand its accent.

'When I heard birdsong, I knew which bird was making it. When I looked across the river to the fields, I could almost see what they contained. It was as if I had a lens that let me look into the earth to the sleeping roots, into the veins of leaves to the green cells growing. That was the day I knelt down and touched the ground, knowing I belonged.'

He laughs softly. 'I was very lyrical in those days.'

The boy rises to his feet. They have survived another Kaba. Their second. He can't believe how quickly the time has passed. Talaia is calling him, and he turns to greet her.

'It's lunchtime, my love,' she says. 'Unless you're thinking of eating the cabbages? Although I don't think they're ready yet. They need to do a little more growing. And sleeping.' Her hand is warm in his. 'Things need sleep in order to grow.' She hesitates. 'I may be doing more sleeping too, but hopefully I won't turn into a cabbage.'

He looks at her blankly. A little shyly she says, 'If I'm eating for two, I hope we like the same things.'

He is vaguely aware of a shadow lifting as the world contracts to a point focused entirely on Talaia's eyes, which are full of anxious joy. He isn't aware of himself or his actions, although an observer would see him throw his arms around his wife, freeze in horror, look at her stomach as she says something that makes him grin a little sheepishly, then give a shout loud enough to wake the mountains.

Of course the family must be told, but not just yet. Time enough to walk beside the river hand in hand, gazing at each other. Then back to the house where he sits in happy stupefaction, looking at Talaia as if she will break, until she gets up and does a little dance, her eyes sparkling with impudence and delight. He has never seen her quite like this. There is only one thing to do. He takes her hands, and joins in.

At Meriem's house that evening, as they eat, drink and celebrate, the boy remains in a state of grateful wonder. Questions are asked, mainly by Meriem, and he hears them as if at a distance. 'When did you know? Well, yes, of course you're wise to wait and make sure. And no sickness, either, that's lucky. So it'll be a summer baby, how lovely, not long after your birthday, Arun, that was good planning.'

At the sound of his name, he looks up. Adri is sitting opposite, and the fleeting sadness on his face makes the boy reflect on the true extent of this family's kindness.

Later, alone in their bedroom, Talaia takes his hand and asks him if he is happy.

'Completely,' he says.

Blossom smothers the trees that year. Buds break like flasks of perfume, flooding the valley with scent. Talaia walks in the orchards, touching branches, brushing her hand across pink and white flowers. Her tunics have been let out and although her belly is rounded, her movements are graceful.

Only one thing clouds the boy's happiness. His sense of unease, almost a stranger to him now, has returned. There is, he tells himself, no reason for it, no cause for worry. Then he thinks it is hardly surprising; he is about to become a father, and reason has little to do with it. If he let himself, he could probably imagine any and every sort of terror that ever beset a father-to-be. But he won't. Nothing will spoil this precious time. He won't allow the past to cast a shadow.

In Meriem's courtyard the flowers are blue jewels, yellow stars, cascades of scarlet silk. 'I've never seen such a display,' she says as they sit on the veranda one afternoon. Later, the boy will wonder why flowers are often described as something other than themselves; as stars or trumpets, feathers or slippers. He will think that no matter what words are used a flower is still, beautifully, a flower.

'This tea is delicious,' Talaia says. She is leaning against him, a faintly distant look on her face, as if she is awake but dreaming.

'It's a special mixture,' Meriem says. 'It was given to Adri by one of his clients.'

There are times when the boy finds it hard to match Adri to his profession, but he has come to understand and appreciate the certainty untainted by arrogance, the deep belief in justice, that lie at the heart of his character. 'Who was it?' he asks.

'Oh, just someone he helped,' Meriem says airily.

The boy has gradually discovered that the family's generosity is not confined to Kaba but continues throughout the year, although it is never broadcast. They are, simply, good people. Like anyone else they have their faults, but their foundations are true and strong.

'I think we need some of this tea,' Talaia says. Meriem immediately promises to go herself, to get the best price. 'I'll go with you,' Talaia says. 'I need to stretch my legs. They're getting shorter by the day.'

A rare frown crosses Meriem's face. 'In your condition, it's probably best you stay here.'

Talaia shakes her head. It is not the first time they have touched on the subject that, as the boy discovered, has less to do with his wife than the condition of those who may be exposed to her.

In the boy's village, pregnant women carried on with their lives as if they were in charge of a melon that would, in due and natural course, transform into a baby. It has come as a surprise to find, in this easy-going city, a certain resistance to pregnant women appearing in public. While not forbidden, it is not encouraged, either. The boy knows it infuriates Talaia, and he shares her view. Meriem does not. It has become a bone of contention – albeit from a very small fish – between her and her cousin.

'It's ridiculous,' Talaia says. 'If the world wants children, why can't it rejoice in the sight of a woman carrying a child?'

'It does,' Meriem says, 'but in private.'

'So it's all about modesty? If everyone was so modest there wouldn't be any babies.'

411

Yentra giggles nervously in the doorway, a plate of cakes in her hand.

'I think,' Meriem says carefully, 'you're feeling a little tired. Perhaps –'

The boy recognises the look on Talaia's face. It comes with four hooves squarely planted, a man tugging vainly at a rope halter as a broad backside lowers itself to the ground. The first time he saw a mule sitting like that, he went up to the man and asked why he couldn't make the animal move. The man had handed him the rope and said, 'He's all yours. If you can get him to the well, there's a coin in it for you,' before going into the White Poplar. When he came out, neither the boy nor the mule had budged. He told the boy to drop the rope. When he did, the man walked away, and the mule followed.

There is no time to be concerned about the less-than-flattering analogy; Talaia and Meriem have fallen into a tense silence.

'Perhaps if we take some tea with us when we go?' he says, and holds his breath. Talaia, he senses, is weighing up her indignation. He blows an imaginary feather into one of the scales. It tilts almost immeasurably.

'That's a good idea, my love,' she says. She gives Meriem a look, and changes the subject.

Which returns when they are at home, having dinner. They are eating some very good cheese when Talaia bursts out, 'It's wrong, whatever Meriem says.'

It is a good thing the boy has kept notes of the conversation, which he silently consults. 'Yes,' he agrees, 'it is. But it's just the way things are here.'

'And that makes it right?' It is a rhetorical question,

which is just as well; he is full of beef stew and too comfortable for an argument, even between people who share the same view.

'Well?' Talaia is looking at him. It isn't a rhetorical question after all.

'No, of course not, but sometimes it's easier to accept things as they are.'

It is the wrong thing to say. 'It's pure hypocrisy,' she bursts out. 'The citizens of Mudaina don't want to be embarrassed by the sight of a woman displaying the results of her activities, that's all.'

An image rises in the boy's mind. He blinks. Talaia makes a small noise and he looks at her, concerned. She is stifling a giggle.

'Even so,' she says as they take the dinner things through to the kitchen, 'it isn't right.'

The following week they go into the city for supplies. Thread, sugar, candles. And tea. The boy worries all the way in, especially when they leave Jena in the family's stables.

The day has a golden edge to it. When Talaia goes into a shop in the main square he waits outside, leaning against the doorway, his eyes half closed. Slowly he becomes aware of a prickling sensation on the back of his neck. Something compels him to look round. As he does, it is as if all activity has been suspended, all noise shut off. His gaze runs unhindered across the square to a figure in a hooded brown cloak. He knows it is looking at him.

Fear rises so fast it almost chokes him. His hand goes to his side, but his dagger hangs on a nail beside the door in the white house. Filled with fury, he starts running. People stare in surprise as he pushes his way through the square.

When he reaches the other side, he looks around desperately. He has lost sight of the hooded figure. No, there it is, ducking down a side street. He follows, running as hard as he can, searching the street, the next one and the next, but it has gone. He bends over, his hands on his knees, gasping.

As he walks back to the square, sunlight, cooking smells, chatter and laughter begin to slow his racing heart.

'I thought it was you,' a voice says, and he nearly jumps out of his skin. 'I saw you from my chambers. Everything all right?'

He turns to see Adri. 'Yes, fine,' he says, 'just running errands.'

Adri gives him a shrewd look, then nods at a large stone building with a wooden balcony running across the upper storey. 'I'm right at the top. It gives me a good view of what's going on. Is Talaia with you?' The boy nods. Adri's response – '*Ah*' – comes with rooms attached.

'It was my idea,' the boy says quickly.

Adri smiles. 'I'm not judging you, my friend. You and Talaia have a right to go wherever you please. If I've learned anything, it's that people can often hold views that overcome good sense. Especially if they come with numbers behind them – the number of people in a city, for example, pretending lovemaking doesn't happen, not to others, at least.'

The boy's face flares. And subsides, since Adri shows no embarrassment. 'Yes,' he says, 'and children appear by magic.'

'It is a kind of magic,' Adri says thoughtfully.

The boy silently kicks himself. 'I'm sorry,' he says, but Adri shakes his head.

'It's just how things are. And Meriem mothers everyone – the household, our friends, and now you.'

This, the boy thinks, is very true. Meriem has supervised the buying of everything from cradle to changing-cloths, has bought so many baby clothes they could open a shop.

'If at times she pops up when you'd rather be alone,' Adri continues, 'it's only through a desire to help. Love can sometimes make a nuisance of people.'

Before the boy can reply, Talaia comes out of the shop. When she sees Adri, she stiffens. He smiles at her. 'After all that hard bargaining, you must be ready for tea,' he says.

That evening after dinner, the boy says, 'I need to talk to you about something. Before I do, please remember that I love you very much, and I only want to look after you.'

Keeping Talaia close has now become imperative. The time for discretion is past, although he knows that no matter how carefully phrased, what he has to say will not be well received.

Talaia's eyes narrow. He takes a breath, the words he rehearsed forgotten. 'I don't think you should go out on your own.' She sits very still. He hurries on. 'I mean, I'd rather you didn't.' She says nothing. 'It would put my mind at ease,' he adds hopefully.

The silence is slowly turning to stone.

'So you agree with Meriem,' Talaia says at last. 'Just

because I'm pregnant – with *your* child – I have to stay indoors, be a prisoner in my own home?'

'No, of course not,' he says quickly, 'that's not what I meant.'

'It amounts to the same thing.' Colour rises in her face. 'I can't believe you'd even think of asking me. Not allowed out unless someone's with me, like a child? After everything we've talked about?' She chokes back tears of anger. 'I'm going outside. I can't bear to look at you at the moment.'

He follows, his world shattering with every step. At the end of the garden she lowers herself into a chair, and turns her face away.

'You do know how I feel about it,' he says urgently, sitting beside her, taking her hand. She pulls it away. 'It's nothing to do with that, I promise.'

'Then what is it?' Her eyes are as fierce as her voice. He is at a loss. He can't add to her distress, especially now. He is already terrified for her and their baby.

'I just need you to trust me,' he says desperately.

'Trust?' Talaia is almost shouting. 'I thought we had no secrets. I thought we were honest with each other.'

'Please,' he says, 'you need to stay calm.'

'Calm? When the father of my child wants to keep me indoors and won't tell me why? And all this time I thought we were equals.' With difficulty she turns her body away from him. Her breath is ragged, as if she is stifling sobs.

Gingerly, he places a hand on her arm. She shrugs it off. 'All right,' he says, 'I'll tell you why.'

He keeps it deliberately vague, saying that ever since their encounter with Ruvek's men in Kerizon he has worried for her safety. And now there is a baby on the way, and he is determined to keep them both safe, whether – his hands tighten in his lap – she likes it or not.

Talaia is motionless for some time. When she turns to him, her face is no longer angry. 'It's not just that, is it? It's about what happened to your family.' She takes his hand. 'Oh, Arun, I know it was a terrible thing, but I don't want our baby growing up with a shadow hanging over them. I want them to have a normal, happy childhood. Otherwise, those people will have won. And I won't let them.' Her eyes are fierce again, and shining with tears.

'Nor will I,' he says, kissing her hands. 'They'll have the happiest childhood they could ever imagine. I just want to protect you both.'

'I know you do, and I love you for it, but we need to look after each other. So no more talk of locking me away, and no more looking over your shoulder. Promise?' He promises. 'Besides,' she adds, 'I'm rarely on my own. There's no escaping the family. Or you.' Her eyes are teasing. When he leans over for a kiss, he is not rebuffed.

But from that day he notices that when she goes out there is generally a reason for him to go with her, and when he starts wearing his dagger again, she makes no comment.

Chapter Thirty

Talaia leans back in her chair, pushing away her plate. 'I shouldn't have had that last fig,' she says.

The boy smiles, stroking her hand. The evening air murmurs with bees. It has been another busy day. While he was out in the fields with the workers, Talaia sat in the shade going over the orders. This year's harvest promises to be even better than the last. Their garden, too, is in full summer splendour, the fig trees bursting with fruit. Talaia has developed quite a taste for them; the boy suspects their child will, too.

The first time Talaia beckoned to him, her face shining with a secret, he hadn't been prepared. When she put his hand on her belly, he'd been alarmed at the soft kick. He was suddenly in a place with no bearings, tied in a knot of anxiety so tight he couldn't speak. Was his reaction unnatural? Was he not meant to be a father?

As if translating, Talaia said calmly, 'You'll be a wonderful father, my love. Don't be afraid.' She gently replaced his hand, and this time it was as if something nudged at his heart.

Talaia groans again. 'What is it?' he asks, concerned.

She catches her breath sharply. 'I think I need to go into the house.'

The boy helps her up, and they reach the living room in a slow hurry. She lowers herself into the chair beside the fireplace, wincing. The boy is almost beside himself.

'I think I need Meriem,' Talaia says calmly. 'The baby's coming. Could you let Rashila know?'

It takes a moment for him to remember the arrangements they made with their nearest neighbour. He starts to move, then stops. If he goes, it will mean leaving Talaia on her own. He is dimly aware of himself as comedy, one foot planted in front of her chair, the other dashing out of the house.

'It's all right, my love, it's not coming just yet,' Talaia says, smiling even as she flinches with pain. His head clears; he runs for the door and quickly returns, telling Talaia that Rashila has gone for Meriem. As fast as she can. Right now. He stands, sits, hovers, until she says, 'I'd love a cup of tea.'

He looks around the room as if he has never seen it before, remembers where the kitchen is, rushes off and returns with a trembling cup. Talaia takes a thoughtful sip. 'It could do with some tea leaves.' She starts rising, majestically.

'No,' he says, alarmed, 'you need to stay sitting.'

'I'm not going to break, my love,' she says. He helps her into the kitchen, where she selects a jar from the cupboard, clutches her stomach and cries out.

'Come and sit down,' he says frantically.

The jar is still in her hand as they go back into the living room. He spoons tea blindly into the cup; flakes drift onto the floor. It is a dark leaf, slightly woody, with here and there threads of stem. He wonders how many berries it takes to make a cup of tea, then why on earth he is thinking this when his wife is about to give birth.

He turns to Talaia, whose face creases from time to time with pain. In his village he overheard terrible things about childbirth, generally accompanied by a shake of the head.

The door bursts open. Meriem is accompanied by Yentra, who has a cloth bag in her hand and is not giggling. With one glance Meriem takes in the scene, and says matter-of-factly, 'It's time, then. Now, my dear, we need to get you into the bedroom and you' – looking at the boy – 'need to stay here.'

He insists on accompanying Talaia. When she is lying on the bed, he stands looking down anxiously.

'Out, out,' Meriem says, flapping her hands.

As he kisses Talaia's forehead, she whispers, 'I'll be fine. Go and do something interesting. Knit clouds. Make needles from rain.'

It takes all his strength of will to leave her. In the living room he almost collides with Yentra, narrowly avoiding upsetting the basin of steaming water she is carrying. As she hurries into the bedroom and closes the door he hears Talaia cry out, and his heart is up and fighting everything that has caused her such pain, including and especially himself. He flees the house, and is standing outside wondering wildly if it is too late to stop it, when someone touches his arm.

'I think I saw some fish in the river,' Adri says. 'Shall we take a look?'

A little way on a dimple appears close to the bank, spreading in rings, each becoming the next. 'There,' Adri says, pointing.

The boy peers down as the water composes a fish. It hangs, silvery green, gills whirring, tail swaying gently. 'Sandlings. Beautiful to look at and, alas for them, good to eat. But not today. You're spared,' Adri says, addressing the fish. Flexing its body, it swims lazily on.

They stand watching the mountains and the clouds passing above. 'I've often wondered what it would be like to fly,' Adri says thoughtfully.

The boy stares at him. It is not what he expected of someone whose natural element seems to be the hustle and bustle of the city.

'As a bird?' he asks carefully.

Adri smiles. 'I hadn't really thought about it. I'm not sure I'd make a very good one.'

'But if you were, you wouldn't know anything else.'

'That's true. And, as a person, I don't know anything else either.' He nods, as if something has been settled.

They are walking back over the bridge when Meriem comes running down the path, waving her arms. 'Come and see!' she cries. 'Come and see!'

The boy starts running, across the bridge, down the path, around the corner and through the door, almost falling over Yentra, who is coming out of the bedroom with a covered bowl in her hands. She shies away, giggles, and inclines her head towards the doorway. On the threshold he hesitates, then goes in.

Afterwards, he wonders what he expected. A mess of heat and blood? But all is calm, and Talaia is sitting up in bed, smiling as if she has never smiled before. She is holding a bundle that coughs, squeaks and makes funny noises. Her eyes are weary, but full of such joy the boy could warm his hands on it. Trembling, he approaches, and she pats the bed beside her. As he sits he takes a deep, ragged breath. He has been so frightened of what might

421

happen he has scarcely allowed himself air.

Talaia seems to understand. 'We're both fine,' she says softly. 'I think your daughter would like to meet you.' She moves aside the lacy blanket covering a tiny face whose eyes are screwed up and whose nose – but her nose is so small it is hardly there. She sneezes and shakes her head like a kitten, surprised. The boy stares in silent wonder.

'Would you like to hold her?' Talaia transfers the warm bundle carefully into the boy's arms, and he peers at the little hand pushing out of the blanket. His index finger seems broad as a tree trunk as tiny fingers clutch it, their nails like the offspring of a perfect shell. The screwed-up eyes slowly open, not quite focused, the eyelids no more than pristine creases; the mouth puckers, and bubbles come out.

'She's very good at that,' Talaia says. Her voice quivers, and the boy thinks of Mirashi's poem about a painter instructed by his master to paint sorrow, and how he finds it impossible because of

a fragment of joy lodged in the throat of the brush.

This room – the entire Suth Valley – can't contain the joy he feels as he holds his daughter in his arms.

'How are you?' he asks, stroking Talaia's hair.

'According to Meriem, I was lucky. It was quick and fairly straightforward, apparently.' She makes a face. 'I won't be able to sit down for a week, but I'm fine.'

'Really?' he asks, needing reassurance.

Her hand covers his, which is still in the custody of his daughter. 'Really,' she says.

It is a busy day, with many visitors. Vezu appears with a

small package in his hand. He gives it silently to the boy, and disappears. Talaia opens it and they gaze at a little wooden mouse, exquisitely carved, holding a nut in its paws.

'Vezu made it himself,' Meriem says. 'He saw how much you liked the mouse on the Kaba bread.' They look at each other in wonder. Later, with ceremony, they place it in the centre of the mantelpiece.

Meriem is the last to leave, promising to return in the morning. The boy sits on the bed holding Talaia's hand, their daughter in his arms, already a necessary weight.

'Well,' Talaia says with a contented yawn.

'Well,' he agrees. Their daughter makes a small noise, somewhere between a purr and a squeak. He looks down in admiration.

Smiling, Talaia shakes her head. 'I can see you're going to be no help to me,' she says.

In bed that evening, they open the notebook to make a record of their daughter's birth. Talaia glances down at the cradle beside her. 'We need to think of a name.' When the boy asks if she has anything in mind, she hesitates. 'I thought Lirriel. After your mother.'

'You do it,' she says when he asks her to write it down. *Lirriel Alesh Persaba.* The date. The place.

He lowers the pen. 'I wish I could put down what I feel. Properly, I mean.'

Talaia closes the notebook and strokes his face. 'You will,' she says.

Arun stares into the pool for a long time. When he lifts his head, he sees nothing around him. 'No,' he says. 'Even now, I can't.'

Chapter Thirty-One

In the week following the birth of a child, it is customary for women to remain indoors. When Meriem told them this the boy expected Talaia to object, but she seemed happy to comply. The house and garden have become, for this time, a small and perfect kingdom to share with their daughter.

Meriem visits every day. Instead of imposing her authority, as the boy secretly feared, she proves invaluable, especially when dealing with visitors. Lirriel's arrival is an enchantment that spreads beyond the white house; a surprising number of workers find themselves outside the door, and each is invited in for a time whose duration is strictly regulated.

After consulting with Jabar, the boy put his foreman in charge of fieldwork for the time being. Jabar was firm about this. 'You don't want to miss out on your daughter's first days,' he said. 'They won't come again.'

From the moment Lirriel saw her great-uncle, a bond was formed. He talked to her gravely, as an equal, and she looked up at him, her eyes wide, in rapt attention.

'This is a cherry tree,' he says as he walks in the garden with Lirriel in his arms. The evening is warm and still. The boy and Talaia sit at the table as Jabar tells her the names of trees and flowers. 'And this,' he says, stopping under the grand old tree whose scent infuses the air, 'is poet's jasmine.'

Lines from a poem come into the boy's mind.

We held a ceremony for our dreams.
The last light presided:
what we said was heard by every living thing.

'Tell me,' Talaia says quietly. When he does, she takes his hands in hers. 'And these are our dreams,' she says softly. They sit with their arms around each other, watching Jabar introduce their daughter to the world.

The wheat has been harvested, and fruit is deep on the branch, when the boy goes back to work. His return is gradual, a few days a week. If Talaia is not with Meriem or the family she joins him for lunch, carrying Lirriel in a soft cotton sling. As they eat their meal, they tell their daughter about the Suth Valley, the land, and what grows on it. She listens with what the boy is sure is a keen intelligence.

Talaia laughs. 'Our daughter is a genius,' she says, 'especially when it comes to winding her father around her little finger.'

Evenings are mostly their own, and they spend them in the garden or, increasingly, beside the fire, where the boy is sitting with Lirriel on his lap. Draped across Talaia's knees is the embroidered cloth Jabar gave them when they moved in. She has been adding to it since their first Kaba and her sewing is improving, but the boy knows she finds it a trial.

'How's it going?' he ventures, laughing at her woeful face as she holds it up. Two silky figures with slightly crooked smiles, one holding a bundle, stand on a half-built bridge. Pairs of stitches fly above. Below is a puddle of blue. 'I think you've discovered the source of the Peluin,' he says.

Talaia puts down the cloth. 'I've been teaching Lirri our names. *Mama. Papa.* I'm sure she understands. And when it's time for her to read and write' – she looks at the boy – 'I thought I could take charge of her education. If you don't mind?'

He feels such pleasure he can hardly speak.

It has rained in the night, and the air is fresh and sweet. The boy stands on the bridge with Lirriel in his arms, telling her the names of things. 'River,' he says. 'Grass. Tree. Mountain. Sky. Sun. The sun is the most important thing. It grows our crops, and you, too.'

Lirriel gurgles, reaching out towards it. If he could, he would take it from the sky and give it to her. But then everything would be dark. He thinks for a moment. 'The sun wasn't always so far away,' he tells her. 'Once upon a time, it was much nearer.'

Shifting his daughter into a more comfortable position, he begins a story about a mongoose and a rabbit. The mongoose is clever and conceited, the rabbit shy and in awe of its friend. In the story the mongoose wants to impress the rabbit, so persuades the sun to come down from the sky. When it does, the mongoose lures it into a cave and rolls a boulder across the entrance. The world goes dark: the rabbit is terrified, the mongoose delighted. Only when a mob of angry animals confronts it does the mongoose let the sun out. Once freed, it flees to the top of the sky and stays there.

'And that's why the sun lives so high up,' the boy says, 'because of a vain and silly mongoose.' He kisses Lirriel's nose, stroking her silky fawn-coloured hair.

'It was a good story, my love,' Talaia says, coming up behind him. 'I particularly liked the voices.'

The boy laughs, putting his arm around her. They stand looking out across the valley, which is slowly fading to blue. The mountains are mauve-grey, tipped with gold.

'This is our home,' he tells his daughter.

'Our home,' Talaia echoes.

They barely have time to recover from Kaba before Meriem and Adri call at the white house. They have come to talk wheat and barley. This winter there is, it seems, a grain shortage in Sert, a neighbouring city. A good neighbour in the sense that it lies in the Neyma Hills. The living room glows with lamplight, and a fire burns in the hearth. The boy and Talaia sit on one side, Meriem and Adri on the other, in a circle of light and shadow.

'It would be a great help to us,' Meriem says, looking at the boy. They have proposed – he suspects Meriem of proposing – that he and Vezu, together with Birith, take their surplus grain to Sert. Even by the reckoning of the city traders it has been a rich harvest, every ear of wheat, every whisker of barley turned to gold almost before it ripened, and Meriem is determined to make the most of it.

'But if we have a surplus, surely they will too?' the boy says.

'They don't grow their own crops. They rely on merchants to supply them.' Meriem looks both satisfied and disapproving, as if their folly profits her in a way that nonetheless causes her pain. The boy glances at Talaia, sensing what she is thinking. The family's grain is also their trust. The spirit becomes the thing.

Lirriel stirs in Talaia's lap, and he sighs inwardly. How can he leave them? He has never been away from them before. Sert may as well be another world. But how can he turn the family down when he owes them so much?

'I know it's a lot to ask,' Adri says, 'especially now, with Lirriel.'

'How long will it take?' he asks.

'Two days, probably, with the weather as it is.'

The boy nods. Winter here has none of the bitter gifts of other parts of the country. The short frosts give heart to the soil and a surface glitter to delight the eye on cold mornings. 'About a week all in, then,' he says.

Meriem glances at Adri. 'I know you'll want to talk it over,' he says. 'Could you let us know tomorrow? If it's a yes, you'll need to set off as soon as possible. Before other traders get there.'

They discuss it later, as Lirriel sleeps in her cradle. Talaia's head is resting on the boy's chest, and he kisses her hair. 'If you don't want me to go, I won't,' he says.

She raises her head. 'That's hardly fair,' she says with a tilt of her mouth.

'Why?' he asks, surprised.

'Because if you don't go and you want to, it'll be my fault. Things like that can bite you on the behind.'

He hides a grin. 'And if I go, even if you don't want me to? Which I don't. Want to go, I mean.' He can feel Talaia struggling not to laugh, so he helps by tickling her.

They have reached a decision. Talaia is satisfied he doesn't want to go, so is happy to agree to it. She has also agreed that she and Lirriel will stay with the family while he is away. 'Meriem will be pleased, and it will be good for Lirri to spend time with them,' is all she says.

Arrangements are made at Meriem's house that afternoon, around the dining table. Yentra serves coffee and cinnamon cakes. Lirriel chirrups and stretches out a hand from Jabar's lap but Talaia says, 'No, little one, you may not have any teeth yet, but when they come I want them to be strong.' It won't be long now before the buds of her gums start to break, and Meriem has recommended a paste Yentra makes from her mother's own recipe.

The boy becomes aware of Adri patiently waiting. 'Sorry,' he says, 'I was miles away.'

Smiling, Adri pushes across a fat little book secured by a silver clasp. 'The travelling accounts. Small enough to carry with you.'

The first line of a poem comes into the boy's mind.

Their lives no more than folded paper

'We record the transactions in here,' Adri says, 'and transfer them into the main ledger when we get back.'

The boy opens the book and studies it. It feels as if there was never a time when numbers weren't familiar to him, and his fluency is both a source of pride and – what? – disappointment, because he secretly hoped he was meant for something else, possibly involving a circle of people in firelight, mouse-quiet as he read his poems?

'As you can see, it's almost full,' Adri says. 'It'll soon

be time for it to be retired to the accounts cabinet for a good rest.'

Meriem shakes her head fondly. 'Now, the horses. We'll need four, and we'll hire them from the usual place.' She smiles at the look on the boy's face. 'Don't worry, my dear, Birith will take care of them.'

Before they go to bed that evening, the boy takes out the Book of Light and looks up the poem he thought of earlier. It is about people in an ancient burial ground. Talaia puts her arm around him, and he reads it to her quietly.

> Their lives no more than folded paper
> small enough to fit a pocket –
> north and south roads meet
> in the lines of their hands.

His voice catches on the final lines, things Mirashi imagined they took with them.

> Warm books
> made from folds of the desert
> a moon's width across,
> clouds of local paper
> rolled up for storage –
> on their faces
> long-forgotten stories of the mountain.

For a moment Talaia is silent. 'Don't be sad,' she says. 'They've lived their lives, but they haven't been forgotten.'

They stand holding each other for a long time. 'It's only a few days,' he says. 'I'll be back before you know it.'

'A few days,' she says, 'yes.'

The sun isn't up yet, and the air is chilly. After breakfast, the boy goes out into the lane behind the white house. Birith and Vezu have already brought the wagons from the end barn and hitched them up, and are checking the harness of the horses. When everything is ready the boy goes back into the garden, where Talaia is waiting with Lirriel in her arms.

'Your father has something important to do,' she tells their daughter, 'and when he comes back, he'll have more stories for you.'

They stand together looking up at the mountains, where a soft blue glow is gathering. Talaia adjusts the boy's cloak and carefully passes Lirriel to him. He holds her close, breathing in her milky warmth as she sits contentedly in his arms, making sounds only she can understand. *Sweet nothings* is what Meriem calls them, *little cakes of the heart.* The boy can almost see his sister rolling her eyes. He seems to recall she had a dim view of babies. Kissing his daughter's fluffy head, he gently detaches her fingers from his cloak.

In the lane, Vezu is waiting on the seat of the leading wagon. Beside it, the reins of Birith's horse rest loosely in his hand. Now the time has come, the boy is gripped with rising panic. As Talaia kisses him he catches her hand, holding it tightly. 'Go safely,' she whispers. He will. He has so much to be safe for, now.

When they reach the turning that will take them through the outskirts of Mudaina and on to the crossroads, he looks back. Talaia is waving; he lifts his hand and waves back. When the white house is out of sight, a deep loneliness clutches his heart. He takes a breath, reminding himself of what he has to come back to.

Travelling with Vezu and Birith is very different from the journeys he made with Talaia and Yorin. Talaia would have pointed out the tiny purple flowers among the heath covering the hillsides, the small, stout birds that burst out in a flurry and disappear with a squawk. Now it is a matter of getting things done as quickly as possible, and the Neyma Hills have become one more thing to negotiate. He can at least be thankful the path is wide and well-kept.

They stop that evening at an inn sitting in a fold of the hills. The boy takes little notice of his surroundings and finishes his lamb stew quickly, as if it will shorten the hours between now and his return. Excusing himself, he stands at the window of his room, looking out. The sky is vast, threaded with stars.

As he sits down on his bed, he reflects that he has become both half and double the person he was. Half, because Talaia is not with him. Double, because she is with him in his heart. And now Lirriel. Together, they make a sum beyond calculation. He stretches out, prepared for a sleepless night.

But sleep has a way of insinuating itself into the sorest hearts. When he wakes, he reaches across for Talaia. His heart jolts in his chest, and he wonders if he dreamed the last years. After a moment of scalding relief he gets up, splashes water on his face, and goes down to breakfast.

The track rises slowly through the hills. It is, Birith says, a well-travelled route.

'Have you been to Sert before?' the boy asks Vezu, who blinks.

After a long pause he says, 'Yes.'

The boy waits for further information. And waits, until realising that, in responding, Vezu has discharged his duty. He glances at him. They have never been on their own together, and he knows nothing about this silent, indispensable member of Meriem's household. Not, he thinks with faint shame, that he has ever tried to find out. But then, he reasons, they could journey round the world and he would probably be no wiser. Shaking the reins, he urges the horses into something more than a walk.

By the following afternoon they have reached the junction where the track joins the main road to Sert. Beyond them, the hills fall away from a series of terraces loosely girdled with undulating grey walls, within which a city spreads and climbs. The boy can see why Sert needs to import grain. Anything planted here would slide back down again.

'Almost there,' he says with relief.

As they crawl along, his impatience starts to rise. From time to time men on horseback gallop past. 'Is it always like this?' he asks.

Vezu shrugs. Birith has proved to be equally quiet, no stories round the fire, no tales of journeys past, and the boy wonders if he has been saddled with the two most tight-lipped souls in the province. But then, he acknowledges silently, he is hardly the most forthcoming of people, unless he is with Talaia.

He wonders what she is doing now. It must be time for tea, and a bowl of softened rice and honey for Lirriel.

Following Meriem's advice, they are slowly introducing different foods to their daughter. 'No need to fret,' she said, 'Lirriel knows what she can manage. And she'll tell you so, in no uncertain terms.'

Dusk is gathering as they reach the city gates and are stopped by officers of the Board of Trade, who prod at sacks of grain before waving them on their way.

Like Vezu, Birith has been here before and knows the city, guiding them to the warehouse district and into one of the cavernous barns. Men help them roll the wagons into a corner, roping them off. Here they will remain until tomorrow, when the auction starts. As the horses are stabled and rubbed down, the boy glances about. High in the rafters are the remnants of nests.

'Mountain swifts. They're small and very fast.' The boy looks round to see a man, heavy-set, blunt-faced, standing nearby. He has never seen mountain swifts, but has heard the air protesting their speed as they tore through it.

'They come every year,' the man says. 'We watch for them in spring.' Introducing himself as Jobe, he asks if they have come far.

'From Mudaina,' the boy says.

Jobe nods. 'A very fertile place. We're not blessed that way, but then again, we have plenty of things to trade. Where are you staying?' The boy mentions an inn, the Cherry Tree.

Jobe considers for a moment. 'You'd be most welcome to have dinner with me and my wife this evening. All of you, of course.'

Birith declines. It is clear he has arrangements of his own, though what they are the boy doesn't ask.

Vezu consults the ground and mutters something about needing sleep.

'I think it'll just be me,' the boy says.

The evening air is still, the streets blue with shadow as he passes grey stone houses with flat roofs. At either side of Jobe's front door, lamps have been lit. Jobe answers the boy's knock and invites him inside to meet his wife, a small, pleasant-looking woman with an unhurried manner. Jobe introduces her as Estel, and she smiles warmly as she welcomes him in.

He follows them down a passageway and into a room in which plates and cups have already been set on a dark wood table. Lamps cast soft light on large woven hangings. He takes the seat Estel offers, and looks around. The hangings fall in waves of many colours blue, from the palest tint of a summer sky to lapis and ultramarine. Having no images or stories running through them, they ask nothing of the observer but to look and enjoy. He finds them strangely soothing.

'You like them?' Jobe asks.

'Very much. Where are they from?'

'They were made by people who live up on the northern coast,' Estel says, placing a bowl of warm water in front of him and waiting as he washes and dries his hands. 'That was the first one Jobe brought back.' She nods at the wall behind him, and he turns in his chair to look. 'It was a gift from a merchant who was pleased with the price his goods fetched.' She offers the bowl to her husband. 'Jobe introduced him to the right person, you see.'

Jobe takes up the story. 'When I brought it home, Estel was so taken with it she asked me to get another one. Easier said than done. No one seemed to know where it came from, and the merchant had gone back home by then. It became something of a quest. I asked everyone I knew, more than once – they started calling me the hanging man. I was such a pest people began to hide when they saw me coming.' He smiles ruefully.

'But it paid off,' Estel says. 'Jobe finally found a trader who knew the people who made them. Well, of course he couldn't go – it was too far away, and he had his work to think about – but the man promised he'd try and find some. He kept his word. Next time he came to the summer fair, he brought them with him. He got a very good price for his turnips.' She smiles. 'Now, if you'll excuse me' – she gathers up the cloth and bowl – 'I need to check the broth.'

When she has gone Jobe says, 'It probably seems like a lot of fuss just for some bits of cloth.'

'Not at all,' the boy replies, 'I think they're beautiful.'

'They have a meaning, too. They represent the curves of life, because that's the way life goes, in curves. Ups and downs. The shuttle is the tongue of the loom, speaking as it weaves.' He looks at the boy. 'You probably think I'm being fanciful.'

The boy shakes his head. He finds it surprisingly easy to be with this blunt-faced man. 'I think what matters to you is what matters in the end,' he says. 'Not above everything else, necessarily, just as much. And there are as many things to see and feel as there are people, or cities. Life isn't all brick and stone.'

Jobe sits back. 'And you are not just a seller of grain.'

After two bowls of chicken broth and enough buttered brown bread to make his belt creak, Estel shows the boy into a smaller room, where a fire burns in the hearth.

Finishing his coffee, Jobe leans back and sighs. 'That's better.' After a pause he says, 'You're not from this province, are you?'

As the boy considers the question, his feeling of quiet contentment starts to fade away. Claims of belonging can turn out to be temperamental. 'No,' he says cautiously.

'Nor me,' Jobe says. 'I was a factor for a grain merchant in Cruseira, in the south. The first time I came here on business, something caught my eye.' He glances at Estel, who smiles back at him. The boy recognises the look. It contains the thing that swims oceans, leaps chasms, scales mountains. A swift in the sky, a keystone.

'I was smitten,' Jobe says with no trace of self-consciousness. 'As soon as I saw Estel, I knew I wouldn't be returning to Cruseira. The grain merchant wasn't happy, but I was.' The story of their courtship is affectionately told and the boy listens with genuine pleasure, at ease in the home of this warm-hearted couple.

'It's late,' he says, declining Estel's offer of more coffee, 'and I've taken up too much of your time already.'

'Not at all, we've thoroughly enjoyed your company. But you'll need to be up bright and early tomorrow to get the best price for your grain. I'm sure you'll have a good day,' she adds with a glance at her husband.

The boy lies on his bed, staring up at the ceiling. He is full of a good meal and good company, but part of him is very much empty. He thinks of Talaia and Lirriel, wondering what they have done today. He hopes they are thinking of him, too.

Arun clears his throat. He tips up the water bottle but nothing comes out. 'May I?' he asks. As he dips it in the pool, the moon shivers into silver pieces. When the bottle is full he drinks deeply, and watches her compose herself again. 'Isn't it cold in there?' he asks.

'She won't feel it,' Night says. 'She never feels anything.'

'And what about you?'

'I keep things hidden. And lay things bare. You should know that by now.'

Arun doesn't reply. It is the time of night when thoughts have worn themselves away and dreams flow on below the surface. It is peaceful, or endless, depending on your state of mind. He knows the torment it has at its disposal. He also knows the sweetness.

Chapter Thirty-Two

The boy feels he has barely touched the sides of sleep as he stands with Vezu and Birith the following morning. The barn is full of people, noisy, expectant. At the far side, Jobe is talking with a group of men. The boy catches his eye, and Jobe gives a short nod. He understands. No favour shown, last night's dinner tucked under his belt.

The air crackles as the auctioneer arrives, a large man in a maroon robe. The auction starts slowly at first, hands reluctant to show, plans held close to the chest. Jobe is standing with a man dressed in a plain shirt and trousers. There is nothing remarkable about him, but the boy has learned that if the inside is well-to-do, there is often no need for the outside to shout about it.

As lot after lot is sold, he tries to keep his impatience in check. The trader belonging to Jobe has yet to bid. At last they come to his wagons. The bidding opens at a price he thinks too low. He starts forward before realising he has no say. He clenches his hands. He has bargained with the best, and beaten them all. But here he can only stand and watch as hands twitch, eyes flicker, heads tilt.

Just as he is wondering how to explain things to Meriem and the family, Jobe's trader moves slightly. The atmosphere shifts. A fractional nod, and the price begins to rise. Up it goes, higher and higher, the boy unable to catch the whole show since it is conducted in miniature in ten places at once, until –

'Done!' The auctioneer brings his hand down, and people start clapping.

The boy wonders why until Vezu tugs his sleeve, saying excitedly, 'You got the best price of the day!' It is more than he has said during the entire journey.

The boy stands numbly amid the tumult. He glances across the barn, but there are people in the way. Not until the crowd starts to drift does Jobe bring the trader over to him.

'That was a hard bargain you drove,' he says. 'I warned Raqui you'd be a tough one to beat.'

The boy shifts uncomfortably. As far as he is aware, he did nothing but stand about feeling useless. Raqui extends his hand. 'I'm told your grain is the best in the province. Let's hope so.'

There is money to be settled, wagons to be unloaded, tallies to be reckoned. The boy completes it in a daze, wondering what happened. He thought he knew most of the merchant's tricks, but this took place in broad daylight under an honest roof.

The barn is almost empty. Raqui's men have taken away the grain. It will, the boy has learned, be used to fill warehouses currently standing empty. He also learned that Raqui was acting on behalf of the city. Gathering his wits, he turns to Vezu and Birith and thanks them for their help. His heart suddenly lightens. It is enough to be going home to Talaia and Lirriel, but now he can bring good news, too.

When he visits that evening, he takes Estel an earthenware pot filled with rich meat paste, a delicacy of the city. For Jobe, a leather belt carved with a pattern of acorns and oak leaves.

After dinner, they sit beside the fire. It takes very little encouragement for the boy to tell them about Talaia and Lirriel, and the interest of his hosts is such that he finds himself talking freely. 'Your daughter sounds like a beauty,' Estel says. 'You'll have your work cut out when she's older.' She offers him small cakes sweetened with brown sugar.

'These are delicious,' he says, taking a bite. 'I wonder – do you have the recipe? I'm sure Talaia would like to try it.'

Estel beams at him. 'Of course. I'll fetch it.'

As she leaves the room Jobe remarks, 'You've made a friend for life.'

The boy smiles. 'There's something I wanted to ask you. About the auction.' Jobe raises his eyebrows slightly. 'What did you –' the boy begins, but Jobe shakes his head.

'I did nothing. Your grain spoke for itself.'

The boy had no idea it was so talented. He looks steadily at Jobe, who shifts in his chair. 'Really, Arun, I didn't do anything. Except drop a hint to Raqui that your valley has the finest crops in the province, and it wouldn't hurt our reputation to be part of it. He's a competitive man. It always helps.'

Even though he is grateful, the boy still feels something is not quite right. He tries again, and Jobe raises his hand. 'My friend, it was fairly done.'

'Then I hope it lives up to its reputation,' he says.

Jobe smiles, looking up as Estel returns with a piece of paper in her hand. 'The recipe. I hope your wife will

441

let me know what she thinks of it. And this is for your daughter.' She gives him a smooth wooden ring adorned with rose-pink ribbons. 'It sounds as if she'll be teething soon. Cherrywood helps with the discomfort.'

Sensing not to ask where it came from, he offers what he feels are inadequate thanks. It is a gift generously given.

That night he sleeps badly, knowing he will see Talaia and Lirriel soon, wishing he could set off right now. He throws back the covers and walks to the window. There is little to see except, dimly, the house opposite. The mind in idleness builds shadows, he thinks. From the table beside the bed he takes the Book of Light, and lets it fall open.

Her song's needle sews goodness in the air.

The poem is about a shaman's daughter creating the fruits of summer while her father's thoughts are elsewhere. When he has finished reading he sits silently for a while, thinking about his family. The weight in his heart is golden. Closing the book, he sleeps away the few remaining hours of the night.

Jobe is already in the barn when he arrives. 'Well, my friend,' he says, shaking the boy's hand warmly, 'everything's ready. Your horses have been persuaded into harness.' He grins. 'On the way back, you'll have to remind them how they earn their keep.'

The way back. Excitement brims. 'If you're ever in Mudaina you must come and see us,' the boy says.

'We'd like that, thank you. And let us know how the cakes turn out, yes?'

Why do return journeys always pass more quickly? He'd thought his impatience would add to the miles but instead here they are, joining the crossroads in fading light. He urges the horses into a trot, and Vezu starts singing. It is so unexpected the boy turns and stares. The song is about a frog and a pond, although he can't work out if the frog is happy or sad. We each have our own song, and we sing it through our lives. He smiles to himself, wondering what Talaia would have to say about it.

They pass into Mudaina under the long porch between the red-roofed towers. His hand trembles on the reins, and one of the horses tosses its head. 'I know,' he says. 'Not far now.'

A dog trots up, sniffs a wheel, trots away. As they turn into the street the boy knows so well, everything is still, as if held in a spell. He hears a cry, his pulse quickens, and suddenly there she is, running towards him with Lirriel in her arms. He jumps down from the wagon and runs to meet them, and now he is holding them both and they are laughing and crying at the same time.

The family leave them on their own that evening, for which the boy suspects he owes Adri his thanks. They will share the good news tomorrow, but tomorrow can wait.

After a huge dinner, they sit beside the fire. Lirriel is sound asleep in her wicker basket, clutching her cloth. Of all her many toys, her favourite is the simplest, a square of soft linen from one of the boy's old shirts. In one corner Talaia has sewn a pair of pointed ears, knots of black silk for eyes and nose, a pink mouth and long black whiskers. When first introduced, Lirriel grabbed the cloth and stuffed it into her mouth. The two are inseparable; its

443

occasional disappearance – behind a cushion, under the bed and, once, behind the chest of drawers – throws the house into a panic until it is found, and all is peace again.

Talaia asks about Sert. The boy tells her about the auction. She brushes his hair from his face. 'It doesn't matter to me whether you make a profit or not, I'd be proud of you anyway.'

As he draws her close he thinks he will never get used to this, and also that it has become wonderfully familiar. Two sides of a coin, each with its own virtue. 'Estel gave me this,' he says, remembering, and fishes the recipe out of his purse. 'I thought you might like to try it.'

'You won't mind if it's not as good?'

'It'll be better. No contest.'

She ambushes him with a kiss.

They are woken the following night by an unfamiliar sound, a long, high strain that has Talaia out of bed in an instant, swooping on Lirriel, catching her up. The boy's heart doesn't know whether to stop or start. He is out of bed too, saying, 'What's wrong? What's wrong?' and finding that repeating it doesn't help.

After an anxious moment Talaia's face clears. 'I think . . .' she says, and gently pushes her little finger into their daughter's mouth. Lirriel looks quizzical, then starts sucking. Talaia's voice shakes as she says, 'I can feel something. A tooth!'

The boy gazes at his wonderful daughter, who has, it seems, produced something from nothing. 'Well done,' he says, 'what a clever girl you are!' She screws up her face and cries. After a moment's frantic thought, he goes to the chest of drawers and takes out the teething ring given to him by Estel. Later, Lirriel will chew it until the ribbons are soggy and it is freckled with teethmarks. But cherrywood and pink ribbons don't interest her yet. She is too concerned about what is happening in her mouth. It isn't yet a tooth, though judging by the discomfort it could be a tusk.

They consult Meriem, Yentra, and Jabar, who remembers Meriem going through the same process. 'It's the gum preparing for eruption,' he says, which makes the boy think of volcanoes.

Lirriel looks at them with round eyes, as if asking why her mouth has suddenly turned against her. They are in agonies until Yentra produces her soothing paste. When Talaia rubs it on Lirriel's gums, she quietens immediately. Such balm, the boy thinks, is worth its weight in gold.

'Look, Lirri,' the boy says, 'cyclamen.' It has become a tradition to walk in the garden looking for the first signs of spring, and now they can share it with their daughter.

'I think that one might be a bit much for her,' Talaia says, and he grins. It isn't only Lirriel's teeth that are preparing to come forth. She has a language all her own, and while it is one the boy and Talaia may never master, they listen carefully as she points to something, makes an utterance, and the thing is duly named. It has been a source of some hilarity; the idea of asking Meriem to sit in the *chuchu* beside the fire reduced Talaia to helpless laughter.

The boy points to a tiny white flower, its head bowed to expose a tender nape. When he names it for his daughter she squirms in his arms, mumbling happily. Somewhere within the sound lies a snowdrop.

That evening, as they sit beside the fire – it is not yet warm enough for the table in the garden – the boy writes about Lirriel and the naming of flowers. Since her arrival he has been writing in the notebook more regularly. He has also been adding to the store of lines and phrases at the back, which seem to come more readily now. Talaia sits opposite, her head bent over the embroidered cloth. When she has finished, she holds it up for the boy to see. He smiles at the tiny child with a white flower in her hand.

'It's supposed to be a snowdrop,' Talaia says, 'but it looks more like a mushroom.' She looks at it thoughtfully. 'I never thought I'd be doing this. It's funny, isn't it, where life takes you?'

He is silent for a moment. He never thought he would be a farmer, or a bookkeeper. Then he reminds himself art comes in many different forms. Apple wine and chutney, the preserved lemons for which the Suth Valley is famous; are they not also created by the lyric of hand and mind?

When he tells Talaia, she smiles at him. 'And what about our bread? When it comes out of the oven it's like a dome with a smaller dome on top. Or coiled around and brushed with sugar. If you go to the next town or city, they'll probably make it a different way. It starts life as flour and yeast, but it's what we make it into that matters.' Glancing at the cloth, she makes a face. 'I know all about suffering for your art,' she says, and the boy starts laughing.

A few days later, he is returning for lunch when an exclamation stops him in his tracks. It is coming from the white house. Seized with dread, he starts to run. Thoughts race frantically through his mind. How could he have been so foolish? Yes, there have been times when Talaia and Lirriel have been on their own, impossible to keep them constantly by his side, and yes, Talaia has sometimes taken Lirriel in the cart to visit the family, but he is never far away, never in the fields too long, the family always dropping in . . . Images flash: a long red-lit passage, a stifling room, a hooded brown cloak . . . He has dropped his guard, and now he is paying the price.

As he bursts through the door, Talaia runs to meet him. 'Lirri's starting to crawl,' she cries, 'come and see!' He stares at her, at Meriem, who is sitting beside the fire, at his daughter on all fours, wobbling across the rug. After a short way she collapses, waving her arms and chuckling.

Meriem starts clapping. 'Clever girl!' she says.

Talaia scoops Lirriel up. 'Well,' she says to the boy, 'what do you think of our marvellous daughter?' She takes his silence as a sign of inexpressible pride.

Arun gazes into the pool. 'It's strange,' he says, 'how I measured time in those days. As a boy at the hut it was the space between meals. In Harakim, the distance from port to port. In the Suth Valley it had been crops and seasons. Now' – he takes a breath – 'it was a tooth breaking through a gum, fat little hands clutching my shirt.'

For a long time he sits with his head bowed. The moon shimmers softly as he looks back to where the boy and Talaia are standing on the bridge. Light falls on the river, which bears it slowly away.

'I don't know,' Talaia says. 'I love them all.' They are discussing their favourite season. She considers for a moment, gazing up at plump clouds drifting in the wide blue sky. 'Whichever one I happen to be in, which means summer.'

He smiles. 'If you could only have one season, which would you chose?'

'Spring,' she says, then with a gasp of horror, 'oh no, what about the apples?'

The boy laughs. He knows how much Talaia loves spiced apple pie. She gives him an impish look. 'A spring in which everything grows, including things that would normally come out later. Or earlier.'

'I think,' he says, 'the rules are changing.'

'Were there rules?'

He puts his arm around her. 'For you, never.'

'Then I choose love,' she says. 'That's the best season of all.'

As they turn to go, a movement catches the boy's eye. Did someone just dart around the corner?

'It's nothing,' he says to Talaia's questioning look. He tries not to hurry her down the path and into the lane. It is empty. With an inward shake of his head, he wonders if becoming a father has made him more jumpy. No, just more protective, he corrects himself as they go into the house, where Meriem is telling Lirriel a story.

They stand in the doorway, listening. Lirriel bounces in Meriem's lap, one hand clutching her cloth, the other grabbing at Meriem's plait. Her yellow smock and trousers embroidered with tiny flowers – a gift from Jabar – remind the boy of the meadow in the northern Tura Lar.

'And then,' Meriem says, 'a bear crept up and – *snap!* – the nose was gone.' The boy starts forward. Why is Meriem frightening their daughter?

448

Talaia puts a hand on his arm. 'Look,' she says quietly.

Lirriel gurgles happily as Meriem approaches, makes a gentle swipe, and lifts her hand. 'Gone!' she says triumphantly. Lirriel chuckles with delight. 'And now' – Meriem swoops down – 'all back again!'

Talaia laughs, shaking her head. Catching sight of her mother, Lirriel stretches out her arms. 'I've fed her,' Meriem says, 'but I don't think she's ready to sleep just yet. I think she wants another story.'

The boy turns to Talaia. 'Why don't you tell her one?'

She blushes slightly, but looks pleased. With Lirriel settled in her lap, she begins a story about a child so small her parents dressed her in brightly coloured clothes, so they could always see where she was. 'She was loved by everyone in the village, and by her parents most of all,' she says, stroking Lirriel's nose. 'One day, a short-sighted crow mistook her for a scrap of silk and carried her off to its nest. The whole village went looking for her, including the local birds.

'She was found by a yellow dove, who returned her to her parents. They were so grateful they set up a feeding table for the birds in the marketplace. But all the time the little girl was in the crow's nest, she was never worried. Do you know why? Because she knew that if she was ever lost, her parents would find her.'

She strokes her daughter's silky hair. 'You see, little one, no matter where you wriggle off to, we'll always find you.'

There is mayhem in the kitchen. The worktop is covered with the rind and seeds of watermelons. Talaia lays juicy slices on a square mesh and covers them with a cloth. The boy has fetched large stones from the garden and scrubbed them clean. As he puts them on top of the cloth, Talaia says, 'It shouldn't take too long. When we've cleared up, I'll start on the cake.'

She glances at Lirriel sitting in the doorway, a scarf around her head to protect her from the sun. She is walking now, a few unsteady steps at a time, supported at first, then gradually on her own, always with one of them at hand. When the inevitable collapse came, she bounced slightly on her bottom and looked up at her parents in surprise. They were ready to fly to her aid, but she chortled and held out her arms to try again. Small steps towards new horizons.

The homemade watermelon juice is for their daughter's first birthday tomorrow. It is a day to be recorded in starry letters in their notebook. Talaia has fretted over the cake for days, making sketches, crumpling them up, starting again. She told the boy it needed to be beautiful enough for a princess, and he agreed. He suspected many fathers viewed their daughters this way, and was happy to count himself among them.

His princess is crawling across the floor, clutching his ankle, blowing bubbles. Her body hasn't yet learned embarrassment, for which he is thankful. It seems to him a child learns all too quickly to restrain, subdue, conceal. Imagination brings everything within the mind's grasp, waiting to be summoned. It is something he wants for Lirriel, the same boundlessness, the instant leap to wherever she wants to go. Another father wishing his dreams on his daughter, he thinks wryly.

The cake is finished. Decorated with fruits and flowers, it is a masterpiece, and when the boy says so Talaia flushes with pleasure. 'Does it mean I can have some?' he asks hopefully.

She pats his hand away, laughing. 'I don't want it nibbled by mice before everyone sees it,' she says with mock severity.

The question of what to give Lirriel for her first birthday has taken a good deal of thought. They had been at a loss until Jabar said, 'At this age, all she wants is food and sleep, so why not something you'll all remember?'

His suggestion caused Talaia to go very quiet. When they were sitting together after dinner she said, 'What about an almond tree?' The boy stared at her. 'You told me, remember. And now Lirri can have one in her family's garden.' She waited anxiously as he tried to find words. Instead he took her hands, and kissed them.

Where to find one was much more straightforward. The boy talked to Halib, a man he had done business with many times. The fruit merchant wore a striped robe – his trademark – and a benign expression that, the boy knew, concealed the soul of a jackal. When he mentioned he was looking for an almond tree, and that it needed to be particularly fine, Halib appeared to think for a moment. 'I have something in mind,' he said. 'It isn't easily come by, though.'

When the boy explained what it was for, the merchant's face changed. Like many others, he had fallen under Lirriel's spell. 'Ah,' he said, 'in that case leave it to me.'

Two days before her birthday, he appeared at the door with a sapling wrapped in damp cloth. As the boy served tea, Halib carefully removed the cloth.

'It's so small,' Talaia said. 'It's hard to believe it'll be a full-grown tree one day.'

Halib smiled at her. 'It will produce the finest almonds you've ever tasted. Have you found a place to plant it?'

They took him through the kitchen and down the garden to the area beside the table.

'It gets sun and shade,' Talaia said.

'Then it will be perfect.'

It is hard to hear what Meriem is saying, since everyone is speaking at once. They are all here, the family, their many friends and neighbours. And, in the middle of it all, the island everyone wants to reach, Lirriel.

Early that morning they took her into the garden, and the boy planted the almond tree. When it was bedded in, Talaia sprinkled it with water. 'May you be to our daughter's eyes as water to a thirsty soul,' she said. 'May the scent of your blossom always perfume our garden. And may your almonds be as plentiful as the milk of a very happy sheep.' The boy laughed, taking her hand, and they stood for a while in silence, looking at the little tree.

'We need more wine,' Meriem says in his ear. 'And we could do with another plate of cheese. No, you stay with your guests, I won't be a moment.' When she comes back she disappears into the throng, returning with Talaia and Lirriel. 'Now,' she says, clapping her hands for silence, 'I think it's time for the birthday girl to have her presents.' Lirriel reaches for her plait and she laughs. 'No, little one, I've got something better for you.'

It is a little horse on wheels with a yellow mane and tail. From Adri, a beautifully illustrated storybook, with tales of bears turning into people, crocks of honey that never run out, a pomegranate that feeds a country. The boy tells Adri they will read the stories to Lirriel every day, until she is able to read them herself. From Jabar, a skein of ribbons the colour of sky and sun. Lines from Mirashi's poem about a weaver ripple through the boy's mind.

On a loom of earth and air
cities grow:
pale Takhara, star of silk;
Imabar, whose ribbon-like passes
she knots by hand.

He thanks Jabar, who smiles and produces a sweetmeat from his sleeve. Lirriel opens her mouth like a little bird, and eats it up.

There are many other gifts. Yentra has made a little dress of ivory linen embroidered with rosebuds and trimmed with lace so fine a sneeze will be its ruin.

'It could have been made for an emperor's daughter,' Talaia tells her, deftly removing it from Lirriel's grasp.

Then Vezu, offering a small package, backing away shyly. The boy unwraps a perfect round pebble on which a scene has been painted. The valley in miniature, made from tiny and particular brushstrokes.

'It's wonderful,' Talaia exclaims.

'It's a work of art, my friend,' the boy says. 'We'll treasure it.' For the first time since the boy has known him, a smile breaks out on Vezu's face.

After Birith has presented Lirriel with a jar of honeycomb, Talaia whispers in the boy's ear and slips away. When he sees her poised in the doorway, he calls for quiet. As she brings in the cake, everyone starts clapping. Meriem gives a slow, considering nod.

'But this is magnificent!' she says at last. 'I had no idea . . .' That she is unable to finish her sentence is tribute enough.

The boy takes Lirriel's hand. 'This is for you, little one. Made by your mother, to celebrate the first year of your life. There will be many more, but there is only one first.'

Jabar makes a short blessing before cutting the beautiful cake. The boy thinks it a shame to destroy such a work of art, but only until he tastes it. As he takes one last mouthful he sits back quietly, letting the conversations move round him like tides. He is filled with deep contentment, and a sharp awareness of a moment that cannot come again. But, he reminds himself, life is made up of many such moments, which are the fleck and colour and flare of it.

He feels Talaia's eyes on him. 'I'm so thankful,' she whispers, 'for you, for Lirri, for everything we have.'

The boy rests his forehead against hers. 'So am I.'

Later, they will record the birthday in the notebook. They will walk up the path to the bridge, and stand looking at a sky overcome by sunset. Clouds will stream dark-grey and purple, pricked with light. The boy will put his hand to his heart, and wonder at its steady beating.

Chapter Thirty-Three

The summer has a fine finish to it, a polished golden light. They walk in the orchards, showing Lirriel the ripening apples. Talaia lifts her up to a branch and she grabs one, an orb for a small princess. She tries to bite it – she has a few teeth now – and slithers down the shiny surface. Perplexed, she stares at her parents, mumbling something. They bend their heads to listen. There it is again – '*Mmm . . .*'

Talaia looks at the boy excitedly, and points to herself. '*Mama,*' she says, '*Mama.*'

Lirriel chuckles. '*Mmmama.*'

They stare at her. Their daughter is finding her voice and they are speechless.

'I see you've come a long way since the library caves,' a dry voice remarks.

For a moment they freeze, looking at each other, then slowly turn around. Framed against the light is Yorin. His grin is doing its best not to break into a gallop. Before he can say any more the boy is hugging him, shaking his head and laughing, hugging him again. Talaia approaches more carefully but her daughter has other ideas, reaching out to grasp his red-gold hair.

'*Mama,*' she says.

Yorin raises an eyebrow. 'I think you need to work on

it,' he says to Talaia, who scolds him, and kisses his cheek.

'And where do you think you've been? All this time, and not a word.'

'Aren't you going to introduce me?' he asks, looking at Lirriel, who cocks her head and coos at him. His face changes slightly. The boy knows the signs.

They walk back through the fields, laughing and talking. There is so much to tell, and Yorin listens enthusiastically. When they reach the crest of the bridge, they stand looking across at the row of white houses. Their house looks much the same as the others, but the boy would know it in his sleep.

'Still standing, then.' Yorin's eyes are dancing. 'By the way,' he says as they reach the door, 'he's still with me, in case you were wondering. We're both stabled at Meriem's.'

'Less chance of being grumbled to death, then,' the boy says.

When they are settled with cups of tea, Lirriel climbs into Yorin's lap. Talaia seems to find it hilarious. 'You're a natural,' she tells him. Putting down her cup she says, 'We've told you about us, now it's your turn.'

Yorin looks down at Lirriel. She is pulling at his belt, and will shortly start gnawing on it. 'There's not much to tell. I've been here and there, done this and that.'

'That won't do. I expect a full account of your adventures. The real ones.'

Yorin's eyes brim with mischief. 'I did go across the Neyma Hills. It's a scrubby country the other side, nothing like here. I needed money, so I became a trader for a while. Pots. Ceramics. Depending on who was buying.' He smiles at the look on their faces. 'I can tell the difference between one maker and another, believe it or not. And if I can't, it doesn't matter. People tend to believe what they want.'

'I hope you didn't cheat anyone,' Talaia says sternly.

Yorin laughs. 'I've missed that look. It tunnels into your conscience and sets up camp. Most of the time I dealt honestly. No, really. I became rather good at it. There was a certain kind of pride involved. People came to me in good faith, and I found myself' – he shakes his head as if troubled by midges – 'unable to be less than almost straightforward.' The boy and Talaia glance at each other. 'At one point I even had a small shop in Ithaldra.' The boy hasn't heard of it. He is learning how easy it is to sink so deeply into a place you begin not to need the world outside.

'I'm glad to see you haven't changed,' Yorin remarks. 'I've always admired your ability to disappear, although I sometimes had to let down a rope to haul you back up.'

No, the boy thinks, not that. Not a well or somewhere underground. More skybound, weightless, beyond the world.

Yorin glances around at the cushions and ornaments, Lirriel's toys, Vezu's mouse on the mantelpiece. A look crosses his face and is swiftly gone. 'You'll be pleased to know it was a great success,' he resumes. 'I was in the shop one day, dusting' – the boy coughs; Talaia tries to hide a smirk – 'when a feeling came over me. It was so strong I had to sit down. I knew it was time to go. I closed the shop, left a note for – someone – and saddled Tobi. It was a narrow escape.'

A note for someone. The boy will wonder about it for

some time. Around it he will construct stories with many branches and fanciful leaves.

'I couldn't get away fast enough,' Yorin says, glancing down at Lirriel. 'I rode until Tobi ran out of puff in a small, shabby village in the middle of nowhere. I asked around, trying to find work, but with no luck. Then it struck me. Most places want to present themselves in the best possible light, neat houses, well-kept gardens. This one looked as if it hadn't seen a coat of paint since the day it was built. I didn't have anything better to do, so I thought I might as well find out why.

'Thank you,' he says, as Talaia refills his cup. 'I talked to the owner of the tavern, and he told me the village had been plagued by bandits for so long they'd just about given up. The idea was that if they didn't look prosperous, the bandits would leave them alone. I'm not sure how successful it was, but it gave me something to work on. I knew what I needed, and I knew who to go to, a man who sold limewash. At least he had, until the village let itself go. When I bought the lot, he almost burst into tears. He left the same day.'

He looks thoughtful. 'It's funny how people believe they can only do something if something else happens. Anyway, I set up a stall in the market – hardly a stall, just a bunch of barrels covered with cloth. People came up to ask what I was selling, but I wouldn't tell them.' Lirriel chuckles, and he strokes her silky hair.

'I did the same thing the next day. The day after that, the headman was waiting for me with most of the village in tow. When he asked why I wouldn't tell them what I was selling, I said I didn't know I had to. From the look on his face, you'd have thought I was some kind of scoundrel.'

He grins. 'I said I'd show him, if he insisted, but I warned him it was dangerous stuff.

'When I pulled off a cloth to reveal a barrel' – his droll emphasis makes Talaia laugh – 'you can imagine the faces. The headman wasn't impressed, so I smirked. That woke him up. He ordered me to open it, so I did. The crowd stepped back, the headman looked down, looked up and asked what kind of trick I was playing. I told him it was no trick, the limewash had a quality so potent I'd been afraid of showing them.

'The crowd muttered, the headman looked sceptical – it was his job, after all. When he asked what was so special about the limewash, I said I'd tell him if he promised not to blame me, as it wasn't my fault. He'd run out of patience by now – his face couldn't get much redder – and said he wouldn't, just blasted well get on with it. So I did. I told him the limewash contained a special ingredient which, when painted on walls, repelled attack.' The boy laughs out loud.

After a sip of tea Yorin says, 'The villagers weren't sure if I was serious or not, so they looked to the headman for advice. He wasn't sure either, but he had a reputation to maintain. At first he told me it was nonsense – not the word he used' – he glances down at Lirriel – 'that limewash couldn't repel attack. At which point I became very serious and asked him if he believed there were things beyond his understanding.

'It took him a while to come up with an answer. He said of course there were; even he didn't know everything, although he knew who'd had the last slice of cherry pie at the tavern last night. It was a good answer; the villagers laughed. In which case, I said, I'd tell him about what happened in the last village I went to. They were sceptical too, but when they painted limewash on the walls, they never had another moment's trouble.

'The headman clearly didn't believe me, but his ears were tuned to the crowd. He asked me to give him my word, and I assured him everything I said was true. The crowd was on my side, we could both feel it. It was like coins falling into an open hand. They bought the lot.'

Talaia shakes her head and raises her eyes to the ceiling. Lirriel gurgles. '*Mama*,' she says.

'They bought it all, little one,' Yorin tells her. 'You see how clever your uncle is? They spent the next few days painting everything they could, every house, every stable, even the chicken coops, until the village was gleaming. I was, too, with the profits I made. I knew it was time to leave, but I wanted to see what would happen.

'I didn't have to wait long. There was a rumour that bandits had been seen in the area, and they obliged. They came expecting to find people so crushed with fear they'd leave whatever the bandits demanded in baskets in the marketplace. Instead they found a village so fired up with limewash – and various sharp implements – that they took one look and fled. That was a good day. I don't think I've ever had so much free beer.'

'You expect us to believe that?' Talaia asks, half smiling.

'They did.'

The five days Yorin spends with them are rich and full. He comes to the house every morning, and after coffee they walk in the orchards, watching the pickers at work. The little almond tree has been admired, Yorin's look telling the boy he hasn't forgotten either. They talk of many things, giving voice to places and times that have become muted in the boy's memory. Distance has transformed them into adventures, almost, and he can hardly believe he was once a part of them. They are not without pain, but the edge is less keen now.

Leaning against a tree he thinks back to yesterday, when he walked up the lane after taking Jena and the cart to the barn. They had returned from a visit to Meriem's, and Yorin was having lunch with them in the garden. The boy stopped at the gate, listening. To the tune of an old lullaby, Talaia was singing

Fly, little bird, fly,
High, little bird, high,
Carry my dreams to the one that I love,
Fly, little bird, fly.

He drank in the scene: Yorin with Lirriel in his lap, her blue smock the same colour as her mother's tunic, her topknot secured with a birthday ribbon; Talaia gazing at her daughter as she sang.

On Yorin's last evening, they gather round the table in Meriem's dining room. It is a loud, happy meal filled with dishes of rich stew, warm breads, spiced beans, roasted squashes. In the centre is a heroic bowl of apple wine that seems to be disappearing very quickly. When Talaia returns from checking on Lirriel, who is in a crib in the bedroom, Yorin says, 'She isn't strong enough yet to knot sheets and lower herself into the city, but give it time.'

461

Meriem laughs. 'You have all that to come,' she says, her eyes twinkling.

Morning has risen softly, staining the sky ochre and coral. Outside the house Yorin is standing in his cloak, holding Tobi's reins and talking with the boy and Talaia, who has Lirriel in her arms. Meriem has given him so much food his saddlebags barely close. Lirriel reaches for his hair and he obliges, leaning over so she can croon at him.

'Where will you go this time?' the boy asks.

He shrugs. 'Over there, perhaps' – he indicates with his head – 'or there' – nodding in the other direction.

'Come back and visit us,' Talaia says.

'How can I not, when I have my niece to bring presents for?' he says, kissing Lirriel's nose. Tobi regards him sourly. He is not a friend of departures, which mean wear and tear to hoof and back. The fact that he has been treated like a prince during his stay at the family's stables has done nothing to soften his eye.

'You love it really,' Yorin tells him. He takes a deep breath, as if inhaling the valley, and coughs. 'Getting soft. The sooner I'm off, the better.'

Talaia gently extracts Lirriel's fingers from his hair and looks at him steadily. 'One day,' she warns.

'But not today,' he says, kissing her cheek.

'There's apple wine for when you get thirsty,' the boy says.

Yorin's eyes sparkle. 'We may find ourselves going up the hills sideways.' For a moment they eye each other, then step forward into a hug.

They walk with him to the end of the lane and watch

him go, under a blue sky, over the clear-eyed river. When he reaches the crown of the bridge, he looks back and waves. The moment is sweet, and bitter.

Talaia takes the boy's hand. 'He'll be back,' she says. He turns to her, and smiles. There are apples to pick, jars to fill. The feeling drifts like leaves, and slowly fades.

Arun stirs, easing a knot in his neck. 'Autumn always felt like a threshold. Looking both ways, forward and back. Although I suppose you could say that of every season. We worked hard – there was always so much to do – but you could feel the stillness coming, the earth preparing for rest.'

'In case you're wondering, my favourite season is winter,' Night says.

Arun is silent for a while. 'In the end, there are only two seasons, life and death.'

He looks beyond the darkness to an autumn long past, when leaves of red and gold lit the orchards, and the air caught its breath in the morning.

They are sitting together at the table, talking. Lirriel is playing on the rug, rolling the little wooden horse to and fro.

'I don't like being away for so long,' the boy says.

Talaia is thoughtful, her face grave. 'I know. I don't like it either. But we did agree.'

'We could always send Vezu,' he suggests, and she laughs.

'He'd turn to soup,' she says affectionately.

The boy smiles, looking at Lirriel, who pulls herself up and makes her way over to him on sturdy little legs.

'*Dada*,' she says, and he catches her up into his lap, where she sucks contentedly on her cloth.

Talaia takes his hand. 'You don't regret it? Staying here, I mean. Not seeing what's over the next mountain, like Yorin.'

'Not for a second. I have all I need right here.'

It is entirely true. There may be times when he stands on the bridge looking at the mountains and wondering, but they are like mist. He came to the valley and stayed first for Talaia, then out of a sense of duty towards her family. Now that duty has been wholly absorbed by love. He thinks of Mirashi's poem about marriage and the differences that can arise within it. It is sad, and hopeful; even as she says

> our love has become a part of speech
> we can't agree on

she adds

> let us fold up
> the corners of our quarrel.

He and Talaia have rarely argued. At times there have been crisp silences or, from Talaia, a crystalline stare. When he tells her what he is thinking she says, 'Whatever differences we have, they take place within a greater space which – I'm going to sound soppy but I make no apology for it – is encircled by love.'

Smiling, he quotes from another poem.

Your temple is only as strong
as the heart it supports

and round it I am constructing a tall fort
of wattles on a timber frame.

Talaia kisses him. 'I'm not sure what love is made from,' she says, 'but I know it'll hold.'

Chalfur is a city beyond the eastern Tura Lar. It is the regional capital, and the boy has never heard of it. The road is well-maintained, but what matters is the time away from his family. Since there are legal issues involved, Adri will be going with him. It will take four or five days to get there, a week, perhaps, to complete the business, and then the return journey. If all goes well, it will mean a very important contract for the family.

It has already involved a great deal of discussion. On a visit to Sert a merchant, Kibula, had some business with Jobe. When he dined with Jobe and Estel they talked about the boy, the Suth Valley, and the family. They spoke so highly of him that Kibula wrote expressing an interest in meeting to discuss the possibility of supplying him with produce on a regular basis.

Jabar was all for keeping things as they were. 'Why change, when we do well enough as it is?' He spoke, the boy thought, from the comfortable chair, and he was inclined to agree. Meriem said that if they supplied the merchant three times a year as he asked, it would move their produce more efficiently and more economically. Her chair had a harder seat, although her bottom was enough of a cushion. The boy drowned the thought in a very deep well.

Finally they turned to Adri. He spread his hands in a familiar gesture, his face thoughtful. 'If it works out,' he said slowly, 'it will be a good thing for all of us.'

And so it was settled. When Adri asked if the boy would be happy to go, his reply was prepared. 'I don't really want to be away from Talaia and Lirri for so long. But' – glancing at Talaia – 'I know it's a great opportunity for the family.'

Adri leans down from the cart, talking quietly to Meriem. Talaia and Lirriel will once again be staying with the family. The boy folds them in his cloak, not wanting to let go. They stand for a while in the comfort of each other's closeness.

The boy takes a deep breath, and Talaia looks into his eyes. 'Go safely, my love,' she says, 'and come back safely. We'll be waiting.'

He wonders if he can in fact leave. Everything has shrunk to a point in which three people stand in utter clarity, and all else is haze. Gently he brushes a tear from Talaia's cheek, and kisses her. 'I love you,' he says softly, and turns to Lirriel to kiss her nose. 'And you, little one. I won't be long, and I'll bring something special back for you.'

'Just bring yourself,' Talaia says.

He climbs up into the cart. If he doesn't go now, he never will. As Jena walks on, he looks back. Talaia is holding up Lirriel's hand, and they are waving.

Chapter Thirty-Four

'I sometimes think,' Adri says, 'we should have to pay to leave. Then people would think twice about it.'

The boy silently agrees, shading his eyes as they cross the bridge and pass through the Suth Valley. He knows Jena well enough by now to loosen the reins and let her walk on.

Adri glances at the horizon. 'In my younger days, I had a notion that the different types of cloud were the different moods of the sky. I even wrote a pamphlet about it.'

The boy looks at him. He knows Adri isn't made of vellum and seals, but clouds seem so entirely opposite in character. 'So what are these ones?' he ventures. They gaze up at white unmoving blossoms.

'They're contented clouds, neither chased off by the wind nor troubled by rain. It was a short pamphlet,' Adri says with a wry smile.

As they wind their way through the foothills of the eastern Tura Lar, the boy looks back. He can't see the white house.

'I miss it already,' Adri says. 'When I was younger, I dreamed of great adventures, all featuring me, of course. Villains fleeing, ladies swooning. No obstacles, everything working out as it should. A paper dream. Not up to a shower of rain.

'When I met Meriem, everything changed. I was apprenticed to an advocate, Locri. To say he was bad-tempered would be doing his temper a disservice. He expected tea at all times of day, and absolute obedience. I didn't have much obedience to begin with, and I hated making tea. I found it incredibly frustrating – there were days when I climbed the walls and chewed the rugs – not at the same time – because I wanted to know everything, and it felt as if I wasn't learning anything at all.

'Everything.' He laughs. 'The truth is, most of it was donkeywork. Bearing the burden of the law into the courts and, depending on the verdict, carting a different load away. Day in, day out. Locri knew it, but he was too clever to let me find out immediately. By the time he was ready to teach me, I was desperate to learn. The driest piece of legislation was suddenly an oasis.'

The boy laughs.

'Funnily enough,' Adri says, 'I took to it immediately. It has its boring bits, of course – what job doesn't? – but it suited me. Which terrified me at the time – no more dreams, everything sewn up. Then, one day, everything changed. I was going to my usual place for coffee – I never drank tea outside Locri's chambers – when I saw Meriem. She was scolding someone for not filling her cup properly. Her hair was shining in the sun and her eyes were glinting.' He is silent for a moment. His profile is softened by the approaching dusk. 'I think we need some light.'

When the lanterns are lit he says, 'Where was I? Oh yes. I visited the coffee-house every day for a week, trying to get up the nerve to approach her. Every time I tried, my feet rusted up. And my mouth. At the end of the week, she beckoned me over and asked if I was going to sit down, as I must be very thirsty by now.' He smiles. 'I remember wondering what on earth I was going to say to her, but from the very beginning I found her easy to talk to.

'When she took me home to meet Jabar and Sireen, I liked them immediately. They were so welcoming I almost forgot my knocking knees. Yentra was there, but not Vezu or Birith yet. It became the custom for me to go to their house in the evenings for dinner. Nothing was said; it just happened naturally.'

'Oh, thanks,' he says, accepting the apple the boy offers. In a few bites he finishes it and tosses away the core. 'Well, one day I left Locri's chambers thinking that if I never went back, I'd be the happiest man alive. He'd been in a particularly foul mood, and I bore the brunt of it as usual. It was a hard day. It made me wonder if I was really made for the law, and if I wasn't, what else could I do? And, if I had to start again, what hope would I ever have of marrying Meriem?

'When I went for dinner that evening, Jabar knew something was wrong. He took me out onto the veranda, and we talked for a while. When he asked what was on my mind, I felt pretty uncomfortable. I wasn't someone who discussed my problems, not then at least, and I didn't want him thinking I was a bad prospect. I didn't know what to say. Jabar did. He told me that trust holds families together just as much as love. He was so patient and encouraging I found myself telling him about Locri, and the fears I had of never being able to set up on my own.

'He asked if I'd been to the courts yet, and I told him I had. When he asked how I found them, I said they seemed a place of two halves, the law on one hand, justice on the other, and they didn't always amount to the same thing. It had come as quite a shock to me. I explained I thought the law provided a structure justice might lack, and that was important, but I'd also seen it used as a shield for those with the money to buy it.

'When Jabar asked who I'd represent if I had my own chambers, I didn't have to think about it. Anyone who needed it, regardless of what they could pay. Naive, perhaps, but true. He thanked me for telling him, and that was that. Nothing more. I went home thinking I'd said too much, or the wrong thing.'

Adri pauses. The only sounds are Jena's hooves, the rumble of wheels, a bird's cry hollowing out the darkness.

'A week later, I was called into Locri's office. He did his usual trick of keeping me waiting while he carried on writing. When he finally looked up, he said he understood I no longer wanted to work for him.

'I was so shocked I didn't know what to say. He told me I had no idea how lucky I was, and asked how well I thought I'd do without him.' Adri shakes his head. 'At that point I was wondering if I'd walked into the wrong chambers. I managed to say that if I'd disappointed him, I was sorry, but I had no idea what he was talking about. He gave me his sizing-up look, shrugged, and said – I remember this clearly – "If that's what you want me to believe."

'That struck a nerve. There he was, sitting in judgement behind his desk, and I had no opportunity to defend myself.

I addressed him formally (in the circumstances I thought it best to call him master), told him I wasn't in the habit of lying, I didn't know what he meant, and could he please tell me. He asked – it was hardly a question – if I really had no idea someone had written to him terminating my apprenticeship.'

Adri brushes a moth from the side of his face. Its wings are wide enough to speak for themselves, a rich, buttery thrum. For a moment he watches it wallow in the arc of lantern light. 'At that point, anger took over. If what Locri said was true, I wanted to know who'd done it, who'd destroyed any hope of a career, of asking for Meriem's hand in marriage. He just sat there smugly until eventually I lost my temper and told him I had a right to know. When he said it was Jabar Astulla, I was speechless. I couldn't believe Meriem's father would do something like that.

'I demanded to see the letter. He took his time unfolding it and pushing it across the desk. It was indeed from Jabar. It did indeed say he was giving notice of termination of my apprenticeship, and enclosed the fee to conclude it.' Adri takes a breath. 'It further informed him that I was now the tenant of a set of chambers on the top storey of the building, and added that the views across the city were spectacular. It concluded by saying that Locri's tutelage had been appreciated, possibly more by the advocate than the apprentice. Then a courteous valediction, and Jabar's signature.

'Even as I was taking it in, Locri made a scornful remark about having fine friends, told me to get my things and go. He wished me luck, told me I'd need it, and that I'd soon find out how it worked. That no one thanks you for what you do; you please one person, the other resents you. He did give me one piece of advice, though. I can still see him squatting in his chair, his hands spread on the desk. He told me to prepare people for the worst. That way, they'd love you for anything you could give them.'

Night has settled round the cart. The lantern sways; the moth labours away. 'He was right. At the time I thought it was the most cynical thing I'd ever heard.' Adri laughs. 'At least he didn't charge me for it.'

For a while they travel in silence. 'Did you mind?' the boy asks eventually.

'I was furious. Jabar's letter said many things to me, none of them flattering. That I'd never stay the course, that I'd never find chambers of my own. That I'd never be able to provide for Meriem without someone else's help. I went to see him that evening, and he greeted me with his usual smile. I, on the other hand –'

He shakes his head. 'It still makes me cringe when I think about it. He knew something was wrong, and showed me into the sitting room. I stood at the window, refusing anything to eat or drink. I was so angry, I didn't know where to begin. In the end, all I could do was hold out the letter.

'He asked me to sit down and I did, with the worst possible grace, perching on the edge of a chair, seething. When he settled himself in his favourite chair, it made me think of the times we'd sat there in the evening, talking, laughing, playing card games. He watched me with those wise eyes for a moment, then said that when he and Sireen were gone, Meriem would inherit everything. He told me it was a great comfort to know she would be provided

472

for, but that she wasn't interested in the administration of the business. He'd tried to teach her, but they'd agreed on a parting of the ways while they were still on speaking terms.' The boy smiles.

'So' – Adri nods as if sitting opposite Jabar – 'he was left with a problem. Who could he trust? He said that those you work with close the door at the end of the day, but your family don't. When he told me he thought I'd be the answer to their problem he looked embarrassed, and a little guilty. He said he'd known I'd make a fine advocate, and apologised for being selfish in hoping he could share some of the running of the business with his future son. He apologised, too, for causing me distress.

'I felt about two inches tall. I didn't know what to say. So' – he takes a breath – 'I did the only thing I could. I got to my undeserving feet, went over to Jabar and stood before him. All I could manage was "thank you", but the look on his face told me it was enough.

'And then' – he laughs – 'the door burst open, and Meriem came in. I knew she'd been listening, even though she still denies it. Her cheeks were flushed, and when she asked if everything was settled, Jabar winked at me.' He falls silent for a moment. 'I was raw as eggs when I went into those chambers. I stood in the main office looking around, wondering what on earth I was going to do. Then Meriem came in, sniffed at the dust, condemned the furniture, and began to organise the place for me. All that and a wedding, too. But she managed, with help from Yentra.

'Jabar never intruded, never insisted on having his own way. But he was always there when we needed him.

As you know, Meriem and I lived in the house in Mirza when we were first married. When Sireen died, we moved into Jabar's house to be with him. He didn't ask us, and he didn't expect it – we wanted to. We love him,' he says simply.

It is time to rest. Under a tall outcrop they secure the cart and settle Jena for the night. After their meal, the boy takes from his satchel a packet of taklaris Talaia made the night before. It contains a note. He has to blink to read it properly. When he has finished, he folds it up and puts it in his shirt pocket.

'We'll be back before you know it,' Adri says gently.

As Jena makes her way along the mountain roads, Adri recounts stories about his clients, some so funny they reduce the boy to tears of laughter. The best one, in which he and Locri meet in court, he saves for last. The passage of time had done nothing to cool Locri's temper, or his opinion of his former apprentice. Although told with Adri's characteristic modesty, it is clear he still relishes the victory.

'He never spoke to me again. All further communication took place in letters. That was a good day.'

They climb still higher, caught between rock walls and a strip of sky. As they come out onto a rocky plateau, a vast panorama fills the boy's eyes, a composition of green hills and wooded plains. Here are villages in peaceful accommodation with the land, hillsides hung with strands of white water and, in the near distance, a great city.

Chalfur. The boy finds it almost too big to take in. 'When I first saw it, I wanted to run a mile,' Adri says. 'It made me realise how happy I was in my own home.'

As they pass through the teeming streets, the boy sees with some surprise that Chalfur is not an elegant city. It is made of many types of brick and stone, with no apparent care for style or order. Wooden buildings, hardly more than shacks, lean out from street corners, their doors peeling, their ironwork rusting. Adri tells him the old city, the original part, is in the centre.

'All this has accumulated over centuries,' he says. 'It means people live very close together, and that can make life interesting. I couldn't live like it, myself.'

As scraps of conversation drop from the upper storeys of houses, as people shout their business with no care for where their words might fall, the boy is inclined to agree. There are children everywhere, running about, clutching improvised toys of sticks and cloth. They chatter brightly, taking no notice of passers-by. It is clear the art of shared living begins very young. The lives of men stream lightly through the streets, he thinks, recalling a line from the Book of Light. The poem goes on to say that

the drone of water underfoot
is time at its deepest pitch.

Time. He shivers, as if it runs cold beneath his feet.

Alone in his room after dinner, the boy sits down heavily on the bed. Recommended by Adri, the Waterfall is their home for the week. He feels suddenly exhausted. Weariness is not the only weight on his heart.

He is so tired he only wakes when someone shouts under his window. He blinks, turns, and reaches for Talaia.

As the room assembles around him, he scrubs his fingers through his hair and tips himself feet-first onto the floor. Opening the shutters, he looks out. The air is mild and crisp, scented with woodsmoke.

After breakfast, they make their way to the trade halls. 'This quarter belongs to the advocates,' Adri says as they turn into a wide street. 'I've been here once before, to settle a matter that couldn't be resolved in Mudaina.'

'Did you settle it?' the boy asks.

'I did.'

They emerge into a large, tree-lined square. To the left is a building with an imposing facade. 'The courts,' Adri says. 'And those' – he nods at the building facing them – 'are the trade halls.' The morning sun dusts the trees, firing the many-coloured stone until it dazzles. 'If you had a window view, you'd never get any work done,' he remarks as they cross the square.

A broad, shallow flight of steps carries them into a wide hall lined with offices. Someone is approaching, a lean man in a tunic of figured yellow damask embroidered with gold thread. His cream-coloured trousers are tucked into boots of tooled green leather.

'We're looking for Kibula,' Adri says, bowing.

The man bows back. 'You've found him.'

Adri introduces himself. 'Then you must be Arun,' Kibula says. The boy steps forward, conscious of appraisal. He meets the merchant's eye, holding his gaze. When the courtesies are over, Kibula invites them inside.

He takes them through his office into a large sitting room arranged with sofas and comfortable chairs, rugs of turquoise silk, lamps of marble and bronze. When they are seated, he pours tea fragranced with lemon and rosewater. The boy accepts a little candied cake.

Kibula is talking to Adri. 'I see,' he says, turning to the boy. 'So you run the business now?'

'With the help of my wife and the family. We all work together.'

'Of course.' Kibula nods. Then, 'Your wife?' The inflection is delicate.

The boy sits hard on his defences. 'I couldn't do it without her.'

'Indeed?' More inflection.

'Yes.' The boy keeps his tone polite and even.

The air and Adri are very still. Kibula sips tea thoughtfully. 'They are the anchor of our ships, are they not?'

The boy can almost hear Talaia's retort. He bites his lip. 'They are,' he says.

It is a long day. Adri warned him nothing would be said about the supply of grain, fruit or vegetables. Kibula shows them around the trade halls, introducing this merchant, that trader. All defer to him. The boy looks about, trying to show interest, but his mind keeps returning to the white house in the valley.

That evening they dine quietly at the inn. 'I thought it would never end,' Adri says with a yawn. 'And tomorrow' – he grimaces – 'we'll probably be taken off to see another batch of magnificent buildings.' He takes a sip of apple juice. 'Not as good as ours.'

It is as Adri predicted. They accompany Kibula to the library to look at scrolls dating back to the founding of the city. 'So you're a family man?' Kibula says.

The boy has never thought of himself in this way before. A warmth fills his chest. There is so much more to it than such shorthand can ever express. But it marks him with the simple pride of love. 'Yes,' he says, 'I am.'

He sits now, on the fourth day, opposite Kibula, in the merchant's substantial office. Paintings and embroidered hangings decorate the walls. On a small table stands an exquisite tree of gold and silver. It is, Kibula explains, a miniature of a full-sized tree he saw once, in a palace. The boy has a sudden desire to stand in the orchards and hear birds singing as the sun comes up.

The time has come. They have gone through Kibula's requirements in detail, and Adri is waiting in the sitting room. The merchant offers tea; the boy drinks.

'You like our city?' Kibula asks.

The boy knows he means the centre, the ancient heart, which is, for the merchant, the only part that matters. 'It's magnificent.'

Kibula nods. 'You see what we have made. A beauty that endures. Our standards are the highest.' He inclines his head. 'My factor, Maru, has inspected the samples you brought. They are' – a fractional pause – 'good. But other people could offer similar things.'

Not the apple wine, not the preserved lemons, not the barley, the boy thinks, then reminds himself that Kibula approached him. There is no need to defend what he has brought.

'You can deliver three times a year?' Kibula asks.

He nods.

'The quality will be as good?'

'Every time.'

'Ah.' Kibula stares out into the main hall. He talks of risk, the importance of a good name, the fragility of reputation. He speaks of the length of time his family have been in business in Chalfur, of grandfathers, fathers, sons.

At last he says, 'I have discussed it with Terek, my advocate, and I have arrived at a figure. I hope it will not be disagreeable to you.'

The boy accepts the folded paper. He unfolds it, reads it, sits back in his chair. He drinks tea, studies it again. Kibula is a scholar of shrewdness, of exquisite guile. But the boy has Talaia at his side and, whether he likes it or not, the merchant and Nissa in his ear.

The morning passes to and fro, in negotiation and polite silences. Finally Kibula shakes his head. 'You ask too much,' he says. The boy waits. Kibula taps his fingers on his desk. Suddenly he smiles. 'Very well. We have an agreement.'

The boy lets out a long inward breath. He extends his hand; Kibula shakes it firmly. 'I think your cousin will want to come in now. There are documents to be signed and witnessed.'

That evening they dine with Kibula and Terek. No wives are present. If Talaia had been there, she would have sat like a firework waiting to be lit. Sack and barrel, bottle and jar may well have gone up in smoke. No, the boy chides himself, my wife is more subtle than that. He smiles, impatient to tell her about it. The contract is a triumph, but what matters is sharing it with his family. Talaia will listen, comment, praise. Lirriel will make bubbles out of it.

Jena stamps, snorting clouds of air. The sun picks out details of rock and tree, the air is cool and clear. Adri hums softly as they travel. The boy thinks of the day he asked Talaia to marry him, and how it will always glow with rose-coloured light. He smiles, touching the pocket of his tunic. Yesterday afternoon he went into the jewellery quarter with Adri, and came away with two velvet boxes. He is already imagining their faces as Talaia and Lirriel open their presents.

The mountains are behind them. As they come down into the Suth Valley, the boy's impatience runs down the reins to Jena, who snorts, tosses her head, and continues at the same pace. He looks about. Nothing has changed; fields, orchards, river, all are in place. As they join the path to Mudaina, the boy urges the horse to a brisker pace. She shakes her mane and plods on.

'Nearly there,' Adri says, smiling as they turn into the familiar street.

The boy's heart leaps. Halfway down, they hear a cry. Someone has been watching for them. The door in the gate opens and Meriem comes running to meet them. Her face is flushed, and she is crying.

Chapter Thirty-Five

Adri jumps down from the cart and runs towards her. When he reaches her, she flings her arms around him. The boy finds himself unable to move. He can hear Meriem sobbing, choking out words. A touch on his arm makes him look around. Very gently Adri says, 'Please, come down, Arun. Come inside.'

Somehow he finds himself in the sitting room with Meriem, Adri and Jabar. The old man's face is ashen. He seems unable to speak. Meriem is crying silently, holding a handkerchief to her face.

Adri takes a breath. 'Please, come and sit down.' He leads the boy to a chair. 'It's Talaia and Lirriel. They –' He tries to say more, but cannot.

'It's my fault,' Meriem bursts out. 'If I hadn't insisted on them going home –' She breaks down. Jabar puts his arm around her.

'There was talk of fever in the city,' he says, 'and Meriem felt – we all felt – that with Lirriel being so young, they would be safer at home.' He rubs his hand across his face, shaking his head despairingly.

Adri's eyes are blank with shock. 'What happened?' he asks finally. 'Was it the fever?'

Meriem answers, her voice shaking. 'No. That's just it.

There wasn't any fever. It was just a rumour. As soon as I found out, I went to tell them. When I got there –' She starts crying again.

'Meriem found them,' Jabar says gently, stroking her hair, murmuring words of comfort.

The room is silent. Adri clears his throat. 'Do you know what it was?'

'The physician wasn't sure, but he thinks it was tainted water,' Jabar says.

Wiping her face, Meriem goes over to the boy and kneels down, taking his hands. 'I am so sorry, Arun. If I'd gone earlier, if I hadn't stayed away –'

Her dress fans out at either side. Her hair has a fine grey parting; he hadn't known she dyed it. He sits very still. If he doesn't move, time will stop too.

Beside the pool, Arun closes his eyes. Night deepens around him. There is utter silence. Finally he lifts his head. Meriem's sitting room has been closed to him for so long he can hardly bear to look, but he does.

Yentra comes into the room. Darting forward, she touches the boy's arm and withdraws. Moments later she returns, carrying a tray. She puts it down, throws him an anguished look, and goes out again.

He stares at the teapot, the cups. They seem very solid and somehow not real. After a moment, Meriem pats his hand and gets to her feet. She pours tea and offers the boy a cup. He presses it against his palms, gripping hard.

'We thought' – Meriem sounds almost fearful – 'you'd like them to be in the garden, under the almond tree. I –'

She hesitates, and the boy senses the word she is trying not to say and almost hates her for making him think it – 'put Lirriel's little cloth with her. I didn't want her to miss it.' She breaks down again, and Adri puts his arms around her as she sobs.

Jabar looks at him. He is about to say something, but the boy has no wish to hear it.

'Would you like to be alone for a while?' Adri asks gently.

Yes, he would, because he is. The conjunctions of happiness, hope and love have come apart. They are words his heart slowly learned to spell, and he wishes now that he had remained ignorant. As he stumbles to his feet and leaves the room someone touches his arm, but he brushes it away. He leaves the house, crosses the courtyard and goes out of the door in the gate. He has to get away because it is a house in mourning, and he is not part of it.

When he reaches the path that will take him to Mirza, he stops. A woman greets him as she passes. The look on his face makes her hurry on, throwing a nervous glance behind her. He forces himself on, ignoring the river, pearl-blue and beautiful.

And there it is, the white house. As he stands at the door, something rises in his heart. Of course they are there, waiting for him. He takes a breath, and lifts the latch.

How do you measure the silence of a place? Nothing has changed, and everything has. The living room holds only the objects it contains. They have no life to them. They never had. He doesn't look at the toys on the floor but walks straight through, into the kitchen. For a moment he stares at the pans hanging from hooks on the ceiling. At the small clay oven in the wall, the fat-bellied pot suspended over a cold hearth. Turning away, he opens the back door.

Autumn has been at work, preparing the garden for sleep. At the far end, in front of the almond tree, is a gleaming white stone. He can see it is made of good marble, and has writing on it. Only when someone touches his arm does he realise how cold he is.

'We'd like you to stay with us,' Adri says gently. 'If you want to, of course. Meriem doesn't want you to be alone.'

After the first week, he starts dreaming. He dreams Talaia is lying next to him and turns to her, crying, saying he thought he had lost her. He dreams he hears Lirriel calling from her cradle, and wakes to find himself alone. So he tries not to sleep. He sits at the window in the room Meriem has prepared for him, hating the world that took his family from him, hating himself because he is here and they are not.

He knows he is the subject of conversation, and resents it. He spends each day in the smaller sitting room, where he is less likely to be disturbed. His eyes have travelled the rugs so many times he knows every stitch and thread.

There is a knock at the door. Adri comes in, carrying a tray. 'I thought you might be hungry.'

The boy looks at the meat pie, the fruit, the cheeses. The jug of cordial, the blue-glazed cup. He wonders why he needs them. The body is a cart pulled by the mind. If the mind becomes a mule and sits down, the body won't move. If the mind is starved, the body will die.

Adri places the tray on a side table and straightens up.

'Would you like me to stay for a while?' he asks. His face is anxious, and boy feels a sudden pang.

'I'm sorry, I'm not very good company.'

'It isn't a social call,' Adri says with a gentle smile. In the hierarchy of smiles, it is not far from the safety of the ground. The boy wonders if the library caves hold a book on the subject. If they did, the old man would surely know. Memory pierces his mind so sharply he recoils. He wishes he had a cloth, heavy and dark, to pull over it. This is the problem. Not the body, but the pitiless mind. Even though it is his own, and has knowledge of his circumstances, it shows no compassion.

'Try and eat something,' Adri says. 'It'll do you good.'

The boy looks at the food on the tray. He picks up a fig. It sits in his hand like a toad.

Adri clears his throat. 'I thought you might like to know we're about to start planting the barley.' It comes back in a stinging rush, the fields, the orchards, the river. He doesn't reply. 'Right, well, I'll leave you in peace,' Adri says. He closes the door quietly behind him.

Later that day there is another knock. The look on Meriem's face is one he is beginning to dread. He forces himself to smile, and she smiles back so warmly he feels another bite of guilt.

'Adri mentioned the barley?' There is about her an air of such delicate concern the boy could reach out and part it like a cobweb. 'We're down on workers at the moment, so we wondered if you –'

'Of course I'll help,' he says.

He helps so hard he exhausts himself. His back aches, his fingers throb, but at last the planting is done, and already spoken for by Kibula. He knows Adri has been afraid to mention the contract, and realises he doesn't want to become one of those people whose presence takes the joy out of things.

He saw it once, in his village. A widow, treated with kindness and consideration in the first days of loss. Then, as if a duty had been discharged, she became an awkwardness. People were suddenly busy when she passed by. Except for his mother. She treated the woman as she had always done, taking to market an extra loaf, a clutch of eggs, to give to her. When the woman moved away to live with relatives, the village breathed a sigh of relief. It was as if a taint had been removed.

He wonders why. Because no one wants to be reminded of what is to come? Because there are things that cause a pain so blinding no one can face it?

The days have become like a house of wattle and daub; if every chink is filled, no feeling can get through. He gets up and goes to the barns, where apples sweeten in the dry air. He records how many bottles have been filled with apple wine. He makes tallies of grain, discusses jars of spiced tomatoes and preserved cherries. Adri takes time off work, and together they go through page after page of accounts. Business is thriving. If Kibula wants more, there will be no problem in supplying him.

In the evenings after dinner he sits with Meriem, Adri, Jabar and sometimes Yentra. Friends call, take coffee, tea or wine with the family. Winter has dug in now; a fire reddens the hearth and throws shadows across the walls. The shutters are closed early against a rosy sunset sky.

They treat him like a wound that needs careful attention. At times he finds himself wanting to shout at their kindness, to see them blink with hurt, and is overwhelmed with shame. He goes to the market, to a tea house, but he cannot leave himself behind. He has become his own shadow, and wishes he could rub it out.

On the first day of Kaba, he attends the feast with the family and their friends. When it is over, he goes up to his room and sits on his bed. Prayers were said for those the year had taken, and as Jabar spoke the boy stared very hard at the floor.

He looks at his hands. Long fingers, slender knuckles. He turns them over and studies the creases, recalling a woman in his village rumoured to be skilled at reading palms. His mother dismissed it as nonsense, but his sister had been intrigued. At market, she disappeared for some time and returned with an air of mystery. At first he wondered where she had been. Then he told himself that was exactly what she wanted.

For the whole day he resisted. By evening he felt like a bullfrog, puffed up with the effort of not asking. He went to her house in the shrubs, barging in, demanding to know. They sat facing each other, neither giving quarter. Such negotiations were delicate; if he broke now she wouldn't tell him at all. So he held his nerve, and waited.

'I saw that woman,' she said eventually. 'The reader of palms.'

He was taken aback. First because of his mother and her views on the subject, and second, emitting a soft jingling sound, the money side of it. 'I thought you had to pay for it.'

His sister seemed quietly delighted with herself. 'Yes,

but she didn't charge me.' When he asked her why, she told him it was because she knew how the woman did it. 'There's a trick to it.'

'I don't believe you,' he said. She shrugged, and began playing with her stuffed animal. He fought with himself in silence, fiercely. 'If you're so clever, why don't you show me?'

His sister raised her eyebrows and gestured for him to hold out his hand. 'It needs washing,' she observed, then examined his palm, frowning. 'Well, there you are, then.'

'Eh?' the boy said. Then, triumphantly, 'I knew it, you don't know!'

He was about to leave the shrubs when his sister said, 'And now you'll go indoors and have some milk and a piece of toasted bread, and then you'll go to bed. Tomorrow, you'll get up after being told to at least three times, then you'll go out and help Father with the potatoes. You'll grumble about it, and then you'll have lunch.

'In the afternoon you'll go to the stream so Father can't find you, and you'll try to catch fish, but you won't succeed. You'll go back in because it's time for dinner, and you'll be scolded for not helping Father. You'll sulk a bit – yes, you do – and then after dinner you'll sit with Mother and me and she'll tell us a story. Then you'll wash your hands, have some milk and toasted bread, and then you'll go to bed.'

She sat back and looked at him. He stared at her. 'What's that got to do with my future?'

'I've just told you what you'll be doing tomorrow, haven't I?' she said, rolling her eyes. He subsided in confusion.

That night he lay in bed feeling something had taken place that wasn't entirely honest. That a trick had been played. 'I still don't think it counts,' he whispered.

'Then the secret's safe,' she whispered back.

With that he had to be content. Much later, he realised she had shown him how the woman used her knowledge of the village to surprise its inhabitants with what they had no idea she knew about them.

The boy closes his hands. He digs his fingernails into his palms, then lies back on the bed listening to the music and chatter below, the celebrations taking place across the city, feeling as if he has never been part of it at all.

The sky is a cloudless blue, the air dry and crisp. In the sitting room, the boy and Adri are talking. It is almost time to go to Chalfur, and they are discussing the forthcoming journey. He will be going without Adri, who is busy with the domestic aftershocks of Kaba, the result, he says, of so many families coming together. Even though the weather is generally dry at this time of year he calls it the rainy season, referring to the way goodwill can be washed away in the relentless tide of proximity. Meriem has her own way of putting it: too many herons nesting in the same tree.

'Well,' she says, brushing her hands on her apron as she comes in, 'it's done. I don't think you could fit any more in. We'll bring the wagons round first thing.' The boy stayed away while the goods were being loaded, grateful for the family's tacit understanding.

'I was talking with Birith,' she says. 'There's no snow in the passes, so the roads are clear. Let's hope it lasts.'

They spend the evening in front of the fire, going over the contract, finalising arrangements. Bandits have been seen in the mountains, and the boy will be taking Vezu,

Birith, and Birith's cudgel with him. Yorin's dagger is in his belt. Let them come, he thinks savagely.

The following morning he rises early enough to avoid even Yentra. For a moment he stands looking around the room. It is the last time he will see it. He will do his duty and go to Chalfur, but he will not return. Instead he will head north, to Kerizon. He can no longer ignore the feeling that has been steadily growing. He couldn't look for her before because he was too afraid of what he might find. He still is. But now there is no one else left. Kara. His last hope. This time he will not give up. He will not fail her again.

In his satchel are letters addressed to Meriem, Adri and Jabar. He will give them to Vezu or Birith on the way back, before he leaves them. He hopes the family will understand. But there is something he has to do first.

Fastening his cloak, he shoulders his satchel and slips out of the house. The night has managed a small frost, and rooftops sparkle faintly. He walks quickly and purposefully, taking the path beside the river, turning down the lane to the white house. The living room is dark and cold as he walks through to the kitchen and out into the garden.

Frost glitters; dew darkens the tips of his boots. At the far end he stops in front of the white stone, staring at the inscription. *Talaia Alesh Persaba. Lirriel Alesh Persaba.*

He wants to kneel, but cannot. He wants to cry, but cannot. They are gone, and with them all human light.

Turning, he walks back, through the kitchen, into the living room. Immediately he knows he is not alone. Someone is standing beside the front door, in shadow.

'It has been a long time,' a voice says, 'but I have been patient. I have waited.'

Chapter Thirty-Six

That voice, soft, lightly accented. A voice he last heard in a place he has tried very hard to forget. Sickness rises. Sweat chills the back of his neck. Even as he tells himself it cannot be true, he knows it is.

'Show yourself,' he says furiously, going to the side window and throwing open the shutters. Light falls on a figure in a hooded brown cloak.

'Do you not know me, Arun Persaba? I know you.'

The figure steps forward, the hood is pushed back, and the boy recoils in horror and disgust. The sides of the face are hideously disfigured, as if something jagged has been drawn down them slowly. But the eyes he would know anywhere. Pale yellow. A viper's eyes.

'It is not pretty, is it?' Magra says. 'But I deserved it.'

The boy's mind works frantically. Not Ruvek's men at all. How could he have been so blind? 'Why have you been following me? What do you want?'

The mouth twists into a cold smile. 'There is a word in my language. *Kochima*. Honour. Because of you, I was cast out from the House of Goash. Because of you, I lost my honour. I was disgraced.'

For the briefest instant Magra's eyes flash with hate. 'The House of Goash is all I have ever known. Drasta raised me; he taught me everything he knew. It took time to earn his trust, but I did. He was like a father to me, and I became his most faithful servant. When he found out you had escaped, he punished me.' He touches his scarred face. 'There were tears in my master's eyes when he pronounced me *efyedi*, outcast. It was only right. I failed him. I failed the House of Goash.

'Men died because of you, Arun Persaba. At first I thought it would have been better if I had died too, but Drasta is wise. He let me live so I could find you and restore my honour. The honour of the House of Goash.'

'Honour?' The boy spits out the word. 'You abducted my family, you sold them into slavery. Because of you, my mother never saw her husband or children again. Because of you, my father died without seeing his wife or daughter again. Because of you –' He breaks off, shaking with rage.

Magra observes him calmly. 'I had a family too. I swore an oath. I made a vow. Because of you, that bond was broken. I would not expect you to understand. It does not matter. I have dedicated my life to righting the wrong you have done, to taking away everything you care about, just as you have taken everything from me.

'I have watched you, all these years I have watched you. Did you really think I would simply let you leave? When you crossed the desert into the Marimvara Hills, I followed. It would have been easy to kill you then, but I told myself the time had not yet come.'

Pebbles slipping underfoot. At the time, the boy dismissed it as the sound of his fear. It is a bitter remembrance. Other times, other feelings, coldly begin to rise.

Magra smiles. 'I watched while you lay sleeping beside the pool of the crescent moon. At the caves of Linshafan, I saw you meet the woman who would become your wife. That was an unexpected gift.'

The boy's mouth is dry. He cannot move.

'The mind is a fragile thing,' Magra says. 'Give it cause to doubt and it will never know a moment's peace. I wanted you to always be looking over your shoulder, to always be wondering. You heard my footsteps in the Eye of Jala. Of course you did. I made sure of it. And then you went into the Green Mountains.'

With sickness in his heart, the boy remembers asking Yorin if there were animals in the mountains.

'When you travelled from Kushtar to Dhurkana, I hoped you would find your mother alive. It would have been pleasing to take her from you again. But watching you kneel at her grave gave me a certain satisfaction. It was right that you should understand what it was to have a part of you taken away. It was right that you should suffer.'

In vivid hindsight, the boy sees a figure standing in contemplation in front of a headstone. A figure in a hooded brown cloak. At the time it barely registered.

Magra licks his lips, as if tasting the air. 'For a time it seemed as if your family was determined to thwart me. First your mother, then your father, broken in the mines of Chanlin and taken to Amala Dyssul. No,' he says, as if reading the boy's thoughts, 'I waited until you left to pay my respects. And I found that a marriage had taken place.

'So, two of your family lost, two remaining. Do you remember Kerizon? A beautiful city. But not for you. You failed to find your sister. Of course you did. You have no courage, no determination. You gave up so easily.'

For a moment the boy closes his eyes, reliving the feeling of being watched as they searched the Velvet Quarter for Kara.

'And now we come to the best part,' Magra says, his soft voice hypnotic. 'The beautiful Suth Valley. The reputation of its apple wine is well-deserved.'

The boy is back in the orchards, experiencing a tug of recognition as a figure in a hooded brown cloak slips away through the trees. His breath fills his throat. He wants desperately not to listen, but is gripped by a terrible compulsion.

Magra licks his lips again. 'The prospect of a child is a wonderful thing. A cause for celebration. I had to go away for a time, on business I think will interest you, and when I returned it did not take long to hear the news. The Astulla family are held in great esteem and everyone, it seemed, was talking about it. The time was finally coming, and the rewards were greater than I could ever have hoped for.'

A dreadful thought is forming. The boy thinks back to that spring, and how he dismissed his growing sense of unease as the formless worries of a father-to-be. A shadow lifting, a shadow returning.

Magra is watching him. 'When you saw me in the market square, were you frightened? You should have been. And when you came after me –' He spits on the floor. 'You are nothing, and deserve nothing. It would have been easy to kill you then, but the time was not right. And then the child came. You had a family of your own.

You see how these things present themselves?' He smiles, as if acknowledging the elegance of the arrangement.

'You kept your wife close, and when the child came you kept them even closer. But I was prepared to wait. It was a challenge, and I accepted it.' He inclines his head, as if engaged in a depraved game. 'The first time you went away, they stayed with the family. Which gave me little opportunity to do what was needed. It had to be accomplished here, in your house, at the appropriate time. It was only fitting. It is the way of such things.

'When you went away the second time, my patience was wearing a little thin. I told myself I had to find a way to bring matters to a close. The opportunity came in a form I had not anticipated. Talk of fever in the city. How quickly rumour catches fire. And so your wife and child returned here, for their safety.'

He puts his hands together and takes a deep, savouring breath. 'There is a plant in the desert known only to the House of Goash. When correctly prepared, it yields a poison so subtle it cannot be traced.'

A rushing sound fills the boy's ears. The room spins. The realisation is almost too monstrous to take in. He turns away, retching. When he straightens, his voice shakes as he says, 'It was you. You murdered them. You came into my house and you murdered my family.'

A look of contempt crosses Magra's face. 'Did you really think I would let you take everything from me without paying a price? How little you know of the world. You deserve to suffer, as I have suffered.'

Bile rises in the boy's throat. 'You bastard!' he shouts, and lunges at Magra, who steps deftly aside, the corner of his cloak flicking out of reach. The boy stumbles past and turns, half blind with hate.

'Patience,' Magra says, 'we are not yet done. There is the matter of your sister. I watched your pitiful attempts in Kerizon. Did you really think you would find her? Did you really think they would tell you what you wanted to know?' A fanatical light gleams in his eye. 'I am of the tribe of the House of Goash. I will not be denied. When I was sure you were settled in the Suth Valley, I went looking for her. That was the business I had to attend to. And I found her. It was not easy – it took some time. She was very skilled at concealing herself.'

The room tightens around the boy. White spots prickle in front of his eyes. His head fills with roaring heat.

'You will be pleased to know she is safe and well, for now. I could have killed her – I was tempted – but I had something more rewarding in mind.'

The boy glances at the door.

'You want to leave right now to look for her. She is the last of your family, after all. But you will not reach her before I do. How does it feel to know that I am going to take away the last remaining member of your family, that there is nothing you can do to stop me? Does it hurt? Does it make you angry?'

The boy's eyes blaze. Fumbling for his dagger, he lunges again, but Magra sidesteps and he finds himself running at the fireplace, grazing his hand as he puts it out to stop himself. Reeling round, he charges, but Magra moves so swiftly he collides with the wall and staggers backwards.

Quickly he turns. Magra is standing beside the table. He throws a contemptuous glance at the dagger in the boy's hand, and pushes back his cloak. A long, curved scabbard hangs at his side.

He studies the boy's face, and smiles. 'I am a fair man. I will give you a chance to save your sister's life. To redeem yourself. When I leave, you will follow. But I will not make it easy. I will be watching every step you take. When you close your eyes, desperate for sleep, I will be waiting. And when your sister is dead, I will attend to you, and the last of your line will be destroyed. Then I will return to my master, and I will take him your head. And he will welcome me back, and all stain will be removed.'

The boy stares for some moments before finding his voice. 'You're the one who's going to die. You're not going back to the desert, or to your master. You'll be dishonoured forever. I'll make sure of it.'

He raises his dagger, gripping it hard. Magra regards him steadily, a look of satisfaction on his mutilated face. 'Yes, good. Remember this feeling when you come after me.'

For a moment – an endless spell of time – they face each other. Then, as if from far away, as if from deep water, there is a knock at the door.

'Arun?' Adri's voice. 'Are you in there?'

The boy looks from the door to Magra, and back again. Before he can move Magra slips past, into the kitchen. The boy turns, but the front door is opening and Adri is coming through.

Chapter Thirty-Seven

'I thought I heard voices,' Adri says. 'Is everything all right?' His gaze falls on the dagger in the boy's hand. There is fear in his eyes. 'Arun?'

'I'm fine,' the boy says quickly. 'I was just checking the blade.'

Adri looks unconvinced. 'Why don't you sit down for a bit?'

The boy clenches the dagger. He needs to leave, to follow Magra, right now.

Adri studies him for a moment. 'I thought I'd find you here. I came to let you know everything's ready. Are you sure you're all right?'

'I'm fine, really.'

'I can always tell them to wait. You don't have to leave right now.'

The boy looks down at his hands. How can he explain?

'I can't go,' he says finally.

'Is it because of Chalfur? I did wonder if –'

'It's not that. There's something I have to do. It's important. I can't tell you any more than that. I'm sorry. But I have to leave.'

Adri is briefly silent. 'Is there anything I can do to help? You only have to ask, you know that.'

The boy shakes his head. Then he says, 'Yes. Would you thank Meriem for everything, and tell her I'm sorry? Jabar, too. I know they won't understand, and I know I can never repay you for everything you've done for me, but –'

Adri's eyes are filled with sorrow. 'I will, my friend.'

Silence stretches between them. There is so much the boy wants to say, but he cannot find the words. 'What will happen with the delivery?' he asks. 'Will Birith and Vezu be able to –'

'We'll manage. You do what you have to do.' Sick with guilt, desperate to leave, the boy says nothing. He is too numb to respond to the warmth of Adri's embrace.

At the door Adri says, 'There'll always be a home here for you, if you want it.' He gives the boy a lingering look, and leaves the white house.

Arun's hand shakes as he drinks from the water bottle. A light breeze stirs the water of the pool, drawing out strands of pearl.

'I unhitched myself from a home, a family, a city, without a backward glance,' he says. 'All I could think of was finding Magra and stopping him before he got to my sister. Nothing else mattered.'

In the stillness of the clearing, he hears a door closing. The boy is coming out of the back door of the house, his satchel slung across his body, a leather sack on his shoulder. He walks quickly down the garden, stopping briefly to touch the white headstone, murmuring something before going through the gate.

'I made them a promise,' Arun says. 'I said I wouldn't let them down, I wouldn't fail them again. I made the

499

same promise to my sister.' A moment's silence. 'I scoured the lane, desperate to find Magra. I had no idea which way he'd gone. I tried the path beside the river, and that's when I saw him. He was standing a little way off, a smile on his face. It was as if he was taunting me. Then he was gone, and I was running.'

He is blind to the river flowing beside him, blind to anyone who might be wondering at a boy at full pelt, a leather sack bouncing on his back. He hitches up the strap and runs faster. There are people in the fields; whether they stop and look as he passes by, or tend to seed and leaf as they have always done, he neither knows nor cares.

The bridge where he once stood with his daughter in his arms flies past; too soon he reaches a junction. He glances to the left – no sign of the hooded brown cloak. To the right – yes, there it is. Through pastureland to the edge of the foothills of the southern Tura Lar they run at punishing speed. He can see Magra clearly, his stride never faltering, moving with the swiftness of a cat.

He pushes himself on. Even as his body strives for breath, his heart is an unquenchable flame. There is one course and one way forward. To stop Magra, to save his sister.

Magra climbs the foothills with no break in stride, running as if possessed. The boy's muscles burn, his lungs are bursting, but grief and rage drive him on. He charges headlong at the slopes, slipping on turf, pulling himself up, keeping Magra always in sight.

The land rises steadily, the ground strewn with small pebbles. A pale sky frames the winter sun. They are following a track across a naked hillside, nothing between them but the pace and will of each. The boy stumbles, falls on one knee, swears, and hauls himself up again. With a backward glance at the Suth Valley, as lovely now as it was when he came over the northern mountains, he runs on.

All day he follows the twists and turns of the track. The hills fold around him; he is buried so deep he can see nothing but slopes of grass. At times he thinks he has lost Magra, and stands with his heart in his mouth, gasping. And then a movement, the flick of a hooded brown cloak, and he starts running again.

The sun is turning to the western horizon as he reaches a fork in the track. One path runs steeply up the hillside, the other goes forward and on. He looks around. Magra is nowhere in sight.

'Where are you?' he shouts. Silence condenses in the still air. He turns a circle, scouring the rutted slopes. 'Show yourself!' Drawing his dagger, he stands waiting.

The sound of quiet laughter sets his heart racing. It feels very close; the cup of the hills brings it to his ear.

'I can see you, Arun Persaba,' a soft voice calls. 'Can you see me?'

The voice comes from somewhere above. The boy turns wildly. He drops the sack and braces himself, holding the dagger out in front of him. As if from nowhere, Magra appears on the hillside. The hood of his cloak is lowered, and he is smiling. 'Have you had enough yet? Do you feel like giving up? Think how disappointed your sister would be.' He turns and starts running.

Swearing, the boy heaves the leather sack onto his shoulder and starts up the hillside. His stride is beginning to falter when the land levels out, widening to a strip of ground between stony slopes. A few pines trees, some bushes and brushwood. At the far side, a wall of rock. In failing light, he follows the track past the trees to its end at the foot of the wall. Frustrated, he looks around. Where is Magra?

The call of a bird quavers on the air. It lingers, and slowly dies. Hairs prickle on the back of the boy's neck. The call belongs to no bird he knows. He stands perfectly still. The bird calls again. The sound is coming from somewhere above and to his right. Slowly, all the time looking about, he makes his way along the wall. At the far end, a crevice opens into a ravine. He peers in, but sheer sides stunt the view. Gripping his dagger, he makes his way in and up, slipping on loose stones. With every step he expects to be knocked to the ground.

The bird calls again, low and haunting. 'I know it's you!' he yells.

The silence that follows is dark and long. His heart pounds in his chest, his palms are wet. But he will see it through to the end because he made a promise, and he will keep it.

With a furious surge of energy he scrambles up the ravine, emerging into clear air. Night has fallen. Cloud covers the moon. He can just make out an expanse of pale ground. Pale walls rise around him. His boots scuff bare stone. He has breached the mountains. He has come this far, and survived.

Weariness takes him, so strong and deep he almost falls to the ground. A bird's call pierces his tiredness, and hatred sparks again. If he has to run through the night he will, and all the days to come. He will never stop following. He will never let Magra harm his sister.

Through darkness he runs, the call of the bird a thread to guide his senses. The ground rises, leading him onto a steep path. He senses walls at either side; sometimes he stumbles, grazing a hand, an elbow, but he feels no pain. Nerve and sinew hold him to a single track, a single vision.

Sunrise holds no pleasure for him. It is valuable only because it offers the light of day. All night he drove himself on, following the call of the bird. Now he stands half-blinded by the corona of light spreading far above. Wearily he wipes his face, and looks about. Towering walls of rock surround the stony clearing. The mountains of the southern Tura Lar are grimmer than their northern cousins, their faces hardened by time.

A movement makes him look up. High above he sees a goat, curved horns sweeping back from its bearded head. It steps nimbly from ledge to ledge, nibbling on something unseen. As he watches, he becomes aware of the strap of the leather sack cutting into his shoulder, and pulls it away from his body.

'You passed a good night?'

Magra stands some distance away. He makes a mocking bow and starts running, following a track the boy hadn't seen until now.

All day he follows, under a misty sun. The track is rising fast. His throat burns, his legs are barely his own any more, but the fire in his head drives him on. As he runs, he pulls his water bottle from the satchel, uncorks it, takes a gulp, chokes, and coughs so hard he has stop. His hands shake as he takes a deep draught, stoppers the bottle and sets off again. Magra must be somewhere ahead; there is no other way, unless he can fly.

He is so intent on pursuit that he doesn't see the sudden bend until it is almost too late. He throws himself back against the wall, his heart thumping wildly. He has nearly run off the cliff. Below is a drop to a gorge so deep he knows there is water only by the sound.

Another sound, from above; a soft, echoing laugh. 'You need to be more careful. If you don't look where you are going, how will you ever save your sister?'

Shouldering the leather sack, the boy sets off again.

He stands on a broad, rocky outcrop. A deep valley lies below. On the far side, a waterfall thunders and fumes, glimmering in the twilight. Here among the shielding stone, Magra has the advantage. The boy finds himself longing for open spaces, a straight line of sight. Turning, he starts to make his way down. He is, he guesses, passing through the middle of the mountains.

The moon is out and full; no clouds cover it. Led by its light he increases his pace, listening keenly, aware that around the next corner Magra may be waiting.

A bird calls. His stomach tightens in answer. He knows the sound by now. Ghost bird, unquiet spirit that goads him on. He longs for the pure clean notes of a blackbird singing at daybreak.

He spends one more night among slabs of moonlit stone, half-sleeping on his feet. An animal shrieks; an owl turns the air to ice. He listens for one sound only, and follows where it leads even as he wishes it forever silent.

Dawn comes creeping in. He pulls his cloak tight against the piercing cold. Tiredness has sunk into his bones. He can barely keep his eyes open. Allowing himself a brief halt, he splashes water on his face and shakes his head vigorously. The coming light unfolds a broader sky. The grip of the mountains is easing.

He listens, hearing nothing. Then a voice, faint but clear, saying that his family were no match for the skills of the House of Goash, and nor is he.

Rage fires him. He sets off again, hard and fast. No matter how great the skills of the House of Goash, they are worthless and always will be, because they do not know love. He increases his pace, running with such fury he skids on loose stones and, unable to stop, tumbles head over heels, all the way to the bottom of a rocky gully. The leather sack tips over his head and goes flying.

He pulls himself to his feet and sees Magra standing above.

'Do you need help? It is no sport hunting a wounded deer.'

The boy runs at the slope, scrabbling wildly. When he reaches the top his cheek is bleeding, his palms torn, but he feels no pain. His body is a means to an end, and whatever injury it sustains it will keep going, because it has to.

In the late afternoon he emerges from the mountains as if shedding a skin of stone. A short way ahead he sees open sky. He slows; he has no intention of falling over another cliff. Crossing a strip of scrub and brush, he stops.

505

A white path winds down a bare hillside. Magra runs as if unhindered by the steepness of the slope. The boy throws himself at the path, skidding sideways, pitching at times onto his hands and knees.

Once, he looks up: grasslands fill the corners of his sight. The grass is parched and yellow, and through it the wind whispers and sighs. In the far distance a group of buildings stand on a long, low hill.

At the foot of the hillside Magra stops and looks back, inclining his head. Then he plunges into the grass. In his haste to follow the boy trips, falls, and finds himself at the bottom, sprawling and winded. Scrambling to his feet, he pushes his way in.

The grasses are much taller than they appeared from the hillside. They are coarser, too, their stems tough and strong. As they close around him, he hears only their seething hiss as they speak with the wind. It is almost as if they feel and resent his presence. Which, he tells himself, is not possible; lack of water is drying his wits.

Pulling the water bottle from the satchel, he shakes a few drops into his mouth. He eats a strip of dried meat, but it sticks in his throat and he has to swallow hard. He looks around. The grasses keep their secrets. Bending his knees, he jumps. A dry yellow sea falls and rises; he jumps again, but sees no sign of the hooded brown cloak. He draws his dagger, recalling tales of great cats whose colouring is so true to their surroundings a man knows he is dying only at the moment of death.

A low call freezes him to the spot. He knows who makes it, but at this moment it is easy to believe in shadows in the grass.

'Can you see me? I can see you.'

Magra's call is a compass, and the boy's every sense is fixed on it. He wades as if through water, following the direction of the voice, heedless of cuts the grasses make as they bend and spring back.

As night falls, he comes to a halt. The wind has dropped; the air holds an unearthly stillness. He has been listening for Magra but has heard nothing for some time now. Even as he wonders which way to go, a low call quavers through the chilly air. His skin crawls. It is the time when the dark imagination begins to stir and, if he lets them, every nameless fear will come creeping through the grass.

Weariness overwhelms him. His legs are sand, his stomach hollow. Unable to go any further, he drops to the ground. His hands shake as he unwraps a piece of cheese and takes a bite. He drinks some water and shakes the bottle. Its stomach is almost as empty as his own. Pulling his cloak around him, he settles down to keep watch.

He is clammy and cold, and his joints are aching. Rolling over, he opens his eyes on a grey morning sky. He sits up, horrified. How could he have let himself fall asleep? He looks about. The grasses are whispering softly, and he is alive and in one piece.

As he lets out a shuddering breath, his gaze falls on his satchel. For a moment he stares. The satchel has been opened. On it, laid out in neat strips, are the letters he wrote to Meriem, Adri and Jabar before he left Mudaina. Their message is clear. Magra wants him to know he could have killed him in the night. That he wants the boy to know his death is also clear.

He gets to his feet, spreads his arms and shouts, 'I'm here! Come and get me, you coward!'

With startling suddenness a figure appears some way ahead, cutting through the grass so fast the boy is caught off guard. Magra is making no attempt to hide. The boy gathers up the sack and satchel and starts after him.

Magra runs as if damnation is at his heels. There is, the boy senses, purpose to his speed. Are they getting closer to his sister? His strength renewed, his heart waxing with anger and determination, he follows.

Morning wears on. All the time he stares ahead, keeping Magra in sight.

He is not prepared for the grasslands to end so abruptly. Running headlong onto springy turf, he steadies himself and looks about. The rock-strewn ground lies bare to the sky and a bleached winter sun. In the near distance is the low hill he saw from the slopes of the southern Tura Lar. Proximity gives the buildings on its crown clearer form. Within a group of smaller ruins, a central structure rises in battered magnificence.

And there is Magra, halfway up the hill, not looking back, knowing the boy will follow.

The top of the hill is much broader than it looked from below. Catching his breath, the boy looks around. He is standing among buildings that must once have been dwelling places. Their roofs have collapsed, their walls decayed. Only the wind lives here now. Is this where he will find his sister? If so, he is ready. He will not fail her this time.

He knows instinctively where Magra will be. He makes his way past the houses to the building that dominates the hilltop and the surrounding land. Though partly ruined, it is still an awe-inspiring sight. Broad steps of grey stone lead to an ornately carved portal. If there were doors – and they would have been mighty – they have long since rotted away. At either side, a series of flat pillars is incised with markings the boy guesses to be some form of writing. Above them, countless bands of grey stone, each narrower than the one below, form a tower that soars to a canopied plinth on which, perhaps, a statue once stood. Each band is decorated with sculpted figures suspended in motion, as if telling a never-ending story.

The boy rubs his arms. For all its splendour, its elaborate craft, there is something unsettling about the building. Dropping the sack and satchel, he draws his dagger and goes in.

Immediately he is struck by the coldness of the interior. Not because the back wall is open to the weather, and water drips down. And not because of the wind funnelling in from above. Time has not mended the nature of this place.

Beyond the wide chamber he stands in, a square-cut arch frames a great block of stone on which is set a thick grey slab. A short flight of steps runs up to it. The sides are decorated with a frieze of figures carrying swords and spears. There are figures underfoot too, some with hands raised in entreaty, others with closed eyes.

Shivering, the boy looks around. Where is his sister?

'This is the Temple of Lakom Essu.' Magra's voice floats down to him. He is standing on a stone balcony encircling the walls. Parts of it have broken off, littering the floor. 'I have long wanted to see it. It was once the heart of a great city, a great civilisation. They are long gone, but their spirit remains.'

The boy looks up, gripping his dagger. Magra has discarded the hooded brown cloak and is dressed in robes of red and black, the same colour as the robes he wore when the boy first met him. His sword is not yet drawn.

'Where is she?' the boy shouts. 'Where's my sister?'

Magra regards him for some moments. 'Once again, you fail to understand what matters. Order. Propriety. Everything is now in place, everything arranged as I wished it to be. I have enjoyed the chase, but now it is at an end.'

He smiles. 'Did you really think I would leave any of your family alive? I left nothing undone. I made sure of it before I came for you. They are gone. Every one of them. I wanted to give you my undivided attention, as you deserved.

'When I found your sister, I told her that her parents were dead, by my hand – I allowed myself that vanity – but that you were still alive. I said I would be attending to you next, and nothing would remain of her family. It would be as if they had never lived at all.' He smiles again. 'And then I killed her.'

The boy stares up at him. His body starts to shake. To have come this far, to have been offered a glimpse of hope –

'You're lying!' he yells.

Magra reaches into his robes, and throws something onto the floor. For a moment the boy stares. With a cry he stumbles forward, and picks it up. It is a red coral button in the shape of a bird.

The stone chamber recedes as images race through his mind: a house in the shrubs; a game of skipstones; a small stuffed animal perched on the pillow of a bed; a young

510

girl running a kite up and down the bank of a stream, her blue-black hair shining in the sun.

'Why?' he shouts. 'Why?'

'Because, Arun Persaba, I wanted to see you dance.' Magra steps forward, a look of burning triumph on his face. 'I have waited for this moment for so long, and now –'

He glances round sharply at the sudden grating sound. The balcony has shifted slightly. With a grinding noise it shifts again, throwing him against the balustrade. Stone chips shower down. Flakes of stone drift in the air.

The boy takes a step back. For a moment there is stillness. Then a sharp crack, a groaning shudder, and part of the balcony breaks away from the wall.

Magra leaps; landing lightly, he rolls, and springs to his feet. Stone slabs hit the floor with a booming crash. A cloud of dust billows up. Even as Magra steps aside, the boy charges. The force of the collision sends Magra staggering backwards. He has barely regained his balance when the boy charges again, slamming him into the wall.

Magra twists round, thrusting his hand at the boy's face. The boy ducks sideways so quickly Magra finds no resistance, and he pitches forward. Instantly he swings around but the boy is already running at him, head down, butting him in the chest. Magra staggers; the boy grabs at the red-and-black robes, twisting them in his fist. Magra kicks out; with a shout of pain the boy falls to the ground, clutching his shin.

Scrambling backwards, he grabs a chunk of stone and hurls it. Magra steps neatly aside and stands for a moment, watching him. He has still not drawn his sword. The boy pulls himself to his knees, panting. His leg throbs, his shoulder smarts, but he burns with all-consuming hate. He hauls himself to his feet, his dagger pointed at Magra's heart.

Magra approaches, his eyes never leaving the boy's face. Then, so quickly the boy has no time to react, he spins round, kicking out. The dagger flies from the boy's hand and lands clattering on the floor. Magra lunges; the boy throws himself sideways but is not quick enough. Magra strikes so hard and fast he falls backwards and hits the floor, the breath forced out of him. Points of light explode before his eyes.

And now cold fingers, like rings of steel, are fastening on his throat. He scrabbles frantically on the damp stone floor, but he cannot find his dagger. He claws at Magra's wrists, but the grip is relentless. His head fills with lightness; his eyes cloud with mist. Images swirl: a spiral symbol, a man whose eyes hold the mineral glitter of stone.

Warm darkness begins to steal over him. Through it he sees a glimmer, a rose-white flicker of petals. An almond tree in blossom.

With a choking cry he draws up his knees and swings his body sideways, heaving Magra away from him. Immediately Magra is on his feet and coming for him, but he is up and throwing himself forward. At the last moment Magra sidesteps, drawing his sword. As the boy runs past, the sword flashes down. He flings himself sideways, and the bite of the blade draws fire from the floor.

As he rolls over, his hand knocks against something cold. His fingers close around the hilt of his dagger. Dragging himself upright, he turns to face Magra once more.

Magra's sword sweeps to and fro, turning at times a graceful arc, as if demonstrating the skill of his hand. He comes steadily closer, his yellow eyes never leaving the boy's face. The sword moves back and forth with the constancy of a pendulum.

The boy wipes the side of his mouth, breathing hard. His hand tightens on the dagger. Yorin's dagger. For a moment he sees his friend as he saw him last, crossing the bridge in the Suth Valley, looking back and waving. He sees himself, too, and he is not alone. His family are with him. The image is so clear that for an instant it obscures the grey stones of the temple and the man moving slowly towards him. As clearly as if she stands beside him, he hears her voice. *Don't be afraid.*

'I'm not,' he whispers. As he looks into the yellow eyes, he smiles. Then he runs, with all the force of grief and love, straight at Magra.

Surprise flickers in Magra's eyes. For barely an instant he pauses, his sword swept out and away from his body. Before he has time to gather himself, the boy comes crashing into him with such ferocity they are carried backwards for some distance until they hit the wall. A sharp gasp as Magra's breath is forced from him, then they slide slowly downwards.

For a moment, everything is still. The boy rolls away and lies panting on the floor. He looks over at the wall. Magra is sitting upright, a thread of blood running from his mouth. He wrenches the boy's dagger from his chest, and throws it on the floor. A spasm wracks his body. When he speaks again, his eyes are fixed on a point somewhere beyond the boy's shoulder.

'I did my best, Master. Let it be enough. I am of the tribe of the House of Goash. Let me go to my death absolved.' He gives a long, shuddering gasp. 'Master –' His head falls sideways. The yellow eyes stare out, seeing nothing.

The boy pulls himself up and sits motionless for some moments. Then he searches on his hands and knees until he finds the red coral button. For a long time he sits holding it in his hand. Then he lowers his head, and cries.

Chapter Thirty-Eight

Beside the pool, Arun wipes his face. 'I got away from that place as fast as I could – it was monstrous to me in so many ways. I don't remember much about the next few days. I was half out of my mind with grief, and everything passed in a blur. I'd had a purpose, and now that purpose was gone. It was as if whatever I'd been holding on to had vanished, and there was nothing to break the fall. If despair was an illness, I think I would have died of it.'

His hand trembles as he drinks from the water bottle. 'When I killed him, I felt no sense of triumph. It was as if I'd completed a task I'd failed before I'd even started. I'd given up on my sister, and because of it she was dead. I'd failed her. I'd failed them all.'

'Have you finished feeling sorry for yourself?' Night enquires after a while.

Arun glares into the darkness. 'Does nothing affect you?'

'Not really. Besides, things aren't always as bad as they seem. There's always hope.'

'What would you know about hope?' Arun says wearily.

The boy has no idea how long he has been wandering, only that he is standing on a high shelf of rock in twilight. Far

515

below, the lights of a settlement twinkle and shine. Beyond it lies a vast, dark body of water.

He stumbles down the turf slope. By the time he reaches the settlement, night has fallen. Skirting the houses, he makes his way to the shore. He drops the sack and satchel and stares out, wondering what it would be like to sink down, to disappear. For everything to be absorbed. He takes one step, then another. He can feel the coolness of the water through his boots. A few more steps, and it reaches his knees. Would it be so bad to let it cover him, to pass beyond sorrow and pain?

He feels a hand on his arm. A voice says, 'It's a bit cold for a swim. Come on, I'll buy you a mug of beer.'

The light is as loud as the music. Someone is playing a fiddle, someone else a drum; a lively tune chases itself into an ending of whoops and cheers. The boy blinks, glancing at the man standing next to him. He has a big, uneven face, coarse black hair lying flat across his forehead, and small dark eyes. A younger man comes through a door directly in front of them. Judging by the sudden gust of voices, it leads to the common room of the inn.

After several beers, the room starts to spin. The black-haired man gives him a shrewd look. 'You look like you could do with a good sleep. You've come at a busy time, the sarling should be arriving soon, but I'm sure Dima will find you a room. I'm Yareth, by the way.'

The boy drops the leather sack and satchel on the floor and looks around. The room is sparsely furnished but the blankets on the bed look clean. He sits down, closing his eyes.

Music rises up through the floorboards, played with some skill on a reed flute. Ripples and reflections, fluent and clear. As the melody ends, there are shouts for more and the flute begins again, drawing from its heart a song so lovely the boy cannot bear it. The rage that drove every step of his pursuit of Magra comes boiling back. Why does anyone dare to love when the consequences are so bitter?

It is a mistake of such magnitude it almost chokes him. At this very moment, people everywhere are committing themselves to loving others. They are either innocents or utter fools. He wants to grab them by the shoulders and say, *Why do it? Why open yourselves to a pain you could never imagine?*

Morning brings a sound the boy hasn't heard since he left Harakim: the keening of gulls. The common room is already busy. In daylight it shows itself to be large, and rough-timbered. Two men are warming their hands on the fire in the hearth. As he finds a space on a bench, a serving-woman asks him what he'd like for breakfast. She offers cham, toasted bread, cheese, meat, fish, eggs, soup, as if reciting the contents of the kitchen.

'Just cham,' he says. 'And tea.'

'With fishermen coming in day and night, they have to be prepared,' the black-haired man says, sitting down beside him. The boy glances sideways, recalling the evening before. Should he thank him or resent him? At the moment he can't even remember his name.

'Yareth,' the man supplies, 'and the fried fish is very good.'

The boy nods, unable to meet his eye. The serving-woman places a large bowl and an earthenware mug in front of him and he eats steadily, hoping to be left alone.

'Come far?' Yareth asks.

The boy stops eating. 'Yes.'

Yareth looks at him. 'Welcome to Shanqa, the city on the lake. We had quite a new year. Shame you missed it. Just passing through?'

The boy shrugs.

'Ever thought about fishing? It's not a bad life, if you don't mind hard work. I started going out with my father when I was young.'

The boy stirs his cham.

'Think about it.' Yareth gets up, nods at the boy, and leaves the common room.

In the street, the boy looks up at the sign hanging above the door of the inn. The Plough. He raises an eyebrow and stands for a moment looking around. The street is as crooked as the wooden houses that form it, tacked together with little sense of permanence, their timbers weathered and flaking. He turns down the street and starts walking. No one is about but he almost stumbles over a cat as it runs past, a rangy animal with ginger fur. At the far end, the street slopes down and round a steep corner, opening out on a breathtaking view.

Lake Sigal. The size of a small sea. Mountains, snow-capped, sweep up at either side, linked by a chain of high green hills. The boy downs the sight in one go, and it leaves him light-headed.

Wooden jetties run out from the stone wharf; boats of varying size jostle in a slight swell. Fishing nets hang like great dark cobwebs on wooden frames. In open-sided sheds women are standing at tables, gutting fish, calling out to the fishermen bringing in their catch. Beyond the wharf, the chilly brightness of the water seems to go on forever. As he stares across at the mountains, the boy thinks of a line from the Book of Light.

He seeks horizons small enough to fit his hand.

The speaker in Mirashi's poem is talking about her father, whose eyesight is failing. In his mind the boy closes the book. He has no heart for poetry today.

All that day he wanders about the settlement. Shanqa is larger than it first appeared. It spreads like silt along the eastern shore of the lake, full of the grit and rot of human existence. The lake keeps drawing him back. He stands on the shore staring out until the light on the water starts to blind him.

'Takes a bit of getting used to.' Yareth's voice. The boy keeps his eyes on the lake. 'We do a great trade in salted fish, export it all over the place.'

The boy takes a breath. 'How long have you fished here?'

'I'm not a fisherman,' Yareth says, 'not any more. I'm a fish merchant. I have my own boats, employ my own men.'

The boy nods.

'You don't give much away,' Yareth comments mildly. 'I'd appreciate a name. Doesn't have to be your real one.'

The boy looks at him in surprise. For a moment he thinks about leaving his name behind. What would it matter? But it does; it was given to him by his parents, and he shared it with two people who were for a time his whole life. 'Arun Persaba,' he says.

'Well, Arun' – Yareth jerks his head at the row of tall warehouses set back from the wharf – 'they're mine. Built from a barrel of dried sarling.' He nods. 'Best get on. Think about what I said earlier.'

The boy watches him make his way back to the warehouses, exchanging greetings with fishermen and the women in the gutting sheds. He is clearly what Nissa would call a *neshinga*, a big noise. She would invariably follow it with a noise of her own, and collapse in giggles. He stares across the lake, wondering if she ever thinks of him.

When he returns to the Plough, he eats his dinner at the same bench. Yareth doesn't come, so he asks the innkeeper, Dima, about him. Dima draws his head back a little, as if assessing the boy. 'He's tough, but he's fair. He won't stand for any nonsense, but if you're in trouble, he's there for you. You thinking of working for him?'

'Maybe,' the boy says. Dima nods, and he knows the information will be stored in the innkeeper's apron pocket. He finishes his stew and goes to his room.

The next morning he is back on the wharf. It is early; the sky is washed with cool light. The water stirs like cold silk, small ripples moving endlessly on. A man tying up a boat calls a greeting, and he nods. Then he turns and makes his way to the shore of the lake.

He sits a little way back, on dry shingle. He scoops up a handful. It gleams in his hand, winking and glittering white, brown and black. He wonders where it came from, and looks across at the mountains. Perhaps it was carried down century by patient century. The thought of so much time depresses him. He lets it drop.

As he gets to his feet he sees Yareth a short distance away on a bank of turf, shading his eyes. He jumps down and greets the boy.

'I'll need somewhere to live,' the boy says, making up his mind.

Yareth nods. 'I expect hard work, and honesty. Other than that, it's up to you. There's space in one of the lofts. You can rent it for the time being, if it suits.'

When he tells him how much the boy says, 'A month? For a loft?'

For the briefest moment Yareth looks taken aback. 'Right,' he says, and names a smaller sum.

It is a good loft, reached by a flight of steps running up the side of the warehouse. Large, high-ceilinged, full of light, dry and clean. A bed, a table and chairs, a cupboard. A pitcher and basin. A blue cotton rug. No ornaments, no books except for Mirashi, kept in the top drawer of a small wooden cabinet. In the bottom drawer he stores his dagger, cleaned of Magra's blood.

That afternoon, Yareth takes him to a warehouse and introduces him to Gef, a master-fisherman and his right-hand man. Small and knotted, he has bad teeth and a cotton scarf at his neck. His face has the cured look of someone who has spent a long time peering into wind and sun.

When Yareth has left Gef says, 'So you want to be a fisherman?' He gives a harsh laugh. 'Let's see what you're made of.'

The warehouse is lined with barrels, and hung with nets of varying sizes. One of them takes up a large part of the opposite wall. 'Thought you'd start at the top, did you?' Gef says. He shows the boy a small, circular net whose edges are fringed with weights. The boy says nothing. Gef shrugs. 'I hope your hands are quicker than your mind.'

He gathers up the net, taking hold of the long cord running out from the centre. 'Handline. Don't let it go. If you do, you'd better go in after it.' With a quick, fluid movement he lets the net fly. Like a flower it opens, spreading gently as it lands.

There is, it seems, an art to preparing the net for casting. By the time Gef has gathered it in, the boy is sure he will never be able to do it. He wonders what he is doing in the middle of a warehouse, being goaded by a man with a permanent sneer on his face.

'Your turn,' Gef says. 'I hope you've been paying attention.' At his command, the boy hurls the net into the air. It bunches up and falls to the floor in a heap. He looks at it. Gef presses his lips together. 'Pick it up, do it again.' The boy hauls it back across the floor.

Gef watches silently as he attempts to prepare it. 'Give it here,' he says. 'Now watch. Properly, this time.'

Again he demonstrates, his hands working swiftly. He offers it to the air; it opens, soars, and falls. 'Now you.' His eyes are challenging. The boy grasps and folds until the net is ready. He turns his body and throws as hard as he can. The net flies up, stutters, drops. 'Again,' Gef says.

And again. Each time he tries, Gef's hands knuckle further into his hips and his elbows stand like out like chicken wings. Even as the boy tells himself it matters not

522

in the slightest, that no one will care whether he can cast a net or not, anger smoulders. What right does Gef have to treat him like this after everything he has endured?

He thinks back to two nights ago, when he almost lost himself to the lake. Whether he was spared by the hand of man or the hand of fate, it makes no difference. In his heart he knows that no matter how hard, his family would want him to go on. Very well. If he is to live, he will honour them in what he does.

Gritting his teeth, he prepares the net, imagines a perfect circle, and throws. The shape is a little lopsided, but the intention is finally clear.

'Well, they won't be quaking in their boots, but it's a start,' Gef says.

All day the boy works. When he has made enough progress for Gef to say, 'That's enough for today. I'll see you tomorrow,' he leaves the warehouse and stands for a moment in the cool air. A breeze makes its way across the lake, chasing small waves. As they meet the shore, the water gathers them back. A misty sun kindles the horizon, flaring as it slowly sinks.

He spends the following day being prodded by Gef, who tells him he throws like a girl. As his hands tighten on the coarse mesh, he thinks of the time he and his sister played a game of catch with a small wooden ball. He was so convinced of her inferior skill that when she threw, he looked the ball squarely in the face. It almost knocked him out. Little stars came out in front of his eyes, and he collapsed on the ground. His sister appeared contrite, but hid a grin as his mother took him inside and bathed his forehead with a cold cloth. Afterwards, whenever he was reluctant to do a chore, his sister would ask if he wanted a game of catch. The memory is scored with pain, but it makes him smile.

'Funny, is it?' Gef says. 'It won't be so funny when you're out on the lake with the fish looking up and laughing.'

Setting his jaw, the boy drags the net back.

On the third day, he progresses to a larger net. How can so many holes add up to so much weight? If this were a ledger, the columns wouldn't balance. Determined to wipe the smirk off Gef's face, he gathers the net, heaves, and flings so hard he takes himself with it.

Gef watches impassively as he untangles himself and gets to his feet. 'Just so you know, the fish can't fly,' he says.

Pushing away his empty bowl, the boy leans back wearily. He and the net have been fighting each other for a week now. He flexes his hands, wincing, wondering if fisherman never die but are transformed into herons, hunched and patiently eternal.

Yareth sits down opposite, not minding the ripple he causes as people squeeze up to accommodate him. 'So, Arun, how are you doing?' The boy shrugs, wondering what Gef has said, and why he should care. Yareth takes a mug from the serving-man, gulps a mouthful of beer and says, 'Don't expect praise.' The boy raises an eyebrow.

'I've had good reports, by Gef's standards. Believe me, when I started, he made me work that net until I wanted to set fire to it.' Yareth laughs. 'Oh yes, I felt exactly the same, but when he's done you'll be more than ready. It's a question of his say-so. I don't move without him.'

Even as he tells himself Gef's opinion is of no importance, the idea of being judged sits badly with the boy. Yareth gives him a shrewd look. 'I was like you once, rushing to do things, thinking I was ready. I found out the hard way.' He finishes his beer. 'It involved a net, a pole, and a near-drowning. The lake may look tame, but it's not.'

'I know,' the boy says stiffly.

'I'm sure you do, but if I'm investing in you I need you to come back with my boat in one piece. Talking of boats' – he gets up, throwing a coin on the table – 'meet me on the shore tomorrow. I've got one that's just right for you.'

The boy watches Yareth make his way through the crowded common room, then raises his hand for another mug of beer.

They stand beside a boat both slender and sturdy, midnight-blue with a flowing white name on the side. *Serryn*. 'It's a bit different from the others,' Yareth says. 'Not as broad but just as stable, and the lightest we've ever made. She won't let you down.'

The boy thinks of the love and care the crew of the *Silver Falcon* showed their ship, the enduring bond formed by sharing the sea's commons.

'Now,' Yareth says, 'let's get you started.'

It is the tradition to launch a new boat from the shore, and return to the wharf for mooring. The boy hops about in the shallows, preparing to climb in as Gef holds the prow steady. Yareth watches patiently. Everything – cloud, sky, water – assumes a supernatural clarity. Aware of Gef's scrutiny, the boy overreaches himself and tumbles into the boat, his face pressed against her ribs.

Embarrassed, he rights himself, and scrambles onto one of the two seats.

'Well done,' Gef says. He slides into the boat like an eel and perches on the other seat. 'She'll keep you safe if you look after her. It'll be up to you, mind. You'll need to check her over every time you return. Flaking, warping, barnacles, weed – they all need attending to. I take it you can swim.'

He is back at the stream on a warm day, when he and his sister were taken to the deepest part of the water by their parents. His father has his arms around his waist and is telling him to put out his arms and legs and move like a frog, so he does. For an instant he is the finest frog in the stream. Until his father lets go. Down he sinks, spluttering and thrashing, until he feels his father's arms around him, lifting him up.

'Not bad,' his father says, 'for a two-legged frog.' The boy blinks, shaking vigorously, spraying him with water. There is for a brief moment laughter in his father's eyes. 'Now, try again.'

This time his father lowers him until he is supporting his stomach with one hand. 'Think *frog*,' he says.

The boy thinks a quick, bright-green frog, and kicks the stream to pieces.

'Again,' his father says. Out and back, out and back – the boy sways on the stem of the current that is also his father's hand. Out and back, out and back – suddenly he is swimming. Water is air, and through it he flies, not body but brilliant light. He surges through the stream, breaks the surface and cries, 'I did it!'

'I can swim,' he says to Gef.

All day they stay out on the lake. Without warning Gef starts rocking the boat from side to side as if encouraging the return of the boy's breakfast. But he is back on the *Silver Falcon*, whose motion became part of every footfall, and his body sways with balanced ease.

Telling him to stand up, Gef grasps the sides of the boat and rocks until it wallows. 'A storm. They can blow up sometimes, without warning.'

The boy rides it out, rolling from foot to foot. Then he wonders what kind of fool would stand up in a small boat in a storm. He sits down. Gef sucks in his cheeks. 'We'll try again tomorrow,' he says sourly.

That evening the boy sits in a chair by the window, looking out. The sky is flushed copper-rose with streamers of palest blue. When all that remains is an amber glow, he goes to bed.

Arun eases into a more comfortable position. His water bottle is nearly empty again. 'I spent every waking moment trying not to think about them. If I could have gutted my mind like a fish, I would have. But at night –' He shakes his head. 'When the beer wore off there was nothing between me and my dreams, so bad I'd be fighting to get out, so good I never wanted to leave. They all ended the same way. I'd wake up alone.'

'It's a good thing I have no heart to break,' Night remarks.

'You have no idea how lucky you are.' Arun turns back to the boat on the lake.

The boy sits under a sky of topaz and pearl into which the sun is slowly stealing. The water is very still, absorbing the

527

colours of the sky. 'Dreaming won't catch fish,' Gef says. The boy glares at him. 'Quick to take offence, aren't you?' Gef sounds almost pleased.

'It's early, that's all.'

Gef shrugs, looks at the oars, then at the boy, who takes them up. They are cool and smooth and weighty in his hands. 'Well, dip 'em in, then,' Gef says. 'And shake 'em out. Always do that first, shake off any bad luck. Right. Now, get rowing.'

There is a look on his face the boy doesn't altogether like. Flexing his wrists, he starts to row, steadily and surely. What Gef doesn't know is that he went out many times with the crew in the tender of the *Silver Falcon*, a bigger and heavier craft than the *Serryn*. He glances at Gef, who looks neither annoyed nor impressed, though the boy suspects the former.

When they are some way out, Gef nods at the net. 'Take it up.'

Standing, the boy feeds it into his hands, and casts. Like spider's silk it floats out, touches the surface of the water and dies away. He waits for nothing from Gef, and receives it.

'Now we wait.' Gef turns his head and studies the horizon.

With sudden horror the boy realises he is trapped here with the fisherman. For a split second he thinks of jumping out of the boat, swimming for the shore and putting it – putting everything – far behind him. An image sways up through his mind, resolving into lines from Mirashi's poem about people returning to their homes on the Day of Remembrance. A train of ghosts, full of life.

From Tahn to Halzen in slow procession they come,
the last an old man breathing gently on the sun in his hand.

He sees them clearly as they rise from the depths, human
and immortal. But they are not the faces he wants to see.
He looks away across the lake.

'For goodness' sake, man, watch your catch!' How long
they have been sitting there the boy has no idea, only that
the handline is straining and Gef is glaring at him. He grasps
the line and, as he has been taught, starts to haul the net into
the boat. It takes every ounce of strength, his arms straining
as he heaves and pulls. Gef sits motionless, watching. He
increases his effort until his muscles are on fire and the net
comes tumbling over the side, a churning silver mass.

'What do we do now?' he asks.

Gef looks at him. 'We take them back. In boxes,
usually' – the boy has seen them stacked on the wharf –
'then gut 'em and salt 'em, put 'em in barrels and sell 'em.'

The boy looks at the gulping mouths, the glistening
eyes. Life that cannot sustain itself in air. 'Don't we – you
know – dispatch them?'

'We give them a last meal as well.'

It is a strange cargo. All the way back the boy avoids
looking at the net, which barely moves now. As he ties up
the boat and climbs out, his legs almost buckle; it takes a
moment to find his feet. A purple haze spreads across the
horizon, turning the water a milky mauve. It is beautiful,
but all he can think is that he took things from their
element and, in doing so, put an end to them.

Yareth hails him. 'A good catch,' he says, smiling. 'Not
bad for your first day.'

Men are already hauling the net away to one of the sheds where women are busy with quick, bright knives. As they toss fish into barrels gulls swirl and dart, snatching, quarrelling. From time to time a woman flicks her arm and the birds rise, fan out, sink back again. Both sides know there is little point, that the birds will return, but the women do it anyway. Habit, the boy thinks, custom. Foundations. Shake them and they resettle.

Gef is speaking quietly with Yareth. Once upon a time the boy would have wondered what they were saying about him, convinced it couldn't be good. He waits numbly until Yareth turns to him and says, 'Come for a drink, Arun, to celebrate your first catch. Always worth celebrating. But then, isn't that the way of life?'

When they are settled in with mugs of beer Yareth says, 'It can be a bit much, the first day. But you did well. Gef tells me you brought the catch up on your own. That's pretty good going.' He looks at the boy. 'I knew I wasn't wrong about you.'

Not knowing what to say, the boy stares at a brown earthenware jug filled with pink flowers. 'They're from the high pastures,' Yareth says. 'Herdsmen graze cattle and sheep up there in winter, bring them down in spring. They're protected from the wind, and green all year round. I've been up there a few times, especially when I start counting fish in my sleep.'

He laughs. 'Try it,' he says, nodding at the mug. 'Buttered beer, imported from Tema. Perfect for the time of year. For any time of year.'

The beer is warm and creamy, flavoured with something – nutmeg? – so delicate as to be hardly noticeable, and yet

530

its lack would be felt. Yareth raises his mug. On impulse, the boy knocks it with his own.

By the end of the evening, they are sliding into a final mug with the kind of grin that neither knows nor cares what it looks like. As they leave the inn, Yareth has his arm around the boy's shoulders in echo of many before them.

The morning sun is peering into his face. He squints, groans, and hauls himself out of bed. A splash of water on his face, and he is done. Yareth is expecting him.

He is greeted with a smile and a large beaker of coffee. The coffee is strong and hot, and goes straight to his stomach, which begs a little mercy. Yareth seems unaffected. 'You'll get used to it,' he says, but the boy hopes he won't. He has never been that drunk before, and feels slightly ashamed.

'Right,' Yareth says, 'time to talk money.' He opens a ledger and shows it to the boy, who notes the neat columns, the meticulous script. 'You get paid every week. I expect a certain weight of catch, depending on the season. If you fall below it, I'll tell you.'

The boy casts an eye over the figures on the page and finds himself making a quick calculation. 'What's the price per barrel?'

Yareth looks at him. 'Depends who's buying. And what the fish is. The sarling bring merchants from as far as Djuna. That's how good they are. Roasted over a fire with lemon and honey –' He kisses his fingers.

The boy nods, but part of him is still doing sums. 'What's your cut?'

Yareth's face changes. The boy may as well have asked to see inside his soul. 'I take what I think is fair,' he says eventually, but he isn't frowning. 'You know something about trading, I think.'

'Yes.'

'Fair enough,' Yareth says. Then, thoughtfully, 'I've seen enough men come and go to know you've been through something hard. Don't worry, I'm not going to ask what it is. Here in Shanqa we don't ask questions. If we knew everything about each other the place would fall apart. All I'll say is that in the end you can't defeat it. You can only learn to live with it.'

The boy looks away. Yareth's observations are neither what he expected nor what he wants to hear.

Yareth underscores a line with his finger. 'This is what you've earned today, after deductions for the use of the boat and the schooling you've received.' The boy stares at him. Yareth meets his eye steadily. 'I run a business,' he says. 'Would you do it differently?' It isn't a challenge; he is too secure in his skin for that.

'No,' the boy concedes.

Yareth nods. 'For that, I'll throw in the schooling for nothing.' As the boy leaves the office he says, 'After a while, you don't notice the teeth.'

He has never felt more removed from things, even though he can still see the settlement, the arc of hill and mountain. The sun sits in a gallery of cloud, water kneads softly against the sides of the boat. Birds cross the sky, and he shifts to watch.

'White-necked geese,' Gef says. In spite of the boy's silent prayers, he is still here. 'They come in autumn, be heading home soon.'

The boy closes his eyes briefly and turns away, a small but telling movement to which Gef seems oblivious. 'They know the right place to come,' he says, 'never gets that cold here. Cold enough for a cloak, maybe, but start walking and you'll soon take it off. Can't argue with the weather.'

Why has Gef decided the best place to start a conversation is in the middle of the lake? No, the boy corrects himself, not the middle – they never go too far from the shore. At the Plough one evening, after several mugs of beer, Yareth said, 'I'll let you into a secret. Lake Sigal may be big, but it isn't that deep. Only at the centre, and there's no need to go out that far. The fish are afraid of heights.'

He shifts a little more.

'It takes patience and wits,' Gef says. 'The fish know we're here.'

The boy imagines a shoal gathered underneath, peering up. He is so absorbed he doesn't notice Gef taking out a cloth-wrapped bundle. 'Want some?' The boy shakes his head. 'Suit yourself.' Gef unwraps the cloth and takes out a plump triangle of pastry. He bites into it crisply. 'My wife makes the best meat patties. Been married twenty-two years. Some going, eh?' Then the question the boy has been dreading: 'What about you?'

He wishes desperately for something to happen, a bird dropping a pumpkin on Gef's head, a monster fish rearing up and dragging the boat across the lake. He looks out across the water, his heart like a bating hawk.

After a short silence Gef says, 'Never happened, then?'

'No.'

'It's never too late, and you're still young. The women here are hard workers – make you a good home, if you let them. Nothing like it, coming back to a hot meal and a smile. Not that it's always like that, of course. That's when I'm thankful to get out on the lake.'

The boy stares so hard at nothing he finally sees it. Pinned to the water as Gef makes unthinking cuts and rubs in salt, he wonders why he ever came to this place where one person's business bumps into the next, like a line of boats in a breeze.

Just as he is working up to making his silence very clear, Gef gives a cry and jumps up. 'They're here!' he yells, pointing at a spot some way from the boat. 'Sarling!'

The sound carries to the wharf where figures start running to boats, jumping in, rowing out. Above the churning mass gulls are screaming, darker birds the boy doesn't recognise diving so fast they enter the water with barely a ripple.

'Come on, man!' Gef cries. The boy plies his mood so fiercely through the oars it takes little time to reach the simmering water.

'Throw!'

The boy scrambles up, the net flies out and rests on the air for less than a moment before sinking down.

'Now heave!'

Together they draw it in. It is teeming with fish, silver-grey with fine yellow and black stripes along the body. Quickly they release it into one of the big wooden boxes slotted between the seats.

'Again!'

The boy needs no prompting. Other boats are reaching

534

them now, and the water seethes with men casting nets, hauling them in, filling their boats with living silver.

Each day is like a holiday of hard work. They go out early, all the boats, laughing and joking, and come back late, the light of their lanterns softly shattering the night water. Then singing at the Plough, rowdy choirs fired with wine and beer, becoming more accomplished by the flagon. The boy sits quietly, a jug of wine at his elbow. He has made a home at a table tucked against the edge of the fireplace. As he watches men and women throwing up their arms and jigging, he wonders where they find the energy. After a day's fishing he is finished. It is only in bed that he wakes up.

The sarling go as quickly as they came, swimming far across the lake to begin their journey to where they were born, to spawn and die. The air is cool and bright. Birds call above, not gulls but smaller birds with sweeter voices.

'Not so many today, eh? Doesn't matter, it's payday.' Gef grins widely.

The boy looks at his teeth and wonders if he is happy, if he ever wants more. He thinks he knows the answer, and part of him envies it.

Later he stands in Yareth's office, waiting to find out how much he has earned that week. It is a not inconsiderable sum, including as it does the sarling catch, and he stores it in the cabinet, where he knows it will be safe. Of all the things he has discovered about Shanqa, the lack of thieving is the one he least expected. It has taken time to see beyond the roughly made dwellings, the trodden-in face of hardship. He is slowly discovering

535

a deep-down honesty and a strong, even fierce, sense of community. Which makes him feel lonelier than ever.

It is almost sunrise. He rubs his eyes and stretches, looking out at the white horizon. He sleeps very little, preferring to spend his time in the chair by the window, watching a view that hardly changes. Which, he reflects, could drive him mad. He thinks about the old man at the library caves, but the memory is too difficult. He wonders about hermits. Are they already mad, or do they drive themselves to it? Or do they become so sane they can no longer live among other people?

He fixes his attention on the horizon, raising his arms as if conducting musicians. *One, two* – on the third beat the sun begins to rise, shimmering, immense. Colours cloud the sky, amethyst, orange, sweet pink. For a moment he closes his eyes. Then he leaves the loft and goes to the boat. With many injunctions Yareth has allowed him to go out on his own, impressing upon the boy that it was not the usual practice.

'It's better to go out in twos,' he said. 'That way, if something happens, one of you can go for help.'

But the boy doesn't want to be a two. Once he was, and then a three, and now he is less than nothing. The morning sky is so clear that if he looks up he can see a bird far above, sketched in by wing and voice. It soars with such grace he finds himself crying, not for the beauty of the bird, but because it is tied neither to the earth nor to the grief of care.

A ripple and a pop. The water bursts softly; fish are rising. He gets up and casts the net. The boat wobbles; he presses with alternating feet until it rolls to his rhythm.

Then he realises what he must look like, alone on the lake, rocking from side to side. He sits down and stares out over the water.

The water bottle is empty. Arun dips it in the pool and takes a long drink. 'I thought being alone would somehow help me heal. Heal!' He gives a hard laugh. 'Day after day looking out across the water, staring at the mountains. The lake, the loft – they were the sum of my days. I suppose it was a protection of sorts.'

He looks back to where the boy is singing under his breath. It is a song his mother used to sing. He bows his head as the boy starts hauling in the net.

Chapter Thirty-Nine

He sits in the boat, a still point on the water. The spring air is soft, the breeze gentle. Birds have returned to the lake in great flocks, flouncing and snapping over the best fishing spots. Their colours are many and lovely, fawn-brown lit with white, fox-red melting into chocolate. A brilliant emerald underwing, a bronze back darkening to sooty black. Eyes ringed with pearl or gold, feet the colour of mustard or salmon.

Although each courtship is singular, they experience the greater world as one. A sudden noise, an eagle's shadow, and they rise in a slow storm. When it is time to roost, they cluster together like lilies on a pond. The boy is particularly fond of the little grey-and-white ducks whose lingering glide as they land on the water makes it gasp.

The birds are used to fishermen and, since he spends much of his time out here now, pay him little attention. Until the catch comes up. They have learned not to overwhelm him and wait with keen, bright eyes as he empties the net. He tosses a fish into the water and watches a bird dart, grab, throw it into the air and gulp it down, swallowing fatly.

For a moment he imagines a country where people plant fish in the ground, believing they will grow just as well as seeds. *Once upon a* – He tries, but he can't. His mind is connected with his heart and there is no way to escape it. He beats the lake once, hard, with his oar. Water crashes up; birds rise, clattering and scolding. Ashamed, he lets the stillness creep back, the birds settle down, before casting again.

The boxes squirm with fish. Sometimes he sees them as the light in a cold country, sometimes he can't bear the sight of them. He can handle them now without wanting to wash, but he still can't get used to the smell on his clothes. Like the other fisherman, he takes them to the woman who runs the only laundry in Shanqa. The big fish, he thinks, surrounded by minnows who scrub and slap and rinse day in, day out. Another kind of purgatory.

But they are invariably cheerful, singing as they work, joking, throwing remarks that should make him blush but slide off him now like water. He knows he is a source of gossip, and has on more than one occasion been approached by a young, a not-so-young, a much older woman introducing herself, her sister, her daughter. He has tried to feel something, indignation, curiosity, interest. Instead he goes away, sinks into a cup of wine and is, for a time, safely numb.

That evening he sits in the chair by the window, a flagon of wine at his feet. He has taken to buying them at the Plough and bringing them back to the loft. Lanterns fastened on posts along the shore cast lines of trembling copper light.

Light is apparent only in the things it reveals, which makes darkness more visible, since it is all there is to see. He is so impressed with his thinking he gets up and goes

539

outside. It is raining, fine needles slanting through the lantern beams. On the top step, he takes a deep breath. The fresh air makes the wine burn harder. He feels happily disconnected. Halfway down, he wonders why he is using the steps when he can spread his arms and fly.

The ground tells him otherwise. He staggers to his feet, wincing. Rain brushes his face as he starts walking. The gutting sheds are deserted but the odour of fish lingers. He thinks of poet's jasmine, of honey and roses.

When he reaches the shore, he picks up a pebble and throws it as hard as he can at the lake. It would have been a fine throw if he hadn't whacked his head with his arm. He starts laughing, finds he can't stop, and sits down smartly – *ouf!* – on the shingle. He scoops up a handful and kneads it wetly in his palm. He knows a little about the way water works, how the doctoring sea examines a bay or a cave, treating it with wave after wave. It has all the time in the world, and even if it didn't it would have no idea, which is a comfort. A blessing. He lets the shingle drop.

The soft crunch of feet can't be his own because they are tucked underneath him. A hand clasps his arm, raising him up. 'Come on,' Yareth says, 'time to get you home.'

The next day is an embarrassment. His head throbs resentfully. The dark bruise spreading down his side speaks for itself, as does his aching left knee. In stages it comes back, the failed flight, the kindness of Yareth as he helped him into the loft and sat him on the bed. His going away and returning with a beaker of hot coffee, which he fed the boy until it was finished. Then falling asleep in his clothes, Yareth in the chair by the window.

He spends the morning in bed, waiting for the knock at the door, wondering why the wine turned on him. In the afternoon he moves to the chair, where he sits with his eyes closed. Inside he boils and rages, hoping Yareth will leave him alone, hoping he will come.

When dusk is in the mountains and the shore glows with lanterns, the knock finally comes. With clenched fists the boy goes to open it. 'I thought you might be hungry,' Yareth says. He is carrying a covered pot from which the smell of beef stew is rising.

The boy's stomach has finally made its peace. 'You want to come in?' he asks. They sit together at the window, Yareth watching the lake as the boy demolishes the stew.

Leaning back, he says, 'That was good, thank you.'

'There's a world of difference,' Yareth says, 'between an empty belly and a full one.'

They sit peacefully for a while as the view slowly fades.

When the boy wakes, the pot and Yareth have gone. He stares out of the window for a long time. Shame makes him tug at the neck of his shirt. He resolves to work hard and not let Yareth see him like that again. He chooses not to notice the built-in escape clause.

The next morning he is back on the lake with a head so clear it aches. Light traces the lines of the mountains, picking out every crag and fold. He casts the net, waits, hauls it up, empties it, casts again. Fish seethe and thrash in the wooden box. Some way off he sees a bird in outline, gliding above the lake. From the length of the neck it must be a crane. He knows they fly south for the winter, and realises he has no idea how far south Lake Sigal is. The part of him that would, in the past, have been interested in mapping it in his head remains unmoved. Is it because he no longer needs mapping, either?

Arun sighs. 'I think I felt there was no south left for me to fly to. Nowhere, in fact, to go. I was terrified this was it, that I'd remain there for the rest of my life. The way the wind quartered the lake no longer held any interest for me. The mountains were hard-faced and remote. Part of me didn't want to feel like that, but it ran too deep. Perhaps if I'd opened up to Yareth, it might have been different.

'I felt humiliated by my behaviour that night, and I let it come between us like a grudge. It's not logical, or fair, but it's true. I was careful never to let Yareth – or anyone else, for that matter – see me beyond the first few drinks. Perhaps he suspected – I'm sure he did, nothing escaped him – but he was tactful, or discreet, or –'

He lifts his hands and drops them despairingly. 'I don't know. Whatever he thought, he kept out of it. I think as long as I brought in the fish, did my job as well as anyone else . . .'

He looks across the clearing. 'Better than anyone else,' he says eventually. 'My father's shadow lived inside me. If I wasn't the best, it meant I'd failed. I know' – he bites his lip – 'she would have put it right, told me I was good enough as I was. But she wasn't there.'

'Someone else could be, if you'd let her,' Night says. 'You're going to have to make up your mind at some point. She won't wait forever.'

Arun stiffens. 'I don't want to talk about it.'

'Suit yourself,' Night says mildly.

Birds roost on the lake, drowsing in the late summer warmth. Gulls coast above. The leaves of the few trees in the settlement are dusty and curling. The boy has been called into Yareth's office, and is barely curious about it. He looks around as he waits for Yareth to finish his business with one of his factors. A small table displays an ornament he hasn't noticed before, a white jade fish so beautifully carved its tail appears to float in the water of the air.

The factor has gone. Seeing the boy looking, Yareth tells him the fish was a gift from a grateful customer. He wonders about this. Although the word *bribe* has more letters than *gift*, it can be made small enough to fit within it. He dismisses the thought immediately.

'You think it's a bribe, don't you?' Yareth says with typical bluntness.

'Of course not,' he replies quickly.

'Don't worry, I only accept gifts from customers I can't help any further.' He smiles at the boy's bewilderment. 'If, for example, I've tried to supply a certain type of fish in a certain quantity, but I can't quite manage it – and believe me, I'll have moved heaven and earth to do it – I'll say so. Sometimes the customer won't really believe me, especially if he doesn't know me, and he'll offer an incentive to make me try harder. He'll think it's part of the negotiations. I, on the other hand, know it isn't, and will tell him so.

'If he still insists on giving me something, it'd be an insult for me to refuse it. So I accept. That I can't supply him with what he asked for – but will find a substitute, of course, since I don't want him going away unhappy – is neither here nor there. I'll have discharged my obligation. He'll know the lengths I've gone to, and will generally beg me to keep the gift.' He glances at the fish. 'Come to think of it, it does look a bit judgemental.'

'But,' he continues, 'we're not here to talk about that. You've been with us for over two years now, and you were good at first – one of the best, in fact – but recently your catch has gone down.'

The boy is immediately back at the hut, being scolded for something he might or might not have done. He reminds himself he is his own man now.

'It's nothing to worry about,' Yareth says, 'it happens from time to time.'

The boy knows the reason why, and suspects Yareth does too. If you stay out longer, come in fewer times to unload your catch . . .

'I'm sorry,' he says. 'I'll make sure I do better.' He declines Yareth's offer of coffee.

'Tell me something,' Yareth says, pouring himself a beaker, 'do you enjoy it?'

The boy frowns.

'It's not a test. I'm just interested.'

'It's not something I've really thought about. I just do it.'

Yareth nods. 'You can go now, Arun. But keep an eye on your catch.'

As he leaves, the boy reluctantly acknowledges a kindness beyond the imperative of business. He returns to the loft and sits looking out over the glittering lake, brooding. Kindness is an open hand, and a fist. Offer it to someone who is hurting, and they will either accept it or drop it as if it were red hot. Act without permission and it will either be received with gratitude, or incite a messier response: *I understand what you did, and I know I should be grateful, but I also didn't want it to be done without my knowledge, so now you have left me feeling uncomfortable and vaguely resentful.*

The sun begins to wane, powdering the sky with silver. A moth shedding its dust. There is something sad about the sunset today, a lingering of light on the horizon, as if trying to leave something of itself behind.

He wonders what he will leave behind. Someone else's book of poems, two half-filled notebooks. On impulse he goes over to the bed, kneels down, and pulls the leather sack from underneath it. His heart is in his throat as he takes out the dark-blue leather notebook embossed with golden suns and silver moons. For long moments it sits in his hands, but he cannot bring himself to open it. Instead he writes himself into a stupor with the help of the only scribe he can rely on, a cup of wine.

The next morning he doesn't get up. He lies in his bed staring at the beams of the ceiling. Part of him is smarting about what Yareth said yesterday. He knows it is ridiculous, since it was only meant to help. With a pang he thinks of Adri, his diplomacy, his quiet wisdom.

There is a knock at the door. He ignores it. Another knock. He waits for a third, but none comes.

That evening there is a rap on the door, followed by Gef. The boy feels a prickle of irritation that Yareth has sent his lieutenant, then annoyed with himself for – what? – wanting his attention?

'I see you're up, then,' Gef says.

The boy looks across from the window, and shrugs.

'Are you ill?'

The boy shakes his head.

Gef gives him a hard smile. 'Couldn't be bothered, eh?'

No, the boy thinks, not that.

Gef comes over to stand beside him, and looks out. The boy wonders what he sees. Is it the same view, or does whatever the mind of Gef contains make it different?

'You'd better watch yourself,' the fisherman says. 'He'll overlook it this time, but –' He turns to face the boy. 'A fine way to repay him. He's set you up, helped you every step of the way, and when you decide you don't feel like working, you don't turn up.' He shakes his head. 'I thought better of you.'

As the door closes behind him, the boy sits motionless. Should he go after Gef, apologise, explain? He gets up, then sits back down.

Arun turns the water bottle in his hands. The leather is soft and cool. 'That was when I decided I was better off without people. It was easier to blame Yareth and Gef for making me feel bad, Yareth because he didn't have a go at me, Gef because he was right. That day gave me the opportunity to do what I'd been wanting to do for a long time, feel sorry for myself. Really sorry. The pig-in-muck variety.

'I went straight to the Book of Light and found the poem beginning "You are no longer with me", the one I couldn't look at in Kerizon. I made myself read it.'

For a moment he is silent. He remembers it all, especially the lines

Your words were made of air –
they passed through sunlight and could not last,

546

they were ghosts and passed over water
so could not rest. How was I to know
each one would be shadowed by silence?

There is shame in his voice as he says, 'When I got to the end, I drank all night. I threw things – luckily there wasn't much in the loft to break – I stamped, I yelled, I smashed the merchant's name into a million pieces, burned the tents of the tribe of the House of Goash to the ground, and wished Magra was alive so I could kill him all over again.

'I ended up on the floor, swearing and crying. The one thing I didn't do was throw myself out of the window, although I thought about it.' He gives a harsh laugh. 'What kind of devotion is that? I couldn't even follow them.'

When he turns back to the boy, it is in the hope that this time will be different, that he will make a different choice. But he knows he will not.

Dawn is on the lake when he goes down to the wharf. Yareth is there, seeing in the nightfishermen. The usual laughter, the joking, the anticipation of going home. A hot meal, someone waiting, perhaps a child to jog on the knee before turning in. The boy slips past to the jetty where the boat is moored, unties the painter and takes up the oars.

As he casts the net and settles down, a breeze stirs his hair, catching the edge of his weariness. He recognises the character of the air. Autumn isn't far away, and he has survived another year. Gradually he settles into stillness. If he moves, it will hurt. So he sits staring out over the water, aware of the occasional boat, a shout of greeting, a settling wake. When he can no longer ignore the prompting of the handline, he hauls up the net. For a moment he watches the fish, sleek, gasping, hopeless. With a sudden movement he releases them. The water seethes white, the fish quicken and fly. Taking up the oars, he starts to row.

The shore is diminishing, the settlement pulling away. He rows until the oars grow warm in his hands. Then he sits, letting the day pass by. Only when his body is shaking with cold does he finally stir.

He is far from the shore, and it is later than he thought. Only the last scrapings of light remain. A bird flies high overhead, and from the keening he knows it is a hawk. Why do they always sound melancholy? Is it because they know their nature, and what they must do to live? He remembers something Nissa once said: *Why do you always have to see the gloomy side? That's just the noise they make. You'll be telling me a cup starts crying when it's empty.*

'Go away,' he mutters, and she vanishes into the mirror of the mountains.

He starts imagining the panic on the shore, people asking where he is – where the boat is – Gef hiding a grin, Yareth frowning with concern. Or are they simply going about their business, impatient for dinner? He shakes his head bitterly. Is he testing them? Is he trying to find out if they care? He would like to think the answer is no. The idea of contentment is a fool's dream, designed to keep men discontented. He thinks of the old man at the library caves, and the peace he made within himself. He wishes he were here to offer words of wisdom. But the old man sleeps deeply, and the library caves are far away.

Land and water are steeped in blackness now. The cold night air makes the boy shiver harder. Enough, he thinks.

Go back or go on. He can either return to the settlement, and the settlement he has tried to make within himself, or abandon them entirely. Telling himself he is cold and tired and could do with a hot meal, he starts rowing for the shore.

He slips in as quietly as he can, hoping not to be seen, but Yareth and Gef are waiting for him on the jetty. His fingers are trembling as he secures the painter, climbs out of the boat and walks straight past them, to the loft.

It is morning when it finally comes. The quiet knock, the courteous silence. He stumbles out of bed, rubbing his face and yawning. When he opens the door Yareth looks at him for a moment. 'May I come in?'

He nods, aware of the empty flagon lying on its side. Without looking at it Yareth says, 'I have to be able to rely on my fishermen.'

The boy stares at his bare feet. One toe is bruised and swollen, and he has no idea how it happened.

'I thought it might help to get out on the water, keep busy, do the things that keep life going,' Yareth says.

The boy has an urge to tell him what happened, to confide, to share the burden. But he says nothing, and the moment passes.

'You're a good man, Arun, and a good fisherman,' Yareth continues. 'I've seen it happen many times – when there's no one to care for, you don't care for yourself either. I don't want it to happen to you. What you did was wrong, but not unforgiveable. But I can only give you one more chance.'

At the door, he turns. 'Get washed, get dressed, and into your boat. If that's what you want.'

Arun looks into the darkness and sighs. 'If I could go back, I would. To thank him for all the help he gave me, the care he showed.' He shakes his head. 'I was too full of anger and defiance. Maybe I wanted him to throw me out, so I could blame him for whatever bad luck came my way. But he was too wise for that, which only made me resent him more. After that, I practically lived on the water, fishing as if my life depended on it. I worked the net until I almost wore it out. One time it snagged, and I pulled so hard it tore.

'The fishermen of Shanqa almost never tore their nets. It was something to do with the way they were made, a secret never shared with anyone outside the settlement. But somehow I managed it. When Gef saw what had happened, he gave me a look of utter disgust. I deserved it. I gritted my teeth and asked if he could help me repair it. I can still remember his words. *Your net, you fix it.* He walked away before I could throw them both in the lake.'

He smiles bleakly. 'All those feelings, and nowhere for them to go. I spent the whole night on the floor of the loft with a needle and thread, trying to mend the wretched thing. In the end I threw it down, went to bed and slept for a couple of hours, then sat and watched the light breaking across the horizon. A herald announcing a queen.'

His face is sad. 'I saw it as a sign of bad faith. It had no right to be there when –' He breaks off, watching the boy take up the needle again.

The houses of the settlement are decorated with garlands of red and white ribbon, clusters of red berries. New year is celebrated not as the week-long festival it was in Mudaina, but a two-day holiday of rowdy and relentless celebration. The air is full of spices, roasting meats and laughter. There is dancing at the Plough, fiddle music, feasting and drinking. Even Gef is relatively good-tempered, managing a twist of the lips when a woman pokes him in the ribs and tells him he is looking well today.

On the first day of the new year, the boy does what he has done for the past two years: rises very early, packs his satchel and leaves the loft.

There is a nip of frost in the air, not enough to harden the ground. No one is up yet, and why would they be, when the morning is cold and their beds are warm? He hugs his cloak around him as he walks the length of the main street and out of the settlement. The lake is faintly luminous, and very still. He heads in the direction of the hills, which are veiled in purple shadow.

When he has climbed high enough, he stops and looks back. Shanqa lies far below, swimming slowly into daybreak. He starts walking again, recalling lines from a poem he has read many times.

She walks the foothills in her skin,
drinking snow water as she climbs
beyond the kingdom of daily life.

Today it gives no comfort. His kingdom is made of ashes and dust. He stumbles, puts out a hand to steady himself, grazes his palm on a nub of rock, and slips to the ground. Suddenly he starts laughing. What is he? A fisherman with a conscience, a never-will-be poet, lost husband and father. He fits nowhere, not even inside himself.

He spends the night and the following day in the hills, returning to the settlement after dark. The holiday is over. All that remains is an abundance of sore heads, an occasional wink and blush, berries smashed underfoot.

After a warm spring, the summer is unusually dry. Cattle and sheep move up to the high pastures, and the boy longs for the simplicity of rain. Out on the lake he ships his oars and watches the little grey-and-white ducks squabble drowsily. They listen to what's inside them, he reflects. They don't question, they just do, without the tyranny of choice.

'To freedom from tyranny!' he shouts as he uncorks a flagon of wine.

He can't remember returning to the jetty or climbing the steps to the loft. It is a warm feeling, set loose from the world. He hums softly, neither happy nor sad. A knock at the door, and the feeling vanishes. He sits very still, hoping his presence won't be felt.

'I know you're in there,' a voice says.

He stiffens in the chair, listening for footsteps, waiting until they die away. What did Gef want?

'Never mind,' he says crossly, and goes to bed. He sleeps fitfully, waking with a dry mouth and a pounding head.

On the wharf, men are standing about in the way they do when something has happened. When they see him, their faces change. As he passes, one of them hisses, 'You've done it this time.' He looks back, startled. And now Yareth is standing before him, his face sombre. The boy follows his gaze to the jetty, where the boat is – not. He stares down, as if the water will part and return it to life. Yareth says nothing. A boat-shaped silence hangs between them.

When he finds his voice the boy says, 'I . . .' and stops. 'But when I . . .' He stops again. Again he tries. 'Where . . . ?'

'I was hoping you could tell me,' Yareth says. The boy experiences a second of pure panic. It is not like causing his sister's vessel to drown when he threw a pebble at it during a sea battle. He has misplaced a full-grown boat.

Laughter rises wildly, and he struggles to keep it down. Yareth looks at him steadily. 'I just hope it hasn't been found by someone else. It has my mark on it, but it can be removed.'

The boy knows he should apologise, but he can't. 'If I don't find it, I'll pay for it.'

'Yes,' Yareth says soberly, and walks away.

The boy can feel men's eyes on him. Ignoring the stares, he makes his way to the shore. He glances back, but people have begun to drift away to their own business. Part of him wants to ask for help, but he knows he can't. There has been so little transaction between him and the other fishermen he has earned no credit at all.

'Did you find it?' Yareth asks when he looks up from the ledger.

The boy shakes his head. 'I couldn't. I didn't have a boat to go out in.'

'It may have drifted further down the shore. I've sent Gef to look for it. If it doesn't turn up, I'll have to take the cost from your wages.' Yareth frowns. 'It'll take a long time to pay it back.'

The boy pulls a small pouch from his tunic pocket. He

pushes it across the desk. 'That should cover it, and a bit more, for the trouble I've caused.'

A look of sadness crosses Yareth's face. 'You're done, then.'

The boy twists his hands together. 'Look, I'm grateful, truly, but –'

Yareth holds up his hand. 'I wasn't after gratitude,' he says gruffly. 'I hoped it might help, that's all. I'm just sorry it didn't work out. I wish you luck, Arun, I really do.'

He holds out his hand, and the boy shakes it with warmth and regret. As he turns to go, Yareth says, 'He liked you, you know. Gef's always hardest on those with potential.'

With a sudden smile the boy says, 'You could have fooled me.'

The smile has gone as he drags the leather sack and satchel from under the bed and takes a last look out of the window. Part of him is already regretting his decision. Under his made-up mind is a chasm so deep he feels sick thinking about it. He knows Yareth would probably take him back. He also knows the time is past.

At the bottom of the steps he stands for a moment watching the fishermen mending nets, hauling barrels, the women at work in the gutting sheds. He turns and walks away, a shadow dissolving in light.

Chapter Forty

He is following a track through a narrow valley. He has been walking as hard as he can, and Lake Sigal is days behind him now. Mirashi writes about a time

> when ships were tuned to the key of stars
> and men sang, spat, turned in their sleep
> as the watch saw things he could never put in words

but he has never been good at reckoning by starlight or the sun. At a guess he would say he is heading roughly south-westwards, and nowhere.

On the far side of the valley, the track feeds into a wider path. As he walks, he notices the sun backing away. He walks faster, but it is too quick for him. He stops; the sun stops too. He turns his back; it hovers overhead. It is too big, too hot, too golden. If he could, he would lure it into a cave and roll a boulder across the entrance, like the mongoose in the story he told to –

He walks furiously away from the memory until he is out of breath and sweating.

Few people pass by. Some nod a greeting, others open their mouths, ready to strike up a conversation, but he walks straight past. That way, there is no chance of misunderstanding.

A little way ahead, a band of air trembles in the afternoon heat. If he runs at it fast enough, will he break through into another world? A child's thoughts, he tells himself, but the deepest part of him knows that to lose the art of dreaming would be hard indeed. He thinks of Mirashi, who never stopped imagining and, with pain, of Meriem, who never knew its loss. To live between the two is an endless balancing act.

A voice, unbidden, tells him it is only a struggle if you make it so, that one doesn't cancel out the other like a line struck through the page of a ledger. There is space enough to live and dream.

'Stop it!' he cries, and falls to his knees, beating the ground with his fist. The packed earth yields tiny pieces of grit. He beats harder until his hand begins to bleed. Then he slumps down in the dirt as dusk collects round him.

He looks up, sees one star, two. He had thought being alone would mean a removal from everything, so why is it not? At least there is a way to escape it for a while. With a shaking hand he pulls a flagon from the leather sack, and drinks until his eyes close.

When he wakes he is still in one piece, although he feels as if he should be dead. Head, mouth, stomach; all are petitioning to leave the body's court. Opening the satchel, he takes out a packet of dried meat and forces himself to eat. A few gulps of water, and he heaves himself up and walks on.

Three days of steady walking take him round a shoulder of hills, brown and scrubby in the high summer heat. He descends into cool shadow, following the curve of a long bend, and stands looking at a lightly wooded country scored by rough tracks, one of which leads to a village. It feels strange to be encountering human settlement again, as if he has been a long time in the wilderness.

A herd of goats roams freely over the short turf. There is something honest about the way they barge and jostle and jump over each other. But there is also something faintly unnerving about the way the pupil slots into the iris. He has heard legends about goats and devils and dismissed them as nonsense, although he has seen them rise on their hind legs to nibble at leaves, at a distance uncannily human. He has also eaten them. He wonders bleakly if it gives him the last laugh.

A little way on, he finds himself among small cultivated plots. Carrots, onions, rows of beans. People are at work in them, mostly women. He nods, instinctively polite, and is startled when they look away.

The track takes him past skinny vines, a few dusty apple trees. On the outskirts of the village he stops, shading his eyes. No one is about. A cart with a broken wheel lies on its side next to a grey stone house. He wonders what the horse is doing with its free hours. Someone comes out, a man with rolled-up sleeves. He stares at the boy. Strangers are clearly regarded with suspicion. The boy feels the man's eyes on his back as he walks down a street of yellow dust, towards an inn.

The lettering provides a helpful prompt to the poorly drawn image on the sign above the door: the Willow. The inn is clean and plainly furnished. He takes a room, orders hot water, and climbs the stairs. Dropping the sack and satchel on the floor, he sits down heavily on the lumpy bed. Another room. Another inn. He is not the traveller Yorin was.

He is spared from dwelling on the last time he saw his friend by a knock at the door.

'Come in,' he calls, and a woman enters. She is wearing a pale-green dress and balancing a jug and bowl on white towels. Conscious of a week's worth of stains and dirt, the boy gets to his feet, tugging at his crumpled shirt. No wonder the women in the vegetable plots looked away.

With quiet efficiency the woman sets the jug, bowl and towels on a chest of drawers and turns, smiling, to tell him the water in the jug is very hot, so be careful, and to ask if he has everything he needs. He takes a breath, aware of long brown hair and a kind face. To answer properly . . .

'Yes,' he says, 'thank you.'

'We're always busy at this time of year. Lots of people travelling to the horse fairs. And Olti runs a good house.'

Her warm hazel eyes hold his gaze. He doesn't reply. 'Well,' she says pleasantly, 'if there's nothing else?' At the door she turns back. 'My name's Lia, by the way. And dinner's being served – come down whenever you're ready.'

He stands at the window, looking out over the houses opposite. Beyond them lie scrubland and stands of trees, a scattering of small dwellings. Turning from the window, he strips off his clothes and has a thorough wash. The feeling of hot water on his skin is so good he almost laughs. He plunges his head into the bowl, draws it up and shakes like a dog, pelting the floor with water. Droplets darken the wood and are quickly absorbed.

Downstairs, in clean linen, he sits at a small table close to the fire, his legs stretched out in front of him. He has demolished two bowls of lamb stew, sunk countless slices of bread into gravy, and put away four mugs of beer. Now all he wants is to drain away into sleep.

'You liked it?' a voice asks, and he lifts his head to see Lia standing beside him.

'It was the best stew I've had in a long time,' he says.

Her face lights up. 'I'm glad. I made it. I do most of the cooking.'

There is no reason why her smile, so warm and alive, should make him feel uncomfortable. He looks down at his bowl.

'Well, I'll leave you to it,' she says.

As he watches her make her way through the busy common room, lines from a poem come into his head. In it, Mirashi notes things that matter to the business of everyday life.

Hairpins and flowers hold things together
as do markets of indigo, black salt, yellow plums.

He wonders if he is losing the ability to talk about plums.

He sleeps through the night and wakes up cloudy-headed and peaceful. A knock at the door; a voice, his own, saying, 'Leave it outside.'

Later, he surfaces in the sunny room and washes in tepid water. He can't remember when he slept so well.

When he goes down to the common room he is greeted not by Lia but by a serving-woman, who asks him if he'd like some – she looks a little confused – 'well, if you haven't had it, it'll be breakfast.'

The bowl of thick, sweet cham is soon empty. Closing his eyes, he sits quietly for a while. Here at the fireside of an inn not so different from any other, he feels strangely calm. Part of him starts asking why, but he shoos it away and lets his thoughts wander.

Into his head comes a long-forgotten story, the tale of a man adrift in the marshes where he went looking for his lost sweetheart. He comes across a gathering of fairy folk who have taken her for the song of her fiddle. He knows that by turning his glove inside-out he will break the spell, so he does, but the magic hops back from the heft of the blow, and shuts. He spends the rest of his life looking for her, in vain.

When the boy leaves the inn, it is with a sense of purpose. A little way out from the village, his pace quickens. He knows where he is going; he saw it from his window.

The path dwindles to a track running past a wooden hut. Leaving the track, he approaches the hut. It looks deserted. The shutters are closed; a rag hangs from the latch.

He tries the door. With a lingering creak it opens, stirring misty air. He looks around at a floor made of wooden boards, a rough stone fireplace with a thick wooden mantel above. A table with a cracked leg. Three chairs, one with no back. Shelves on the walls. A lopsided bed. On the floor, a pile of rags that may once have been

560

a rug. Two windows, one beside the door, the other in the left-hand wall.

The boy goes to the side window and opens the shutters. One of them falls to the floor with a mighty crash, and the sun crowds in. Dust flies in streams of light. He sits on a chair, absorbing the room.

After a while he goes outside to look around. The ground is dry and scrubby. Behind the house he finds a well. When he heaves off the thick wooden lid, a wave of dampness hits his face. Peering down, he catches a gleam of water. Beside the well, a length of rope lies next to a broken bucket. The rope is cut through and has started unravelling. He wonders who did it, and why. A final act of spite between a parting couple? Revenge for a deal that fell through?

He raises his eyebrows. It is a rope, and won't speak. But he can speak for it, so he picks it up and reattaches it, making a knot Yareth would be proud of. He tugs, and it holds, but he can't draw up water because the bucket is broken.

A dog barks, a goat bleats. The air is softening round him, drawing dusk across the hills. When he returns, the inn is already busy. He goes to his table and waits for someone to serve him. It is Lia, smiling in welcome.

Abruptly he says, 'The hut outside the village, do you know who owns it?'

'It's been abandoned for quite a while. I think it was used by goatherds, then a family lived in it before they moved away. Why? Are you interested?'

The boy looks at her warily. 'I'm not sure.'

When Lia returns with his food, she asks if she can sit down for a moment. He shrugs.

'About the hut,' she says as he cuts into meat and potato pie, 'I don't think anyone would mind if you wanted to live in it. Mending it would be fair payment. And Kandra's a good village. Small but sound.'

She stays with him as he eats, and he finds himself not minding. More than that, he finds it comforting. It has been so long since anyone took the trouble to spend time with him. Or is it the other way round? Frowning, he stabs at a piece of pie.

'Is it that bad?' Lia asks with a slight smile. He assures her it is very good.

When he has finished, she takes his empty plate, excuses herself – 'hungry mouths to feed' – and wishes him a peaceful evening. He watches her go, slender in a simple blue dress, and finds himself wondering how long she has been here, and where she came from.

In the market the following morning, the boy finds a man who seems to be made of many trades. He buys an axe and other tools, kitchen utensils, blankets, and a ladder, which he will need if he is to mend the roof. He buys other things too, and the trader, Min, lends him a mule to carry his purchases out to the hut.

The boy tucks the ladder under his arm, regarding the animal with suspicion. Its eye is limpid, innocent. As he approaches, the mule slowly turns its head towards him. He knows the look. Turning to Min he says, 'I'll go on ahead. If it wants to follow, let it. I don't have time to waste,' and walks away. After a moment the mule snorts, ducks its head and follows, panniers swaying at either side. The trader's face slowly breaks into a smile.

The boy reaches the hut just before the mule. When the goods are unloaded, he takes a carrot from a sack. The mule's nostrils quiver. 'Thank you for helping me,' the boy says formally. The carrot is gone in a single crunch. 'I'm sure you know your way back,' he adds politely.

As it turns and starts plodding along the track, he reflects that there is no lateral thinking in a mule.

When everything is unpacked, he takes up his new axe and goes in search of wood to use as timber. Lia suggested white pine, plentiful in the area. Not far from the hut, he sets to work. By the time he is done the sky is violet-blue, the air pleasantly cool. When he has finished stacking the wood he puts his hands on his hips and stretches, his back aching slightly. It is a good feeling. He makes a cold dinner, pouring himself a beaker of red wine from a flagon bought at the market.

He is lying on the floor of the hut, staring up at sunlight coming through holes in the roof. He isn't sure how he got here, only that his head is a thundercloud, his mouth a desert. The mule's revenge, he thinks, pulling himself to his feet and going outside.

Morning has started without him. At the well, he lets down the bucket and hauls it up hand over hand. It is surprisingly light, and as it breaches the rim he sees it is empty. 'Of course you are,' he mutters, and takes it back to the hut, squinting against the light. Choosing some pieces of wood from the pile, he carries them to the front of the hut, and drops them with a clatter.

He has never mended anything before, and it is not as easy as he thought. After a few false starts he finds his stride, working intently. When he is finished, his shirt is soaked, the top of his head burning. The air swims; the bucket shimmers like water.

He wakes to find himself on the ground. A pleasant coolness trickles down his neck; someone is pressing a cloth to his forehead. Groaning, he tries to sit up, but a hand gently pushes him back. Warm hazel eyes look down at him.

'Not yet,' Lia says, 'you need to do it slowly.' She holds a beaker to his mouth. Too ill to feel embarrassed, he drinks. The liquid is cool and sweet. She tells him it is ginger wine, good for sun-sickness. 'There's no alcohol in it.'

His head begins to feel as if it belongs to him again. Another drink and the ground, which has been tilting beneath him, starts to settle. Lia puts down the empty beaker. 'Can you stand?' she asks. He tries, but his legs are like sand. She helps him up, puts an arm around his waist, guides him into the hut and onto a chair.

'How are you feeling?' she asks.

'Better,' he says.

'I brought you this. I thought you might need it.' It is a basket covered with a clean white cloth. She puts it on the table. 'Now, will you be all right, or would you like me to stay?'

'I'll be fine. I've taken up enough of your time already.'

When Lia has gone, the boy removes the cloth to find a stone bottle, a large pie, a loaf of bread which, judging by the warmth, is freshly made, and a slab of butter wrapped in paper. With both hands he picks up the pie and takes a bite. Buttery pastry melts in his mouth. Beef, herbs, gravy.

When every crumb has gone, he uncorks the bottle and takes a long draught of ginger wine before attending to the bread. He finds the knife he bought, saws off a chunk, smears it with butter and crams it into his mouth.

When he can eat no more he sits back with a contented sigh, wiping his hands on his shirt. Drowsily he looks at the chair with no back. 'You're next,' he says. But first, sleep.

When he wakes, it is dark. A clerical dark, working by moonlight to copy the holes in the roof onto the floor. He rubs his head, looking round for the lamp. Where did he put it? Pulling himself to his feet, he fumbles on the shelf next to the fireplace until his hand knocks against something metallic and cold. When the lamp is lit, it casts a soft beam across the room, fraying into shadow. Hungry again, he sits on the floor and finishes the loaf.

The wooden boards are cool and sound. At least he hopes so. An army of munching creatures could be working away beneath him. He remembers his father heaving up a large stone from the ground next to the hut, exposing an ants' nest. As the boy peered down at the intricate construction, its angry citizens streamed out and up his leg.

'Stamp, boy, stamp!' his father said, and he did, leaping and waving his arms wildly. Afterwards, when he was in a particularly bad mood, his sister would perform what she called Arun's Ant Dance, and he would end up laughing.

He smiles faintly, but his face is sad as he pulls a blanket from a pile beside the fireplace, throws it around himself, blows out the lamp and curls up on the floor. Sometime later he wakes, and lies for a moment wondering where he is. Darkness presses in; he turns over and closes his eyes. It is no use. Getting up, he lights the lamp and takes a flagon from the shelf in the corner.

The next morning he promises himself no more late-night drinking. It is another fine day, the sun high in a blue-white sky. He trudges to the well, hauls up a bucket of water – the mended parts hold – and empties it over his head.

Indoors, he rummages about and finds a bag of raisins. The shrivelled brown pellets look like ancient rabbit droppings. He has never paid much attention to raisins, considering them a waste of a grape. There are, he knows, whole shelves of verse extolling the pleasures of the vine, but he has never come across a poem dedicated to dried fruit. Holding one between thumb and forefinger, he studies it. If he did write something it would have to tactful, with no reference to desiccation. He pops it in his mouth.

All day he works, cutting planks to patch the sides of the hut. His head is covered with a damp scarf; he has no wish for Lia to find him on the ground again. He wonders where she is, thinks, of course, she's busy at the inn, and hammers harder. If he makes enough noise it will drive out everything else.

In the Willow that evening he pulls a brimming bowl towards him. He has earned this. There is a blister on his thumb, and his back aches. The bowl is soon empty, the gravy mopped up with slices of bread. Sitting back, he loosens his belt and closes his eyes. After a while he senses someone near him.

'You look as if you enjoyed that,' Lia says. 'Can you manage another helping?'

He smiles, shaking his head. 'But it was excellent, thank you. Oh, and I've brought your basket back.'

Lia smiles. 'How did it go today?'

He finds himself inviting her to sit down. She is a good listener, attentive and interested as he tells her about his argument with a particularly stubborn piece of wood.

'When you've finished, it'll make a good home,' she says.

The room feels instantly colder. She seems to sense his change of mood. 'I'm sorry if I said something wrong. I didn't mean to upset you.'

It would be easy to let himself find comfort in the warmth of her voice. 'It's late,' he says abruptly. 'I'd better get going.'

No headache today. Which would be a good feeling, but he is still thinking about last night. Lia showed only understanding when he left, which made matters worse. He resolves to stay away from the inn this evening, telling himself he would not be good company.

There is little left to eat. Frustrated by his lack of planning, he makes his way to the village. The market is already busy. He follows his nose to a woman in a meal-coloured apron.

'Is the bread fresh?' he asks. She stares at him. Quickly he says, 'I'm sure it's the finest in the province.'

It is excusably extravagant praise. Her expression softens. 'I don't know about that, but here –' Breaking off a piece, she offers it to him. It is warm, and begging for butter.

He buys two loaves, and wanders through the stalls. Meat, fruit, vegetables, spices, herbs, milk, pastries, candles, pottery, toys for children, even a stall selling wooden chests, one of which will do for clothes. All in all, a surprisingly good market. The one lack is fish, for which he feels no regret. All the same, he can't help asking about it.

The man wrapping his final purchase says, 'If you want dried fish, go to Min. Fresh fish is generally too expensive. Traders come from time to time, but we're too small to make it worth their while.'

When he has put his shopping away, the boy uncorks a stone bottle. He has been looking forward to this. The beer was brewed by someone he met outside the Willow. A stocky man with short dark hair, his name was Fulda and he was making a delivery to the inn. He explained that he made the beer in a room in his house in Raksal. 'It stinks to high heaven,' he said with a laugh. 'My wife holds her nose when she brings me tea.' He offered the boy a taste. Gratified by his response, Fulda pressed a couple of bottles on him as a gift.

The beer is as good as he remembers, golden-brown, nutty, stomach-warming. As he drinks, he thinks of Yorin, who once declared that he travelled simply to taste every beer in every inn this side of the world.

He finishes the bottle and wipes his mouth. There is a chair to be mended, and a table to set straight.

Chapter Forty-One

The light has no business worming its way through the holes in the roof. Surely it was only moments ago that he was toasting the mended chair with Fulda's beer? Groaning, the boy throws off his blanket, pulls himself up from the floor and goes out. He almost trips over a basket covered with a clean white cloth.

Rubbing his eyes, he tries to ignore the feeling it inspires, telling himself he has no reason to feel guilty. He didn't go to the inn last night, he inflicted himself on no one, and has hurt no one's feelings. And today he will start patching the roof. But first – catching up the basket, he takes it indoors. If someone has gone to the trouble of bringing it, he can at least see what it contains.

It would have been rude not to eat it, he tells himself as he hammers a plank into place. The fact that the honey tasted delicious on the white rolls, and what is left of the round spiced cake will do for his mid-morning break, is neither here nor there. It is after all hungry work, mending a hut.

'Ow!' The ladder wobbles dangerously, the hammer falls through the hole and clatters to the floor. He nurses his thumb in his fist before inspecting the damage. It will wear a fine bruise, but it will live. And if returning Lia's basket this evening proves he is neither ungrateful nor mannerless, and prevents another accident, then that is what he will do.

The pie is flaky and golden, crammed with pieces of succulent chicken. He is served by a young man who looks as if he has better things to do. He sets down the plate distractedly, almost misses the table with the mug of beer, and departs without a word.

'Thanks,' the boy mutters to his back. He glances round the common room, but he can't see Lia.

He is finishing his beer when he hears her voice. His pulse quickens, but only because she startled him.

'I was wondering if you'd come,' she says, wiping her hands on the apron she is wearing over a dress the colour of barley. He notices a pair of freckles on her sun-warmed nose, and wonders when she found the time to collect them.

'I'd have come over sooner but we've been very busy. How are you?' she asks. He finds himself unable to put one word in front of another.

'May I?' She indicates the chair opposite, and he nods. 'I was hoping to see you,' she says. 'I was worried I might have scared you away.' She tucks her soft brown hair behind her ear. A nervous gesture. The last thing he wants is to make her feel anxious.

'The cake was wonderful. It all was. Thank you. And I brought your basket back. Again.' The words come out in a rush.

Lia smiles. 'You're very welcome. But' – her face changes – 'what happened to your thumb?'

The morning air is crisper now. The boy wears his cloak when he walks to the inn. Every evening he updates Lia on his progress. The pleasure she takes in his work is infectious; he finds himself looking forward to telling her what he has accomplished each day.

She showed particular interest in hearing about the pains he took to mend the table, planing and polishing until the old wood glowed again.

'There's nothing like a good table to serve food on,' she said. 'It makes everything taste better.' She made a face. 'You probably think it's a silly thing to say.'

When he assured her it wasn't, that good food deserved respect, she smiled and touched his hand, saying she thought he would understand. The gesture was not flirtatious, but a faint shock flared through his skin.

When he returned to the hut, he took a flagon from the shelf and drank so fast that wine spilled on his shirt, staining it red. When he finally slept, he saw her clearly for the first time.

She was wearing her favourite tunic, rose-coloured, embroidered on the collar and cuffs with tiny silver lilies. Her hair was loose about her shoulders and she was smiling. When he told her he thought he'd lost her, she touched his face, saying, *You'll never lose me, my love, I'll always be with you.* As he reached for her, she vanished.

He dreamed harder, trying to find her again, but lost his way in winding alleys and long passageways, emerging onto a wide sandy beach. Salt spray wet his face as he ran up and down looking for her. A gull glowed ruby-red in the rising sun. He held up his hand but it flew past him, into the sea.

My mother said fish breathe water, he told it, *but you are a bird and need air*, and he ran to the shore and dived in. The sea closed over him. As he took his last breath, gentle hands lifted him and laid him on the sand. He had found her. She had saved him. Joy flooded his heart. He looked up into warm hazel eyes.

All that day he worked furiously, barely noticing when he stunned his thumb again. By the time evening came, he had thought his way out of not going to the inn. Lia had shown him only friendship and kindness. How he responded had nothing to do with her. It had been so long since he felt a woman's touch it was hardly surprising he reacted as he did.

That evening he kept his hands on his side of the table, although there was no need, since Lia made no attempt to touch him again.

Someone is sitting at his table. The news he has for Lia is briefly forgotten. He hovers, shooting looks at the man who, when skins were being handed out, grabbed the thickest. Eventually he gives up and finds a vacant spot in the corner, under the window beside the fireplace. He sits facing the wall, where a lamp glows softly.

Lia is threading through the crowd, a jug in her hand.

'A change of scenery?' she says.

'My usual place was taken.' He treats the man to a resentful glance.

Smiling, she says, 'He's here for the sheep.'

'They asked for him by name?' It is out before he can stop himself.

Lia starts laughing. 'Don't tell them, but it's mutton broth this evening. With dumplings. A new recipe. Let me know what you think.'

When she returns later he invites her to sit down,

and she looks at him expectantly. He knows what she is waiting for. 'Words don't do it justice,' he says, and her face lights up.

'I'd offer you some more but it's all gone. I'd no idea it would be so popular.'

The boy says he is not surprised. 'And – I've finished. It's done. The hut, I mean.'

Lia's reaction couldn't be more gratifying. 'That's wonderful. You must be pleased.'

He says he is, and then, a little hesitantly – he has thought about it since he hammered the last nail into place and stood back to appraise his work – he asks if she would like to come and see it, tomorrow morning, if she's not too busy?

'I'd love to,' Lia says. 'Thank you.'

A fire burns in the hearth, a kettle hangs above. He has rearranged cups and plates a dozen times, and sits at the table with his hands in his lap. He gathers himself before answering the knock at the door.

'I brought something to commemorate the occasion,' Lia says, offering him a basket. Her smile puts him at ease. As she looks around, he sees the hut through her eyes, no longer threadbare or neglected but warm and cared for. Mirashi writes about a house

> made from the green wood of summer
> and furnished with swallows

but he finds himself content with what he has as Lia walks round, touching the mended shutters, glancing at

573

the satchel hanging on a nail on one side of the door, the dagger on the other. She takes time admiring the table – 'It's even nicer than I thought' – the chair, and the low, round-seated stool he made before starting on the thing he is most proud of.

The stool gave him somewhere to sit as he worked in the shade of the hut, preparing wood for the sides and shelves of the cabinet. Making the pegs to hold it together was harder than he thought, and it took a fair few curses and a deep cut in his forefinger to knock them into shape. When the cabinet was finished, he carried it into the hut, set it against a wall and inspected it. He'd let the grain of the wood sing out, and its voice was pure and strong.

'It's beautiful,' Lia says. 'It must have taken quite a while to make.'

'The walls' ears were burning by the time I'd finished.' He offers her a chair.

When tea is prepared she says, 'May I?' Removing the white cloth, she takes from the basket a large round cake. 'I hope it's all right, I made it last night at the inn.'

'I'm sure it'll be delicious.' He smiles.

Lia cuts through the sugared crust and puts a pale golden slice on a plate. It is moist, subtly flavoured, and very quickly gone. As she cuts another slice she says, 'There's something I want to tell you, but it can wait. First, a toast to your new house.'

There is one last bottle of beer in the cabinet. 'Just a drop,' she says as he pours. 'I want the lamb stew to be edible. Otherwise Olti will never forgive me. Especially –' She breaks off. 'What about the toast?'

'You do it. I'm not very good with words.'

Her eyes tell him she thinks otherwise, but she raises her mug. 'I hope your time here is happy, and the rain never gets in.'

'I'll drink to that.'

'Let me,' she says later, when he offers more tea.

'You're the guest.' He has finished the beer, and a warm feeling runs through his body. Lia holds up her cup and he carefully fills it. Her head is tilted upwards; the pair of summer freckles have faded away.

Slowly, almost as if he is detached from himself, he leans down and kisses her. She sits very still, holding her cup. He kisses her again, and this time he feels her respond. He has almost forgotten what it is like to experience for the first time the delicate exploration of shared pleasure. The first time –

His body flames with guilt. He pulls away so quickly he spills tea on Lia's dress. What was he thinking? How could he even have contemplated it? What kind of husband does it make him?

He is barely aware of himself or his actions as he shouts, 'Get out! Get out!'

Only when he hears the door closing does he begin to realise what he has done. He wants to run after Lia, to apologise, but he cannot. He can only stand staring at the door as shame overwhelms him.

He wakes fully clothed on the bed. Groaning, he puts his feet on the floor and leans over, resting his head on his knees. As blood rushes in, he slowly uncurls and waits for the room to stop revolving. He avoided the inn last night, unable to face Lia. Instead he sat beside the fire until it died, trying not to look at the plates and cups on the table, the basket whose clean white cloth loomed whiter as the room grew dark. Finally he got up, threw away the remains of the cake, put the basket in a corner and opened a flagon of wine.

As he draws water from the well and plunges his head into the bucket, he tells himself he can't avoid Lia forever. He shakes his head vigorously, and takes a deep breath. The morning air is like a blade to his lungs. Coughing and swearing, he goes into the hut and slams the door.

It has taken all his courage to get here. There is a sick feeling in his stomach as he enters the common room, half-expecting to be set upon by angry customers. But no one takes any notice as he makes his way to the table in the corner. Someone is approaching and he looks up quickly, but it is only the young man. With barely a glance, he tells the boy if he wants the lamb stew he'd better be quick, it has almost gone. Lamb stew. It was what Lia was making yesterday.

Where is she? He has worked himself up to an apology, but his nerve is about to break. 'Isn't Lia serving this evening?' he asks.

The young man shrugs. 'No, she's gone.'

'Gone?'

'That's right.'

'Where?'

'No idea.'

'When will she be back?'

'Search me.'

If he could, he would. But he can only sit in a pool of self-loathing, wondering where Lia has gone, and why.

Was it because of him? He suspects it was, and despises himself even more.

Looking round, he catches Olti's eye. The innkeeper gives a curt nod and turns back to his work. Something crawls coldly down the boy's back. What if Lia told Olti about the way he behaved towards her? If she did, the innkeeper is hardly likely to divulge her whereabouts. And he can ask no one else, since he has made neither friends nor conversation with anyone apart from Lia.

After his meal, he sits for a long time staring at the lamp on the wall. Finally he stirs. Very well. If he is to be damned, he may as well do it properly. He calls for more beer, Fulda's this time, only to find that Olti's customers have drunk it dry. No matter. Any beer will do.

The temperature has taken a dive. He walks quickly, thinking about the lamb stew. Stew. What a poor name for something so delectable, so sublime. He finds himself singing at the top of his voice. 'L-a-m-b-d-i-v-i-n-e, r-a-v-i-s-h-i-n-g-l-a-m-b!' No matter that it comes out as 'ravshing'. Tonight he can lose as many vowels as he likes. He has lost everything else, after all. He spins in a circle and ends up on his back on the ground, laughing. But something is burrowing through layers of beer-fuelled warmth to ask how he could have behaved so badly, especially towards someone who has shown him nothing but kindness. Has he come so far from the light?

'Always the light. I've never understood the attraction.' The voice is dry, and faintly ironic.

The boy hauls himself up on to his elbow, looking around. An owl hoots close by, making him jump. A glimmer of pearl and it is gone, low and swift over the

577

ground. Did he just hear it speak? If so, what it said would make sense, since it works with the night, winnowing the dark for the living grain.

He lies back, looking up into a deep blue sky. Stars are like eyes opening, he thinks, and wonders if the night feels a pinprick as each one comes out. The question is on the tip of his tongue, but he rolls his eyes and struggles to his feet. The thoughts of an owl are enough for one night.

Beside the pool, Arun watches the boy weave his way back to the hut. He looks away.

'That was almost the first time we met,' Night says, 'and you thought I was an owl.' A snort of derision. 'I almost gave up, but you know me. I stick at things. I persevere.'

'I'd noticed. Well, do you feel something?'

'About what?'

'When the stars come out. And you're not ducking the question this time.'

'In which case, I choose not to answer.'

'You never do.'

In a dignified voice Night says, 'Not at all. I answered by telling you I chose not to answer.'

There is a complicated silence.

'If I'd known then what I know now, I'd never have started this,' Arun says.

'And think what you would have missed.'

Arun shakes his head. 'Always the last word.'

He looks from the moon in the pool to where it stands in cold reflection above the hut.

Chapter Forty-Two

The common room is crowded, as usual. He sits at his table nursing a mug of beer. Lia has not returned. He has succeeded in driving her away.

'It's not always about you, you know.' The voice again, dry, sardonic, close to his ear. He glances around but everyone is occupied, eating, drinking, talking. He peers into his mug. Whatever inspiration it contained has dried up. He gets to his feet, throws down some coins and leaves the inn.

Inside the hut he sits on the mended chair and looks up at the roof. No holes remain. No light can get in. 'Ha,' he says smugly.

The following morning there is little to be smug about. He groans, rolls over onto a bottle, rolls back and out of bed. He goes to the shelf in the corner and peers into the bread crock. When did he eat the last of the loaf? The idea of another trip to market irritates him.

He glares at the crock. 'If this was a fairy tale, you'd never be empty.'

Wishing plants and creatures made of spice and earth. Her teasing voice comes back to him. He drops the lid with a clatter.

He walks to the village in a state of resentment, buys

what he needs, and returns. He spends the afternoon lying on the bed. A narrow bed, no need to be any wider. The reason why flashes up from the depths of his mind. He throws a stone and it darts away.

The only problem, he thinks as he walks back to the hut, is the walk back to the hut. The night air, the pinching breeze, wake him up again. He stands for a moment, looking up. A hazy moon drifts across the sky. He corrects himself. Clouds cross the moon, the moon appears to move. He is done with starlit skies of darkest velvet. The night is for poets, not for him.

'Night makes poets of you all.' The voice sounds amused. He shuts the door firmly behind him.

He wakes with a thirst only Fulda's beer can satisfy. Rubbing his face, he sits up in bed, thinking. If the beer won't come to him, he will go to the beer. The idea is pleasing in its simplicity. Fulda lives in Raksal, beyond the shoulder of hills. If there are arrangements to be made, he needs to be clear-headed. It will be water all the way.

Raksal obliges by being where he thought it would be. It is larger than Kandra, and looks more prosperous. Evening has drawn folk indoors, and the main street is quiet. Halfway down he finds the inn, its sign depicting a pair of swans, foreheads touching, their graceful necks enclosing a heart of air. He tells the innkeeper he is looking for Fulda, and is directed to a house on the corner. He decides to take a room for the night and call on the beer-maker in the morning.

After breakfast, he walks slowly down the street. When he knocks on the door of a house with blue shutters a woman answers, her face flushed. Apologising for disturbing her, he introduces himself.

She gives him a flustered smile. 'I'm Imah, Fulda's wife,' she says. 'Please, come in.'

In a large, light room two children are sitting on the floor, playing with a toy horse. One has a serious face, the other a determined look as he tugs the horse away from his brother.

'Play nicely,' Imah says automatically. The boy looks away, and follows her into the kitchen. She knocks on a door in the right-hand wall and receives a mumbled reply. 'Go in, my dear,' she says.

Fulda looks up as the boy enters. The room is spacious but cluttered, its open window failing to dispel the impressive pungency. Not unpleasant but warm and yeasty, with a slight edge to it. The smell of gestation. Fulda gets up from his stool and offers the boy his hand.

'I remember you. We met in Kandra.'

'You have a good memory,' the boy says.

'I don't forget people who like my beer.' Fulda smiles. 'Please, come in, sit down.'

The boy skirts round a collection of bottles as Fulda sweeps a pile of sacks from a chair. 'I grow the hops, but I buy the bottles from a man in Mestra,' he explains. 'Now' – he looks at the boy expectantly – 'what can I do for you?'

The boy tells him he was so impressed with Fulda's beer he had to come and see where it was made. Not entirely true, but timing is important. It wouldn't do to show his hand too soon. Fulda beams. 'It's taken a long time to get this one just right. It hasn't been easy to find the right blend, but when I did . . .'

He lowers himself onto his stool with the ease of one who knows exactly where everything is. 'When I first started brewing, it was just for myself. I'm fussy about beer, and when Imah said if I thought I could do better I should have a go, it was all the encouragement I needed. She's always encouraged me.' He rubs his ear. 'I started by finding out how to grow hops. That took some doing.'

He laughs. 'Everyone thought I was mad. Even me, at times. But I didn't give up. I studied the climate – really studied it – the soil, the wind, the water. It took a long time, but it was worth it. There's water under there' – he nods at the floor – 'if you know where to look.'

He reaches for a bottle, and offers it to the boy. 'Try this. I think I've just about got it right.'

'It's very good,' the boy says appreciatively, wiping his mouth.

Fulda smiles. 'If you knew how many attempts it took me – I was cross-eyed by the time I'd worked it out, and Imah was just cross. She's a good woman, though, and I'm lucky. How many wives would let their husbands disappear for hours on end to study the way the wind's blowing, tending each vine as if it were dearer than his children, going out each morning to check if the buds are in flower?

'Ah, flower of the hop! It took two years and a lot of patience before I found the right one.' He nods at the bottle. 'Star of the Desert. It's hardier, able to withstand drought. Although I found a way around that, too.' Getting up, he leads the boy through another door, into a long garden.

Beyond tall rows of trellised vines the boy sees an elaborate construction of wooden pipes. Inside, water softly sings. 'I invented it myself,' Fulda says. 'It's quite simple really, based on water being drawn up from an underground spring.' He explains it to the boy, who wonders if there are different levels of simple, and whether he is doomed to remain at the lowest.

There is something gentle in Fulda's face as he looks at the vines. 'I could stay out here for hours, but I have a family to think of. Twin boys keep you on your toes.' In sudden uproar, his children come running out of the house to fold themselves around his legs. The boy turns away and studies the irrigation system.

Someone is tugging at his trouser leg. One of the little boys is gazing up at him. 'You're honoured,' Fulda says. 'Tref's normally shy. Unlike Tarius.' He picks up the other little boy and starts bouncing him up and down. Tarius squeals and giggles. Tref has spotted Imah coming down the garden, and runs off to be enveloped in her apron.

Fulda glances at the boy. 'You wait. When you have your own, you'll wonder what you ever did without them. Now, I think it's time for some tea.' The boy's head fills with a black buzzing, as if a hive has taken up residence.

'Go through,' Imah says at the door, 'I've lit a fire.'

In the living room, the toy horse lies abandoned on the rug. A low square table holds cups, plates and a large platter of cakes.

'You made them!' Fulda exclaims. 'Cinnamon and orange,' he tells the boy as they sit down. 'Nothing beats them.'

Fulda's pride has a firm root. The boy eats too many, and drinks four cups of tea flavoured with lemon. Sighing contentedly, Fulda puts down his plate. 'Imah always keeps some back. She knows I'll eat them all otherwise. I don't eat children, though,' he says in a louder voice, reaching down, fishing up Tref and sitting him on his lap.

The boy examines his cup. It is made of fine white material into which tiny blue-headed flowers have been pressed. A subtle glaze creates a film of dew.

'A wedding present,' Fulda says, 'from my parents.' He looks down at his son. 'They're not with us any more, but they lived long enough to see these two into the world.' The boy leans back from the heat of the fire and pulls at the neck of his shirt.

Fulda sets Tref gently on the floor and strokes his hair. 'Go find your brother. See what mischief he's up to.' A muted bang comes from the kitchen, and Tref runs towards it. 'See what I mean? I came home once to find two little ghosts. They'd got into a sack of flour and were throwing it at each other with great enthusiasm.'

The boy is aware he is failing as a guest. 'They get into everything,' he says politely.

'They do,' Fulda nods. 'Now, you didn't come here just to taste my beer.'

The boy explains he would like Fulda to supply him with beer. Fulda looks troubled. 'I'd like to oblige, Arun, only . . .'

The boy guesses the reason for his discomfort. In business transactions, the line between good and bad faith is finely drawn. He thinks for a moment. 'What if I talk to Olti about it?'

Fulda looks relieved. 'I think that would be a good idea.' He offers more tea but the boy declines. He has a sudden urge to leave. At the door he thanks Fulda and

Imah for their hospitality, and says he will send word when he has it.

It is dark by the time he reaches the outskirts of Kandra. A wasted journey, a wasted day. He has no intention of talking to Olti about Fulda's beer. If Lia told him what happened – the innkeeper's demeanour contains as yet no discernible clue – any hope of a favourable outcome has already expired. Even if she hasn't – which, from the little he learned about her, he believes more likely – he feels unable to make the approach. There was a time when he blew through a group of merchants like a storm – he smiles faintly at the image – but that was another life. To make such an arrangement would require connection, a continuing attachment to something he no longer wants to be a part of. Besides which it would create an obligation, so no, he is not going to talk to Olti.

'I'm glad you've sorted that out.'

The boy looks around, but sees no one. He shakes his head hard, as if the voice will come tumbling out. Is he finally going mad?

'Nowhere near, in spite of your efforts.' It is everywhere, and yet only in his ear.

'How would you know?' he retorts, but receives no reply. 'Suit yourself,' he mutters, and walks on.

His satchel clinks softly as he hangs it on the nail beside the door. Before he left, Fulda pressed on him half a dozen bottles of beer and a warm invitation to return. He starts to take one out, changes his mind, and throws himself down on his unmade bed.

At the inn the following evening he avoids Olti's eye, as if news of his visit to Fulda is written on his forehead. So what if it is? he tells himself, glancing up as the young man approaches. His clothes are more fitting for a feast or a celebration. The boy orders his meal, and watches the young man as he leaves. Perhaps he has decided he is made for better things. And perhaps those things are more likely to take notice if he makes himself conspicuous.

'I've only just got here, and I'm already exhausted.' The voice again, tinged with amusement. 'But you've given me an idea for our first topic.'

The boy sighs. He is too weary to wonder about his lack of curiosity. All he wants is a quiet meal, but he senses the voice won't go away. 'Which is?'

'Which is, why are men always striving, always looking for something more?'

He has no intention of responding, but as he waits for his meal he finds himself thinking it isn't so apparent in women, the striving for something more, and tries to decide if it is because they are more content with what they have, or – he suspects this is closer to the truth – because they are not always given the opportunity.

'I'd say your second guess is nearer the mark.'

The boy sets his jaw and stares at the wall.

'I've been watching you for some time now.'

'Don't worry,' the boy says sarcastically, 'I don't feel special.'

'Oh, but you should. I don't talk to just anyone. And it would only be polite to invite me to join you. Or have you forgotten your manners?'

With a heavy sigh, the boy waves his hand at the table. 'Please, be my guest,' he says with exaggerated courtesy.

The lamp on the wall is briefly obscured. 'Sorry about that,' the voice says.

The young man returns with the boy's meal, and departs. 'It looks delicious,' the voice says. The boy spoons up chicken broth and holds it out to the wall. 'I won't, thank you,' the voice says politely.

Tearing off a chunk of buttered bread, the boy dips it in the broth. It receives the liquid in an almost sensual way, becoming soft and full.

'If the land behaved that way with the sea you'd all drown.'

The boy's face heats up. 'It's rude to listen to other people's thoughts,' he says.

'I can't help it, although believe me, sometimes I wish I could. On the other hand, it can be very entertaining.'

The boy gulps beer and starts coughing. He puts down his spoon with a clatter and glares across the table. 'If you're so keen on manners, why don't you introduce yourself?'

'Why don't you guess?'

The boy groans. He was never any good at riddles.

'Have a go,' the voice says. 'I'll make it easy.'

'Fine. Anything to shut you up.'

'Right then, first clue. I fall but never break.'

The boy thinks for a moment. 'Water?'

'Not bad, but wrong. Clue number two. I fill the world, but take no space.'

'Air?'

'Wrong again. You really aren't very good at this, are you?' The boy folds his arms. 'One last clue. The more of

587

me, the less you see. That one's normally for children,' the voice adds helpfully.

Nettled, the boy puts his elbows on the table and thinks hard. Finally he looks up. 'You're night.'

The lamplight gutters, as if something has brushed against it. 'Pleased to make your acquaintance, Arun. And note the initial capital,' Night says.

For some reason, the boy is not as surprised as he feels he should be. He sits back and drinks some beer.

'No need to say what an honour it is,' Night remarks. 'People are always wanting to talk to me. In me, to be precise. It's generally wishes and prayers. I don't know why. Whether they're answered or not has nothing to do with me.'

The boy stares across the table. 'What do you mean?'

'What do you think I mean?'

Question and echo. It is something the boy will get used to. He is silent, thinking. Night presses him; tiny white stars prickle behind his eyes. 'Don't do that,' he says sharply. Night draws back; the lamplight grows stronger.

'I think,' he says eventually, 'I've had enough of wishes. They don't get you anywhere.'

'I knew I was right,' Night says smugly. 'You see yourself as someone with no time for dreams. Which isn't true. I've watched you, and believe me, you're a dreamer.'

'I hardly dream at all,' the boy retorts, trying not to think of the many times he has woken up and instantly closed his eyes, desperate to return.

'Remember the time your mother was a day late back from a trip? The only trip she made when you were living in the valley, as I recall – and your father stomped about, making a lot of noise, drinking a bit too much? You managed – mostly because of your sister – but your dreams were terrible. Darkness – not that there's anything wrong with it, of course – and cliffs, and falling –'

The boy is there, descending into a blackness he knows will be neither soft nor warm.

'Stop it!' he says. He gulps beer, finds himself at the bottom of the mug, and bangs it down on the table. With raised eyebrows the young man appears, filling it from the jug in his hand.

When he has gone the boy whispers angrily, 'Don't do that again.'

'I do apologise, but there's no need to be so dramatic.'

'I don't like dreams, that's all,' the boy mutters. He wonders about the things Night must see and hear. It must require either unshakeable resilience or an utter lack of compassion. Otherwise –

'Otherwise,' Night interrupts, 'I wouldn't be able to do my job. You may not like what I offer, but other people do. A good me works wonders.'

The boy snorts into his mug. 'It's hardly a skill. You're just there, you can't walk away.' There is a stiff silence. He doesn't know whether to laugh or cry. After all he has been through, he has now managed to insult half his daily life.

'Look,' he says eventually, 'I'm sorry. I'm just not used to talking to –'

'Anyone. Although someone was willing to give you a chance.'

The boy glares at the wall. 'What would you know?' he snaps.

After a moment he says cautiously, 'Are you still there?'

'It'll take a lot more than that to offend me.' Night sounds unruffled. 'People have been trying for centuries. Torchlight processions, dancing round bonfires – everyone has a go at some point. I don't know why, I'm very easy-going. We can talk about anything you like. There's just one Rule.'

'Which is?'

'You can't ask me anything personal.'

'About you?'

'About you.'

'I know far too much about myself already. Why would I want to know more?'

Night gives a suffering sigh. 'I mean anything relating to your life. You can ask, but you won't get anywhere. My lips are sealed.'

The boy begins to protest, but stops. He is sure Yorin is doing very well without him, and as for Lia –

'The Rule,' Night says severely, 'is not to be broken. And note the initial capital.'

'Fine.' Glancing away, the boy notices the young man hovering near the doorway of the common room. He is clearly waiting for something. No, someone – and there she is, the reason for the young man's overzealous clothes, coming through the door in a green dress with a yellow bodice, pushing back her hair and blushing. The young man looks as if he would like to throw his tray into the air and let it fall where it will. Instead he puts it down on the nearest table, and turns to Olti. The innkeeper nods, the young man offers the girl his arm, and they leave the common room.

The boy rests his head on his arms. In the past it would have embarrassed him; now, he no longer cares.

'It still happens, you know. It won't stop just because you don't want to see it.'

The boy raises his head and stares at the wall. 'Don't want to see what?'

'You know what.'

The boy is beginning to wish he had never started the conversation. He lifts his mug for more beer, and a serving-woman fills it.

'You people,' Night remarks, 'always drowning your sorrows.'

The boy looks into his mug. 'They wouldn't fit.' He finishes his drink. 'I'm going home. Good – you.'

Night says nothing, but the air ripples with amusement.

Arun's mouth is dry. He takes a drink from the water bottle. In the pool the moon shimmers serenely.

'Our first proper conversation,' Night says fondly, 'and wasn't I marvellous?'

'You were arrogant and opinionated.'

A chirping cricket breaks the silence. 'Wretched creature,' Night says testily, 'it's been going for hundreds of years. You'd think it would come up with another tune by now.'

Arun peers through the darkness. 'The same cricket?'

Within the clearing, all sounds fade. Suddenly Night laughs. Stars flicker; a meteor shower dissolves into rain above a plateau ever afterwards flecked with silver. For a while, time drifts. As the small sounds of night resume, Arun looks back to the hut. Brightness is growing around it, but the shutters are closed.

The boy wakes with the day behind him. He gets up, has a quick wash, and goes to the inn, where he is served by the young man, now in working clothes. He is whistling as he sets down the plate. Breaking his golden rule, the boy asks him why.

'Why not? It's been a good day.'

'Good for some,' the boy says under his breath. He picks at his rice and lamb. It is not as good as Lia's. He finishes his beer, picks some more.

The lamplight flutters. 'That's no way to treat good food,' Night says.

'Good evening to you too.'

'Drink up, we've got things to talk about.'

The boy looks into his mug and sees a warm road to wherever he wants to go. Across the room, someone starts to sing. Another man finding talent at the bottom of a mug. He is joined by a group of friends whose ears have also been dipped in beer.

'Oh, for goodness' sake!' the boy exclaims.

'You're turning into the resident grouch,' Night observes.

The boy frowns. Should he feel ashamed, or is it something to be proud of? Either way, he has no intention of apologising.

He stirs rice around his plate. It lacks the golden warmth of saffron, and he knows why. Saffron is costly; it was served at the merchant's finest dinners, and he made sure his guests knew how many flowers had been pressed into the service of his kitchen.

'Bastard,' he mutters. All the beer in the world can't dull the feeling of anger and pain. If confronted about what he'd done, the merchant would have offered a smooth explanation. It would never have occurred to him to apologise. In his eyes, he had been the boy's saviour.

'It takes strength of character,' Night comments.

The boy looks up. 'What does?'

'Apologising. Acknowledging you're in the wrong.'

The boy consults his mug. 'What about someone who never apologises?'

'Because they can't, or won't?'

'Either. Both. I don't know.' When Night doesn't reply he says 'All right, what if they won't apologise, even when it's clear as day –'

The lamp on the wall flickers wildly and goes out, the boy's hand slips and knocks over his beer. Glowering, the young man appears, mops up, relights the lamp and refills the mug.

When he has gone, the boy looks across the table. 'What happened?' he asks.

'Never,' Night says icily, 'mention that name again.'

It takes a moment for him to work out what Night means. When he does, he bursts out laughing. The idea that a single word can throw something so vast and omnipresent into a blind panic is irresistibly funny. Wiping his eyes he says, 'I'll bear it in mind in future.'

'I'm not sure we have a future,' Night says stiffly.

'Suit yourself. But you never gave me an answer.'

As he suspects, Night is unable to resist. 'Why waste your time? They won't change.'

The boy waits, drinks, waits. 'That's it?'

'No point trying to move a mountain. Although I once saw a flea try. It succeeded, too.'

The boy raises an eyebrow. Curiosity wins out. 'Well, go on then.'

A theatrical pause. 'A girl was tending her goats; she sat down for a rest and fell asleep. One flea made a bet with another flea, the latter flea bit the girl and she leapt to her feet. The flea succeeded. She moved.'

The boy shakes his head, exasperated, amused. 'I'll remember that next time,' he says.

'Remember what?'

'That you don't play fair. That you shift the scenery.'

'I didn't say what kind of mountain it was.'

The boy walks home through the chilly dark, stumbling a little. His mind, too, is pleasantly wrong-footed. At the hut, he opens the door and stands looking up into a sky strewn with lights. If he lifts his hand, he can touch a star. He clenches his fist and goes inside.

Arun opens his hand and examines his empty palm. 'Don't you ever get tired of being everywhere at once?' he asks.

'Dear me,' Night says, 'whatever did they teach you? You may find it hard to believe, but in some parts of the world I'm currently' – a pause – 'resting.'

Arun rolls his eyes, feeling foolish. But then, he reminds himself, he was schooled to columns of figures, not the geographies of the world.

Nissa once told him about a globe she saw in the house of a merchant with whom her father desired a better and more profitable acquaintance. She said it was bigger than a pumpkin, painted with many colours and set on a polished wooden stand. Through the centre ran a decorative spindle topped with a golden ball. It was girdled by a thick wooden band, also highly polished.

'She came back and told me she made the world fly.' Arun smiles briefly. A thought strikes him. 'You must know where she is now. What she's doing.'

'You know I can't tell you that,' Night says primly.

'Yes, I know. The Rule.' Arun's face is thoughtful. One part of his life, at least, will remain unchanged. For a while he sits thinking about alphabets and sacks of rice, a dish of chestnut cream. In a strange exchange of shadows, he is there in the hut with the boy. One flickers through the other; the boy starts as if he has been stung, Arun feels the heart and soul of the boy and closes his eyes.

Chapter Forty-Three

'Birds won't work. What would they carry it in?'

'Their pouches,' Night says. 'Have you never seen a pelican?'

They are discussing how to bring water from the well to the hut. They have talked about cities, and water flowing in long cool lines of culvert and gutter. The boy has bought paper, made drawings and notes, devised a system of troughs ending in a snug hole in the wall of the hut, with some kind of receptacle underneath. But how can he draw up the water? It has no legs to climb, and he has no intention of crawling down to investigate.

He spoons up the last of the vegetable stew. It is good, but Lia's was better. 'No, I haven't,' he says, imagining a bird with a beak so large it topples over.

'Not bad,' Night says, 'but make it tubbier.'

'Just one problem. They can fly away.'

'Fine. Birds are out.'

The boy glances shrewdly across the table. He has learned by now that if Night's opinions are not accepted, they are cut adrift. Or blown on gently until they end up bobbing at the boy's sides. 'There must be a way,' he says. 'Rain falls down. Waterfalls – fall. So how do you make them go the other way? Some kind of pump?'

The darkness pulses. 'You know, don't you?' he says. 'You know the answer and you're letting me flounder about, casting my net in places fish haven't swum for years.'

'Intoxication certainly brings out the metaphor in you.'

'Someone must have studied it,' the boy persists. 'It must be written down somewhere.'

'Your faith in human endeavour is impressive, but you're a long way from the library caves.'

'Fine, don't tell me. I'm going home.' The boy gets up, sits back down, puts his head on his arms and goes to sleep.

Arun looks away. 'Not my finest hour,' he says.

'No,' Night agrees, 'but I saw you home, with a little help from the moon . . .'

. . . whose radiance softly lights the path. As he walks, the boy murmurs to himself, 'A pump, that's what I need. A pump. But how?'

He is woken later by an insistent buzzing. There is something inside the hut. He opens an eye. A bee is bumping against the shutters. He tips himself out of bed, and stumbles across the room to the cabinet for a beaker. Cautiously he approaches.

'I'm not going to hurt you,' he says, gently trapping the bee, whose voice assumes unnerving magnificence.

Now for something to contain it. In a cloud of abstraction he sees himself sliding a smooth thin sheet of wood under the beaker, tipping it upright as the bee howls

597

harder, carrying the beaker outside, whisking away the piece of wood and, like a thistle-head, the bee floating out and away. He has given it freedom.

Instead he stands with an aching arm and an increasingly bilious bee. His head is thumping, his mouth parched. There must be an easier way. How about opening the door and letting the air waft it away? But what if – he has some experience in these matters – it lumbers about growing angrier and angrier? Will he have to hide in a corner until it finds its way out and, on leaving, makes a lightning strike and stings him?

Closing his eyes, he sees a smile. A smile with answers in it. *Why not open the shutter?* His fingers tremble as he fumbles for the catch and lets the bee fly away.

When he wakes again, desire lingers in his blood. At times the ache is so strong he finds himself longing for any human touch. He has learned to deaden the feeling, but sometimes his dreams betray his living heart. He gets up, throws on some clothes and goes out to the well.

The morning sun is hazy. Looking about at the dun-coloured landscape, he realises it is almost winter. How has he not noticed? Has grief become his sole season? He stares blindly into the well, thinking about the conversation at the inn yesterday evening. Either Night knew the answer or let him make something greater from the silence.

Determined to return with a solution, he pretends he is two people discussing the problem. 'So,' he says aloud, 'you want water in your hut? You don't want to keep trudging out here, dropping the bucket down the well, lugging it back? But you have no idea how to set up a pump, which is governed by physical laws of which you have no knowledge?'

He turns to face himself. 'Exactly.'

He turns back. 'Then use your noddle. Your nut. Your –'

'Yes, I get the picture. I've tried, but it hasn't worked. Maybe there isn't a solution.'

'Of course there is, or the country would be littered with the remains of people who've died of thirst. And I'm sure they didn't have to think about suction, pressure, light of sun, light of moon, in order to work it out.'

Nor did the boy, until now. Thanking himself for making things worse, he slides down until he is sitting with his back against the cool brick of the well. A small black beetle is toiling over the ground and will shortly arrive at his boot. Instead of lifting his foot, he waits to see what the beetle will do. With barely a break in rhythm it marches up, across and down the other side, taking the line of least resistance.

He frowns thoughtfully. The line of least resistance. Make it simple. Make it –

'I'll make it,' he says, dawning on himself. 'A barrel – I'll make a barrel.' Then, afire with inspiration, 'Why not buy it?'

It wasn't the easiest thing, rolling the barrel back from the village, one shoulder hunched to stop the handle of the new bucket slipping down his arm. This he will fill with water and keep inside the hut, next to the door.

He goes back and forth, hauling up bucket after bucket of water. When the barrel is full, he dips in a beaker and takes a long, sweet drink. Before replacing the lid, he looks down into the glittering depths. Wood and water. It reminds him of Mirashi's poem about a sea spirit.

> The food at her table
> is the grain of the sea –
> she looks out on a wood of water.

Needing to read more, he goes indoors, takes the Book of Light from under his pillow and brings it outside.

> Her words are stepping-stones
> to bays where the heart can set down in bad weather.

> When storms break the bindings of the shore,
> she turns the last page and reads what's written there.

He wants to ask Mirashi about the final line, but she is three hundred years from where he stands beside a barrel, a book of poetry in his hand.

'Took you long enough to get there,' Night says that evening, 'but I'm glad to see you solved your supply problem.'

It was easier than he thought, asking Olti if he could refill his flagons with wine and beer.

'I'm not surprised,' Night remarks. 'You're his best customer.'

'If I am, it's paid off,' the boy says. The landlord's agreement finally convinced him that Lia had said nothing about what happened.

'So,' Night says, 'what's the topic this evening?'

'Nothing while I'm eating.'

'You can eat and think at the same time. Eating takes up your mouth, not your thoughts. Rather, your mouth takes it up. The food, that is.' Then, dramatically, 'Save me! I'm turning into you. Never leaving things alone, rushing at them from behind, leaping from above and knocking the stuffing out of them. No wonder you drink so much beer.'

'Not enough,' the boy mutters, holding up his mug for more.

He is beginning to wake later, and wonders if his interior time is changing. If he peered into his head, would he see a timepiece hanging there? If it were, he'd never get a moment's peace. Unless it was a sundial, silently collecting the hours.

He moves about the hut, gathering food for a meal. He has come to rely on dinner at the Willow as his main meal, and never cooks for himself now. He took pride in it once. The first time he baked a cake it was a messy business, full of laughter and spilled sugar.

He looks down at his hands, the long fingers equally suited to picking apples or writing in a notebook. She liked his hands. He shoves them in his pockets and looks around. The day stretches before him like an ocean. He eats his meal and goes back to bed.

A mug or two of beer before he ventures out sustains him against the chill. In his village it was believed that unless you were wrapped up to the eyes at night, taking small sips of air as you walked, you were destined for the grave. He takes a deep breath. So what if it fumes into his lungs?

'My air is perfectly good,' Night says, 'and mind the shrub.'

The boy swerves, grinning. 'See? Heightened awareness. Comes of walking at night. In Night.' He laughs.

'I'd pull myself together if I were you.'

'Why, are you coming apart?' the boy asks, finding everything hilarious.

He piles through the door of the inn, and makes his way to his table. It is the second time he has been served not by the young man but someone else.

'Who, Iblis? He's gone off,' the serving-man says when he asks.

'Gone off?' the boy echoes.

'With his girl. Her parents didn't like him, so they ran away. And good luck to them.'

First Lia, now the young man. The boy's mood of hilarity vanishes. The serving-man returns with his meal, a hearty lentil stew. He eats in silence, ignoring the atmosphere gathering opposite.

When he has finished, he puts down his spoon and looks at the wall. 'Is there anything in particular you want to discuss?'

'Yes,' Night says. 'If you know something that will affect someone else's life – a friend's, say – but will also cause them pain, should you tell them?'

'Of course.'

'Every time? No exceptions?'

The discussion that follows is neither elegant nor particularly well-reasoned but conducted with great intensity. On the boy's side, a good deal of indignation and incredulous laughter as Night's arguments grow more wildly preposterous. On the other, darting gibes, the whipping of a rug from under what the boy considers a devastating rebuttal, and a short sulk.

When they have dug so deeply into their respective positions they are in danger of disappearing, the boy pushes back his chair and takes a gulp of beer. There are many ways of looking at things, and at the moment he feels unequal to any of them.

'Why do you think men flee to the wilderness?' Night asks.

Is it fleeing or finding? The boy is no longer sure.

'Take your pick,' Night says. 'I've lost count of how many I've seen holed up in caves. Each to his own.'

'Or her own.' The boy thinks of Pera. Far from anywhere, and yet so much a part of life. 'Maybe nothing is fixed, unless we choose it to be. No, that's not quite right. We have choices made for us as children. And that's probably not a bad thing. If my mother hadn't made me wash, I'd have been the most pungent boy in the valley. And if my parents hadn't taught me manners, I wouldn't have been fit company for –' He looks at his hands.

'So how do you see yourself now?'

'I don't.' The boy stares into his mug. Within it, something glitters. A star. 'Take it out.'

'What?' Night asks innocently. He looks again; the star has gone.

'You probably drank it,' Night says.

As winter deepens around him, he is beginning to think

Lia will never return. And if she doesn't, it is no concern of his.

'No indeed,' Night says. 'One less thing to worry about.'

'I wasn't talking to you.' The boy spoons up soup, swallows, puts down his spoon. 'Don't you ever get tired of minding everyone's business? Of always being here, of never being able to –'

'Die?' Night finishes for him.

The boy looks sharply across the table.

'You're all so touchy about it.' Night sounds amused.

'It's not a funny subject.'

'Not for you,' Night agrees.

There is a tense silence. Shoving back his chair, the boy throws down some coins and leaves.

As he walks, his breath keeps ragged pace with him. He wonders why, since he has wished it gone many times. It is like a guest who outstays his welcome, causing hosts to whisper behind closed doors. *You tell him. No, you.* There should be some sort of handbook offering means of tactful escape. For example: *I'd love to see you. Sadly, it can only be for a short time as I have appointments outside the city.* That should do it. Unless, of course, you were worrying that your forehead had somehow become transparent, revealing your inner thoughts.

He thinks harder. Under cover of darkness, then. Another snag. With the focus solely on the voice, dissembling would be harder to conceal. The faintest whiff of a lie, and –

'Oh, for goodness' sake!'

He stops dead, throws out his arms and shouts at the top of his voice, 'Mad at last! Happy now?'

Then he wonders who he is talking to. Not Lia, who has gone away and is not coming back. Not the overdressed young man, who is with his sweetheart and happy because he loves and is loved.

'No,' the boy shouts, 'I renounce it – I renounce love!'

Beside the pool, Arun laughs sadly. 'As if you can,' he says.

Night has suggested the topic of fishing. The boy suspects the choice is deliberate; he dips a piece of bread into barley broth and tries not to think of Lake Sigal.

'Steady on,' Night says, 'no need to wolf it down.'

'I'm merely appreciating good food.'

'I'm sure in some countries guzzling counts as a compliment.'

The boy lifts his spoon and points it across the table. 'No games tonight.'

'No, indeed. Given how hard you worked today, it's a wonder you have any energy left to think.'

'How would you know? You weren't there.'

'You're a creature of habit.'

The boy opens his mouth, and closes it again. He woke in the dark, not a chink of light. He wondered if he missed it, and decided he didn't. There must be a hinge in his heart, a trapdoor through which all good things had fallen. Getting up, he made a late breakfast: a piece of bread, a smear of honey. The floor needed sweeping; dirty plates and beakers piled up on the table. He felt a brief, perverse pride. Then he caught sight of Lia's basket, the one she brought before she left, the white cloth folded neatly over the handle.

'I am not responsible for anyone or anything,' he said. In the silence it sounded hollow. 'Oh, shut up,' he muttered, taking a flagon from the cabinet. Uncorking it, he swung it up by the handle, twisted wildly to avoid hitting his forehead, tripped, fell, and ended up on the floor with the flagon in pieces around him. The smell of beer flooded the hut. Swearing, he gathered up the remains, threw them outside and slammed the door.

'If you're trying to make me feel guilty, don't bother,' he says. 'It won't work.'

'Perish the thought. I was merely observing.'

The boy wipes his mouth with his sleeve, reflecting on how closely observation is related to criticism. Phrases swim fishily into view: *I thought you ought to know . . . I mean this with the greatest respect . . . it's none of my business, but . . . don't take this the wrong way . . .*

'Why can't people say what they mean?' he asks crossly. Then, after brief consideration, 'If they did, everyone would end up falling out with everyone else, and no one would speak to anyone again.'

'And the world would be a much quieter place.'

'You'd hate it. You'd have no one to listen to. Besides, it's up to me what I do.'

'And when your money runs out?'

The boy folds a piece of bread and presses it into the dregs of the broth. 'Not that it's any of your business, but I'm fine. I've still got money from – before – and I hardly spent anything when I was fishing.'

'Do you miss it?' Night asks.

The boy retrieves the soggy bread and eats it, frowning. 'No, I don't. It became too –'

'Fishy?'

'Constricting.'

'You had the entire lake. And beyond that . . .'

Beyond that the boy never went. He wishes now he'd rowed out of Lake Sigal to wherever it took him.

The cold bites deep now. There is one consolation, at least; the new year comes in heartily, but stays only for the night.

This evening he has decided not to get drawn into endless argument. He eats potato pie and drinks beer without looking up.

'I can wait all me, you know,' Night says. The boy shrugs, and carries on eating. 'I know why you're ignoring me. It must be hard, always coming off worst.'

Don't rise to it, the boy tells himself, silently recalling the many times he has ended up on his back with his feet in the air, as if he'd ridden headlong into an overhanging branch. He smiles briefly, remembering Yorin's comment: *You've heard of headless horsemen? They're just idiots who weren't looking where they were going.* It had been the prelude to a fierce argument about whether there was an explanation for everything.

'Did you ever come to a conclusion?'

'Yes.'

'Yes what?'

The boy sighs heavily. 'Yes we agreed that no, there isn't an explanation for everything. We also agreed that if we couldn't find an explanation, we'd make one up.'

'That's hardly original.'

'So what?'

'I expected better of you, that's all.'

The boy is lost for words. Is Night disappointed with him? The lamplight blurs and shakes. 'Are you laughing at me?' he asks angrily.

'Of course not,' Night says. 'Although it wouldn't be a bad thing.'

The boy spends the following day smarting about Night's comment. After a brief lunch he sleeps away the afternoon, getting up at sunset and leaving for the inn.

The common room is crowded, the fire high and bright. He can't help it; he has to ask.

'Why wouldn't it be a bad thing?'

'I knew you wouldn't forget,' Night says complacently.

'You haven't answered the question.'

'How about a game of dominoes?'

The boy stares at the wall. 'Fine.' Then, sternly, 'The spots aren't supposed to move.'

'You still haven't let it go, have you?' Night says.

Arun looks across the clearing. 'You said something I felt was unfair, and you never explained it.'

'I didn't see the need then, and I don't now. I seem to recall a conversation about how pointless it was trying to get someone to change. You clearly weren't listening.'

For a while Arun sits thinking about the people he knew, the times he wished they were different. For the first time he wonders if they ever wished he were different.

'I am as I am,' he says firmly.

'Indeed you are,' Night agrees.

Chapter Forty-Four

It is mid-morning, and spring. The boy is trying to ignore them both. A knock at the door makes him open an eye. 'Go away,' he mutters. Another knock, and he sits up and slides off the bed. When he opens the door Fulda is standing there, smiling.

The boy stares, coughs, tries to smooth down his hair.

'Olti told me you lived here,' Fulda says. 'I hope I'm not disturbing you?'

'Er . . .' he says, then, 'no, of course not, it's good to see you.' He asks Fulda in before recalling the state of the hut. There is nothing he can do – he can't unword himself – so he says, 'You'll have to excuse the mess.'

He opens the shutters, pushes unwashed dishes to one side of the table, and offers Fulda a chair. As the water boils, he finds clean cups and frets about the state of the hut. Fulda sits looking perfectly at home. When the tea is made, the boy puts it on the table with some biscuits he found in a jar.

'I was wondering how you are,' Fulda says. 'We both were. Imah still talks about your lovely manners.'

The boy's face heats up. He remembers his promise to send word when he'd spoken to Olti about Fulda's beer. 'I'm sorry I can't offer you any cakes,' he says.

'It's probably a good thing.' Fulda laughs. 'I eat far too many.'

The boy sits awkwardly until Fulda says, 'I can't believe it's that time of year again. I dropped off the barrels before I came here.' He smiles. 'I've made a new blend, something I haven't tried before. I'd really like your opinion.'

The boy ends up inviting him for lunch, explaining he has to go to market first. They go together, the boy in yesterday's clothes, Fulda in a tan-coloured cloak over a brown tunic and trousers. 'I feel the cold nowadays,' he says. 'I went to Jessa once, to see about supplying one of the inns there. It took six days and a steady drop in temperature. By the time I got there, I'd almost frozen to death. I hadn't realised how near it is to the snowline. I ended up buying thick gloves and boots.'

He laughs. 'Amazing how many of their shops sold them. I suspect they forget to tell visitors how cold it is. Well, you have to make a living, I suppose. In the end I decided against it. They wanted a written contract, which made it feel too much like a business for me. Besides, it was a long way to travel – I didn't want to be away from my family for so long.'

As they walk, Fulda talks steadily, and the boy finds himself listening with interest. He learns that Imah has insisted on Fulda building a wooden shed at the bottom of the garden for his beer-making, and that Tref and Tarius now have a patch of their own to grow flowers and vegetables. Of the boy's promise Fulda makes no mention.

When they reach the village, Fulda goes to the inn to see Olti. The boy is finding the light particularly trying. The sun stands against the sky, ring after ring of melting silver.

Keeping his head down, he makes his purchases and sets off for the hut. His arms are laden with packages of vegetables, meat for stew, bread, cheeses, fruit, cakes, milk and ginger. He isn't sure why he bought so much, or why he bought ginger. Perhaps Fulda will have a recipe for ginger wine.

A fragrant warmth steams out as he opens the door. 'Smells good,' Fulda says appreciatively, stamping his feet on the threshold.

At the table, the boy uncorks the bottle Fulda gives him, dividing it between two mugs. Water from his still-damp hair drips onto his clean shirt. Raising his mug, he makes a toast. The beer is fruity, with a whisper of honey, and leaves a comforting warmth in his stomach.

'This is really good,' he says.

Fulda looks pleased, and asks what he can taste. When the boy tells him, he beams. 'That's exactly what I was hoping for. Would you say it's a spring beer?' It reminds the boy more of summer. Fulda takes another mouthful, considering. 'You know, I think you're right.'

The boy fills a bowl with stew, and puts it in front of his guest. He waits anxiously as Fulda swallows, closes his eyes and sighs.

'My friend, this is heavenly.' He takes another mouthful. 'There's something else, something extra.' The boy can see him running through a list of spices in his mind. 'No, I can't put my finger on it. You'll have tell me.'

The boy smiles. 'Ginger.'

Fulda's response is gratifying. 'I'd never have guessed. And subtle enough to warm your tongue rather than biting it off. You'd make someone a very good husband.'

The boy stiffens. He dips his spoon into his bowl, hardly tasting what he eats. Fulda appears not to notice. 'Imah will never forgive me if I don't get the recipe. If you don't mind, of course. I know for some people it's a matter of life and death. Imah's mother, for instance. She wouldn't tell Imah what she put in her fruit bread until we were married. Perhaps she thought my courtship was a way of finding out, and as soon as I knew I'd be off to the nearest market to set up my own business.'

He laughs. 'It worked. We were married three months after we met. Well, there's no point waiting if you've found the right person.'

He finishes his stew, and the boy offers more. After a second bowl Fulda leans back in his chair, his face shining with contentment. For a while they sit in peaceful silence.

Stirring, the boy says, 'Would you like some cake? It's very good – you normally have to get there early to avoid the stampede.'

'I'd be failing in my duty as a guest if I refused.'

The boy slides the cake onto a plate and puts it on the table. It is a fat, round honeycake, bursting with fruit and pieces of crystallised orange, the domed top glittering with a crust of light-brown sugar.

'It seems a shame to cut it,' Fulda says, his eyes gleaming.

The boy hands him a knife. He brings it down slowly, crunching through the sugar. He repeats the action, sliding the knife under the cake and withdrawing it, leaving behind an empty wedge. The boy offers a plate; Fulda tips the slice onto it.

'You first,' the boy says.

Fulda takes a bite. His eyes close; he looks blissful. 'Truly a queen among cakes. One moment –' Reaching down, he opens his bag and pulls out a slender bottle. 'This will go perfectly with it.'

The boy brings beakers; Fulda pours an amber-coloured liquid. 'Try it,' he says.

The boy sips the sweet wine. 'It's excellent. It is yours?'

Fulda tells him he buys it from a merchant who comes to Raksal a few times a year. 'He won't tell me what he puts in it,' he says, anticipating the boy's question, 'and that's as it should be. I won't tell anyone what I put in my beer. Except Imah, otherwise I'd have to get my own dinner. And as you know, I'm no cook.'

The afternoon glides on. They have demolished the cake, leaving behind a scattering of spicy brown crumbs. The wine bottle is almost empty. They sit at either side of the fire, whose flames roar softly.

'That,' Fulda says, 'was one of the best meals I've had in a long time. But don't tell Imah.' After a comfortable silence, he stretches and yawns. 'You're a most unusual man, Arun. You seem to have many interests. And yet – forgive me if I'm speaking out of turn – you stay here, away from others.'

Tightness gathers in the boy's stomach.

'I say this because I like you, my friend,' Fulda says. 'If you want me to shut up and doze, I will.'

The boy finishes the last of his wine and looks into the fire. Spires and clouds of orange, blue and yellow, a spit of green. He finds himself saying, 'I wasn't always on my own.'

For a long time Arun sits motionless. Finally he says, 'I told him. I kept it brief, but I told him. In a way, it was a relief. He said nothing, just listened. He was a good listener. When I'd finished, he just nodded. I couldn't have stood it if he'd shown kindness or sympathy, and I think he knew that.

'We sat there for a little longer, then he said he had to get back before it got too dark. We clasped hands, and he said' – he makes himself go on – '"Suffer the heart to love." That's all. I can still see him walking away through the dusk, turning once and raising his hand.'

For a while he stares at the moon in the pool. 'When I woke up the next morning, I knew I'd never see him again. I couldn't. It would be like standing naked in the marketplace with the whole world looking on. It was as if he'd become the embodiment of my pain.'

He gives a heavy sigh. 'After that, I found out from Olti when a delivery was due, and went off into the hills. I wonder if Fulda knew. Probably.' He shakes his head. 'He could have been a good friend, if I'd let him. But I couldn't. I couldn't even go and see him when –' Shaking his head, he falls silent.

Spring has come to Kandra once more, tipping the trees with bud, greening the hills beyond. For the boy, its return is simply a nuisance of light, something to endure on the walk to the inn.

This evening, it is raining. He shakes droplets from his hair as he comes through the door. Olti nods at him briefly. He is talking with someone, his face grave. As the boy passes, he hears Fulda's name. He looks around quickly, but cannot see him. With a twinge of guilty relief, he lingers in the doorway of the common room.

'I hope he gets better soon,' Olti says. 'Give him my best regards. And thank him for this, won't you?'

They shake hands, and the man leaves. Turning, Olti sees the boy. He shakes his head. 'It's a shame,' he says. 'I've got a lot of time for Fulda, and not just because of his beer. He's a good man.'

The boy can't help asking what has happened.

'He's been ill. Pretty bad, by the sound of things. A friend of his brought the delivery. Fulda wanted to make sure we got it. Typical of him, always thinking of others.'

'How is he?'

'Better than he was, but he's still not able to work. He's thinking of giving up beer-making, apparently. It'd be a shame, we'd miss it sorely, but it's up to him.' He looks at the boy. 'I know how much you like it. Best make the most of it. It might be the last chance you get.'

The boy doesn't order Fulda's beer. He pushes potatoes around his plate.

'Not hungry?' Night asks.

The boy puts down his fork and looks at the wall. 'I suppose you knew about Fulda.'

'Judging by the way you nearly jumped out of your skin at the mention of his name, I wouldn't have thought you'd want to know.'

'You wouldn't have told me anyway.' He prods moodily at a piece of chicken. Part of him wants to ignore the waiting silence, to make his resentment clear, but what would be the point? They are here on Night's terms, and if he wants their conversations to continue, that is how it has to be.

'It must be bad if he's thinking of giving up beer-making,' he says eventually.

'You know what people are like. Something happens, and they start thinking about everything else. An internal avalanche. I've seen it countless times.'

The boy has seen it too. Usually it begins with something unexpected or unprepared for, an illness, perhaps, or a piece of bad luck. Something inside begins to stir, working quietly away until finally it erupts, and someone is giving everything up and moving to another town, another country. Or abandoning someone else, and that someone is left wondering what happened. Or they go together, leaving behind a line of shaking heads.

He spears a chunk of potato with his fork and holds it up, studying it for a moment. The fire crackles softly; thoughts of Fulda press on his mind. He knows some people can toss things aside, including cares and worries, and he envies them. But is any life ever really like that, no backward glance, nothing to clutch at hand or heart?

'It's nothing to do with me,' he says.

'Of course not.'

He hadn't reckoned with the power of his conscience. In bed he tosses and turns until he sits up and says, 'It's not my problem. I can't do anything about it. His family will look after him.'

When he wakes, his conscience wakes with him. He stumbles out of bed. The bread crock is almost empty. He remembers reading somewhere that gods live on nectar, requiring no solid food. Lucky them, they never have to go to market, he thinks crossly. As he makes tea, his mind idles on a question. If they did, what would they buy?

'If they shopped anywhere, they'd go to Darat Market,' Night says that evening.

The boy has heard of it. The largest market in the country, sitting at a great crossroads like an endless temptation. It is rumoured that anything can be bought there, including a new character.

'But what would they want?' he asks, looking thoughtfully at the wall. 'If anyone knows, it's you. You cover the sky, the sky is full of gods. To some people, at least.'

Part of him wonders if he should be introducing the topic at all, since it seems to have been designed to send men up in flames. But he has come to understand that Night generally has a pot to stir, not a drum to beat.

'Have you finished?' Night enquires. 'Good. Then I have no idea. And, just to be clear, I've never met any. Although if I were a god . . .'

A prompting silence gathers. 'No,' the boy says emphatically, 'I'm not discussing it.'

'Another win.'

He lies awake until he senses the rising sun, then covers his head with a blanket until his face heats up. He throws off the blanket and sits up. The thought he had last night hasn't left him. If he says it aloud, perhaps it will leave him in peace.

'If I were a god, I would bring them back.'

His stomach turns; he breaks into a sweat. Getting up, he goes to the bucket and splashes water on his face. On impulse, he opens the door and looks out on a morning speechless with mist. In the Suth Valley, the orchards will be in blossom. His throat constricts. He goes back in and slams the door.

Arun takes a deep breath. 'I failed him. I let Fulda down. I never found out what happened to him. The beer kept coming, so I told myself he must be all right. I was a coward. I still am.'

Guilt becomes a fortress from which the boy rarely ventures. He walks to the inn and enters their discussions with increasing vigour. Night has suggested this evening's topic: the fable of art. The flame in the lamp quivers expectantly. The boy eats, and thinks.

Eventually he says, 'If it's a fable, what's the point of discussing it?'

'That, if you don't mind me saying so, is a rather childish response.'

'It's as good a response as any.'

After a short silence Night says, 'It puts me in mind of something I overheard outside a coffee-house once, between two women. One of them, a teacher, was telling her friend about what happened at school that day. Picture, if you will, a classroom in a country much hotter than this one . . .'

. . . and rows of desks with girls attached, silently wilting. Their heads are bent as they put sentences together and take them apart again. They are at an age when they believe it will serve no useful purpose, but are as a rule obedient. Their minds, however, keep straying to cups of iced pomegranate juice and slices of melon so cold they crunch between the teeth.

One girl, usually the last to speak, raises her hand. The teacher looks at her enquiringly.

'*Baravha*,' she says – she is a very polite girl – 'we're dying in here. Please, can't we have the afternoon off?'

The teacher stares; the girls stare too. Some are shocked, others suppress glee at the scolding to come.

The teacher appears to be thinking. At last she says, 'Is there any particular reason why I should give you the afternoon off?'

The classroom holds its breath. Frowning, the girl looks down at her desk, then says, 'Because Shala's goat has died, *Baravha*.'

The teacher consults with herself before saying gravely, 'That is as good a reason as any.'

'That girl went on to great things,' Night says reflectively.

'I'm sure she did,' the boy says through a mouthful of lamb, 'but I'm choosing the next topic.'

'*Socks?*'

The boy laughs out loud at the look of disgust in Night's voice. 'Socks. By the way, this pie is excellent.' He cuts through buttery pastry and forks a piece into his mouth. 'Onions, leeks, cream – it's amazing how well it works.'

'Ever the gourmet,' Night says sourly. The boy keeps eating. His cup of wine is red, spiced and warming.

'I happen to know,' Night says, 'of a woman in a very cold place who has dedicated her life to the knitting of socks. She takes pride in varying the patterns and colours, and no two pairs are ever the same.' After a thoughtful silence: 'If people keep mending them until finally there's more new than old, is it the same sock?'

'No idea,' the boy says, finishing his pie, 'but I'm sure you'll tell me.'

'I'm asking your opinion. You know how much I value it.' Night's voice is coaxing.

'Perhaps the spirit remains, and that's all I'm prepared to say.'

'You're the one who suggested it.'

Draining his cup, the boy resolves to go barefoot to the inn the following evening.

Twilight arrives so gracefully he is hardly aware of it. Above him are stars and a slip of moon. He walks to the Willow and drinks wine as he waits for his dinner, thinking about a poem in which a tall stone marks the fall in battle of a warrior-prince.

> Here is a young man who is part of a dream:
> the wind binds him,
> around him cattle make marks
> unwritten by rain.

He wonders who the young man was, and whether he is still remembered. Then he wonders if anyone will remember him.

'Feeling sorry for yourself?'

He starts. Night has stolen in. 'No, just thinking.'

'And has it helped?'

'It passes the time and occupies my mind.'

'It's amazing how much occupying the mind can do.

I've known it to pitch its tent on the same thought for years. Then again, I've known minds with the soul of a vagabond.'

The boy spoons up red bean stew. 'Aren't you confusing things?'

'You tell me.'

The boy eats stew, drinks wine. 'Minds can't have souls. They're separate things. One's the machinery, the other is –' He stops, confused. 'It can't be the heart, because that's – well, something else.'

Night deepens with amusement.

'All I want is to eat my stew and drink my wine,' the boy says at last. 'The soul can wait.'

'But can it?'

The boy feels a fire smouldering inside him. Pushing his plate away he gets up, throws down some coins and leaves the inn.

As he walks, each step fans the flames. He walks so fast he can almost feel tatters of heat streaming from his back. When he reaches the hut he falls through the door and slams it behind him. What happened? How did the evening turn into something so hard and unpleasant?

Taking a flagon from the cabinet, he throws the stopper on the floor and drinks. Wine slops down his shirt, staining it red. He can hear his mother saying, *Slow down, what's the hurry?*

'No!' he shouts, thumping the table. 'You have no right to tell me what to do! You left me! You all did!' He drinks until the flagon is empty, then goes to the fireplace and kneels down, staring at the cold grate.

On impulse, he thrusts a hand into the grey-white ash, pulls it out and examines his fingers. He smears ash over his forehead and across his cheeks. Then he sits with his back against the chair until he falls asleep.

He wakes from a dream in which he is out in the middle of Lake Sigal, with no means of rowing back to where his sister stands unspeaking on the shore. A faint glow tells him it is early morning. Pulling himself to his feet, he finds a rag and stuffs it under the door.

'There,' he says with satisfaction, 'no more light.'

Arun's hands tighten in his lap. 'After that, I did everything I could to avoid going outside during the day. I asked the market traders to bring what I needed to the hut. I paid for it, of course – money always makes people obliging. I didn't care what they thought of me. All that mattered was staying behind the door.'

'You still went, though,' Night points out. 'To the inn. Because of me, no doubt.'

Sighing, Arun says, 'Yes, I still went. There must have been a part of me that couldn't quite let go. Well, at least I gave them something to talk about. If they talked about me at all.'

He forces himself to look hard at the corner where the boy is sitting, as if through someone else's eyes.

He sees a long-haired, slightly scruffy man eating, drinking, holding intense conversations with the lamp on the wall. His hands flare in gestures of impatience or excitement; he frowns in concentration or shouts with incredulous laughter.

He slumps back against the tree. 'Is that me?' he asks, appalled.

'Who else would it be?' Night says.

Chapter Forty-Five

'I'm not surprised you slept so badly,' Night says. 'You got yourself into a real pickle.'

The boy concentrates on his soup. Last night he'd lain awake, thinking again about the soul. Where was it? In the head, the tips of the fingers, the stomach? Did it stay in one place or move around? Did it grow with you and, if so, did it die with you?

He thought about tortured souls – the old man at the library caves told him about someone who came for a visit and never left – and souls that couldn't rest. A woman in the village calling someone a poor old soul, her tone divided between condescension and pity. A restless soul – that could apply to Kerel the plant-hunter, always searching, always looking for something more extraordinary.

And what about those with a gift – musicians, craftsmen, artists? *He has the soul of a poet.* Where did he hear those words? Wherever it was, he was sure it hadn't been said about him. But what haunted him most was the fear that he once had a soul, and now it was gone. Left him, perhaps, in disgust or despair. He knew it was there when he loved. What did that tell him? That love and the soul were the same thing?

He threw off the blanket and sat up, fighting for breath.

Shadows shifted and curled, indistinct yet clear. 'Go away!' he cried. 'Leave me alone!' Sudden panic overwhelmed him. Would he only know he had a soul when he died? But if he were dead, how would he know?

'And what did you conclude?' Night asks.

The boy is silent. Contemplating the soul is one thing; discussing it with a cynical darkness is another.

'I'm not cynical.' Night sounds hurt.

'You are.'

'Suit yourself. Anyway, it's up to you to decide if you have a soul or not.'

The boy stirs his soup. 'They've forgotten the bread.' He catches the eye of a passing serving-man. 'Is it me, or is the service getting worse?'

When the bread arrives, he tears off a piece and dunks it in the soup. 'If souls were made of food, yours would be very large,' Night observes.

The boy grows thoughtful. 'If you didn't know about it, would it still be there?'

Night chuckles. 'Now you're drowning. If I were you, I'd jump into your bowl and paddle off as fast you can.'

The boy is still thinking as he walks back to the hut. If there were such a thing as a soul – and he believes, on the whole, that there is – and it were made visible, it would surely have to be under a night sky. An owl's cry pierces the darkness. He seems to recall people believing that owls embodied the departing spirit.

At the door of the hut he looks up into a sky charmed with stars. It is a night of exceptional beauty.

'If you're expecting me to be grateful, I'm not,' he says, and slams the door.

'I've finally made my mark,' he announces a few days later. There is a polite silence. 'The path between my hut and the village. Made by me. My feet, to be precise.' He toasts himself with his cup of wine.

With a sigh Night says, 'Another human preoccupation. Being remembered. The world is full of palaces and temples, statues and plaques. So-and-so lived here for a time. He or she did this or that, the world was amazed and put up a stone to commemorate it.'

'What's wrong with that?' the boy asks through a mouthful of carrots. 'People do good things. They should be remembered.' He thinks of Mirashi, of the shrine at Lar'kan.

'They also do terrible things, and they're remembered too.'

The boy thinks he knows where this is going. 'Doesn't it depend on the way it's done?'

The corner remains silent, so he answers himself. 'Yes, Arun, it does. They can be celebrations, or warnings.' He frowns. 'I seem to remember they honoured the founder of Harakim with an annual holiday.'

'How interesting. And did you know that as a young man he embezzled money and wasn't particularly nice to his family?'

'Why did you have to tell me that?'

'Because it's true. Their glorious founder foundered badly in youth.'

'But look what he did later.'

'Granted, and to be fair, he did eventually pay the money back, and his family forgave him.'

'Don't you ever get dizzy, always looking both ways?'

He waits for Night to take dramatic offence, the lamp to gust wildly, but the flame remains true.

'I was simply extending our discussion into what lies between,' Night says primly.

Grey areas. The boy hates them. And yet part of him feels Night is right. People are rarely entirely good. Or entirely bad.

'We all have our weaknesses,' he says shortly.

'And should we forgive them?'

The boy takes a sip of wine, refusing to be drawn.

'What about not being there when those you love are taken from you?' Night says slyly.

The boy sits in frozen silence as a serving-man clears away his plate and refills his cup. 'Yes,' he says in a shaking voice.

Arun stares into the pool. 'Yes,' he says sadly. Then, with sudden bitter fury, 'I should have protected them. I went away when I should have stayed. It was all my fault.'

The moon shivers as a light wind crosses her face. A star winks; a bird cries as it circles the upper air.

'Do you know what I do every night when I go to bed?' he says. 'I pray for forgiveness. I pray to be able to forget. I pray they are happy and safe and waiting for me.'

Each day the sun is called earlier to the horizon, and the boy feels it like a weight. Even though no light can get in, he checks the walls for warping and cracks, examines the shutters, stands on a chair and runs his hands over the boards of the roof. He treats summer like an infectious disease, but at its most joyous height there is little he can do.

Just once he woke with a fierce thirst for sunrise, and opened a shutter to see it on the crown of the hills, spilling out waves of glorious radiance. For a moment he was back in the white house, standing at the window with his daughter in his arms as the sun, a halo of stone and flame, rose in the Tura Lar Mountains.

Autumn is the hardest time, not for the shortening days, which he welcomes, but because it offers the prospect of settlement. Meat is cured, grain is stored, spiced red wine is heated and drunk from tall beakers in firelight. No matter how hard he has tried, the boy has not succeeded in curing his heart.

He crumbles bread into thick tomato soup. The tomatoes have been dried until their juices stand still. When cooked, they quicken richly.

'I'm glad you're enjoying that,' Night says. 'Now, where were we? Ah yes, we were talking about the ups and downs of love.'

The boy picks up his mug. 'No, we weren't.'

'I think you'll find we were.'

'No, *we* weren't.'

'I do apologise.' The flame in the lamp twitches slightly.

'Never mind,' the boy mutters. He finishes his beer and signals for more.

The sky is moonstruck as he walks back, as if it has found what it was looking for and regards it with grateful wonder.

'Surely the joys must outweigh the sorrows,' he says aloud, 'otherwise what's the point?'

'I knew you wouldn't be able to resist,' Night remarks.

A long silence. 'There is a garden,' the boy says quietly, 'in which an almond tree was planted. It will be grown now. I think about it every day. But I can't make the joy add up to more than the sorrow.'

There is no point trying to sleep. He sits at the table, staring into the darkness. Abruptly he gets up, goes over to the bed and pulls the leather sack from underneath it. The cloud of dust makes him cough, so he takes a bottle from the cabinet and drinks it down. Then he lights a lamp and stands it on the floor. After a long moment, he unties the cord. Very slowly he takes out:

two notebooks, one green and salt-stained, the other covered in dark-blue leather and embossed with golden suns and silver moons

a pouch containing two rings of beaten silver, each set with three stones, two blue, one white

a bookmark of silky dark-blue cloth, embroidered with two sets of initials

a box of dark wood inlaid with sprays of flowers. In it are a necklace of rose quartz, a silver belt buckle, an unopened letter and a red coral button in the shape of a bird

a rose-coloured pouch containing a pair of deep-blue silk velvet slippers embroidered with gold and silver thread a carved wooden mouse with a nut in its paws

a peach stone wrapped in a cloth

the feather of a mountain finch

a dried arylindra flower

a ring made of cherrywood, adorned with pink ribbons

a little horse on wheels

a picture book

the last of a skein of ribbons

a little dress of ivory linen embroidered with rosebuds

a round painted pebble

a note found in a packet of taklaris

two velvet boxes bearing the mark of a jewellery house
in Chalfur

a tattered map

a piece of paper containing a list of coded accounts

a docket confirming receipt of twenty sacks of rice

a bill of sale for the purchase of a boy.

Replacing each item carefully, he knots the cord tightly and pushes the sack as far back under the bed as he can.

He is alone, which is how he arranged it. But he is not lonely. It is an important distinction. He has chosen to be by himself. He is a man of solitude. *Sol-i-tude*. A song-like word. Unlike *lone-ly*, which seems to depress the voice. As he walks, he tells himself he has accomplished his solitude much as one would create a work of art. It is an achievement entirely his own.

Music is playing when he reaches the inn. Passing musicians, he thinks as he goes through the door. He is right; a man is playing the fiddle and singing as the common room keeps time with its collective foot. There is barely room to stand up. Reminding himself he is man of solitude, he pushes his way through the crowd to his table. Three people are sitting there. He stands glaring until one of them shifts in her chair. It is Lia. Without a word he turns and walks away.

Chapter Forty-Six

He is hardly aware of slamming the door behind him, uncorking a flagon of beer and pouring it into his mouth. He drinks until the flagon is empty, goes to his bed and throws himself down. Why is she here? Why has she come back? She has no right to, not now. Everything is arranged as he wants it to be, nailed down tight, letting nothing in.

Is it? He sits up angrily, scrubbing his face. He can't blame Night; the question is all his own.

'It is,' he says loudly, getting up and pacing around the hut until he boils out and onto the track. He walks until he has made good distance. When he comes to a large boulder, he climbs up and perches there.

He sits for a while, his eyes closed, as the night air flows over him. After a moment of chilly calm his agitation returns. It comes, he realises, as much from seeing Lia again as being reminded about the way he behaved towards her. He has worked very hard to bury it, but this evening has shown him how shallow the soil is.

He tells himself she won't want anything to do with him, not now, so there is nothing to worry about. It is simply an inconvenience. But – he sits up straight – how can he return to the inn? He lies back, staring blindly into the sky.

In the morning, he peels himself stiffly from the boulder and drops to the ground. The air is fresh as water on his face. He stands and stretches, clasping his hands above his head. The sky glows with early light. Here is the world at ease with itself, one bird calling to another. Do they notice the beauty of the day? Perhaps it is enough to get on with the business of living, raising young, finding enough food to survive. His hands fall to his sides and he starts walking rapidly back to the hut.

A basket covered with a clean white cloth is sitting at the door. He stares as if he has never seen a basket before, then picks it up and goes inside.

Under the cloth he finds sweet rolls glazed with brown sugar. A round loaf with a split floured crust. Wedges of yellow cheese wrapped in white paper. A disc of golden butter stamped with a spray of flowers. He puts the basket on the table and eats until his stomach aches. He allows himself no thought but the simple pleasure of eating. Then he goes to his bed, and sleeps.

It is a good sleep, filled with nothing but rest. When he wakes, the shutters are open, the floorboards banded with light. He sits up, stretching comfortably. Pink and gold clouds swell the early evening sky. Outside, he pushes the lid off the barrel, dunks his head in and comes up gasping. Instead of going back into the hut, he settles down and looks about.

A little way off, a small brown-striped creature speeds across the ground and suddenly disappears. He wonders how it knows the exact location of its burrow, and what would happen if it miscalculated. Is there a branch of stripy creatures with crooked noses? He is still smiling when his eye catches a movement. As Lia approaches, her gentle greeting brings him to his feet.

The embarrassment he feels is quickly lost in the warmth of her smile. Her eyes hold neither judgement nor blame. Something inside him eases a little.

'I'm sorry about your table,' she says, 'there was nowhere else to sit.'

'It doesn't matter,' he says quickly. She asks him if he enjoyed the rolls. 'I did, thank you.' He finds himself inviting her in.

Lia sits at the table as the boy fills the pot with water, then realises the fire has gone out. Apologising, he lights it again, aware of his shaking hands. He is beginning to regret his invitation. Lia is slender and gentle, but her presence in the hut feels large and difficult. As does what happened the last time he saw her. He is also trying to ignore the dusty floor, the rags tacked to the shutters, the empty flagons piled in a corner.

Lia seems unaware of them as she tastes the tea. 'This is very good. Where did you get it?'

'In the market,' he says, and falls silent. Then, in a tumbling rush, 'I'm sorry. The way I behaved towards you was unforgiveable. I'm not surprised you left.'

Lia studies him for moment. Taking a package from the pocket of her dress, she says, 'This will go nicely with the tea, if you don't mind?'

'Er, yes, of course,' he says, gathering himself, and fetches a plate from the cabinet. He watches her unwrap a rich dark-brown cake, rectangular in shape, studded with raisins and sultanas. She cuts into it, releasing an aroma of apples, nutmeg and cinnamon.

'Try it,' she says, and he eats, aware of her eyes on him.

When he has finished she says, 'It wasn't unforgiveable, and I didn't leave because of it.' He waits. 'I've thought about it a lot since I left. I don't know much about you, Arun, because you never talked about yourself at the inn, but I guessed you'd been through something very hard. I thought that if you wanted to talk about it you would, and if you didn't, that was fine too. I just enjoyed your company.'

He wants to say he enjoyed hers too, but sits in silence.

'I knew there must be a reason why you reacted as you did,' Lia continues, 'and I wasn't upset, just sad. I'm sorry if I caused you pain.'

He can find no words to match the generosity of her understanding, so he offers more tea.

She takes a sip. 'I was going to come back because I didn't want to leave things as they were, but a messenger came to the inn that evening with a letter from Samiros. It's my home town. My aunt was ill, and asking for me. She's not the sort of person to complain so I knew it must be serious. I left almost immediately.

'It was a long illness, and now it's over. I know I should look on it as relief from her suffering, and part of me does, but . . .' She takes a breath. 'Aunt Terise was my mother's sister. She lived with us, and she was the one who taught me to bake. When I was a child, I made mud-cakes until my mother decided she'd had enough of cleaning up after me, so my aunt stepped in and taught me properly.'

She smiles at the boy. 'At least I was there to take care of her at the end. It meant a lot to me, being able to give something back. And spending time with her made me realise I wanted to go back to Samiros. While I was there, I made some good friends.' She tells him she will be returning to live in her parents' house. 'I'd been in Kandra for three years before I left, and I enjoyed it, but it's time to go home.'

Which answers the question the boy had been about to ask. He crumbles cake on his plate.

'I'm here for a few days,' Lia says. 'I have some things to sort out. But I'd like to see you again before I go. Only if you want to, of course.' Her gaze is steady, but he senses the vulnerability behind the words.

'Yes,' he says, 'I'd like that.'

He watches her walk away down the track, a basket on each arm – he has finally returned the one she left behind – before closing the door. He sits at the table, thinking. When he stirs, he has made a cautious peace with himself. Since Lia will only be here for a few days, there is no reason not to enjoy her company.

It was long overdue, he tells himself as he sits back and surveys his work. The dust had been developing a family tree. He put the empty flagons in a sack to take to the inn, scrubbed the table until the wood came up shining. Using the broom he bought when he first came here, he almost swept the floor out of the door. He washed down the shelves of the cabinet and polished it inside and out. Then he stoked the fire, boiled water and made tea.

By late afternoon he is beginning to think she isn't coming. The knock comes as he is smoothing down a rough patch he found on the side of the mantelpiece. Lia explains that she can't stop, she has a meeting with the notary, and asks if she can come back in the morning.

When she has gone, he investigates the basket she left behind. It contains a cluster of small, syrup-glazed rolls. After eating every one he gets up and goes out, taking the track to the boulder, climbing up and stretching out with his arms behind his head.

Afternoon glides into evening. For a while he is lost in time, gazing up at a sky composed of a million stars. The moon is new-bladed and yellow. Only when he starts to shiver does he realise how cold it is. He scrambles to his feet and stands looking out. From here, Kandra is a dark huddle threaded with yellow lights, like fireflies. *Stars on a necklace of leaves.* That was what she called them, one night long ago.

The following morning he inspects the hut and finds himself pleased with what he sees. It is weatherproof and snug, more than enough for his needs. His needs. Is a man simply the sum of his needs? If so, has he made himself into what he is?

He is still frowning when he answers the knock at the door. Lia looks at him questioningly. 'Just thinking,' he says, and welcomes her in.

At the table, she removes the cloth from her basket to reveal small savoury biscuits flavoured with cheese and sweet red pepper powder, a dense golden-brown loaf, a pat of butter and a mound of tiny round cakes, crisp on the outside and creamy within, as the boy will shortly discover. He pours tea for Lia, for himself, and cuts thick slices from the loaf. The butter is cool but spreadable.

The bread is as good as it looks, with a hint of

sweetness. 'Syrup,' Lia explains. 'It gives it that colour. I did some baking yesterday evening. Olti was very accommodating – it might have had something to do with the cakes I made him.' So that was what she'd been doing. He'd waited at his table, but she hadn't appeared. 'And I've been making the final arrangements about my house. Hence the notary.'

House? The boy assumed she lived at the inn. 'I did, but I also have a house I've been renting out. My tenants are going to buy it. They've become very attached to it. They were with me at the inn that night.'

The boy stares at her, wondering where to start. With the fact that she owns a house, or where she found the means to buy it, or . . .

Lia smiles. 'My parents left me a little money, but I saved most of it myself. I've always worked, ever since I was old enough. I love cooking. It makes me happy to see people fed.'

The boy thinks she is fortunate to have found what she wanted early on. 'Yes,' she says with simple gratitude. When he asks what Samiros is like, she tells him it is a city to the south-west of Kandra, very green, famous for its gardens, and that it sits on a natural spring.

'What made you leave?'

A little sadly she says, 'In the end it wasn't enough. My parents knew it, and they didn't stand in my way. They always encouraged me, whatever I did.'

After a short silence, the boy asks where she went. 'To Harmat, a much bigger place, very different from Samiros, which is why I chose it. I found work almost immediately, as a cook in a tavern. After I'd worked there for a while I started experimenting, in my own time and with my own ingredients.'

For a moment she looks away. 'It turns out some freedoms are resented. The son of the owner found me deep in pink batter and decided I was some kind of sorceress.'

The boy stares. The larger the town the greater the sense, surely? 'Pink batter?' he asks.

'Crushed strawberries. I thought if I made them part of the mix rather than adding whole fruits, it would taste even better.'

They both start laughing. 'Did they really think you were a sorceress?' the boy asks.

'The son did, and that's what mattered. I was dismissed. I had to leave Harmat, of course – no one would employ me after that. It took quite a while to find somewhere else.'

The boy refills her cup, offers more bread. She drinks, and eats half a slice. 'As soon as I arrived in Chelar, I knew. Not so much the look of it as the fact that it felt right.'

The boy remembers a saying he heard once, that the fortunate man may go to a mountain or a desert, pitch his tent and call it home.

Lia nods. 'Exactly. I looked for work, and found it in a bakery. It meant a lot of early mornings, and the hours were long, but I was happy there.'

Chelar. The name sounds familiar. The boy recalls Olti saying, *Best bread, no contest*, and understands why he was so pleased to have Lia as his cook.

'So you were the baker?'

'Not quite. I was chief underbaker to Beigan. And not without a fight. There was a strict hierarchy. I was only promoted because Soriyal – Beigan's wife – said she'd wrap him in dough and bake him if he didn't.'

The boy laughs.

'There's a lot to be said for early mornings,' Lia says. 'I lived a few streets away from the bakery, on the edge of town. You get to know the birds as they wake up: who sings first, who comes in later. You have the company of the moon, and the sun.' The boy asks how long she was there. 'Six years. Good years.'

Judging it time for the savoury biscuits, he freshens their tea and offers Lia the plate. 'You first,' she says. 'I'd like to know what you think.'

He takes a bite, and the biscuit melts on his tongue, leaving a tang of cheese and the faint warmth of pepper. 'It's wonderful. Is it your recipe?'

Lia looks pleased. She tells him she experimented for quite a while before she found a way to preserve the flavours but keep the biscuit light. 'Sorry, I could bore you for hours. It's hardly the most interesting subject.' The boy assures her it is, then asks why she left.

Lia cradles her cup and studies it for a moment. 'I was restless. Although I was happy where I was, I kept feeling there was more to see and do. I tried to stay, but in the end I knew I had to go.'

She drinks tea, looking upset. 'I hurt them. Soriyal and Beigan. I know I did. They were so kind and understanding. In a way, it would've been better if they'd told me how ungrateful I was, shouted, perhaps, or shown me the door. But they didn't. They just wanted me to be happy. Leaving Chelar was hard.'

She looks at the boy. 'There are times when you'd give

639

anything for someone to make the decision for you. You go round in circles, worrying this, arguing that, scrutinising the other until it becomes half dead. Then, just when you think you have the answer, the nagging doubt comes puffing up beside you and collapses at your feet. What does it want, praise? "Well done, you got here. Have a biscuit."'

The boy stares at her for a moment, then starts laughing. 'You sound as bad as me,' he says.

She smiles, then her face becomes serious again. 'In the end it was almost a relief to leave. I had to go where the work was, so I travelled out of the province, to Tandesh. I found a post in a household, good pay, but hardly challenging. The woman I worked for had a delicate stomach, so I had to prepare bland food. If she even suspected a spice, she wouldn't eat it. It was a waste, really, so I started giving away the leftovers at the back door to people who needed them. She never knew, and I never felt bad about it. That was when I started making things again. And giving them away, too. They had to be portable, hence the little cakes. Easy enough to smuggle in a pocket.

'I'm not sure what happened, but I think someone told my employer something was going on.' She stops, as if the memory is painful. The boy waits. 'She jumped to the conclusion that it wasn't cakes I was giving away at the door.'

She says no more, but her fingertips press against the sides of her cup. Indignation heats the boy's face. He is about to say something unflattering about the woman with the deservedly delicate stomach when Lia says, 'I don't blame her. She had enough worries with her husband.' He fills in the gaps.

'I was going to try Belisi next.' He has heard of the town, to the west of Kandra. 'I broke my journey here, and stayed at the Willow. When I arrived, Olti was in flap – his cook had just left, and he was desperate for someone to replace him. I didn't intend to stay, but he gave me free rein. No pink batter, though.' She smiles at the boy. 'And when the house came up for sale – they're normally passed down through families, but there weren't any surviving relatives – I bought it. I've been very happy here.'

Sunlight slants across the floorboards. It is almost lunchtime. The boy invites Lia to stay for a meal of cold meats, a slab of yellow cheese. He brews more tea and offers her some of the tiny round cakes. Afterwards they sit contentedly beside the fire. The boy finds no need to fill the silence; it is doing very well on its own.

Eventually Lia sits up, stretching. 'I've enjoyed this very much, Arun, thank you, but I need to get back, there's still a fair bit to do.'

'I've enjoyed it too. Perhaps tomorrow . . . ?'

'Tomorrow I'm meeting my tenants and the notary, to sign the contract. But that's in the morning. Could I come later, in the afternoon?'

'Yes, of course.'

He stares into his dinner, wondering about the colour of guilt. A sick yellow-green, perhaps.

'Enough of that,' Night says briskly. 'I want to talk about whether a butterfly has more brains than a gnat.'

The boy lifts his head. 'Really?'

'No, but it got your attention. There's no need for this, you know.'

641

'For what?'

'You know what.'

The boy lifts his mug and drinks. The beer tastes a little thin. 'Same beer,' Night says, 'and don't change the subject.'

'Leave it.'

'You've been leaving it for so long you wouldn't know if it's still breathing. So, are we on for the butterfly and the gnat?'

The boy drops his fork on the plate with a clatter. Getting up, he leaves the inn.

He sits at the table eating the last of the tiny round cakes. When he has finished, he spends some minutes sweeping up crumbs, rinsing his plate, drying it and replacing it in the cabinet. When the fire is up and running, he sits staring into it.

He enjoyed himself today. What was wrong with that? He has heard of people who lost someone they loved, and remained alone for the rest of their lives. He remembers thinking how miserable it must be to shut your heart away for good. But they didn't, he corrects himself. They loved in other ways. Their relatives, their friends, the interests they had, the work they did. They climbed over the full stop and carried on.

His shoulders slump. He did, too, for a time. After he lost his family, she – he still can't bring himself to say her name, even in his head – helped him convert it into a semicolon. Which became a sentence, a paragraph and, finally, what it was meant to be. A story. Which ended.

He sighs, looking around. Nothing has changed. He

wonders what would happen if he took the leather sack from under the bed and left without looking back.

A lemon-coloured light fringes the hills. He moves restlessly about the hut. By the afternoon he is ready to snap. A knock at the door; he surprises himself with the warmth of his greeting.

He shows Lia to a chair beside the fire. She has brought a ginger cake dusted with an intricate design of powdered sugar. The boy admires it as he pours tea.

'I cut a pattern out of paper, lay it on top, and sprinkle it with sugar,' she tells him as she cuts the cake. 'Flowers are my favourite.'

'You like decorating things.'

'I always like something to look its best. Even if it disappears very quickly.' The boy looks guiltily at his half-eaten slice. 'Oh, no,' she laughs, 'that's the reward for my labours.'

For a while they eat in silence. 'How's your packing coming on?' he asks.

'Nearly done. Olti's been very helpful, although he keeps trying to persuade me to stay. Just a few more things to load up. It's taken less time than I thought.' The boy asks when she will go. 'The day after tomorrow.' Firelight catches a gleam of gold at the neck of her dress, drawing his eye.

She sees him looking and fishes up a pendant on a gold chain. It is a little owl, carved from a white opaque gemstone. A little cap of beaten gold narrows into a long beak; the turquoise eyes are rimmed with gold. Two short, thick bands of gold clasp the shoulders, like folded wings.

The plump oval body flares into a short tail; golden claws grip a golden branch.

The boy stares in wonder. He has never seen such a thing before, not even in the merchant's house.

'It was a gift from someone who's become a very good friend,' Lia says. 'She's called Ruen, and she's a jewellery-maker. She's married to Edern – he's an architect – and they have two children, Erissa, who's five, and Mihal, who's three. They came to Samiros a few months after me. They were staying at an inn while they looked for somewhere to live. I'd heard that a couple a few streets away were about to move, so I took Ruen and the children to see the house.

'They fell in love with it immediately. It's very pretty; there's a flower-filled courtyard and plenty of space for Erissa and Mihal to play. Ruen was so grateful, she gave me the owl. I refused at first – it's hardly fitting for someone like me – but she insisted. I'm glad she did, I love it. It goes everywhere with me.'

The boy is intrigued. He refills their cups, puts another slice of ginger cake on Lia's plate, and waits for her to tell him more.

She met Ruen in a bakery. 'I always bought my bread there. I'd come to know the baker, Kri, very well. Ruen had brought Erissa and Mihal to buy cakes. It took ages for them to decide. They were in agonies over what to choose.'

She smiles. 'To Erissa, they weren't just cakes. A cinnamon bun was a sleeping cat all curled up; the fruit in an apricot tart came from a special tree. When I asked her where the tree was, she looked up at me with big brown eyes, tugged at my dress so I'd bend down, cupped her hands and whispered in my ear.'

The boy understands Lia will never reveal what was said. 'Kri was telling Mihal what went into the various cakes, and he was listening very carefully. Ruen was watching them – it was as if the bakery was filled with the light in her eyes. There are times when I wonder what it would be like to have children,' she says thoughtfully. 'Mostly, I've been too busy to think about it. But when I see the joy they bring, it gives me such pleasure. Someday, I hope. You never know.'

The boy feels strangely honoured by Lia's frankness. For some reason, hearing her talk about children is not as painful as it might have been.

Lia breaks off a piece of ginger cake. 'There are chairs and tables outside the bakery, and when the children had made their choices, Kri offered Ruen tea. Ruen asked me to join them, and that was when she told me she was looking for a house for her family. It needed to have a workshop for her jewellery-making. What struck me was the way she included Erissa and Mihal in the conversation, as if their opinions mattered too. I liked that. I told her about the house, and we arranged to meet there later that afternoon.

'As soon as I saw it, I knew it'd be perfect for them. It has a white-painted front with large windows covered by pretty wrought-iron grilles, and pale-green shutters. It's set back from a courtyard shaded by trees: peach, plum, cherry and pear. There's a large pond full of water lilies, and stone benches to sit on. When you go in, there are rooms on both sides of a long hallway, and a broad stairway going up to the four bedrooms. The back bedrooms look out on a smaller courtyard filled with flowers. It's known as the evening garden. And, behind that, outbuildings, any

645

of which was big enough to be made into a workshop for Ruen.'

The boy laughs. 'You've done a good job of selling it to me,' he says.

Lia smiles. 'While they were looking around, I had a chat with the couple. The husband told me they were returning to his wife's home village to look after her mother. They had no regrets, they were going willingly, and she was particularly looking forward to it. It's funny, isn't it, how sometimes no matter how far you go in a straight line, it turns into a circle.'

She looks at the boy, who glances at the fire. 'It was all arranged that afternoon. The couple were delighted to find someone to rent their house, and when it was settled I walked back to the inn with Ruen and the children.' She laughs. 'They were so excited, tugging their mother's hands, arguing about which bedroom would be theirs and what games they'd play in the courtyard.

'It's funny, it felt as if I'd always known her. Ruen, I mean. As if we'd met somewhere before. We became friends almost on the spot.' She pauses. 'I'm not normally like that. I don't tend to make friends easily.' The boy silently disagrees. He can see why people are drawn to Lia. 'They're a lovely family,' she says. 'Edern is a kind, thoughtful man, and he adores Ruen and the children.

'Those children!' Her eyes are shining. 'They have such imaginations – they named the plum tree the Shaking Tree Ship, and the pear tree is now the Fox Ship. Woe betide anyone who tries to board them. It was when we were in the courtyard, being repelled, that Ruen gave me this.'

She touches the little owl briefly, her face thoughtful.

'What struck me first about Ruen was her sense of calm determination. Although she's never said anything, I have a feeling it's hard-won.' She stirs. 'I've been talking far too much. I really must make tracks.'

The boy wants to hear more about Ruen and her family, but he gets up and walks Lia to the door. She tells him she has enjoyed his company, and asks if she can come again tomorrow afternoon. She looks at him for a moment before setting off for the village.

He stands for a while, staring into space. It is strange, this feeling, as if a spring of clear water has found its way out of the ground. For the time Lia was with him, he gave no thought to sadness or loss.

Chapter Forty-Seven

Lia has brought a round cake decorated with flowers made from lemon slices and curls of rind. 'A good cake to go away to,' she says as she puts it on the waiting plate. The boy says nothing. Settled by the fire, she cuts the cake. It is truly marvellous, infused with lemon, sweet, tart, moist and sticky. He shows his appreciation by wolfing it down.

'Ruen's husband Edern does most of the cooking,' Lia tells him. 'He's very good. He was taught by his mother. She raised her children to be equal to whatever was put to them. They all had the same schooling too, never mind that one was a girl, the other two boys. Quite right.' She nods approvingly.

'They met in Haisan. It's the biggest city in Pular province. Edern – did I say he's an architect? – had been commissioned to prepare a report on a very old building called the Artisans' Hall, which was on the verge of falling down. The foundations were sound, but that was about it.' She smiles. 'They met backwards. He was looking up at the roof, making notes, stepping back; she was leaving her workshop, locking the door behind her. When she turned, she went straight into him.

'The tray of jewellery she was carrying went everywhere. He was full of apologies, gathering up the scattered pieces and, as he told me later, going to pieces himself.' She studies a slice of crystallised lemon. 'You'd think it would have a sour disposition, but show it some sugar and it leaps about happily.' The boy finds himself grinning.

'Well,' Lia continues, 'Ruen thanked Edern, took the tray and went back into her workshop. When I asked her why she went back in, she said she'd forgotten what she was going out for. Edern told me that when he got home and looked at the measurements he'd taken, they didn't make sense. As you've probably gathered, it was an interesting courtship. It took quite a while for Ruen to invite Edern into her workshop.'

Her eyes are full of affection. 'When they tell it, they make you feel as if you're there. I never get tired of hearing it.'

The boy listens, absorbed, as she paints a word-picture so clear he can almost see Ruen putting the finishing touches to a necklace of seed pearl, topaz and sapphire commissioned by a man for his daughter's sixteenth birthday. Edern is watching, trying his best to look at ease, his hands gripped behind his back.

The warm, low-ceilinged workshop is lined with shelves overflowing with pots and jars, the workbench crowded with tools, from large pliers to slender little fine-tipped gravers. Edern shifts a little, aware of the closeness of Ruen's sleeve to his own. When she is done, she holds the necklace up to her throat and asks him if he likes it. The word feels as if it has lain untouched in a cellar for forty years. *Yes.*

The moment is sweet, and stinging, but the boy won't wish love from the world because of what happened to him. He clears his throat and waits for Lia to continue.

She tells him Ruen was lodging in a small and very respectable house run by two unmarried sisters, Kelyn and Tibesa, who had at one point given the city pause for thought. When they first set up the lodging-house, there were mutterings about the propriety of a household without men, the unspecified depravities it would lead to. With some disappointment it was discovered that not only did the sisters run an excellent establishment, they also taught people to read and write.

They started quietly, with their neighbour and her daughter. The neighbour was a widow whose husband had taken care of everything. At the reading of his will, she was informed by the notary that she was left with almost nothing. She took the will to a friend, who studied it, made enquiries, and informed her that the notary had shifted a good deal of her husband's estate into his own pocket.

The widow looked at her daughter and became a lion. She threatened to report the notary to the local magistrate, and suddenly there was money in her purse and a roof over her head. It was at this time that Kelyn and Tibesa moved into the house next door. She took them bread and fruit; they offered homemade mint tea and currant cake.

The friendship was sealed when the sisters offered to teach the widow and her daughter to read and write. Every afternoon they would bring out a series of cards, each one containing a letter and a beautifully painted picture. Once word went forth about what they were doing, other people started coming to the house. Quietly at first, and generally at dusk. Then more openly, until the house became, as someone remarked, the first letter of the alphabet.

Ruen found them by accident when she was looking for somewhere to stay. Hearing children chattering and laughing, she stopped outside to listen. Some kind of lesson was taking place, guided by a woman's patient voice. When Kelyn came to the window for a breath of air, she saw Ruen standing there and, with typical generosity, invited her in.

Once the lesson ended, Kelyn and Tibesa asked Ruen where she was staying. When she told them she hadn't yet found anywhere, they offered her a room. She accepted, a price was agreed for bed and board, and they took her out to explore the city.

Lia puts down her cup, and the boy refills it. 'They also introduced her to a friend of theirs, a jewellery-maker,' she says. 'He had a workshop in the Artisans' Hall. Ruen used to go there and watch him, until one day he offered her an apprenticeship. She became very fond of him. I think he was one of the few people she trusted. When he died, he left her the tenancy of the workshop. They were generally lifetime tenancies, passed down from father to son. It raised a few eyebrows – she was young, a woman, and unmarried – but Kelyn and Tibesa had taught the sons of the cousin of the official responsible for the Artisans' Hall, so that was that.

'I've always envied people who can make things,' she adds with a rueful smile. 'I'm hopeless. Give me a piece of clay and it remains a piece of clay.'

The boy laughs. 'But you make wonderful cakes.' Her eyes fill with pleasure.

'You were telling me about the workshop,' he says after a moment.

'Yes, of course. Ruen settled in very quickly, as she did in the sisters' house. That's what made me wonder if she was used to moving from place to place.' She breaks off a piece of cake. 'It's interesting how one thing can change the fate of another. Take the Artisans' Hall. When Edern first went in, he saw a building so full of holes it could have doubled as a sieve. When he met Ruen, he realised the holes were there to let the stars shine through.'

'I said it was an interesting courtship. It took a lot of persuasion on Edern's part. He'd hover at the door of Ruen's workshop, asking if she'd like to take tea with him, and she kept turning him down. She was too busy, she had too many orders, it was never quite the right time. Eventually he stopped asking, but discovered an area near the workshop that required particular attention.'

She laughs. 'One day he was standing outside, reading his notes for the twentieth time, when Ruen came out, told him she was about to have tea, and that if he wanted to join her, he could. That's when she showed him the seed pearl necklace.'

She gazes into the fire for a moment. 'Although Ruen's never said anything, I think something happened in her past, something so painful she can't talk about it. It's made her very wary of people. It generally takes time for her to trust someone. But I don't think I need to explain that to you,' she says gently. The boy feels curiously like a flame in the fire, of discernible colour and shape, yet also translucent.

'I've often wondered if it's one of the reasons she works so hard,' Lia says. 'She was in that workshop every day, from first light to sunset. The piece that really started things off was a pendant. I didn't see it, but she keeps a coloured sketch of everything she makes. It was exquisite.'

She describes a golden ship, its hull enamelled with scales of cobalt blue, a large ivory-coloured flower at the centre. Pearl-coloured sails unfurling from masts rigged with delicate gold. A peacock-blue pennant flying from the main mast. White enamel waves curling up the prow, a white-and-gold flag billowing from a bowsprit of gold.

'It was snapped up by a man looking for a present for his mother's eightieth birthday. He said she was the ship that steered the family, so it was perfect for her. Commissions flowed from it, but Ruen was always choosy. She'd only take so many, and set aside time to make what she wanted. She's developed a whole menagerie of animals. They've become her trademark. My favourite is the owl, of course.'

She touches the pendant briefly. 'Others – well, whatever she makes is beautiful. A turtle of dark-green jade with silver flippers and eyes of jet. A dove carved from mother-of-pearl, with an emerald leaf in its beak.

'Her little cats and dogs are always in great demand, especially with children, so she makes them from more affordable materials. There's even a dragon. It's about this high' – she opens a gap between thumb and forefinger – 'made of bronze, every scale in perfect detail, and a wicked green eye. It's not for sale. She keeps it on a shelf in her workshop. She calls it the Spirit of Creation.' The boy wonders what his creative spirit would look like.

Lia is quiet for a moment. 'It's funny, Ruen makes such beautiful jewellery, but the only thing she wears, apart from her wedding ring, is a bracelet of blue thread. I've never seen her without it. I think it must mean something to her. Maybe one day I'll ask her about it.

'Sorry, I'm off again.' She shakes her head, smiling. 'Where was I? Oh yes. Well, if Edern was to do his job properly, the problem with the area outside Ruen's workshop couldn't last forever. When the time came to make his report to the official in charge of works, he knew he'd be recommending a complete renovation, and he wasn't sure if the city purse would be deep enough. If it wasn't, the Artisans' Hall would have to be demolished, and he was determined not to let that happen.'

The boy feels strangely anxious as Lia's quiet skill brings the scene to life. Edern is waiting in a long corridor. He sits, stands, paces, wonders if time can be given a kick up the backside, sits down again and hooks one leg around the other. When his name is called, he gets up so quickly he almost falls over.

The official has read the report and made a decision. He knows the Artisans' Hall has a special place in the hearts of the people of Haisan. He also has an eye on the forthcoming elections. It is a lucky day for Edern. Stamping the report, the official tells him to make sure it is the most beautiful building in the city. Edern is just happy to know it won't fall down. He goes straight there to tell Ruen the good news.

It seems she isn't the only one waiting on the decision. As Edern goes in, people crowd round to ask how it went. When he tells them, they start shaking him by the hand, patting his back, offering him thanks, cakes, tea. He is aware of none of it. He is looking for Ruen. And there she is, her face serious, her eyes shining.

'It's funny,' Lia says, 'how at times like that a place seems to have its own breath.'

Which stops as Ruen walks towards Edern. She stands in front of him with an appraising look. Then she holds out her hand. Her fingers are closed. He opens them gently. In her palm is a ring, a wide band of beaten silver, at the centre of which is a raised gold star. Edern stares – everyone stares – and takes it from her. A moment of awkwardness – what should he do? – then Ruen takes his left hand and slips the ring onto his finger. The place is in uproar as he takes her in his arms and kisses her.

'Then of course there was singing, dancing, food, wine, and a lot more laughter.' Lia smiles. 'I asked Ruen later how Edern felt about being proposed to.' The boy has been wondering too. 'Apparently it was a great relief. He'd been working up the courage to ask, but every time he saw her, he fell apart. He couldn't have coped if she'd refused him. I think she knew, so she took matters into her own hands.'

She glances into the fire. 'They were married shortly afterwards. Nothing fancy, just a simple ceremony. Ruen's ring is very similar, a band of silver set with a gold heart. It's unusual, I know, a man wearing a ring, but it's right for them, and that's what matters.'

The boy thinks of another ceremony, two other rings.

He gulps a mouthful of tea as Lia's voice leads him back to where Ruen and Edern are sitting on chairs outside her workshop. They are talking quietly, their faces serious. It is, he gathers, some time after the wedding, and the Artisans' Hall is transformed. The roof, a soaring pyramid of glass, sends light through the building. The walls are decorated with paintings and sculptures, the air croons with roosting pigeons. People wander to and fro, going into workshops, coming out with packages. It is a place whose beauty and purpose has been remade.

Lia describes the scene with care. Ruen has one hand over Edern's, the other in her lap. No, not her lap, but resting on her belly, tender and protective. The boy's throat closes. He can almost see Edern's face transform with joy.

He starts; Lia is touching his hand. 'I'm fine,' he says. 'Please, go on.'

Lia tells him Erissa was born first, Mihal two years later. When Erissa was three and Mihal one, Ruen and Edern made an important decision. They'd lived in Edern's house since their marriage, and had now outgrown it. Ruen wanted to look for a bigger house somewhere greener and quieter than Haisan, with space for the children to play. It would mean leaving all they'd worked hard to establish, but what mattered was that they were together.

'It took a while for them to find a suitable place. They discussed various towns and villages near Haisan before deciding to look further afield. Ruen asked the artisans about it, and one name kept coming up – Samiros, my city.'

She looks thoughtful. 'When Ruen told me about it, I could sense how hard it had been for her leave the place she'd come to call home. I think it was the first time she'd felt truly settled. For me, of course, it was a blessing. Her friendship – the family's friendship – has been a real comfort to me, especially during my aunt's final months.'

Lines from a poem drift in the boy's head.

She thinks of her mother taking the days carefully,
the months resting in their leaves.

He speaks without thinking, immediately regrets his lack of caution and sits staring at his hands. Lia's calm presence slowly settles the heat in his chest.

'Did you write it?' she asks.

'It was written by someone called Mirashi,' he says. Warmed by the encouragement in her eyes, he tells her about the Book of Light.

'I wish I could meet her,' she says. 'Invite her in, share some cake.' The boy explains it might be difficult, since Mirashi is long dead. 'But not her poems,' she says.

'Not her poems,' he agrees. Then, impulsively, 'Poems shouldn't be kept silent. They should be recited, passed down, discovered all over again, one generation to the next.'

'Your face changes when you talk about it,' Lia says. 'It lights up.' The boy wonders aloud if he is turning into a lantern. She bursts out laughing. 'Maybe it'll shine your way into the unknown.' Then, in answer to his questioning face, 'What I mean is, there are so many things we could do but don't, because the pitfalls seem more real than what might actually happen. And so we close the door each evening, and congratulate ourselves on escaping disaster. But when you actually face it, it often turns out to be a mouse in a very large hat.'

The boy is still smiling when she asks, 'Have you ever written poetry?'

He thinks of words and phrases scribbled in the back of a notebook. Of lines written later, in despair. And out of them, not a single poem. He hesitates. 'I thought it would be easy, just a matter of putting down what I feel. What came out was a flood, and just like floods it brought everything with it, including the rubbish.'

'It'll come when you're ready,' Lia says gently. The idea appeals to him. And if it never does, he can at least tell himself he had potential.

'I wish you could see Samiros,' she says. 'It sits among low green hills and small rivers and streams. In the evenings, the sun catches the tops of the towers and turns the roofs golden.' She stirs. 'It really is time for me to get back. Just a few more things to sort out, and I'll be ready to go.'

At the door she says, 'I'm leaving at daybreak, from the Willow. I'd really like it if you came to say goodbye.'

The boy watches her go, aware of a pulling sensation in his stomach. He must be hungry.

He is so hungry he eats nothing for the rest of the day, fails to go to the inn and lies in bed listening to his stomach grumbling until he gets up, makes a bowl of cham and sits in the middle of the night stirring it with a spoon. He has no intention of seeing Lia off. He is clear on this, at least.

He stands beside the wagon, watching Olti give a final tug to the thick hemp cord securing the blankets protecting Lia's belongings. 'Won't budge an inch,' Olti says gruffly. 'See you all the way to Samiros.' He nods, and goes back into the Willow.

They are left alone in the breaking light.

'I have something for you,' Lia tells him, 'and something to say.' She hands him a small cloth-wrapped parcel, 'to open later.' She looks at him for a moment. 'You have a lot to give, Arun. I know you think you're protecting yourself by shutting yourself away, but it also means shutting yourself off from people who would care for you.'

She touches his face gently. 'I won't be returning to Kandra, but I'd very much like it if you came to Samiros, for a visit, or longer, if you decided you liked it. You'd be most welcome, in my city and in my home. I'd like you to meet my friends, especially Ruen, Edern and the children. And I'd like to see you again. That's all.'

The boy can't speak. Lia kisses his cheek. She steps into the wagon and takes up the reins of the dark-brown horse. The horse's ears prick as it pulls away. He watches until they are out of sight. Then he turns and starts walking back to the hut.

Chapter Forty-Eight

A star trembles at the heart of the pool. 'I see you're wearing it,' Night remarks.

'How . . .?' Arun begins, then, sighing, fumbles at the neck of his tunic. A glint of gold: the little white owl turns slowly on its chain, luminous in the moonlight. 'It was too late to give it back to her,' he says defensively. 'She'd gone by then.'

'But you thought about what she said. You thought about writing again.'

'Yes, I thought about it.'

He watches the boy pull the sack from under the bed and take out the green leather notebook, its corners eaten by time and salt. His handwriting is as precise as the ledgers he kept. *We left in the afternoon, and people were waving on the quay. Kumbar and Nissa saw me off. Minu was there too. The sea is very blue.*

Seeing the merchant's name written there in what now seems like shocking innocence makes the boy get up, go to the cabinet and take out a flagon of beer. He settles back down. *I am sitting in my cabin and I am not seasick.* He smiles bleakly. Turning the page he reads, *It is a clear day, and the sea and sky are very blue* – 'Yes, we've established that,' he mutters – *and there are gulls overhead.* He uncorks the flagon. Perhaps his writing needs a drink.

'It did get better,' Arun says, 'once I stopped feeling so self-conscious. But all the time, in the back of my mind, I could see the other notebook, the one she gave me. I tried opening it once before, at Lake Sigal, but I couldn't. I thought it would be different this time. I don't know why. When I took it out, it was like touching a wound. I put it back, and finished every bottle in the hut.'

He takes a deep breath. 'All that, and the only thing I came up with . . .'

He takes the Book of Light from his tunic pocket and opens the front cover. A slip of paper flutters out. He unfolds it, smoothing out the creases. In a low voice he reads,

I have seen the shining tree of gold and silver,
held night-and-day tablets engraved
with the world.

He stares at the paper for a moment before folding it up and replacing it in the front cover. When the book is once more in his pocket he says, 'That's as far as I got. I wanted to say that what matters in the end isn't works of astonishing beauty but' – he catches his breath – 'a white house with a red roof. Someone coming to meet you with a child in their arms. They're the body's light, the things that make the heart beat faster. But I couldn't find the words.'

'You don't seem to be doing too badly,' Night says. 'Perhaps you just need to be in the right place. Samiros, for example. How long has it been?'

Arun looks down at his hands. 'Four months.'

'Not that you're counting. She won't wait forever, you know.'

Arun shakes his head. 'Look at me. I have nothing to offer.'

'Not true. If Samiros ever has trouble with the Leatherworkers' Guild, it'll know where to come.' It takes a moment for Arun to realise Night is talking about Liso, the man he was once apprenticed to. 'Not to mention more self-pity than you can shake a stick at.'

'You have no right to say that,' Arun says angrily. 'You don't know what I've been through.'

'I think I've got a pretty good idea, since you've just told me,' Night points out. 'I've also seen people abandoned by their parents and left to fend for themselves. People driven off their land because someone decided it would make good grazing for sheep, so their wells were poisoned and their houses burned to the ground. People –'

'You've made your point,' Arun says, 'but they mean nothing to me. They're not –' He lowers his head.

'All these years feeling sorry for yourself, and where has it got you? No wife, no child, no friends, no family. Except beer and wine, which seem to be your beginning and end. None of my business, I know, but is it any way to honour their memory?'

Arun looks up swiftly. 'Don't you think I've asked myself that? Don't you think I'm ashamed of what I've become? Please, just leave me alone.'

'You're forgetting who you're talking to. And, as I said before, there's always hope. You still have a decision to make. You can either give up, or go on. It's up to you.'

Arun slumps back against the tree, covering his face

with his hands. The idea of leaving terrifies him. The thought of going back fills him with despair. He has no idea what to do, and no one to turn to for advice. Certainly not Night; he has learned that already.

'You wouldn't even make one exception to that damn Rule,' he says. His anger at Night's refusal to tell him where Kara was buried resulted in the only time Olti suggested, with a firm hand on Arun's arm, that he'd had enough to drink and would better off at home in bed.

'I seem to recall you accusing me of being utterly heartless, a shockingly ignorant thing to say. Have you any idea how many hearts are beating in me this very minute?' Night sniffs. 'Always quick to condemn, always jumping to conclusions. After spending so much time with me, I'd have thought you'd know better by now.'

'What's that supposed to mean?'

'What?'

'Always jumping to conclusions.'

'Did I say that? You'll have to excuse me. I'm feeling a little light-headed.'

A breeze stirs. There is a shift in the quality of the darkness. With surprise, Arun realises it must be nearly daybreak. He frowns. He is no mood for Night's games. Nor is he any nearer to making a decision.

Far away, a cockerel crows. Across the clearing, shadows are resolving into trees.

When Night speaks again, Arun strains to hear. 'I feel quite exhausted. I could do with a break. I think you've worn me out. See you later, same place, no doubt, still going round in circles, trying to work out what to do.'

'Go away.'

The cockerel crows again.

'Have you gone?'

Silence.

Arun sits perfectly still as the sounds of morning collect around him. Birdsong flutes through the trees, branches rustle. *See you later, same place, no doubt.* He tightens his jaw. One thing he is sure about: he won't be here this evening. He has no intention of giving Night the chance to be even more insufferable.

As he stares into the pool, a frog looks back at him. The moon has vanished. He wonders if the frog has eaten it. Then he wonders what Lia would think if he told her. What was it she said, about how fear of the unknown can prevent you from doing things? *When you actually face it, it often turns out to be a mouse in a very large hat.*

The memory makes him smile. Very well. Since he has nothing better to do, he will go in search of the mouse. He takes a last drink, packs away his water bottle, gets up, slings the satchel across his chest and shoulders the leather sack. A deep breath, and he is ready.

The dawn light hurts his eyes. Even though the air is cold, he is sweating. Why did he not bring any beer? He skirts the pool and leaves the clearing. Beyond it, a small track winds through trees and bushes. He comes to a halt, shaking. Part of him wants to run back to the hut and into the nearest flagon. But he takes a step, and then another, and soon he is keeping pace with the rising light.

He walks steadily, fixing his gaze on the way ahead, thinking of nothing but the track. Which, he tells himself, is all that is required. He is a moving point on a brown dirt line, neither here nor there, but somewhere in between. Nothing is fixed; he can at any time decide to stop, go back, go on to somewhere that is not famous for its gardens, and has no natural spring.

By late morning he has run out of breath. His head is throbbing. He steps off the track, into the grass, dropping the sack and satchel. Too tired to eat, he collapses on the ground, stretches out and stares up at the sky.

A low rumbling sound wakes him. He sits up, rubbing his face with his hand. By the look of the sun, it must be mid-afternoon.

'I hope you don't mind me asking, but are you all right?'

A man is looking down from the seat of a wagon pulled by a stocky grey horse. The man is bald, but he wears a short, brindled beard. 'Lora said we'd better check, just to make sure.'

Arun looks from the man to the woman sitting beside him. Her brown plaits fall to her waist, and her face is round and smiling.

'It's a safe road,' she says. 'We've travelled it many times. But you never know.'

Arun gets to his feet, tugging down his tunic. 'I'm fine, thanks. Just having a nap.' He waits for the wagon to move on, but it remains standing.

'I'm Fasir,' the man says, 'and this is my sister, Lora. We've been visiting our brother in Hadra, and we're on our way home to Lasou. Do you know it?'

He doesn't.

'I don't suppose many people do,' Lora says. 'It's only a small village, but it does for us. We grew up there. We've never wanted to go anywhere else, have we?'

'No,' Fasir says. 'I've never understood this moving from place to place. I don't mind a visit, but after a few days I'm ready to go home. And I don't like leaving the chickens. Our neighbour looks after them, but it's not the same. They fret if we're gone too long.'

Arun nods politely, shifting from foot to foot.

'Where are you heading?' Fasir asks.

He debates whether to tell them. Why not? The thought of a city full of people coming and going is sure to send them hurrying back to their chickens.

'Samiros?' Lora exclaims. 'But that's on our way. You must travel with us. Of course you must, mustn't he?' Fasir nods warmly. 'That's settled, then. Fasir will put your bags in the back.'

Arun watches silently as Fasir loads the leather sack into the wagon. 'I'll keep this with me, thanks,' he says, pressing the satchel to his chest.

The grey horse switches its tail as the wagon moves off. Arun clutches the satchel. The thought of making conversation with strangers, sharing their company and their questions, makes his palms sweat. He tells himself that when they reach Samiros he can always wave them off and head elsewhere. They will never know.

Fasir and Lora turn out to be good companions, which is to say each is as talkative as the other, filling every space, leaving him little to do. Having established his name and where he has come from, they tell him about their village and their chickens.

'The finest in the district,' Lora says. 'They lay the best eggs you'll ever taste.'

'Which make the lightest cakes,' Fasir adds.

That night they stop beside the track, and make a cold dinner of mutton pie. Lora sleeps in the wagon, Fasir underneath. The grey horse snorts, flicking its ears. Arun lies back in the grass and thinks of other journeys, other horses. At least he has been given no room to dwell on what lies ahead.

Shivering, he turns over, trying not to think about beer. The Book of Light presses against his chest, prompting the last lines of Mirashi's poem about a man who wakes from a dream, knowing the path he has to take.

He will make his final journey
as the sun is rising.

He wonders if this will be his final journey, or if he will ever find rest.

By the following evening he has had his fill of chickens, no matter how exceptional, of neighbours whose dog barks until the cows come home, of brothers who never visit the village they were born in. Why did he ever leave Kandra? He has grown the hut around him, and feels its absence. Although, he reflects, not as much as he thought he would. He realises too that he has given hardly any thought to Night, or their conversations at the inn. It is as if the part of him he has worked hard to suppress is starting to come up for air.

'We should get to Samiros around mid-morning, all being well,' Lora says. 'Did you say you were visiting someone?'

He hasn't said anything. Fasir and Lora have

surrounded him so thoroughly with their hospitality that nothing has slipped through. 'A friend.'

'That's nice. Are you staying long?'

'I'm not sure.'

Fasir nods approvingly. 'Keep it open, that's the best way. Then you can always leave sooner without causing offence.'

The light plays on Arun's nerves as they set off again. He concentrates on his surroundings. Low hills rise all around them. Shrubs are in flower, trees in bud. Fir, spruce and juniper light the slopes with soft green fire. It is a land of gentle riches.

'Lovely, isn't it?' Lora says. 'I never get tired of it. Why would you? It has all you could ever want.' And she is away, talking about the time it has taken to make their house just right, 'a place you never want to leave, and a pleasure to return to.'

Arun listens with half an ear. Lora's chatter serves to take his mind off what is to come. If he chooses. It is up to him, after all.

They turn a corner; the wagon slows. They have come to a junction with a broad, paved road flanked with trees. It runs for some distance, ending at the chalk-white walls of a city whose entrance is marked by a graceful archway.

'Samiros,' Fasir says. 'This is where we turn off. Or we can take you a little further, if you like?'

Arun thanks them, saying he would like to walk, it will do him good to stretch his legs.

'Of course, my dear,' Lora says. 'It's been a pleasure

having your company. It made the journey go so much quicker. I hope you enjoy your visit.'

Thanking them again, Arun collects his leather sack. He waits until they are out of sight, then joins the paved road. With each step he reminds himself he still has a choice.

Within the shadow of the archway, he stops. People pass by, greeting him, wishing him good morning. He tells himself there is no reason not to go in. Lia has no idea he is here, and he can always take a look around and leave.

At the far side of a pleasant square, low hedges frame a wrought-iron arch. Beyond the hedges, people are taking the air, sitting on benches, chatting beside a large fountain. Paths paved with white stone wind past deep beds filled with flowers and shrubs.

Arun crosses the square and goes through the arch, into the gardens. People nod and smile at him. He finds a bench, and sits for a while. Children play on the grass, mothers call them back for a drink, a bite to eat. The atmosphere is calm, unhurried. It reminds him of Amala Dyssul. The thought makes him leave the bench and start walking. He follows a path out of the gardens, into a broad street shaded with trees. He looks at the doors. Could one of them be Lia's?

A man passes by, stops, and turns. 'You look a bit lost,' he says. 'Can I help?'

Arun gives him the name of Lia's street. He'd found her address on a piece of paper tucked in the parcel with the little owl.

'Oh yes, it's not far. Take the next turning on the left, go all the way down to the end of the street, turn left again, and there you are.'

And here he is, standing outside a blue door, his mouth dry, his heart failing. He would give a very great deal for a bottle of beer. What was he thinking?

He turns to go. He turns back. He raises his hand. He drops it. Night's words echo in his head: *Still going round in circles, trying to work out what to do.*

He knocks.

Chapter Forty-Nine

And knocks again. No reply. She is not in. The decision is made. He has tried, and now he can leave. Turning to go, he sees Lia coming down the street. She is wearing a sage-green dress, and has a basket on her arm.

Her face breaks into a smile. 'Arun – I thought it was you. What a wonderful surprise!'

He stands motionless as she kisses his cheek. As he looks into her warm hazel eyes, something inside eases a little.

'You must be tired,' she says. 'Please, come in.'

He follows her through the door. She puts the basket on the floor, and looks at him. 'I can't believe you're here. I'm so glad. Let me take your cloak. You can leave those there for the moment.'

He drops the leather sack, and takes off the satchel.

'Why don't you sit down, and I'll make some tea.'

Seated on a sofa draped with a pretty shawl, Arun looks around the room. Another sofa faces him, also covered with a shawl. An oval table sits between them. There are smaller tables too, and lamps, and colourful rugs. It is a cosy and comfortable room whose atmosphere of restful welcome softens the edge of his anxiety.

He sits back, looking at the pictures and sketches covering the walls, wondering if Lia did them. Above the fireplace hangs a painting of a garden. It is the garden he walked through earlier. A woman sits on the sill of the fountain, her face turned away as she gazes into the water. There is something about her that makes him get up to take a closer look.

'Do you like it?' Lia comes through the doorway at the far side of the room, a tray in her hands. She puts it on the oval table and goes to stand beside him. 'I've just finished it. It's for Ruen. That's her, sitting beside the fountain. I wanted to live with it for a while before I gave it to her, to make sure nothing needs changing. I started painting when I came back. I'm not sure how good it is, but I love doing it.'

'It's very good,' Arun says. He finds himself wishing the woman would turn her head.

'Come and sit down,' Lia says. 'I'm sure you must be hungry. I made this yesterday, with a little help from my new apprentice.'

She serves Arun tea and a slice of fruit cake, and sits on the sofa opposite.

'Apprentice?' he asks.

'Mihal, Ruen's son. I don't know if you remember me telling you about him?' He does. 'Well, at the ripe old age of three, he's decided he wants to be a baker. Strictly cakes, mind you. I think it might have something to do with the fact that he can eat the end product.'

Arun smiles.

'I'd like to hear about you,' Lia says. 'How are you? How have you been?'

He glances down at his cup, then at Lia. Her eyes are gentle, encouraging. 'There's not really much to tell. The hut's still standing, and I go to the inn every evening.' He can feel his anxiety creeping back. He must be the worst guest in the world.

'I'm sorry,' she says. 'I didn't mean to make you feel awkward. Asking someone to talk about themselves can sometimes have the opposite effect. Although with some people it can be like unblocking a dam – if you're not careful, you end up being washed away.'

Arun laughs. 'Do you know people like that?'

'I do. I've learned how to keep my feet dry.'

He smiles. Lia's natural warmth begins to steady him again.

'How's the Willow?' she asks. 'Is Olti still cross with me for leaving?'

'It's hard to tell. He doesn't give much away. He hasn't found a permanent replacement yet, though. The food's not bad, but it's not as good as yours.'

Lia sips her tea. 'How was the journey? How long did it take you get to here?'

He finds himself telling her about Fasir, Lora and the exceptional chickens.

She starts laughing. 'Do you think they'll barricade themselves in when they get home? Well, at least you had company. It must have made the journey more' – her eyes sparkle – 'interesting.'

'It did. But I have a feeling I know why the brother never visits, no matter how light the cakes are.'

Lia watches him for a moment. 'I think it took a lot for you to come here,' she says gently. 'I didn't know if you would, but I'm very glad you did. It's so good to see you again.'

He is silent. Before he came, he wasn't sure how he would feel, but now he has no doubt. 'It's good to see you, too,' he says. 'Oh, I forgot – I brought this back for you.' He ducks his head, slips off the gold chain, and holds out the little white owl.

'Oh, no, it's for to you keep. Besides, Ruen's given me something to replace it. She noticed I wasn't wearing it, and when she asked me about it, I told her about you. She was very interested.'

'She didn't mind you giving it to me?'

'Not at all. I think she was hoping you'd come, so she could meet you. We talked for quite a while – your ears must have been burning.'

Arun touches the side of his face. 'Still are.' He smiles. 'How are you? You look well.'

'I am. I can't believe how quickly the time has passed. It seems like only yesterday that I was leaving Kandra. But I'm very happy to be back.' Her face glows with contentment.

'And you've taken up painting?'

'Among other things. Apart from teaching Mihal how to bake, I've also started making cakes for Kri. He owns the bakery where I first met Ruen.'

'I remember you telling me about him.'

'You have a very good memory.'

'How could I forget? It involved cakes.'

Lia laughs.

'And the rest of Ruen's family? How are they?' he asks.

'All well, thank you. Erissa has decided she's going to be a jewellery-maker like her mother. Which naturally means trying on all the rings and necklaces.'

She offers him another slice of cake. 'Do you remember me telling you about the blue thread bracelet Ruen wears?' He nods. 'I finally asked her about it. We were sitting in the courtyard, and it seemed like the right moment. It wasn't long after I'd told her about you, and maybe that had something to do with it. An exchange of confidences, perhaps.'

Arun wonders what Lia confided.

'At first I didn't think she'd tell me, because she went very quiet. But then she said she'd been given the bracelet by a girl she once knew. She didn't say where, or why, but I was just grateful she trusted me enough to tell me. Apparently they'd left somewhere together – she didn't say so, but I don't think it was a good place – and were about to go their separate ways. Before they did, they exchanged gifts. Tokens of affection.

'Ruen's friend gave her the bracelet, and Ruen gave her – well, you can see for yourself. It's what she made to replace the little owl. It's a copy. The original belonged to her grandmother, and Ruen's mother passed it down to her. I was very touched. It obviously means a great deal to her.'

She opens the neck of her dress and draws out a red coral pendant in the shape of a bird. The eye is a tiny pearl. 'It's beautiful, isn't it? It looks as if it's about to fly away.'

He can't speak.

'Arun? Are you all right? You've gone very pale.'

He sits motionless. Lia kneels in front of him, taking his hand. 'You're shaking. Would you like some water?'

It takes some moments to sort through the turmoil in his head, to ask what he needs to know.

'You said it was a copy. Of another pendant?'

Lia thinks for a moment. 'No, it was a button.'

'And she exchanged it with this girl?'

'Yes.'

His mouth is dry. He swallows. Lia comes to sit beside him, her face anxious. After a moment he leans down, opens the leather sack, and finds his mother's box. From it he takes the red coral button in the shape of a bird.

Lia's eyes widen. 'Where did you –'

'I need to see her. Ruen. I need to see her.' His voice is shaking. 'Will you take me?'

'Of course. She'll probably be in her workshop. Arun –'

But he is already at the door. He waits for Lia to join him, and follows as she leads him through the streets.

He walks blindly through wide green spaces and tree-lined avenues. Thoughts swarm in his head. He sees Ruvek, her eyes glittering with spite. *Ah, you mean Luana. Of course I remember her . . . She was very fond of that button. She wore it on a thread around her neck.*

Ruvek again, speaking to Voll: *It wasn't the only mistake you made. But you learned your lesson . . .* Was Ruvek referring to the fact that Voll had also let another girl escape? That Kara wasn't on her own when she left the Perfumed Garden?

What if – what if Magra found out about the button, perhaps from Ruvek, perhaps from one of the girls who worked there, and used it to identify Kara?

He stops. His stomach is churning, and he feels feverish.

'Arun –' Lia puts her hand on his arm. 'Would you like to sit down for a moment?'

676

'No. Thank you.' He is aware of her worried face, the concern in her eyes, but he cannot explain. Not now. Not yet.

As he walks, more thoughts come. Magra again. There is no need to wonder why, in the white house, he told Arun that Kara was alive. It was what he had planned. One last game, to make the ending sweeter. Leading Arun to the Temple of Lakom Essu was no idle fancy. It was the setting in which Arun was meant to die. But before he did, there was one final agony to inflict.

He sees Magra standing on the stone balcony, looking down. *Once again, you fail to understand what matters. Order. Propriety. Everything is now in place, everything arranged as I wished it to be . . . Did you really think I would leave any of your family alive? I left nothing undone. I made sure of it before I came for you. They are gone. Every one of them. I wanted to give you my undivided attention, as you deserved.*

It wasn't enough that Magra took away his wife and child. He held out hope, and destroyed that too. He told Arun his sister was dead. That he had been chasing a ghost. The red coral button had been proof of his word. His moment of triumph had been all too brief; the balcony had given way, and he and Arun had fought, and he had died, but he did so believing he had killed Kara.

But if she had given the button to her friend, then he had been wrong. He had searched for the wrong girl, had found her, and –

He stops again, breathing hard. They have come into a broad street lined with trees.

'Arun? This is where Ruen lives. Her workshop's round the back. Shall I take you there?'

He is afraid to move. Can it really be true, or is it just a cruel coincidence?

Something Night said beside the pool comes back to him. *Always jumping to conclusions.* It was after he mentioned Night's refusal to tell him where Kara was buried. What if he'd been mistaken in his belief that the refusal was based on an unwillingness to break the Rule? What if – he can barely let the thought breathe – there could be no revelation because there was no grave? If Night had known Kara was still alive, and said nothing . . .

He shakes his head. That Night has no conscience, no moral scruple, is something he has always known. There is no appealing to Night's better nature because Night contains neither good nor bad nor any other human quality. Night was merely being Night. Letting down a hint that cost nothing because it would probably never be taken up. Besides which, if Arun had known about his sister, he would have gone in search of her, and Night would have lost a source of amusement, an entertaining companion. Which, he reflects, is all he ever was.

'Arun?'

He stares blankly at Lia.

'The workshop's this way.'

He follows her down the street and around the corner. A little way along, a wrought-iron gate opens into a yard containing a number of outbuildings.

'That's Ruen's workshop.'

He looks across at a building made of chalk-white stone. It has one large window and a sloping roof. There are toys on a bench outside. His throat tightens. He is not sure he can go any further.

Lia puts her hand on his arm. 'Would you like me to go with you?' The calmness of her voice gives him courage. Whatever is to come, Lia is with him. He is no longer alone.

'No,' he says finally. 'I'll be all right. Thank you.'

He walks slowly towards the workshop. When he reaches the window, he hears singing.

Rose in the garden, bird in the tree,
Love in my heart when he comes to me.

Love and pain catch his breath. It is the song his mother sang to him and his sister, long ago.

He looks in.

A woman is standing at a bench, polishing a small silver cup, singing as she works. Her blue-black hair gleams softly. As she holds the cup to the light her sleeve falls back, and he sees on her wrist a bracelet of blue thread. As if sensing his presence she turns her head, her eyes velvet-dark in a heart-shaped face.

Arun's eyes widen. He could almost be looking at his mother. 'Kara?' he says hoarsely.

She stares blankly, then her face changes. She drops the cup.

Arun takes a step forward. He lifts the latch, and opens the door.

I have seen the shining tree of gold and silver,
held night-and-day tablets engraved
with the world. I have watched the moon
drown her light in the crescent spring,
draw from the water's throat that which
water would leave unspoken. I have been
to the place of no return, where a girl
found the key to a house of treasure
made by a god for a weeping soul –
and what have I learned? That love
is the body's light: the heart beats faster
to see four white walls and a tiled roof,
a woman running down the road
with a child in her arms.

About the Author

Zeeba Ansari has worked as a poetry tutor in partnership with Cornwall Adult Education and Library Services, and on a freelance basis. Her debut poetry collection, *Love's Labours*, was published in 2013 by Pindrop Press. *The Hut* is her first work of fiction.

Notes and Acknowledgements

Many of the poem excerpts, or versions of them, are taken from *Love's Labours*, by Zeeba Ansari (Pindrop Press, 2013).

The crescent spring and the library caves were inspired by real places, both in China: the Crescent Lake, or Yueyaquan, in Gansu Province; and the Mogao Caves, also in Gansu Province.

Grateful thanks to: Carcanet Press Ltd, for kind permission to use phrases from Robert Graves's translation of Apuleius's *The Golden Ass* in the poem 'Love's Disciple', an excerpt from which appears in this book; Faber Academy; Ryan Guillou, Mona Bourell and the team at San Francisco Botanical Garden; Tony Pawlyn at the Bartlett Maritime Research Centre and Library, National Maritime Museum Cornwall; Hugh Jackson; Susan Hunt; Frances Wood, whose book *The Silk Road: Two Thousand Years in the Heart of Asia* is a continuing inspiration. I am grateful to Dr Wood for allowing me to use phrases from her book in some of my poems, excerpts from which appear in this book; and the amazing team at Troubador, for their tireless guidance and support.

Special thanks to: Robert Wilton, whose patient guidance, instinctive understanding and whole-hearted encouragement have made such a difference; Victoria Field and Alison Munro, whose insight and support have been invaluable; Lauren Humphries-Brooks, for her perception and attention to detail; Judy, for being there through it all; my wonderful parents; Jenny, for kindness and crosswords; and Deeba, for love and chocolate.